DAUGHTER OF ASH

BOOKS 1-3 OF THE BITTER ASHES SERIES

SARA C. ROETHLE

Copyright © 2019 by Sara C. Roethle

All rights reserved.

No part of this book may be reproduced in any form or by any electronic or mechanical means, including information storage and retrieval systems, without written permission from the author, except for the use of brief quotations in a book review.

❦ Created with Vellum

DEATH CURSED

BOOK ONE

PROLOGUE

Hot breath steamed across the side of my neck, tickling the tiny hairs. At first I snuggled deeper into my pillow, thinking it was a dream. Then the bed shifted as someone climbed up beside me. Fully awake now, I froze, my thoughts racing for an explanation. I lived alone, had no pets, and didn't have the type of friends that would stay the night. Whoever was sidling up beside me had broken in.

I opened my eyes to mere slits, not wanting to alert the intruder that I was awake. The room was nearly pitch black, but the curtained window let in enough moonlight for me to see the outline of a second form standing beside the bed. Judging by the build, I was pretty sure it was a man, though I was still unsure about the person in bed beside me.

I squeezed my eyes shut as the standing intruder bent at the waist, placing his hands on either side of my pillow. He continued to lean down until his face was only inches from the large artery in my neck. The one who had climbed onto the bed shifted a little closer to my feet.

The man hovering over me took a deep breath, almost like he was scenting me, then the presence lifted away. I let out a quivering breath that turned into a scream as suddenly both figures grabbed me. The one on the bed wrapped strong hands around my ankles, as the other pulled me up by my armpits into a vice-like embrace. A large, masculine palm clamped over my mouth to stifle my screaming, overwhelming my nostrils with the scent of soap and skin. I thrashed violently, but both men held fast.

My ankles lifted as the one at the foot of the bed reached the edge and stood. The intruders began moving toward my bedroom door. I screamed against the hand covering my mouth and struggled to kick my feet, hoping to loosen their grasp. I only succeeded in straining my back and a few other muscles as the figures carried me effortlessly through the dark house. I squinted to see in the dark as we neared the back door. Unable to take full breaths with the hand pressing against my mouth and nose, my screams degraded to whimpers. The other hand pulled painfully beneath my armpit. Trying to even out my body, I flung my free arm upward, but barely managed to slap at my captor's face.

The figure carrying my feet put them both under one arm so he could fling the back door open, bathing us in a wash of chilly air. I tried to make out the features of the person holding onto my bare feet, but the clouds covering the moon stunted my vision. All I could see was the outline of broad shoulders and possibly wavy hair.

I turned my eyes skyward and began to cry, soaking the hand that covered my mouth. Stars twinkled serenely above me as we entered the woods that bordered my house. I gave up on my thrashing and let my body go limp, but it didn't slow my attackers any more than my previous strategy.

My captors continued gracefully through the foliage. I began to shiver with the cold, but it didn't seem to bother the man carrying my upper half. He radiated warmth, even though I could feel only the fabric of a thin tee-shirt against the back of my head and neck.

It seemed like we ran on for ages, but the men carrying me never tired. I closed my eyes and told myself that I was dreaming, yet the bite of cool wind and the ache in my back did their best to shatter the illusion. Eventually, we came to a stop, deep within the darkness of the woods.

I felt dizzy from moving horizontally so quickly, and didn't immediately react as I was lowered to the damp ground.

My back sank into a raised mound of earth, soft, like it had recently been turned, with loose rocks jabbing into me here and there. Moisture soaked into the back of the tee-shirt and underwear I'd gone to sleep in, chilling me further.

I tried to sit up, but hands instantly pushed me back down. Something slithered across my arm. My panicked breathing brought in the scent of damp earth and growing things while my two captors crouched over me. My first thought as the cold, rough skinned creature made its way toward my neck was *snake*.

My heart pounded in my throat as more things slithered over me. I pushed against the restraining hands, but I couldn't budge them. I screamed, and one of the hands lifted from my shoulder to cover my mouth. It wasn't an improvement since now my head was being forced against the earth, hard enough that the soil scratched my scalp. Within seconds I was covered entirely with slithering objects. Some of the objects started reaching up toward the sky like tiny hands trying to grasp the moon.

The spindly creatures unfurled toward the dim light, casting eerie moon shadows onto my face. Something was wrong with them though. They had no heads, and instead branched off at the ends like no creature I'd ever seen. I wasn't covered in snakes. They were *vines*. I was glad the things weren't snakes, but being slowly engulfed in living vines did nothing to ease my panic. I screamed against the hand covering my mouth until my throat went raw. I fought against the vines with increased desperation, a last ditch effort to not be buried alive, but they only bound me tighter, until I could no longer move at all. They crushed my lungs, forcing out my last gasping breath. In that moment I knew I was going to die. I managed to catch one last glimpse of stars as the last of the vines covered my face, obscuring my view completely.

CHAPTER ONE

My eyes snapped open. I sat up in bed with a deep, aching breath, clutching at my chest. The last thing I remembered was vines encasing my entire body, then pulling me into the cold, moist earth. I had been buried alive while my attackers pinned me down.

I glanced around. The first thing I noticed was firelight flickering nearby, then the bed. It was *not* my own. *My* bed was back in my small house in a suburb of Spokane, Washington where I lived alone, and had lived alone for many years. It had been a long time since someone had been in that bed with me. I hadn't expected for it to finally only happen when someone decided to kidnap me.

I looked up at dimly-lit fabric above my head, realizing this unfamiliar bed was one of those four poster monstrosities with a princess canopy. I reached out and touched the nearest post, half expecting to wake up out of this nightmare at any moment. The wood was smooth to the touch, thick and obviously expensive.

My distorted reflection peered back at me from the dark, gleaming wood. What I could see of my long, dark brown hair was a snarled mess. I looked back into my blurry blue eyes numbly, and couldn't seem to think of anything beyond my messy hair.

I shook my head in an attempt to clear the fog. I had to escape. My bare feet slid to the edge of the burgundy comforter as I lowered myself to the ground. The floor and surrounding walls were made of strange gray stone that made me feel like I was in a castle.

A thud to my left caught my attention. I jumped, ready to fend off my attacker, then realized the sound was a log tumbling in the simple stone fireplace behind me. I turned to stare into the flames, wondering if they could be used as a weapon, but I had nothing to wield them with. That was just like my attackers to not leave me a torch.

"I didn't expect you to be awake yet," a male voice said from across the room.

I nearly stumbled as I tried to turn around too quickly. A man stood framed in the now open doorway, leaning against the frame casually. He wore black slacks and no shirt or shoes. It was an odd look that made it seem as if he simply hadn't finished dressing yet . . . or perhaps he just hadn't finished *un*-dressing.

I grasped at the ends of my oversized gray tee-shirt and tried to cover at least a small portion of my bare legs. I realized as I looked down that my legs were still covered in dirt from my experience in the woods, verifying that it had all been quite real. Perhaps this man was one of my kidnappers. I backed toward the fire, not wanting him near me.

He stepped into the room, casually observing me. His straight, black hair fell well past his shoulders to frame his pale skin and dark brown eyes. My mouth went dry with fear as he took another step forward. He was tall, I placed him around 6'2", given that I'm 5'9" and still had to look up to meet his eyes as he came even closer.

I held up a hand in front of me and took another step back. "S-stop," I stammered. "Where am I?"

He cocked his head. He was attractive in an ethereal sort of way. Something about the slope of his jaw or the narrowness of his nose made him seem almost feminine, though he was clearly *all* man. "Where do you think you are, Madeline?"

"It's Maddy," I corrected reflexively, still gripping my shirt with one hand while I pushed my hair out of my face with the other, "and how do you know my name? Who are you?"

He met me step for step until my back was against the hard stone wall. When I couldn't back away anymore he stopped, not closing the final space between us. His eyes danced with amusement.

I craned my neck to look up into his deep brown eyes, feeling like a deer in the headlights.

I flinched as he reached a hand out to twirl the ends of my hair around his fingers. "Don't you want to know *my* name?" He smiled widely, and if I didn't know any better I would say I saw the points of little fangs where his canines should have been. Then again, I had just been pulled through the earth into some sort of windowless castle by vines. Maybe I didn't know any better.

"No," I gasped, side-stepping against the wall until I was out of reach, "but directions to the nearest exit wouldn't hurt."

He smiled again, flashing his little fangs. "I like a girl who can joke when she's terrified."

I gulped, unsure whether or not he was just toying with me. "I wasn't joking," I said, voice barely above a whisper.

He grinned. "Neither was I, but I'm afraid I can't show you the exit when you've only just arrived."

"Leave her alone, Alaric," a woman's voice snapped from the doorway.

The fanged man stepped aside to reveal a woman that looked startlingly similar to him. She strode into the room confidently, trailing the ends of her gossamer-thin red dress behind her. Her black hair hung nearly to her waist, intermingling with the loose red fabric like oil on blood. There was something else about her that I recognized, though I couldn't quite place it. It tickled at the edges of my memory, letting me know I had seen her before.

Alaric left me to stand by the woman I had to assume was his sister, given their strong resemblance. He tugged on her long hair playfully like they were children, eliciting a steely glare from her dark eyes. I watched the woman's face, searching for any sign that she might recognize me as well, but she only returned her gaze to eye me coolly.

"Out," the woman ordered her brother sternly, pointing a finger behind her toward the door.

Alaric gave her a mocking salute, then winked at me. I stared back at him as he turned and glided toward the door. *Glide* was the only word I could think of to describe his walk. He moved like a cat, with light steps and limber, balanced grace.

The woman came toward me, taking my attention off Alaric's sinewy back as he left the room. She looked annoyed, yet I still instantly preferred her company to that of her brother. At least she wouldn't hit on me . . . probably.

"I'm Sophie," she introduced.

The introduction would have been nice had it been accompanied by a smile, but I decided to keep my opinion to myself. I caught a glimpse of dainty, sharp canines in her mouth as she sniffed the air around me. I gulped, suddenly glad that I'd chosen not to speak.

"You need a bath," she said with a sneer, revealing her sharp teeth more clearly.

"What am I doing here?" I asked, ignoring her statement. "I know I've seen you before."

"We've never met before, Madeline," she replied flatly. She said my name with harsh emphasis on the *e*, and something once again tickled my memory.

I saw a flash of her in my mind, sitting behind a large, wooden desk. *"This time will be different," she said with a warm smile. She wore a modest skirt suit, with her black hair pulled back into a tight braid.*

"You were my case-worker!" I blurted as realization dawned on me.

I had sat on the other side of that desk so many times growing up, and those moments were thoroughly ingrained in my memory. In fact, I was surprised I hadn't recognized her sooner.

"I don't know what you're talking about," she snapped, though her eyes shifted nervously.

I almost believed her despite the nervous twitch. She hadn't aged a day, and I'd been out of the foster system for nearly ten years. Yet, the resemblance was just too much to be a coincidence.

"Why am I here?" I repeated, beginning to panic again. "Don't lie to me, I remember you. I was in and out of your office often enough to remember."

I knew I was right. Sophie had been my case-worker as I was bounced around from home to home all those years ago. Now that I'd made the connection, I remembered distinctly how she'd said my name each time she told me that the next home would be different. A few weeks, or a few months later, I'd go back and call her a liar, but she'd never get angry.

My thoughts came to a screeching halt as my memories of

childhood led to where they always led, a memory I'd done my best to block out entirely. My knees went weak.

"Wait," I said as I felt the color drain from my face, "am I here because of what happened back then? You said it would all be okay!"

Sophie's expression softened, showing just a small hint of sympathy. She knew exactly what I was talking about. I tried to shut my mind off to the memory, but I wasn't successful.

"This has *nothing* to do with what happened," she explained evenly. "I swear it. You will face no repercussions for that day."

"Um," I began weakly, my heart thudding in my throat, "then would you mind telling me why I'm actually here, and why *you're* here?"

"That is none of your concern," she snapped, leaving me to wonder if I'd only imagined the sympathy in her eyes.

"It *is* my concern," I argued. I fought them, but tears began to stream down my face. "In fact I find it very concerning that I was ripped from my bed at night, and pulled into the ground by vines! Not to mention that I'm now faced with my old social worker who hasn't aged a *day* in nearly ten years."

"Come with me," she said, then turned around, expecting me to follow her.

"I'm not going anywhere until you tell me what's going on," I replied, trying to keep my voice steady as I backed away from her.

My legs felt numb and shaky, but I managed to move my bare feet across the floor, step after step. I was sure that I was in a mild state of shock, which was probably a good thing, because it kept me from collapsing into a screaming heap on the floor.

She turned back to me with a frustrated sigh. "Do you still sense the emotions of others?"

I felt my face shutting down. She was one of the few people I'd ever told about my secret. I'd been able to sense what others were feeling since I was a child. It had made foster living absolute hell.

"Do you, Madeline?" she pressed.

I shook my head. "Is *that* why you brought me here? I was just a kid, making stuff up." *Lies*. All lies. Lies I'd learned to tell to survive. Psych evaluations are no fun.

"You made nothing up," she said matter of factly. "And that man's death? It was *your* fault, just as you've always believed. Now come with me, and I might tell you what else I know about you."

I stared at her in shock, forcing painful memories away. A fresh tear dripped down my face, then another.

"Come, Madeline," she demanded. "I promise, we mean you no harm."

I wiped the tears from my eyes, and took a deep breath. For people that meant me no harm, they sure had a funny way of showing it. "Where are we going?"

Sophie looked me up and down, a wry smile on her full lips. "You're covered in filth. We're going down the hall to the bathroom."

I stared at her a moment, looking for any sign that she might be lying. Not that it mattered. I glanced past her to the open door. She and I were about evenly matched physically, I could probably escape her . . .

"Don't," she warned. "Try anything and I'll have my brother carry you to the bathroom kicking and screaming."

I bit my lip. I could try to run now, or I could wait for a better opportunity. I didn't want her, *or* her brother, touching me.

Seeming to sense my defeat, she gestured toward the open doorway. "Run, and I will catch you."

Giving her a wide berth, I hurried toward the door, exiting into a long stone corridor. I glanced both ways, but saw nothing but gray stone one way, and a wooden door the other. Sophie walked past me, heading toward the door. Upon reaching it, I noticed that the hallway continued on to the right. So there was empty corridor behind me, and this new path. Two possible routes of escape.

Sophie opened the door and gestured for me to walk in ahead of her.

I obeyed. Against the far wall of the over-sized space was an ornate, claw-foot bathtub made of white porcelain, standing on tarnished brass feet. To my left were the sink and toilet.

"Bathe," Sophie ordered.

"I don't-" I began, but she cut me off with a stern look that said *I know you're unhappy, but you have to listen to me regardless*. It was the same look she used to give me when I called her a liar.

She finally offered me a hint of a smile. "I will keep my brother at bay, if that is your concern. I know you are considering the best time for you to run, but I assure you, it would not be a wise choice. You will not escape this place easily."

I crossed my arms, glanced at the tub, then back to her. I was *not* going to get in that tub. "I never knew you had a brother."

It wasn't actually strange for me to not know. Most caseworkers kept their lives private from the children they worked with. It just seemed weird to me that I'd never seen him, or heard any mention of him at all.

"Well I do," she replied. "Now please, stop stalling and bathe, and I'll be back to fetch you soon."

With that, she turned and left the bathroom, shutting the

door gently behind her with a soft click. As soon as I recovered from the surprise of being left alone, I ran to the door and quickly twisted the lock. I did a frantic scan of the bathroom, but didn't find anything that could aid my escape.

There was no shower, just the bathtub, a toilet, and a sink surrounded by a pale pink marble countertop. Another fire burned in a fireplace set in the wall behind the bathtub. The room, ceiling, and floor were all made of stone, with no modern ventilation that I could see. There was also no visible lighting, yet the room was somehow well-lit. I scanned the walls and ceiling, but couldn't tell where the light was coming from. Eventually, my panic took over. I collapsed to my knees and closed my eyes, willing the whole situation to be a dream. It *had* to be a dream. Vines didn't move on their own, people aged and didn't have fangs, and rooms couldn't be lit without light bulbs or candles.

I sat like that for several minutes, but when I finally opened my eyes, I was still in the strange stone bathroom. I rose shakily to my feet and looked at the bathtub again. I briefly considered just doing what Sophie told me, but couldn't bring myself to do it. Not seeing any other options, I turned toward the door.

I wasn't about to trust Sophie just because she'd been my social worker. In fact, it made me trust her even less. I had to get out of here, *now*.

Knowing Sophie was likely waiting right outside the door, I grabbed a small basket of wrapped soaps from the counter beside the sink. It wasn't much as far as weapons went, but if it could distract her long enough for me to run, I'd take it.

Not giving myself time to consider the consequences of my actions, I balanced the basket in one hand, flipped the lock with the other, flung open the door, and chucked the soap basket at Sophie where she waited outside.

I barely registered her shocked expression as I took a sharp left and fled. My bare feet pounded harshly against the hard stone, sending little jolts of pain up through my shins and into my knees. I didn't look back to see if she was chasing me. The narrow, high-ceilinged hallway seemed to stretch on forever, with no discernible landmarks to tell me where I was or how far I'd gone. I ran past several closed doors and turned another corner.

I had only taken a few more steps when I ran straight into someone who'd been walking down the hall in my direction. We'd both hit the corner at the same time, and had no time to react. I bounced off his chest and fell to the ground with a thud. The man wasn't even shaken by the impact. He looked down at me and let out a good-natured chuckle. He wore a hunter green tee-shirt and jeans that seemed out of place in our castle-like surroundings.

The man leaned down to offer me a hand, causing his chin-length, golden brown hair to fall forward.

I scuttled away from him, stumbling to my feet to run the other direction. I managed one step before he grabbed my arm and jerked me back to face him.

He lifted a golden brow, his fingers digging painfully into my arm. "Are you lost?" He had a slight southern accent, but it was faint enough that I couldn't really tell which state it came from. He looked me up and down, lingering on the fact that my bottom half was only covered by underwear.

My heart pounded in my ears. "Just looking for the front door," I growled, swinging my free arm toward his face.

He caught my fist effortlessly.

I balked, not understanding how he'd moved so fast. I opened my mouth to beg him to let me go, but my words caught in my throat as I finally looked directly into his icy blue eyes, so pale they were almost white. The rest of his face was handsome enough: a strong nose, a jaw just wide enough to be masculine . . . yet those eyes. I'd seen eyes like that before, and they hadn't belonged to the living. A flash of memory shot through me like lightning, raising the tiny hairs on my entire body. I shook away the horrifying image of a young man's eyes just as his life had left him. It had been a long time ago, and there were more pressing matters to worry about.

"Are you going to behave now?" he asked, his grips on my fist and arm unyielding.

I nodded, unable to look away from his eerie eyes.

Slowly, he released me. "Now let's get you back to Sophie—"

The moment my arms were out of his reach I dropped to the ground, narrowly avoiding him as he made another grab for me. Once I was down, I did the first thing I could think of and kicked him in the kneecap. The move would have worked better if I wasn't barefoot. As it was, all I got for my effort was a grunt of annoyance. Recovering, I tried to push away, but he grabbed me again. This time he lifted me like I weighed nothing and threw me over his shoulder.

I was so shocked by how fast he'd moved I went limp for a moment, blinking at the back of his shirt and wondering how I'd gotten there, then I started screaming, pounding my fists on his back and kicking with my bare feet.

Not seeming to mind, he carried me down the hall. "You're lucky that I like it rough," he laughed.

I pulled up the back of his shirt and raked my nails across his back. The pain I caused echoed through me. Another little secret I'd kept as a child. If I caused others damage, I'd feel that too. He dropped me to the ground on my butt, knocking the wind from my lungs. He pulled me back up, this time pressing my back against his chest, forcing me to stumble forward. Still relearning how to breathe, I dragged my feet in vain, bruising them on the hard stone floor as we went back the way I'd come.

We rounded a corner, and Sophie came into view. She stood near the bathroom looking regal in her red dress, tapping her foot impatiently. The basket of soaps was neatly arranged under her arm. She hadn't even tried to chase me.

She approached, then grabbed my arm with her free hand, taking me from the man without a word. Moving her hand to my back, she shoved me into the bathroom. This time when she shut the door, she stayed inside with me.

"I told you not to attempt escape." She braced herself against the door and let out a shaky breath, betraying her show of confidence.

I leaned against the wall, my battered body screaming at me. "You can't really blame me for trying to escape," I wheezed back at her.

Seeming to regain her composure, she locked the door and walked over to the bathtub to start the water. I glanced at the locked door, then at Sophie's turned back, surprised that she was leaving me the opportunity to escape again.

As if reading my thoughts, she glanced back at me. "Trust me when I tell you that you are much safer in here with me, than out there with James."

James. A third kidnapping accomplice. Scariest one so far. "Safe?" I questioned. I was feeling a lot of things, but safe wasn't one of them.

Sophie shrugged. "Relatively so. I will not hurt you unless you make me. James would very much like to hurt you." She shivered and I wondered if James had very much liked hurting her too.

I stood up straight and pushed my back firmly against the wall as she left the tub to walk toward me.

"Please tell me why I'm here," I pleaded one last time.

She pinched the bridge of her nose like I was giving her a headache. "*Please* take a bath," she countered. "It is not my place to answer your questions. You will simply have to wait on that." She breezed past me, returning to her post by the door without another word.

I looked over at the slowly filling bath. It had an old-fashioned, slender faucet that didn't let out a great deal of water at once, and the basin was filling painfully slow. Feeling awkward, but definitely not wanting to go back out in the hall with James, I undressed, wishing I'd just listened to Sophie the first time. At least that way I wouldn't have had her watching me while I bathed. I couldn't even remember the last time I'd been naked in front of *anyone*, and I really didn't like being that vulnerable in front of someone I was afraid of.

Wrapping my arms around my chest, but having nothing to cover the rest of me with, I dipped a toe into the bath. I quickly withdrew the toe, then added more cold to the water flow so that I wouldn't end up scalding my skin off. Once the temperature was bearable, I took a step in, then slowly sat, hissing through my teeth as I adjusted to the heat.

I watched the black soil swirl off my skin into the steamy water for a moment, then glanced at Sophie. Despite the circumstances, she still seemed like the same old Sophie. At one point, I'd even considered her a friend. "What did James do to you?" I asked.

She didn't answer immediately, and I was left with several moments of silence to ponder my situation. I was pretty sure I was, in fact, in shock, because all I could think about was how strange it felt to be around Sophie again, in a tub of now-dirty water no less. I'd spent so much time talking to her in my youth that it almost felt natural, even though we were now meeting under far different circumstances.

Eventually she snorted, the gesture somehow elegant, as she came out of her own private thoughts. I'd previously thought that snorting elegantly wasn't a thing, but that was exactly what Sophie did. She moved away from the door to perch on the closed toilet seat, folding her long legs underneath her in a position that didn't look at all comfortable.

"James would never dare offer me violence," she explained, "but I've seen what he likes to do to people." She turned the full power of her dark stare onto me. "The things I've seen would make a nice girl like you want to cut out her own eyes, though it wouldn't stop the nightmares."

I leaned forward to shut off the faucet, then huddled in the hot water, wincing at the bruise forming on my tailbone. I had to admit the warmth felt good, even if taking a bath was the last thing I wanted to be doing. "I've seen plenty of things to give me nightmares."

She startled as if she'd fallen deep into thought. "I know," she answered finally. "I know much more than you'd think. The world has not been kind to you."

I swallowed past a renewed sense of panic. She knew what had happened with my last foster family, but she couldn't know about Matthew. I'd met Matthew years later, and that event was for my nightmares alone. I flashed on his dead eyes again, eyes that had looked so much like James'. I'd done it to him. I wasn't sure how, but Matthew's death was my fault. Sophie had no way of knowing anything about that.

She smiled at me like she knew exactly what I was thinking. I looked away quickly, suddenly more frightened than I'd been before, if that was even possible.

I watched her out of the corner of my eye as she reached

toward the basket she'd replaced beside the sink, retrieving a new bar of yellow soap, still in the wrapper. She took off the plastic and handed the soap to me. It looked handmade, and smelled like vanilla.

"Wash," she demanded. "Once you're dressed, I'll take you to learn why we brought you here."

I began to wash myself, wishing I could wash away more that just dirt. Matthew's dead eyes were still at the forefront of my mind.

The world would be a lovely place if we could wash away fear and bad memories, but it wasn't a lovely place. I'd seen the ugliness of the world long before I'd learned to live in fear of making it worse.

CHAPTER TWO

At one point during my bath, someone delivered some clothes for me. Sophie had only opened the door a crack, so I hadn't seen who it was. I'd ended up standing in the middle of the bathroom, dressed in a slim-fitting black dress that encased my legs down to the tops of my knees. Black boots covered my calves and left just a sliver of flesh to be seen below my kneecaps.

The boots had much higher heels than I was used to. Okay, they were only three inches, but I never wore heels. I got my height early, and therefore have the tall-girl syndrome of not wanting to tower over everyone. In the boots I was 6'.

I stole a glance at myself in the bathroom mirror as Sophie leaned against the door. In addition to the uncomfortable added height, the black made my normally deep olive coloring a little washed out. Back in the real world, I never wore black without a little bit of makeup. At that moment though, my coloring was on the bottom of my list of concerns. The woman standing by the door was somewhere near the top.

"Are you done primping yet?" Sophie asked impatiently. Her earlier show of camaraderie must have been a fluke, as she had already reverted back to the steely bitch persona.

I looked in the mirror again. My hair was only partially dry, and felt heavy and snarled. It was thick enough that it would be hours before it dried completely, and Sophie hadn't offered me a blow dryer.

"Where are we going?" I asked yet again, even though I knew my efforts were futile.

"I cannot tell you," she sighed, leaning more heavily against the door.

I looked back to the mirror. The dress was tight enough that it was a little hard to breathe. "Then tell me why I'm dressed like this. I feel like a lamb being led to slaughter."

Sophie crossed her arms and cocked her hip to the side. "The sooner you stop asking questions, the sooner you'll know the answers."

On that cryptic note, she opened the door and walked out, expecting me to follow her. Not wanting to risk another run-in with James, or with Alaric for that matter, I did as I was told. Sophie was the lesser evil, at least for now.

She glided down the hallway ahead of me, moving gracefully like her brother. Though I was slightly taller than her with the heels, I felt like I had to take twice the number of steps to keep up. Our heels clicked on the stone floor as we headed in the opposite direction from where I'd run.

We didn't have to go very far before the hallway expanded into a larger walkway, opening into what I could only think of as a throne room. There was no actual throne, but there was a dais against the far wall that was just begging for a gilded throne. We walked across the barren, open space and went through a doorway into a private room.

My confusion increased. Seated in front of me was a small old man. His long gray hair draped across the loose, deep blue clothing he wore, and continued on to pool on the floor in a silvery mass. With his apparent age and hair color, it seemed like he should have a beard as well, like some sort of diminutive wizard, but his face was clean shaven.

He sat at the head of a simple table made of heavy wood. There were enough seats for ten, but no one else kept him company. He turned his weighted gaze to Sophie, who still stood beside me.

"Leave us," he said simply.

With a curt nod, Sophie did just as he asked. I turned to watch her go, nervous to be left alone with the man.

"Face me, Madeline," he said softly.

I turned around slowly, somehow more nervous now than I had been since first waking up. Maybe the shock was finally wearing off, or maybe I was just losing my mind. Most likely it was the latter. Upon closer observation, I placed the man as slightly younger than I had originally thought, maybe late sixties instead of seventies. His face was dappled in only slight wrinkles that increased a bit around his pale gray eyes. His eyes seemed to radiate a *knowing* as he looked me up and down. I'd learned to read people pretty well in my younger years, and I instantly knew that this was a man that I would never try to fool.

"Forgive us for capturing you so abruptly," he began, lifting his eyes to meet my gaze. "I would have liked to leave you be, but I am afraid our need is simply too great."

I wiped my sweaty palms on my dress. I had the distinct feeling of insects crawling across my skin. "What need?" I managed to ask.

What could this man possibly need from me? A million

thoughts raced through my head, none of them rational. My intuition was begging me to get far away from him.

"What do you know of the *Vaettir*?" he asked, his expression pleasant despite what my instincts were telling me.

I took a deep breath, trying to calm myself. "I don't know that term." I answered cautiously. He'd pronounced it *vay-tur*, and it sounded slightly Swedish. "Should I?"

He smiled patiently, making me feel like a child back in school. "Two more common terms for what we are would be Wiht or Wight."

"What do you mean *we*?" I asked. "Why am I here?"

"I'm attempting to explain," he replied sourly. "If you'll please answer my original question."

"I don't know anything about Wights," I answered, but that wasn't entirely true. "Aren't they similar to zombies?" I asked, still not sure what mythological creatures had to do with anything. I shifted my weight from foot to foot, glancing around the room for possibly routes of escape. He hadn't threatened me, but I had a feeling this man was the reason I'd been kidnapped. I needed to get away from him.

Not seeming to sense my unease, he continued, "In more common renditions, I suppose. Those myths began in the 1800s. Corpses would reanimate, but most were actually Vaettir. But I assure you, the Vaettir are not undead. Quite the opposite, actually. We are beings of nature, Fae, for lack of a better word. We are more alive than any others who walk this earth. In ancient Norse culture, we were revered as patrons of the land, though in later years, a less favorable picture was painted. Hence, our solitude."

I laughed, a nervous bark of sound in the quiet room. The sound seemed to startle me much more than it did the old man. In fact, his face didn't change at all. He simply waited for me to speak.

"Wait," I said finally, "you're trying to tell me that you are this Vaettir thingy?"

I was beginning to sweat profusely, and had the feeling if this conversation didn't end soon, I was going to start screaming.

The old man nodded, quite serious. "As are you," he replied simply.

The rigid smile wilted from my face. "You're kidding, right?"

His face still didn't change.

I didn't know much about Norse mythology, but I knew I wasn't part of it. "Why am I here? I don't know anything about zombies or anything else." I laughed nervously. "Next thing you'll be telling me is that I'm some sort of long-lost fairy princess."

Finally the old man smiled wickedly, turning my stomach to ice. "No my dear, you are definitely not our long-lost princess. You're our executioner."

I started laughing again, and it sounded psychotic, even to me. I couldn't help it. The old man was obviously serious, but he was talking nonsense. Feeling weak in the knees, I sat in a chair several seats down from him. "You people are insane," I breathed.

He tilted his head to the side and smiled. "What do you know of your parents?"

"That doesn't mean a thing," I replied instantly, knowing that Sophie had probably filled him in on my history. I wouldn't let them prey on the fact that I had been a foster kid. Enough people had done that already. "Not every abandoned baby ends up being a wizard, or a fairy, or . . . something out of ancient myth," I finished coldly.

"No," he chuckled. "But in your case . . ."

I stood, deciding that I'd rather take my chances with

James or Alaric than sit around listening to crazy stories. The old man slammed his hand on the table, and my legs collapsed underneath me. I barely managed to aim my butt toward the chair to keep myself off the ground. I tried to stand again and didn't even make it halfway out of my seat before being forced back down.

"I apologize," he said serenely. "This was not how I hoped this meeting would go. This is a homecoming, not a kidnapping."

I looked around the room frantically for an explanation. My legs wouldn't work. This had to be some sort of trick. Maybe they'd drugged me.

"What's happening?" I demanded, my breath catching in my throat.

"If you would stop trying to stand," he said with a condescending smile, "I would not have to force you to sit."

My eyes widened. He was claiming that he could make me sit . . . with what, his mind? Of course, I *was* sitting against my will with no other explanation to go on.

"Who are you?" I asked, panting with exertion while I clutched at the edges of my chair.

"My name is Estus," he replied. "I am Doyen of this clan."

I gritted my teeth, unable to stave off the tears that began to flow down my face once again. "I don't know what that means."

A hint of impatience flickered in Estus' eyes, cracking the kind old man act, not that I'd believed it to begin with. "We should never have left you to the humans for so long," he sighed.

"So why did you?" I asked, unable to think of anything else to say. If you can't beat 'em, then you may as well play along.

"A clan only needs one executioner," he explained. "Any others born with the specific qualities of an executioner are exiled. It would be chaos otherwise."

Each crazy thing he said made my tears flow more quickly. This had nothing to do with my years in foster care. These people were completely insane.

"Too many executioners over the centuries have ended up killing each other," he went on, ignoring my tears. "If we continued to let them live together, we'd end up without any executioners at all, and that would be very, very bad. Now, if we send the extras out into the world, we may call them back when we are in need of a replacement."

I moved my tongue around in my mouth to try and get some saliva going, but it was no use. I swallowed around the lump in my throat. "And you're in need of a replacement *now*?" I panted, still straining to stand.

"Precisely," he answered, seeming relieved that I understood. "Our clan cannot function properly without you."

If these crazy people wanted me to be their executioner, that meant they were going to try keeping me with them. It also likely meant they were going to expect me to kill people. I could never do that. Someone would have to come looking for me eventually. They had to.

I mean, people don't just disappear without the police being notified. Of course, it might take a while for them to get notified. I had no parents to report me missing, and no spouse. I had a few friends, but the scenario of them not hearing from me for a few weeks wasn't unheard of. Events in my past had led me to a life of near-solitude, keeping people at a distance for fear that history would repeat itself. My history was dark and sad, and not worth repeating.

Normal people would have at least had a boss to miss

them when they didn't show up for work, but I did freelance writing for a living, so there were no coworkers or bosses to report me missing. I had a landlord . . . but seeing as it was only the 8th of October, he wouldn't be expecting a rent check for a while. He probably wouldn't sound any alarm bells until his pockets were feeling empty. Being alone was hard, but I'd never thought that being antisocial would come back to bite me in such a major way.

Estus gave me several minutes to digest everything. I still didn't believe anything he'd said, though the fact that I was quite literally glued to my seat definitely gave me pause. Regardless, it definitely wasn't the time to argue. I was better off going along with whatever Estus said until they left me alone again.

"I can see that you are having some trouble believing what I say," he stated finally.

"No," I lied quickly. "I understand."

Some of the smile slipped from Estus' face. "I will not tolerate lies, now tell me what happened with Matthew."

A searing feeling of cold shot through me at the name. My breath caught in my throat. "How do you know about that?" I croaked.

Estus eyed me steadily. "Just because we left you on your own, does not mean that we let you go. Not entirely. Now tell me."

"No," I replied. "That's private."

I gripped the edges of my chair until my hands ached as I tried to push away the memories. That specific story was one I never planned on sharing with *anybody*, let alone one of my kidnappers.

"It was not your fault," he consoled. "It is your nature."

I was beginning to shake as I held back more tears, but the memories weren't held back as easily. We'd been in a car accident. Several cars had been involved. Others had died, but we weren't overly hurt. Matthew's wrist was clearly broken, but that seemed to be the extent of it. Good Samaritans had helped us out of our car to wait on the side of the road for the paramedics.

We were sitting in the grass, and it was killing me to see Matthew gritting his teeth against the pain. I'd always been highly affected by the pain of others to an extent that made me avoid hospitals like the plague. If I saw an injury on someone else, my mind made me feel like I had it too. Even strong emotions affected me. At one point I'd gone to therapy for it, but nothing helped.

The old memory played out in my head like a movie. *I reached out and smoothed my hand across Matthew's face, hoping to soothe him just a bit, and in effect soothe myself. He looked at me, suddenly not just in pain, but frightened. His fear made my heart hammer in my throat, but I continued holding my hand to his face, not sure of what had changed.*

I felt a rush of energy as it left him, that spark of life. I watched as it left his eyes. I was so shocked as he slumped over that I didn't even scream. Later I would try telling myself that he'd damaged something internally in the accident, but I knew it was a lie. I'd stared at him as the paramedics arrived and rushed over to us, and knew for a fact that there was nothing they could do.

I still rode next to his dead body in the ambulance as they did their best to resuscitate him. I was later told that they couldn't find the exact cause of death. They wrote it off as a small brain hemorrhage, but I knew otherwise. Some tiny voice screamed in my mind that it was me. I'd killed Matthew.

"You are probably starving," Estus said sympathetically, watching the emotions play across my face. "Sophie will escort you to the kitchens. We will speak more when you are at full strength."

As if on cue, the door opened behind me, and Sophie re-entered the room. I turned wide eyes to Estus to see if I was allowed to stand.

He smiled warmly, then lifted his hands, shooing me away.

I took a deep breath and stood without any unseen force impeding me. I turned and numbly followed Sophie's slim form without another word to Estus. I felt shaky on my feet, but I kept walking. That's all we can ever really do.

We went back through the throne room and down another narrow hallway. Sophie looked back several times, but didn't say anything.

Eventually I stopped walking, feeling like I might throw up. "That man—" I began.

She stopped, then turned to face me. "Estus," she corrected.

"Did you tell him about me?" I asked. "Is he like, a mental patient?"

Sophie's eyes widened. "Do not ever let anyone hear you say such a thing," she hissed. "Estus is Doyen. All here obey him."

The urge to vomit increased. I felt like I was motion sick, but it was probably just another symptom of shock. "You're not really a social worker, are you?"

She shrugged. "I like to think I was pretty good at it."

I just stared at her, at a loss for words.

"Chin up," she said with a sudden smile.

She turned and began walking forward again, and I quickly followed, resigning myself to whatever fate might befall me. The queasiness dissipated as we walked, only to be replaced by an icy, shaky feeling that wasn't much of an improvement.

I attempted to distract myself by taking in my surroundings, and noticed with a start that I had not seen one single window in any of the thick, stone walls. The entire place was illuminated just like the bathroom, with no visible source of light. It didn't make any sense.

I trotted to catch up to Sophie and walk beside her. "Where does the light come from?"

She gave me another sympathetic look, then explained, "The Salr provides its own light."

"The sah-what?" I asked, not knowing the term.

"Salr, *Sah-lur*," she sounded out for me. "It is where we live."

"I don't understand," I replied. "How can a place provide its own light without any windows?"

Sophie stopped walking again and put a hand on her hip. "Estus explained to you what we are, yes?"

My pulse picked up again at the mention of Estus. What he'd done in that room... "Kind of," I answered. "But—"

"You still don't believe him," she finished for me. She suddenly gripped me by my shoulders and looked straight into my eyes. "Watch," she instructed.

Not sure what I was supposed to see, I looked into her eyes. As I watched, her dark irises flashed to golden, with large flecks of green. Her pupils narrowed until they looked like cat eyes. I tried to jerk away, but her hands held me iron-tight. A moment later, her eyes returned to normal.

"What the hell was that?" I whispered, utterly still in her unyielding grip.

She abruptly let go of my shoulders and started walking again. "My brother and I are Bastet," she explained, as if it made all the sense in the world.

I knew that Bastet was the cat-headed Egyptian goddess of warfare, but I didn't think Sophie was claiming to be a goddess.

"That man, Estus, said that you're Vaettir," I said, feeling extremely silly for discussing it so seriously. "Like zombies," I added.

Sophie smirked at me as we walked. "We are Vaettir, but we are not *zombies*. Sometimes the Vaettir reanimate after death."

"Uhh," I began, "you know that's basically the definition of zombies?"

Sophie grunted in frustration. "Perhaps, but we are not the zombies portrayed in all of those silly movies. We sometimes reanimate because a piece of our soul is left in our bodies. It gives the bodies life, but the person who inhabited that shell is gone."

I bit my lip, thinking about my reply, then tried to not sound condescending as I said, "That's still pretty much the definition of zombies."

Sophie huffed in annoyance, but didn't try to convince me further. If zombies actually existed, that would be it for me. I would lose my mind and run screaming into the dark, never to return.

We passed through a large dining area and into a kitchen the size of what a large restaurant would have. Monstrous pots brimming with boiling liquids sat on the industrial sized stove, filling the room with savory smells. Sophie retrieved a large bowl and began filling it with what looked like beef stew.

"I don't eat meat," I said quickly.

She stopped ladling and dumped the stew back into the pot. "Of course you don't," she said with a touch of sarcasm. "Because a vegetarian executioner totally makes sense."

"I'm not an executioner," I said nervously. "You've all made a mistake."

"Whatever you say," she replied. She picked up a knife and began hacking away at a large loaf of bread that had been sitting out on the counter. "Cheese?" she asked.

I nodded my head. "Yes, cheese is fine, just no meat."

"Not ever?" she asked as if she didn't quite believe me.

I shook my head.

She snorted. "Well that's irritating."

Setting down the knife, she ventured to the far side of the kitchen, opened a large, walk-in refrigerator, and disappeared inside, eventually emerging with an armful of produce. She returned to the cooking area and placed a tomato, an avocado, some lettuce, and a package of alfalfa sprouts on a cutting board. She began chopping haphazardly while I looked at the rest of the kitchen.

Large, gas station style coffee pots took up a counter to my left, and in front of me along the far wall was bar style seating, along with a few small tables and chairs set out of the way.

Within a few minutes, I was seated at the shiny counter built into the far wall with a veggie and cheese sandwich placed in front of me. Sophie had left out mayo and mustard, but the sight of her wielding the large kitchen knife had prompted me to keep my mouth shut.

My stomach was groaning painfully, arguing with my mind for not wanting to eat. When my stomach won out, I picked up the sandwich and prepared to take a bite.

"How is our little executioner doing?" Someone whispered right beside my ear, though no one had been there a moment before.

I jumped and dropped my sandwich back to its plate. It

fell apart, looking pathetic and unappetizing. I turned to find Alaric staring at me from just a few inches away.

My pulse quickened as he reached out his hand, then swept my hair away from my face to reveal my neck, turning my initial annoyance into anxiety. "You know, there's no meat on your sandwich?" he asked, looking at my neck instead of my face.

I scooted my stool a few inches away from him. He didn't seem offended. In fact, he pulled another stool up close and sat with his knee touching mine. I was glad that he'd at least found a shirt somewhere as he leaned against me.

Sophie cleared her throat behind us. She sat near the door, drinking a cup of coffee. I would have loved some coffee, but I didn't really want to ask her for anything else. I already had the feeling that she hadn't appreciated having to make a sandwich for me.

Seeing my longing gaze, Alaric rose from his seat and walked past his sister to pour two more cups from the coffee maker's spout. He returned and placed one cup beside me, then sat in his original position.

Leaning away from him, I sipped the coffee, feeling instantly more stable as the warm liquid poured down my throat, thawing the icy pit that had formed in my insides. Alaric sipped on his own coffee as he watched me.

I glanced at him, feeling increasingly awkward. "Do you have to do that?"

"Do what?" he replied as he picked up a piece of my hair to play with.

"Be creepy," I answered, gathering up my sandwich once again. I leaned as far away as I could without falling off my chair.

He laughed and dropped my hair, but didn't scoot away.

He watched me take the first bite of my sandwich like he'd memorize every movement.

"You know," he said. "A lot of women don't like being watched while they eat."

I washed the first bite down with a sip of coffee. Without any condiments on the hard bread, the sandwich was a little dry. At least the coffee was good. Definitely not the cheap stuff.

"I don't care if you watch me," I replied. "Just don't touch me."

"Well you two are obviously getting along," Sophie quipped, "so I'll just let Alaric show you back to your room."

I turned. "No!" I blurted. "Please don't leave me," I glanced at Alaric, then reluctantly added, "with him."

She smirked. "He's only teasing you, Madeline. He's not going to eat you."

I opened my mouth to argue further, but she simply turned her back and left the kitchen. I had to snap my gaping jaw shut as I turned back to Alaric.

"Eat your sandwich," he said good-naturedly, obviously not upset with the current arrangement. That made one of us.

I took another bite of the dry sandwich and had even more trouble swallowing than before. It had seemed like a good idea to eat, if only to gather my strength, but now each bite was beginning to feel like heavy lead in my stomach. I put the sandwich down on the plate, suddenly disgusted with it.

"Black isn't your color," Alaric commented. "I tried to pick your clothes, but I was over-ruled."

"Who picked them?" I asked, feeling uncomfortable that he cared what I wore.

"Sophie," he replied. "She chose them before you arrived. I take it you will be staying with us?"

I pushed my sandwich plate away. Yeah, definitely done. "Like I have a choice," I answered bitterly.

Alaric laughed as he spun down off of his stool in one liquid motion. "I suppose not."

I suddenly felt the tears welling up again. I didn't know why they chose to hit just then, a delayed reaction I guess. I looked down at my uneaten sandwich and cried, because I didn't know what else to do.

CHAPTER THREE

*A*laric had waited while I cried. He didn't try to comfort me, and I was grateful. It would have been just a little too strange having one of my captors showing that type of compassion.

My tears had left me numb and thoroughly without an appetite. I left the sandwich on the counter so Alaric could walk me back to my room. He reached my door first and held it open for me, the picture of a perfect gentleman. *Yeah right.* I turned and looked at him once I was inside, wondering if he was going to leave me alone in the room. He didn't.

"I'm tired," I said, hoping to appeal to his sense of mercy.

"I know you've been through a lot-" he began.

"That's a vast understatement," I interrupted.

"And I know you probably don't have warm, fuzzy feelings toward any of us right now," he went on.

"Keep going," I sighed weakly, feeling unsteady on my feet. "You're on a roll."

He laughed. "Your ability to be sarcastic under the direst of circumstances is quite impressive."

"Would you rather I screamed and begged for my life?" I questioned.

"It might be interesting," he replied. "Though your life is in no danger."

I left him and walked further into the room to sit on the foot of the ornate bed, smoothing the thick comforter with my hands. "You don't have to die in order to lose your life," I said quietly.

He raised an eyebrow as he left the doorway and slunk toward me. "And your life was so great before?"

I glared at him. "It was nothing special, but at least I had a choice in what I did."

"And you chose to shut yourself up in your little house," he said softly. "No, I don't think we took you away from very much at all."

"How long were you people watching me?" I hissed. "I'm beginning to think that this wasn't just some random kidnapping."

"You *know* this wasn't a random kidnapping, Madeline," he replied. "Just as deep down, you know what you are."

"My name is Madeline Ville, and I'm a human being," I answered sarcastically.

Alaric kneeled in front of me, putting us at eye level. It was an oddly intimate position, but he hadn't left me room to stand, so it was either scoot back onto the bed and give him room to follow, or stay where I was. I stayed.

"Sophie told me what happened with your foster family," he admitted. "I helped cover the incident up. It must have been difficult for you to deal with at such a young age."

I shook my head in disbelief. "That's not possible. That's —" I paused, not sure what to say.

The last family I'd been placed with had been a couple in their late thirties, Ray and Nadine. They both suffered from alcohol issues, and used the foster system as an easy paycheck. It hadn't been terrible, not compared to some of the other places I'd been.

I was seventeen at the time, and they let me do what I wanted as long as I didn't rat them out for not being real parents. I was content to stay there until I was eighteen and finished with high school.

It was all fine, until one night they came home completely hammered. Nadine passed out, and Ray turned his *attentions* to me. I tried to fend him off, and things got violent. He ended up falling on the corner of the kitchen table, neck first. It sliced him open, then he hit the ground. There was a lot of blood and I panicked. I could admit to myself that I didn't care about his well being, but I knew if anything serious happened I'd be blamed for it. Plus, I could *feel* his neck wound on my own neck. It wasn't as bad as some of the other pain I'd felt, but it was still unpleasant. I'd put my hands on his neck and tried to stop the blood flow. His eyes turned up to me, frozen in terror, then suddenly, he was dead.

I had thought his death was caused by blood-loss at the time, and had dismissed the strange rush of energy I felt when he passed as adrenaline. Then Matthew died, and I had to admit that neither death had been normal. They were both *my* fault.

The night Ray died I'd called the police, and ended up in Sophie's office as the sun began to rise the next morning. I'd frantically pleaded with her to not let the cops take me, that it had all been an accident. She'd told me not to worry, that it was all taken care of. There would be no questions. I would simply wait for my eighteenth birthday in a women's shelter, rather than with another foster family.

"The police saw him," I said out loud, returning to the

present. "There was no way it could be covered up. I should have at least been questioned."

"You don't need to worry about that anymore," Alaric assured.

I curled my legs up underneath me and huddled in on myself. "What really happened?" I asked in a strained voice. I didn't want to believe any of this was real, but if there was even the slightest chance I could learn the truth . . . "Why did Ray die? I've been over that memory so many times. He hadn't lost enough blood. He was conscious and cursing at me as I tried to stop the blood flow."

Alaric placed his hand on my shoulder. "It is your gift, Madeline."

I pulled away, shaking my head over and over. "I don't understand."

He stayed kneeling in front of me, but didn't try to touch me again. "You have the power to release the lives of those who are suffering."

"I don't believe you," I said petulantly, though part of me did.

I'd stayed up far too many nights wondering what had happened with Ray and Matthew to not have considered that there was something different about me.

Alaric sighed. "You'll see in time."

"And what do you have to do with any of this?" I asked suddenly. "I still don't understand why I'm here."

"You'll understand soon enough," he explained seriously. "I promise I'll do what I can to help."

I laughed, but it turned into more of a hiccup because of my tears. "You know, I preferred you when you were flirtatious," I said, suddenly embarrassed by my breakdown.

He wiggled his eyebrows at me. "As my lady commands."

I smiled, then quickly wiped it away. A girl shouldn't

smile at her kidnapper, even when he was trying to cheer her up.

"I'm tired," I said again.

He nodded. "I wouldn't go wandering," he advised. "Many things less pleasant than my sister wander these halls."

With that ominous advice ringing in the air, he stood and left the room, shutting the door gently behind him. I leaned down and took off the high-heeled boots. Apparently I'd just been dressed up to meet with Estus. He was their leader, in some way, so I supposed he merited proper attire.

I paced around the room, feeling sick and dizzy, and none too happy to be left with only the form-fitting dress to wear. There were a few dressers in the room that matched the bed, and as a last ditch effort I started going through them. Many of the drawers were empty, but eventually I came to two drawers filled with clothes. I found some silky red pajama pants with a matching shirt, but passed them over. I didn't actually want to go to sleep. I *couldn't* go to sleep. I had to find a way out.

I searched through the clothes a little bit more and came out with a pair of black jeans and an indigo blue tee-shirt. The jeans fit me like a glove. My imprisonment had obviously been well-planned. Gre-at.

I dressed quickly, nervous that someone would come calling while I was naked. I felt slightly better in normal clothing, more like myself. There was even a pair of black running shoes underneath the dresser. It was as if they actually *wanted* me to run. I was happy to oblige.

When I could find nothing else of use in the room, I sat on the bed to wait. Hopefully everyone would go to sleep and I could search for an exit unhindered. I wasn't sure how anyone could even tell that it was night-time without windows, but I felt tired enough for it to be night. That meant that it had already been a full day since I'd been taken.

I tried to just wait on the bed, but I was too nervous to sit still. Instead, I began examining the room, even though there wasn't much to it. Wood had been added to the fire before I was re-delivered to the space. The flames crackled happily as they gave off their warmth, contrasting drastically with my mood.

I stood by the fire for a while, because it beat sitting on the bed. Eventually I went through the dressers again, even though I knew I'd find the same things, and looked underneath the bed as well. There was nothing under the bed, not even dust bunnies.

Finally I'd had enough, and went for the door. I reached for the knob and hesitated, then placed my ear against the door to listen. I couldn't hear anything on the other side, but the wood of the door was so thick that it didn't mean much. I took a deep breath and grabbed the knob, opening the door before I could think better of it. I let out my breath when it was revealed that no one was waiting on the other side.

With a steadying hand against the wall, I tip-toed out into the hallway, almost wishing I would have gone with bare feet rather than running shoes. I crept down the hall, cringing at the little tip-taps of my steps on the stone.

The lighting in the halls was more dim than it had been earlier, but still enough to see by, luckily. Not sure where to go, I finally decided to go back down the hallway where I'd had my encounter with James. I did *not* want another meeting with him, but it seemed the most likely place for an exit. From what I'd seen of the opposite direction, the other halls led deeper into the compound.

I glanced over my shoulder every few seconds, wanting to run, but afraid of the noise my feet would make. I was mid-step when I heard a low-throated growl that raised the hairs on my arms. I turned around in what felt like slow motion to see a dog the size of a grizzly bear creeping up behind me. It must have come out of one of the rooms, else I would have noticed it approaching.

I stood perfectly still as the beast took a slow step toward me, scraping its long nails across the stone floor. I swallowed the lump in my suddenly dry throat. Maybe it wasn't a dog. It had a face similar to that of a Rottweiler, but with an elongated snout. Something about its stance was wrong as well. I took a slow step back, realizing its neck was far too long, and what I could see of its tail was too thick. It had the body of a bear, the head of a dog, and the neck and stance of a giant lizard. Dark brown fur flowed over its face and body, blending the aspects of the different animals seamlessly.

The thing cocked back its head and sniffed the air, then let out another low growl. It shifted from paw to paw, preparing to pounce. Knowing that I would have no chance if it jumped on me, I turned and ran.

I was no longer concerned about my footfalls as I rounded a corner in the hallway, my heart thudding in my chest. I grabbed the knob of the first door that I saw, praying to whatever I should be praying to that it wasn't locked.

The door came open and I practically fell inside. I felt the air shift behind me as the creature went barreling by. I slammed the door shut and slid the deadbolt into place, not waiting to see if the creature came back. I was suddenly very glad that all of the doors in the place seemed to be made of heavy, sturdy wood, though it was a little strange to have a deadbolt on an interior door.

I turned to look at the room I was now trapped in as I tried to regain my breath. The room was made of stone, of course, but something dark stained the walls and floor. I couldn't tell what the substance was, as the room barely had enough light to see by, but I could tell it had been a thin liquid, spattering the walls lightly, then pooling in large puddles on the floor. I waited by the door for a moment, listening for the return of the creature, but heard nothing.

My shoulders relaxing, I walked toward the nearest wall and touched the stains, smoothing my fingertips across the stone. My fingers came away with something thick and sticky. Older, dry stains were spread underneath the more recent ones, flowing in patterns like water. I stepped away from the wall, rubbing my fingers on my jeans as I went. I still hadn't heard a peep from the other side of the door. The creature wasn't trying to come in after me.

My sneakered feet stuck to the floor as I explored the dimly-lit room a little further. Large cages with thick steel bars came into view as I approached the far wall. The refuse inside of the cages hinted to the fact that they had once been occupied, but they were all empty now. I wondered if the cages were for other beasts like the one I'd seen. The room stank of rot and a strange burnt smell.

A scratching at the door caught my attention. My heart leapt into my throat at the thought that the creature had realized where I was, but then I noticed that the scratching was coming from somewhere beside the door, not outside of it.

I crept toward the sound, barely able to hear the scratching over the thudding of my heart. There was something small moving around where the floor met the wall, but there wasn't enough light to quite make out what it was.

I crouched down and reached out a hand to try and coax the thing into the dim light. It worked. Too fast to follow, the thing lunged for me. It was only the size of a very large rat, but it flew into my chest with such force that it knocked me to the ground.

The moist stickiness of the floor seeped into my clothing. I half sat up, frantically trying to grab at the thing that was now scratching its way up my torso. I wrapped my hands around it, but the creature was wet and slippery. It slipped right through my fingers and went for my throat, pinning me back to the ground. It wrapped tightly around my neck.

My breath wheezed in and out shallowly as I pried at the thing's fingers. Fingers? It felt like a hand around my throat. Flashes of fear and rage pulsed in my mind, just like the other emotions I could sense from people. I saw blurry scenes that I knew had nothing to do with my own memories, they were somehow coming from the creature. The scenes faded as my vision began to go black from lack of oxygen. I forced away my panic, focusing on removing the thing at my throat. I felt a small rush of energy and the thing suddenly went limp. I threw it off me and pushed myself backwards across the floor.

My vision came back in stages as I caught my breath. I could see the dark shape of the thing a few feet away, but it didn't move. I got to my feet and ran forward as steadily as I could manage in my panicked state, then stomped the creature with my heel as soon as I reached it. I jumped on it until I heard bones crunch. Sure that it was now dead, I leaned down to examine it again. It *was* a hand.

The hand was now bruised and misshapen from my stomping, but that wasn't the worst of its injuries. Right above the wrist bone, the hand had been severed from its owner. Bone gleamed in the dim light as blood continued to gush forth. There shouldn't have been that much blood in just a hand, but the thing was covered in it. That was why it had been so difficult to keep a hold of.

Yet, none of those things had been what killed it. I had killed it, just like I did Matthew. I knew it with a sickening surety. I had felt the same rush of energy when Matthew died. I had somehow stolen whatever life force had animated it.

I pushed myself away from the hand, just before I lost what little dinner I'd eaten. My vomit and tears fell to commingle with the substance on the floor that I now realized was blood. The whole room was covered in congealed blood.

I quickly got to my feet and tried to wipe my hands off on my jeans, but the blood was too sticky and I couldn't get it all off. I stumbled back toward the door, ready to take my chances with the creature in the hall if it meant I could just get out of that room. How had the hand even moved to begin with?

I glanced back at the hand in question, half-expecting it to have disappeared, but it was still just lying there. My own hands were shaking so badly that it took me several tries to undo the lock. When I finally managed to open the door, I had to jump back because someone was in the doorway. I ended up slipping and falling hard on my tailbone.

Alaric's hair fell forward over his shoulders as he looked down at me. "I thought you might try to run again. I figured I'd make sure you didn't get eaten."

"Great job," I replied shakily, on the verge of hysteria.

He crouched down and picked me up effortlessly into the cradle of his arms. He stood and carried me out of the room of horrors without a word, and I let him.

"You need another bath," he commented once we were walking down the hall.

"W-what was that room?" I stammered. I wrapped my arms around his neck to feel more secure. In that moment, I didn't care that he was one of my captors as long as he got me the hell away from that room. "There was a hand," I added.

He chuckled. "Sometimes parts get left behind. They can be a little cross about what happened to their bodies."

For a moment I thought I might vomit again, but I managed to hold it in. "And what happened to their bodies?" I asked weakly.

"Did Estus tell you why you were brought back to us?" he asked rather than answering my question.

"He said you needed a new executioner," I answered breathlessly, as if it were a normal thing to say.

Alaric stopped to hoist me up and get a more firm grip around me. "You just met the hand of our last executioner."

"You killed him!" I exclaimed, trying to wriggle out of his grip.

"Not me personally," he replied holding on and not letting me drop. "Though I would have. He was a traitor."

The struggling was getting me nowhere, so I stopped. "What did he do?"

Alaric looked down at me with a cold expression. "He was a traitor, and we cannot afford traitors in times like these."

"Times like these?" I prompted.

"My dear executioner," he replied. "We are at war."

My next question froze on my tongue as I considered the complexities of what he was saying. Who would want to go to war with people that dismembered their victims, and let enormous, furry lizard beasts run loose in their halls? More Vaettir? Were there other places like the one we were in, with more crazy freaks populating them? I began to feel dizzy again.

"What was that creature?" I asked suddenly, remembering why I'd run into the bloody room to begin with. "It was like a dog, but not a dog. Kind of like a lizard."

"Ah," Alaric observed, "you must mean Stella. She's James' . . . pet. A lindworm, one of the few left."

Alaric let me down to my feet as we walked into the bathroom. He gave me a scrutinizing look. "I assume you can get back to your room from here?"

I looked at him as he prepared to leave me while visions of lizard dogs and bloody hands danced in my head. "Please stay," I said before I could think it through.

He looked surprised, then smiled. "You mean, *stay?*" he drew out the word as if it meant more than just staying.

My eyes widened. "Oh no," I corrected. "It's just. What if there are more body parts wandering around?"

"You handled that hand all on your own—" he began.

"Please," I interrupted.

He shrugged and entered the bathroom fully so he could shut the door behind him, then went to sit on the closed toilet seat.

"You have blood on your clothes," I observed, suddenly feeling uncomfortable.

He raised an eyebrow at me. "You have much more on yours."

I looked down. He was right. The sticky, congealed blood had soaked into the back of my jeans, and there were smears of it all over my shirt.

I knew I should ask him to leave, but I could feel bruises forming on my throat from the hand. I'd nearly died in there. "Close your eyes please," I said, making up my mind. I was more than ready to get out of the soiled clothing.

"And what if I said no?" he asked with his eyes still wide open.

"Then I would take my chances with the severed body parts," I answered bluntly, refusing to show him just how rattled I was.

He laughed at me, but still obeyed and closed his eyes. I peeled the soiled clothing off and hopped quickly into the tub. Instead of just filling it right away, I ran the water and splashed off any of the blood that was on my skin so I wouldn't have to soak in it. The pinkish water running toward the drain would have almost been pretty if I didn't know that it was from a man who had been brutally murdered. When I was clean enough, I plugged the drain to trap the hot water.

I glanced at Alaric, his eyes still closed. Really, the tub was tall enough to hide anything I'd want hidden unless he stood up and looked down, but I still felt uncomfortable.

"Can I open them yet?" he asked in a tone that implied that I was being very silly.

"Yes," I answered. "But keep your gaze forward please." If modesty was silly, then baby, call me the queen of slap-stick.

"You know it would be much more efficient if I could just hop in there with you," he joked. "At this rate I'll never get to bed."

"I'll be out soon enough," I grumbled.

The water had filled enough for me to start scrubbing myself with the vanilla soap. As I washed I realized I had blood in my hair too. I scootched forward enough to lean back and dunk my hair into the water. When I came back up, the water was pink. I quickly turned off the faucet and unplugged the drain.

"I was only kidding," he said.

"I need to refill the water," I explained, turning to look at him. "Hey, avert your eyes!"

He looked away with a laugh. "Why do you need to refill the water?" he asked, obviously trying to distract me.

"There was blood in it," I answered.

He laughed again. "It will be interesting to see how you adapt among the Vaettir."

"Why?" I asked. "Do you enjoy bathing in the blood of thine enemies?"

"Something like that," he answered soberly.

"You can't keep me here forever," I added.

He turned to look at me, but he seemed so serious that I just hunched down to cover my breasts rather than telling him to look away.

"It would have happened again," he said cryptically. "The taking of life is your gift."

"The taking of life is not a gift," I snapped, once again thinking of Matthew.

"Not always," he replied, finally averting his eyes. "Nor is it always a curse."

I shook my head. It *was* a curse. There was no way around it. I plugged the drain and renewed the water flow, then slipped down into the tub, fully prepared to sulk. *It would have happened again*, he'd said. I couldn't bear what had happened with Matthew happening with someone else.

"Tell me about this war," I said, needing to change the subject.

He sighed. "We are just one clan of many. We fight for power, land, age-old vendettas . . . " he trailed off. "Aislin, the Doyen of a clan predominantly residing in Scandinavia, and Estus have been at war for years. As far as I can tell, they're both searching for something."

I turned my shocked expression toward him, but he was still looking away. "You mean you're fighting a war without knowing what you're actually fighting for?"

He smirked at me, then quickly turned away. "You believe the wars of humans to be any different? I am simply trying to live my life in relative safety. I do as my Doyen bades, because that is the way it has always been."

I washed my hair and scrubbed my skin nearly raw in silence. These people were absolutely nuts.

"You have lovely skin," he commented, pulling me out of my thoughts. "You should probably try not to scrub it all off."

"Stop looking!" I exclaimed as I sunk down into the tub to ensure everything was covered.

"I can't protect you from severed hands if I can't *see* you," he argued, laughter in his voice.

I smiled in spite of myself. He was being a lech, but he was also trying to cheer me up again. I had to appreciate the latter, at least a little.

"If you died," I began, then cringed when I realized how inappropriate the statement sounded.

Alaric turned wide eyes to me. "Do you have plans that I'm not aware of?"

I glared and removed one of my hands from my chest to gesture for him to look away. "If you died," I began again, "would you reanimate just like that hand?"

Alaric kept his eyes firmly forward, for once. "As would you."

I gasped. I hadn't thought about *that*. Part of me believed that Alaric actually would reanimate. I could no longer argue with all of the evidence laid before me, especially when one of the pieces of evidence had just tried to kill me. Yes, I mostly believed that Alaric and the others weren't exactly human, but me? I still couldn't wrap my mind around *that*.

"What if I had died last week? Would my corpse have walked right out of the morgue?"

Alaric laughed. "We had more than one reason for keeping an eye on you. If you had died, your body would have been brought here."

I somehow didn't find that comforting. "What if I had died in a plane crash, and my body ended up at the bottom of the ocean. What then?"

Alaric glanced at me in surprise, then looked away quickly. "Then I suppose we'd hear of sightings of zombie mermaids in the news."

He'd meant it as a joke, but the idea of my corpse walking around after I was dead gave me goosebumps. I shook my head, then dunked my hair in the water again, trying to get warm. I stayed that way for a while, but couldn't seem to wash away the cold, because it wasn't *that* kind of cold.

When I was finished, Alaric handed me two towels, one for my hair and one for my body. It was oddly considerate. Then again, with the length of his hair he probably had to use two towels too.

He turned his back so I could step out of the tub and dry off. It only dawned on me as I finished drying myself that I didn't have any clean clothes to change into. At a loss, I wrapped the towel I'd used on my body tightly around me, then tapped Alaric on the shoulder.

Now, when someone turns around to see you, you usually expect them to take a step back to make room. Alaric turned around without the step back, and was suddenly very close to me. His pants brushed against the bottom edge of my towel, moving the fabric ever so slightly. Luckily the smaller amount of blood he'd gotten on him was already dry and didn't transfer to the clean towel.

I slowly moved my eyes upward, feeling nervous and perhaps a little bit of something else. Alaric looked down at me with a knowing smile, eliciting goosebumps up and down my arms once again. I eyed him warily, feeling small and vulnerable, but he didn't move out of my way.

"If my gift is death, like you say," I began carefully, "then shouldn't you be afraid of me?"

"You would bring a swift death to a human," he replied. "But I would only fear you if I were severely weakened." He smoothed a hand down my bare arm.

"You're really going to kidnap me, then hit on me?" I asked, pulling away from his touch.

He smiled, not in the least bit offended. "I am simply letting you know your options. The choice remains yours."

"So I have the choice of whether or not I sleep with you, but not the choice of leaving this place?" I asked, now with a hint of anger in my tone.

Alaric raised his hands in an *I give up* gesture. "That second choice is not mine to give. I would not offer you a lie."

A subtle throbbing was beginning to grow between my eyes. I pinched the bridge of my nose to ease the pain.

"I'm very tired," I said, hoping to end the conversation.

This time when I was left in my room, I really would sleep. I felt unsteady on my feet just standing there. Alaric nodded and led me out of the bathroom and back down the hallway toward the room I'd been given.

He stayed in the doorway of my bedroom, forcing me to squeeze by him in order to go inside. I half-expected him to follow me in, but he remained in the threshold. After a moment he stepped back to close the door for me, though he left it open long enough for him to peek his head back inside and leave a standing offer for him to be my "snuggle buddy".

I refused his offer. I needed a snuggle buddy like I needed hepatitis.

CHAPTER FOUR

I fell asleep almost instantly, and if I dreamed, I didn't remember. I woke up confused as to where I was, until the memories of the previous day came flooding back.

Had all of that occurred in just one day? I thought about my little house, and the fact that no one would have yet noticed that I was missing from it. No one knew that I hadn't spent the last two nights safely tucked into my bed.

I was still sitting in bed dazed and confused when Sophie flung the door open without a knock. She glared down at me still snuggled in bed, annoyance clear on her face.

"Get dressed," she ordered. "Breakfast first, then you have a job to do."

The *job* they had brought me here for was the position of executioner. Did they want me to kill someone?

"I, um, I don't feel well," I stammered. "I should probably just stay in bed today." I had to get the hell out of this place.

Ignoring me, Sophie walked to the nearby dresser and started pawing through the drawers.

I watched her in apprehension, dressed in flannel pajamas I'd found underneath the red silky ones.

Straightening her back, she threw a pair of blue jeans and an olive colored tank top at me. Next came a clean bra, underwear, and a pair of socks that nearly hit me in the head. Once she was finished flinging fabric, she stood at the foot of my bed with her arms crossed.

"Well?" she prompted.

I rolled out of bed and got dressed quickly, not wanting her to throw something more substantial than socks at me.

When I was finished she looked me up and down, then said, "You know where the bathroom is. You'll find a toothbrush and whatever else you might need. I'll be waiting in the kitchen."

With that, she was gone, leaving me to fret over just what the "job" might be by myself. I peeked out into the hall to verify that the coast was clear, then hurried into the bathroom where I promptly locked the door behind me.

I debated my options. Escaping at night hadn't worked out too well for me, nor had running blind with no idea where I was going. I'd be better off going along with things until I could figure out where the exit was.

My decision made, I scanned the expansive countertop until my eyes landed on the basket where Sophie had retrieved the soap the night before. In it was a toothbrush still in its packaging, a brand new tube of toothpaste, lotion, and deodorant. I was in a B&B from hell.

I brushed my teeth and put on deodorant, then stared in the mirror. Deep bags had formed under my eyes, marring my skin. I felt vaguely unreal, like I wasn't truly there. I didn't want to leave the bathroom, to face Sophie and the others, but eventually I had to admit to myself that I couldn't just stay in there forever. I needed to plan my escape.

I sighed, knowing I needed to be honest with myself. I was grudgingly beginning to not just think about escape, but of learning everything these people might know about me. The Vaettir had verified what I had always somehow known about Matthew. That experience had kept me chaste and alone for fear of it ever happening with someone else. Maybe there was some way to control when it happened. If I could control it, I would be free to live an actual life. That was, of course, if I could not only learn control, but then escape my captors in one piece. The latter was seeming less and less likely.

Finally, I took a deep breath and went out into the hall, heading straight for the kitchen, memorizing every turn in the hall, and every shut doorway. Did more of the Vaettir live behind the doors? Or were there just more bloody rooms with dismembered body parts . . .

I picked up my pace, soon entering the kitchen. Sophie was waiting as promised, but so were Alaric and James. Sophie and Alaric were both dressed in all black again. It would have almost been cliché if it didn't look so good on their tall frames. They were also both sipping on coffee, while James had tea. I couldn't tell what kind it was, but the little green leaflet hanging from the string hinted at herbal tea first thing in the morning. I liked him less and less.

I moved to stand by Sophie, who handed me a mug of already poured coffee. The division between the coffee drinkers and the non was highly apparent.

I eyed James nervously and he eyed me right back, sipping his tea with a secretive smile. The smile made me more uncomfortable than a thousand angry glares ever could. His golden hair was still damp enough from his shower to leave small dark stains around the collar of his charcoal gray shirt.

The dark color of the shirt made the icy color of his eyes even more pronounced.

I suddenly felt nervous enough to throw up, and had to take a sip of coffee to keep it down. As the liquid was sliding down my throat I considered the possibility it was drugged since I hadn't seen it being poured. I choked on it, lowering the mug as hot coffee sloshed over my fingers.

James smiled a little wider.

A woman I hadn't met yet came walking into the kitchen. She was shorter than me, around 5'4", and had dark hair cropped closely to her head. She turned large, honey colored eyes to me, gave me a look of dismissal, then turned her eyes to James.

"Estus wants her now," she announced, as if I was no longer even there.

James winked at me. "Looks like breakfast will have to wait."

I simply stared at him in response. I wouldn't have been able to keep any food down regardless. I looked to Sophie to lead the way, but she only shrugged apologetically at me and nodded toward James.

When I still didn't move, James took hold of my arm and pulled me forward. I managed to set the coffee mug back by the industrial-sized pots before more of it could spill, though I was still craving more of it despite my fears.

Alaric watched us quietly as I was pulled away, having not said a word since I'd arrived. He seemed somewhat . . . sad?

I turned away as I was pulled out into the hall. The nameless, short-haired woman went ahead of James and I, then disappeared around the next turn. I looked over my shoulder for one final glance at Alaric and Sophie, but they had turned to speak quietly to each other, and didn't see me.

Turning forward, I tugged my arm out of James' grip and

continued walking on my own. He gestured each time we were to turn down a new hall, and I went along willingly, wanting to avoid being hoisted over his shoulder again. Judging by the path we took, I began to suspect that we were going to the room where I'd been attacked by the hand. Call it intuition, but I had a feeling that was a room James frequented. My feeling of dread increased as we approached the door, but we ended up going past it and into the room immediately after it.

This new room was cleaner than the one I'd visited, but just barely. This room also had a full man, and not just a hand. The man hung limply from a set of manacles hammered into the wall. His chest was bare except for a decoration of deep cuts and bruises across his tanned skin. Blood had soaked into his blue jeans, staining the fabric.

I glanced to the side and jumped, realizing the short-haired woman was standing against the wall, just inside the door.

I turned my shocked gaze back to the manacled man as he looked up from under sweat-matted hair. At first the look was distant as if he didn't truly *see* us, then his eyes focused on me.

"No," he breathed, his gaze filled with horror. He struggled against his manacles, clanking the chains against the stone wall. As his head thrashed back and forth, I realized he was missing an ear. All that was left in its place was a bloody hole.

"No," he pleaded more firmly, his gaze now aimed toward the other side of the room. "Please. I told you I had no choice."

It was only then that I noticed Estus standing in the corner, looking dispassionately at the man. He was still in the loose, blue outfit he'd worn during our meeting. The clothing made him look like some sort of monk, but the tortured man begging him for his life kind of ruined the picture.

I began backing out of the room, but James grabbed my arm and held it, tight enough to bruise. The short-haired woman stood silently on my other side. She didn't speak, but it was obvious by her expression that she wasn't enjoying the show any more than I was.

"Please," the man pleaded, looking at me now. "Please don't do this."

I looked away from the fear in the man's eyes. The fact that I was the source of that fear, and not the people who had tortured him, hurt my heart, even though I couldn't quite understand it. I could feel what had been done to him just as I could often feel the wounds of others, and I could taste his fear like cloying perfume on the back of my tongue.

James dragged me forward, and the fear and pain increased. By the time I stood directly in front of the man, his emotions were almost unbearable. In addition to his fear, I felt sadness and loss. He loved someone, and now knew that he would never see her again. I closed my eyes and shook my head over and over, trying to diffuse the emotions before they overcame me.

"What is she doing?" the short-haired woman asked. "Why isn't she finishing this?"

"It will come with time," Estus explained. "Her nature will take over. This is what she was born for."

I heard someone saying, "No, no, no," over and over again, and realized that it was me. His pain was too much. Something within me ached to release it, just like I'd done with Matthew. I *wanted* to reach out to him.

The man sobbed, and I could feel his defeat.

I forced my eyes open, the rest of my body frozen in fear.

"Just do it!" the man broke down and shouted, flinging spittle in my face.

His pain was palpable. I thought that if I could reach out and touch it, I could ease that pain. I *wanted* to reach out and touch it. It pulsed in front of me. I had taken several steps toward him without even realizing it. I began to reach out a hand. No. If I touched him, he would die.

James pushed me forward so that the man's face was only inches from mine. The man could have tried to kick me or head-butt me, but he didn't. I felt his bitterness. He had given up.

"Please," the man whispered right against my face. "Please just let it be over before my body gives out. I know I'm not getting out of here alive, and I don't want to be stuck in a corpse like all the others."

"Stuck in a corpse?" I questioned distantly.

"If we kill him and you do not release him," Estus said from across the room. "A part of his spirit will remain in his body, forever."

It was just like what Sophie had said, but the gravity of it only hit me just then. His body wouldn't just be animated like a zombie. Part of his soul would be trapped for eternity. What would happen to the rest of his soul if it was missing a part? I felt sick. I wasn't even sure if I believed in souls.

I met the tortured man's pained gaze. His eyes were a light brown with flecks of green in them. He obviously believed what Estus said. His eyes pleaded with me to act.

I reached a trembling hand toward him, cradling his face. I knew what to do even though it had never been taught to me. Images flashed through my mind of a woman, and I almost pulled away. I felt his love for her, and his sorrow in knowing he would never see her again. I did my best to take that sorrow away. I held the man's gaze as the light faded from his eyes. His energy soaked into me in a warm rush as it left him.

"Thank you," he whispered with his last breath.

I lowered my hand, then turned back to the room, awestricken. I noticed a figure in the doorway. Alaric stood framed in the light of the brighter hallway, watching me calmly.

He offered me a solemn smile and said, "Not always a gift, but not always a curse either."

I wanted to run out of the room, but seemed incapable of moving my feet. I had just killed a man, and didn't even know what his crime had been. I had felt his emotions to the very end.

"What did he do?" I asked to no one in particular.

"He fought for the wrong side," Estus answered apathetically.

I glared at him, anger bubbling up inside of me. I felt giddy with the man's residual energy, and I could still taste his bitterness on the back of my tongue. It spurred my rage on. His memories clung to me, chastising me for what I'd done, even though he'd asked me to do it.

I walked toward Estus, pointing an accusatory finger. "You took him away from someone who loved him!" The dead man's loss felt like my own. I thought of the woman who'd survived him, and how I'd felt when Matthew died. "What did *she* do to deserve this?"

Estus held his ground and stared back at me, daring me to act.

"How could you possibly know that?" James asked from behind me.

I spun on him. "I felt it!" I cried. "I *saw* her. She was the last thing he thought of. His greatest concern was the idea of never seeing her again."

"Interesting," Estus commented. "An empath and an executioner. I do not envy you, my child."

I turned back to the old man. I said very slowly, emphasizing each word, "I *will not* be doing *that* again."

"This is war, Madeline," he replied. "We all do what we must."

"What war?" I spat gesturing back to the corpse on the wall. "I don't see any battles happening! All I see is torture."

Tears were running steadily down my face, and I couldn't seem to stop them. The man's last emotion was just too much for me to digest. The images of the one he loved were already fading from my mind, but the emotion was as fresh as ever.

"Not all war is battle and bloodshed," Estus replied, finally letting a hint of his own emotion show through. "And I will not let my people be slaughtered because of one squeamish executioner."

"What do I even have to do with it!" I shouted. "I'm not part of this!" I knew I was bordering on hysteria, but I just couldn't stop myself.

Estus walked forward. "Without an executioner," he said very carefully. "We do not truly die. Would you leave us all to that fate?"

"This can't be my responsibility alone," I sobbed. "There must be another way."

Estus sneered, making me wonder if the kindly old man act had ever even existed. "We could have chopped that man up and put him in ten different boxes, and still some part of him would have lived. He would no longer have thought or spoken, but the life force would have remained."

A horrifying realization dawned on me. "Is that what you did to the last executioner?" I asked. "Is the rest of him still alive in a box somewhere."

"It is a fate befitting his crimes," James said from beside

me. I hadn't noticed how close he was standing to me until just then.

I took a step away from him. "Take me to him," I demanded.

Estus smiled. "So, you would kill another?"

"You owe me for *this*," I gestured wildly to the dead man. "Now take me to him."

Estus simply nodded and walked toward the door. I followed him, but everyone else stayed put. Alaric stepped out of the doorway as we walked by to give us space. I followed Estus out into the hall, then into the room where I'd found the hand.

"I see you have already met with part of him," Estus commented as he kicked the dead hand aside.

He walked to the wall with the cages and felt across the stones. A brush of his fingertips revealed a handle I hadn't seen before. Estus gripped the handle and pulled, causing the stone to come out of the wall like a drawer.

I didn't want to look into the drawer. I knew it would be something horrific and bloody, but I also knew that the life, or soul, or whatever you wanted to call it, was still trapped inside this man's dismembered corpse. It wasn't right.

Estus stepped away from the drawer to make room for me. Before I could think better of it, I walked forward, avoiding blood puddles as I went, and looked down into the box. Inside was a human heart. It didn't beat, yet blood seeped steadily out of the severed ventricles. The box wasn't sealed at the edges, and the blood dripped through the cracks onto the floor. I felt rage and betrayal radiating from the heart, and somehow knew that it could sense my presence.

"The heart is the key," Estus informed me. "Release the heart and the soul is free."

Not thinking about what I was doing, I reached down and

stroked a finger across the heart. I should have been horrified, but I was more intrigued by the heart than anything else. The muscle that composed the thing felt thick and alive. I willed the life out of the heart, but nothing happened.

"It's not working," I whispered to myself.

"Do what you did in the other room," Estus advised as if I'd been talking to him. "Do not will the life away. Take its pain."

Feeling like I was in a trance, I reached out again and felt the soul's hatred and pain. Yet the emotion that outweighed everything was betrayal. If this man was a traitor, it was not by choice. He was killed by the ones he considered kin. I took a shaky breath. This time, instead of willing the life away, I focused on taking the heart's pain, and taking away the feeling of betrayal.

The heart gave a final shudder, then collapsed in on itself. More blood leaked out as the heart deflated and then was still.

Estus shut the drawer and dismissed me with a wave of his hand like he was tired. After a mostly sleepless night and no food, I should have been exhausted, yet I was filled with energy. Electric currents ran through me to collect in my fingertips, which felt heavy like they were filled with too much blood.

I left the macabre room to find Alaric waiting for me in the hall. He looked at my expression carefully, attempting to judge my mood.

I did my best not to cry, but something must have shown in my face, because he wrapped me tightly in his arms. I didn't know him well enough to receive that sort of comfort from him, but I didn't know where else I was going to get it, so I returned the hug. A sob racked my entire body, releasing some of the emotions I'd absorbed from the dead man and the executioner's heart. I clenched my eyes shut, and did my best to slow my breathing. We stayed that way until I had gathered myself, then Alaric gave me a final squeeze and pulled away.

"Let's get you some breakfast," he said softly.

I shook my head. "I don't think I could eat. I feel . . . strange."

Alaric placed his hand gently at the base of my spine and guided me forward. "Let us at least distance ourselves from these rooms."

I could tell by the tone of his voice that he was just as appalled by the torture rooms as I was. I felt oddly relieved at the sentiment.

We had only traveled a few steps when a screeching roar sounded in the hallway, grabbing both mine and Alaric's attention. I turned wide eyes up to him for an explanation.

"Get back to your room and lock the door," he ordered.

"Wha—" I began to ask, but he had already left me to run down the hall.

Estus, James, and the short-haired woman all ran by before I could even move. They all disappeared around the next bend, and suddenly I was alone.

I glanced around. It was the perfect opportunity to search for an exit, yet something kept my feet glued in place. I was horrified by what had happened to the man in the torture room, but I was even more horrified by my part in it. I had killed him, and part of me, just a tiny *dark* part, had liked it. Could I really return to the normal world without learning more about my terrifying *gift*? Without learning how to stop it?

I stood frozen in the hallway until I heard the sounds of distant fighting as the others reached whatever the original sound had been. My mind snapping into the present, I started to run in the opposite direction that they had gone, but stopped beside the room where I'd taken the life of the first man.

His body was still hanging against the wall, limp and lifeless. How could I return to my safe little house, when I could accidentally take someone's life with a touch, just like I'd done to the poor man hanging on the wall?

I wrapped my arms tightly around my stomach, feeling ill. The people down here were monsters, but maybe, just maybe, I was a monster too.

CHAPTER FIVE

I stood outside the torture room, questioning my own sanity. These people had just made me kill a man. I couldn't stay, not even to gain knowledge of my curse. With the sound of fighting in the distance, I turned and ran the other direction. I had nearly reached the end of the hall when I heard a blood-curdling scream. Goosebumps erupted across my arms. My feet slowed. Somehow I knew the scream had come from Sophie. Even through the stone walls and space between us, I could sense her pain. Sophie, who had helped me through my childhood, and who I was pretty sure was *still* trying to help me. Well *shit*.

I turned and ran the other way. I kept going toward the sound of fighting, cursing my choice even as I made it. I had no idea how I might be able to help, but I couldn't just think about myself and ignore what was happening. I knew deep down that Sophie was a good person. When I'd been in foster care, she was someone I'd actually almost considered a friend. She'd made me feel safe in a world of chaos and pain.

I went around several bends in the hallway and came to the room that I thought of as the throne room, already slick with blood and littered with corpses. I skidded to a halt, then ducked out of view, clutching at my stomach as the pain in the room hit me. Leaning against the wall, I resisted the urge to vomit, instead taking deep breaths to distance myself from the violence. Mixed emotions sang through me—fear, pain, bloodlust . . . I shivered, forcing them to the back of my mind. I'd come to find Sophie.

Releasing my stomach, I gripped the wall and peered around the corner. The intruders, at least I guessed they were the intruders as I watched James slash a throat with a long knife, were dressed in ornate leather armor. The pieces of armor reminded me of insect carapaces, and didn't fit at all with the modern day attire everyone else wore.

The dog/lizard creature I'd encountered in the hall the previous night darted across the room to crash into one of the intruders, and suddenly the shrieking roar made sense. The creature must have been the one to find them. I assumed the intruders were other Vaettir, though everyone in the room appeared human.

I stared in utter shock, unable to move. I corrected my original thought that the attackers looked *human*. Only half of the violence was done with weapons. The other half was done with what I could only refer to as magic. A woman swiped her hand in front of a man's face, and his skin erupted with blood like he'd just been sliced by invisible claws. One of the male intruders pushed another man to the ground and climbed on top of him, pinning down his arms. The man struggled to free himself, but slowly his body iced over until he could no longer fight. I looked away from the frozen man as his icy pain shot through me. Corpses fell quickly, painting those who still fought with their blood.

Finally, my gaze fell upon someone lying in a heap in the far corner. *Sophie.* I couldn't tell if she was breathing. I leaned a little more into the hall, then realized my folly. One of the intruders quickly spotted me, then started in my direction. His movements reminded me of a snake as he wove through the chaos with his eyes focused solely on me. As he got closer, a long, serpent-like tongue flicked out of his thin lips. I froze in place as the man drew near. I glanced around for help while backing toward the hall, but everyone else was engaged in the fighting.

My mind screamed at me to run, yet fear held my limbs rigid. I could hardly even breathe. The intruder came to stand in front of me, but only remained there for a moment. In the blink of an eye a black shape barreled into him and sent him flying back into the thick of the fighting.

I didn't take the time to see who had saved me, and instead hurried to hide in one of the nearby rooms. I should have closed the door, locked it, and piled every piece of furniture in front of it, but I couldn't make myself do it. I still needed to reach Sophie.

I peeked back out into the fighting, which had suddenly all but halted as the last of the intruders were put down. The furry lizard tore into the stomach of one of the dead, splitting the armor like the delicate petals of a flower. The creature found the intruder's spinal cord and tore a chunk of it free. Its dog-like mouth munched happily, flinging dribbles of blood down its face.

I forced my gaze away and found Alaric, crouched over the now-dead snake-man. Blood and thicker bits ran down Alaric's face and onto his chest. As I watched, he spat a thick glob of flesh onto the ground. He'd bitten the man's throat out. Alaric looked over at me with eyes that had turned entirely feline, and I was horrified to see the teeth to match.

He turned away from me, assessing the dead and injured. James still lived, though his arm hung limply at his side, and

Estus seemed completely unharmed. Sophie was still lying in the corner.

I stepped out into the room, feeling almost as if I was floating. I didn't feel anything else, and wondered vaguely if I was going into shock again. Alaric cast one final glance at me with a face that had returned to normal, then hurried to his sister's side.

I started to step around a body, then made the mistake of looking down. It was the short-haired woman that had led James and I to the torture room, now lying completely still. The side of her head was a bloody mess, the skull damaged. Though she was dead, the pain of the blow hit me like an icepick, doubling me over.

Without a thought I reached down and smoothed a hand across her face, releasing her life force. I was instantly horrified that I'd done so without thinking. What if she could have been healed? If these people could maintain their lives when they were chopped up in little boxes, maybe her head would have healed.

I withdrew my trembling hand and straightened, then noticed Alaric seated against the wall, rocking his sister back and forth like a child. Her body hung limp and unresponsive in his arms.

James came to stand beside me, though his gaze was all for Alaric and Sophie. "You need to release the dead," he instructed. "Do it now."

"But what if they can heal?" I asked, unable to take my eyes off Alaric and Sophie.

"They will not heal," he said darkly. "Once we are dead, we do not come back, but we do not fully die either. It is our curse." His voice shook as he said it, surprising me.

I closed my eyes. There was so much pain in the room that it was almost unbearable. The dead man nearest to me was the one that the lizard creature had half-eaten. As I looked at him, the pain in my stomach made me ill. It was only a small fraction of what he'd felt. My feet swayed beneath me, and I fell to the ground, curling up to shut out the pain. My cheek was in a pool of blood and I didn't care. I just wanted the pain to go away.

I forced my hand out toward the man and took his pain. As soon as he was truly dead, my own pain eased, but there was still plenty more to go around. I forced myself to my feet. If I released them, the pain would go away.

I went around the room and took the lives of the fallen one by one. Each life that I took seemed to stick to me, leaving a little bit of itself behind. As I went, the collective pain lessened each time, just as the remnants of life force remaining with me grew.

Finally, all that was left was Sophie. I could tell that her throat had been cut without even looking at her, since it was the only physical pain left that was strong enough to ring though me. The wound was not nearly as brutal as some of the others, but her pain hurt my heart more than anything else.

I could feel Alaric's pain too, like a heavy weight on my soul, mourning the loss of his sister. The others left living felt pain, but nothing like what was coursing through Alaric's veins at that moment.

I came to stand before him, and he looked up at me with human eyes, his tears streaming down to mingle with the blood staining his mouth. I crouched across from him and looked down at Sophie. Her blood was beginning to congeal in her loose, black hair. She looked pale and very dead.

I reached my hand out slowly, looking at Alaric rather than Sophie. His loss was almost unbearable. I touched her shoulder, meaning to soothe her pain, but instead tried to soothe his.

I focused on taking that sense of loss away while I stroked my hand down Sophie's arm. I felt the clinging remnants of the lives I'd taken leave me while I touched her. At first they slowly dripped off like water, then they leapt from me in a mighty torrent. I looked down, surprised at the sensation, to find that Sophie's eyes had opened. She took a deep, rasping breath and sat up in her brother's lap. The wound in her throat was gone.

Alaric looked stunned for a second, then laughed, hugging his sister to him. Pushing his arms away, she scooted out of his lap, seeming rather cranky, so he turned to me instead. Before I could react he pulled me against him and kissed me. I could taste the blood and salty tears on his mouth, but underneath that I could taste him. I was too shocked and overwhelmed to pull away.

After a few seconds I managed to gather my wits about me and pushed my hands against his chest. I fell back from my crouch, landing on my butt. I took a shuddering breath, then looked into Alaric's eyes, sparkling with joy. He laughed, and I found myself laughing with him, or maybe I was crying, but there was still a smile on my face. We laughed together, covered in blood, and surrounded by corpses, and I knew with a surety that my life would never be the same again. Maybe I didn't want it to be.

No one said a word as Alaric helped me to my feet, then guided me around the carnage. Those who watched looked at me with wide eyes, like they didn't quite know what I was. Alaric continued to smile, paying them no heed.

I met Estus' gaze just before we left the room, and he gave me a small nod of recognition. I didn't like the nod. I wanted as little of Estus' attention as possible, and I had a feeling that I'd just gained his undivided interest.

I shivered as we walked out of sight. "Why do I get the feeling that I did something highly out of the ordinary?" I whispered, my voice sounding distant to my own ears.

Alaric raised an eyebrow at me. "Should we not be amazed that you just brought my sister back to life?"

Hearing him say it out loud made things seem all too real. I was just coming to terms with the idea that I could kill with a touch, but people killed things all the time. Bringing someone back to life was a little more difficult to digest.

"I mean, can't you all do things like that?" I asked, knowing it sounded dumb.

"No, Madeline," he said softly as we neared my room. "I've never even seen an executioner perform such a feat."

"Maybe it was just a fluke?" I suggested. "Like some sort of miracle?"

"Miracles don't happen in our world," he stated as the smile finally slipped from his face.

I shook my head and looked down at the ground. "They don't happen in my world either."

We reached my room and kept walking, though since I really didn't want to be left in my room alone, I didn't question it.

"Why didn't you run?" he asked suddenly as we took another turn in the hall. He still huddled close to me, as if he was afraid I might run now.

"What?" I asked, startled because my mind had began to wander.

"Why didn't you run when we were attacked?" he clarified. "We were all distracted. You'd think it would have been the perfect opportunity to escape."

I shrugged, feeling suddenly uncomfortable, and maybe a little embarrassed. "I thought about it."

"But?" he prompted when I didn't elaborate further.

I sighed. "I don't know how I can go back, knowing what I know now. Knowing that I could kill someone with a touch. If there's some way to control it . . . " I trailed off.

"You would regret not staying to find out," he finished for me, "because if you could control it, you could have a normal life."

I nodded as we stopped beside a closed door that looked like all the others. Alaric opened it to reveal a bedroom more modern than mine. The bed was simple, with a deep blue bedspread and several fluffy pillows. The rest of the room was taken up by a large dresser, a desk, and a bookshelf, the contents of which had overflowed onto the floor.

As we walked inside, I crouched down and picked up one of the books, but it was in a different language. I put the book back down quickly as I noticed the blood on my hands. It was probably on my face as well. I felt sick and dizzy enough that I had to sit on the edge of the bed before I lost my feet. Alaric shut and locked the door, then came to sit beside me.

"Is this your room?" I asked numbly.

"I figured you might want some space," he explained. "If I had put you in your own room, you would have been bombarded with visitors and questions soon enough."

I took a shaky breath. "Good thinking, but don't even think about trying anything now that we're alone."

I scooted back on the bed and pulled my knees up to my chest, my thoughts a jumbled mess. I was beginning to question everything I knew, and everything I thought I was. Alaric sat beside me, watching me quietly and not complaining that I was getting blood on his bed.

I met his eyes as the gears slowly clicked in my mind. I

was no longer a part of my old world, and I wasn't sure I really ever had been. I knew with a surety that I was going to remain among the Vaettir long enough to learn more about my gifts.

"I won't kill anyone," I stated. "If someone is already dead, I will—" I hesitated, *"release* them, but that's it. I won't release someone's life while they're still alive."

Alaric nodded. "I will state your terms to Estus," he hesitated. "And Madeline?"

I blinked up at him, still shocked I was actually considering staying.

"Stay away from James."

I tilted my head. "Why?"

He reached out a hand as if to touch me, then stopped, letting it fall to his lap. "You may be our clan's new executioner, but James is the *questioner*."

I didn't have to ask what that meant. I'd seen that man's battered and burned body.

I let out a shaky breath, then nodded. I would learn what I needed to learn, and find an escape route in the process for when I was ready to leave. While I was there, I would grant the Vaettir their final deaths. Anything to be able to live a normal life again, eventually.

Did that make me a monster, or did it just make me practical? Who knew.

CHAPTER SIX

"It's time," Alaric announced, way too chipper first thing in the morning. He was dressed in gray sweats and no shirt. I would have felt more comfortable if he was wearing a shirt, but I suspected if I said anything, he would only tease me. His long black hair was tied back in a low ponytail, making his dark eyes stand out.

"I don't think this is a good idea," I began.

I had been waiting in my room, already dressed in my own workout attire of black yoga pants and a matching sports bra, but now my nerves were kicking in. The previous day's events had left me reeling, and now Alaric wanted to teach me to fight. If there was another battle, I wouldn't be utterly defenseless.

"Of course it is," he replied happily. He took my hand and pulled me up off the bed.

We hesitated for a moment as he held my hand, and I almost thought that he might kiss me again, but then he simply led me out of the room. I trailed behind him with a nervous flutter in my heart, which I instinctively squashed.

Alaric was part of a dark world that I didn't belong in, not really. Once I learned to control my *gifts* . . .

My thoughts lingered on our kiss. The sight of him spitting out the gob of flesh that had once been a man's windpipe was a bit unsettling. More unsettling still, was the fact that I had almost enjoyed the bloody kiss afterward.

James came into view down the hall, clearly waiting for us. I found the golden-haired, handsome man way more unsettling than anything else put together, and that was really saying something.

"What are you doing here?" I asked, sincerely hoping that he wasn't planning on joining us.

James laughed. "Like I would miss the little mouse receiving her first lesson in combat."

"Just be careful that she doesn't turn her training on you," Alaric commented. "You might have all of the torture techniques, but Maddy has the follow through."

James looked down at me smugly. "I'm okay with follow through. Be sure you save some of it for this evening."

My heart stuttered to a stop. "This evening?"

"We have another traitor in our midst," he said ominously.

My stomach lurched at the news. Part of me had been hoping the man I'd killed had been a fluke, and that perhaps I wouldn't be needed again unless we were attacked. Even if the body was actually dead before I arrived, the final pain and emotions lingered. I'd felt every excruciating moment of the last man's death. His pleading eyes haunted me more deeply than anything I'd seen during the battle.

James watched as the emotions played across my face, then seemingly satisfied, turned and walked away. Alaric glared after him.

I tapped his shoulder, but he kept glaring, deep in

thought. I could feel the edges of his anger dancing across my skin like tiny flames.

Remembering his warning from the previous night, I muttered, "I'm sensing some sort of rivalry there."

Alaric still didn't look at me. "No rivalry," he corrected, "just moderate hatred. I told you what he does."

I nodded as we began walking again. "Yes, but how can hatred be moderate? Hatred is the extreme."

He finally glanced over at me, his expression unreadable. "That's not true. There are many different types of hatred. I doubt you've felt most of them."

I stopped walking and put my hands on my hips. "What the hell is that supposed to mean?"

Alaric turned to me, still looking angry, then his expression softened. "I meant it in a good way. You don't seem to be the grudge-holding type. Hatred gets you nowhere, but even knowing that, it's difficult to avoid."

"That's not true," I growled. "I've felt plenty of hatred in my life."

He shook his head. "You're an empath, Madeline. While I can't begin to understand how that feels, I know you can sense the deeper emotions of others. How can you hate, when at least a part of you can understand where everyone else is coming from?"

I frowned, annoyed that he was right. I hated, sure, but I also understood. I couldn't hate blindly. I was yet to meet someone purely evil, purely deserving of hate. Evil usually sprang from long-hidden pain.

"Well I can at least hold a grudge," I grumbled. "I'm still angry about being kidnapped. *That's* a grudge."

"Yes," he replied, "but you're also still here. You could have tried to flee when we were attacked, but you came back to help instead. You're angry and confused, but you don't hate us. You don't even hate Sophie, and that's . . . uncommon."

"I appreciate Sophie," I admitted. "She doesn't try to tell me pleasant lies. She never has."

Alaric looked surprised. "And I do?"

I started walking again. "I'm not sure yet, but you do pretend like nothing is wrong when your people are in the middle of a war."

"*Our* people," he corrected, catching up to me.

Our people. I still hadn't quite processed the fact that I was one of the Vaettir myself. To sound monumentally cliché, I'd always known I was different, but I never would have guessed I was a member of an ancient race populated with people and creatures that were quite literally the stuff of fairytales. Being a little empathic was one thing. Living in a magical domicile with people that killed each other for being *traitors* was quite another.

"Our people," I agreed slowly, "but you've distracted me. Why do you hate James? It can't just be his . . . occupation. I'm sensing something else."

"It doesn't matter," he replied. He stopped next to a door and held it open for me, gesturing for me to walk inside. "Just as long as you don't trust him."

"Well I don't really trust *anyone* here." I flicked my gaze up to him. "No offense."

A hurt look passed across Alaric's face, but he didn't comment. I considered telling him that I trusted him, maybe just a little, but it would have been a lie. I might not be a very hateful person, but I'm also not stupid. At least not stupid enough to trust someone that had participated in my kidnapping and subsequent imprisonment. He might have been nice and protective since then, and he may have cheered me up when no one else could, but it didn't cancel out the original act.

I walked through the doorway ahead of him to take in the room beyond. I had hoped that my combat lessons would take place outside, but I was apparently out of luck. The room we entered was large enough to be a banquet hall, and boasted numerous racks of weaponry, but not the open blue sky I'd been craving. Humans needed sunlight. The lack of it was depressing, and a bit maddening. Maybe that was the real reason the Vaettir were killing each other.

I walked around and perused the weapon racks, wondering if I'd be able to sneak one out of there. The floor of the room was covered in thick exercise mats that squished beneath my feet. It was a nice change from the hard stone floors of the rest of the compound.

"Isn't there an outdoor area to practice in?" I asked hopefully.

Alaric retrieved a blade the length of his forearm from one of the racks. "No part of the Salr is outside," he explained, moving the weapon from hand to hand, testing its weight.

"Well can't we just walk out the front door?" I asked.

Alaric laughed. "Have you seen any front doors since you've been here?"

"Well no—" I began.

"The Salr isn't fully aligned with the human world," he explained. "Do you remember how you got here?"

"I was *kidnapped*," I said hotly. "I told you already, I haven't forgotten that."

He had the grace to look abashed. "What I'm trying to say is that we have no front door," he explained, giving his weapon an experimental swing. "The Salr is a protective enclosure. A place cannot be a sanctuary if people can just walk right through the front door."

Watching the sharp edge of the blade, I took a step back. "But those Vaettir that attacked us found a way in."

He sighed. "They found the way that you came through. It has since been sealed."

Sealed? Did that mean there was no way out at all? "Are you telling me I never get to go outside again?" I gasped.

"You will," he answered. "When it's safe."

My shoulders relaxed, just a bit. "Do *you* get to go outside?" I pressed.

He spun the blade around in his hand like he knew what he was doing. "I'm beginning to think that you're just trying to distract me from giving you your lesson." He walked toward me with the blade.

My heart thudded in my chest. "Last question, I promise," I blurted.

"Yes Madeline, I get to go outside." He swung the blade at me. I was so shocked that I almost didn't move, but at the last moment instinct kicked in and I dropped to the ground to avoid the blade's razor sharp edge.

I looked up at him wide-eyed. "You could have killed me!"

He tsked at me as he spun the blade casually in one hand. "I was only testing your reflexes. I wouldn't have hit you."

I believed him, because if he'd wanted to hit me, I'd be dead, reflexes or no, but I wasn't about to stand so he could swing at me again. "I don't think it's fair for me to have to spar with someone that outweighs me by at least fifty pounds, especially when that someone has a blade and I don't."

"Would you rather learn from Sophie?" he asked, swinging the blade aside to offer me a hand up.

I thought of Alaric's hot-tempered sister teaching me to

fight. The size was the only less intimidating thing about her. If I had to choose, I'd say I'd end up with many more bruises if Sophie were my teacher.

I grabbed Alaric's hand and got to my feet. "Can we at least not start out right away with the sharp pointy objects?"

He laughed and dropped my hand, then went to put the blade back into the rack. I followed him with my eyes, and couldn't help but watch the smooth muscles work in his back as he walked away. I've always been a sucker for a nice back. I quickly averted my gaze as he turned around to face me, but his small smile let me know that I'd been caught.

He came to stand in front of me once again. I was relieved that he was empty handed this time, but my relief only lasted for a moment as he suddenly lunged for me. In the blink of an eye, I ended up on the ground for a second time that day. Alaric came down with me as I hit the mat, straddling my hips and pinning me to the floor.

He grabbed my wrists in one hand and held them against the mat above my head at an angle that was almost painful. I'd made the mistake of leaving my hair loose, and now it was pinned underneath me, making the position even more awkward.

I struggled against him, but it didn't do much good. "How is this helping me learn how to fight?" I huffed.

"The best way to learn is to do," he explained. "Now do your best to get me off of you."

"I already did," I replied hotly.

He still didn't move. "Try getting your legs underneath you," he advised.

I did as he instructed. Rather than doing it slowly and asking for approval, I got a firm planting then bucked my hips upward. When I had a little bit of room to work with, I flipped over onto my stomach. I managed to turn my wrists enough in his grip that I could somewhat comfortably bring my knees up under myself. With my new vantage point, I rolled him off me, then scuttled away out of arm's reach.

Alaric sat on the mat smiling at me. "See? Now what did you learn?"

I glared at him. "I learned that you're an ass."

He rose to a crouch then lunged for me again.

Despite my best efforts, I was on my back within a few seconds. This time he stretched his body over me, pinning me more fully.

His mouth was only inches from mine when he asked softly, "Now what would you do in this situation?"

I smirked, beginning to enjoy the game in spite of myself. "I would probably headbutt you. Or," I decided, "I could seduce my attacker into kissing me so I could bite out his tongue."

"Well I like the first part of that second option," he said, bringing his lips even closer to mine.

My pulse sped, sending shivers through my entire body.

"This isn't like any combat training I've ever seen," a woman's voice stated from the doorway.

I craned my neck to see an upside-down Sophie as she came to stand over us. I tried to wiggle out from underneath Alaric, but he wasn't budging.

"Sure it is," he argued, looking up at her. "I think any attacker coming after Maddy would definitely try to put her in just this position."

Sophie snorted. "*You* are such a lech."

Alaric finally rolled off me and helped me to my feet. "Well if you can manage to spar with her without being the least bit tempted, then be my guest."

I took a few steps back, not wanting to spar anymore with anyone. Sophie turned toward me with a mischievous grin. That grin was the only warning I had before she jumped me with much more force than her brother had used, though she only pinned me for a moment before letting me go.

Alaric side-stepped out of the way as I got to my feet and fled from Sophie, only to be knocked to the ground again.

"You can't just leave me here," I groaned, curling up on the mat so Sophie couldn't knock me down again.

"Just try the kissing maneuver!" he called out as he left the room.

With my cheek on the mat, I rolled my eyes, then stood to continue my lesson.

With Alaric gone, Sophie actually began to instruct me as she attacked me. Just as I'd guessed, she was a much more aggressive fighter than Alaric, and she was *fast*. She darted and dove around like a cat, which was an accurate description given her and her brother's . . . feline qualities.

It was nearly impossible to fend her off as she continued to tackle me over and over again, shouting out instructions on what I should be doing to avoid her. The only problem with her method was that since she was telling me what to do, she knew how to counter my movements before I made them. I eventually stopped listening to her instructions in an attempt to get one step ahead of her, but it didn't do me much good.

Finally, she knocked me down one too many times and I refused to get back up. My entire body ached like I'd been hit by a truck. I expected Sophie to try and force me back up, but instead she sat down beside me.

"You're developing feelings for my brother," she observed without warning. She didn't look like she just had an hour long workout. I probably looked like I'd been working out for a week straight.

I sat up. "No, I'm not." Sure, we had chemistry, but chemistry and *feelings* were two very different things.

"Well I'd advise against developing any," she replied bluntly. "Not for his sake, but for yours."

"What do you mean?" I pressed, suddenly very interested in the conversation.

"I like you," she said. "You're very sweet, and Alaric would only hurt you."

I crossed my legs so I could lean forward. "I can take care of myself."

These people obviously all just thought I was some mushy cream puff. I was really more of a muffin, or some other moderately firm baked good.

Sophie rolled her eyes. "I'm trying to be nice here," she chided. "Alaric's attention tends to shift quickly. I don't want to see you get all goo-goo-eyed just to have him shift his attention to someone else. Plus, the only reason he's drawn to you is because you are an entity of death."

I raised my eyebrows at her. "What the hell is that supposed to mean?"

"Really, Madeline," she sighed. "One would think you would have thought more deeply on your gifts. Yours is the power of death. Alaric and I are Bastet, we were born in her image."

"And?" I pressed, still not getting it.

"Bastet is a goddess of war," she explained. "War, and death. Alaric likes you because your energy resonates with him. It is why I feel a certain kinship with you as well. Like attracts like."

I thought about what she was saying, feeling a little sick at her explanation, but grateful for it as well. I was more drawn to Alaric than I'd ever been to a man, even though the rational side of me knew I shouldn't be. Still, it was hard to argue with the feeling of comfort I felt when I was around him. Maybe it was artificial, but I still *felt* it.

Sophie frowned, watching my thoughtful expression slump into disappointment. The feeling in my heart might have been hard to argue with, but that wouldn't stop me from trying.

"I hope I didn't burst your bubble," she apologized.

I shook my head. "I know better than to try living in a bubble."

"Good," she nodded to herself. "Very good."

Yeah, I knew better. The world was full of rusty needles just waiting to pop all of the shiny happy bubbles that came rolling along.

CHAPTER SEVEN

I wanted to ask Sophie more, but James entered the room. He didn't actually say anything, or even approach us, but his presence was enough to halt our conversation. He looked so harmless standing in the corner with his golden hair and country boy charm, until you got to his eyes. You could see the dark soul, or lack thereof, in those eyes.

Sophie glared at him. "You don't get her until this evening," she said coolly.

"I need her now," he said in a tone that made Sophie's iciness seem like mid-summer. "Maya isn't talking."

"That doesn't explain anything," Sophie snapped.

I could sense intense emotions from her. Something about this Maya person had her on edge.

James sighed. "I just need Madeline to *scare* her. No one is going to die . . . *yet*."

I raised my hand to join in the conversation. James and Sophie both turned their attention to me, and I wished I'd just sat quiet.

"Um," I began, turning toward James, "no offense, but I'm guessing if *you* can't scare her, then I won't be of much help."

Sophie laughed bitterly, but James answered, "The final death is a greater threat than any damage I can do. If she sees you, she'll know we mean business." He didn't seem happy about the admission.

I glanced at my bare stomach, then back to him. "Can I at least change first?"

He scanned my attire. "Make it quick."

With a final long, somehow meaningful look at Sophie, James retreated from the room in a whirl of angry energy. That he didn't make any quips about my state of dress, or about Sophie and I "getting sweaty" together, made me think that this Maya woman had him seriously annoyed, but the look on Sophie's face told me there might be another reason.

She glared at the space where James had been, reminding me of Alaric earlier, except there were tears in her eyes.

"You both really hate him, don't you?" I asked.

"Both?" she questioned, turning her gaze to me as she quickly wiped the moisture off of her cheeks.

"You and Alaric," I amended. "Your brother wears a very similar look when James is around."

"Hate is a very complicated word. Mostly, I just don't trust him," she answered quietly.

"There seems to be a lot of that going around," I mumbled, "but I get the feeling there's something else."

She looked at me for several seconds, and for a moment I thought she might actually explain the raw pain in her eyes, then she shook her head and turned away.

"You should get dressed," she ordered curtly. "I have things to do."

With that, she stood and fled the room. I stared at the empty doorway, then stood. Whatever was eating at Sophie would have to wait. My issues were a bit more pressing.

I was supposed to go and threaten this woman with

death. I'd never honestly threatened anyone before. It just didn't feel right, even though what I was threatening to do felt natural to me. Releasing pain was instinctual. Yet, growing up around humans and not knowing what I was had given me a different moral scope than what seemed common among the Vaettir.

I exited the room to find one of the Vaettir waiting to escort me. He was tall with black hair and large features. Giving him a wary glance, I headed back to my room to change, not looking forward to finding something else to wear. Almost everything Sophie had picked out for me was black, tight fitting, and expensive.

I reached my room, glanced once more at my escort, then shut the door behind me. I pawed through the dressers, searching for something appropriate to wear. The jeans I ended up with were a perfect black, not the faded gray that most black jeans turn to, and the long-sleeve shirt was a deep purple that almost managed to be as dark as the jeans.

After getting dressed I looked around for something else to delay my journey to the torture rooms, feeling ill at the remembered scent of blood, death, and burned flesh. I found myself wondering if the hand that had attacked me had been severed while the previous executioner was still alive.

Shaking my head, I tugged on a pair of low heeled boots and exited the room. My silent escort waited outside. I ignored him.

When I reached the chamber where I was expected, I paused to push my ear up against the thick wood, heedless of the man watching me. I could hear someone speaking quietly, but the door was too dense for me to make out the words.

I was leaning against the door with my ear pressed firmly

to the wood when it suddenly swung inward. I stumbled into the room and nearly bit it on the stone floor.

Estus offered me a small smile that made the slight wrinkles decorating his face bunch up. His long gray hair was twisted into an intricate braid that trailed all the way to his ankles. He looked like a diminutive, jolly, Santa Claus, but I was quite sure he was the scariest thing I'd met in the Salr so far.

I steadied myself, wondering with a shiver if Estus had opened the door using the same power he'd used to glue me to my seat. There was a twinkle of laughter in his pale blue eyes that said *yes*.

James stood near his latest victim, watching me with interest. His hands were covered with fresh blood, and there were little spatters of it on his handsome face. The blood had come from the woman I'd come to intimidate, though she hardly seemed broken despite her wounds. The name Maya suited her. Her proud eyes and aura of calm made her seem like some sort of fallen goddess.

She was in plain white underwear that had been stained with sweat and blood. The fabric of her bra was also singed at the bottom corner, drawing my attention to the fact that her dark skin was covered in what looked like brands, though they had no specific shape to them. The smell of burnt flesh wafted off of her, making the room smell like an acrid campfire. I tried to breath shallowly through my mouth, but it was a mistake. Even when I returned to nose breathing, I couldn't get the taste of burnt flesh off the back of my tongue.

I looked down the length of Maya's muscled body to see that she was also missing a foot. The skin at the stump of her ankle had been cauterized. My stomach threatened to crawl out my throat. This woman had been undergoing torture for a while if James had gotten to the point of cutting her foot off, yet she still eyed me defiantly. I backed away. I couldn't be a part of this. This was *wrong*. I didn't care what this woman had done, no one deserved this.

My steps slowed as I noticed something else strange about Maya. I couldn't sense her pain. Not that I minded the lack of pain, but if she was feeling it, I should have felt it.

"I don't feel it," I said to myself, not expecting anyone to reply.

"Yes," Estus replied. "We've come to the conclusion that she does not feel it either."

I looked down at the woman's missing foot again, then to James' frustrated face. It must have really chaffed his hide to have his intimidation tactics nullified.

"Madeline is our executioner," Estus announced to Maya.

Rather than showing fear, she only laughed. "She doesn't look like an executioner," she observed. "Just look at those innocent blue eyes."

James grabbed my arm and pushed me forward.

I struggled against him, not wanting to get closer.

He yanked my arm hard enough that I thought my shoulder might dislocate and I stumbled forward, unable to tear my gaze away from Maya.

She looked down at me. Her black, curly hair had been ripped out of her scalp on one side, leaving a bald patch to slowly ooze blood as she watched me with a predatory expression. "Have they told you what they want to know from me?" she asked as if the men were no longer in the room. "Do you know what all of this is for? Why you're here?"

James squeezed my arm tightly, obviously wanting me to lie.

"No," I answered honestly.

Maya smiled. "Not an obedient pet after all. Maybe you'll be smart enough to run away before you end up like their last executioner."

"What do they want to know from you?" I asked.

James began to jerk me away, but Estus simply shook his head. James let his hand fall from my arm, though he obviously didn't like it.

"Come closer," Maya said with a smile. "I'll tell you a secret."

I obeyed hesitantly. I didn't feel her pain as I stepped closer, but she could still try and injure me once I was within reach. Yet, something in her face made me trust her. I stepped close enough for her to reach her mouth down toward my ear. The manacles she was shackled to held her slightly off the ground, but I was tall enough and she was short enough that we ended up face to face.

She leaned in a little closer until her lips touched my ear and I had to force myself to not jerk away. "Find me tonight," she whispered.

The sound was barely audible to my own hearing, so I knew James and Estus would not be able to hear. "Listen to what I have to say," she continued, "and I'll tell you everything that your *friends* want to know. It will be up to you whether or not they get to know it. Not everything is as it seems in this place."

I stepped away and tried to hide my shaking hands. I balled them in fists at my sides and turned toward Estus.

"She's not afraid of me," I announced. "I can't help you."

Estus nodded, as if he'd known all along, which made me suspicious. Why summon me at all, and why allow Maya to whisper in my ear?

"We will call you once she has spoken," he assured.

"But—" James began, but Estus cut him off with another look.

I backed out of the room while I still could. The woman kept her gaze focused on me as an eerie smile crept across her face. I made it out into the hallway and shut the door behind me with a thud. I almost leaned against it, but then remembered how Estus had made me fall inside the first time, and walked a few steps down the hallway to where my escort awaited.

Ignoring him, I leaned against the stone wall and tried to think. Maya's words echoed in my mind, *not everything is as it seems*. I didn't know how things seemed. I didn't know anything at all, so how could she tell me any different? After growing up in foster care, then living a life of solitude, being confused and alone was nothing new, but it was time for me to stop accepting my fate. I needed answers if I ever hoped to take back my life.

The odd thing was, for the first time in a very long time, I felt like I somewhat belonged. Alaric and Sophie were stronger than normal humans. I wouldn't accidentally kill them with a single touch. But what if this was all some scheme to use me, and then discard me when I was no longer needed? Would I end up just as alone as before, with no real answers?

I had seen a few other Vaettir within the Salr, but most gave me a wide berth. At first I thought they knew about my gifts, and it made them nervous, but maybe they didn't fear me. Maybe they just feared I'd find them out. I had to know for sure. Even if I couldn't escape, I at least would not be led like a lamb to slaughter. If this so-called traitor could give me answers, then I would be an idiot to not listen.

"Are you okay?" someone asked from behind my turned shoulder, opposite my escort.

I jumped, as I hadn't heard anyone else approach. I turned and had to look down to see the woman who had spoken. She couldn't have been more than 5'2", with wispy white-blonde hair and large lavender colored eyes. She wore a spider-silk thin dress that matched the bluish-purple of her eyes.

"I'm fine," I answered instinctively.

She offered me an innocent, closed-lip smile. The bones of her face were so delicate that I thought they might crumble with the movement. She flicked her gaze to my escort, then shooed him away.

To my surprise, he obeyed.

I turned to fully face the woman. "I'm surprised you're actually speaking to me."

"Most are afraid of you," the woman said, still smiling.

I licked my dry lips. "Why are they afraid?"

"Your gifts can be dangerous for those who are weak of will," she explained. "I am not weak of will, and so I am not afraid. My name is Sivi." She held out a dainty, bony hand to me.

I took her hand, careful to not squeeze. Her fingers seemed longer than they should have been, and wrapped around my hand with more force than I expected.

"Maddy," I replied, wondering what this tiny creature wanted from me.

"I know," she said cheerfully. "I'd actually like to bestow a favor upon you." She looked around the hallway as if someone could have snuck up on us. "But not here," she added.

She switched her grip from my hand to my wrist and pulled me down the hall toward an area of the Salr that I was yet to visit.

"Where are we going?" I asked as she rushed me along.

Instead of answering, she stopped suddenly to open a door and pull me inside. The room we entered smelled of moss and mildew, which probably had something to do with the giant pond that took up most of the floor. Vines and lichen grew out across the stones surrounding the reflective water, framing the surface in shades of green.

Sivi pulled me toward the pool, then dropped down into a seated position, forcing me to follow suit. She curled her dainty legs demurely and smiled at me, then ran her hand across the surface of the water while her other still gripped my wrist. As the water rippled, the vines began to shiver. She swirled the water more and the vines came to life and grew outward, searching for something to grab onto.

I flashed back onto the experience of being pulled by vines into the ground, and tried to pull my wrist out of Sivi's grasp as my pulse sped. Her grip was like iron, and she didn't seem to struggle at all as I continued my attempt to pull away.

"Look," she said pointing down to the water.

I looked down automatically. Before, the reflection had been of the stone ceiling, but now I could see trees and blue sky, as if I was in a lake looking up through the water, rather than looking down.

"What is that?" I asked nervously. One of the vines crept across my jean-clad leg, then continued its blind search.

She grinned, exposing pointy little teeth. "It's a way out. For *you*."

"Alaric said the only way out was sealed," I argued, though I couldn't really argue with the scene in front of me.

"Sealed from people coming in," she countered. "Not from going out."

"Why are you showing this to me?" I asked, suddenly suspicious. "What do you want?"

A thousand thoughts competed in my mind. I could escape and go back to my little house. No one would even know that I'd been gone. I would never have to see Estus or James again . . . until they found me and stole me away once more. Maybe I could go into hiding.

"I am only trying to offer you your freedom." She continued to smile, though now the smile seemed slightly strained. Her lavender eyes flicked to the door then back to my face.

"Why?" I pressed, more to delay making a decision than anything else.

She sighed and let the smile slip from her face with another glance at the door. "Are you always this ungrateful?"

I shook my head. "Not ungrateful. Suspicious."

"Yet you are not suspicious of Alaric and Sophie," she snapped. "Where does your suspicion draw the line?"

"I'm suspicious of everyone," I answered honestly. "It's nothing to get offended over."

"Do you not want to go home?" she asked, seeming increasingly impatient.

"I do," I answered. "But—"

"But what?" she interrupted. "Either you do or you do not."

"It's not that simple," I interjected. "It's not safe for me to be around humans. I want to know who—*what* I am. I *need* to know."

Sivi cocked her head like she didn't understand me. "You've spent your entire life in that world—"

"And it was fine at first," I finished for her. "I didn't kill anything, not until . . . " I hesitated, not wanting to say Ray or Matthew's names out loud. "Eventually I had to be alone," I finished. "If I go back, I'll have to be alone again. I can never touch anyone again."

"And you hope Alaric can help you with this, alone-ness?" she questioned. "The Vaettir can die just like humans. There is no safeguard against being alone."

"Well he's a lot less likely to die," I replied sullenly, "and I won't be the one to kill him."

Sivi laughed. "How many have died since you came to us? Will you be able to give Alaric the true death when his time comes? You would not need to do so for a human."

I shook my head. "At least if I did bring him death, it wouldn't be an accident."

"If you went home," she began anew, ignoring my argument, "you could learn to control your gift. Now that you know what you are, you can learn to interact with humans. There is no need for you to hide in the dark any longer."

I shifted uncomfortably, gazing down at the pool. I *wanted* to go, but why did Sivi want me gone so badly, and why hadn't she offered this before?

"I'll think about it," I said, hoping to escape her until I could think things through. She seemed to want me to jump in the pool right that moment, but I wanted to talk to Maya first. If she could tell me what I needed to know, I might be able to leave.

Sivi eyed me as if she didn't fully believe me. "See that you do," she answered finally. "I may not want to help you so much tomorrow, and the next day I may want to help you even less."

She stood, then crossed her arms and turned her back, dismissing me. I stood slowly and backed away from the pool, watching the vines warily. I backed all the way into the hall until I could no longer see Sivi's tiny form, then turned and ran back to my room. Panting and feeling shaken, I shut and locked the door behind me.

I was becoming increasingly unsure of who my true

enemies were. It was funny how small things could change your perspective. In a few short hours I'd had cryptic warnings, I'd threatened a footless woman, and I was offered an escape through a vine-filled, magical pool. You know, small things.

CHAPTER EIGHT

I stayed in my room for the rest of the day. No one bothered me. Laying with my back on the bed, staring up at the stupid canopy, I began to grow anxious about finding Maya. I highly doubted the escort awaiting outside my door would let me go wandering. I'd have to figure out some way to escape him, but first, food. My stomach growled painfully.

I sat up. I knew the way to the kitchen, but really didn't want to leave the solace of my room. What if another attack occurred, or what if James wanted me to torment someone else?

My stomach growled again.

Giving in, I stood and made my way to the door. I opened it a crack to peer outside, then stifled a groan. Sure enough, the same dark-haired man from before waited for me. I opened the door the rest of the way then walked out, dutifully ignoring him as I turned toward the kitchen.

Shouts echoed down the hall as we neared. I almost turned around and fled, but I recognized Sophie's voice. Curious, I peeked into the kitchen.

Though I didn't make a peep, Sophie froze and turned a tight-lipped frown my way. James wore a similar expression that said, *Oh great, here comes naïve little Madeline, she really has some nerve interrupting us*. I tried to back out of the kitchen, but Sophie stormed past me before I had the chance.

Well, now that I'd butted in, I might as well eat. I ended up slurping on a bowl of mushroom soup while James watched me like I was a new toy that he might purchase . . . though really he was more of the shoplifting type.

"Maya was even more smug after she saw you," he said suddenly.

"Maya?" I questioned, startled that he had finally spoken.

"The woman you met earlier," he explained.

"Oooh," I said, though I already knew who he was talking about. "The woman whose foot you cut off."

"I had to make her talk," he replied as if it justified his actions. "And I don't see that you're in any place to judge."

"I've never tortured anyone," I replied coolly, though my thoughts echoed, *Murderer*.

I could take people's lives and still be morally righteous . . . at least that's what I kept telling myself.

He laughed. "Give it time. You'll be one of us soon enough."

I laughed right back, though mine sounded tired. "So you're saying everyone else here is an egotistical sadist like you?"

"The sadist part at least," he said with a smirk. "Even Alaric."

"I'll be the judge of that," I mumbled, not meeting his eerie white-blue eyes.

He laughed again. "We all have the same nature Madeline. Some just hide it better than others."

When I didn't reply, he watched me in silence. As it

became obvious that I was now ignoring him completely, he stood and left the kitchen. I let out a breath at his departure.

I stood and threw the rest of my soup into the large kitchen sink. I didn't bother washing it. Let my silent watcher wash it if it bothered him. Crossing my arms, I met his gaze. How to escape him . . . I drummed my fingers on my arm.

"I imagine you can find your way back to your room on your own?" he asked.

I raised my eyebrows at him. He was actually just going to leave me alone? Staring at him blankly, I nodded.

He turned and left the room.

Debating my options, I wiped sweaty palms on my jeans. Something was fishy. Why escort me around all day, only to leave me to my own devices now? Was it a test? Maybe Estus wanted to see if I still planned to escape. Maybe Sivi's offer had been just a ruse too.

It probably didn't matter. My priority in that moment was Maya. She seemed the most likely person to help me make sense of everything.

The hall was empty as I left the kitchen. I strode confidently forward so that if I encountered anyone, they wouldn't think I was up to anything. When in doubt, act like you know what you're doing and people usually won't question you.

I went around a corner and let out my breath as I saw that the next hall was empty as well. Despite the fact that I was lucking out, I still felt a little bit wary that I wasn't seeing anyone. While I'd interacted with few of the Salr's inhabitants, I'd seen others during the battle. I knew they were around . . . somewhere.

By the time I came to stand in front of the door to the torture room I felt queasy and cold. I took a deep breath and grabbed the knob. If someone was inside with Maya, I'd simply lie and say I was checking to see if they needed me. It was my *job* to be there, kind of, so they couldn't really question me.

I strode into the room, fighting an overwhelming sense of revulsion, to find it empty. Completely empty. The manacles that once held Maya hung loose against the wall. Panic shot through me. What if James had killed her? Would he have mentioned it? I shook my head. That wasn't right. He wouldn't kill her until he got what he wanted from her. Plus, if she was dead I would have been called to release her spirit . . . unless Estus decided to put her heart in a box.

I searched the room for any evidence as to where she might have gone, but came up empty. Other than the blood staining the floor and walls, there was nothing to see. She could have been moved anywhere within the Salr, and I hadn't even explored the entire compound to know how big it was, or how long I'd have to search.

I walked back into the hall, feeling numb and not knowing what to do next. At a loss, I crouched down and leaned against the wall of the hallway. Then I saw the blood. There wasn't a lot of it, but there was a definite trail of blood drips leading farther down the hall.

I stood and followed the trail through a few twists and turns of the hall, all the way to a gargantuan stairway leading downward. The stones composing each step were larger than my torso and had to weigh a few hundred pounds a piece. Speckles of blood decorated the large stones all the way down into the darkness. I paused to consider my options, then hurried down the huge steps awkwardly, straining my knees as I went.

The steps ended in a narrow corridor. Where the rest of the Salr was lit by means that weren't visible to me, this corridor was lit by torchlight, and the torches only went so far. Roughly twenty feet in front of me, the darkness was complete. I grabbed one of the torches off of the wall to light my way and almost dropped it, not expecting it to be as heavy as it was.

As I got a better grip on the torch, I began to tremble with anticipation and fear, but still I forced myself forward. I crept along, crouching every so often to hold the torch near the floor to make sure the occasional spot of blood could still be seen. The corridor began branching off into hallways on either side of me, but the blood drops led straight forward.

There was absolutely no light as I went deeper, and I began to fear that my torch wouldn't last long enough to lead me back out again. I almost turned back, but then I felt the pain. Not Maya's pain, as I couldn't feel anything from her, but old pain from others that had been kept down there. This place had to be where prisoners were kept when they weren't being tortured. The walls practically ached with despair. I blocked the pain out as much as possible and hurried onward, now sure that I was going in the right direction.

Just as I was thinking that I was lucky to only be going straight, as I probably wouldn't get lost, the blood drips took a turn to the right. I veered off and trotted down the new corridor, hoping desperately that I wouldn't have to make any more turns.

The corridor ended with a final turn that led to a cell. Behind the thick metal bars was Maya, who had to quickly cover her eyes at the sudden light. She looked even worse than when I'd left her. One of the hands that she held in front of her face was missing several fingers, and the left side of her face was a mass of swollen bruises.

"I'm surprised you came this far," she rasped. "You didn't happen to bring any water, did you?"

"I'm sorry," I said quickly. "I didn't think-"

She waved me off then lowered her hands as her eyes adjusted to the light. "I suppose I should just be glad that you aren't stupid enough to believe everything you're told."

"Why are you being tortured?" I asked, itching to escape the dark corridors as soon as possible.

"Estus wants a certain object," she said, "and I may or may not know where it is."

That lined up with what Alaric had said. Estus and someone named Aislin were searching for something, and they wanted it bad enough to kill. "What is it?"

"If he had this object," she went on, ignoring my question, "the war would be over, and Estus would be the sole man in charge."

"Is that the worst possible outcome?" I replied. "At least no one else would have to die."

Maya let out a laugh that ended in a hacking cough, making me wonder if James had damaged one of her lungs. "Tired of your job already?" she asked.

I frowned. "Can you blame me? I didn't ask to come here. I was *kidnapped*. The second I learn what I need to know, I'm getting out of here."

She shook her head. "Don't say that to anyone else. You'd be a fool to believe that the last executioner was actually a traitor."

My mouth went dry. "How do you know about that? Do you know why he was killed?"

She shrugged. With her injuries, the shrug should have hurt, but she didn't so much as cringe. "Word gets around, but we're getting sidetracked. You implied that letting Estus win might be a good thing, but you're not looking at the big picture. Of course having one leader cuts back on the bloodshed, but what if that leader is a tyrant?"

I shook my head. I didn't really care who led the Vaettir. "I don't know . . ." I trailed off.

"No, you don't," she replied. "The Vaettir withdrew from the human world for a reason. They called us wights, the undead, and burned many of us alive."

"So you—" I hesitated, "*We're* hiding so that they don't kill us?"

She laughed again. "Things are different now. The Vaettir have grown in number, and they've become twisted things. The humans were right to be afraid. We are not what we were meant to be."

"And what was that?" I prodded, desperately hoping that what we were meant to be wasn't the terrible picture of the Vaettir that I was forming in my mind.

"We're nature spirits," she explained. "We're supposed to be guardians of the land, created in the image of the old gods. In all of history we've never gathered together like this. The Salr is supposed to be a sanctuary, not a home, and definitely not a fortress."

I let out a sigh of relief as some tension within me eased. Perhaps my nature wasn't what I'd been led to believe after all. The idea of some part of me being like James made me ill, but maybe James was the exception and not the rule.

"What does Estus want?" I asked, filing the information away. "Please, they could find me down here soon," I added to hurry her along.

She shook her head. "Estus wants a lot of things, and none of them should you give him."

I looked over my shoulder again. "Why shouldn't I give anything to him? How can I trust you? Everyone seems to have a different idea of who I should trust. Sivi said—"

"*Sivi?*" Maya interrupted

"She tried to get me to leave," I explained. "She showed

me a way out of here." I bit my lip, feeling stupid for not taking it. "Maybe if I could get you out of this cell we could—"

Maya shook her head. "There is no getting me out of this cell, and I wouldn't trust Sivi either. If you want an example of what the Vaettir are supposed to be, she's it."

"But isn't that a good thing?" I asked. "Just a moment ago you were telling me that we've been twisted away from what we're supposed to be."

"She *is* what we're supposed to be. She has maintained her connection to the land, even down here." At my blank stare, she went on, "Let me guess, this alleged way out had something to do with water?"

"How did you know?"

My torchlight was beginning to seem dim, but I wasn't sure if the fire was actually getting lower, or if my fear was playing tricks on me.

"She can travel through water," Maya explained, "because it is the element that she's associated with. She is descended from Coventina, goddess of wells and springs. She has maintained that connection, making her less interested in power plays, and more interested in restoring the natural order. Sivi is very, very old, and hasn't changed much over the centuries."

"Centuries?" I laughed. "You're kidding right?"

Maya shook her head. "Her age isn't important. All you need to know is what Sivi would *do* if she could convince the other Vaettir to follow her."

"The natural order doesn't sound bad—"

Maya cut me off with a sharp motion of her mutilated hand. "The *natural* order would mean far fewer humans and Vaettir alike. She would try to knock the world back to medieval times."

My eyes widened as my mouth formed an "oh" of understanding.

Maya glanced around as if she could hear something that I couldn't. "You're running out of time," she said quickly. "Listen to me very carefully. Sivi is only looking out for her own well-being. The Vaettir by nature are solitary creatures, and she holds to that. Your escape would benefit her and only her. If you stay, you can work against both Estus and Sivi. Trust me, it's the right thing to do. Now get out of here."

I shook my head. "Wait, there's so much more I need to ask you."

"No waiting," Maya snapped. "The answer that Estus is looking for is right under his nose, only he can't find it. Only someone with a connection to death can find it. *You* can find it. Just like Sivi is a guardian of water, you're a guardian of death. Estus recently figured that part out, and that's why he suddenly wants you. That's the real reason you were brought here. I think that the last executioner failed, and so he was killed. Soon it's going to be your turn, and I'm going to help you do it."

"Why?" I asked, growing more confused by the second.

"This thing would grant Estus complete control. He'll make you find it eventually, even without my help. At least if you find it without him present, before he even knows that you're looking for it, you can decide what to do with it."

I could hear footsteps in one of the nearby corridors. "How do I find it?" I whispered.

"Estus believes that only someone with a connection to death can see the object he seeks, but he's not quite right. In truth, only the dead know where it is, so someone with a connection is needed to ask them."

The footsteps had stopped, but Maya looked around again as if she could hear something that I couldn't. "There is a place within the Salr where the worst of traitors are kept," she continued, barely loud enough for me to hear. "Their punishment is to have their souls trapped forever within their dead bodies. Only the dead can show you the way to this object, so you need to go and ask them."

"How am I supposed to ask them questions?" I rasped. "They're dead!"

The footsteps sounded again, closer this time. We both froze at the sound as someone came to stand in the cross-section where I'd turned to find Maya. I blocked as much of my torch with my body as I could and waited. Whoever it was paused for a moment, then walked on.

"Just go and try," Maya whispered, barely loud enough for me to hear at all. "It's the only chance we have. Now *go*."

I waited until the footsteps got far enough down the hallway that I could no longer hear them, gave a final apologetic look to Maya, then ran to the end of the corridor. I looked both ways down the hall, but my torch didn't cast enough light to see more than a few feet. Things seemed to echo more harshly down the main corridor, so despite my instinct telling me to run, I crept back slowly the way I'd come.

I knew I was almost back to the stairs, though I couldn't yet see them, when I heard the footsteps again. Whoever it was had walked farther down the corridor, and now they were walking back at a much faster pace than I was going. I paused for a moment, not sure what I should do, then decided echoes be damned, I needed to run.

I took off at full speed and could tell instantly that whoever was behind me had heard. The heavy footsteps quickened just as the stairs became visible ahead of me. I dropped my torch onto the ground as I used my hands to speed my progress up the giant steps.

I reached the top and ran at full speed down the hall, refusing to look back. I ran that way until I reached my bedroom, unsure if whoever was down there had actually seen me.

Not wanting to be caught in the hallway huffing and puffing, I let myself quickly into my bedroom, only to be caught huffing and puffing by the two people sitting on my bed waiting for me.

"Where were you?" Sophie asked. "We looked everywhere."

She and her brother sat at the foot of my bed with matching worried looks in their dark eyes. The symmetry was continued by the fact that they both wore their long, dark hair loose, and they were both dressed up in black evening wear. They looked like the poster children for *Goths R Us*.

"I was just walking around," I lied, stepping away from the door. I did my best to keep my voice even in spite my racing pulse. "I can't just stay shut up in this room all of the time."

"If you were just walking around the halls we would have found you," Alaric countered. "We looked everywhere."

"I don't see why it's any of your business, either way," I snapped, feeling like my nerves were about to snap as well. I thought about what Maya had said. Part of me wanted to trust Alaric and Sophie, to believe they were different from James and Estus, but how could I? They might not have tortured Maya, but they hadn't tried to stop it either.

"Something has happened," Sophie said calmly, though it was an obvious effort for her to not snap back at me. "Estus called a gathering this evening to tell us."

So that's why the halls had been so empty. "And I was the only one not invited?" I asked, though in truth I didn't mind the exclusion.

"You tell her," Sophie growled at Alaric. As she stood, she turned to me and said, "You really shouldn't be so impossible when people are trying to help you." With that she left the room, slamming the door behind her.

Alaric stood as well, but it was to walk closer to me. I wrapped my arms around myself, suddenly feeling more nervous than I had been while running back to my room.

Alaric circled me. "Estus has asked us to search for something. It's very important."

I turned with Alaric, trying to keep him in my sights. "And what something is that?" Could this be the same something Maya had mentioned? The something that might get me killed?

"It's a small charm," he replied, stopping just a step away from me.

Did he know I'd gone to see Maya? I was finding it hard to breathe, but managed to glare at him regardless.

"Estus asked me to speak with you," he went on. "He believes that you of all people can find the thing he's looking for. He'd like your help."

My breath caught in my throat. *Bingo.* It was just like Maya had said. "Why me?" I pressed, curious to see if he would give me the same explanation that Maya had.

He shrugged. "Trust me, I'd like to know myself, but Estus is Doyen of this clan, and when he asks, I obey." There was a tightness around his eyes as he said the latter, making me think that he wasn't entirely happy with the arrangement.

I took a step back, effectively putting myself out of reach. "And what is so special about this charm?"

"That is not for us to know," he replied. His brow creased a little further.

I crossed my arms, the hint of a smug smile creeping across my face. "You don't like taking orders, do you?"

He smiled bitterly. "No one likes taking orders, but these are the times we live in. We are not free to choose our own paths as we once were. Estus says find this elusive thing," he waved his hand in the air, "and I must find it. He says use Madeline, and I must use you."

"Well I'm not going to help find it until I know what it is," I replied, "and I don't like the idea of being *used*. I'm not a tool."

Alaric took a step toward me. "This is how things work, Maddy. It's how they have always worked. We are all just tools in our little microcosm. To be here means safety, but it comes with a price."

How they had *always* worked? Not according to Maya.

I stared up into his dark eyes. "Don't lie to me," I said evenly.

He smiled again, but this time it was sad. "It seems you've been gathering information on your own, haven't you? It's how things work *now*," he corrected, "and how they have worked for a very long time."

I stood rigid, refusing to move. "Define *a very long time*."

"For as long as I've been around," he answered cryptically. "I've known no other way." He grabbed a lock of my hair and began twirling it around his finger, distracting me. "And I don't see it changing any time soon."

"And how long have you been around?" I asked softly. Maya had claimed that Sivi was several centuries old. I wouldn't have believed her, except I'd seen that magical pool. I'd sensed Sivi's power. That meant that any of the Vaettir might be older than I'd originally guessed.

He leaned in close and whispered, "Long enough."

I opened my mouth to ask more, but he delicately pushed his hand under my chin to shut my jaw. He then used that hand to guide my face up toward him. Suddenly the situation took on a whole new tone.

I blinked up at him, wondering why the hell I wasn't stepping out of reach.

He leaned down and kissed me.

I froze as too many emotions collided inside of me, then pulled away. "Is what Sophie said true?" I gasped.

Heat danced in his eyes. "What did she say?"

I licked my lips. "She said I'm drawn to you because death goes with war, and vice versa."

He shrugged. "Does it matter?"

I took a shaky breath. My hands rested on his arms, and I didn't quite remember placing them there. I needed to do what Maya had told me. I needed to figure out Estus' evil plan. I needed to—

Alaric leaned down and kissed me again.

My hands slid up under his shirt to feel the smooth skin underneath. I had so many unanswered questions, but I couldn't seem to pull myself away long enough to ask them.

Washed away on a wave of anxiety and fear, my palms smoothed over his chest nearly up to his throat. As the kiss intensified, I drew my hands down to either side to caress the bones of his ribcage. Suddenly I slid my hands back out of his shirt and pulled away from the kiss, surprised and embarrassed by my actions.

His fingers caressed my waist, pulling me closer. He kissed a gentle line down my throat, leaving a pleasant, burning sensation in the wake of his kisses.

My thoughts raced, telling me that I shouldn't trust Alaric to touch me, but my doubts were outweighed by the fact that it had been a very long time since I'd been touched. I hadn't been with a man since Matthew. *Matthew.* The sobering thought stopped me, and I was able to pull away completely.

Alaric let his hands fall from me, and I regretted the loss as soon as it happened. His dark eyes observed me curiously. In his eyes I saw the remnants of the heat from just a moment before, but also some sort of sadness that I didn't understand. The sudden loss of heat left me with only cold memories.

"I killed the last man I was with," I blurted out, as if it explained everything.

Alaric nodded and raised his hands as if to touch me again. "You will not be able to kill me in the same way."

I stepped back. "Someone told me that I could still harm the weak of will, even if they are Vaettir."

Alaric smirked, letting his hands fall back to his sides. "And you believe me weak of will?" he asked playfully.

I crossed my arms. "I don't know you well enough to judge," I answered. "Which is another reason why we shouldn't be doing this."

Alaric smiled and raised his hands in an *I give up* gesture. "In that case, I will have to leave the next move to you."

Despite his statement, he stepped close to me so that his chest touched my crossed arms.

"I'm tired," I lied, stepping away from his touch once again, and feeling instant regret just as I had before. Hadn't I been wanting him to kiss me again? I chastised myself for ever giving in to *that* fantasy. I barely knew him. He had been kind and protective, if a bit of a pain in the ass, but he was also one of the people holding me captive for reasons I couldn't fully comprehend.

Alaric's shoulders slumped with a heavy sigh. As he turned to leave, he opened his mouth like he might say something, then closed it. He left the room without another word.

I regretted everything as soon as the door was shut. I regretted the kiss, and I regretted ending it. Being alone with only memories was a terrible thing, even if it was the thing I was most used to.

If I'd known what I was sooner, Matthew wouldn't have died. If I'd been raised among the Vaettir from the start, maybe I'd have had some idea on how to live my life. Maybe I'd actually know how to have a normal romance with someone, not supernatural chemistry with my kidnapper. My *ifs* were more torturous than James or any of the other Vaettir could ever be.

Even as I half-wished that Alaric would come back, Maya's words still rung clearly in my mind. I didn't fully trust her, but she'd given me enough information that I didn't trust anyone else either.

I couldn't trust Alaric with my heart, just as I couldn't place my fate in Estus' hands. There was nothing I could do about Alaric, so I'd focus on Estus. If I could find what he was looking for without him or Alaric knowing, then I would have the upper hand. It was time to stop being such a willing prisoner.

I crawled into bed fully clothed, though I knew a nap was unlikely. The large, four-poster bed and burgundy bedspread still felt foreign to me, and I found myself missing my little house and my small bed. I'd only been gone a few days. Sadly, it wasn't likely that anyone back home had even noticed I was missing.

I sighed and thought about the kiss, trying to convince myself that I was right to end it. Yet, even with my rational thoughts laid before me, my conclusion marked me as a total idiot.

CHAPTER NINE

I awoke, surprised that I'd managed to fall asleep in the first place. I was even more surprised by the fact that someone was crouched over me in my bed. At first I thought maybe Alaric had returned, but the form was far too small to be him.

Tensing, I lunged at them, but they dove easily out of the way. My room slowly lit up of its own volition, as if noticing I was awake, and I blinked against the sudden brightness.

Sivi crouched beside me, eyeing me like a pale bird of prey. The light shining through the curtain of her hair made me realize that it wasn't actually white, it was translucent. Her strands of hair looked like impossibly thin lengths of fishing line. Her violet eyes stood out in the paleness of her skin like amethysts.

"Time is up little one," she whispered. "Will you stay or go?"

I crept backward out of bed, putting some distance between us. "I haven't decided yet."

"Well I might not want to help you later," she taunted from her perch on my bed.

"And why do you want to help me now?" I asked. "Why is it so important to have me out of the way?"

"You ungrateful little wretch," she hissed. "I've seen countless executioners die one after another over the centuries. What makes you think you're so special?"

"Well," I replied, "you sneaking into my bedroom for a private conversation was my first hint. Like you said, you've seen countless executioners die. Why would you finally choose to help one?"

She smiled ruefully. "If only you knew the creatures you've chosen to align yourself with. In time you'll wish you had taken my offer, but it will be too late."

I crossed my arms. "I haven't aligned myself with anyone."

She crawled off my bed with snake-like grace and went for the door. With her hand on the knob, she stopped to regard me one last time. "It will be interesting to see which one of them kills you, once they get what they want. I'd like to see your face in that final moment of betrayal."

The slamming of the door made me jump. I blearily wondered what time it was. Did the lighting of the room mean I'd slept half a day and an entire night? It sure felt like it. I stretched my arms, then hurried to my dresser to get a change of clothes, shaking my head at the surreal encounter. Estus expected me to look for the charm today. I'd look for it alright, though I hadn't yet decided what I'd do when I found it. Maybe it was a like a weapon of mass destruction and suddenly I'd have power over them all. Fat chance, but I still wanted to find it.

Estus obviously knew that someone of my talents was needed to find it, but he didn't know as much as Maya. If he did, he would have sent me straight to the corpses of the alleged traitors to *ask* them. No, he thought I'd somehow be able to *see* the charm where others could not. That thinking was probably what had gotten the last executioner killed.

I picked out an outfit to suit my mood: black jeans, black silk top, and low-heeled black boots that went up to my knees. That morning I was beyond caring how black looked with my coloring. Clothes in hand, I ventured out into the hallway toward the bathroom. If I was lucky, no one would get in my way. Unfortunately, I'm rarely lucky.

"I don't get it," James said, reaching an arm in front of me to block my way.

He had been waiting in the hall, still in his clothes from the previous day, letting me in on the fact that he was yet to get any sleep.

I tried to push past his arm, but didn't have much success. "Don't get what?" I huffed, giving up on forcing my way through.

"I don't get why Estus is so fixated on you, and I *really* don't get why Sivi was in your bedroom a few minutes ago. I think I might have to dedicate a bit more time to finding out what's so special about you."

I took a step back, but he instantly closed the gap. Instead of stepping back again, I met his eyes with a glare. "Is that a threat?"

He smiled, and I was reminded of the first time I'd met him, and how he'd callously thrown me over his shoulder. Sophie had improved since that night. James had not.

"Is my attention such a frightening thing?" he asked playfully, putting an arm on either side of me, trapping me against the wall.

"Yes," I answered honestly. I dropped down out of the circle of his arms and wiggled my way to freedom.

I backed away from him toward the bathroom, even though I knew he wouldn't let me go so easily. He matched me step for step until he had me pressed against the bathroom door instead of the wall. This time he put his whole body into trapping me. He wasn't as tall as Alaric, and being tall myself, I could nearly meet his eyes directly. I tried to remain calm in front of his icy blue eyes, but it was hard to keep my panic down below the surface.

"Get away from her," a voice said from behind James.

I peeked around James' broad shoulders to see Alaric walking down the hallway toward us. He'd changed into clothes more casual than what he'd worn the night before, but the entire outfit was still black. James looked back at him, giving me enough room to maneuver. Repeating to myself, *I'm not a cream puff, I'm not a cream puff,* I took a deep breath and drove my knee up into his groin.

His pain echoed through me, but it was worth it. He grunted in surprise and backed up a step, hunching over. Giving in to the fact that I was being a bit of a masochist, I punched him with every ounce of oomph I could muster. The punch didn't rock him back much, but the satisfying crunch I felt told me that maybe I'd broken, or at least damaged, his nose. The sudden pain in my own nose verified it.

I resisted the urge to rub my sore nose. "I'm not your plaything," I said calmly as blood dribbled down his shocked face. "Don't ever touch me again."

I opened the bathroom door and went inside. Before I shut it, I noticed Alaric as he held up a hand in front of his face to hide his silent laughter. His eyes met mine for a brief moment, and then I was blissfully alone in the bathroom. I quickly turned the lock before I took a second to catch my breath.

I would have preferred a quick shower, but I only had the tub. Still, not willing to forgo bathing, I turned on the water and stripped down. I half-expected James to start pounding on the door, but the hall outside was silent.

I washed myself quickly and got dressed, the whole time nervous that someone would interrupt me. Fully clothed, I was finally able to breathe easy as I went for the door.

Alaric stood leaning against the wall directly outside of the bathroom. "About time," he said. "You're not the only one who takes baths around here."

I glared at him, suddenly embarrassed about our kiss the night before. "I'm sure there are other bathrooms."

He grinned as he walked in and I walked out. "But I like this one."

"You were protecting me," I observed, turning back to look at him. "I think I proved that I can handle James on my own."

"You proved that you're dumb enough to piss off the world's biggest bully," he countered, "and I was not protecting you. I was simply waiting to take a bath. Speaking of, if you for some reason didn't get clean enough, you're welcome to hop back in with me."

I smiled sweetly. "Let me get my coffee, then I'll get back to you with a clever retort."

I turned to saunter away, trying very hard to keep my mind off of the idea of Alaric in the bathtub. It didn't work, and I simply had to be grateful for the fact that no one could see me blush as I walked away.

I could feel him watching me, and it took a great deal of self control to not simply scurry to the nearest hallway where I'd be out of sight. Finally, I heard the bathroom door shut. I picked up my pace, eager to get on with my search. It seemed I'd been relinquished of having a constant escort, and I didn't want to press my luck, but I really needed some food first, and I *definitely* needed coffee.

I had a well-thought idea of where I'd look first, but there were drawbacks to my plan. I stood a good chance of running into James again if I went to the room where Estus had shown me the executioner's still-beating heart, and he probably wasn't happy about his nose. Still, since there'd been one heart hidden there, there were probably more. I wasn't sure about somehow *communicating* with them, but I'd sensed the magic and pain in that first heart. I had to try.

I reached the kitchen to find it already occupied by three people I'd never seen before, sitting at the counter together drinking coffee. I gritted my teeth, hoping none of them would note the fact that I was alone. They watched me silently as I poured myself a cup from the massive coffee maker. I turned my back to them, but could feel their eyes following me as I went to the large pantry to find something to eat. I couldn't help feeling that they were just waiting for me to slip up like the last executioner, but maybe that was just my own fear speaking.

When I emerged from the pantry, bread in hand, they all averted their eyes and pretended like I wasn't even there. I put the bread into the toaster and slammed the handle down loudly, looking pointedly at their turned backs.

The oldest looking of the three cleared his throat, and they all stood to file silently out of the kitchen. I shook my head as I waited for the toast to pop up, and just took it dry when it did, wanting to get out of the kitchen before anyone else showed up. Something strange was going on beyond my comprehension. I was being allowed to wander around alone. No one wanted to talk to me except James and Alaric. It felt like a trap.

I left the kitchen, wondering what would happen if I hurried across the Salr to Sivi's magical pool. I could escape and go home . . . but it wouldn't be that simple. Even if I managed to hide, I could never touch another human again, and I'd always wonder if I could have learned enough within the Salr to lead a normal life.

I scarfed down my toast as I walked through the hall, nearly choking on the half-burnt dryness, then scalding my throat when I tried to wash it down with the too-hot, black coffee. By the time I reached the first interrogation room my toast was gone and I only had a half-cup of cooling coffee left to sooth my scratched and burned throat.

I took a deep breath, then reached for the doorknob and turned it. I had nothing but horrifying memories of the room, and wasn't looking forward to seeing the blood-stained walls once again, but I wanted to ensure no one was next door to catch me searching for more hearts.

I pushed on the heavy door and it opened slowly with a long creak, just like a door out of a horror movie.

"What are you doing?" someone asked from behind me.

I nearly jumped out of my skin, then turned to see that Sophie had come around the corner, catching me as I took my first step into the room. I'd been so intent on not getting caught by someone inside the room, that I'd completely ignored the possibility of someone walking behind me.

Cursing my hesitation at going into the bloody room in the first place, I turned to fully face her. "I think I lost . . . a bracelet," I lied.

"I picked out all of your clothing," she snapped, instantly sensing my mistruth. "You haven't had a bracelet since you came to us. Now tell me what you're doing."

I crossed my arms and stayed in the doorway. "Why do you care?" I asked sharply, irritated that she was snapping at me for no good reason.

She crossed her arms across her chest to mirror me,

completely ignoring my anger. "Why has Sivi been lurking around your room?"

"I don't know what you're talking about," I lied, stepping out of the room to close the door.

I wasn't going to be able to look with Sophie around, so there was no reason to stay in the morbid room any longer than I had to.

Sophie narrowed her eyes at me for a moment, then brushed past me to walk down the hall. For a fleeting second I thought I was off the hook, but then she snapped, "Come with me," as she continued walking.

With a heavy sigh, I followed her tall, black-clad form down so many twists and turns in the hall that I wasn't sure if I'd be able to remember my way back. Finally, she went into a room and left the door open behind her for me to follow.

The room inside was done in deep grays and other neutrals, though rather than being bland, it was cozy. There was a large bed similar to the four-poster in my room, only it didn't have a canopy. I personally liked the canopy-less bed better. The canopy made me feel like a little girl playing princess.

As soon as I stepped inside, Sophie turned on me. She pointed. "Shut the door."

Sophie's fangs were peeking out, and her nervous energy elicited goosebumps on my arms. I debated trying to bolt before she unleashed her temper on me again, but so far Sophie had seemed to genuinely be on my side, and I didn't want to lose that just yet. I shut the door.

Now that we were alone, I expected Sophie to start talking, but instead she just stood with her arms crossed, shifting her weight from foot to foot. It was only then that I noticed that she was still in her clothes from the previous day, just like James.

She bit her lip as if she wanted to say something, but was holding back. "I don't know who else to talk to," she finally blurted out, her anger melting away like a poorly done disguise.

I took a few steps closer to her. My instinct was to reach out and comfort her, but I wasn't sure if Sophie and I were on that level. She solved the problem for me by sitting on her bed and patting the spot beside her with her palm. I sat next to her and waited for her to speak, shivering as her nervous energy touched me.

She turned her worried, dark eyes to me. "Swear to me that you'll keep your mouth shut. It could be very bad for me if anyone knew what I was thinking, and I could make it very bad for you as well."

I frowned. "You know, threatening people really isn't the best way to get them to help you."

She waved me off. "I know, I know. I'm sorry. I had a long night."

When she didn't say anything else, I cleared my throat.

Sophie glanced at me, then took a deep, shaky breath. "I need to help Maya escape." She instantly looked horrified that she'd said what she was thinking out loud.

I tilted my head, wondering if she was tricking me. Sensing she was genuine, I replied, "I think that's a wonderful idea."

"What!" she rasped. "You can't. We can't go against Estus. He is Doyen. He'll have us all killed. You're on thin ice as it is." Tears streaked down her face.

"Okay," I said soothingly, wondering what I'd gotten myself into now. "First start by telling me why you want to free Maya."

Sophie looked at me with red-rimmed eyes and bit her lip again. "She was my lover," she said finally, "and then she left.

She no longer wanted to live in the Salr, but she's not a traitor. Estus claims that she's sided with Aislin, but I know she wouldn't. She wouldn't do anything that would hurt me."

"Who's Aislin again?" I asked, feeling like I wasn't fully comprehending what Sophie was trying to tell me.

"Aislin was once Doyen of a small clan," Sophie explained. "But now she has gathered many clans together. They all answer to her. Estus is afraid that she'll come for us next, and if he's afraid, it means such a thing is likely to happen. They both want this object you're supposed to find. Estus claims it is the only way to protect us."

"So let me get this straight," I began. "Aislin was the one who sent those Vaettir who . . . killed you. Was Maya with them?"

"I told you she's not with them," Sophie sobbed. "She's going to die simply because she did not want to live like we do. Obeying orders and hiding from the sun."

I sighed. I really needed someone to trust, and Sophie had just put her trust in me.

"When I first met Maya she offered me information, but she would only tell me if we were alone. I waited until evening, then went to visit her in her cell. Some of the things she told me . . . " I let my words trail off, still not sure what I thought about everything Maya had told me.

"So you believe me?" Sophie asked like my answer mattered a great deal to her.

I shrugged. "I don't know who to believe, but I'm going to tell you what Maya told me, because I need someone to help me understand what's going on."

I filled Sophie in on everything Maya had said. About half-way through She seemed to calm down as she processed all that I was telling her.

When I finished, she looked worried. "Estus told us about

this object, this . . . charm, but only told a select few of us know he wants *you* to find it. Now we know why."

"So you believe what Maya said?" I asked. "She doesn't know me. She might not have been telling the truth."

She gathered her long hair over her shoulder and started stroking it like it was her favorite pet. "We need to tell my brother," she said finally.

I was both glad and worried that she wanted to tell Alaric. He'd been a lascivious tease, but he'd also been kind to me. Yet, the idea of telling him was troubling. He was loyal to Estus, but I could tell he didn't fully enjoy taking orders. If I had both Sophie and Alaric on my side . . . well, I might not only escape with my life, but I'd have two allies to help me figure out everything else.

"What if he doesn't believe us?" I asked.

She glared at me, though the effect was lessened when she had to sniffle her nose and wipe more tears away. "He may not believe us, but he will also not turn us in. He would never betray his own sister, and well you . . . he has a certain affection for you, even if I do not approve of it."

"How will we get him alone?" I pressed, ignoring what might have been a subtle insult.

Sophie rolled her eyes. "I imagine he'll solve that problem for us soon enough. He's developed a habit of lurking around your bedroom door."

The thought of Alaric hanging out around my bedroom brought a nervous flutter to my stomach, but I decided it would be best not to comment on it. "So *I* have to tell him?" I asked weakly.

Sophie smiled as if she was enjoying some secret thought. "Yes, you'll need to go back to your room and wait for him there. It will work out beautifully actually."

"Beautifully?" I questioned, not liking her tone.

"Well," she answered, "he's much less likely to take his anger out on *you*. So, you can break it to him, and your discussion will lead the way for me to discuss matters more fully with him."

I bit my lip, anxious to find some way out of being the one to tell Alaric. "I don't want his anger either," I argued weakly.

Sophie sighed. "He won't hurt you, and likely won't even get mad at you at all. He would, however, be extremely angry with me, so you telling him first gives him some time to calm down before I speak with him."

"Fine," I agreed sullenly. "I guess I should probably go wait, though I'm not as sure as you are that he'll just show up."

I stood to go, but Sophie grabbed my wrist to stop me. "How was Maya?" she asked, concern back in her voice. "What did James do to her? Estus won't let me see her."

"She's alive," I replied, not wanting to tell her the gruesome torture that Maya had endured. "Let's do our best to keep her that way."

Sophie nodded to herself. "Okay," she said distantly, "now go break the news to Alaric. If he gets angry . . . well, I'm sure it will be okay."

Great, I was off to play the sacrificial lamb, and the look in Sophie's eyes told me that despite her claims, I was about to get roasted.

I left Sophie and went back to my room to wait. I waited so long that I ended up falling asleep. When I awoke, the only indication of time I had was the lighting of the room. It had dimmed to almost darkness, evening, but not the middle of the night, else it would have been pitch black. Panic gripped me. I had slept the whole damn day away again. The stress must have been affecting me more than I'd realized. I'd wasted so much time.

I felt the bed shift and I froze, thinking that Sivi had decided to pay me another visit. I waited for more movement, but nothing happened. Finally, I sat up in bed and shifted my gaze to find Alaric sitting on the side of the bed next to me. He was slumped forward with his elbows on his knees and his hair thrown over one shoulder.

When he made no move to acknowledge me or say anything, I asked, "What's wrong?"

"Well," he began, "I was going about my evening when my sister found me, and she was very upset that I had not yet visited you. Now, I love my sister, but she is not really one to watch out for other women. I pressed her about it, and eventually she told me a very elaborate story."

He turned and leaned toward me enough to make solid eye contact in the dim lighting. "You do realize these allegations can be very dangerous?"

I clenched my fists in the bedding. "I'm not making any allegations. I just told Sophie what I'd been told."

"Sophie's judgment is clouded on this matter," he stated.

I sat up straighter and pulled my knees up to my chest as I watched him. "So you're not going to help us then?"

He laughed bitterly. "Well I can't just let you get caught now, can I? Sophie is determined to see this through, and if I don't agree, she'll just do it without me and get herself killed."

"So . . . you don't believe us, but you'll still help us?" I pressed.

He met my eyes again. "Something like that."

He continued staring into my eyes long enough that I finally looked down, feeling uncomfortable with the pressure of his gaze.

He reached out a hand and lifted my chin up so I would

meet his eyes again. "Why does Estus believe that only you can find the charm? I've heard little of the thing until now, and suddenly it's in the Salr and only our new executioner can find it. It seems far too convenient to be true."

So apparently Sophie didn't tell him *everything*. "Maya thinks that I can somehow use the spirits of the dead to find it. She thinks that I might be able to communicate with them. I don't know how much Estus knows, but I don't think he's figured out that piece of the puzzle yet. He thinks if I search I'll be able to *see* it."

"And when the hell did Maya get a chance to tell you that?" he asked in surprise. "I doubt she'd say all of that with James around."

I blushed and was glad that he probably couldn't see it in the dim lighting. "I might have made a trip down to her cell," I admitted.

He placed his palm against his forehead in a sarcastic *now why didn't I think of that?* gesture. "Of course you did," he sighed, then turned back toward me. "You know, it would be easier to keep you out of trouble if you bothered to tell me your schemes beforehand."

"I hadn't planned on telling anyone my *schemes*," I explained. "I only told Sophie because she took a risk telling me about Maya. I figured it was safe."

He stood and started pacing in the dark. "And what makes you think that you're so unsafe here?" he asked as he walked.

I stood, finally feeling agitated myself. "What is there to make me think that I *am* safe? I was forcefully brought here, if you don't remember. Sophie almost died, and that was only from an outside attack. James seems to be torturing someone new every day. You people killed your old executioner. What did he even do to deserve it? If I can't find this charm for Estus, will I be next?"

"I'm here because I don't want you to be next!" Alaric hissed. He moved to stand in front of me. He seemed shocked at what he'd just said. Finally, as if coming to terms with his admission, he lowered his voice and added, "I don't want to see your heart in a box with all the others."

"So I ask you again," I began calmly, "How could I ever feel safe?"

He smiled bitterly, and I realized that he had gotten rather close for me to be able to see it. "You have a point, I suppose," he admitted.

"Darn right I do," I seconded.

He smiled mischievously, "Though you would probably feel safer if you had someone to sleep in this big, lonely room with you."

I looked up at him innocently. "Do you think Sophie would have a slumber party with me?"

"Sophie," he said as he took a step closer, "was not who I was referring to."

I placed my hand against his chest and pushed. "I don't think so, *buddy*. We may all be in this together now, but don't go getting any funny ideas." My words belied my racing heart.

He didn't step back.

I gulped. Damn it all, I was drawn to him. Maybe it was all the mystical death and war stuff Sophie had told me, but it was hard to think straight. "There's something else," I said breathlessly.

Alaric nodded for me to go on.

"When I was first summoned to see Maya," I explained, trying to keep the quaver out of my voice, "she wasn't afraid of me at all, and it was like Estus knew that was the case. He even let her whisper in my ear. That's how I knew to go find her in the dungeon. There were no guards around her cell to keep her from speaking to anyone. Why would Estus let an alleged traitor tell me anything, when he's so intent on keeping me in the dark? And why was I allowed to walk around alone all morning?"

Alaric's eyebrows raised. "Maybe because he wanted you to do exactly what you're doing now." He paused in thought. "If Estus knew that Maya had information on how to get the charm, and knew she wouldn't tell him, he would logically turn to tricking someone else into finding out the information."

Icy fear shot through my gut, speeding my heart rate even more than Alaric's closeness. I was an idiot. I'd expected a trick, but I hadn't expected to fall for it. "So why hasn't he come to get it out of me then?"

His brow furrowed. "Because it would make much more sense to just wait for you to find it. Then he could take it from you and be done with it."

I shivered at the thought.

"I won't let anything happen to you," he assured.

I shook my head. "How can you promise that?"

He reached out his hand, rubbing it absentmindedly up and down my arm as his gaze turned distant with thought. After a few uncomfortable seconds, a smile crossed his face. "I have a plan."

My thoughts were becoming increasingly jumbled at his touch. "Care to share it?" I breathed.

Alaric smiled even wider. "Nope."

He placed his other hand on my free arm and pulled me against him. All of my arguments slipped away. All I could think of was that the room was dark and cozy, and Alaric's body felt warm and exhilarating. I looked up into his eyes and felt like a field mouse caught by the big, predatory, barn cat.

He had managed to distract me from what we were originally discussing, and I wasn't sure if he was really going to help us, or just not tattle on us. Did he really have a plan, and if so, why wasn't he telling me? I suspected he was distracting me on purpose, and I should have pressed the subject, but the warm electric feeling in my chest made the fear I'd been feeling just a short time before irrelevant.

Alaric leaned down and kissed me, just a soft caress. That small touch drew out my years of solitude and sadness. The softness was nice, but I wanted more. If matters were really as bad as they seemed, I wasn't going to waste my time with gentle niceties.

I wrapped one hand around the back of Alaric's neck and the other around his waist, pulling him tighter against me. He let out a sound in his throat that made me pull even harder.

He put his hands underneath my butt and lifted, giving me the choice of either hopping up and wrapping my legs around him, or keeping them straight to be held off of the ground awkwardly. I hopped. He held me up and carried me toward the bed effortlessly.

Being carried like that was a new experience for me. Matthew and the few guys I'd dated before him had been my height or just an inch taller, which meant if they lifted me up, my torso would tower above them.

With Alaric's height, the once-awkward position was comfortable. Well, it was comfortable for the few moments it took to reach the bed. I was no longer thinking about comfort as he laid me gently on the bedspread and smoothed himself over me.

As he kissed down to my collarbone, he glided his hands up from my hips to the sides of my chest, then ran the barest of touches over my bra. I tried to hold still, but the anticipation was too much.

I pushed at Alaric's shoulders and rolled him off me. At first a look of confusion crossed his face, but it was soon erased with a wry smile as I slowly crawled up his body until I was straddling him.

I grabbed his arms and pinned them over his head, much like how he had pinned me during my sparring lesson. His smile turned into something dark and feral, just as I felt the same smile creep across my face.

See? I told you I'm no cream puff.

CHAPTER TEN

I had reveled in the feeling of touching and being touched. It was a relief to know that I could still feel that way at all anymore. Since Matthew, I had closed myself off, not even allowing myself the simple pleasure of a kiss for fear of harming someone again.

To go past a kiss and have everything thrown at me in one heaping punch of passion left me nearly delirious. Beyond that, was the feeling of actually drifting off in someone's arms. It was delectable, but something still itched at me. I couldn't stop thinking about Maya wasting away down in her cell, or even worse, about James taking another shot at her.

I believed what she had told me more than what anyone else had said. She stood nothing to gain in meeting with me, and even told me the very thing that she'd kept from James and Estus. She had tried to leave the Salr, and they brought her back and tortured her. Even the possibility of her choosing to work with our supposed enemies wasn't excuse enough for what had been done to her.

Alaric drifted into what seemed a deep sleep as I worried over a woman I barely knew. Of course, I was in bed with a man I barely knew, so I couldn't judge Maya based on that fact alone. I stayed in bed a moment longer, saying in my head *just do it, just do it*, until I finally sat up and gently placed my feet on the floor.

Alaric turned onto his side and reached toward my now-empty spot, but his eyes didn't open. I wanted to reach out and touch him, but I couldn't risk waking him. Instead, I crept around the room, picking up the pieces of my clothing that had been thrown haphazardly about. When I had everything, I dressed quickly in the corner as I watched Alaric for any signs that he might be waking up.

After quietly putting my tennis shoes on, I took one more moment to observe Alaric in my bed. It was strange seeing him in such a defenseless position, when normally it seemed like nothing could touch him. I left him there as the warmth of his embrace left my skin.

The halls had a little more light than my room, which I was thankful for, but it also meant that I would be easy to spot. Of course if Stella, the Lindworm, was out and about, she would sniff me out regardless.

I wasn't sure if I should try to find Sophie, or if I should just look for the charm. Maya had said that there was no way for me to get her out of her cell, but there had to be a way. If someone could put her in, then I should be able to get her out, especially with Sophie's help.

I hurried down the hallway, following the twists and turns that led to Sophie's room. She opened the door before I even had a chance to knock and pulled me inside.

"What did he say?" she whispered as soon as the door was shut. "I didn't mean to tell him before you could, but he forced it out of me."

She'd changed clothes with the obvious intention of not getting any sleep, and was now dressed in skin-tight black leather pants and a billowy black blouse. There was one of those battery-powered touch lights illuminating the room, answering my question as to what we were supposed to do when the Salr decided that it was lights out. I felt a bit bitter that no one had given me a touch light.

"Well, he doesn't fully agree with us," I explained, "but he doesn't want us to get ourselves killed either. I'm not sure how much he'll help, but he'll do his best to make sure we don't get caught."

Sophie's eyes narrowed at me. "And what took you so long to come here?" she asked suspiciously. "I've been waiting *forever*."

My face suddenly felt hot. "I um-" I stammered.

Her eyes widened. "You slept with him! I told you not to."

I shrugged. "Sorry."

"Don't be sorry," she snapped. "Just don't come whining to me when he breaks your heart."

I didn't know how to respond to that, so instead I asked, "What do we do now?"

She turned away from me and started pacing, reminding me of Alaric. All I wanted was to crawl back in bed with him.

"Focus," Sophie ordered, glancing at me. "We need to help Maya escape, and we need to find the charm. The problem is which one first. If we help Maya escape, then everyone will be looking for the traitor that did it and it will become more difficult to find the charm in secrecy. We could try finding the charm first, but who knows how long it will take? I don't like leaving Maya down there."

"Maybe we just shouldn't find the charm at all," I offered. "If it's such a dangerous thing . . . "

Sophie shook her head. "If Estus wants it, it will be found. He's already figured out that he needs an executioner to find it. He *will* eventually discover that using the traitor's hearts is the key, even if Maya won't tell him. If he discovers what to do, then we'll have no chance of keeping the charm from him."

"So you agree with Maya then?" I asked. "She thinks that Estus would be a tyrant, but isn't he kind of one already?"

Sophie snorted. "He's only a small scale tyrant right now, and he's kept it hidden well. Most of our people love him. I've never held any love for the man, but my time spent here has been mostly comfortable. I was content, until I found out about Maya. Now I can't ignore the fact that I could end up in a cell just as easily. If what Maya says about the charm is true, then Estus would be a uniting leader amongst the clans. He wouldn't have to worry about keeping up appearances in order to keep his numbers strong. He would have *all* of the numbers, so what would a few extra deaths mean?"

The implications were making me dizzy. I shouldn't care what happened to the Vaettir, but if all these freaks were banded together, what might that mean for the world at large? I slumped onto the bed. "But what would he do with the numbers?" I asked weakly. "World domination? Is he *that* power hungry?

Sophie's gaze went distant. She spoke like she was standing on the edge of a cliff. "I believe that Maya thinks he would have us on the outside world again, but not how we were before. I am not sure of that. As far as I'm concerned, Estus only wants power. Keeping his people underground under close supervision would give him that. The only thing we know for sure, is that whatever he plans, it isn't good. No one strives for such power for noble reasons. We need to find that charm and get rid of it."

I stood, my mind made up. "We need to help Maya first."

"It could ruin any chance we have—" Sophie began.

"We help Maya first," I said again. "We would still be in

the dark if it weren't for her. We can't just take her information and let her rot."

Sophie eyed me very carefully, then suddenly pulled me into a hug. She whispered, "Thank you," then let me go abruptly.

She opened a large closet and started clanking around inside while I waited. I went to the closet door to watch her as she pawed through several large wooden crates.

"I have something in here that could help cut through the bars of Maya's cell," she explained. "If we can get down there with no one seeing us, we should be able to get her out."

"Are there no keys?" I asked, puzzled.

Sophie shook her head. "The Salr listens to the Doyen of the clan. If he wants someone to be imprisoned, the cell will not open without his say-so."

I nodded, creeped out by the idea of the Salr listening to Estus, or anyone for that matter. Buildings were not supposed to be sentient, even when they were magical underground sanctuaries.

I wondered if the Salr knew what we were doing, and would tattle on us to Estus. Of course, if that were the case, Sophie likely wouldn't be talking about things so openly, and we would have already been thrown in cells ourselves.

"So what do we do with her once she's free of the cell?" I asked. "If the only way out is Sivi's pool—"

"That's not the only way out," Sophie sighed.

I put my hands on my hips. "But Alaric—"

"He lied," she interrupted, finally turning to look at me. Her face softened at my hurt expression. "He had no choice. He was only following orders."

Confusion replaced a bit of the hurt, but only a bit. "Did Estus really get that specific? Why would he want me to believe there's no way out? It's not like my escape attempts were successful."

"Orders concerning you were very clear," she said bitterly. "He's not going to risk you getting snatched away. Executioners aren't exactly a dime a dozen, and we've already lost one."

I crossed my arms. "He already *killed* one you mean."

Sophie rolled her eyes like it made no difference. "What I'm saying is that he wants to keep you here, badly, and from what you've told me, Sivi wants you to leave just as badly. It all backs up what Maya said." She stood with a small, perfectly round stone in her hand.

I eyed it skeptically. "And that's going to get Maya out of her cell?"

"Yes," she replied. She closed her fingers around the stone and looked me up and down. "Are you ready?"

"W-what?" I stammered. "You want to go *now*?"

She nodded. "Isn't that what you came here for?"

I shook my head rapidly. "I came here to *plan*. Shouldn't we wake Alaric?"

Sophie's eyes narrowed again. "You left him sleeping in your bed, didn't you?"

I looked down at the floor, embarrassed. In an attempt to change the subject, I asked, "I thought we told him everything because we needed his help. Shouldn't we tell him what we're doing?"

Sophie sighed. "The purpose was to have him willing to help *you* should anything happen to me tonight."

It was my turn to narrow my eyes. "You planned on helping Maya tonight regardless of what I chose to do, didn't you?"

Sophie blushed, not quite meeting my accusing gaze. "I can't leave her there. I can't risk Estus storing her heart with all of the others. If you had chosen to find the charm first, I would have tried to help her on my own."

I clenched my jaw in frustration. At least she was honest. "So if something *does* happen to you, then what?"

"You flee the scene," she instructed. "If anyone sees you, you tell them I forced you to help me. Then you and Alaric can find the charm and get rid of it."

I shook my head. "If I blame you like that, you'll end up just like Maya."

Sophie's lips twisted into a wry smile. "If we get to the point of you needing to blame me, I will already be dead or on the run. Just promise me that if the former occurs, you'll find a way to release me. I don't want to be stuck in a box."

I nodded. "I promise."

Sophie hugged me again, then pulled away, blushing harder. "Are you ready?"

I took a shaky breath. Alaric probably wouldn't forgive me if I let his sister get killed, but it was a risk I was going to have to take. "As ready as I'll ever be," I sighed.

Sophie looked at me like she didn't quite believe me, and she shouldn't have. I wasn't ready at all. A silly, childish part of me thought that maybe with Alaric I could be happy. Sophie might argue that, and she might be right, but I could still try. Now I was going to risk the first man I'd been able to touch without the risk of killing him. Sophie thought I could get away without blame, but there was no guarantee. Just the thought of being under Estus' scrutinizing gaze made me shiver.

I could have tried forming a semblance of a life with Alaric, but instead I was about to risk it all for a woman I'd just met. It was stupid, but I couldn't just leave her there to rot, and I couldn't be blindly happy while people were being tortured for no good reason. Ignorance was bliss, and I already knew far too much.

Maybe at first I could have believed that what I was expected to do was just a casualty of war, but what did the other side think about that? It would have been nice to ask the last executioner what he thought about it, but he had been tortured and killed by James, all on Estus' orders.

Even if I didn't want to save Maya, I couldn't just wait idly by for the same fate to befall me. I shook my head at my own foolishness. I should have just left when Sivi gave me the opportunity. I was in way over my head, and sinking fast.

CHAPTER ELEVEN

The dungeon was just how I remembered it: dark, scary, and filled with pain. We found Maya right where I had left her, but not *how* I had left her. At some point James had taken one of her hands to match her already missing foot.

Sophie started crying the moment she saw Maya curled up in the corner of her cell. The battered woman now reached her one hand through the bars for Sophie to hold while she knelt in front of her.

Sophie's back shook with silent tears. "I'll kill him for this," she rasped.

"It wasn't James' fault," Maya muttered. "He may be a sick bastard, but he was just following orders. Estus is the one who did this to me."

Sophie raised her head to meet Maya's gaze. "And that is who I mean to kill."

Maya's shoulders slumped with a sigh. "Sophie—"

I couldn't help the feeling that there were eyes on my back. I felt for both of them. *Literally*, I could feel Sophie's heartache, but we needed to get out of the dungeon before someone caught us. "Umm, not to interrupt, but we really should get this show on the road."

"What show?" Maya asked sharply.

"We're busting you out," I explained. I offered a hand to Sophie. Her fingers trembled as I helped her to her feet.

"No," Maya rasped, shaking her head in disbelief. "You can't. You'll just end up down here too."

Sophie ignored her as she fished the small stone out of the pocket of her leather pants. Before Maya could protest further, Sophie placed the stone against one of the bars. At first nothing happened, then sparks began to fly out from underneath the stone. I watched in awe as Sophie withdrew her hand, leaving the stone in place. After a few seconds the sparks stopped, and she reclaimed the stone to reveal a clear cut through the bar.

"What the hell was that?" I asked.

Sophie didn't acknowledge me, and instead set to placing the stone on each bar until a perfect cut went about two feet across. Next she cut the bottoms of the bars, instructing me to hold each one so it wouldn't fall when it came loose. The bars were much heavier than they looked, and my arms felt like pudding by the time we had a hole big enough for Maya to fit through.

Once the bars were all set aside, Sophie crawled through the opening, then helped Maya up, balancing on her remaining foot.

"I wish we had something to help with the pain," I commented without thinking as they maneuvered through the opening.

"Maya doesn't feel pain," Sophie explained.

"How did you manage to keep that information from Estus until now?" I asked.

It seemed pointless to torture someone who couldn't feel

pain. Of course, I suppose the threat of losing a foot could make a person talk regardless of whether or not they'd feel it.

"I knew better than to share my secrets around here," Maya said, looking pointedly at Sophie.

"I've learned that lesson too," Sophie said quietly.

Maya nodded and we all started forward. Eventually I went to Maya's other side to help speed our progress. She reeked of burned flesh and other smells, and I had to hold onto her scabbed skin more tightly than I would have liked, but it was necessary.

We were lucky that Maya was small, or we would have had trouble carrying her out. I couldn't help but wonder how she'd even survive out of the Salr with the condition she was in.

Sophie's eyes caught mine over the top of Maya's head. The look in her eyes was sad, yet determined, and told me exactly what she was thinking. She was going to go with Maya and leave me to find the charm on my own, even if we managed to get Maya out undetected. Sophie watched as the realization played across my face. She bit her lip, waiting for my reaction. Doubting that I really had much choice in the matter, I nodded that it was okay.

As we reached the stairs, the three of us looked up with concern. The tall steps were strenuous enough to climb in the best of conditions, and these were definitely not the best of conditions. Our worries about the stairs were erased as a new worry stepped into view. A tall figure came to stand at the top of the stairway, clearly intending to block our way, though it was too dark to see his face.

"I'll try to keep whoever it is busy," I said quietly. "You run with Maya."

"You'll be killed," Sophie replied harshly. "Or worse, you'll end up in Maya's cell, only *you'll* be able to feel the pain that

James will cause you. Run to whoever it is for help. Tell them I forced you to do this."

The figure took a step down the stairs, then another. "We're caught now," I said through gritted teeth. "And me turning you in won't do any good. I'll try to take them down, then I'll follow you. I'll leave too."

The thought of leaving without telling Alaric sent an uncomfortable squirm through my heart, but it had to be done. I couldn't involve him any further. If Estus hunted Maya down, he would hunt anyone else that left too. I ran out of time to think as the figure drew closer. It was clearly a man, but I still couldn't see his face.

I let go of Maya and prepared to charge.

"Maddy?" a man's voice said. "Is that you?"

"You idiot," Sophie chided, relief clear in her voice. "You scared us half to death."

"You should be scared," Alaric whispered back. "What the hell are you two doing down here?" He eyes turned toward me as he stepped close enough for me to see in the near dark. "First you ask for my help, then you sneak out of bed while I'm sleeping and run off, once again not allowing me to help. What happened to letting me in on your schemes *before* you carry them out?"

I shrugged, at a loss for words.

Obviously frustrated, Alaric walked past me and effortlessly lifted Maya up into his arms. "The North Breach?" he asked.

"Yes," Sophie answered simply as she started forward, leading the way.

I wanted to ask what the North Breach was, but kept my mouth shut as I followed our party up the stairs, then started down the hallway silently. We walked unhindered for a while and I was just starting to feel a little less nervous when I heard clicking behind me, then something poked into my back. I jumped forward and bumped into Sophie. The forward jump wasn't enough to get me out of the way, as the next thing I knew I was on my back with a tremendous weight on top of me.

Stella's rottweiler face panted inches from my nose, forcing hot, steamy breath into my sinuses. I gagged, but didn't try to scoot away. She could have easily crushed me with her thick middle, but instead she hovered above me with her legs to either side, only placing enough weight on me to keep me in place.

"Stella!" Sophie hissed.

Stella looked up at Sophie and growled. I watched upside down as Alaric gently let Maya down to her foot. She leaned against the wall as if only having one foot was a perfectly normal thing for her.

Alaric glanced at Sophie. "I'll grab Stella, then you grab Maddy."

Sophie replied with a curt nod. As Alaric stepped closer, Stella lowered her belly more firmly against me, still not crushing, but making it obvious that she didn't want me to go anywhere.

Alaric stepped behind Stella so that I could no longer see him.

"Be ready to grab her quickly," he whispered. "I don't want Stella's claws to get to Maddy when I lift her."

I thought the idea of Alaric lifting Stella questionable in itself, since the beast had to weigh several hundred pounds. Even more questionable was the idea that Sophie could get me to my feet quickly enough to avoid getting skewered by Stella's large, bear-like claws.

"One," Alaric counted down.

"Two," Sophie said.

Before anyone could say three, Alaric and Sophie both lunged toward the creature. Suddenly I was on my feet, and Stella was thrashing around in Alaric's arms as he tried to hold her aloft.

"Go!" he grunted.

Sophie shoved me forward ahead of her, then picked Maya up in a less-than-graceful fireman's carry. It was either run or block Sophie's way, so I forced myself forward. I looked back over my shoulder as we took a nearby turn. The last thing I saw was Stella turning around in Alaric's grasp to slash him across the chest just as she let out a loud bellow.

"We have to go back!" I cried as Sophie used her free shoulder to shove me forward.

"He'll catch up!" she yelled back.

I cringed at her shout, but after Stella's warning shriek, we were no longer concerned with silence. Our only hope now was speed, and I was hindering us.

I tried to force my way around Sophie to go back to Alaric, causing her to nearly drop Maya. Sophie blocked me and got in my face as she repositioned Maya over her shoulder. Eyes that had gone full-feline stared me down. "He *will* catch up. Now *go*."

I went, not sure where I was running to, but trusting that Sophie would guide me. Tears streamed down my face as I thought of Alaric getting cut up by Stella. What if he didn't catch up? Would Estus blame everything on Alaric if Sophie and I left?

"Wait!" Sophie shouted.

I came to a skidding halt in front of a door to my left as Sophie stopped right beside me. She still had Maya over her shoulder, and her little stone was in her free hand. Sophie placed the stone against the lock on the door until it became a melted hunk of metal. She pushed the door open, then gestured for me to go inside.

I staggered in, then stopped, expecting a room and not a long, narrow hall. I forced myself to run again, even though my muscles and lungs were screaming at me from over-exertion. Sophie's steps echoed behind me. Clean stone walls whipped by, eventually showing signs of erosion. We hit an expanse of vines creeping up over cracked stones. I couldn't tell for sure since everything was a blur around me, but it seemed like the vines were moving.

The hallway ended suddenly in a writhing mass of vines. Sophie set Maya gently down amongst the serpentine tendrils. The smaller tendrils crept forward and instantly began to envelop her, just like they'd done to me when I was first brought to the Salr.

I watched in awe as Maya's form disappeared from view with barely a sound. I was so entranced that I only heard the footsteps a moment before someone grabbed my wrist and whirled me around. I came face to face with James. He watched my fear for a moment, then tugged my wrist again, bringing me toward him. My back thudded against his chest and his arm looped around me, tight enough to constrict my breathing.

"I've been dreaming about having you chained to a wall," he grunted as I struggled against him. "It looks like my dreams are about to come true."

Sophie watched us as she backed herself toward the vines. I realized what she was going to do as the first tear crept slowly down her face.

"I'm sorry, Maddy," she said softly before turning her sad eyes to James.

"I'd stop you," he began, "but what I'm going to do to your

brother will cause you so much more pain than knives and fire ever could."

I started struggling again as Sophie lowered herself into the vines. She met my eyes until the vines reached her face and pulled her down into the swirling mass.

I continued struggling as James pulled me back away from the only route of escape. "You can't kill me," I grunted, gasping for a full breath. "Estus needs me."

James laughed. "Accidents happen," he said happily, forcing me back down the hallway. "An accident happened with the last executioner, and we found a new one just fine."

My mind raced at his admission. "So he wasn't a traitor then?" I breathed, already knowing the answer.

James laughed. "He couldn't figure out how to find the charm. I had hoped to inspire him, but I might have gone too far."

"So you knew?" I gasped. "You've known what Estus was looking for since the beginning?"

We had reached the door with its melted lock just as Alaric came into view. His bare chest and neck were a bloody mess. I squirmed in discomfort, feeling every little cut on his body.

Ignoring his blood dripping onto the floor, Alaric sneered his unnaturally elongated teeth at James. I had only seen his teeth look like that one other time, and that was right after he'd bitten a man's throat out. Even as injured as he was, he still planned on a fight.

James tossed me aside like I weighed nothing.

I staggered, thudding into the wall.

"You better not have hurt Stella," he hissed.

I turned as Alaric glared at James defiantly, then spit blood onto the ground. Whether it was his own blood, or someone else's, I wasn't sure. "You'll have to get through me to find out."

James took one step forward.

"*That*, will not be necessary," Estus said as he came into view behind Alaric.

Alaric stepped aside, repositioning himself in front of me.

Estus cocked his head to one side. His loose gray hair streamed over the shoulder of his dark colored robe like silk.

"Truly Alaric," he said calmly, "you could have at least *tried* to keep your sister here."

Alaric dropped to one knee and bowed his head. "I was preoccupied," he apologized, "but at least you still have your executioner."

I looked from Estus to Alaric's hunched back in confusion. Just a moment before he had been ready to fight James, and now that Estus was here, he was just handing me over? I stared down at Alaric, willing him to turn and look up at me, but he just knelt there as a small pool of blood formed underneath him.

"Take her to a cell," Estus ordered.

James looked just as shocked as I felt. "He was helping them," he stated, pointing at Alaric's still form. "I should be bringing *him* to a cell."

Estus looked directly at me when he said, "Alaric was working on my orders. Madeline is the only prisoner here."

James growled and grabbed me again, shoving me forward harder than he needed to. Alaric kept his head bowed as Estus approached him, then we turned a corner and I could no longer see the true traitor in my life.

CHAPTER TWELVE

My bones ached from the cold as I slowly lifted myself to a seated position. I had no idea how long I'd been left alone in the dark, but judging by the pain in my stomach, I'd say at least 24 hours. The side I'd been lying on slowly regained feeling as I groggily peered around in the darkness.

I reached forward blindly until my hands met with cool metal. I snaked my grip around the bars as everything came crashing back once more. Sophie and Maya, James, Estus . . . and Alaric. He had betrayed me, and now I was in the same dungeon we had rescued Maya from. Poetic justice at its best.

With nothing to comfort me in the pure darkness, I resorted to curling up in a corner with my back pressed against the wall. I squeezed my eyes tightly shut. The darkness was much worse than the hunger or cold. I laid there for what felt like hours. Every time I tried to open my eyes, I would panic from lack of bearings. Realistically I knew I was in a cell by myself, but when you can't even see an inch in front of your nose, you constantly feel like something is going to reach out and grab you.

A noise somewhere down the long hall that ended in my cell startled me back into full awareness. My eyes snapped open before I could stop them, only this time I wasn't assaulted by the oppressive darkness. The light at the end of the hall crept closer, and a sliver of hope made my heart race.

That hope sank to the pit of my stomach when I saw who was approaching. James eyed me thoughtfully with his cold, pale eyes as he came to stand in front of my cell. His eyes reminded me of the eyes of a corpse . . . cold, dead, and unfeeling. Not liking the feeling of him looking down on me while I huddled in my corner, I forced myself to my feet.

He eyed me for a few more silent moments, as if he'd memorize the pitiful sight of me, then smirked. "I just don't see it," he said, shaking his head.

"See—" I rasped, then took a moment to wet my throat. "See what?" The words felt foreign on my tongue after the prolonged silence of my imprisonment. Emotions that I'd been avoiding came flooding into reality now that I had a target for them.

"Why Estus won't let me kill you," he stated bluntly as he pushed his golden hair out of his face.

His hair was that annoying length where it's almost long enough to tuck behind the ears, but not quite, so it always just fell forward instead. His hair and faintly tan skin gave the image of someone who spent a lot of time hiking, or doing other outdoor activities, yet his favorite activities were reserved for dark rooms, behind locked doors. A dungeon cell was close enough.

I leaned back against the wall with my hips slightly jutted forward. I'd only done it because I was ready to lose my feet, but James didn't need to know that. When in doubt, try to look tough.

"What do you want?" I asked coolly, ignoring his insult.

James put his free hand on one of the bars of my cell so he could lean forward and leer at me. "Just because Estus won't let me kill you, doesn't mean I can't harm you. I wanted to see you so that I could picture clearly what I'm going to do to you."

I glared at him in response. The idea of being left to James' tender mercies made me want to scream. I'd seen what he liked to do to his victims. I doubted I would come out of the ordeal mentally or physically intact.

"It must have hurt when Alaric let me carry you off," he said suddenly.

I knew he was just trying to get a reaction out of me, but I couldn't help the hurt expression that crossed my face. It *had* hurt, but even more than that, it had been humiliating. I never should have trusted Alaric, and I was paying for that mistake ten-fold.

I corrected my expression to one of extreme distaste and grumbled, "Fuck off."

James lifted his hands in a mock expression of fear. "Oooh, the little girl has some teeth after all."

I staggered closer to where James was leaning and pushed my face against the cool steel, inches from where his hand gripped the bar. "Come closer and I'll show you my teeth," I taunted.

James laughed at me, but he pushed away from the bars instead of leaning closer. "All in due time, darlin'. All in due time."

With a final laugh he walked back down the hall, taking the light with him. I slumped back into my corner, feeling utterly defeated. Sophie had abandoned me, Alaric had betrayed me, and the only person who cared enough to visit my cell was a deranged sadist. I had heard that things start to go downhill when you neared thirty, but this was just ridiculous.

The darkness eased again sometime later as someone I didn't know came into view with a torch. The woman slid a hunk of bread and a single, small cup of water through the bars of my cell, then silently walked away.

As I devoured the bread so fast that I almost choked, I thought of what the food delivery might mean. Estus obviously wanted me alive, at least for the time being. He still needed an executioner to find his stupid charm, though I'd be damned if *I* was going to find it for him. He'd kill me as soon as I did. After I died, there would be no one to release my spirit, so some part of me would be stuck in my dismembered corpse forever.

The thought almost made the bread come back up, but I forced it back down with a gulp of water. By this point, I was pretty sure that Estus kept many hearts in the same place he'd shown me the heart of the last executioner. I would not be surprised if there was a drawer reserved in that room for me. There probably was one for Sophie too, if she ever came back. Alaric's heart was safe, if he even had one.

I tried to turn my thoughts away from Sophie and Alaric, but the bitter feeling of betrayal flooded in regardless. I had helped Sophie free Maya, and the two of them left me to rot. I should have never trusted Sophie or Alaric. I shouldn't have trusted anyone. To the Vaettir, I was a tool, and nothing more.

I couldn't help but feel like everything that had happened was punishment for being what I was. I could trash talk the other Vaettir as much as I wanted, but it was *my* curse to take life. It was *my* curse that had gotten me into this position. It seemed so much worse than having telekinesis or turning part feline from time to time.

I couldn't blame the humans who were frightened of us centuries ago, forcing the Vaettir to go into hiding, if I were to believe what I'd been told. In hiding was where we deserved to be. It was where *I* deserved to be. Still, if I had the opportunity, I would go live amongst the humans again, even if it endangered them. Call me selfish all you want. You'd be right.

I was startled as another light came into view. I had already been fed, and James had already taunted me, so there was no reason for anyone else to visit.

My heart pattered nervously, hoping in spite of myself that this new visitor would be Alaric. He would come and tell me that it had been an elaborate ruse. He had been on my side all along, but couldn't let Estus know. I would be freed at once and we would run away together.

I was overwhelmed by a sinking feeling in my gut as Sivi came into view. The pale, fairy-like creature swayed toward my cell, though her feet didn't make a sound. Her violet eyes and translucent hair were illuminated by a small, hovering light in the palm of her hand. I wasn't even surprised by the free-floating ball of light. I'd seen things more astounding ten times over.

Sivi cocked her head, observing me. "I told you not to trust them," she chided. "You could have been free."

"Lack of foresight is a real bitch," I grumbled. "What do you want?"

"I want the charm," she said simply. "I will free you in return."

"What would you do with it?" I asked, actually considering the offer. Sivi probably wasn't the best person to be granted ultimate power, but I'd take her over Estus any day of the week.

"I would put us back where we belong," she answered.

"We are guardians of nature. To live in the cage of the Salr is blasphemy. It is not meant for this."

"And what of those who would resist?" I pressed. "Many of the Vaettir enjoy their current existence."

Sivi shrugged and made it clear by her expression that I was boring her. "They will die. Those who choose this life are abominations. This is not what we're meant to be."

I rose to my feet and walked toward the bars of my cell. I towered over Sivi, and I felt a little better looking down at the tiny woman rather than looking up at her.

"What about the humans?" I asked. "The world is not how it used to be."

Sivi spat on the ground in disgust. "The Vaettir are far greater in number now. We will not be hunted as we were in the past. Humans will grovel at our feet and beg forgiveness for what they have done."

"And that is our natural place?" I asked skeptically. "Nature guardians who rule over humanity?"

"The humans have destroyed the home granted to us by the gods," she said almost sadly, then her face contorted back to anger as she added, "and they will pay."

I shook my head. "I don't think I'll be helping you."

Sivi pressed her face close to mine and sneered so that I could see her tiny, pointed teeth. "You would rather rot here than be free?" she snarled. "You're a fool."

I shrugged. "At least this way, I'll be the only one to die."

Sivi let out an ugly laugh. "An executioner that values human life, how precious. You're as twisted as the rest of them."

I didn't really like being lumped in with *the rest of them*, since they had only brought me grief, but I kept quiet. I was more concerned with the fate of humans than I was with the fate of the Vaettir. Plus, I was beginning to believe that the

Vaettir really were all evil. I didn't particularly want to help any of them. If I was going to die a gruesome, torturous death, I might as well do it with a bit of dignity.

Sivi glared at me for a moment longer, then turned to go. I watched as her slender form seemed to levitate down the hallway silently. She stopped half-way down and looked back over her bony shoulder at me with a malicious grin. "Remember when it comes time to choose sides, that one ruler locked you in the cell, and the other would have had you freed."

I fell back to the ground as she disappeared from view, regretting my decision, but knowing I could have done no different. I'd done enough harm already. While I'd take freedom if it was offered under other circumstances, I'd be damned if I was going to sacrifice countless human lives just for a chance to see the sun again. A few, maybe, but not the large scale bloodshed Sivi had in mind.

CHAPTER THIRTEEN

It seemed like a full day had passed before I once again saw the light of a torch. A man and a women I had never seen before removed me from my cell, and held me up by my arms as we walked down the hall, then ascended the enormous, stone stairway leading away from the dungeon. I was weak enough that I didn't argue or try to escape. I was just happy to be out of the darkness.

The man glanced at me nervously as we walked. He looked young, with dark hair cropped close to his skull, making his blue eyes seem wider. He seemed unsure of himself. I almost thought about trying to reason with him, but then I saw the woman's face. Her lovely hazel eyes looked at me with an expression that said it all. I was the scum of the earth, a traitor, and I deserved what I had coming to me. She tossed her ginger colored hair over her shoulder as she looked away, a gesture perfected by mean girls the world over.

I was beginning to see that Estus' power didn't only extend to telekinetic feats and a little mind reading. His real power was in the sway he held over his people. If he told them that jumping off a bridge would help their clan, I had little doubt that most of them would do it.

The couple brought me to a bathroom I'd never been to, though it was nearly identical to the one I'd used on a regular basis before my imprisonment. They shoved me ahead of them, then shut the door behind us. The woman gestured to the bathtub.

I glanced at the clean, white, tub, having no desire to hop in. I turned toward her and crossed my arms. "What's the point of bathing if James is just going to kill me?"

The woman wrinkled her nose at me. "You stink."

I looked at the tub again, then back to the man and woman blocking the doorway. I could try getting past them, but I doubted Estus would send only two people to guard me if they weren't fully equipped for the task.

Deciding that it wasn't my time to escape, I turned my back and began undressing. My black silk top was in surprisingly good shape for all I'd been through, as were the black jeans. I *did* stink though. Sweating during the attempted escape with Sophie, then lying in a dungeon for several days had taken its toll.

I slipped down into the bathtub before even filling the water, wanting to cover my nudity as quickly as possible. The man and woman watched me dispassionately, not interested in my state of undress either way.

I plugged the drain and turned on the faucet, then turned back to my prison guards. "So," I began casually, "what lies has Estus told you about me?"

The woman glared at me. "You are a traitor, working for Aislin. You freed a valuable prisoner, and so, have been sentenced to death."

I gulped, feeling sick. I'd known I was likely going to die, but hearing it out loud made it seem a little more real.

"Is that where you're taking me once I'm clean? To be killed?"

The woman shook her head, but kept her eyes forward. "You must be questioned first."

The man beside her was beginning to sweat profusely. Either he was nervous to be around a *traitor*, or he didn't like what was happening. Perhaps Estus' sway wasn't as complete as I'd originally thought.

"To what end?" I pressed. "I know nothing of value."

When the woman didn't answer, the young man finally met my eyes. "That is not for us to know."

I smirked at him, though my insides were filled with sickly acid. "Your Doyen says jump, and you say how high?"

The woman sneered at me. "Hurry up and bathe. Your very presence taints us."

I tsked at her and began washing myself as I mumbled, "There's no need to be insulting."

She gave no sign that she heard me, and instead stared straight ahead. A good little soldier.

I finished bathing, and stepped out to dry myself off with a nearby towel. My guards both still stood directly in front of the door. The only way I might escape them was to try it after we left the bathroom, but at that point they would both have a hold on me again, and I was almost too weak to stand.

The female guard reached down to the floor toward a pile of folded clothing I hadn't noticed until then. She straightened, unfolding the fabric to reveal a loose-fitting, black, spaghetti strap dress, and a black bra and panties to match. I didn't see any shoes among the offerings. Not bothering to ask for any, I took the clothing and got dressed. The dress fell below my knees and seemed a size or two too big.

I looked back up to my guards to see that the young man now held a length of rope in his hands. I began to back away, but there was nowhere to go. The woman lunged for me. I darted back, then slipped on a puddle of water, landing hard on my butt. The woman grabbed both my arms, then the man knelt and secured my wrists in a quick, efficient manner. Maybe he wasn't such a novice after all. All I could do was groan in pain and curse the pair's existence.

Once I was thoroughly bound, my escorts each gripped one of my arms, tugged me up off the ground, then opened the bathroom door to lead me back down the hall. As hard as I tried to stare down the young man on my right, I was given no further explanation of where I was going . . . though I didn't really need one. I knew exactly where I was going. I was about to end up where all prisoners ended up. We were going to the place I lovingly thought of as the torture room.

Though I was still stinging from my fall, this was my last moment to fight. Soon I'd be in shackles. I feebly threw myself backward, managing to free my arm from the young man, but not from the woman. He panicked, but the woman did not. She let go of my arm and punched me square in the jaw. I reeled away from her and nearly fell, then before I knew it, both of the guards had a hold of me once more, and I could feel a welt forming on my cheek.

They half dragged, half carried me the rest of the way to the blood-stained room where I'd first met Maya, chained to the wall, and covered in cuts and burns. I'd done my best to save her, but I doubted anyone planned on doing the same for me.

James was already in the room, dressed in a skin-tight, white tee-shirt and dark jeans. His eyes sparkled with excitement as my escorts chained my bound hands to the wall above my head from one of the manacles. The woman had to stand on a stool to reach, and I would have kicked it out from under her if I'd had the strength. Too weakened to fight, all I could do was glare into James' eerie, white-blue eyes while I tried not to cry.

Unlike Maya, I was tall enough that even hanging from the manacle, my feet still touched the ground, though just barely. Once I was secured, James nodded to my attendants and both left the room without a word. The sight of the door shutting behind them made the last sliver of hope drip from my body like icy water.

I narrowed my eyes in the dim light toward a small medical table at James' side. James stroked the gleaming metal instruments on the table as if they were his favorite pets. In a way, they were.

"I've been waiting for this since the moment I met you," James taunted as he left his table behind to approach me, "though it would be nice to see some of the fight you had in you yesterday."

"Now, now," I replied weakly. "I wouldn't want to go and make this enjoyable for you."

James laughed and took another step forward, rubbing a hand up my arm. "I'm going to enjoy this either way, Madeline."

I stifled a shiver as James moved his hand slowly toward my breast. He smiled as he watched my face. I tried to keep my expression blank, but I'm sure some of the horror I was feeling showed through. He stopped short with his hand on my ribcage. With a another smile, he let his hand drop and turned away from me.

He looked toward the door as it opened, seemingly of its own volition, to reveal Estus. James dropped to one knee in acknowledgment of his omnipotent leader, but Estus only had eyes for me.

The small man approached, surveying me with eyes even paler than James'. His impossibly long, silver braid slithered from the front of his shoulder to fall against his back as he came to stand directly in front of me. I would have given much in that moment to strangle him with it. He was dressed in his usual ensemble of dark colored, loose fitting shirt and pants.

I looked down at the elderly man and felt more fear than James would ever manage to cause me. While James was a sadist, I was beginning to sense that Estus was a complete sociopath. One might expect to feel pity, anger, or a myriad of other emotions from the person condemning them to torture, but I looked down at Estus' impassive face and knew that he felt nothing beyond his sick obsession with power.

"I will need her relatively whole," he said as he looked up at me, though obviously he was speaking to James. "She still has a task to perform."

Movement in the doorway drew my attention as Alaric came into view. My heart stopped at the sight of him, looking tall and handsome, and none too concerned with my fate. His dark hair was tied back at the nape of his neck, giving it the illusion of being shorter than it actually was, and leaving the shoulders of his black dress shirt bare. His dark brown eyes flicked to me briefly, then landed firmly on Estus as the old man turned to face him.

"Ah, there you are," Estus said, sounding like a jovial grandfather who just caught sight of his favorite grandson. "I thought you might like to see Madeline one last time in her current state. It's always a pity when we have to ruin pretty things."

The muscles in Alaric's jaw and neck tensed, and for a moment I thought he might actually be against me being tortured, but then the moment was gone, and his face was apathetic once more.

James watched the whole scene carefully, and seemed

disappointed by the results. His disappointment was nothing compared to mine as Alaric gave me one long, cold stare, then turned back to Estus.

"Will that be all?" he asked blandly.

Instead of answering, Estus motioned one small, bony hand toward James.

James' face erupted into a toothy grin as he turned his attention back to me. He sauntered over to his table and lifted a dainty scalpel into his meaty palm. He twirled the delicate knife in his fingers as he walked back toward me.

My eyes flicked around the room, looking for something to help me. Coming up with nothing, I settled on meeting Alaric's eyes as panic bloomed in my stomach. I stared at him, daring him to drop his gaze as James stroked the dull side of the knife gently down the side of my throat.

I couldn't help it as my breathing sped, but I kept my eyes glued on Alaric. As far as I was concerned, he'd tied me up to the wall himself. I cringed as the knife turned to bite into the flesh of my collarbone, but my eyes remained on Alaric. Other than a certain tension around his eyes, no emotion was visible.

I was so focused on Alaric's unreadable expression that I was shocked when James stabbed the knife into my side. I shrieked at the sudden pain and closed my eyes. Panting, I forced my eyes open to glare at the man who'd betrayed me.

I hoped to whatever deity might help me that he could read my thoughts, because if I escaped my imprisonment alive, I was going to make Alaric pay. In that moment I didn't care about hurting James, Estus, Sophie, or anyone else.

I looked at Alaric as pain screamed through my body, and I hoped he knew the hole he'd dug for himself. Normally I found the idea of leaving the soul in someone's dead body abhorrent, but for Alaric, I would gladly make an exception.

Not liking the lack of attention, James stabbed the knife into my side again. I screamed, my body reflexively jerking away, but I only managed to slam my head back against the hard stone wall. I opened my eyes long enough to see Estus smile, then he turned to go, with Alaric following close behind him. The door shut on its own, leaving me alone with James once again.

He stood inches from me, his knife at his side. His face was a bit lower then mine, but I could clearly see the satisfied look in his eyes. I took in one ragged breath after another, refusing to scream. When he didn't move away, I let out a sob and spat in his face.

He laughed, wiping the spit away with his free hand. "Now there's the fight I was looking for."

My vision began to go gray. "Well sorry to disappoint, but you won't be getting much more of it," I rasped.

I could feel blood trickling down my side and onto my leg, growing cooler as it went. James smoothed his hand against my leg, smearing the blood across my skin as his hand searched upward underneath my dress.

At first I thought things were about to get sexual, but his fingers continued on to poke at the wounds in my side. I let out a grunt of pain, knowing that his fingers were pressing on the damaged flesh, but unable to feel exactly where because my pain-receptors were going haywire.

James reached his other hand beneath my dress to grip the clean side of my waist. "I'd like to offer you a deal, Madeline," he said softly.

I was feeling so woozy that I almost didn't understand what he was saying. "W-what?" I questioned weakly.

James smiled. Bracing himself with my waist, he leaned against me so he could put his mouth against my ear. "I want you to find the charm," he said softly, "and give it to me."

"You want to lead?" I groaned, feeling dizzy and confused, but not really surprised.

James chuckled. "No, you're not getting it, Maddy. This whole time Estus has been looking for a traitor."

My head was spinning, but I managed to put together the pieces. "You're working for Aislin," I panted.

James had been the traitor all along. Apparently Estus was correct in his fear that Aislin would try and take his clan from him. The proof was quite literally staring me in the face.

"Bingo, kiddo," he replied, removing his hands from underneath my dress.

"Why are you telling me all of this?" I asked. "I could easily turn you in to Estus."

James shook his head. "I'm your only hope of survival, Maddy. You might be stupid, but I know you're not *that* stupid."

"Couldn't you have offered this *before* you stabbed me?" I rasped. I was actually considering his offer, though it was probably just the blood loss talking.

James pouted at me, and the pout seemed wrong since his hands were covered in my blood. "I had to put on a good show for Estus. Plus, I *really* wanted to stab you."

I took a deep, aching breath, then cringed from the pain. "Well if I die, then I won't be helping anyone."

James snickered. "You are Vaettir, Madeline. We are not so easily killed."

I swallowed the lump in my throat, feeling like I might vomit from the pain. "And what would I get in return for this deal?" I whispered, barely able to speak.

"Your life," James answered simply, as if surprised that I would ask for more.

I shook my head slightly. "Someone else has already offered me that. Keep trying."

James sighed. "I cannot speak for Aislin, but I'm sure she could find a place for you in one of her clans."

"I want a guarantee," I hissed. "I want a guarantee of protection from Estus."

James raised an eyebrow at me. "You're not exactly in a place to bargain, little mouse."

I tried to laugh but it came out as just a shaky breath. "I told you, I've had other offers. Now give me a reason to pick you."

James eyed me with a look of what might have almost been respect. "I'll be back," he replied.

He left me hanging, literally and metaphorically, in the darkness. Part of me wished I had simply taken Sivi's offer right off the bat, but I couldn't do that. James didn't know that though. Perhaps Aislin planned on being a better ruler than Estus or Sivi. If so, I'd be happy to give her the charm if it meant I wouldn't get stabbed anymore.

Beyond that, I wasn't sure how I felt about getting involved with another clan. It would have been nice to just go back to my little home in the above-ground world, but I knew Estus would only recapture me. I needed protection. Plus, I couldn't help hoping that another clan would be different. It was only in that moment that I'd realized just how close I'd been to my breaking point back home. Even after all I'd been through, I didn't want to go back.

Years of solitude out of fear of hurting someone had taken a toll on me. Even though Alaric was not the person I'd thought, my one intimate night with him had shown me just what I'd been missing. I wasn't sure if I could go back to my old life after that.

I'd accidentally killed my lover before Alaric, and now I

was seriously considering killing Alaric on purpose, but perhaps there could be another lover in yet another new life. Third time is the charm, right? Of course, I'd have to escape the Salr alive first. With the blood dripping steadily down my side, my chances seemed grim.

CHAPTER FOURTEEN

The door opened again a short time after James left me. I thought perhaps he was back with whatever offer Aislin had for me, but the silhouette in the doorway was too tall and slim to be James.

Rage washed over me as Alaric came into view. He watched me cautiously as he approached. His caution was unwarranted, as I couldn't have even lifted a leg to kick him, no matter how badly I wanted to.

When I made no attempt to attack him, he closed the distance between us. He wore a worried expression, but he didn't say anything as he lifted the side of my dress to examine my stab wounds. His fingers hovered over the damaged area, but didn't touch. I felt like I should have been offended that he lifted my dress without asking, but given everything else, it seemed a relatively petty argument.

"James wouldn't have hit any vital organs," he said softly. "You'll be okay."

My head was throbbing so loudly that I could barely see Alaric's face, but I'm pretty sure I managed to glare at him.

"That's all you have to say!" I choked out. "I'm going to rip your lying, deceitful head off!"

Alaric took a step back. I felt his shock and hurt at my sudden outburst.

"Don't you dare look hurt at me," I rasped. "You betrayed me. You left me in a cell to rot. *You* let James stab me. You better hope Estus kills me, because so help me, I will make your death *slow*."

Hot tears streamed down my face. The pain in my side was nothing compared to the stabbing sickness in my stomach.

"I had no choice," he interrupted before I could go on. "It wouldn't do much good if we both ended up in shackles. This was the only way, Maddy."

I shook my head over and over. It wasn't the only way. He had a choice, and he chose to save his own hide. I wouldn't have done the same to him.

"Estus knew," I sobbed. "He knew I was going to help Maya. You told him the entire plan."

He shook his head. "I didn't tell him anything. He had already figured it out, don't you see?" He reached his hands toward me, then let them fall away. "When I realized what you were doing that night, I did my best to get you out of here. If you only would have told me your plans, I could have protected you. Once Estus found us it was too late. I did the only thing I could that would ensure I had some chance of saving you."

"I don't believe you," I said coldly. I tried to hold in my tears, but they just kept coming.

He raised his hands as if to cradle my face, but I turned my head away the best I could, and his hands dropped.

"You will see in time that everything I've done, I've done

to protect you," he replied sadly, "and you haven't made it an easy job."

I turned back to him, anger drowning out my sorrow once more. "Well I didn't feel very protected when you let James drag me off to a cell, and I'm sure I won't feel very protected when I die from infected stab wounds."

"The Vaettir do not contract infections," he answered, ignoring my actual point. "You're not going to die."

I opened my mouth to argue, but given I'd never had an infection in my life, I couldn't. I'd always just chalked it up to a healthy immune system.

"How can you be so calm about this?" I asked, exasperated. "How could you just stand there while James tortured me?"

"I had *no* choice," he replied vehemently. "I knew he wouldn't kill you."

I turned my gaze away from him, tears still dripping down my face. "There is always a choice."

Alaric stepped closer to me again. "I'm going to get you out of here, Maddy. You just need to be patient."

I looked down at Alaric's handsome, angular face. Part of me still ached to kiss him, and I hated it. "I'm going to get *myself* out of here, and you had better hope that we do not cross paths again."

"Maddy—" he began.

"No," I cut him off. "Please leave."

"Maddy, I couldn't save you if I was dead!" he rasped.

I managed to stop crying and glared at him. "I told you, I don't *need* you to save me. I don't need you at all. Now *leave*."

Alaric opened his mouth to say more, then closed it. A tidal wave crashed into my heart as he turned and left. The water coursed through my veins, wiping away my thoughts, then all was silent.

By the time James finally returned, my hands and arms had lost feeling, and my feet felt like ice cubes. I'd stopped bleeding, and the blood that I'd lost had gelled to a sticky, cold mess on my side.

"I've spoken with Aislin," he began, then paused as he looked me up and down.

I noticed that he held a pair of hiking boots in his hands, and I sincerely hoped they were for me.

"And?" I asked quietly.

"*And*," he continued, "she says to name your terms."

"I don't understand," I replied.

James shook his head and smiled. "Neither do I, but that was her reply. I'm pretty sure that beats any other offers you have at the moment . . . if you really do have other offers."

I glared at him, but my eyelids were so heavy it probably just looked like I was about to fall asleep. "Get me down from here," I demanded.

James didn't move. "So we have a deal?"

"Yes," I sighed before I could think better of it.

It was probably a bad idea putting my trust in a woman I'd never met, but it was an even worse idea to wait for Alaric to save me.

Instead of letting me down, James put the boots on my feet and began lacing them.

"If we have to run, I don't want you complaining about your poor, girly feet," he explained.

I didn't reply. Having shoes to run away in would be nice. I could suffer a few insults if it meant shoes on my feet.

James unshackled my hands, then had to take most of my weight to keep me standing as he untied the rope around my wrists. My limbs felt like jelly, and my torso felt hollow.

When it became clear that I couldn't stand on my own, he finally just lifted me up into his arms.

"We have to find the charm before we can leave," he stated.

"Take me next door," I ordered.

James didn't move. "Next door?"

I sighed. I was starting to feel like I might throw up. "No one tells you anything, do they?"

James grunted. "I'm the hired muscle. All I need to be told is who to torture, and when, not why." He said it like it was something he had been told, but not necessarily something he agreed with.

"I'm going to use the hearts of all of the people you tortured to find the charm," I explained.

James nodded, either not picking up on my disapproval or not caring. I was betting on the latter. Regardless, my explanation got James to move, and it also confirmed my suspicions that there were more hearts.

I had to wrap my arms around his neck to brace myself while he used one hand to open the door. The feeling was returning to my limbs, making them ache more than my side, which was beginning to go numb in contrast.

We walked through the doorway like nothing was out of the ordinary. As the resident torturer, no one would question James moving one of his victims to the adjacent torture room, unless they noticed the boots on my feet.

We made it to the next room without a hitch, and suddenly I was nervous. The wall where I'd seen Estus remove the heart of the previous executioner looked smooth and solid, but there had to be other drawers within the stone. Of course, there could have only been the one, and the other hearts might be somewhere else. If that was the case, we were screwed.

"What now?" James asked.

I turned my head to look up at him. "Do you know how to open the drawers?"

He stared at the wall. "Who do you think put the hearts in there to begin with?"

He carried me over to the wall without another word, then wrapped one arm more tightly around my legs so he could use the other to smooth a finger around one of the wall's stones. I could hear a soft click from within, then the stone popped out of the wall. James pulled on the drawer to reveal a fresh-looking human heart. It didn't exactly beat, but the smooth muscle of the heart rippled and twitched in irritation at being disturbed.

I looked down at the heart, not sure what to do. I could feel the heart's physical pain distantly, as if it was stuck in the memory of having its body destroyed. Beyond the pain I felt hatred, violence, and jealousy. If I had to venture a guess, I'd say that the heart had belonged to a terribly unpleasant person.

I unwrapped one of my arms from James' neck, forcing him to put both of his arms around me once again to keep me aloft. I hovered my free palm over the heart, searching for . . . something. At first all I could feel were mixed emotions, then I heard it. It was like a soft voice whispering in my ear, but I couldn't make out anything that it was saying.

"Open them all," I demanded.

"What?" James asked, seeming startled that I'd finally spoken.

"Open all the drawers," I replied.

I wasn't sure what I was doing, but some sick compulsion told me that I needed to see all of the hearts. I could feel them fluttering within the wall like caged birds.

James let me down to my feet and helped me to lean

against the wall. It hurt to use the muscles in my side to keep myself erect, but it was a distant pain, drowned out by the whispering of the hearts as James began to open the drawers.

I could feel their pain, but it was more than that. Most of the hearts had been taken from their bodies years ago, some over one-hundred years ago. I could feel each heart's age along with its plea to be released.

As soon as James opened the final drawer he retracted, rubbing at the goosebumps on his arms. "What are you doing to them?"

"I'm not doing it," I replied softly. "They want to be released."

"Well you better do whatever you plan on doing quickly. If this energy continues to grow, Estus is bound to feel it."

I knew the thought should have worried me, but my brain didn't seem to be working right. All I could think about were the hearts. Their whispers were becoming more clear as they begged me to set them free. My body ached to answer them, but I needed to find the charm first.

As soon as I thought it, the hisses and whispers grew together until I could hear just a few clear voices calling out to me.

A picture formed in my head of a place I had never seen before. A great tree was surrounded by what appeared to be burial mounds. The mounds throbbed in my mind like something alive. The voices of the hearts began to whisper in unison, *"The Key."*

I nodded my head and could feel myself smiling. The charm was a type of key, and it was in this secret place, protected by the mounds of the dead.

"I can hear footsteps," James rasped. "We need to go."

"Not yet," I said distantly.

"Maddy, *now*," James ordered.

Ignoring him, I walked closer to the hearts, no longer feeling the pain in my side. I reached my hands into the drawers and started releasing the hearts one by one. Each release was a relief to me, yet at the same time, pressure began mounting in the air. I could feel energy swirling around me as each heart was set free. A part of each spirit left, while a part remained behind to swirl around me.

The door opened just as I touched the final heart. I turned to see Estus framed in the doorway, with two nameless men at his back. Their forms seemed foggy to me as I tried to look at them through the pulsing energy.

"What have you done, Madeline?" Estus asked calmly.

"I've undone your wrongs," I said simply.

With a thought, I sent a portion of the energy rushing forward. It collided with Estus and his men, hitting them like a semi-truck. The three of them flew backward into the hallway, hitting the stone wall with enough force to make it shudder.

"The charm isn't here," I said to James. "We need to go."

He rushed over to pick me up, but I stopped him with a palm on his chest. "I can run," I said simply, and it was true.

The energy from the hearts had healed the wounds in my side. In fact, I felt like I'd just woken up from a perfect night's rest.

Taking me at my word, James darted forward and I followed. We ran past the crumpled, groaning forms of Estus and his men, and further down the hall. We were going in the same direction we'd gone when Sophie and I helped Maya escape. I remembered the vine-filled room vividly. I also remembered Sophie disappearing through the vines, abandoning me to my fate.

James and I reached the door that led to the vine room to find a new, shiny padlock on it. Sophie had melted the last one, but she had taken the tool she used with her. I extended my hand toward the lock. It popped open without a hitch.

"How did you do that?" James balked.

"It won't last long," I explained. I could feel the energy from the hearts dissipating with each use. Knocking Estus down had taken a far greater deal of energy than healing my side or opening the lock.

James threw the lock to the ground and pushed open the door. This time, he pushed me to run ahead of him as more footsteps thundered down the hallway behind us.

He turned around, bracing himself against the door. "Don't wait for me," he ordered.

"I wasn't planning on it," I replied, then took off toward the vines.

I could hear someone banging on the door behind me as I ran at full speed down the hall. A few tendrils of vine became visible amongst the broken stones of the hallway, letting me know I was getting close to my destination. Adrenaline pulsed through me as I entered the room, then nearly burst into tears. The vines had been destroyed. Giant heaps of cut foliage littered the room, and the thick stumps of the vines were scorched black.

I shook my head, refusing to give up. I was getting the hell out of there. Not knowing quite what I was doing, I threw the last of my borrowed energy at the burned stumps. For a painful second, nothing happened. Then a shiver of movement pulsed through the vine stumps. Slowly, they began to writhe and grow before my eyes, healing just like my stab wounds.

James reached my side as the vines finished filling out. He grabbed my hand and flung us forward, just as more forms piled into the room. I braced myself, worried that we would go face first into the stone, but the vines reached out and caught us. Within seconds we were engulfed in the swirling mass. I held onto James' hand for dear life as a tingling sensation overcame my entire body, and then I was sitting on my butt in the middle of a forest.

James offered me a hand up. "We need to move." He was a mass of cuts and bruises from holding off our pursuers, but none of his injuries looked serious.

Reluctantly I took his hand, feeling shaky as I rose, but I knew I needed to keep moving. Forcing my feet into motion, I ran off ahead of him, not really worried about what direction I was heading, as long as I was heading away from where we'd arrived. Using the last of the heart's energy on the vines had taken a toll, and my legs and lungs began to burn with exertion. The forest was chilly. Distantly I remembered that it was October in the real world, so the cold, autumn air made sense. We ran with no signs of pursuit until we reached a large, icy-looking river.

"Get in!" James demanded as he reached my side.

"We'll freeze to death," I argued, but it did me no good as James grabbed my arm and threw me into the river.

Icy water clamped around me, driving the breath from my lungs. My head went under, and I had to fight frantically toward the surface with heavy, stiff limbs. I gasped as my head emerged, only to flinch away as James dove in right beside me.

Not bothering to ask if I was alright, he began swimming downstream with perfect swimmer's form.

Still in shock, it was all I could do to doggy-paddle after him and keep my head above water in the strong, rushing current.

We went downstream for what seemed like hours, but was probably only ten minutes, traveling swift and far, profoundly exceeding the speed of foot travel.

Relief flooded me as James finally swam over to the bank and lifted himself out of the water, but I overshot the area where he had gotten out as the current rushed me too far forward. James had to run along the side of the water and snatch me out when I finally got close enough.

I curled up into a shivering heap as soon as I was free of the river. My lungs and skin burned painfully. I shut my eyes against the tears that stung my skin like mini drops of fire.

After a minute, I opened my eyes to find James standing perfectly at ease above me, completely unaffected by the cold.

"What are you, superman?" I asked through my chattering teeth.

"I am Vaettir," he said simply, surveying our surroundings.

"Yeah well so am I, but I'm also currently an ice cube."

James looked down at me with a raised eyebrow. "We all have our gifts," he said cryptically. "Let's keep moving."

I just stared at him. My body had given all that it had to give. There would be no more moving for me for at least a few hours, and that would only be after I got warm.

When I didn't move, James sighed and crouched down to lift me into his arms. He took off at a steady jog away from the river. It was strange being carried around by someone I'd grown to thoroughly loathe. He'd taunted me since I'd first arrived at the Salr, and that was the least of his sins.

The hands that held my body aloft had tortured and killed countless people. He might have been acting on orders, but that didn't change the fact that he'd enjoyed every bit of it.

Now this sadistic murderer was my only lifeline. He was the only person I had left to trust. It was just me and the Devil, running through the woods.

CHAPTER FIFTEEN

James ran with me in his arms for hours, never seeming to tire. My black dress was finally almost dry, but the remaining dampness from the river still made me shiver. I attuned myself with the bumping up and down of James' gait, finding it surprisingly tolerable, though it would have been nice to know where we were going. I imagined at some point I would be delivered to Aislin so we could find the charm, or key, or whatever it was, but I was too weak and delirious to ask.

I felt myself slipping in and out of consciousness, and my bleary thoughts turned to Alaric. He'd claimed that his betrayal was the only way to save me, that if we both ended up in a cell, he wouldn't have been able to rescue me. I called bullshit. We could have fought our way back to those vines to follow Sophie and Maya out into the human world. I'd made the right choice in taking James' offer. He might terrify me, and he might have tortured me, but he worked for the other side. From what I'd seen of Estus' little clan, any side was better than his.

The trees above us faded in and out of view as I warred

with my heavy eyelids. The October air of the forest that would have been pleasant had I been dry, chilled the damp parts of my clothing in an almost painful way. The only warm part of my body was the side pressed against James.

It seemed odd that he was carrying me like a bride on her wedding day, rather than in a fireman's carry, but the uneven weight distribution didn't seem to fatigue him, and I was more comfortable that way, so I didn't complain. My long hair was caught between our bodies, but I didn't complain about that either.

We seemed to run on for days, though the sun never fully set, and I was only partly conscious when he finally set me down on the ground. I looked at him in confusion, wanting to ask for an explanation, but I couldn't form the words.

"We'll stay here for the night," he explained as he walked around, observing our surroundings. "Once you've . . . recovered, we'll find the charm. I'm assuming you know where it is," he added with enough menace to let me know that what he actually meant was, *you better know where it is, or else*.

"The hearts showed me an image of where it is," I explained dizzily, "but we might need Aislin's help in finding the right place."

"They just showed you a *picture*?" he asked incredulously.

"Yes," I replied, my gaze partially focused on the light slowly fading from above the trees. It would have been nice to argue with James from a safe, standing position, but my legs felt like congealed pudding. "It was a very unique picture, and it gave me a feeling of *distance*. The charm is far away. With a little research we could probably find the right place, and I think if we get close enough, I'll be able to sense it. If Aislin is as old as Estus, she might even know where it is."

"We'll need to have the charm in hand *before* I take you to Aislin," James replied.

I mustered the strength to turn my head in James' direction. "I thought you said—" I began.

James shrugged like it didn't really matter. "I lied. Aislin wanted me to sneak another executioner into the Salr to search for the charm. I thought this way would be easier, though I'm beginning to reconsider my choice."

"What!" I asked again as a surge of adrenaline enabled me to sit up. "So there's no deal for me? You lied about everything?" I pulled my legs up to my chest and curled around them. I was in deep shit.

James rolled his eyes at me. "Trust me. If you and I can deliver the charm to Aislin, we'll both be given whatever we want."

"*Trust* you?" I snapped. "You just admitted to lying to me about everything. Why the hell should I trust you now?"

James laughed. "Do you have any better options?"

I was fuming, but he was right. Aislin was still my best chance. It wasn't a very good chance, but given that the other option was to just wait around for Estus to find and kill me . . . Alaric and Sivi had both probably lied about their offers of help too. Of course, Sivi's offer of *well, you'll be alive while I murder everyone*, didn't have enough sugar coating to be a lie, and Alaric, he'd betrayed me after fully gaining my trust. At least James was upfront about being a scheming, sociopathic jackass.

"The charm can be found inside a giant tree," I explained with anger still tinting my voice. "The tree is surrounded by large burial mounds that protect the charm. The place is very old, and hidden. I got the feeling that you could walk right by it and never know. It might even be underground."

James stood with a huff. "That's it?" he asked sharply. "That's all you got? You couldn't have asked for a map?"

I let myself slump back to the ground, curling up on my side in the dry leaves. "It wasn't like I was just discussing things with the hearts over a nice cup of tea. I seem to recall you urging me to get things done before Estus came to kill us. We had a bit of a time constraint."

James sighed and came to stand over me. "It's fine," he said, more to himself than to me. "Our plan is still the same."

"So you know how to find the tree?" I asked hopefully.

"No, but I know someone who might be able to help. We'll visit her in the morning." He began to walk away. "I'd tell you to wait here," he added, "but I doubt it's necessary."

"Where are you going?" I asked, suddenly nervous.

"I'm going to find us some dinner," he replied, his voice already a good distance away.

With a tired sigh, I curled up into a ball on the ground in an attempt to get warm. I sincerely hoped that dinner would come with a fire. I hadn't quite recovered from our swim in the icy river, and the increasingly chilly air was not helping matters. Not only that, but I felt like I had expended myself a little too much back in the Salr, like using the lifeforce from the hearts had taken a bit of my lifeforce along with it. At the time, using the energy had felt marvelous, almost as good as it had felt to release all of those long tortured souls, but I must have overdone it. I raised a shaky, pale hand in front of my face and could barely even force my eyes to focus on it. Yep, definitely over-did it.

I was still curled in a ball on the hard ground when footsteps alerted me to James' return. I peeled my eyes open to see that he carried a dead rabbit in one hand, and some kindling for a fire in the other. I had no idea how he had killed the rabbit, and I didn't want to know.

Without a word he set the rabbit down and began building a fire near me. His back was to me, but with a few motions of his hands, the dried grass he'd gathered underneath the kindling began to smoke. Maybe he'd had some sort of flint.

"You're like a giant boy scout," I commented.

"Ha ha," he replied sarcastically. "Not all of us spend our entire existence among the comforts of the Salr."

James turned his attention back to his task at hand, and soon the dried grass and small twigs went up in flames. He began expertly stacking smaller logs over the flames before the small fire could go out.

I let out a sigh of relief as the fire roared to life and engulfed me in its warmth. My eyes slipped closed, allowing me to feel a measure of peace for a time as my numb extremities came back to life, then I smelled cooking meat and came to a horrible realization. The only thing we had to eat was rabbit.

"I don't eat meat," I commented weakly with my eyes still closed.

"Then you won't be eating," James replied, like it didn't matter to him either way.

"Good luck finding the charm after I die then," I replied just as casually.

"You already told me where it is," he replied. "Your death wouldn't be much of an inconvenience."

My heart climbed up into my throat for a moment, but I managed to force it back down.

"The charm is protected by death magic," I explained. "You'll never be able to get to it even if you find it."

"And when did you become so wise?" he asked sarcastically. "You only just found out what you were a few weeks ago."

"The hearts told me," I lied.

My theory was actually just an educated guess. The images the hearts had shown me had been muddled at best, but through them I could feel the mounds. I somehow knew that if I reached them, I would be able listen to them, just like I had with the hearts.

"If you won't eat the rabbit, then you'll just have to wait until morning," he said finally.

"Fine," I mumbled. I edged closer to the fire. If I was going to starve, at least I'd be warm.

I thought about my situation as James ate the cooked rabbit meat. An entire clan to choose from, and the person I disliked the most was the one I ended up with. I was beginning to think my whole life was just a cruel joke. I'd had an ounce of happiness with Matthew, then I took his life away. After years of solitude, I'd had about two seconds of happiness with Alaric, then he betrayed me. I'd killed the man who was good to me, while the bad one was still alive and well.

"How long did you serve Estus?" I asked suddenly, wondering why James was so willing to betray him, while Alaric was not.

James turned thoughtful eyes to me. I almost thought he wouldn't answer, but then he said, "Thirty years, give or take."

"So what?" I questioned skeptically. "You served him since you were a baby?"

James' eyes glittered with amusement. "For a know-it-all, you know very little."

I frowned. "Enlighten me."

"The Vaettir age slowly, some among us get to be very old indeed."

I rolled my eyes. "I know Estus is like, really old, and Sivi too, but you can tell that they're older."

"How could you tell that Sivi is old?" he asked, though I had a feeling he was trying to prove some sort of point to me.

Come to think of it, I wasn't sure. Maya had told me a bit of Sivi's history, but I'd sensed she was ancient upon first meeting her, even though she appeared around twenty-five.

"I could just sense it," I replied, not sure of how else to explain it.

"The more powerful Vaettir can live for centuries," James explained. "Some even longer. Sivi is nearly eight-hundred years old."

The news was shocking, yet I wasn't terribly surprised. I sat up and gathered my legs to my chest. The last hints of cold had been chased from my bones, and I was feeling better despite the lack of food and water.

"Then Estus must be over a thousand," I commented, trying to sound like I knew what I was talking about.

James shook his head. "Estus is younger than Sivi."

I scrunched my face in confusion. "But he looks so much older than her."

"It's a power thing," James explained. "Most of us have become more and more human as we become disconnected from the old gods we were once connected to. The change ages us. Some are even born with less power than the generations before. Sivi remained what she always has been, and so, has not aged."

It all made sense in a theoretical kind of way, though my mind didn't quite want to embrace what James was telling me. I'd seen too many things over the past weeks to ever believe the Vaettir were similar to humans, but the idea of someone living eight-hundred years and not aging past twenty-five was difficult to stomach.

"So why is Sivi serving Estus, and not the other way around?" I questioned. "If she's powerful enough that she looks a good fifty years younger than Estus, why is she stuck scheming behind his back?"

James shrugged. "Estus is beloved. He is a seemingly human figurehead for a race that has become all too human. Our people would never follow a creature like Sivi."

The woodsmoke was beginning to sting my eyes, but I still wasn't ready to lose the warmth of the fire. Instead, I rolled over so that my back was to James and the fire, and squeezed my eyes shut.

"Is Aislin a seemingly human figurehead as well?" I asked, suddenly wishing that I could still see James' expressions as he spoke.

"More or less," he replied. "She's more powerful than Estus, but is struggling to gain control since many of our people were born during less enlightened times, and are unwilling to follow a woman."

The statement had me rolling back over toward the fire so I could give James a look of disgust.

He raised his hands in surrender. "Hey, *I* follow her. Don't shoot the messenger."

With an irritated sigh, I scooted away from the fire to keep an eye on him. The silence stretched out, only to be broken by the hoots of a distant owl, and the chorus of crickets that surrounded us.

"So back to your time spent serving Estus," I began again, still curious about the whole arrangement. "Thirty years seems like a big investment just to find a charm, especially when the charm wasn't even in the Salr to begin with."

James stared into the woods. "It wasn't always about the charm," he admitted.

"What was it about then?" I pressed.

He'd lived with those people for such a long time. It was hard to imagine sacrificing thirty years just to be a spy.

"That's no longer relevant," James answered quickly, almost as if he was nervous about the line of questioning.

He rose to throw a few more logs onto the fire with more force than was necessary. I had to scoot back to avoid the sparks he created with each new log.

I glared at him. "Suit yourself. Just trying to make conversation."

He returned to his original seat in the dirt. "And why is that? I'm well aware of your . . . distaste for me. Why even attempt conversation at all?"

I shrugged, not entirely sure of my answer. "I'm not going to argue that I think you're a monster, but not everything is black and white. I could throw stones at you for enjoying your work, but . . . " I trailed off, not wanting to complete my thought.

"You enjoy yours too," James finished for me.

I stared into the fire, regretting starting the conversation to begin with, because he was right. I hate what I was, but the actual taking of life, the release, felt like nothing else. I'd been frightened when I'd accidentally killed one of my foster parents, and I'd been devastated when I'd accidentally killed Matthew, but the Vaettir I'd released, and the hearts . . . it felt amazing. I was pretty sure that it made me evil, or a sadist, or . . . something, but I couldn't help it.

I glanced back at James with his icy eyes that practically promised death all on their own and shook my head.

I could avoid thinking about the monster at the door as long as I wanted. The monster in the mirror was another story entirely.

CHAPTER SIXTEEN

I awoke to the sound of fighting. Not huge, battle-style fighting, but the distinct grunts and curses of a one-on-one fight. I opened my eyes to see that the fire had burned down to embers, but I didn't get to look at it long as I was pulled roughly to my feet.

Someone gripped my back tightly against their chest, with their arms wrapped around my shoulders protectively, not quite pinning me. I recognized Alaric's voice immediately beside my ear as he said, "She's coming with me. I don't know what lies you've been telling her, but she won't want to stay with you once things have been set straight."

James came into view with blood dripping from his nose. "She's just about the only person who knows the truth, actually." He looked at me when he said it, though he spoke to Alaric.

I shoved Alaric's arms off me, and took a few steps to give myself some space, putting us all into position for a three-way standoff. If only I had a gun.

Alaric turned his dark gaze to me. His black hair was tied

back to leave his face bare, and he wore casual clothes perfectly suited to the woods.

I could sense his anger, but his voice was hurt when he asked, "How could you trust *him*, of all people? I would have gotten you out of the Salr, if you'd only given me time."

I snorted and crossed my arms. "Sorry, I got tired of starving and getting stabbed while I waited."

"But *he* stabbed you." He gestured toward James. "Surely my crimes are not worse than his?"

"He never pretended to be something he's not," I countered, "and when he decided to help me escape, he actually followed through on it."

Alaric's shoulders slumped in defeat. "I've only tried to ensure your survival, Maddy. You must believe me."

"No, I mustn't," I replied haughtily.

James watched our exchange with an annoyed expression. When no one had spoken for a moment, he stepped forward.

"We need to get going. There's no telling who could have followed *him* here," he said with an irritated nod toward Alaric.

I glared at Alaric. "How *did* you find us so quickly?"

"He's Bastet," James answered before Alaric could say anything. "He sniffed us out."

I'd seen the teeth, eyes, and claws, but I'd never considered that Alaric might have a heightened sense of smell too.

Alaric just stood there looking miserable while James snuffed out what remained of the fire. Once he was finished, he walked away through the trees wordlessly. I took one last look at Alaric, then began to follow.

"Maddy, please," he begged.

I stopped, then turned to look over my shoulder at him. "I've got things to do. I'd appreciate it if you would keep this meeting to yourself, but I'm sure you'll run to Estus the moment my back is turned."

I started walking again, hoping that he would go back to where he came from, but he quickly caught up to my side. I was out of luck it seemed. Not that I had any to begin with.

I stopped walking and glared at him. "What are you doing?" I asked sharply.

"I'm coming with you," he answered, looking forward at James' back in the distance instead of at me.

With a huff, I began walking again, and Alaric kept pace wordlessly beside me. As we made our way through the woods, Alaric unbuttoned his navy flannel, then took it off and held it out toward me. Although I was still quite cold in the lightweight dress I was wearing, I ignored the shirt and walked a little faster.

"I don't want you to come with," I pressed. "I think I've proven that I don't want, nor do I *need*, your help. You're lucky I'm too tired and fed up to attack you."

Alaric snorted and let his hand with the shirt fall to his side as he trotted to keep up with me. "Well if you've chosen to trust James, then you *do* need my help. It wouldn't surprise me if this was all some elaborate plan orchestrated by Estus to trick you into to finding the charm."

That stopped me dead in my tracks. I'd trusted James because he was willing to risk his life to help me escape, but what if he wasn't risking his life at all? Estus could have easily assigned James the task of making me believe he was an ally, so that I'd be willing to find the charm. Then once James had the charm, he could just give it to Estus instead of Aislin.

"Didn't think about that, did you?" Alaric asked with a bitter smile.

I started walking again, trying to brush off my reaction.

"Of course I thought of that," I replied, "but he's helping me at the moment, and if he *does* turn on me, I'll be prepared."

He caught up to walk at my side. "Well since we're being so logical, I'm sure you can see that your best option lies in having me join you as well."

"On the contrary," I replied, "I'd rather only have to watch my back against one traitor, not two."

Alaric laughed, annoyingly delighting in our repartee. "If one of us is a traitor, then the other one can help you escape. You'll have the odds of two against one either way."

I glared at him, then quickly turned my eyes forward. "Unless you're both on the same side, and Estus sent you *both* to trick me."

Alaric shrugged. "Do you think I'd be Estus' plan A, or plan B?"

"Plan B," I grumbled.

Alaric shifted his gaze quickly to me, then back to the woods ahead of us. "And why is that?"

"Because Estus would have to be an idiot to believe I'd ever trust you again," I answered. "He wouldn't waste Plan A on the underdog."

Alaric was silent after that, though he stayed by my side. When it became clear that I wasn't going to take his shirt, he put it back on. The moment he did, I shivered and wanted the shirt even more, but I refused to ask for it.

We followed James for several hours. The protests from my stomach grew louder as my feet began to drag, and I grudgingly accepted Alaric's help as I stumbled and almost fell several times.

Just when I thought I couldn't go on any further, James stopped. At first I was unsure of why we'd come to a halt, as all I saw were more trees ahead of us, then the air went all shimmery. As the shimmers dissipated, a small cottage came into view.

I balked at the cottage's sudden appearance as James confidently opened the front door, walked through, and shut it behind him.

"Son of a bitch," I grumbled under my breath, hurrying toward the door. I eyed it, wondering what to do. At a loss, I raised my fist and knocked.

No answer.

Feeling irritated because Alaric was watching me with a raised eyebrow, I grabbed the doorknob and turned it, then pushed the door open and went inside. I scanned the interior for any sign of life, but it seemed abandoned. Where was James? Given his absence, I desperately hoped that who or what ever might live in the cottage wouldn't try to eat us, and would possibly offer us food instead. I stepped inside, my too-big hiking boots echoing on the floorboards.

Alaric followed me in, keeping close to my side. I could feel tension radiating off him like tiny ants marching across my skin.

"This should not be possible," he said quietly, peering around at rickety furniture covered in a thick layer of dust.

I stepped out of the way as a mouse scampered past my boots. "What should not be possible?"

"The Vaettir are forbidden to live above ground," he explained. He crept around the room, running his fingers along the wall as if looking for a secret panel.

"I don't think anyone lives here," I whispered, following his progress around the room.

He traveled down a nearby hallway, forcing me to either follow, or stay in the creepy, dusty room by myself. I followed.

"It's an illusion," he explained, "a facade to turn away any who might discover the nature of whoever lives here."

"Forgive me," an elderly female voice said from behind me.

I whipped around to find an old woman standing in the middle of the living room. The room she stood in was the same one we'd just left . . . only different. The dust had all been lifted to reveal spotless furniture, and a few candles were lit to make the place cozy.

"I needed a moment alone with James," the woman explained. "It is not often I receive visitors, especially other Vaettir."

The woman was dressed in a long, pale blue robe that obscured any other clothing she might be wearing underneath. The hood of the robe was pulled up to cover her short, curly, gray hair.

"And where is James now?" I asked suspiciously.

"He's fixing you supper, little mouse," the woman said with a smile. Her eyes were the vibrant green of fresh-leaves, and looked out of place in her pale, deeply lined face.

"I really wish people would stop calling me that," I grumbled.

The woman chuckled to herself, casually removing the hood from her head. "I am Diana," she introduced, "and I offer you refuge for the evening."

"Um, thanks," I replied hesitantly. "I'm Madeline."

James entered the room from the hallway opposite us. He carried a large tray stacked with sandwiches on one side, and several teacups on the other. He set the tray on the low coffee-table that stood in between the couch and two comfy-looking chairs. He sat in one of the chairs, followed by Diana, who sat in the other.

Alaric sauntered past me and took a seat on one side of

the couch. The three of them watched me as I considered where to sit. With a final pointed look at Alaric, I sat cross-legged on the floor in front of the coffee table. The position I'd chosen put me closer to Diana than I wanted to be, but it was the spot farthest from both James and Alaric.

"Sit by your man, child," Diana scolded. "There's no need to sit on the floor."

"He's not *my* man," I replied politely. "I much prefer the floor."

Diana huffed. "Just because you're mad at him, doesn't mean he isn't yours."

The woman was obviously senile, but I humored her none-the-less. "I'm not just mad at him," I explained. "He had me put in a cell, and then he watched while *James* stabbed me. Mad doesn't even begin to cover it."

Diana tsked at me. "You will see things differently in time."

James stared at her. "What else do you see?"

Diana turned toward him. "You know better than to ask," she chided. With that, she took a cup of tea into her bony hand and settled more comfortably into her chair.

Confused by the conversation, I turned my attention to the sandwiches lying only a few torturous inches away from me. I smelled peanut butter and jelly. While it was a strange choice for supper, I was just glad there wasn't any meat in them. Noticing my gaze, Diana gestured toward the sandwiches with a smile.

"Now, about this charm," Diana began as I snatched a sandwich and bit into the hearty bread.

My mouth half-full, I interrupted, "James sure told you a lot in that short amount of time, didn't he?"

She set her teacup on the table, then laced her hands in her lap. "He told me very little, though he did mention your current quest. I wanted a moment with him before I met you so that I might scold him for not warning me of his visit."

I narrowed my eyes at her, suddenly feeling very uncomfortable. I had a suspicion that Estus could sometimes read the thoughts of others. Perhaps this woman was the same.

"Then how did you—" I began, wondering how she'd known about me and Alaric.

"I see things," she interrupted. "What has been, some of what will be, but only sometimes what *is*."

Well that explained her observations about Alaric, which I'd have to think more upon later. At that moment I was more concerned with the look in Diana's vibrant green eyes as she stared at me. It was a look that said she was imagining peeling my skin off layer by layer.

"Could you please stop looking at me like you want to eat me?"

"I have offered you sanctuary," she replied. "You are safe from my appetites . . . tonight."

I gulped. I hadn't actually thought she wanted to eat me, but I had seen a similar, predatory look from James.

Diana turned her attention to Alaric. "Now my dear," she said, "I haven't seen you since you were a boy. Where is Sophie? You two were never far from each other as children."

Alaric looked truly surprised. "I'm sorry, do I know you?"

Diana smiled. "I asked my question first."

"Sophie is . . . " Alaric paused, seemingly at a loss for words.

It only occurred to me in that moment that I wasn't the only one Sophie had abandoned. She had never even planned on telling Alaric that she was going to leave with Maya. It had to hurt.

"Sophie is away on business," I answered for him. That was a whole can of worms we didn't need to open.

Diana cocked her head at me. "You're not lying," she began, "but you're also not telling me the truth."

I shrugged and took another bite of my sandwich.

Diana sniffed and turned her attention from me. I glanced up at James, who was sitting stiffly with an unreadable expression. Something told me that we didn't want Diana to know that Sophie had left the Salr, though I wasn't sure why.

"I will help you find the charm," Diana said suddenly, "but I want to share in the credit when you deliver it to my sister, Aislin."

"Aislin?" Alaric sputtered as he choked on his tea at the same time I asked, "Sister?"

Alaric turned to me for verification. "Why would we give *her* the charm?"

"Because Aislin didn't have me hung from a wall and tortured," I answered sweetly.

Diana chuckled, her glittering eyes on Alaric. "I see someone has yet to choose the correct side."

Realization dawned on Alaric's face as he stared at Diana. "Aislin knows that you're living above ground, doesn't she? And she allows it?"

Diana's smile grew. "Like I said, the *correct* side."

Alaric turned his glare to James. "I wonder which side you *actually* work for," he mused darkly. "In the end, which will you betray?"

Diana snorted. "James would not abandon his own grandmother, and I have no intention of betraying one as powerful as Aislin, sister or no."

I was doing my best to figure everything out while the attention was off me. If Diana was James' grandmother, then that made Aislin his great aunt. Given the family connections, James was probably telling the truth about working for Aislin during his time with Estus. The family ties lent him credibility. Then again, lies might run in his family as well.

I started eating another sandwich as Alaric and Diana continued to bicker. I felt like a little kid, sitting on the ground while the grownups talked about grownup things. I might have even been offended if I wasn't so bone-achingly tired.

James watched me with a small smile on his face throughout the exchange. Eventually he nodded toward the hallway, then stood. Not particularly wanting to remain in Diana's presence, I rose to my feet as he walked past me and down the hall. I followed warily, still expecting some sort of trick.

A moment later the bickering stopped, and Alaric was following close behind me. James pushed open the first door he reached, revealing a small, clean bedroom. He stood to the side of the door while he waited for Alaric and I to walk through.

Once in the room, I turned and looked a question at James. "I hadn't hoped for a private room, but separate beds would have been nice."

James regarded me with an evil smile. "I figured I'd let you two lovebirds have the honeymoon suite. I'll sleep on the couch."

I glared at him. "I knew you would betray me."

James gave me a little salute, then shut the door in my face, leaving me alone in a dark room with a man I once could have loved.

I hugged my arms tightly around my stomach, not wanting to turn around and face Alaric again. Sure, I'd spoken to him in the woods earlier that day, but we hadn't been alone. Being alone made me nervous.

The room was small, and fit with the rest of the cottage-style decor. The single bed stood ominously, lit by the moonlight shining through the room's only small window.

I jumped when a hand landed gently on the side of my arm. Alaric's long fingers gripped my bare skin, turning me to face him. I moved stiffly, not wanting to look at him, but knowing I couldn't avoid it.

"We shouldn't stay here," he whispered. "We need to look for Sophie. She can give us a place to hide and regroup until we decide what to do."

"There is no *we*," I hissed. "There is only *me*, and I'd like to get some rest, if you don't mind." I looked at the lower half of his face while I said it, not wanting to feel the full pressure of his gaze.

He put his fingers underneath my chin and raised my eyes up to him. "You're putting yourself in the middle of a war, Maddy. You don't understand what you're doing."

I took a step back out of his reach. I'd thought my anger was exhausted, but I was wrong. "*You* put me in the middle of a war. I had no choice in the matter."

Alaric's shoulders slumped as his hand fell to his side. "Nothing would have happened to you if it weren't for Maya."

"Maya?" I scoffed. "You mean the woman who was being *tortured* right in front of me?"

Alaric raised his hands in frustration, but seemed to calm as he closed his fists, then dropped them back down. "Maya's problems weren't your fight, Maddy."

"Then whose were they?" I countered.

"You're defending a woman who abandoned you!" he growled. "I didn't see Maya coming back to risk herself when *you* were the one in the cell."

"Well I didn't see you risking yourself either," I snapped. "Just because Maya didn't save me in return, doesn't mean I shouldn't have saved her to begin with. I didn't help her because I thought she deserved it. I helped her because that is the type of person I want to be. I don't want to be the person who leaves others literally hanging from manacles."

"That type of person does not exist among the Vaettir," he replied coldly. "Do not risk yourself for others, because they will never risk themselves for you."

"And yet here you are," I stated blandly, "*risking* yourself for me."

"So you believe me?" he asked, instantly jumping on what I'd just said.

I shook my head. "I don't believe anything anymore. Not without solid, indisputable proof."

Alaric took another step toward me, and this time I didn't back away. "I'll prove it to you in time," he said with an almost smile, "that is, if we live long enough."

"You think Estus will come after us?" I questioned, though I already knew the answer.

"He will. Especially after you released all of his hearts. He put two and two together, and he would rather die than let you hand the charm to Aislin."

"And you would let me give her the charm, even though your Doyen forbids it?" I pressed.

"I left the Salr against his wishes," he answered. "He is no longer my Doyen. The life I had is gone."

"You didn't need to follow me," I stated coldly. I'd be damned if he'd make me feel guilty for his loss.

He shook his head. "I was already planning on leaving once I managed to free you. If we would have been more swift, or if *you* had bothered sharing your plan with me, I would have left with you the night Sophie escaped with Maya."

I shook my head. "I don't believe you. You would have had

no reason to make such a sacrifice for me. You barely even know me."

"You keep insisting that I've made some huge sacrifice," he replied, his head tilted slightly to one side.

The movement made his now loose, dark hair fall over his shoulder. I didn't know at what point he'd untied it, but I had the overwhelming urge to reach out and run my fingers through the soft tresses. Repressing the impulse, my hands balled into fists at my sides.

"You left your home," I explained. "Leaving home is always a sacrifice."

He shrugged. "I've had other homes, and I'm sure I'll have more in the future."

It was my turn to tilt my head in confusion. "It was my impression that you and Sophie grew up in the Salr."

He laughed, the abrupt sound startling in the darkness. "Sophie and I grew up in a very different world from the one we know now."

"James informed me that the Vaettir don't always look their age," I said as an idea formed in my mind. "How old are you, exactly?"

He shrugged. "Old enough."

I shook my head. "No. No more lies. I'll need two forms of I.D. before I'll believe anything you say."

He sighed and turned to wander around the room. He ran his fingers along the quilted bedspread, then went to fiddle around with the bedside lamp like it actually interested him.

"I've lost track of the exact time," he said finally, "but I was born around the year 1500, give or take a few years."

"You're trying to tell me that you're over five-hundred years old?" I scoffed.

He flicked the lamp on and off absentmindedly. "Don't

believe it, if you wish. I wouldn't have told you if you would have let the subject go."

I went to stand in front of him with my hands on my hips. "And why wouldn't you have told me?"

He smiled. "You don't seem like a woman who'd be interested in a much older man."

I laughed, and it felt strange after the past few days I'd had. "It *is* a little creepy, now that you mention it."

He held a hand to his chest dramatically. "Oh Madeline, you wound me."

I laughed again, and it felt a little more natural. "We should get some rest," I said finally. "I hope you find the floor comfortable."

He let out a dramatic sigh. "I suppose arguing tonight would be a moot point?"

I nodded, "Just in case you're lying, I'd rather not revert to snuggle buddy status."

He cringed. "I suppose I deserve that."

I nodded again, then stood on my tippy-toes to plant a kiss on his cheek.

"And what was that for?" he asked in surprise as I took a step back.

I shrugged and climbed into bed. "For the possibility that you're telling the truth."

"Would another truth earn me a pillow?" he asked hopefully.

I tried to look as disinterested as possible when I said, "It might."

He was standing far enough back that all I could see was his silhouette as he said, "In all of my five-hundred years, letting James stab you was the most difficult thing I've ever done."

Tears started to well up in my eyes, and they were tears

that I didn't want to share with anyone. I grabbed the extra pillow off the bed and tossed it to Alaric, then I laid my head on the other pillow with my back turned toward him.

I listened as he lowered himself to the floor. A long while later, his breathing slowed to the even rhythms of sleep. Finally I let a few, silent tears slip out. They weren't tears for Alaric, or for anyone else but me. They were tears for the life I'd lived thus far, and for what might lay ahead. Sometimes you just have to cry for yourself, because no one else will.

Moments later, loud snoring that could only belong to James echoed through the wall, and I wished I had the extra pillow to sandwich my face. Instead I pulled the quilt over my head in a futile effort to muffle the noise. And here I thought there wasn't supposed to be any rest for the wicked.

CHAPTER SEVENTEEN

I woke up early to find Alaric already wide awake, sitting at the foot of my bed, watching me with a distant sort of look. He perked up as I struggled my way out of the tangled mess I'd made of the bedding.

"How long have you been sitting there?" I groaned.

He shrugged. "A few hours. I couldn't sleep."

"You know, a normal person would have found a book or something else to occupy their time," I chided.

He shrugged again, then stood and offered me a hand to get up. I ignored his extended hand and stretched my arms over my head. I had to put them back down quickly though, as it dawned on me that I hadn't showered in a while.

"I'm going to find the bathroom," I announced, hoping that Alaric hadn't caught a whiff of me, but knowing that he had.

"Would you care for some company?" he asked with his eyebrows raised.

"Absolutely not," I mumbled, then made a beeline for the door.

The bathroom was just across the hall from the room

we'd been given, so I was able to make a quick escape. I locked the bathroom door behind me, thinking that I should have asked Diana before I went to take a shower. Oh well, I wasn't about to go back into the hall in my state of stench, so I found a spare towel rolled in one of those little towel baskets and started the water.

I stripped out of the black dress, immensely displeased that I'd have to put the tattered thing back on after my shower. At least the river had washed away the blood from my stab wounds.

I observed my naked side to find two small scars where the knife had punctured my flesh. In that moment I realized how someone with my particular gifts could abuse such a power. The ability to take lives in order to heal others should never have existed.

Feeling more cold than the temperature of the room could account for, I stepped under the hot stream of water. I used the shampoo and soap that had been left in the shower, but couldn't find any conditioner. I scowled. Long, unruly hair needs conditioner. I'd be a total poofball by noon.

By the time I finished my shower and emerged from the bathroom in my shabby dress, coffee and breakfast had been made. We all sat at a small kitchen table like a nice, dysfunctional little family. James and Alaric sat to either side of me, leaving me to look directly at Diana as I sipped my coffee.

Diana was dressed more normally today, in khaki slacks and a pale green, floral blouse. The green of the blouse made her leaf-green eyes stand out vibrantly in her pale face. She watched me carefully as I ate my french toast.

I had been mildly surprised the night before when James made sandwiches. When I'd found out that he'd also made the french toast, I was shocked. It was perfectly cooked, the outside crispy, and the inside sog-free. I was also pretty sure that I detected a hint of cinnamon and nutmeg. Maybe torture was just James' day job, and he secretly moonlighted as a chef. Then again, maybe not.

"The place you seek is not on this continent," Diana said suddenly.

It took me a moment to figure out what she was talking about, then I realized that James had probably filled her in on what I'd told him.

"Please tell me you're joking," I replied with my mouth full of french toast. I looked to James for confirmation.

He shrugged, like it didn't really matter. "It looks like we'll be taking a trip. Passports and IDs are all taken care of in case Estus tries to track us by more mundane means. Your new name is Nicole, FYI."

I blinked at him. A sudden international flight? Fake passport? Was I working with spies?

"But we'll need to find Sophie first," Alaric chimed in.

I turned my dimwitted stare over to him. "Why do we need Sophie?"

"Strength in numbers," James replied plainly. "Plus, I already had a passport made for her. I'd hate for it to go to waste."

I sighed, dropping my fork onto my plate. "And you two just planned this whole thing out while I was in the shower?"

"You should not be so remiss to visit your homeland," Diana interrupted.

"I was born in California," I countered. "I've visited my homeland plenty."

"The Vaettir originated in Scandinavia," Alaric explained. "She's not referring to where you were born."

"Scandinavia?" I asked incredulously. "You expect me to believe my ancestors are Scandinavian?" I gestured to myself. "I might be tall, but blonde I am not."

Diana tsked. "Truly, have you boys taught her nothing?" Addressing me, she continued, "When our race first came into being, Scandinavia is where we originated, but we come from many pantheons of gods with different ethnic origins."

"Okay . . . " I trailed off, wondering what pantheon *I'd* come from. "So skipping over all that confusing information, if this charm is in another country, why did Estus ever believe it was in Washington?"

"The Salr is not in any one place," Alaric explained. "The entrances are stationary, but the actual structure resides on its own plane of reality. It's not really in Washington, nor is it anywhere else, and there are many more Salr spread out across the world."

"That doesn't make any sense," I replied slowly. I knew that the Salr was a place of magic, but it had to *exist* somewhere real.

Alaric shrugged. "The Salr were created long before my time. I cannot explain any more than I know. All I can tell you is that they are a place of refuge. They came into being where they were needed."

Dianna nodded. "Yes, originally the Salr were meant as places of sanctuary, but clans began moving into them permanently as our numbers dwindled. Those who did not have a clan were left out in the world alone. Leaders stepped forward to rule over those who resided within each Salr. Those rulers became Doyen, like Estus and Aislin."

I shook my head. I understood the theory of what I was being told, but the mechanics didn't make sense at all. "Okay, so Estus became Doyen over a Salr, how, just because he wanted the job? Was there another Doyen before him?"

"Enough chit chat," James interrupted irritably. "We need to get moving."

I tilted my head. This was more information than I'd been

given previously by a long shot. I wasn't about to stop questioning now. "So say we hop on a plane, and end up in Finland or wherever. How will we find the charm once we get there, and how can we be sure that it is even there?"

"Because I know the place that you were shown in your vision," Diana replied, "and I will be going with you."

"Couldn't you just draw us a map?" I asked hopefully.

Diana bared her teeth in an unpleasant smile. "Do you not desire my company?"

"It's not that," I corrected quickly, though really it was. "I just don't see the need for everyone to drop what they're doing to fly to Scandinavia."

Diana stared at me until I finally looked down. Strangely, I was much more nervous about the idea of traveling with one little old woman than I was about traveling with my almost sort-of ex-boyfriend and a man who might very well be a psychopath.

I averted my gaze and ate the rest of my french toast in silence, even though it felt like cardboard in my stomach.

"I should find Sophie before we all leave this place," Alaric announced, breaking the silence. "We are well hidden here. It makes no sense to risk Madeline being out in the open until we are ready to depart."

"So we should just let you run off to Estus while we wait here for the ambush?" James countered.

Alaric glared back at James. "If my sister sees us together, she'll hide. I have a better chance of talking to her on my own."

"Sophie won't hide from me," James muttered, looking down at his plate.

I snorted. "Wanna bet?"

"You don't know what you're talking about," he snapped.

I looked back at him, too surprised to be angry. Normally James could take any insult I had to throw at him.

I turned to Alaric. "What exactly am I missing here?"

"James and Sophie were once lovers," Alaric explained, "and he is somehow deluded enough to believe she still cares for him."

"You don't know what you're talking about either," James said to Alaric. "What happened between Sophie and me is our business. Period."

I held up my hands before an argument could begin. "I'm still having trouble grasping the fact that Sophie would ever even look at James to begin with. How recent was this?"

"The breakup occurred roughly one year ago," Alaric answered while still looking at James.

I was beginning to understand all of the tension between James, Alaric, and Sophie. Both siblings had told me not to trust him, but wouldn't give me a reason. My guess was that James had betrayed Sophie's trust, and Alaric had gotten protective of his sister. It was all a moot point as far as I was concerned. I'd never trusted James regardless.

"It doesn't matter," James snapped. "You're still not going alone to find her."

"And I'm not going to let you two run off and kill each other," I added. "Plus, Sophie owes me an apology."

"I'll wait here," Diana said calmly. She rose from the table and walked toward the sink to fill her tea kettle.

"It's settled then," I stated flatly.

"It's not settled," Alaric argued. "We don't need to risk your life any more than we have to, and our best chance of recruiting Sophie is if I go alone."

"First," I replied, holding up a finger dramatically in the air, "I don't think Sophie will run from me. She may have deserted me, but she's no coward. Second," I said as I held up another finger, "you've risked my life plenty. There's no need to start getting squeamish about it now."

"I agree with Madeline," James added.

"I don't care if you agree with me," I snapped. "I'm the only one here that can find the charm, so we're going to start doing things on my terms. I don't know if either of you realize this, but I'm no longer a prisoner."

"Maddy—" Alaric began.

"She's right, you know," James interrupted with an infuriating smile.

"Why is it," I began as I looked at James, "that even when you're on my side, I still want to slap you?"

"Oooh, please do," he taunted.

"Enough," Alaric said, bracing his hands on the table. "If we're all going, we may as well get on with it. If I know Sophie, she'll be hiding in the city. She wouldn't go far until she knew whether or not I'd be following her, and she sure as hell wouldn't hide out in the woods."

"So we go to the city, and what, sniff her out?" I asked.

"Yes," he replied, "but we might run into a problem."

"Which of our myriad of problems are you referring to?" I asked tiredly.

Alaric looked at me like I was being silly. "You're technically a missing person, Maddy. Someone must have noticed that you're gone by now. Walking openly around Spokane is probably not the best idea."

"Well then we should probably get me something more to wear than this stupid dress," I said irritably. I didn't feel the need to point out that I probably wasn't a missing person yet, given that there would have been no one around to miss me.

"We'll be sure to stop at *Nordstrom*," James sniped.

Alaric took a deep breath to say more, but Diana cut him off with a tsking sound. "Enough bickering, children. We have things to do, and time is short. Estus may not know where the charm is, but he'd be a fool to discount the possibility of Madeline finding it. Do what you must, then meet me at the airport."

I had to wonder just how old Diana was to be referring to Alaric as a child, but I wasn't about to ask her. Instead, I straightened my dress and got to my feet like a good little girl.

Soon we'd be off to somewhere in Scandinavia. Though it was true that I needed a vacation, I would have been happy with a beach in Mexico. Something told me I wouldn't be getting any margaritas with Diana around.

CHAPTER EIGHTEEN

*O*ur only choice was to leave on foot, which was fine, except that Spokane was a good five miles away from Diana's hidden home. Normally I'd be fine with a five mile hike, but a five mile hike in boots that were a size too big, with two very grumpy hiking companions was not my idea of a good time.

Also, it was *cold*. Fall had just begun in Spokane when I was snatched out of my bed and taken to the Salr, but it felt like winter had taken over in the relatively short time I'd been gone. I knew winter would get much colder before the year was through, but normally I would be properly attired for the occasion.

I'd grudgingly accepted Alaric's long-sleeved shirt, and he didn't seem fazed as he walked bare-chested in the chilly air beside me. I'd have to remember to give him his shirt back before we made it to civilization. I was pretty sure a bare-chested, 6'2", ethereally gorgeous man walking through town would draw more attention than a woman who may or may not have been reported as a missing person.

I did my best to keep my eyes off of his bare skin as we

walked, but I might have lagged behind a few times just to get a good view of his back for a while. Of course, every time I lagged behind, he would turn and wait for me, dashing my plans to bits.

"You two are pathetic," James commented from behind us as Alaric stopped to help me over a fallen log.

"It's a good thing that I don't value your opinion at all," I replied, "or I might have some hurt feelings right now."

"That's all well and nice for you," Alaric said with a smile, "but I think I need to go cry in a dark corner for a little while."

James snorted. "Mock all you like, but *I'm* not the one acting like a teenager with their very first crush."

"I *saw* you as a teenager," Alaric replied without looking back, "I'm not sure I could ever match how ferociously you flirted with Sophie."

"Wait," I said as I stopped walking, "Sophie was an adult while James was a teenager, and she still dated him?"

Alaric laughed. "Well it was much later that they dated, and he was as much of an adult at the time as he is now . . . which is, of course, debatable."

"Oh you guys are just barrels of fun to be around," James muttered, picking up his pace to walk past us.

"You started it!" Alaric called after him.

When James was a good distance ahead of us again, I turned to talk to Alaric as we walked. "It almost seems like you guys are friends."

Alaric shrugged. "Perhaps once, but things change, and some things are unforgivable."

"And those unforgivable things have to do with Sophie?" I pressed, my curiosity getting the better of me, as it often did.

"Sophie and James were together for two years, just after Maya left, and then Sophie lost interest. Sophie was unfazed, but James had taken their relationship very seriously," Alaric explained.

"Why was Sophie so unfazed?" I asked. "Two years is a long time to spend with someone."

He shrugged. "Two years to someone who has only lived a human lifetime can seem like a lot, but when you live long enough, two years seems like a blip on the radar. Sophie tried to explain the concept to James, who is much younger than us, but he wouldn't accept how casually he'd been brushed aside. My sister admittedly could have had more tact, but she has a short attention span, and moved on almost immediately with another man."

I glanced at him with an eyebrow raised, then glanced at James in the distance to make sure he wasn't close enough to hear us. "You know, that's exactly what Sophie said about you when she warned me not to develop any feelings."

"That I moved on immediately with another man?" Alaric joked.

"The short attention span," I replied without mirth, though I was pretty sure he knew what I meant.

He peered at the ground as we walked. "My sister needs to learn when to keep her mouth shut."

"Was she telling the truth?" I prodded, not willing to let the subject drop so easily.

He sighed. "Perhaps, but the past is not always a predictor of the future."

We walked in tense silence for a moment, then Alaric said, "But back to my story."

I blushed, because I'd completely forgotten that we'd originally been talking about Sophie and James. I cleared my throat. "Yes, do go on."

"James couldn't handle seeing Sophie with another man,"

he continued, "though he never admitted it. Instead he befriended the man, Sammael was his name."

"Well that was big of him, I suppose."

Alaric shook his head. "James spent a good deal of time befriending Sammael. They became quite close really. Sammael would have trusted James with his life. It was at that point that James tortured and killed Sammael. This happened roughly six months before you came to us. James later admitted that he spent the time to gain Sammael's trust in order to make his vengeance more rewarding. He also wanted to allow Sophie enough time to grow attached to Sammael, so that the loss would hurt her more."

"And he was allowed to remain in the Salr?" I asked, shocked.

"That was the day James became Estus' pet torturer," Alaric replied distantly. "Estus claimed that James would prove to be the very best man for the job."

I let out a slow breath. "Well, Estus was right on that count, I suppose."

"Though he was wrong to ever trust him."

"Wasn't he wrong in trusting you as well?" I countered. "You didn't exactly hold up well on the loyalty meter either."

Alaric glanced over and offered me a small smile. "I suppose you're correct."

I shrugged. "It still seems too simple to me . . . " I trailed off.

"That Estus would put so much faith in any of us?" he questioned, reading my mind.

"Escaping shouldn't have been as simple as it was," I elaborated, "and even after James and I escaped, to let you go as well?"

"I've considered that," he replied.

I rolled my eyes. "I'm going to need a little more feedback than that."

"I've considered the fact that perhaps we are doing exactly what Estus hopes. Perhaps he knew all along that the charm was not in the Salr. He couldn't trust us to go free and find it for him out of loyalty, so instead he set us up to do it out of a need to defeat him," he explained.

"What if that's all true?" I asked. "We could very well be doing exactly what he wants us to do."

Alaric's expression turned somber. "We must continue on regardless, and hope that we can defeat Estus when the time comes."

I let out a huff of breath, fogging the chilly air. "I'm not doing it to defeat Estus. I'm doing it to join Aislin's clan."

"And why would you want that?" Alaric countered quickly, like he'd been wanting to ask for a while. "You're out here, free. You could just move somewhere far away and live your life."

"And have to look over my shoulder forever?"

He shook his head. "That's not why you're doing it."

"What is it that you want me to admit, exactly?" I snapped.

I wasn't sure why I was getting angry, I just knew that I didn't like being pressed on things I didn't want to talk about . . . even if I didn't know why I didn't want to talk about them.

Alaric shrugged. "Nothing at all. I'd only like you to consider the fact that not having a clan does not automatically mean you will be alone."

That was it. He'd hit the nail on the head with the word *alone*. I looked ahead again to see how far James had gone. He was barely visible in the distant trees ahead of us, but I lowered my voice none-the-less. "What exactly are you saying?"

Alaric moved closer to me so that we were walking shoulder to shoulder, except my shoulder was quite a few inches lower than his.

"I propose that we destroy the charm," Alaric whispered. "Our people are not meant to be ruled. Destroy that power, and perhaps we can escape them all."

"Just a few days ago you were all, *Estus is Doyen, he asks and I obey*," I argued, shocked at what Alaric was suggesting.

"He pushed too far," he said simply.

"Really?" I balked. "Was it the assigned kidnapping, the maiming of your sister's girlfriend, or the maiming of your own girlfriend that caused you to finally draw the line?"

"My *girlfriend*?" he asked with a lascivious smile, ignoring everything else I'd said.

I rolled my eyes. "You know what I mean. What finally changed your mind?"

"My mind was changed as soon as you and Sophie decided to leave the Salr, as I no longer had much reason to stay," he began. "The only reason we were there to begin with was because I wanted to protect Sophie. I thought it the safest place. But when James harmed you . . . " he shook his head, as if reliving the moment. "I will not again put myself in the position of obeying one leader blindly."

Now that I understood his reasoning, I couldn't argue with him. He was right to assume that I'd give the charm to Aislin just so I wouldn't have to be alone again, even though I didn't relish the thought of becoming another clan's pet executioner. I didn't trust myself around humans, but any Vaettir I might associate with would be impervious to my gifts. I'd thought joining another clan the only solution... but if Alaric would hide with me, if he would be willing to teach me more about my curse . . .

"Please tell me what you're thinking," Alaric said after I'd been silent for a while.

I glanced up toward James again. "I'm thinking that this could very well be the biggest decision of my life, but you're acting like it's an easy choice for you and Sophie."

"You're young," Alaric stated. "My sister and I have been part of many clans, and we have been on our own as well. The centuries change things. Eventually big decisions become inconsequential."

"Well that's depressing."

"It is something you'll learn to deal with, in time," he said with a small smile.

I snorted. "Barring the fact that I'll probably be killed off any day here, I doubt I'll live anywhere as long as you have."

He blinked at me. "Why would you say that? You are Vaettir, just like the rest of us."

"James explained about the more powerful Vaettir aging slowly," I answered. "I imagine I'll be aging rather quickly."

"It is not as simple as that," he sighed. "My sister and I are long-lived not because of our power level, but because we are more closely linked to our goddess than others. Many no longer even know from which god they descend."

"So you're like, part god?" I asked incredulously.

Alaric shook his head. "I am Vaettir. We come from the earth, just as the gods and goddesses of old. We embody their energy."

"Then where do I come from?" I asked, perplexed.

He shrugged. "A death goddess, I imagine. You inherit your gifts from your mother's side."

"And what about my pesky penchant for empathy?" I asked.

He shrugged again. "Now that, I have no explanation for, and it was clear that Estus did not expect you to come with such interesting gifts."

"Okay," I began, reverting back to our original line of conversation. "If I am a *denizen of death*," I said spookily, "and other Vaettir like Sivi identify with the elements, what exactly do you, as Bastet, embody?"

"War," Alaric replied simply. "I believe Sophie mentioned this to you."

I bit my lip, thinking back. "She said something about me being attracted to you because war and death go together, but how can you *embody* war?"

"Well, I'm very good at killing."

"Well that's comforting," I mumbled.

He laughed and pushed against my arm playfully. "Since when is death intimidated by a little bit of war?"

My legs were beginning to tire from all of the walking, and my brain was tired enough that I didn't quite know how to answer him. Sure, death was a part of war, but death wasn't supposed to feel the pain and emotions of those who were to be claimed.

I took a deep breath, and gave Alaric the only answer I could think of.

"Since death grew a heart."

CHAPTER NINETEEN

I felt like my feet were about to fall off by the time I first heard sounds of traffic. The sun was making its slow descent past the trees, robbing us of the last of its warmth. James had eventually fallen back to walk with us, though he'd remained silent by my side.

I unbuttoned Alaric's shirt, not looking forward to baring my arms to the chilly air. He took the shirt absentmindedly and began putting it on as he sniffed the air, reminding me of a lion, or some other large cat.

"Anything?" James asked as he eyed our surroundings.

Alaric shook his head. "I know a few places she would go. We might have to search for a while."

"We don't have much time," James replied sternly. "That we're yet to see any sign of pursuit from Estus is shocking, to say the least."

"There's probably time for food though, right?" I chimed in.

My stomach was cramping terribly from the lack of food over the last few days. Alaric and James didn't seem affected by it, but they didn't seem affected by a lot of things. Me, I needed food and a nice warm coat.

Alaric pulled me toward him and wrapped an arm around me. My first instinct was to fight, but I was freezing, tired, and hungry. I simply didn't have any fight left, and his body heat was one small comfort I wasn't willing to refuse.

James gave us an irritated look, but didn't comment. Instead, we all began walking again, following the sounds of traffic.

Soon we started seeing houses here and there, and our footing transitioned from dirt and pine needles to sidewalk and asphalt. I didn't recognize where we were, but Spokane is a large city, and there was no way for me to be familiar with all of the suburbs.

As darkness fully fell, we reached a small strip mall. The smell of cooking food wafted out of a few restaurants, but the few clothing stores had already closed. Maybe it was Sunday. I'd completely lost track of the days.

"Get her something to eat," James instructed, his attention on Alaric. "I'll find her a coat."

I raised a finger in the air. "And some socks . . . if you don't mind."

James sighed loudly, then turned and disappeared into the darkness of the nearby storefronts, presumably to steal me a coat. Alaric ushered me across the street, then toward the nearest restaurant, a small pasta/pizza place.

"It's like we're going on our first date," he intoned happily, his arm still snug around me.

I glared up at him, my feet dragging as he gently urged me toward the restaurant. "The first date usually occurs before the breakup, and it definitely occurs before the . . . " I trailed off, not wanting to say what I had originally intended.

"The sex?" Alaric finished for me. "So we like to do things backwards," he went on, "it's part of our charm."

"There is no *we* or *our*," I corrected, "and this is *not* a date."

"No roses, no wine," Alaric joked. "Got it."

"Wonderful," I grumbled.

Alaric held the door for me as we went inside the small restaurant. Nervous, I pulled my hair forward to cover my face. The chances that someone would recognize me as a missing person were slim, but it was still a possibility that I'd rather avoid.

I received a few odd glances at my tattered dress, though the glances were probably more because of the small amount of fabric I was wearing in the cold weather than the state of my clothing. Grunge was in again, or so I'd heard.

With no sign of a hostess, we slid into a corner booth with our backs to the wall. Even with a full view of the restaurant, I felt like Estus would pop out and nab us at any moment.

I fiddled with my place setting. "Maybe we should have gone with fast food."

Alaric slouched against the backrest like he hadn't a care in the world. "I don't eat fast food. That stuff will kill you."

I snorted. "If five-hundred years of living among the Vaettir doesn't kill you, the fast food surely will."

He smiled and raised an eyebrow at my joke, then turned as a young waitress came to the table for our drink orders. Her eyes lingered on Alaric for longer than was polite, and she looked a little confused as she took in my disheveled, frizz-haired appearance.

I ordered an iced tea and gave the waitress an uncomfortable amount of eye-contact. Alaric ordered a glass of red wine and gave the waitress a cheerful wink, completely undermining the hopefully intimidating stare I had going on.

"I thought you said no wine," I grumbled as the waitress walked away with a smile on her face.

"I lied," he said simply. "I'm supposed to be a liar, remember?"

"And here I'd thought you'd changed," I sighed.

Alaric feigned a hurt expression. "Well at least you're talking to me now."

I opened my mouth to argue that I was only talking to him since he was the only company present, but the waitress came back and placed our drinks in front of us. I hadn't had time to look at the menu, but it would have been a moot point as Alaric started ordering for us: fettuccine, spinach lasagna, mozzarella sticks, fried mushrooms, a pizza, and three different deserts.

I looked at him in astonishment as the waitress walked away. "Are we expecting guests?"

He winked one dark brown eye at me. "Who knows when our next meal will be? We should enjoy ourselves, for tomorrow we might be dead."

I stared dejectedly at my iced tea, unsettled by Alaric's way of thinking. Suddenly I wished that I'd gotten something more extravagant like a strawberry daiquiri or a milkshake. If I was going to die soon, I really didn't want to waste my time with bland iced tea.

Alaric used his index finger to slowly scoot his glass of red wine in front of me. Not needing any more of an invitation, I wrapped my fingers around the stem of the glass. He smiled as I took a long sip, then offered the glass back to him.

He reached out for the glass, brushing his fingertips across mine as he took it. His expression had lost its playfulness. The look in his eyes made me gulp, and I quickly turned my gaze back to my iced tea.

Movement caught my eye, and I let out a sigh of relief as

James entered the restaurant. I didn't know how to deal with the heat in Alaric's eyes, and James was a welcome distraction. He approached our table and handed me a knee-length black coat with a fur-lined hood that I sincerely hoped was faux.

"Put it on and keep your face covered," he said quickly. "We need to go."

Alaric stood immediately, taking James' mood seriously. I stood and wrapped the coat around me, wanting to cry at the fact that I was going to miss another meal.

"Socks are in the pocket," James said to me, "but you'll have to put them on later. Now move."

He grabbed my arm and pulled me forward so that I was walking in front of him. Our waitress watched us leave with what looked like our appetizers in her hands. In fact, the whole restaurant watched us leave. Hopefully we'd be long gone before they noticed we hadn't paid for the wine.

So much for not making a scene.

"We were tracked," James said as we spilled out into the parking lot. "Marcus confronted me. He's dead, but there will be more."

My eyes darted around the half-full parking lot as we walked, but everything in the night was still. Who the hell was Marcus?

"If Marcus was here, then Siobhan won't be far behind," Alaric said.

Since I didn't know who they were talking about, I kept my mouth shut and allowed myself to be led down the dark sidewalk and past more closed or closing businesses. We crossed the street, then went into the parking lot of a large, abandoned warehouse. The yard was strewn with refuse, and didn't look like it had been used in many years. Whatever suburb we were in, the place had definitely seen better days to leave such a space right in the middle of town.

"Give up the girl," a female voice said from behind us.

The three of us turned in unison.

A man and a woman stood under the illumination of a streetlight. The woman's long, white coat made her strawberry blonde hair stand out vibrantly in the light. The man looked out of place beside her in his casual street clothes and knit winter cap.

"I don't want to hurt you, Siobhan," Alaric replied, "but the girl you cannot have."

As the girl in question, I didn't like being talked about like I wasn't there, but I'd complain later. The mismatched pair left the sidewalk and approached us warily, sizing up the odds, then everything exploded into chaos.

James shoved me out of the way as the man rushed us, and Alaric had already collided with Siobhan.

I stumbled aside, then turned to see James' grappling with the man. Within seconds he had him pinned, then I smelled burning. James' hands seemed to melt through his attacker's chest. I clutched at my own chest as searing agony hit my skin. Lesser pains I could block out, but this was too much. My vision blurred. I couldn't quite make sense of what James was doing to the man, then the smell increased. I was pretty sure I'd just figured out how James had started the fire in the woods.

Miraculously still alive, the man bucked his legs, throwing James off him. He staggered to his feet, then lunged at James as if he didn't have two palm-shaped, scorched craters in his chest. I panted against the pain as the pair tumbled to the ground again, then James lifted the man up by his neck. I didn't have much time to contemplate James' apparently super-human strength as his hands burned through the man's neck, cutting off the sound just as he tried to scream. I was glad that it was a quick death, because the moment of pain I'd felt in my throat was almost unbearable. His hands now gripping a charred mass of flesh, James cast him aside like a rag doll.

"You burned him," I croaked in astonishment.

"How else did you think I cauterized my victims wounds?" he replied, brushing his hands together to remove the man's charred flesh.

I didn't have time to answer, as Alaric drew my attention with a loud bang against a large, metal dumpster. The woman, Siobhan, had him pinned against it with fingernails that had grown to be as long as daggers at his throat. They seemed sharper too, more like claws than nails.

I opened my mouth to speak, hoping to draw her attention, then someone with a black curtain of hair moved behind them. Siobhan's pain echoed through me as a blade sliced into her flesh, pushing up through her abdomen into her heart. I made a grunt of pain, then Siobhan slumped to the ground, dead. Sophie stood before her brother, bloody blade in hand.

"I never liked her," Sophie commented, peering down at Siobhan's body.

"I was *trying* not to kill her," Alaric answered hotly.

I personally was stunned to see Sophie, but judging by Alaric's expression he was not at all surprised that she'd found us first.

Sophie rolled her eyes at him as James and I approached. "Don't be so sentimental," Sophie chided, "the two of you dated, what, two-hundred years ago?"

Ignoring Sophie and Alaric's bickering, I kneeled down and released the spirit from Siobhan's body, averting my gaze from her bloody wound. She was pretty, and I felt like maybe

I should be jealous that Alaric had dated her, but really I just appreciated the fact that he didn't want to kill her. Maybe he could be sentimental after all. With that task done, I went to the man, once again not looking too closely at his wounds, lest I lose the meager food in my stomach. I stood and flicked my hands, hoping to cast away the little thrill the fresh energy sent through me.

"Do I not even get a hello?" Sophie said in irritation at my back.

I turned to glare over my shoulder at her. "Do I not even get an *I'm sorry?*"

Sophie had the grace to look abashed. "I did what I had to do, and Maya left me anyway." I stood and stepped away from the now lifeless corpse, feeling much better with the new burst of energy in spite of myself. "Seriously?"

"She was working for Aislin all along," she explained. She didn't let her pain show in her expression, but I knew that she felt it none-the-less.

"Sorry to break it to you sweetheart," James interrupted, "but so are we."

Sophie glared at James for a moment, then turned to her brother. "Is this true?"

Alaric shrugged. "I couldn't really argue with the decision."

Sophie snorted at his answer, but seemed to accept it as well. "We need to move," she instructed. "I could smell you from a mile away, and there will be more where these two came from." She gestured to the two corpses on the asphalt.

"Plus," I added, "we might want to run away from the corpses before someone calls the cops. We're not in the Salr anymore."

For once everyone listened to me, and we made our way past the abandoned warehouse and into the alleyway behind it, but something still nagged at me. If Maya was working for Aislin, why didn't James know the information she'd held, and why had he tortured her? Unless . . . unless James *wasn't* actually working for Aislin. I eyed him askance as we walked, but his deadpan expression gave nothing away.

Sophie and Alaric began whispering in a language I didn't recognize. I knew it was probably just so they could talk freely around James, but I didn't appreciate the exclusion. For all I knew, they were talking about running off and leaving James and I to find the charm on our own. *Or*, they had reached the same conclusion I had.

I caught Alaric's gaze, attempting to convey my worry.

I wasn't sure if he understood, but he lagged behind to take my hand. "It will be alright," he whispered. "I promise."

I knew I shouldn't trust him, but my shoulders relaxed at his words. It hit me then that I'd been expecting Alaric to leave since he'd first found us. I'd expected at some point he'd decide that I simply wasn't worth the trouble, and he'd abandon me.

Yet, when we reached a busy street and hailed a cab, Sophie took the front seat, and James and Alaric each slid in on either side of me. When we reached the airport and boarded a plane with Diana, who met us there as planned, Alaric was still by my side. When I fell asleep on his shoulder during the long flight, I vaguely sensed him as he craned his neck to give me a kiss on the top of my head.

It was strange, because in that moment, while we were flying to another land, with danger at our backs, and plenty of more danger to face, for the first time in quite some time, I felt like I was going home.

※

Later, I woke up groggy, sometime mid-flight, and glanced back at Diana and James. They whispered to each other conspiratorially. I knew with surety in that moment that they were both playing us. Neither was working for Aislin. Only Maya was her actual spy.

I settled back into my seat, glancing at Alaric, who was dead asleep. I'd share my fears with him later, or maybe I wouldn't. Not just yet. We needed Diana's help to find the charm. Once it was found I'd be damned if Diana, Estus, or maybe even Aislin got a hold of it. Something that caused so many lies had to be protected. If it was as powerful as Maya said, even the fate of humanity might be at stake. A protector was needed.

Unfortunately for humanity, all they had was me.

COLLIDE AND SEEK

BOOK TWO

CHAPTER ONE

The sensation of the plane bouncing on the tarmac woke me. It had been a trying few days, and the extra sleep on the plane was a welcome reprieve. I didn't mind lying on Alaric's shoulder either.

I still wasn't quite sure how to feel about him. Okay, I knew exactly how I *felt*. I just wasn't sure what to do about it. As much as I wanted to ignore the fact that he'd misled me about many things, and had allowed my torture, those two facts still ate at me.

Forgiveness is one thing. I'm great at forgiveness. Being an empath means I'm a seasoned pro at putting myself in the shoes of others. At some point I had relented to *mostly* forgive Alaric, but I couldn't forget what had happened, and I sure as hell couldn't trust him.

Betrayal is a funny thing. The sting of it often sticks with us longer than the thrill of love, the fire of hatred, or the emptiness of loss. Betrayal eats at us when we know we should be happy, and it overwhelms us when we're already sad.

I raised my head up from Alaric's shoulder as the plane

came to a slow stop. He smiled down at me, unaware of my thoughts, and I couldn't help but smile in return. Despite everything, it felt good having him by my side. It would have felt even better if we were on a plane to some romantic destination, but we weren't.

Although, I suppose Norway *could* be romantic, given the right circumstances. The pictures I'd seen were gorgeous and fairytale-esque, and I was traveling there with a handsome man, but I'm pretty sure romantic vacations aren't supposed to include being hunted by supernatural beings while looking for a charm that's guarded by the dead. Running for your life is a major mood killer.

We waited while the rows of people ahead of us stood and un-stowed their luggage. I shifted uncomfortably, feeling trapped. Once there was enough room, I stood and glanced back toward James and Diana, wondering why each of them *really* wanted the charm, and to what lengths they would go to get it.

James pulled Diana's luggage down from the storage compartment. He had none of his own. In fact, he was still wearing the white tee-shirt he'd worn while he tortured me, just as I was still wearing a black dress with holes in it where he'd stabbed me. Luckily James had stolen me a long, black winter coat with faux fur trim around the hood. It hid my dress, but looked slightly out of place with my too-large hiking boots and thick winter socks.

Sophie waited in her seat across the aisle for James and Diana to get out of the way, pushing them closer toward me. Her original seat had been next to the unwelcome pair, but she'd managed to flirt her way into a seat trade, leaving James to sit next to a man who could have easily taken up two seats on his own. The man in question was still asleep in his seat by the window.

Squeezing past me, Alaric woke the man with a gentle shake of his shoulder, then signaled for him to move, much to the chagrin of the people behind us who would now have to wait even longer.

The line ahead of me moved and I scurried forward, eventually exiting the plane. It was a surreal feeling leaving the West Coast a few hours after dark to arrive in another country where evening had already come again. I'd never traveled such a long distance. Heck, I'd never traveled much at all. Living as a recluse with meager monetary means had prevented me from seeing much of the world.

My next shock came after we went through security and emerged into the cold night air. My coat was warm by West Coast standards, but it could not contend with the icy temperature of Oslo in late October. I clutched the meager protection closer to my body, but my bare legs still erupted in almost painful goosebumps.

James and Sophie stepped ahead of the rest of us, scanning the busy street like a pair of vengeful angels, dark and light, illuminated by the halo of a streetlamp. I could sense their nerves. We all knew Estus wouldn't let us escape so easily.

Alaric, seeming unaffected, smiled and put an arm around me.

Diana tsked at us like we were all being silly children and went to the curb to hail a cab. She clutched a modern black cape around her small form, the fabric swirling around her legs in the cold breeze like it had a life of its own. Though she was small and elderly, with perfect gray, granny-styled hair, I would never mistake her for anything less dangerous than she was.

She was the sister of Aislin, ruler of several clans, which made her old, and we're talking centuries, not decades.

Though I was yet to see her do anything out-rightly scary, the threat was always there. She was twenty times scarier than James, and he'd stabbed me and tormented me for fun.

A cab pulled up, and it became readily apparent there were five of us, and only four available seats.

"We'll wait for the next one," Alaric announced, clearly referring to him, myself, and Sophie.

James smirked. "I don't think so. Madeline will come with *us*."

My heart sped at the idea of being left alone in a cab with James and Diana, but Alaric stepped forward before I could move. "*I'll* go with you, and Maddy and Sophie will catch the next cab. You can kill me if they don't show up."

My eyes widened, but I wasn't about to argue.

With a curt nod, Diana climbed into the front seat of the cab while James put her suitcase in the trunk. Alaric gave me a quick kiss on the cheek, then slid into the backseat after James. I touched my cheek where he'd kissed me, feeling a mixture of annoyance and apprehension.

Diana rolled down her window and relayed the address of the hotel, then suddenly we were left to wait for another cab by ourselves. It was the first time Sophie and I had been alone since she'd rejoined our party after leaving me to be tortured in her place. I crossed my arms and turned away from her, half-wishing I would have just gone with the others, leaving her to catch a cab on her own. It wouldn't compare to her leaving me in the Salr to face punishment for her crimes, but it was a start.

She sighed dramatically at my back. "How long are you going to ignore me? Maya left me. I think I've paid for my actions."

I looked over my shoulder at her. "So because someone

betrayed your trust, it makes it okay that you betrayed mine?"

"I said I'm sorry," she snapped, quickly losing patience.

I turned away from her again and mumbled, "Barely."

Another cab pulled up to the curb. I turned and followed Sophie as she opened the back door and climbed in. The heat inside was almost stifling, but felt good after standing on the chilly curb.

I would have been tempted to take my own cab, but one, I had already forgotten the address, and two, I had no money to pay the cab driver, so I was stuck with Sophie.

The driver barely even looked at us as Sophie told him where to go. I crossed my arms again and stayed silent as he drove the cab through a few roundabouts leading out of the airport, then onto the highway. I had no idea how far away the hotel was, but I hoped it was close. Sophie was staring at me intently, her face a pale oval in the darkness of the cab, and I wasn't sure how long I'd be able to maintain the silent treatment.

"You would have done the same," she said eventually.

I looked into her dark eyes, so similar to her brother's, and could see she really believed what she'd said.

I shook my head. "Not everyone is like you."

"Look," she sighed. "I said I was *sorry*. It's not something I say often, and I wouldn't have said it if I didn't mean it. What else do you want from me?"

Her emotions were intense enough at that moment that I could sense her frustration, and underneath it, guilt. She really did feel remorse over leaving me. It might not make up for the original act, but it was a start.

"Okay," I replied.

She narrowed her eyes at me. "Just . . . okay? Why don't you seem angry suddenly?"

I shrugged. "I know you regret leaving me. I'll get over it . . . eventually."

Sophie's eyes widened. "You empathed me! That's not fair."

I rolled my eyes. "You know I can't help it. Strong emotions leak through whether I want them to or not."

She harrumphed, then glanced at the driver as he swerved to the right and cut several people off so he could exit.

She turned back to me. "So you've forgiven my brother?"

I shook my head. "Not quite. Maybe with time."

She shook her head in return. "I don't know how you do that."

"Do what?"

"Forgive so easily," she explained. "If I were you, I'd have already tried to kill me, and Alaric would have been dead the moment I saw his face. Not that I'm not grateful that you're not attacking me . . . "

I shrugged again. "It's the empath thing. Trust me, I did want to kill Alaric, but guilt is a very strong emotion. So is fear. It's hard to blindly judge someone's actions when you can literally *feel* what they are feeling."

It was Sophie's turn to cross her arms. "I am *not* afraid."

I laughed. "Oh please, you're terrified, and you're sad."

She glared at me as the cab pulled into the parking lot of a large, well-lit, resort-style hotel. "I don't think I like you very much."

I grinned. "And here you were just begging for my forgiveness."

The cab halted, and I quickly opened the door and climbed out, leaving Sophie to pick up the tab.

"I was not begging!" she shouted after me.

I laughed as I walked across the asphalt toward the hotel.

Torturing calm, cool, and collected Sophie with my empathic abilities was far more rewarding than snubbing her.

Alaric and James, who had been waiting outside the hotel lobby for us, came striding forward to meet me. The warmth I'd collected in the cab was quickly fading, and the expanses of surrounding near-darkness made me nervous. Anyone could be out there watching us, and we wouldn't even know. I gazed at the hotel longingly as the men reached me.

"Ms. Moneybags has us staying at the most expensive hotel in the country," Alaric explained. He was still just dressed in his navy flannel and black jeans, unfazed by the cold.

"I wouldn't let Diana hear you calling her that," James chided.

Sophie reached us, then breezed on by without a word, like a tall, dark, angry cloud.

Alaric watched his sister's back, then whispered, "You *must* tell me what you did to make her so angry."

I wrapped my arms tightly around myself, fighting shivers. "You wouldn't be able to pull it off. Now can we please go inside before I freeze to death?"

Alaric placed a hand at the small of my back and guided me forward. The building rose up in front of us as we neared. I counted ten stories, the exterior done in a crisp white that matched the surrounding patches of snow on the ground.

James strode past us toward Sophie.

Alaric smiled down at me. "We have our own room," he said with a waggle of his eyebrows.

I stopped walking, though my bare legs were burning with cold. "Why?"

He shrugged, placing his hand against my back again to keep me walking. "If I didn't know any better, I'd say Diana is trying to play matchmaker, but I think she has much more nefarious plans in mind."

My stomach lurched, but I kept walking. She *was* planning something, I knew it. But why the room? "If she's manipulating us, shouldn't we, I don't know, *not* go along with it?"

"Why would I argue with plans that benefit me?" he said happily as the automatic glass doors slid open in front of us.

Some of the tension seeped out of my body once the doors slid shut behind us. The bellhop waiting inside gave us a strange look, probably due to our lack of luggage. The young man shrugged his narrow shoulders and sighed, then led us to a row of elevators. James and Sophie had already gone up, leaving us to ride up with the bellhop alone.

Alaric put an arm around my shoulders as the elevator lurched into motion.

I dutifully removed it, then took a step away, thinking that it was a really bad idea for us to share a room. Not only was Diana up to something, but I didn't fully trust myself. It had been impulsive to fall into bed with Alaric the first time, and I didn't want to be that stupid again. Of course, we still might die tomorrow. Normally it was wise to err on the side of caution, but was it really wise to make good life-choices when my life might not last much longer? Shouldn't I just enjoy being alive while I could?

Alaric could act like we weren't in danger all he liked, but I knew better. If Sophie was scared, it meant we were up a very smelly creek with no paddles, with plenty of holes in our boat. I'd seen first hand how Estus dealt with those who opposed him. If he found us and sent more of the Vaettir to capture us, we would all suffer very ugly ends.

The elevator came to a stop and the doors slid open. Without a glance in our direction, the silent bellhop led us down an extravagantly decorated hall to our room. He used a key card on the door, then handed it to Alaric as we entered. The room was bigger than my old house, with a full sitting area, king-sized bed, and a kitchenette partially obscured from view by bar-style seating, all done in delicate gold and pale blues.

My eyes scanned the room, then came back to rest on the bed. They lingered there, then went back to the couch. It looked comfortable enough.

Alaric tipped the bellhop, then urged him out of the room. Once we were alone, Alaric walked past me to flop down on the bed. He laid on his back with his arms behind his head, watching me as I took a closer look around the room.

"So what do you want to *do*?" he asked eventually, putting emphasis on the word *do*, to make it seem dirty.

I walked past one of the cushy chairs on either side of the couch to peek into the bathroom. "I *think* we're here to find the charm, so that's what I want to do."

"Diana claims the location is very near, but she doesn't know exactly how near," he explained, "she needs time to pinpoint it, which means we have some time to *kill*."

I glared at him. "Stop emphasizing random words to make them seem sexy."

He grinned. "Is it working? Are my words . . . *sexy*?"

I shook my head and turned away from him.

In an instant he was up off the bed and at my side, moving a lock of my dark brown hair behind my shoulder to bare the side of my neck, grazing his fingers across my skin as he went. It might have been a sexual gesture if he wasn't watching me with such a concerned look on his face.

"I take it your attitude means I'll be sleeping on the floor again," he said softly.

I glanced at him, but didn't pull away. I had to audibly gulp before I could answer, "I'll take the couch this time. It's only fair since I had the bed at Diana's."

He let my hair fall from his grasp, then took my hand into his grip instead. He kissed my knuckles one by one, then answered, "As you wish."

I slowly pulled my hand away. "Why are you being so agreeable?"

He glanced into the large bathroom that boasted a full-size jacuzzi tub as well as a glass-walled shower. "I think I'll take a bath."

I crossed my arms. "You didn't answer me."

"I don't suppose you'd like to join me?" he asked, still not answering me.

"We don't have any clean clothes," I commented. If he wasn't going to answer me, I wasn't going to answer him either.

Alaric shrugged and walked into the bathroom. "It's late. We'll buy you a whole new wardrobe in the morning."

I stayed where I was standing and glared at his back. "Some jeans and a sweater would suffice."

He began to unbutton his shirt with his back still to me. As the fabric fell to the floor, I blushed and turned away, marching dutifully over to the couch to turn on the TV. The screen came to life. The commercial that came on was in Norwegian, obviously, but it didn't matter because I was so distracted by the sound of Alaric filling up the bathtub that I wouldn't have been able to concentrate on it regardless.

"Maddy?" Alaric called out.

"Yes?" I asked hesitantly.

"Come keep me company."

My mouth suddenly went dry. I cleared my throat. "I don't think so."

"Do you really find it entertaining to watch a show in a language you don't speak?" he pressed.

I glanced at the TV screen again, then back to the open bathroom door.

"I'll be a perfect gentleman," he added. "Scout's honor."

Silently cursing myself, I stood and made my way to the bathroom. Keeping my eyes dutifully averted from the bathtub, I entered the steamy room and took a seat on the closed lid of the toilet.

I could feel Alaric's eyes on me, but refused to look. "There are plenty of bubbles," he assured. "You won't see a thing."

With another sigh, I rolled my eyes as I turned my head to look at him. There were indeed plenty of bubbles, but I could still see the top of his chest, slick with water. He'd wet his dark hair, pushing it away from his face to make him look even more ethereal than usual.

I did my best to maintain eye-contact as Alaric slipped a little further down into the bubbles. "You know, it seems like a waste of water to fill this gigantic bathtub just for one person," he commented.

I smirked. "Well you're the one that did it, that's on your conscience." Desperately wanting to change the subject, I added, "I thought Diana said she knew of the place the hearts showed me. Why does she need time to find it now?"

"Norway has changed a great deal since she was last here," he explained, "and this is not a place you can see, it's a place you have to *feel*. She's using her connections to at least get an idea of the general area so we can go there and search."

"So what do we do until then?" I questioned.

A small smile curved across his lips. "You could get in the bath with me."

I stared at him for several heartbeats, then sighed, "Fine."

His eyes widened. "Fine? I was expecting a lot of things, but *fine* wasn't one of them."

I shrugged and tried to act like my heart wasn't racing. "We're stuck in a hotel in a foreign country," I explained, "waiting for a very scary old woman to lead us to a place that you can only *feel* and not *see*. Meanwhile, we have an angry, sociopathic Doyen thirsty for our blood. Normally, I would be appalled by your offer, and I would snub you to the fullest extent, but I'm scared, and I'm cold, and I have no idea what tomorrow will bring, so I say *fine*."

Alaric raised his eyebrows in surprise. "You are a very strange woman, Madeline."

I smirked as I stood and began undressing. "Says the guy with cat fangs."

He grinned to show his dainty, pointed canines, then watched my every move as I took off the holey dress, bra, and panties. I quickly slipped into the tub on the side opposite him, inhaling sharply at the heat of the water. I let out my breath slowly as my skin adjusted to the temperature change, then settled down until the bubbles nearly reached my chin.

Alaric's smile turned mischievous, and I eyed him warily. Before I could react, he reached through the water and grabbed my arm, then spun me around in one fast movement so that my back was pressed against his. A little wave of water splashed out of the tub a moment later to soak his towel where he had set it on the tiled floor.

"I said I'd take a bath," I replied coolly, "I didn't say I was going to snuggle with you."

"Shh," he breathed as he lowered his lips to the side of my neck.

He laid gentle kisses all the way up to the base of my ear, making my chest and upper arms erupt in goosebumps, despite the warmth of the water.

"I—" I began, but he cut me off by turning my face to the side with one damp hand so he could kiss me.

My thoughts were a jumble of emotions, ranging from nervous excitement to guilt. The guilt was all for me, like I was letting myself down somehow, but it was drowned out by the feel of Alaric's free hand making its way down my ribcage.

I pulled away from the kiss and looked up into Alaric's eyes, which looked even darker surrounded by his wet hair. "Desperate times call for desperate measures?" I questioned weakly, looking for an excuse for my actions.

He chuckled. "Something like that."

He pulled my face back up for another kiss and I gave in. I would probably regret everything tomorrow, but that was tomorrow. This was tonight, and Alaric's soapy body felt far too good against mine to just go to bed.

Some time later we ended up on the king-sized bed with the covers pulled partially up. Alaric was lying on my lower body with his head cradled on my stomach while I stroked his drying hair. My original plan of sleeping on the couch seemed pretty silly now, and seemed even sillier as Alaric's hand slowly slid up from my hip to the side of my waist.

His fingers found the little scars where James had stabbed me. His entire body seemed to tense. When I didn't react, he relaxed, and began running his fingers back and forth across the scars.

I could sense he wanted to say something, but was probably afraid of opening up a can of worms since the scars were kind of his fault.

"What is it?" I prompted.

"How did you know I wanted to say something?" he asked with a hint of laughter in his voice.

"I'm an empath, remember?" I reminded him, though really I was just going off intuition.

He chuckled and ran his fingers over the scars again. "How did you heal them so quickly?"

It was a good question. In theory I knew how I'd done it, but I wasn't sure if I could replicate it, or even explain it. "I used the energy from the hearts, just like I did when I healed Sophie after the battle."

He moved his arms underneath my lower back and squeezed me tightly. "You know executioners aren't supposed to be able to heal, right?"

I smirked, but he couldn't see it. "Actually, I don't know much about executioners at all."

He lifted his head to meet my gaze. "And you know nothing of your parents?"

"N-no," I stammered, taken aback by the question. "Do you?"

He shook his head. "No. There's a chance I may have met them at some point, but I don't know who they are. Estus probably knows."

I shifted to put another pillow behind me so I could see him better. "Would they be executioners too?"

I'd gone so long without thinking about who my parents might be, I hadn't considered that they might be still be among the Vaettir. The thought was both intriguing and terrifying.

Alaric lifted one shoulder in a half shrug. "We inherit the traits of our mothers, but some lines are more specific than others."

Confused, I nodded my head for him to go on.

"Since Sophie and I are descended from a goddess of a

major pantheon, we have similar gifts to our mother. Other smaller deities are simply embodiments of nature, and the gifts inherited may vary. Your mother could have been descended from a major death goddess, in which case your gifts would be similar to hers, or she could have come from a lesser nature deity. Death is a part of all things, and can be inherited at random."

"So what about my empathy?" I questioned.

He laid his head back down on my stomach, rubbing his hair across my skin to cause a delightful shiver. "I do not know," he answered finally. "It should not be, just as your ability to heal should not be. Few among the Vaettir are true healers, and they usually descend from major deities."

I sighed. He spoke like all of these gods and goddesses actually existed. I would never have believed it before, but I'd had a rough few weeks. I was willing to believe most anything now. I thought about my next question, then asked, "What would other executioners do with the leftover energy of releasing someone's life force?"

He kissed my stomach, sending another shiver up my spine. "They would keep it, or use it as a weapon."

I took a shaky breath, then decided to ask a question I'd been wanting to ask ever since I found out what I was. Really, I'd been wanting to know the answer since the first time I'd killed. "Do you think I'm evil?"

Alaric lifted his head and looked up at me again, surprised. "How long have you been holding onto *that* one?"

I stared back at him. "Just answer it, please."

He eyed me seriously. "You're not evil, Maddy." I felt a moment of relief, but it was short lived as he added, "but you're not entirely good either."

At my horrified expression, he rolled off me so he could sit by my side and pull me close.

"I don't mean that how you think I do," he explained. "In nature there must be polarity. A forest fire may kill many trees and creatures, but it also brings new life and fertility to the land. Death is neither good nor bad, just as you are neither good nor bad. You simply *are*."

"But I'm a person with emotions and a moral compass," I argued. "I'm not simply *death*."

"Ah," he said with a coy smile, "but you were not asking me about your moral compass. You were asking if you are innately evil, because of your gifts."

I took a moment to think about what he'd said. "I guess I understand, but what about you? How could war ever be viewed as a good thing?"

He pulled me in a little closer, nestling me in the curve of his arm. "You are thinking of war in terms of bloody battles and rotting corpses. While that is part of what I am, that is not what war is in its purest form."

"Okay," I commented, "you've lost me again."

"It goes back to polarity," he explained. "Without one side, the other does not exist. Without conflict and chaos, there can be no victory nor peace."

"I suppose that makes sense. Without darkness, there's no light, and so on and so forth."

He gave my shoulders a squeeze. "Precisely. Now we should probably get some rest. Come morning we will likely have work to do."

I turned, my expression utterly serious. "Well then it's probably time for you to move to the couch."

His eyes widened in surprise, and he opened his mouth to say something, but no words came out.

I snickered.

Realizing my joke, he lifted me off him and pinned me to the bed with a wicked gleam in his eyes.

"I thought we were going to bed!" I exclaimed, still laughing.

He smiled wide enough to flash fang. "Not quite yet."

My laughter died down as I gazed into his now serious eyes. He leaned down and kissed me, and as he pulled away, I smiled. I'd already made one bad decision that night, so I might as well make another.

As he kissed down my chest, I glanced over at the heavy curtains covering the window. It likely wouldn't be long until the first light of dawn edged along the corners. Early rising Diana was going to be *pissed* if we weren't up and ready when she was.

Pissing people off seemed to be fast becoming a hobby of mine, but it was better than a lot of the alternatives.

CHAPTER TWO

*A*loud banging at the door woke me, not like someone knocking, but someone trying to break in. Alaric was already up out of bed, struggling into his dirty clothes next to the bathroom door. I held the sheets up to cover myself and rose to search frantically around the room for my dress, until it dawned on me that I had left it in the bathroom. The banging grew louder until the door slammed inward, hitting the wall with a startling *thwack.*

I froze halfway to the bathroom while Alaric faced whoever stood in the doorway. He had managed to get his pants on, but no shirt. Before I could react, a woman barreled into him, sending them both to the carpet at my feet. I caught a quick glance of her bright blonde hair and black clothing, then turned to face four more people rushing into the room.

They all wore black, like the woman, and I didn't recognize any of them. Shouts and the sound of fighting echoed through the walls from the next room over, letting me know we weren't the only ones being attacked.

Two of the intruders, both men, went to help the blonde-haired woman with Alaric, while the other two, a man and a woman, slowly approached me.

"She's the executioner," the man commented with a glance to the woman.

I looked back and forth between them, weighing my options. Sparring with Alaric was the only fighting experience I'd had, and I doubted I was any match for the pair in front of me.

One of the men attacking Alaric went flying across the room. He hit the wall hard enough to dent the drywall, then slid to the ground and was still. Five-hundred years of fighting experience had obviously done Alaric good. The man's pain was only a dull throb to me, which meant he was either dead, or unconscious.

I darted my attention back as the pair in front of me finally started to close in. My eyes shifted from side to side while I hiked the sheet up around my body like a dress. My body felt strange, like I was feeling emotions and injuries from too many people, and it all just condensed into a huge wave of pain and anxiety. It made it difficult to move or even think. I closed my eyes and took a deep breath, attempting to shut everyone else out. A measure of calm reached me, then my own emotions came flooding in. I opened my eyes just as the pair reached out in unison to grab me.

"Stop this at once!" a booming voice called from the doorway. The three of us turned to see Diana, looking a little mussed but unharmed, holding out both arms in a dramatic stance.

The two intruders that had approached me let their outstretched hands drop, then turned to face the new threat. Seeing an opportunity, and still blocking out a measure of the emotions around me, I ran to the man Alaric had thrown into the wall.

He was unconscious, but I couldn't tell how injured he was. I reached a hand hesitantly toward him, hoping that if he was near death, his spirit would reach out to me. The energy from one death wouldn't be much, but Alaric had claimed other executioners used that energy as a weapon. Maybe I could too.

I turned as one of the male intruders started shrieking to see Diana standing over his hunched form, one hand held out like she was *Darth Vader*. I searched for Alaric, but it sounded like much of the fighting was now happening in the hall. I wasn't sure what Diana was doing to the man, but he dropped to his knees and began clawing at his skin, leaving deep craters to fill with blood. I clutched at my own face, clenching my jaw against the sudden pain.

The horrifying sight was taken from my view as the blonde-haired woman that originally attacked Alaric darted around her tortured colleague and came to stand in front of me.

"I'm not going to hurt you," she assured, "but I need you to come with me."

I reached out to the unconscious man again, guiltily hoping he was near death. I could feel his life force, but it felt solid inside of him. I reached out mentally, trying to connect with the energy, but it wouldn't budge from his body, meaning he wasn't badly hurt.

With a glance at her prostrate colleague, the woman grabbed my arm and hauled me to my feet. It was all I could do to use my free arm to keep the sheet around me. I tried again to pull at the unconscious man's life force, but another answered. The energy came rushing out of the man Diana had tortured, ready to be released. It flowed through me as the woman began hauling me toward the door.

Rather than assisting me, Diana tilted her head as a

strange smile crossed her face. I looked at her in panic as the blonde woman jerked me forward. She turned, raising her free arm like she was going to hit me, and I reacted by shoving the energy at her, much like I had done to Estus when I escaped the Salr with James. The woman went flying back, losing her grip on me as she shot out into the hall.

I stared at her crumpled form, dumbfounded, until James stepped into view in the hall. He was covered in soot and ash, letting me know he had probably burned a few people to death.

He looked at the woman, then over to me and chuckled. "Little mouse has some teeth after all." He walked into the room, smirked at the sheet covering my body, then walked up to Diana. "Thanks for the *help*," he said sarcastically.

"Madeline is what's important," Diana replied coolly.

Not taking the time to ponder the harsh statement from Diana, I ran out into the hall in search of Alaric. I found him being helped to his feet by Sophie, surrounded by several dead people.

Seeing me, Alaric pulled away from Sophie and closed the distance between us, engulfing me in a tight hug as soon as he reached me.

Diana came into the hall, followed by James. "Release them quickly, Madeline. We must go before the human police come."

"But they're not all dead," I argued, reluctantly pulling away from Alaric.

"They will be," she said apathetically as James crouched down and slit the unconscious blonde woman's throat with a knife.

My stomach lurched at the sight. He must have picked up the knife sometime after we landed. I looked away as the woman's blood flowed onto the fancy carpet. The rest of the hallway was utterly still, but I knew the chaos had to have been heard by others. I wasn't surprised as police sirens suddenly wailed in the distance.

Snapping into action, I gathered my sheet tightly around myself and ran past Diana back into the room, then dashed straight into the bathroom. My wrinkled, tattered black dress was on the floor where I'd left it, looking unappealing and a little damp. Knowing I had no other options, I slipped the undergarments and dress back on, cursing the fact that we were yet to get me anything but a coat.

I returned to the main room to find James finishing off the unconscious man. In total we had five victims, the blonde, the two Alaric had killed in the hall, the man Diana had taken down, and the latest one, although I still had no idea what happened in the other rooms.

The sirens grew nearer.

"There's no time," Diana barked. "Leave them."

"I can't leave them like this!" I shouted, panicking as Diana put her iron cold grip around my arm and began to drag me out of the room.

Sophie had followed us in, and grabbed my coat off the couch as Diana pushed me in front of her so she could shove me into James' grasp. I began to struggle, horrified at the thought of leaving life in dead bodies, but Sophie cut in and quickly helped me into my coat.

"They're right," she snapped. "Now *move*."

When I didn't react, James threw me over his shoulder and carried me into the hall. Alaric had been busy checking the other rooms, but as we neared him James tossed me onto his shoulder like a rag doll.

"I have to free them," I pleaded from my awkward perch, knowing Alaric would at least listen to me, but he continued walking forward as the others entered the stairwell.

"There's no time," he explained as the door to the stairwell slammed shut behind us. "Besides, you'd be doing nothing for them once the police arrested you."

I knew he was right, but I could feel the souls of the dead reaching out to me, pleading to be released. "We have to go back!" I shrieked, unable to listen to reason as the spirits cried out in my head.

Alaric jogged a little faster down the stairwell. We were five stories up, but no one had even glanced at the elevators. The sane part of me knew that we were taking the stairs so we wouldn't be entirely trapped should the police show up too soon, but the rest of me could only think about the corpses we'd left behind.

I cried in vain as Alaric took the stairs in great bounds. If I fought to go back, I would likely get us all killed, or at least jailed, though something told me James and Diana would not go down without a fight.

We reached the bottom stairwell and continued into the lower parking garage. From my backward vantage point on Alaric's shoulder, I couldn't tell who was leading us, I only knew we were last in line. The sirens grew louder as another door slammed shut behind us, and Alaric lowered me to my bare feet, but my legs buckled. He caught me with an arm under my shoulders before I could fall. I felt like I wanted to cry. We'd forgotten my damn shoes. No one else standing in our little semi-circle seemed to notice.

"They're already outside," James stated calmly.

"We'll split up," Diana instructed. She turned her vibrant green eyes to Alaric. "Get Madeline out of here. Without her, our efforts are useless."

I had one confused moment before Alaric lifted me back up over his shoulder and started running. Everyone else ran in opposite directions. There were several exits to the parking complex that I could see, but Alaric chose one that led to the back of the hotel.

I couldn't decide whether I was happy or sad as Sophie and the others disappeared from sight. Neither I suppose. Mostly I was just worried about escaping the police, and about trusting my fate to the man running effortlessly underneath me.

The door thudded against the building's exterior as Alaric carried me outside. The cold was a sudden slap in the face, or rear, considering how I was being carried. I pushed away from Alaric's back to get a better view of our surroundings as he sped across the back parking lot. There were no police in sight, which meant that likely only one or two patrol cars had been dispatched to investigate the disturbance. They hadn't surrounded the place.

Shouts echoed in the distance, followed by loud banging then more shouts.

It was only then that I looked down and realized Alaric wasn't wearing shoes either. Without hesitation, his bare feet hit the snowy ground past the parking lot.

The commotion continued in the distance as we ran, but all I could think about was the cold and distantly, the souls I'd left trapped in their bodies.

Alaric quietly cursed under his breath as he carried me into a forested area. There didn't seem to be any businesses or other buildings around, from what I could see. Just shadowy, dense forest. Thoughts flashed through my mind of cops with well-trained dogs hunting us down in the woods. We'd all been seen by the bellhop, so the police would quickly learn how many of us there were, and what we looked like. Of course, none of it would matter if we froze to death first.

I let out a yip of surprise when someone came jogging up to our side, then sagged in relief when I realized it was Sophie. I would have really liked to run on my own, but the no shoes and freezing cold aspect kept me quiet.

"James and Diana?" Alaric asked as they ran side by side, only sounding slightly out of breath.

"I don't know," Sophie replied, "but I'm glad to be rid of them."

I sucked in a breath despite the bumping pressure of Alaric's shoulder against my abdomen. "Don't we . . . need . . . Diana's help?"

Alaric and Sophie were both quiet for a moment, then began speaking to each other in a different language, the same one I'd heard them use before we left Spokane. Great, just great. Not only was I going to either freeze to death or go to jail, I was also going to be left out of any planning involved in attempting to prevent either of those outcomes.

Alaric and Sophie continued talking like I wasn't even there. I clung to Alaric, resigned to listen for signs of pursuit. I could no longer hear the sirens, but I almost thought I could hear the souls screaming back in the hotel for me to release them. The sound would probably haunt me until I died, which given my luck, would likely be within the next few hours.

Eventually Alaric and Sophie slowed and I was let down to my feet. I hissed at the cold, tip-toeing to a snow-free spot near the trunk of a massive tree. My entire body ached from cold, and from being held over Alaric's shoulder. Along the way, I had continuously replayed the entire hotel scene over and over in my mind, and still couldn't push the disturbing imagery from my head.

By now, the dead Vaettir would have been put into body bags and carted away by the police. They would likely reanimate, and Norway would be awash with sensationalized stories about a zombie rampage.

Alaric and Sophie both paced, crunching icy pine needles under their feet. Sophie was the only one of us lucky enough to be wearing shoes, and she was fully clothed in her normal black attire. Alaric wore only his black jeans, leaving his dark hair to trail over his pale, bare chest.

I crouched down to cover my legs with my coat, then glared up at both of them.

Sophie glared right back. *"What?"*

I sighed."If you both are done ignoring me, I have some questions."

Alaric stopped pacing and came to crouch beside me. "I'm sorry," he said, wrapping an arm around me. "We didn't mean to ignore you."

Accepting his body heat, but not his apology, I leaned against him. "What's going to happen when the dead bodies we left in the hotel room reanimate?"

Sophie moved to stand beside us, her dark eyes scanning the distance. "I'm sure their clan will take care of it."

"Their clan?" I questioned.

"It's the whole reason we formed clans to begin with," Alaric explained, "and why we are supposed to stay within the Salr. It is the Doyen's responsibility to make sure things like this don't happen."

I closed my eyes against a budding headache. "But whose clan were they part of?"

"That's the part I do not like," Sophie commented. "They were not from Estus' clan, and James claimed they did not belong to Aislin, either."

My shivering increased, and it wasn't just from the cold. I

didn't understand the world of the Vaettir like Alaric and Sophie did, and I was getting tired of being left in the dark.

"So what do we do now? If Diana thinks the charm is somewhere near here, should we try to find it without her?"

Alaric and Sophie both looked at each other instead of me, like they were passing thoughts back and forth in front of my face.

Finally Alaric turned to me. "We never planned on finding the charm *with* her. We just needed her help to locate the exact area."

My mouth formed a little "oh" of surprise that soon turned into a tight-lipped grimace. "You could have let me in on that plan at some point," I chided. "Here I've been worrying over exactly when she and James would betray us all."

"We didn't want to give Diana any reason to doubt your intentions," Sophie explained, "but her obsession with you and Alaric has given us pause."

I exhaled an annoyed huff of breath, fogging the air in front of me. "Stop talking like you're the *hive mind*. What do you mean her *obsession* with us?"

Alaric gave me a tight squeeze as Sophie explained, "Her obsession that the two of you be together. She would not do it for selfless reasons, and I highly doubt she's a die-hard romantic. She somehow wants to use that bond, and I do not like it. She's more invested in this than she's letting on. When we were attacked in our rooms, she left James to go after you. She chose you over her own grandson."

"But there are other executioners out there," I countered, "Surely I'm not *that* important."

Sophie shrugged. "I have no explanation for it, but I vote we leave this place and forget all about the charm."

Alaric scoffed. "And hide forever? I've no doubt Diana will

do her best to hunt us down, as will Estus. Aislin is Diana's sister, which means we'll have the two largest clans among the Vaettir scouring the earth for us."

Sophie glared at her brother. "We've hidden before . . . " she trailed off.

I shook my head. "I agree with Alaric."

Sophie aimed a venomous glare at me. "Of *course* you do. So what do you suggest, Madeline, since you seem to know everything?"

I would have been offended by her sarcasm if I couldn't feel the fear wafting off her like heat waves. "The only conclusion I can come to in regards to Diana, is that she wants us to find the charm so she can either use it herself, or claim credit for its delivery to Aislin. I vote we find the charm and give it to Aislin ourselves in return for protection. Short of killing Estus, there is no other way to stop him from hunting us."

Sophie blinked at me, then shook her head. "You don't even know Aislin. What makes you think she'll keep her word?"

"Do you have any better ideas?"

We sat in silence for several minutes before Sophie said, "Fine, but we better get moving if we're going to keep ahead of James and Diana."

I nodded and stood, though pulling away from Alaric's warmth and re-baring my legs to the cold took way more willpower than I'd like to admit.

After a few minutes of me hobbling on the cold ground like a newborn horse, Sophie even gave me her boots and kept just her socks on, proving she was a much tougher woman that me, which I was more than okay with.

I had no idea how we would find the charm before anyone else found us. My hope was that Alaric or Sophie would be able to sniff it out, but there was one fall-back option. The charm was sealed in a place guarded by the dead. If the spirits still remained within the burial mounds, I would be able to sense them . . . hopefully.

It was a long shot, but at least we would probably freeze to death before Estus or anyone else could kill us.

CHAPTER THREE

*A*fter several hours stumbling through the wintery woods, there was still no sign of James or Diana. There was also no sign of the place we were looking for. My borrowed boots crunched over dead twigs and patches of snow haphazardly as I forced myself onward, feeling numb from cold and exhaustion.

I glared at Alaric and Sophie's backs, moving with graceful ease through the snow. Neither had expressed worry about the implications of being lost in the freezing cold woods without food or shelter, and I had to trust that they would keep us alive. We had other more imminent worries anyhow.

Unable to contend with my burning lungs, I staggered toward a tree and leaned against it. I knew we needed to keep moving, but the cold air and altitude were making me lightheaded. It wouldn't do anyone any good if I passed out.

Likely noticing the lack of labored breathing behind him, Alaric stopped, turned, and walked back to me. Sophie watched us with hands on hips, clearly annoyed.

Alaric moved to lift me into his arms, and I was ready to

let him, but something caught my eye in the air beside his head. A slight shimmer disturbed the still scenery. I was about to write it off as a hallucination, then a faint whisper shivered across my brain. Soon, more whispers joined it.

I held out a hand to halt Alaric's progress. I couldn't tell where the whispers were coming from, but it was obvious he and Sophie didn't hear them. They both watched my changed expression warily.

"You guys don't hear that, do you?" I asked, wanting confirmation.

Alaric shook his head, still watching me cautiously.

"I hear only the birds and the wind," Sophie added, "and my hearing is likely *much* better than yours."

Alaric closed the distance between us and placed a hand on my arm. "What do you hear, Maddy?"

The volume of the whispers increased.

I crouched to the ground, pulling Alaric with me. As I suspected, the whispers grew louder still.

"I hear voices," I explained distantly, utterly absorbed.

Alaric cleared his throat. "You know, that's what crazy people say..."

I bit my lip, trying to think of a witty reply. I opened my mouth to speak, then the air began shimmering around us, distracting me. I inhaled sharply as I finally realized what I was feeling. *Spirits.* Or at least their energy. The air felt alive with it. It was clear Alaric and Sophie still felt nothing, even as my own sense of things increased.

I scraped my bare hands across the icy ground, clearing soil and dead pine needles near the base of the tree. I still couldn't get a direct sense of where the voices were coming from, but I knew they were somewhere below us. I could feel their heavy presence reaching out to me.

Alaric watched me for a moment, then began clearing more of the hard soil away. Sophie stood back and waited.

The whispers became almost unbearable, seeming to egg me on. With a sigh to let us know how irritated she was, Sophie joined us in our digging. The pulsing energy was thrumming so desperately that it shook my bones as my hand ran across a small, metal ring amidst a yellow clump of grass. I dug my fingers into the grass and pulled the loop free. It hinged upward, connecting to something in the ground. I attempted to tug on it as Alaric and Sophie came to crouch on either side of me, but it wouldn't budge.

With a look of wonder on his face, Alaric took the ring from me, then gave it a pull, using his knees to lift with more force than I had to offer at the moment. When it still wouldn't budge, I wrapped my hands around his wrists while Sophie grabbed his waist, and the three of us pulled together.

A large trap door pulled free from the earth. I fell onto my butt and Sophie toppled on top of me. Quickly righting ourselves, we moved around the now open door to crouch in front of the opening. I leaned over the edge and looked down, but it was dark. Damp and rot filled my nostrils as the voices filtered back in through my mind, louder now.

"How on earth did you find that?" Alaric asked breathlessly, peering down beside me.

"I could hear them," I replied cryptically.

I reached my hand into the cavern, searching for some way to climb down inside. The trap door was wide enough for two of us to fit down at once, but the straight drop down made it a less than practical mode of entry.

I continued patting around the inner lip of the entrance until my fingers scraped across a bar of rough wood, hopefully the top rung of a ladder. I turned around and stuck a foot into the darkness, ready to climb down, trying not to think about the dangers that might lurk within. Alaric wrapped a hand around my upper arm to stop me, worry creasing his brow.

He opened his mouth to speak, probably to suggest he go first, when a dark shape barreled into his back. Alaric and I fell with our attacker into the darkness.

I landed, *hard* on loamy earth, with a squirming weight on top of me. I'd distantly registered the echo of the trap door slamming shut, sealing us in darkness. I strained to get up, thinking I had injured my back, but then whoever was on top of me rolled off and I was able to sit up with a groan. I didn't think it had been Alaric, they weren't big enough.

Banging and shouting above us let me know Sophie was still outside. The sound of her shouting suddenly moved away from the door, but I could still hear her, like she was shouting at something, or someone, else. I wanted to call out to her, but I hadn't entirely regained my senses.

"Maddy?" Alaric whispered.

"I'm here," I groaned, wanting to stand and move toward the sound of his voice, but the darkness was so complete, it held me immobile. Plus, whoever had landed on me might still be nearby, and I didn't want to accidentally run into them instead.

I jumped as a hand landed in mine.

"It's me," he whispered.

I nodded, then realized he couldn't see it as he pulled me to my feet. Standing gave me an overwhelming sense of vertigo, and the smell of mildew and damp earth made me feel like I might throw up.

"Someone is in here with us," Alaric whispered, pulling me against his side.

"I know. Whoever it was landed right on top of me."

I became further disoriented as we began to move. Even

with my free hand held out in front of me, I felt like I was going to run my face into something at any moment.

"What about Sophie?" I whispered. I could no longer hear any commotion from above ground, and I was worried something had happened to her.

"Sophie can take care of herself," he replied. "Plus, I think she's probably safer than us at the moment. Now we should probably stop talking. Try to step lightly."

I ran my hand along the damp, rough wall, feeling the varying pits and grooves of natural stone.

I knew I should be silent, but questions burned within me until I quietly blurted, "Do you think this is the right place?"

Alaric tightened his arm around my waist. "Don't you?" he whispered. "Or did you have some other reason for pawing around in the soil, then trying to climb down here without even thinking about what might lie below?"

My hands slipped across rough wood mounted in the stone corridor. A doorway. We stepped through, then turned a corner, following a faint illumination in the distance.

"What is that?" I whispered.

"There's only one way to find out," Alaric whispered in reply, removing his hand from my waist to my arm.

We crept toward the light. While the small amount of light eased some of my tension, the feeling of eyes on my back gave me chills. Why would someone push us into the cavern, only to hide in the dark?

The light intensified as we neared, revealing a hunched form, sitting in a rocking chair with its back to us. Surrounding the chair was a rather cozy room complete with upholstered furniture, and a large woven rug. The cozy scene was thrown off slightly by the surrounding darkness. I couldn't tell where the light was coming from, but it should have touched that darkness. Instead the black was like a solid wall.

At first I thought the figure in the rocking chair was an elderly woman, since all I could see was the hump of her back and the lackluster fabric of her loose clothing, but then she left her chair to turn and rise before us. At her full height, she stood a good foot taller than Alaric, and that wasn't including the antlers protruding from her skull. They were the antlers of a deer, and they somehow complimented her strange, narrow face. I wasn't quite sure how I knew the creature was female. She just had a certain femininity about her.

"She's a Norn," Alaric muttered in disbelief.

I knew that Norns were creatures of Norse myth, and that they controlled the fates, but that was about it. Suddenly I wished that I had finished the book I'd started on Norse myth in college. I might have remembered whether or not Norns ate human flesh.

The Norn blinked large, up-tilted eyes at us. It was difficult to tell in the soft light, but I was pretty sure her glistening skin was a pale shade of green.

She spoke to us in a harsh guttural language that I didn't understand. I was about to ask the creature if she spoke English, when Alaric replied in the same language. I realized with a start that it was the same language I'd heard him and Sophie speaking.

"She asked us why we're here, and in such a poor state of dress," Alaric explained. "I told her what we seek, and that we were attacked."

"Was it wise to just blurt it out like that?" I asked as the creature stared at us intently.

"Lying to a Norn would do no good," Alaric replied with a small smile.

The Norn said something else that made Alaric look over his shoulder.

"What is it?" I asked, whipping my gaze to the near-darkness behind us.

"She said that someone else is approaching. Probably whoever pushed us down here."

The Norn said something else, something that made Alaric's face go rigid.

"What did she say?" I asked when he didn't explain. When he still didn't answer me, I shook his arm, not liking the look in his eyes.

"She asked who will claim the charm after we've sacrificed ourselves," he explained evenly.

My eyes widened. *"What?"*

Someone stepped up on my other side. I stumbled away from Diana, looking a little disheveled in her black cloak. She said something in the Norn's language.

Alaric let out what sounded like a curse word in that strange language, then grabbed my arm, pulling me away from Diana and the Norn.

"What's happening?" I gasped, stumbling backward.

"It's a trap, Maddy," he growled. "A sacrifice is needed to release the charm, and we're it. This is what Diana was planning."

The whispers started up again, almost drowning out Alaric's words. With all the excitement, I hadn't even realized they'd been quiet until then. I pulled away from Alaric and clamped my hands over my ears, but it did nothing to stop the sound, because the voices weren't coming from around me, they were inside my head.

Alaric lifted me and carried me toward the entrance. The Norn and Diana did nothing to stop us. I found out why a moment later as the darkness in front of us solidified. I could see no wall or barrier, but whatever we stood in front of was solid, as if the darkness had been given form.

"Let me down," I hissed. We weren't getting out of here, and I wanted to face Diana on my own two feet.

We both turned back to her, our backs against the solid wall of darkness.

"The least you can do is explain why it had to be us," Alaric said coldly.

I glanced at his icy expression and wanted to yell at him for just giving up, but the voices in my head were making me dizzy, especially since I couldn't understand what any of them were saying.

Diana chuckled. She looked like a dwarf next to the Norn, but stood so confidently that she still looked imposing. A small smile crossed her aged lips. "The charm is sealed by ritual. Six of the Vaettir died to seal it. Each pair loved each other dearly, a trait rare amongst our people. The woman of each couple killed her mate, and then herself, first sacrificing her heart, and then her life. That kind of magic is not easy to undo."

The voices surged in my mind. I fell to my knees. I was doing my best to understand what Diana was saying, but I could barely hear her voice over the voices in my head. Alaric crouched beside me, but kept his eyes on Diana.

"I needed an executioner to release their spirits, so that they would no longer bind the charm," she continued.

"We had assumed that already," Alaric snapped, "but that does not explain the need for sacrifice."

Diana chuckled again, and I would have walked forward and hit her had I been able to stand. "Magic is a funny thing," she explained. "To fully undo a ritual, it must be repeated in some way. It seemed much more simple to just use the two of you, rather than finding another couple."

The voices stopped abruptly. I could sense the dead, paying close attention to us. Their apprehension was palpable. Though I saw no burial mounds, I knew the place from my vision was near. I could feel each of the corpses pulsing like I had seven heartbeats.

Alaric rose and stepped in front of me. "She does not love me. Cutting out my heart might hurt her, but it would not be akin to sacrificing her own heart. Putting us together in a hotel room for a night was a feeble plan, at best. The ritual will not work."

I was finally able to peel my eyes away from Diana at that. Alaric glanced back at me.

"Maddy?" he said weakly. "I'm right, aren't I?"

"She already loved you, you fool," Diana chided, "but another night to increase the bond couldn't hurt, now could it?"

Ignoring Diana, Alaric continued to stare at me. "Tell me she's wrong, Madeline."

Was she wrong? I honestly hadn't considered the possibility of loving Alaric. I knew that I could grow to love him, given the time, but did I love him already?

My eyes widened in horror as I realized the answer. I did love him, at least in some odd, twisted way, and now we were probably going to die for it.

The look on my face was enough of an answer for Alaric. "Find a way out. I'll hold them off."

I rose shakily to my feet and moved to his side. "I won't leave you. There's two of them and two of us. This isn't over yet."

The Norn said something else in her language, then Diana said, "Neither of you will be leaving. The room is sealed. The ritual will be completed whether you volunteer, or not."

At her words the voices in my head started anew. I crumpled back to the ground, hands covering my ears though I knew it would do no good. I watched helplessly as Alaric charged Diana and the Norn, and then my vision went black. My last thought was, *I hope I don't wake up.*

CHAPTER FOUR

I woke lying on my back. I scraped my hands across the ground, touching damp soil. I rolled my head to the side and saw Alaric chained up to a tree, and it all came rushing back to me. The Norn. Diana. *The sacrifice*. We were still underground, so the tree supporting Alaric shouldn't have been there, yet its limbs stretched up into the darkness, covered in healthy green leaves. Candles surrounded the tree's base, holding back the darkness.

I rolled onto my stomach and pushed myself up to my knees. More candles lined the cavern walls. I staggered to my feet. I needed to get to Alaric.

I stumbled as I realized I was right next to one of the burial mounds from my vision. The mounds were unmarked, and covered in dark soil. The same soil now covered much of my skin. The only reason I even knew that the mounds were graves at all was because I could feel the dead below. They were all silent. *Waiting*.

I looked back to Alaric, who appeared unconscious, hanging limply from his bindings, then hurried toward him, praying to whatever forces might be listening that he was just unconscious and not dead.

I reached him and placed a hand on his pale neck, searching for a pulse. It was there, but faint. I pulled my hand away, leaving a mark of black soil on his skin, then turned to search the rest of the room for a way to free him. The chain that held him was composed of dark steel with no lock that I could see.

At the edge of the cavern, the Norn stepped out of the darkness with Diana a few steps behind. I could have sworn there had been a solid wall where they stood just moments before.

"I won't do it," I stated, sounding much stronger than I felt.

Instead of replying, the Norn raised her hand and the voices started up again. She blinked her strange, large eyes at me, completely devoid of compassion as the spirits called out. I couldn't understand their language, but being this close to them broke down other barriers.

Images flashed through my mind of their sacrifice. There had been so much blood when the men's throats were slit that it seeped into the soil, enriching it, though nothing would ever grow in such a place. Nothing but the tree in the center, because it was composed of the magic of sacrifice. I saw each of the women falling to the ground, having slit their own throats, and then my view was from the ground as well, looking out from the eyes of the final woman as she died. The images faded and I was left with nothing but a sense of time. The spirits had been trapped there for centuries, alone and in the dark.

I opened my eyes without even realizing I had closed them to find myself kneeling on top of one of the mounds, my hands pressed against the dirt. The woman inside had been the one to show me the images. I recoiled instantly with the realization that I had been only moments away from releasing her spirit.

At my hesitation, the images started again, taking away my other senses. I saw war. I tried to push away images of rotten corpses strewn across vast battlefields, and women and children burned alive for living along the wrong trade-route, but it was like watching a movie inside my head. I couldn't just close my eyes to shut it out.

My mind reeled away from the memories, but they stuck with me as if they were my own. I was back on the mound, with my hands buried in the black dirt. I could feel the soul within begging for release. She had died for a cause. The charm was evil, and had to be locked away, lest her children and her children's children suffer the same fate as their elders. Yet she was tired, and her children were likely dead. Why should she have to protect the charm any longer? Hadn't she sacrificed enough?

I shook my head as I reached out toward her spirit. My mind was warning me to stop, that if I set her free I would have to help the others, and then Diana would try to make me kill Alaric.

The other corpses pulled at me as I hesitated. It wasn't fair for them to stay trapped while I lived. I shook my head, knowing that last thought was not my own.

"Get on with it," Diana demanded impatiently, snapping me back into reality.

My hands felt glued to the earth, like the woman's soul would not let me go. She would hold me there forever if I made her. The connection deepened the longer I knelt there. Suddenly I could feel not only her memories, but her body, withered and decayed, and I could feel the pain of her brutal death. The pain seared through my body, but it was nothing compared to the pain of killing the one I loved. I shook my head. The one *she* loved. My thoughts were blurring together with hers. Unable to bear the pain any longer, I released her, then fell sobbing to the ground as I felt the other dead shift in anticipation.

All I could think as the woman's energy rushed through me was, *fuck this*. I would not die like this woman had, and I would not let her sacrifice be in vain. If I let Diana have the charm, those in the earth below me would have died for nothing.

Not really knowing what I was doing, I took a deep, shaky breath, then shoved the woman's energy back into the ground through my hands. The power ignored the woman's now-empty corpse and forced its way through the ground until it found the others.

I stumbled to my feet as the ground began to shake. Diana no longer looked cocky, she looked terrified. "What are you doing!" she cried. "Release them!"

I could no longer hear the voices of the dead, but I could *feel* them. They were rising to the surface, animated by the energy I'd given them.

I ran back to Alaric, unsure of what I had just released, and clung to his limp hand. The soil of the nearby mounds began to shift. First came their skeletal hands, clawing at the air. Decayed corpses pushed their way up through the soil, pulling free to rise slowly to their feet. Most were just skeletons with tatters of cloth and a few dried ligaments, but some had retained a measure of dried skin.

Something squeezed my hand and I flinched, then I realized that Alaric had regained consciousness. I glanced at him, but he had eyes only for the dead.

I turned back to the corpses, all facing me. Having their eyeless skulls staring at me should have been the most horrifying sight I'd ever seen, but I wasn't scared. Though they did not speak, I could sense their emotions. They were still not free, and they would do anything if only I would just release them.

I smiled as inspiration hit me. I would let them go, but they would have to do me a favor first. I squeezed Alaric's hand. "Tell them to kill Diana and I'll release them," I ordered.

"What?" Alaric asked, confused.

"I don't speak their language, tell them."

With a shriek of frustration Diana began marching toward us, leaving the Norn to wait by herself.

"Tell them!" I pleaded.

Alaric spoke quickly in the strange language.

The corpses turned toward Diana in unison, freezing her in her tracks.

"No," she breathed, realizing her predicament.

She backed away, pleading with the corpses in their language. They shambled toward her, backing her into a corner until she reached the Norn. Diana reached out her hands, and I knew she was trying to harm the corpses like she had harmed the man back in the hotel room, but nothing happened. These Vaettir had already felt all the pain they would ever feel.

Diana turned wide eyes up to the Norn. "Stop them!" she pleaded, but the Norn only glanced down at her, then turned her gaze back to me.

I couldn't be sure from the distance, but I thought I saw a satisfied smile creep across the Norn's face.

Diana screamed as the dead reached her. Her fear was more palpable than any other emotion in the room. It stabbed me in the gut like a knife.

"You'll feel me die, Madeline!" she threatened as skeletal hands clamped down on her aged skin.

She was right. I could feel people's wounds like they were my own, and even muted, Diana's death was going to be a horrible one. Alaric squeezed my hand hard enough to make my knuckles pop and I was able to look away from the scene.

"Focus on me," he whispered.

There were tears in my eyes as I nodded, and then the dead began their work, tearing Diana limb from limb. I fell to the ground with the pain of it as she continued screaming in vain, but Alaric kept my hand gripped tightly in his.

I focused on him, and felt a measure of calm, but Diana's emotions of pain and fear were much stronger than calm, and they leaked through until I was screaming with her. I curled up into a little ball, with one arm raised above to retain my hold on Alaric.

Suddenly her screaming stopped, and mine cut off just as abruptly. The only sounds that could be heard were the thuds of Diana's body parts dropping to the ground.

My entire body trembled as I staggered to my feet, still holding onto Alaric.

The corpses turned empty eye-sockets to me. The Norn, still smiling, was motionless behind them. I noticed blood on skeletal hands and tatters of clothing as the corpses began to shamble in my direction. They had done their part, now it was time to do mine.

I swallowed the lump in my throat and kept my eyes averted from Diana's remains, which wasn't really difficult with what equated to mostly decomposed zombies filling my vision. I pulled away from Alaric as the first one reached me. It was a man's corpse, and I wasn't just judging by the size of the skeleton. I could still feel the energy of who he once was, trapped inside his bones.

Sick curiosity got the best of me, and I leaned down and forward to look through his ribcage. Sure enough, a perfectly preserved heart gently pulsed inside, long since abandoned by the other organs. Estus had once told me that the heart was the key to it all. Release the heart, and the spirit could fully move on.

I reached out and placed my palm against the man's ribcage. As I did so, the heart within reacted. Instead of the fear and rage I was used to from Estus' victims, I felt an overwhelming exhaustion, tinged with sadness. My knees almost buckled at the sensation. Without thinking about it, I released the heart, willing away its melancholic hurt. The bones crumbled to the ground, no longer possessing whatever magic had held them together.

The expected rush of energy wiped away my fatigue, then the next corpse stepped forward. I released each of them, the energy building inside me as each set of bones fell to the dark earth. The Norn watched it all impassively, making no move to interrupt.

When I was done, I turned back toward Alaric, feeling almost drunk on extra energy. It was even more of a high than what I'd felt after releasing all of Estus' long tortured hearts, letting me know the people who'd died to keep the charm in place had been very powerful indeed.

He looked down at me with a mixture of awe, and maybe a little bit of fear as I touched my fingers to the chains binding him. They fell away at my touch, and I had to help steady him as his feet hit the ground.

He wrapped his arms around me and held me for several seconds, tight enough that it was hard to breathe, not that I really minded.

"You are a little bit amazing," he whispered against my hair.

"Just a little bit?" I whispered back, still feeling giddy.

We turned, hand in hand, to face the Norn. The tall creature inclined her head in our direction, then said something in her strange language.

I looked to Alaric for a translation.

His expression was thoughtful as he said, "She asks that you approach her, *alone*."

I oddly wasn't afraid. I was still riding on waves of stolen energy. It was dizzying, yet made me feel safe, and maybe a little bit powerful. I let go of Alaric's hand and approached the Norn, maintaining eye contact with her as I went. Once I reached her, I had to crane my neck upward to still be looking at her face.

She smiled and reached her long fingers toward me. It was only then I realized she only had four of them, and her hand was actually shaped more like the talons of a hawk with three fingers in front and one in the back, each ending in a gleaming black point.

Three talons came to rest on the side of my face, finally causing my pulse to quicken. I only had a moment of fear, though, as images began to flash through my mind. She might not speak my language, but she could communicate in pictures, just like the corpses.

The images flashed so quickly, I couldn't make out half of them. I saw many faces I didn't recognize, violence, and scenes of ritual. At the center of the chaos was a tiny key. *The charm.* Releasing it would bring its chaos upon the world, but it could no longer remain sealed away. It had to be destroyed, and it would take magic like mine to do it. Finally the images stopped to rest on a gathering of other Norns like the one standing in front of me. They were the guardians of the key.

As the final image faded from my mind, the Norn pulled her talons away and moved past me toward the tree. I turned to watch as she stopped in front of it, looking much like a tree herself with her tall, narrow form, and loose, shape-stealing robes.

I made my way to where Alaric had gone to stand, close to the wall and off to the side so we could see the Norn's face as she reached her talons out to the tree, caressing the bark. My breath hissed through my teeth as her other clawed hand dove suddenly into her lower chest, the talons cutting easily through her skin and clothing. She staggered against the tree, her spindly arm contorting to reach underneath her rib cage.

Alaric and I watched in horrified silence as she withdrew her hand to reveal her still-beating heart, perfectly removed to remain whole. Blood seeped into her robe as she fell to her knees, then extended the heart in our direction.

I rushed to her side with Alaric following on my heels. I had no idea how she was still alive, but the Norn blinked up at me, pain furrowing her brow.

Her pain shot through my chest, stealing my breath. I would have fallen, but Alaric caught me.

She held the heart up, then bowed her head. Understanding what she wanted me to do, I clung to Alaric with one hand while I stroked trembling fingertips across the heart, releasing it.

The antlers on her head touched the soil as she slumped to the side, dead, then I was hit with energy like I'd never felt. Alaric released me with a hiss of breath and I fell to my knees by the prostrate form of the Norn. Her pooling blood dampened my bare knees, but I barely noticed as I looked around frantically for some way to release the energy.

It felt like it was scorching my brain, and filling my lungs with hot steam, far too much for me to hold. Seeing no other option, I placed my hands against the nearby tree and willed the energy away. I didn't picture something happening like I normally would, I just *pushed*, desperate to feel normal again.

The energy left me in a steady current, and we had just a moment of stunned silence before the world started moving again. The tree shot upward with new growth, twisting like a serpent as its bark expanded, too fast for the eye to follow. I collapsed in a panting heap beside the tree, too tired and delirious to move away.

Suddenly Alaric was there, pulling me into his lap and wrapping his arms protectively around me as we both stared up in awe. Where the branches reached the ceiling of the space, they diverged away from each other and began curving back down toward us.

Thoughts of being impaled by the tree hit me just as Alaric rolled me closer to the trunk, sheltering me on my back with his body, but the branches slowed and stilled, all except for one. One tiny, hair-thin branch reached down until it was mere inches in front of my face. At its end was a small, black metal key.

Alaric and I reached out together. His hand closed around mine, as mine closed around the key. It pulled away from the branch easily, and our hands came back down. I observed the key in my palm. It felt so small and mundane in my hand, but I was pretty sure we'd found the charm everyone was searching for, far more dangerous an item than I could have imagined.

Alaric stared down at it. "Now that we have it, what on earth are we going to do with it?"

I glanced over to the Norn who had given her life to release the key. Her sacrifice had shattered the ritual binding it to smithereens.

I gripped the key so tightly the edges cut into my skin,

thinking of the images the Norn had shown me. "We destroy it."

"As my lady wishes," he replied, half-joking, though I knew he meant what he said. He pulled me in a little closer, cradling me in the cool soil, surrounded by bones.

I knew in that moment that this whole ordeal had only just begun. It would have been easy to use the key as a bargaining chip for our own lives and freedom, but after what first the corpses, then the Norn had shown me, I couldn't just give the charm away. The tiny key had the power to cause massive wars and chaos. So much death.

Destroying it would not be easy, but I knew it was possible. That was why the Norn wanted me to have it. My particular brand of magic was needed, but I'd need power. I'd need many, *many* deaths. I paled at the thought, but those deaths would be nothing compared to what would happen if the charm fell into the wrong hands. It was a tool of chaos, and needed to be destroyed. The only question was, did I have the heart to do it?

Alaric kissed my cheek, his lips lingering against my skin. "How will we destroy it?"

I pulled my head back so I could look up at him. "We're going to start a war."

He grinned, and it was a little frightening given the context. "Why Maddy," he said mischievously, "that just so happens to be my specialty."

"War and Death," I breathed. "Partnership at its best."

I rubbed my thumb across the key in my palm as I considered the possible consequences of such a plan, and all I could think was that things looked bleak, but . . . didn't they always?

CHAPTER FIVE

"I break all of my nails getting down here, and you two are just lying in the dirt!" Sophie stood at the edge of the cavern, hands on hips.

I sat up and pulled away from Alaric, but still didn't feel steady enough to stand. I gripped the charm in my hand, feeling oddly protective over it, and not liking the feeling one bit.

Alaric laughed. "It's about time you came to the rescue. Maddy nearly killed me."

Sophie sighed as she glanced around the room, undisturbed by the piles of bones that had once been Vaettir. Her eyes came to rest on the Norn.

"Is that what I think it is?" she asked.

"It *was*," Alaric corrected.

"*She* was," I corrected on top of his correction.

I felt oddly sorry for the Norn, even though she had nearly let Diana sacrifice us. I was pretty sure the Norn knew all along what would happen. Norns were supposed to be weavers of fate, after all. Maybe she knew I would come, and knew I cared enough about the world to not want such a horrible magic to be released once more. Hopefully that meant I actually stood a chance of destroying it, since the Norn had given her life for that purpose.

"Can we please get out of here?" I asked weakly.

Alaric stood, then helped me to my feet.

"Where's Diana?" Sophie asked, eyeing us both expectantly.

Alaric gestured with the hand that wasn't around my waist to the bloody pile in the corner of the room.

Sophie's lip lifted in distaste.

"Any sign of James?" I asked.

She looked back at us and shrugged. "I left him unconscious up above. When you guys fell in the hole, the door slammed shut and wouldn't budge. I had to dig the damn thing out and rip it off its hinges."

Well that explained the broken nails. "Can we *please* get out of here?" I asked again.

"Did he attack you?" Alaric questioned, ignoring my question as well as Sophie's griping about the door.

Sophie snorted. "No. He actually acted like he wanted to help me, but I wasn't about to leave him at my back."

Alaric smiled knowingly at his sister. I wasn't sure what the smile was about, and at that moment, I didn't really care. I looked at them both expectantly, hoping we could finally leave.

Sophie kicked a nearby bone. "We should search this place for supplies first," she glanced at me, "unless you care to give me back my shoes?"

I cringed. Supplies would be nice, but I wasn't sure it was worth it if it meant I had to stay there a moment longer. I was rather disturbed by the whole ordeal, especially with the part I'd played, and what it meant for me in the near future.

I finally really *looked* at Sophie and realized with a start that there was now a way out of the room, since she had walked in so easily. I looked behind her to see a shadowy doorway, previously solid wall. The Norn's death must have unbarred the room.

"Let's go," I instructed.

Sophie turned and led the way out of the room, but I gestured for Alaric to help me over to the bloody pile that was once Diana instead of following Sophie out.

His eyes widened when he realized my intent. "Are you sure she deserves to be released?"

I shook my head, thinking of the souls that had guarded the charm for far too long. "No one deserves that fate."

With a nod, Alaric helped me to kneel beside Diana's remains. Her limbs and head had all been ripped free of her body, but her torso was still mostly intact, wrapped in the bloody fabric of her clothing and cloak. My limbs ached with the pain of her death, but it was a subtle pain, as most of her life was gone. Only the energy within her heart remained. I reached my hand out toward where her heart should be, but stopped as I felt something tickling at my bare leg.

I looked down in horror, hoping to whatever I should hope to that a mouse or some other creature had made its way into the underground lair.

My hope was dashed as Diana's hand, still attached to most of her petite arm, wrapped its fingers around my leg right above my boot and dug in. In an instant, Alaric was on my other side, prying the fingers off my leg one by one, face calm. Resisting the urge to vomit, I ignored what was happening to my leg and turned back to Diana's torso.

Her emotions coursed through me as I reached my hand out toward her chest again. I had expected anger and hatred, but all I felt was fear and confusion. She had been alive a very, very long time, and had not expected to die, especially in such a simplistic way. She didn't want me to release her soul, because she was still clinging to whatever life she might have. Alaric pried the last of her fingers away, freeing my leg from her grasp, but I barely noticed.

I shook my head, wondering how I could read a dead woman's emotions so clearly, while at the same time hoping that this increased feeling of empathy wasn't permanent. It was bad enough feeling someone's wounds as they happened, did I really have to share in their darkest fears?

Gritting my teeth, I released her spirit, and was relieved of her emotions simultaneously. Part of me felt a little smug that even in doing what was right for her, I was able to go against Diana's wishes, but most of me just felt confused and afraid. Maybe I had only felt Diana's emotions so strongly because they so closely mirrored my own.

I stared down at the now lifeless corpse pieces, feeling melancholic about the whole ordeal.

Alaric touched my arm to get my attention, and I turned to him, feeling as if I'd just woken from a dream. "We should prepare to leave," he said softly. "Estus' people are still out there looking for us, and the human police may be as well."

I nodded and stood as all of our future concerns came rushing back.

We left the dark room, and I ended up waiting in the Norn's comfortable sitting room while Alaric and Sophie searched for clothing and supplies. The entire scene from the attack in the hotel room all the way up to the Norn's death played over and over in my head. For some reason, the scene that stuck out most to me was Alaric finding out that I maybe loved him, and him begging me to not let it be true.

The rational side of me assured that his fear and astonishment came from the fact that the revelation meant Diana would force me to kill him, but some small, scared part of me said he was afraid for other reasons. Reasons like me being a cursed death machine. I couldn't even begin to think about the idea that I might be in love with him. I didn't have time for love, especially when it could easily be ripped away at the flick of Estus' hand.

The supply search didn't take long, fortunately, as the underground complex was small. Alaric and Sophie returned to save me from my thoughts, and they saved me from the cold as well with a pair of roughly made pants and too-large winter boots. The clothes seemed like they came from a different century, and smelled like they had been stored for just that long. It was a marvel that they even held together, but I wasn't going to turn my nose up at anything that would protect me from the harsh weather above.

There was no food to be found, even though the Norn had likely stayed in that little sitting room alone for ages. Perhaps Norns didn't have to eat, but I did. My stomach growled painfully as I put on the offered clothing and followed Sophie and Alaric back to the trap door, then climbed the ladder out into the daylight.

James was still lying unconscious in a patch of snow above. The three of us stared down at him.

"Leave him," Alaric suggested. "I'm sure he'll find his way back to civilization."

"That's what I'm afraid of," Sophie countered. "He'll likely realize we have the charm, and he'll run to tell Aislin, or perhaps even Estus. The search for us will quadruple in strength."

"Do you suggest we kill him?" Alaric asked with a smirk.

Sophie looked down at James with an odd mixture of emotions on her face.

"Or was there a reason you left him alive up here to begin with?" Alaric added like he already knew the answer.

I hoped Alaric had some idea of what was going though Sophie's mind, because I sure didn't.

"Not that you guys ever listen to my opinion anyway," I said sarcastically, "but I really don't want to be around when he wakes up and discovers I killed his grandmother."

Sophie blinked rapidly and shook her head as if coming out of a dream. "He's our only *in* with Aislin. Perhaps we might need him."

I twisted my lips at her logic. "Diana was also Aislin's sister. I think that option is lost to us. Besides, weren't you the one who suggested we remain clan-less?"

Sophie glared at me. "And what of the charm? I imagine you have it?"

"We're going to destroy it," I replied, not taking a second to think about it.

Sophie crossed her arms. "What if we could use it to protect ourselves? If it could grant one of the Vaettir the power to rule, could it not grant us a little diplomatic immunity?"

"We destroy it," I said again, unable to put into words what the Norn had shown me. "Now back to James."

I could tell she didn't fully accept my answer, but she did turn back to the man in question. "We take him with us," she stated.

Alaric and I both looked at each other in surprise as Sophie continued to stare down at James.

"Do you really think that's wise?" Alaric asked, turning back to his sister.

Sophie didn't look up. "We can't have him telling anyone we have the charm, or leading them back to this place," she explained.

"And you can't kill him," I said with a soft smile.

She snapped her eyes up to me and practically snarled. "I *could*," she argued.

"But you *won't*," I finished. "And here you all were thinking *I* was the cream puff of the group."

Alaric held a hand up to his mouth to hide his grin.

A low growl trickled out of Sophie's throat.

I grinned wider. "I'm sorry, you're not a cream puff. You're a sweet, cuddly little kitten."

Alaric snickered.

"If you're done being comedic," Sophie growled, "you could make yourselves useful and help me carry him."

Alaric did as his sister bade him, still laughing as he went. I watched as they lifted James to standing.

The three of them looked an odd picture. Alaric had found a shirt that was the same old-fashioned style as my pants and similar boots to mine. They clashed with his modern jeans and the modern clothing Sophie and James wore. The scene was made even more odd and slightly humorous by James' head lolling around as they moved him.

I was dreading the moment when I'd have to explain to them everything the Norn had shown me, though they would likely be more practical about it than I wanted to be. Alaric and Sophie were descended from a goddess of war, after all. What were a few more corpses for the greater good?

CHAPTER SIX

I shifted from foot to foot in my brand new, low-heeled boots. My leather pants creaked softly, making my pulse quicken since I was supposed to be quiet. I was *never* letting Alaric choose my clothing again. The simple, long-sleeved black top was a little more practical, but it didn't matter since it was covered by my stolen, knee-length black coat.

My long hair threatened to come loose from the braid I'd put it in as the chilly, Norway wind buffeted against me. I glanced over my shoulder, anxious for Alaric and Sophie to finish *procuring* whatever final supplies we might need so we could head back to the woods where we'd left James.

My anxiety doubled as I thought about James. Sophie had knocked his head too hard, because he didn't remember a thing. While his amnesia complicated things, I guiltily hoped his memory would remain lost, then I wouldn't have to tell him that I'd killed his grandmother. On the other hand, I didn't enjoy acting as though I actually liked him.

He'd been so confused when he woke, knowing who and what he was, but little else, that we'd all agreed a little bit of pretend was in order. His most recent memories occurred over thirty years ago, so he wouldn't understand if we all just let our hatred shine through.

I braced myself against a particularly forceful gust of wind, thinking that maybe it would be nice to lose that much memory. James didn't remember killing Sophie's lover, and he didn't remember all of the people he had tortured. Heck, he didn't even remember torturing me.

I jumped as two dark shapes appeared on either side of me, then tried to quiet my breathing as Sophie and Alaric hurried me away from the store they'd just robbed. They each had brand new black backpacks slung over their shoulders.

"You know," Sophie whispered, "the *look-out is* supposed to *actually* pay attention."

"I was," I whispered back. "It's not my fault you two move as quietly as cats."

I glanced at Alaric to see his pale face grinning in the moonlight. He was like a kid in a candy shop any time he stole. I guess after living five-hundred years, you had to take your thrills where you could find them.

I looked down to hide my frown as we made our way through the quiet streets. We still hadn't talked about the possibility that I might love him, and I wasn't sure if I wanted to. I hadn't yet concluded the notion. I reflexively reached up to fondle the key at my throat, secured by a length of leather cord.

I felt oddly attached to the little black key, my own little tool of chaos. It wanted war and conquest. I was going to give the charm what it wanted, if only to ultimately destroy it.

The charm seemed to pulse with energy, as if it had read my thoughts, then we reached the edge of civilization, and it was all I could do to keep up as Sophie and Alaric began to run.

They darted over the snow and around trees. To anyone listening, they would only hear my clumsy footfalls, as my companions were as quiet as they were quick.

After a time I slowed, then stopped and hunched over, trying to catch my breath. Alaric circled back around to me as Sophie continued on. Within seconds, she was out of sight.

Alaric grinned down at me, flashing his dainty, feline fangs, then scooped me up in his arms. He began to run effortlessly with me in his grasp.

Heat radiated from my body despite the cold, making my usually useful heavy coat a bit of a hindrance. I looked up at Alaric's face, which didn't appear strained or flushed at all, and suddenly felt greatly inadequate. Sophie, Alaric, and James were all unnaturally strong, with way more endurance than I'd ever have.

"How do you do that?" I asked.

"What?" he replied, his voice not hitching in the slightest.

"Run without tiring, even while carrying me. James can do it too, but I'm stuck with sucky human speed."

He grinned, his eyes remaining on the path ahead. "My gifts are mostly physical. I have little innate magic, except for my ability to shift my hands, teeth, and eyes. Those with more obvious magic usually tend to be physically weaker. Estus is like you."

"So some get to be scary in the magic department, but in a fist fight, shit out of luck?"

He snorted. "Something like that."

He slowed as we reached our campsite where Sophie was already waiting with James, then let me down to my feet. What I could see of James' face by the light of the campfire was morose. His elbows were on his knees, hands propping up his chin. He sighed as he rolled his near-white eyes up to us, then let his chin-length, golden hair fall forward in defeat.

Sophie grunted in irritation, then unrolled her previously stolen sleeping bag. Her new black backpack rested beside her, and I couldn't help but wonder what it contained. We had already stolen clothing, camping supplies, and food. What else was there?

Alaric nudged me playfully with his shoulder. "Let's go find some firewood."

I nodded and followed him as he walked away. I eyed the backpack still slung over his shoulder with interest, then caught up to his side. The backpack blended in with the black of his clothing, but still looked somehow out of place. It made him seem younger, like a teenager on his way home from school, only most high schoolers weren't 6'2" and well muscled, and they didn't look at you with their dark eyes like they were thinking about eating you.

"So," I began as we ventured further into the darkness, "about what happened with Diana . . . "

"You're regretting killing her?" Alaric joked, avoiding the actual subject I was attempting to broach.

I rolled my eyes. "I'm referring to what happened *before* that."

He crouched down and snagged a few fallen branches.

I suddenly wished I hadn't brought up the subject at all. I took a deep breath as I looked down at his dark hair. I knew it was unbelievably soft, and had the sudden urge to run my fingers through it, but I resisted.

"When I said that I loved you, I was put on the spot," I grumbled. "I'm not really sure how I feel. I'm not even sure how much I *like* you. You did let me get tortured, after all. I just don't want the idea of love hanging in the air like some big, foreboding thing that we're both avoiding talking about."

I let out a harsh breath. I hadn't expected my words to tumble out so haphazardly, and now my pulse raced as I waited for him to reply.

He smiled and stood back up, firewood in hand. "I see you've been holding on to some things," he joked. "Has it really been bothering you?"

"Yes," I answered quickly, "or no." I took another deep breath, then explained, "I just thought we should talk about it."

"And you want to know if I love you back," he finished.

"No!" I exclaimed, though really I did. "I just want to be clear on the fact that if I love you, it's in some weird, twisted, *Stockholm Syndrome* type of way."

He quirked an eyebrow at me. "Isn't that the one where captives begin to love their kidnappers?"

I blushed. "Well you *did* kidnap me."

He frowned. "I was acting on orders."

I shook my head, then started walking. "Be that as it may, I'm not about to just blindly love you without taking into account everything we've been through."

"So you *do* love me?" he asked from behind me. Before I could answer, he caught up to my side and tugged on the end of my braid playfully.

He let go of my hair and brushed my shoulder as he walked ahead of me to where I assumed there was more firewood. I, for one, couldn't see anything. Night vision must have been another perk of physical magic.

I reached his side again and stopped while he picked up more wood. "That's not what I meant. I just meant that I'm not some silly, naïve girl that falls in love despite all the evidence the guy might not be good for her."

Alaric stood and looked down at me with a strange expression.

"What?" I asked, when he didn't speak.

He sighed. "Have you ever stopped to consider that maybe *you* might not be good for *me?*"

My jaw dropped. When I managed to close it I asked, "How so?"

"Well, Madeline," he began in a lecturing tone. "Since we met, I abandoned my home, became a fugitive, almost got sacrificed *by you*, and now I'm about to risk my life to start a war because *you* want to destroy that little key around your neck. I think you've been much worse for me than I have for you."

My stomach churned. I knew that most of it hadn't been my fault, at least not directly, but he *had* gone through a lot by simply being associated with me.

He began walking again, and I had to jog to catch up with him. "Then why even pursue me at all?" I asked weakly.

He stopped and flashed a lascivious smile. "Because I *like* things that are bad for me."

My mouth went dry as he dropped the firewood he'd been carrying and closed the distance between us.

"But do you love them?" I managed to say.

"Perhaps," he said slyly as he reached his hand up to cradle my jaw, "but I would be loathe to admit it, especially after they've worked so hard to convince themselves that they don't love me in return."

He leaned down and kissed me before I could say anything in reply. I kissed him back, not sure if our conversation had actually accomplished anything. I had a feeling that it hadn't, but at the moment, I didn't really care.

Alaric pulled one hand away to unzip and reach into the backpack behind him. A moment later his hand returned to hook something onto the side of my belt.

I pulled away from the kiss and looked down to find a

huge hunting knife at my hip. I looked back up to meet his eyes. "Are we planning on stabbing people?"

He quirked his lip into a crooked, half-smile. "Hopefully not, but as the saying goes, 'Speak softly, and carry a big stick.'"

I raised an eyebrow at him. "Or in this case, complain loudly, and carry a big knife?"

His expression turned thoughtful, then he nodded. "Something like that, now come here."

He wrapped his arms around my waist and pulled me against him. Sophie and James were probably running out of wood for the fire, but my concern over the situation was minimal. My greatest concern at that moment was the man holding me close, looking devilish with his long, black hair, and eyes that had at some point shifted to feline.

CHAPTER SEVEN

I pulled away from Alaric at the sound of shouting. Sophie's voice rang out clear in the night, while James' was a mere murmur in reply.

Alaric rolled his eyes. "Even with his memory gone, they're still fighting."

I took a step back, feeling silly for getting absorbed in a makeout session literally seconds after trying to explain to Alaric that I didn't love him.

"We should probably get back before their arguing alerts the police and any Vaettir looking for us," he continued.

I didn't argue, and instead waited while he regathered his firewood, then followed him as he led the way back to our campsite, glad that he couldn't see my blush.

We still had no idea if the cops were even after us, but we'd decided to play it safe and stay out of sight. The hope was that the local Doyen had cleaned up our crimes. It was standard protocol for the clans, but we weren't banking on it.

I might have been more skeptical than I was if I didn't already know what the clans could accomplish. There should have been questions when I accidentally took the life of one of my foster parents, but the questions never came. Estus had covered it up.

However, this time there were multiple bodies instead of one, and we had no idea what had happened between Diana, James, and the police when Alaric, Sophie, and I had made a run for it. We likely never would know, unless James regained his memory or Diana miraculously came back to life.

I stumbled across felled branches and rocks as we went, feeling tired and hungry. I'd been so worried about getting my convoluted point across to Alaric that I hadn't realized how far we'd walked to find firewood.

I breathed a sigh of relief when the campfire came back into view, a tiny beacon of light in the darkness. I could no longer hear Sophie and James arguing, and as we approached I saw that they now sat on opposite sides of the fire, not meeting each other's eyes.

Alaric walked ahead of me to dump the extra firewood near James, then went to sit by his sister. Feeling embarrassed about how long we'd been gone, and a little bad for James in his current state, I took a seat next to him instead of the others.

He turned and gave me a sad smile. I *almost* reached out and patted his shoulder in encouragement, then reminded myself that he was still *James*, the man who had stabbed me and enjoyed it, even if he didn't remember it. He didn't deserve my sympathy.

Feeling uncomfortable, I scooted a little bit away from him.

Alaric turned to his sister. "Was there a reason you were trying to alert anyone within a five mile radius of our presence?"

Sophie scowled, then gestured at James with a sharp nod.

"Mother Theresa over there thinks that we should make peace with the local clan so we can all live happily ever after."

James frowned and looked down at the fire, obviously not wanting to argue with Sophie any further.

I pushed my boot-clad feet a little closer to the fire. "It's not the most absurd idea, especially for someone who has no clue what's going on."

"*If* he has no clue what's going on," Sophie added.

I stared back at her, confused.

"She thinks I'm faking," James explained.

"Ah," Alaric cut in. "Well that explains the yelling."

I shivered. Even though the area we'd chosen was well-sheltered by trees, the earth was still damp from residual snowfall. The moisture was yet to soak through the leather pants, but it was still cold.

"It's something he would do," Sophie muttered.

Everyone went silent.

"It doesn't change our plan either way," I said finally. "Tomorrow we contact the local Vaettir, and we take them by force."

"You say that so casually," Sophie replied hotly, "like we aren't about to all risk our lives on the slim chance that you can make the charm work to your advantage. That's if we can even get the locals to talk instead of jumping straight to killing us."

"Do you have a better plan?" I sighed, knowing for a fact that she didn't.

She crossed her arms and glared at me. "No, but I'd like you to take things seriously."

"You're not my case worker anymore," I snapped, "and I'm no longer a scared teenager hoping for some worthwhile advice. I know you're unhappy with this whole situation, and I know you're hurt that Maya betrayed you after you risked your life for her, but neither of those things are my fault. Stop taking your bad mood out on me."

Alaric grinned as he watched our exchange, but made no move to cut in. James looked down at his feet miserably.

Sophie took a deep breath. "You're right, I'm sorry," she replied, sounding pained. "We will contact the natives, and meek, little Madeline will assert herself as their omnipotent leader."

I bit my lip at her sarcasm, but let it go.

"The natives are already here," came a heavily accented female voice from behind where Alaric and Sophie sat.

All of us except for James jumped to our feet. James remained seated, terror clear on his face. Either he wasn't faking his memory loss, or he was an exceptional actor, because the James I knew never looked scared.

Three people stepped forward out of the darkness. Two stood beside Sophie, and the third beside Alaric. I assumed the person standing beside Alaric had been the one to speak, as she was the only female of the group. At first I thought we might stand a fighting chance, then several more shapes came into view.

"I assume you are the ones who killed our people at the hotel, though I was told there were five of you," the woman who'd initially spoken continued.

She seemed confident even though we had killed several of her friends just a few nights before, or maybe it was just her height. It was hard *not* to look confident when you were around 6'4" with a mane of pale blonde hair and a perfect, creamy complexion. She had a warrior's body, all muscle, but lithe enough to move quickly.

Her light eyes flicked to each of my companions, then settled on me. "Am I to assume that you are the one who will be swooping in to take us over?" she asked as a smile curved her lips.

"Well there's a long story behind that," I began, but she held up her hand to cut me off.

"We've been searching for you, Madeline," she explained. "I'm to bring you to our Doyen."

"She goes nowhere without us," Alaric stated, sounding more serious than I was used to.

The woman glanced at him briefly, then turned her gaze back to me. "*Fine.*"

She gestured with her hand and the rest of her people moved forward. As they came into view, I noticed that many of them were extremely tall and blond, just like their leader. It felt like we were being taken captive by a Viking clan, and the effect was increased by the large amounts of leather and fur most of them wore.

Two hulking men who looked like twins each tried to grab onto Alaric and Sophie, but their hands came up with empty air. Moments later Alaric was at my side, and after glaring at her would-be captor, Sophie joined us.

James allowed one of the few dark-haired people, a woman, to help him to his feet. The blonde Amazon calling the shots watched the whole display like it was the most amusing thing she'd ever seen. Since the Vaettir aren't exactly a cheerful people, maybe it was.

She turned and walked back the way she'd come, confident that we would follow. Alaric and Sophie both stopped to pick up their backpacks, which I presumed held more weapons like my knife, then sandwiched me like bodyguards. In a way they were, since I was fairly helpless until someone died, and the knife at my hip would do little against a trained attacker.

The cold seeped in as we left the heat of the fire behind,

and the light touch of Alaric and Sophie's shoulders offered no warmth. James followed behind us like a dejected puppy as the rest of the Vaettir fanned out around us, many of them disappearing from sight in the dark woods just as suddenly as they'd appeared.

The blonde's tall form walking in front of us was little more than a shadowy silhouette in the dark forest. I tried to catch Alaric's eye as we walked, hoping for an explanation to why we were following the blonde's orders so willingly, but both he and his sister kept their expressionless gazes ahead on our captor.

After a painfully cold ten minutes trudging through the woods, the blonde stopped in front of a massive tree. I stopped and waited, confused. The only way I'd ever entered a Salr was by way of magical vines, but I didn't see any vines in the snowy landscape.

The blonde hadn't moved that I could see, but suddenly the earth began to tremble. I watched in awe as the tree in front of us shimmered like a mirage in the hot sun, only it was nighttime and freezing. The shimmer dissipated, revealing a dark doorway in the middle of the tree, tall enough for the blonde to walk through comfortably, and wide enough for two people to walk side-by-side. Alaric and Sophie did not appear impressed, but I sure was.

The blonde disappeared into the darkness within, while our other captors waited for us to move forward. I resisted the urge to clutch the charm near my throat as I took a hesitant step. Sophie dropped back behind us, leaving Alaric to walk by my side into the tree. Unable to help it, I reached out and touched the rough bark of the doorway, needing to reassure myself that it was real. The bark was cold, and left my fingertips damp.

I took another step forward, disoriented by the act of

walking into a tree and not hitting the other side. The darkness remained solid as we walked further

Alaric abruptly grabbed my arm. I froze in alarm, but then he moved and I realized he was just signaling that there was a step down in front of us. I followed Alaric's lead down several more steps, blind in the darkness, until we reached the landing and the gentle lighting of the Salr.

This new Salr was startlingly similar to Estus'. There was no apparent source of lighting, yet the hall was filled with a dim glow, illuminating the same gray stone that composed the other Salr.

The blonde had gotten several steps ahead of us as I stumbled on the steps, and now turned to wait further down the hall. Alaric held out his arm to me. I stared at his arm, not sure I understood the gesture, but it became clear as his other hand guided my arm through the bend of his elbow. He then moved his guiding hand to grasp my fingers, placing them delicately onto his forearm.

The blonde chuckled, then turned and started walking again, boot heels clacking on the stone. The other Vaettir shifted impatiently behind us, and I quickly hopped forward then started walking.

I felt awkward being escorted rather than walking on my own, though I would have taken other forms of closeness. I was part of the hand-holding or arm around the shoulders generation, and being led around like a *lady* felt weird.

"Why all of the formality?" I whispered, keeping my gaze forward.

"Shh," Sophie warned from behind us.

I bit my lip, wanting to argue. We'd had no time to plan, and I had no idea what courtesies we were supposed to observe when going into a foreign Salr. Then again, we were there to take them over, so maybe we weren't supposed to be courteous at all.

I glanced over my shoulder to see Sophie and James walking side-by-side, and the rest of the Vaettir walking in pairs behind them. Perhaps we'd be observing some ceremonies after all.

We were led though multiple twists and turns, until eventually we came upon a large throne room, similar to the one in Estus' Salr. It seemed odd that a place of refuge, which was what the Salr were, would come with a throne room, but it also seemed odd that they came with dungeons, unless the features had been added once the Vaettir began to live in them full time. Maybe the Salr shaped itself to suit its inhabitant's needs. I'd seen enough crazy stuff lately that anything seemed possible.

Unlike Estus' throne room, which held a dais, but was barren of decor, this one was accented with heavy tapestries done in rich colors, and thick, Persian rugs. The Vaettir who'd escorted us went to stand on either side of the room in orderly lines, while the blonde went to stand by the simple, wooden throne. At first I thought she might sit in it, but then a man emerged from a nearby doorway and stole the show.

He looked just as Viking-esque as the rest of them, except with rich, chestnut-colored hair instead of blond. His roughly 6'5" frame was covered by a heavy robe done in gold and garnet red. Our eyes met, and he smiled, then he moved his gaze to the blonde by the throne. His eyes had been a startlingly bright reddish brown that contrasted interestingly with his armpit-length hair.

The Vaettir surrounding us knelt as he walked past them. I watched them stupidly until Alaric tugged me down to my knees. I glanced at him, but his expression was unreadable, so I turned my eyes to the reddish-haired man instead.

He lowered himself onto the throne, seeming somewhat out of place in the regal setting, likely because he looked around thirty years old. I had expected an older person as Doyen, just like Estus, but it was a silly expectation. The more powerful the Vaettir, the less they aged. To have become Doyen, this man was likely old, and to look so young bespoke his power. Estus was scary powerful himself, but not powerful enough to halt the aging process as much as others.

Of course, he might just be descended from a major deity, like Alaric. Less power, but no aging. The man gestured for us to stand, but stayed seated himself.

"I am Mikael," he announced as we stood, "Doyen of this clan. You must be Madeline."

I realized with a start that he was talking to me. I had expected him to start with Alaric or Sophie, or anyone else who actually might know what was going on.

"Y-yes," I stammered. "That's me."

He cocked his head and raised an eyebrow at me. "I'm told you've come to take over my clan. Forgive me, but you don't seem well-equipped for such a task."

I bit my lip. The blonde had been with us the entire time, so someone else must have raced ahead to rat us out.

When I didn't deny nor confirm his accusation, he asked, "Do you have the *lykill*?"

My eyes narrowed in confusion. The word was pronounced *ley-kik*, and sounded like the language I'd heard Alaric and Sophie speak.

"The ley-what?"

"It means *key*," Alaric whispered, finally deciding to be helpful.

He didn't elaborate any further, which made me think we didn't want Mikael to know we had the charm.

"I'm not sure what you mean," I replied loud enough for everyone in the room to hear.

"She's lying," the blonde stated immediately.

Mikael smiled, and it was a bit unnerving. "I cannot let you take my clan from me," he announced, "but I can offer you sanctuary from your pursuers."

"But why?" I asked at the same time Alaric said, "I don't think so."

I had been so focused on Mikael, I only then noticed the anger emanating from Alaric.

"I could simply take the key from her," Mikael commented as his gaze moved to Alaric. "Your choice."

The charm in question was pulsing at my neck like something alive, as if it sensed all the excitement. Before I could think better of it, I reached my hand up to my throat to touch the little key through the collar of my shirt.

Mikael turned his gaze back to me, quirking the corner of his mouth into a half-smile. "Unless she knows how to use it . . ."

I could have cut the tension around us with a knife. All the Vaettir had gone rigid, waiting for their Doyen to signal the attack. The only person who appeared calm was Mikael, still slouched on his throne with one leg now dangling casually over one of the chair-arms.

I continued to clutch at the charm, unsure of what to do. I had no idea how to use it, but Mikael didn't know that. I flicked my eyes to Alaric, hoping for some subtle advice. What I got was not subtle at all.

"I hope you can figure this out quickly," he began, his eyes only for me, "because I won't be able to hold them off for long."

At a sudden flick of Mikael's hand, the Vaettir surrounding us surged forward. Alaric and Sophie were nothing but blurs as they darted around me, flinging our attackers aside like rag dolls. I smelled burning flesh somewhere behind me and knew that James had joined the fray.

I stood frozen as I clutched the charm. I briefly thought about the knife at my waist, but dismissed it. My eyes found Mikael, who still sat casually upon his throne. He gazed at me with his head tilted downward in challenge, daring me to act.

Feeling like I was in a trance, I untied the cord that held the charm, removing it from my neck, then dangled it out in front of me. Accepting the taunt, Mikael stood, then strode confidently toward me. Somewhere in the back of my mind, my thoughts raced, asking me what the hell I thought I was doing, but the front of my mind was calm, and didn't feel like it belonged to me any longer.

A part of me knew I should be sensing the pain of those getting injured around me, but it was somehow blocked out. All I could focus on was the charm in my hand, and Mikael's determined gaze as he neared me. Distantly I knew his people were attempting to capture, not kill my companions, as we were greatly outnumbered, but remained unharmed. Whatever had taken me over rejected the idea of capture. It was not an option.

I didn't feel in control of my own limbs as I yanked the cord up, then caught the charm in the palm of my hand. The charm's pulsing grew stronger. The distant back part of my mind realized the charm was feeding on the chaos around me. I could feel it sucking the energy in, much like I did when I released a soul, except I only took a portion of the energy, the charm was taking all of it.

Alaric flashed for a moment in front of me, then was gone, tumbling to the side as he kept another one of our attackers away from me. We were extremely outnumbered, but having two five-hundred year old embodiments of war fighting on our side helped to even the odds.

Mikael reached me, and it was like everything around us went still. I knew that mere seconds were passing, but the scene was playing out before me in slow motion. The charm's stolen energy began to trickle down my arm, filling me up with more power than I would get from one hundred simultaneous deaths.

Mikael reached out, just as the charm's consciousness suddenly ripped through my mind. It didn't want to go with him. Our powers were the same, and I would be able to use it to its full potential.

Energy shot from the fist I'd closed around the charm. I wasn't sure if it was my doing, the charm's, or a mixture of both, but it brought Mikael to his knees. He gritted his teeth against the force of it, but was unable to regain his feet.

Words trickled out of my mouth that I didn't quite understand. "You will kneel until I tell you to stand, Mikael Agnarsson."

"I . . . did not . . . expect this," he spat through gritted teeth.

Finally he bowed his head, and the torrent of energy stopped, just as the key's consciousness left me all at once. I looked around the room, truly freaked out, having no idea how I'd known Mikael's surname.

Those who still stood were silent. Alaric and Sophie both waited within arm's reach, but neither reached out to touch me.

I looked back down at Mikael, who had raised his head to glare at me. "I suppose this alters my plans," he stated calmly. I was pretty sure he could have stood then if he wanted to, but he stayed kneeling. "What would you have of me, *mennskurð?*"

I glanced at Alaric and whispered, "What is *mennskurð?*"

He looked a little green as he answered, "It means *the lady*, but refers to a woman of high standing, sometimes a seeress."

I looked back to Mikael, who waited patiently with an odd smile on his face. The smile wasn't exactly bitter or unhappy, maybe *rueful,* or . . . calculating?

All of the Vaettir waited with their eyes glued to me. Some looked worried or confused, some angry, and some apathetic.

"What should I say?" I whispered again.

"You know, I can hear you," Mikael teased. For someone who was losing control of his clan, he didn't seem terribly upset.

A catty remark froze on the tip of my tongue. It probably was a bad idea to antagonize even a fallen Doyen while his people waited ready to pounce.

"I would like to hold a private audience with you, *and my advisors*," I added quickly. "We have delicate matters to discuss."

Mikael's smile widened, a hint of challenge in his reddish eyes. "Wise choice, *mennskurð*. May I stand?"

"Yes," I replied as I took a step back, "and please, just call me Madeline."

He rose, taking a step forward to close the space between us, then offered me his arm. "Shall we?"

I looked down at the offered arm, then to Alaric, who nodded. Sophie was paler than usual, but fully determined as she kept her eyes trained on the other Vaettir around us. James just looked scared.

I looped my arm through Mikael's and allowed him to escort me, much like Alaric had done earlier. The fabric of his ornate robe was scratchy underneath my palm. He led me toward the door he had originally emerged from, and had to hold up his free hand to stop the blonde from following us. She did *not* look happy.

We went through the door unhindered, with my three companions following behind us. James shut the door, and I felt instant relief, even though it was still uncomfortable to have Mikael at my side. The room we entered was done up like a sitting room, with large, cushy chairs and a gleaming coffee table in the middle. It seemed like a good place for a private meeting, but Mikael kept walking.

We went through another door, down the hallway for a while, then through a final door into a room with a large table and chairs all around. It would have looked like any other conference room, except the walls and floor were made of stone, and the table was made of rough-hewn planks of wood as thick as my torso.

Mikael dropped my arm, then pulled a chair out for me. After I sat he went around the table to sit across from me, leaving everyone else to get their own chairs. Alaric took the chair to my left, then Sophie and James took the next ones down. I was glad they still wanted to sit near me after what had happened with the charm. I wasn't sure if *I* even wanted to sit near me.

"That was quite the display," Mikael stated, breaking the silence. "I have a feeling things will be much more interesting this time around."

"This time around?" Sophie questioned.

Mikael grinned. "Yes, my dear, last time the *Lykill* surfaced, it fell into the hands of an earth spirit. She caused a great deal of destruction, but earthen spirits at their core embody stability and patience. Really, she had no business wielding a tool of chaos. Executioners, or simply *Dauðr* in the old tongue, can control massive amounts of energy, the same type of energy controlled by the charm."

His gaze landed solely on Alaric and Sophie as he said, "The only thing more interesting would have been if the charm had chosen one of you. A being of chaos and war to wield a powerful tool of, well, chaos and war."

"So let me get this straight," I interrupted. "You were around when the charm was last used, when all of those terrible scenes of bloodshed and misery occurred?"

Mikael raised an eyebrow at my question. "You speak as if you witnessed those scenes with your own two eyes."

"One of the women who gave her life to seal the charm away showed them to me," I explained, feeling suddenly angry, though I wasn't sure why.

He steepled his fingers together in thought. "Interesting, very interesting," he mused.

I glared at him. "You didn't answer my question."

"He was there," Alaric answered for him.

I looked back and forth between the two men. "You two know each other?" I asked, perplexed.

Sophie met my eyes as I scooted back so I could view everyone at once. She looked just as confused as I felt.

"We've *met*," Alaric replied, clipping his words in irritation.

"But that's a tale for another time," Mikael finished for him, then turned back to me, "What is it you plan, *mennskurð?*"

Unsure of whether we were divulging our actual plans or not, I turned to Alaric.

His jaw was clenched in irritation. It reminded me of how he'd looked when he allowed James to torture me. I was beginning to realize that look was reserved for situations where he was forced to follow decorum when he really, *really* didn't want to.

When it became apparent that I wasn't going to get any

advice, I turned back to Mikael. "We're going to start a war, and I need you to instigate the first battle."

Mikael chuckled. "And for this task, you've chosen one of the smallest clans in existence?"

My mouth opened into an *oh* of surprise. "It was kind of a choice of convenience," I said weakly. I glanced at Alaric again, then back to Mikael.

"Who were you hoping to start a war with?" he pressed.

I eyed him suspiciously. "Why are you being so cooperative? Just a short while ago, you were threatening to take the charm away from me."

His slight cringe was the only sign that he'd minded the exchange. "You quickly proved that it was not an option," he explained. "The key has chosen you as its wielder, and will protect your right to it."

"You speak like it has a mind of its own," I accused, feeling uncomfortable in the hard, wooden chair.

He laughed so suddenly that I jumped in my seat. "Would you argue with such a claim?"

I thought back to the energy flowing through the charm, and the foreign thoughts and emotions that had raced through my head. "I guess not."

"We will start a war among the two largest clans of the Vaettir," Alaric cut in, saving me from Mikael's calculating gaze.

Mikael's smile was wicked as he turned back to me with a look of excitement in his eyes. "Well then," he replied. "This shall be very interesting indeed."

Interesting wasn't how I'd describe it. I'd go with terrifying, sad, or maybe guilt-inducing. I'd have no qualms if Estus died in the process, but many others would die too. Innocent people with no choice but to follow orders would be sacrificed unwillingly for our cause. Now to add to everything, we were going to do it with one of the smallest clans around. If we made one wrong move, Estus or Aislin would wipe us out.

I looked around the table, doubting everything. It was obvious that Mikael didn't share my sentimentality, and I doubted Alaric or Sophie would either. Maybe James and I could cry together about it over a shared bottle of wine. Now *that* would be interesting.

CHAPTER EIGHT

We were given rooms and food. Everyone was extremely courteous, and I didn't trust it one bit. My empath abilities allowed me to sense the confusion and fear wafting off any Vaettir who neared us. They had no idea what was going on, or why their leader was catering to the people they'd taken prisoner.

Alaric, Sophie, and James all currently occupied the room I'd been given, though they'd each been allotted rooms just as grand. They looked out of place in their black clothing against the royal blue and gold decor. The artfully carved oversized furniture, colorful tapestries, and thick, cozy bedding must have cost a pretty penny.

I sat on said bedding, waiting for someone to tell me what we were supposed to do next, but all they could do was argue.

"Why have I never heard of Mikael?" Sophie snapped at Alaric as she stalked back and forth across the carpet. "How do you know him? We would have planned this whole thing differently."

"Sophie," Alaric replied calmly. "We didn't plan any of this.

It's not like we were taken prisoner on purpose, and I had no idea Mikael was Doyen here."

"Well tell me how you met him, at least," she said, somewhat deflated.

Alaric glanced back at James, still uncomfortable divulging information in front of him, even though James likely wouldn't think twice about any of it.

I raised my hand to speak. Sophie glared at me, but Alaric gestured for me to proceed.

"While I'd like to know more about Mikael, and what it means for us that his clan is so small," I began, "what I'd most like to know, is what the hell happened to me when I used the charm? How did I know Mikael's surname?"

Sophie's glare softened. "I'm not sure," she replied.

"But Mikael likely knows," Alaric finished for her. "Not that he'll tell us."

"Yes," Sophie growled as her gaze turned once again to her brother, "back to *Mikael*."

"Because it felt like I was possessed," I went on, not willing to let the subject drop.

The charm began to pulse gently against my throat, like a cat purring. Feeling uneasy, I pulled the little key out from my collar to rest on top of my shirt. It continued to pulse, but at least now the feeling was slightly dampened.

James looked at the charm like it might jump off my neck and bite him. "Maybe you should take it off," he suggested.

"She can't take it off," Sophie chided before I could respond. "Mikael would have taken it if he could, and I've no doubt he's still after it."

"Now *you're* talking like you know him too," I observed.

"I'm just not an idiot," Sophie grumbled. "I saw the look on his face when you went all creepy and pulled the charm out. He wants it."

"I'm going to bed," James announced solemnly, obviously hurt by Sophie's reaction to his suggestion.

I started to say "good-night" but only got out a "goo—" as he stood and let himself out of the room, shutting the door behind him.

I gave Sophie a tired look. "Do you have to be so mean to him?"

"He's still *James*," she argued.

"And you're still the one who made us keep him," Alaric argued back.

Sophie crossed her arms and looked back and forth between the two of us. With a final huff, she left the room without another word.

I looked to Alaric with an eyebrow raised. "Are you off to bed now too?"

His lips curled into a smile. "If you think I'm about to leave you alone with Mikael lurking around, you are sorely mistaken."

"So how *do* you know him?" I asked as he took a step toward me.

He stopped short, his shoulders hunched in defeat. "You just *had* to ask, didn't you?"

I nodded excitedly as he took a seat next to me on the bed.

"He knew my mother," he admitted, "and he inadvertently caused her death."

My eyes widened in surprise. "That's why you didn't want to tell Sophie?"

He nodded without looking at me. "She would have marched right out of this room to kill him."

"But you said inadvertently," I replied softly. "She'd kill him for an accident?"

At that, he turned his dark eyes up to regard me.

"Wouldn't you want someone to pay for your mother's death, even if it had been an accident?"

I waited for him to remember the little detail he had forgotten.

Almost immediately he cringed. "I'm sorry, Maddy. I forgot you never knew your mother."

I shrugged like it didn't matter, and in many ways, it didn't. It was a pain I had dealt with long ago. "I guess I'd still probably want to avenge her . . . "

Alaric sighed and looked back down at his lap. "I tried to avenge my mother, but I was rather young and stupid at the time."

"What happened?" I prompted when he didn't continue.

He glanced at me with a rueful smile. "You're not going to let this drop, are you?"

I gave him my most innocent look. "If you don't want to talk about it . . . " I trailed off.

He gave me a playful look that said, *I know you're manipulating me, but I'm just going to go with it,* then he put an arm around my shoulders and pulled me backward. Our backs hit the bed, then I turned to nestle into the curve of his shoulder, pulling my feet up to curl against him while his legs remained dangling off the edge of the bed.

"It was during the *Thirty Years War*," he began.

"So in Central Europe?" I questioned.

He patted my shoulder. "Yes, now no more interruptions."

"I was just a child of roughly one hundred years," he went on.

"That's not exactly a child," I cut in incredulously.

He playfully put a hand over my mouth, then continued, "It was a time before the Vaettir had fully withdrawn from the world, though many had started living full time within the various Salr. We would often become involved in politics to better our financial standing. As a descendant of *Dolos,* Mikael was an expert at such politics."

"Dolos?" I questioned against the hand that still gently covered my mouth. The name sounded somehow familiar to me, but I couldn't remember where I'd heard it before.

"The god of deceit and treachery," Alaric explained, finally removing his hand.

The wheels began to turn in my head, but I kept my thoughts to myself.

"It is due to Mikael's nature that he was able to remain among the humans much longer than the rest of us. He's an extremely difficult man to pin down," he continued.

"Or so you found when you tried to avenge your mother?" I guessed, attempting to lead him back to the point of the story.

Alaric pulled me a little closer, then took a deep breath before continuing, "When Christian IV invaded Germany, Mikael was by his side. Christian IV had been a successful ruler, and had amassed a great deal of wealth for Denmark. Even so, the incursion into Germany was funded by the French Regent Cardinal Richeleau. Mikael betrayed Christian to the Germans, and the Danes were defeated."

"And Mikael got rich?" I questioned, finding the story fascinating, but not seeing what it had to do with Alaric's mother.

"And the money was supposed to go to Mikael's Doyen," Alaric added, "but Mikael was not fond of the idea of serving someone else. He fled, and my mother helped to cover his tracks."

I scrunched my face in confusion. "Why would she help him?"

Alaric shrugged. "He and my father had been old friends. I think she did it because my father would have wanted her to, had he been around. My mother was blamed for his treachery, and she was beheaded."

I gasped. I knew where the story was leading, but I hadn't expected the telling to be so . . . blunt.

"I could not stop my mother's death," Alaric stated, voice void of emotion, "but I thought I could avenge her. I went after Mikael, and found him even. I never told Sophie, and neither did the few who knew the truth. She believes our mother died in battle. I knew Sophie would have gone after Mikael herself, but if he had bested me, he would best her as well."

"He bested *you?*" I asked, slightly shocked. I'd seen Alaric fight, and I didn't think anyone stood much of a chance against him. He was an embodiment of war, fighting was an innate part of him.

He sighed. "I told you, I was but a child at the time, and Mikael was many centuries old at that point, now he's positively ancient."

My pulse raced at the very thought of someone even older than Estus, or Sivi, the frightening water elemental who wanted to kill, well . . . everyone. "Just how old?" I asked weakly.

"He was a Viking led by Ivar the Boneless in the 800s," Alaric explained, "though I do not know when he was born."

With that information, my heart nearly stopped. He was a 1,300 year old Viking . . . and I had forced him to kneel. How stupid could I be? Or really, how stupid could the charm be? Why on earth would it choose me when it could have an ancient Viking as its host?

"So is there a reason why he hasn't killed us all yet?" I asked, my voice barely above a whisper.

"In Greek Mythology, Dolos was an apprentice to the Titan Prometheus," Alaric began in a lecturing tone. "He was not particularly powerful, but he was clever. While Prometheus was sculpting *Veritus,* a being who would influence humans to tell the truth, Dolos secretly replicated the sculpture, only he ran out of clay for the feet. Prometheus happened upon Dolos' replica, but thought it so perfect that he wanted to take credit for both statues. He fired them both in his kiln, and Dolos' statue became *Mendacium,* or lies, while Prometheus' became truth. In effect, Dolos created lies, and became the god of trickery and deceit."

The explanation made my head hurt. "That doesn't tell me why Mikael hasn't killed us yet," I groaned.

"Because you don't kill your pawns," Alaric said coldly, "you use them to your advantage, then let your enemies kill them."

Suddenly I felt cold. I pressed my body more firmly against Alaric's, but his warmth didn't help. It wasn't *that* kind of cold. "Do you think what happened with the charm was a trick? Did he willingly kneel?"

"No," Alaric replied, "but if anyone can find a way around something as powerful as the charm, Mikael can."

"Then why are we still here?" I whispered as I lifted my head up to look at him. "Why aren't we trying to find a way out?"

Alaric smiled wickedly, surprising me. "Because this is my chance to finally best him, and I am no longer *any* man's pawn."

My eyes widened as I stared at him. Alaric might not be a pawn, but I sure was, and I'd never been very good at chess.

CHAPTER NINE

*A*fter Alaric's little revelation, I had definitely wanted to discuss things further, but we were interrupted by a knock on the door. We both rose to answer it, but Alaric beat me to it.

The tall blonde whose name we still hadn't learned stood framed in the doorway. She wore the same outfit she had earlier, only minus a few layers. The muscles of her bare arms flexed imposingly as she regarded us.

"The Doyen would like to invite the Executioner for a nightcap," she announced.

Alaric feigned a hurt expression, then said, "And no invite for little old me?"

The blonde smirked. "Not quite."

"But I imagine you'll be standing guard at the door?" Alaric asked.

The blonde answered with a curt nod.

Alaric smiled. "Then so will I."

The blonde glared, then turned on her heel and walked away, obviously expecting us to follow.

Alaric followed her, and after standing shocked for a moment longer, I hustled to catch up to his side.

"I don't want to be *alone* with him," I whispered. "What happened to not being a pawn?"

Alaric smiled wide enough to flash fangs, but kept his eyes on the blonde's back. "It is a game, Madeline. He will not openly confront you yet. He's simply testing the waters."

I hurried to keep pace with him, then whispered, "I'm not good at games."

"The mouse doesn't need to be good at games," he replied, "because she has a cat to protect her."

"I'm not a mouse!" I protested.

"It's good to be a mouse," he said almost cheerfully. "You can scurry out of harm's way." He stopped suddenly and looked at me squarely. "And that's exactly what I expect you to do."

He waited for me to nod, then continued walking to catch up to the blonde. She'd led us to the door of the comfortable sitting room that was attached to the throne room, then held the door open for me. I walked through, feeling vulnerable and nervous. Alaric gave me a nod of reassurance, then the blonde shut the door behind me.

I hesitated near the entrance, but the room appeared empty, so I took a step further in. There was a fire crackling happily within the stone fireplace that was the centerpiece for the seating arrangement. I walked toward the fire and reached out a tentative hand to touch the velvety fabric of the cushy, burgundy couch.

A hand suddenly alighted on my shoulder and I froze. Pulse thudding in my throat, I slowly turned my head to see Mikael, standing slightly off to the left behind me.

He'd exchanged his regal attire for silken pants and a smoking jacket. The outfit looked just as strange to me as the robe he'd worn earlier, but at least he looked more comfortable. I envied his comfort, because I was anything but.

He let his hand drop and walked past me toward the fire, taking the cushy chair closest to the heat and crossing his legs casually. One bare foot bobbed in the air as he turned his deep amber gaze to me.

I swallowed the nervous lump in my throat. "I wasn't aware that this was such a . . . casual meeting."

"Having a night cap is usually a more intimate event," he replied. He gestured for me to sit. His face remained impassive, so I couldn't tell if he was hitting on me, or if he'd used the word *intimate* in a more casual way.

Erring on the side of caution, I walked around the arm of the large couch and sat on the side farthest from him. Doing my best to avoid his too-intense eyes, I looked around the room. Everything was done in burgundy and other dark tones, and reminded me of something out of the late twenties.

I caught movement out the corner of my eye and whipped my head toward Mikael, suspicious of anything he might be doing while I was distracted. Instead of lifting some previously hidden weapon to kill me, he lifted a bottle of bourbon from a drink table beside his chair. In his other hand he balanced two glasses, each of which he filled effortlessly while his eyes remained on me.

He placed the bottle back on the table, took one glass in his now free hand, then held out the other glass toward me.

"No thanks," I mumbled, looking at the amber liquid like it might jump across the room to burn my skin off.

Mikael rolled his eyes at me. "This is kind of the whole point of a nightcap, and I poured both drinks from the same bottle, so I'm not trying to poison you."

I let my eyes linger on the glass, unsure of what I should

do, then looked back at him. Alaric had said Mikael was just testing the waters, but still . . . "You could have poisoned the glass itself," I offered.

He rolled his eyes again, then retracted the offered glass only to then hold out his own. Out of a desire to get the strange situation over with, I stood and moved toward him to take the glass. He rose as I reached him, then pulled the glass close to his chest.

I eyed him cautiously, pretty sure by that point that he was flirting. When I didn't come any closer, he held the glass out to me again. I snatched it from him, then retreated to my seat.

He sat as well and sighed. "I imagine Alaric had many *wonderful* things to say about me."

I shrugged and took a sip of my drink, but didn't reply.

"He was but a child at the time, and had little understanding of what really happened," he continued.

"Living for one hundred years doesn't make someone a child," I commented, keeping my gaze firmly on my lap.

He chuckled. "And how old are you?"

I glared at him. "By your standards, I'm still inside the womb."

He laughed again. "You're quite hostile for one so young. Has the world been so very cruel to you?"

"Look," I snapped feeling defensive. Sure, the world had been cruel to me, but it was cruel to everyone. "I don't know what game you're playing, but it's not going to get you anywhere, so cut it out."

He cocked his head to the side as a strange smile crossed his face. "Okay, Madeline. What game would *you* like to play?"

"The one where you tell me what you want," I replied, then added, "*really* want."

He gave me an innocent look. "I want to help you, *my lady.*"

I snorted, slowly gaining confidence since he was yet to attack me. "Alaric told me who you're descended from, so I'm not inclined to believe anything you say."

"Then why even ask?" he countered.

I shrugged and took another sip of my bourbon. It was good, *really* good. "Wishful thinking?"

He laughed again. "I'm beginning to think this little game will be more fun than I'd imagined."

I glanced at the door, wishing Alaric would find some excuse to come barging in. "I told you games will get you nowhere."

He set his glass on the table beside him, then steepled his fingers in front of his face. "I was referring to this little war game you're playing."

Starting to get nervous again, I looked down at my drink. Maybe if I chugged it, the *night cap* would be over. Worth a shot.

I downed the glass, then held it up for Mikael to see. "Does this mean I can go to bed now?"

Instead of answering, he stood and walked toward me. I jumped up from the couch to get away so quickly that I stumbled, and his hand was suddenly there on my wrist, keeping me standing.

I dropped my glass in surprise and it thudded harmlessly to the thick rug. Mikael didn't release my wrist, and I looked up at him, feeling like a rabbit cornered by a snake. In my sudden burst of fear, I realized that I'd left my knife in my room, and I had nothing else to protect myself.

"I *will* help you," he said, face entirely serious.

"Let me go, please," I squeaked, feeling silly for being rude to the one-thousand plus year old Viking.

He obliged, but remained standing *way* too close. He towered over me, making me feel small, even though I was used to being one of the tallest kids in class.

"If Alaric told you that much of my history, I imagine he told you of my lineage," he said evenly as he stared down at me.

Yeah, he told me you were a friggin Viking, I thought, but what I said out loud was. "He didn't really tell me much."

I wanted to take a step back, but was afraid he'd grab me again. He saved me from making a decision as he sat on the couch, then looked up at me expectantly. Not knowing what else to do, I sat, then waited for him to get to his point.

"It doesn't matter," he sighed. "All you need to know is that I am not content here, hiding in a dark hole waiting for someone to come and take my small clan from me."

I cleared my throat uncomfortably, since that had been my intent before he decided to cooperate with us. I glanced out the corner of my eye to see him smiling again.

"I will help you, Madeline," he stated again. "Not for you, or out of fear of the charm. I will do it for me, and for the look on Aislin's face when *I* take her clan from *her*."

"You want to rule," I stated, not knowing why it came as any surprise.

The barest incline of his head was my only answer.

I stood abruptly. "Then you want the charm."

He stood again as well, then reached out to move my hair away from my face. I jerked away, making him laugh. "Now Madeline, why would I try using the charm myself, when I already have the perfect tool to control it?"

I craned my neck upward to narrow my eyes at him, suddenly wishing I was wearing heels so I wouldn't feel so small. "I take it I'm the *tool*?"

He quirked an eyebrow at me. "Does that offend you?"

I shrugged, then took a step back. "A bit, yes. It seems that's how most everyone views me these days."

"Well if not a tool," he said as he once again closed the distance between us, "then how about a partner?"

I looked down to see his hand held out for me to shake, then looked up to meet his gaze. "I have no desire to rule."

"That simply cannot be true," he said with a hint of laughter in his voice.

"And why's that?" I asked, having the feeling that he was mocking me.

He grinned. "Because *Every-body-wants-to-rule-the world*," he sang.

Not expecting the joke, I inhaled to laugh so suddenly that I choked on my own spit. Mikael made his way back toward his chair, retrieved his still-full glass of bourbon, then returned to hand it to me.

I accepted it gratefully and took a sip to quiet my coughing.

"Now *that* glass was, in fact, poisoned," he commented as I took another sip.

I spat liquid all over the floor and began sputtering again, dropping the mostly full glass to the ground. It missed the carpet and shattered on the stone floor. I clutched at my throat in horror as I looked up at Mikael.

His face was impassive for a moment, then he burst out laughing just as the door to the room flew open. Alaric came rushing in, followed closely by the blonde.

Alaric glanced around the room, then took in Mikael and I standing way too close to each other. Laughter still coated Mikael's face, and I was pretty sure mine had turned beet red.

Alaric's eyes narrowed. "I heard a glass break."

Alaric and Mikael stared at each other, while the blonde crossed her arms in irritation.

"So that wasn't really poison, right?" I questioned weakly, feeling perfectly healthy now that my coughing had subsided.

Mikael turned his gaze from Alaric to me. "If I wanted to kill you, *mennskurð*, I would think of something much more fun than poison."

I swallowed the lump in my throat, then took a step back. "I'm going to bed," I stated.

Mikael was looking at Alaric as he said, "We haven't finished our discussion."

"So finish it," I demanded, completely out of patience.

He looked back to me. "I will help you because I want to rule. I will not be told by others that I must live in a hole in the ground. You will help me because you want to survive, and you need a ruler who doesn't give a rat's ass if you want to run off with your little kitty cat to live happily ever after."

Alaric cleared his throat at being called *my little kitty cat*, but didn't speak.

"And what do you plan to do as ruler?" I questioned, unable to agree until I knew if he was like Sivi, and wanted to *punish* everyone.

Mikael smiled mischievously. "I plan to eat a lot, *drink* a lot, and bed *a lot* of women." He placed a hand to his chin thoughtfully. "And perhaps I'll get back into politics. Much has changed since the *Thirty Years War*."

I blinked at him, a bit stunned. It was a lot better than what Sivi or Estus planned, and it seemed like he'd kill fewer people. Of course, many would have to die *before* he became ruler. The charm pulsed against my skin, excited by Mikael's plan. That made one of us, at least.

"I'll consider your proposition," I stated blandly.

Mikael bowed his head slightly. "Then we shall speak in the morning, *mennskurð*."

I inclined my head in return, then made my way toward

Alaric as he held out his arm to me. I was quite tired of being escorted around, but if it meant I'd get to go to bed, I'd take it.

As we left the room arm in arm, the blonde began to yell at Mikael in that gutteral language that everyone except me seemed to speak.

"I have to ask," I whispered to Alaric as we walked, leaving the sounds of arguing behind. "What is that language, and why do you all speak it?"

He smiled down at me, even though he still looked pale and slightly irritated. "It's Old Norsk. The Vaettir originated in these lands, and for many of us, Old Norsk was our first language."

I stopped walking. "Explain something to me. Everyone keeps mentioning that the Vaettir originated here, but most of us don't look very Nordic." I gestured up and down my body. "Especially me."

"We are not human, Madeline," he replied. "You must not hold us to human standards. The Vaettir were made in the image of the old gods from varying pantheons, and those genetics were passed down, but they are nothing like human genetics."

"Now when you say *made* . . . " I trailed off.

He shrugged and continued walking. "That is like asking humans the origin of their species. Some believe the old gods were embodiments of different aspects in nature, and that we came from that same energy. Others believe the gods created us themselves."

I shook my head, supposing it didn't really matter since we were here now. "So my ancestors are from this region," I concluded, "but since I never knew my parents, I'll likely never know any more than that. So, back to Old Norsk. Can you teach me?" I asked hopefully.

A look of surprise crossed his face as we continued walking down the stone hall. "You just finished making a deal with the devil, we're in peril, and your primary concern is learning a new language?"

I shrugged. "I didn't make the deal with him yet, and I wouldn't mind having something a little more normal to focus my attentions on from time to time."

He waggled his eyebrows at me. "And I'm not *normal*?"

I laughed as the tension from my meeting with Mikael finally seeped away. "No, my *little kitty cat*, you are not."

"Can I have your attentions anyway?" he pressed jokingly.

I shrugged. "Once we get back to our room, sure."

Alaric dropped my arm, only to wrap his arm around my shoulders instead. "In that case, I'll teach you Old Norsk, if you'd really like to learn. It would probably be useful regardless if you're going into politics."

"I'm *not* going into politics," I pouted.

"Then I can kill Mikael?" he whispered conspiratorially.

I gave him a side-long glance, not sure if he was joking. "Let's deal with the creepy little key around my neck first," I replied slowly. "Then we'll worry about your centuries old vendetta."

Alaric leaned over to kiss the top of my head as we reached my room. "As you wish, *mennskurð*."

"Don't you start calling me that too," I groaned.

His arm left my shoulders to open the door in front of us. "How about my little *bani*?"

"That all depends on what that word means," I replied as I walked past him into the room.

He followed me in and closed the door behind us. "It means slayer, *one who kills*."

I turned and narrowed my eyes at him. "That's not exactly what I'd consider a term of endearment."

He paused, as if really considering his answer. "How about my *land-skjálpti*?"

I crossed my arms. "Let me guess, it means *destroyer* or something equally romantic."

He smiled, showing me his pointy little canines. "It means *earthquake*, since you came along and shook up my entire world."

I sighed as I walked over to drop down onto the bed. "You're not very good at this pet-name business," I observed, staring up at the stone ceiling.

The bed shifted as Alaric plopped down beside me. "I've just never understood why someone would want to be called *my little flower*, or *cupcake*, or something silly like that. Flowers have short life-spans and are easily crushed, and cupcakes are eaten without a second thought."

I reached my hand out to pat his arm. "When you put it that way, earthquake doesn't sound so bad."

"It's settled then," he said with a yawn. "Just don't let Sophie know. Growing up, our mother called her *veðr*, which means storm. She'll be jealous if she learns there's a new natural disaster in town."

I moved to lay my head on his shoulder, and he wrapped an arm around me obligingly. "Do you think Mikael will really help us?" I mumbled, fighting the call of sleep.

He turned his head so that his lips were near my forehead. "For now," he whispered against my skin, "but our plans will only suit him for so long."

"And what will we do then?" I pressed.

He was silent for a long while, and by the time he finally answered, I was drifting off to sleep. I could have heard wrong in my delirious state, but I was pretty sure that Alaric had replied with, "We'll kill him."

CHAPTER TEN

I woke up feeling like someone was watching me. At first I thought it was Alaric, but I reached out to find the bed empty beside me. I rolled over, forcing my eyes open, to find impassive hazel eyes staring down at me.

Mikael's blonde lackey pursed her lips and crossed her arms.

I sighed and sat up. "If we're going to be spending this much time together, I should at least know your name."

"Aila," she grunted in her thick accent as she continued to stare down at me.

Aila had been much more animated when she was taking us prisoner, but apparently having us as *guests* had put a giant bee in her bonnet. Wanting some distance, I scooted to the far side of the bed before standing. Aila stood immobile, staring at me across a sea of rumpled bedding.

"Where's Alaric?" I questioned. I wasn't sure at what point he'd left me, and Aila's stoic expression had me worried.

"With Mikael," she said with a sneer, "*planning.*"

I crossed my arms, allowing myself to get irritated now

that I knew that Alaric was at least relatively safe. "I get the feeling that you don't want us here."

Her sneer deepened. "You should be killed for having our Doyen kneel before you."

I smirked. "He doesn't seem terribly upset about it."

She smiled suddenly, though it was more a baring of teeth. "If you say so," she hissed, then turned and walked toward the door, expecting me to follow.

"I need to get dressed first," I stated.

She looked over her shoulder at me. "Then do so. I'll wait outside."

She left the room and shut the door behind her, and I was able to let out the breath I'd only then realized I'd been holding. I also only then realized that at some half-asleep point during the night I'd lost the leather pants and black blouse, and was now only in my black bra and panties.

I sighed, thinking that Aila probably viewed me as a rather ridiculous creature, while wondering why I even cared. I started searching the room for my clothes, and eventually found them on the floor near the head of the bed. I struggled into the pants, once again cursing Alaric for his fashion choices. Who the hell buys leather pants for a vegetarian?

Fully dressed, but cranky, I went into the adjoining bathroom. Though the décor was spartan and somewhat medieval, there was a fresh toothbrush waiting with a full-sized tube of toothpaste. Vikings who appreciated oral hygiene, who'd of thunk it?

I brushed my teeth and tamed my wavy hair back into its braid. A shower would have been nice, but I really didn't want to leave Mikael and Alaric alone together any longer than necessary.

I returned to the bedroom, then opened the door leading

out to the hall. Aila was waiting for me, as expected. She began walking almost instantly, and I had to practically jog to keep up with her, feeling like a dwarf next to her long, long legs.

After a few twists and turns down the hall, I suspected we were heading back to the little conference-style room with the big wooden table. My suspicions were confirmed as Aila led the way through the sitting room then stopped beside the interior door, gesturing for me to enter.

I raised an eyebrow, my hand halfway to the handle. "You're not coming?"

She moved her back against the wall, then stared levelly away from me. "I am *Merkismathr*. I have no say in matters of politics."

I had no idea what a *merki-whatever* was, but Aila didn't seem terribly happy about it, so I didn't question her further. Instead, I opened the door and walked into the room without another word.

All eyes turned to me as I gently shut the door behind me. Alaric and Sophie sat together at one end of the table, frowns on both of their faces, and Mikael sat on the other end, his face unreadable.

Feeling awkward under the pressure of their gazes, I lifted my hand and waved feebly. "Um, hi," I mumbled.

Sophie rolled her eyes at me. "Sit down, Madeline."

I did as she asked, taking a seat on the other side of Alaric.

"A message has been sent to the clan leaders," Mikael announced, his strange, amber eyes all for me.

My eyes widened. "Already? I never even agreed to a partnership."

Mikael smiled. "Well since I've used you as bait, you might want to make up your mind."

I turned to Alaric in shock, who sat stony-faced. He obviously already knew the score, as he didn't seem at all surprised. Sophie watched me, waiting for my reaction.

I turned back to Mikael. "I thought you said you were going to *help* me."

Mikael raised an eyebrow at me. "As I recall, this is exactly what you wanted."

"To be used as bait?" I questioned. "I don't think so."

He rolled his eyes. "How else did you intend to draw them out? Tell them that my tiny clan was looking for a fight?" He looked around the table to each of us, then settled back on me. "No. We tell them you have the charm and you know how to use it, and that you will side with the more powerful clan."

I clenched my teeth as I considered what he'd said. As a plan, it wasn't half bad . . . unless Estus just sent assassins to kill me quietly.

"Estus would never believe that I'd side with him," I argued.

Mikael quirked the side of his mouth. "Perhaps not, but he will also not allow Aislin to swoop in and claim you."

I opened my mouth to argue, but couldn't. He was probably right.

"So what do we do in the meantime?" Sophie cut in. "Just wait here while they kill each other?"

Mikael stood. "Not quite. We can't risk that either of them might send people to claim Madeline. We will need to remain on the move, always one step ahead."

Alaric finally looked surprised. "So you will just pack up your entire clan and abandon your Salr?"

Mikael's smile was more of a snarl. "There is no pride in hiding in a hole. A small group of us will remain together, while the rest of my people disperse. An entire clan is too easy to track. When the moment is right, we will come back together."

His energy was so ferocious in that moment that I almost didn't speak, but there was something we needed to get straight.

"I need to be near the battle," I stated.

Mikael's expression softened with slight confusion. "Why?" he asked suspiciously.

I couldn't tell him that I wanted to destroy the charm. His whole plan was banking on me using it to make him ruler, but I needed a lot of death in the same area to do what the Norn had shown me before she died.

"It's the only way the charm can gather enough power," I lied. "It draws its energy from chaos and war."

"And you draw yours from death," he added, still sounding suspicious.

I schooled my expression to be as cold as possible as I said, "Do you want to rule or not?"

He cocked his head. "I do," he answered finally, "but I will require that you swear allegiance to me."

I cocked my head in return, doing my best to play it cool. "You offered me partnership. If any oaths are to be sworn, we'll *both* be swearing them."

Sophie and Alaric gave me identical approving nods, though I could sense they were surprised by my tact. Their reactions bolstered my confidence regardless, and let me know I was hopefully taking the conversation in the right direction.

Mikael on the other hand, was looking at me like he wanted to eat me. "Clever girl," he commented. "We will swear our oaths, then we will depart. I'll leave you to prepare yourself."

He walked around the table toward the door, then let himself out. I could hear Aila speaking frantically as they both ventured down the hall. Soon all was quiet.

I turned to Alaric and Sophie. "Um, what exactly does this oath require?" I asked, feeling nervous at the idea of needing to *prepare* myself.

Sophie smirked. "And here it sounded like you actually knew what you were doing for a moment. I thought perhaps the charm had taken over."

Alaric appeared solemn. "It is a blood ritual. Normally when fealty is sworn, the swearer will offer their blood to the Doyen. In this case you will both offer blood, and the ritual will be bound to the earth."

"Is it magic?" I questioned weakly, terrified of what the consequences of such an oath might be.

"Of a sort," Alaric replied. "A simple blood oath would not mean much, and would only serve to establish a connection. When an oath is bound to the earth, the terms are quite different. Breaking such an oath would result in the earth coming to claim you."

I gulped. "Claim me?"

"You would die," Sophie clarified.

My eyes widened. "You know, one of you could have stepped in before I put my foot in my mouth."

Sophie shrugged. "We're probably all going to die anyway. I'd rather be claimed by the earth than by the blade of my enemy."

I shook my head, not agreeing with Sophie's viewpoint. "What will the oath be, and what would I have to do to break it?"

Alaric stood and moved behind my chair so he could put his hands on my shoulders. He rubbed gently, attempting to sooth my panic. "I don't imagine it will be anything extreme, as Mikael will be swearing it himself. It will likely be an oath of no direct harm, which as far as I know, you aren't planning on killing him yourself, and it would be good to have such a promise for your own well-being."

I took a deep breath and let it out. An oath of no direct harm didn't sound so bad, though I was still a little shaken at the idea of *offering blood*. The Vaettir didn't do anything half-assed, and it would more likely be a pint than a thimble full. Not to mention that being bound to Mikael in any way gave me the serious creeps.

Alaric leaned down and kissed my cheek, startling me out of my thoughts. "We should prepare," he said softly.

I nodded a little too quickly. Things beyond my comprehension had been set in motion. I pictured Estus plotting within the confines of his Salr, vying for my blood, planning an assault on Aislin's clan so they wouldn't get to me first. So many innocents would die, and it was my fault. I flashed back to the scenes of bloodshed I'd seen the night Diana tried to sacrifice us, and tried to picture those same scenes as they'd apply in modern times. The thought made my stomach turn.

What was to come made one little blood-oath pale in comparison. After all, what was a little blood between acquaintances?

The members of Mikael's clan gathered around us as we stood in the woods outside the Salr. Fresh snow had fallen, blanketing the ground and making the world seem soft.

I stood across from Mikael with Alaric, James, and Sophie at my back. At his back stood Aila and two clan members I had only just met. The man's name was Faas, and the woman, Tabitha.

An elaborate design had been carved into the ground, deep enough to turn the soil underneath the snow. It looked a bit like a circular labyrinth, but with jagged edges making it imperfect, but no less mesmerizing.

Both Mikael and I held small, ornate knives in our hands as we stood mirroring each other. He'd traded in his robes for traveling clothes, and looked a little more normal in leather and fur attire that matched his clanmate's, though not as normal as he would have looked in street clothes. The four foot long sword strapped to his back seemed natural, and I had no doubt he knew how to use it.

The oath we had decided on was an oath against betrayal. I was walking a thin line with it. Technically I had never said I *wouldn't* destroy the charm, so doing so wouldn't be a betrayal, but it still made me nervous. Alaric had assured I'd be fine as long as I didn't lie outright, or intentionally put Mikael in harm's way.

The preparation had consisted of me memorizing a few words in Old Norsk, that basically meant loyalty, honor, and truth. I had dressed in the leather pants with a new burgundy sweater. It felt nice to wear something other than black, but I wasn't really thinking about my clothes at that moment.

"*Hollr,*" we both said in unison as we poised the blades above our open palms.

"*Mannvirðing,*" we muttered as the blades slid across our skin, sharp enough to cut with only the weight of the metal as pressure.

"*Sannindi,*" we finished as we tilted our palms to let our blood fall to the snow.

I could feel energy dancing around me as my blood trickled downward. A little shock went through me once the first drops hit the earth. I could sense the ground below me like it was something alive, and in a way, it was.

Our blood began to flow through the paths carved into the snow. There wasn't enough blood to build momentum, but it seemed to flow forward of its own accord. I watched in awe as the two streams of blood rushed forward, searching for one another, until finally they met in the middle of the design.

My eyes found Mikael's as our blood merged. He smiled, watching me with his head tilted slightly downward, framed by his loose auburn hair.

Something told me that I'd bitten off more than I could chew and then some. The moment our blood fully intermingled my ears popped with pressure, and the blood sank down into the earth. I watched as the design filled itself in, sucking soil then snow down into its lines. After a few seconds the only sign anything had happened were a few bloodstains on the pure white snow.

Mikael clenched his fist around the knife wound, then inclined his head toward me. I stared at him, resisting the urge to gulp. As he turned away to speak to his clan I stood frozen, looking down at the blood on the icy ground.

Alaric stepped forward and helped me into my coat, then began tying a bandage around my hand. I turned worried eyes to him, hoping for a little reassurance.

He shook his head with a small, bitter smile on his face. "He's mad that trusts in the tameness of a wolf," he quoted.

Unfortunately I knew my Shakespeare. I bit my lip before replying, "Things didn't exactly end up well for *King Lear*."

Alaric raised an eyebrow. "Yes, but who is the King in this situation?"

With that confusing question, he took my uninjured hand and led me forward to join the rest of our traveling party.

I still felt uneasy with Alaric quoting King Lear. Shakespeare either wrote comedies where most everybody lived, or tragedies, where most everybody died, and King Lear was a tragedy. It didn't really matter who was in charge if everyone still died.

If it was just a question of dagger, asp, or poison, we were all screwed.

CHAPTER ELEVEN

I had to hand it to him, Mikael had eyes and ears *everywhere*. Given his Viking heritage, I had assumed we would be roughing it in the freezing forest, but Mikael had other plans. We would hide amongst the humans, where his network of spies could easily pass messages to us.

He'd also theorized that should enemy forces find us, they would be hesitant to attack within the confines of civilization. I'd argued that *his* people had attacked us in a hotel in broad daylight, but that ultimately only proved his point, because they had been *his* people, and unlike Estus and Aislin, he didn't want to preserve our secretive existence within the Salr.

Once we reached civilization, we'd learned that Mikael owned several houses, spread out across different towns, and some in different countries. He'd even changed into normal clothes once reaching one of the aforementioned houses, though it was obvious that he did so grudgingly.

We'd stayed at the house for several days, but would be leaving soon. To where was anyone's guess.

I peeked out through the heavy-curtained window,

waiting for my turn in the shower. Our current hideout rested in a quaint, residential neighborhood. It was the kind of neighborhood where elderly people walked hand-in-hand, and children played in the streets without fear. The house was set back from the road, with large trees in the front yard, but I could still see a young couple walking happily down the street. I would have given a lot to be as carefree as they seemed, but my life had never, and would never be that way.

I suppressed goosebumps at the idea of Vaettir invading the small neighborhood in search of us with their cold and violent ways. The young couple would have plenty to care about then, if they even survived.

A hand touched down on my shoulder, and I turned to see Alaric smiling down at me, not sensing my worried thoughts.

"Our turn for the shower," he announced.

I blinked up at him innocently, pushing the feeling of dread to the back of my mind. "*Our* turn?"

Without answering, he scooped me up in his arms and carried me toward the bathroom, past floral couches, lace doilies, and other décor just as quaint as the neighborhood. Not exactly a house suited for a Viking, but I think the idea was to blend in more than anything else.

Sophie, with her long hair twisted up in a towel, and another towel wrapped around her body, rolled her eyes as she breezed past us. I turned and stuck my tongue out at her, unwilling to let her spoil my small moment of comfort amidst a sea of troubles.

We entered the cozy bathroom and Alaric used his foot to shut the door behind us. The bathroom was small, with a pedestal sink and toilet to the left, and a shower/bath combo to the right. There was still leftover steam from Sophie's shower fogging up the mirror. I hoped she had saved us some hot water.

As soon as Alaric set me on my feet I locked the door, pausing to listen for any movement outside.

Alaric grabbed my shoulders and gently turned me to face him. "Expecting an attack?"

I pursed my lips. "Something like that."

More like I was expecting a Viking siege. Things had been weird with Mikael since we'd taken our oath. He had given up on hitting on me after his initial attempt during our *night cap*, but he was still giving me a strange vibe.

I knew he wasn't plotting, since he'd taken an oath to not betray me, and I didn't think he was wary of me or the charm. In fact, he seemed quite comfortable with *that* situation, unlike me. The vibes were more . . . portentous, like something big was coming and only the two of us knew it. Whatever it was had him excited, and it was like he was watching me, waiting for me to set events into motion.

Alaric brought me back to reality as he moved behind me, then pushed my hair aside to rain soft kisses down my neck.

"Focus, Madeline," he whispered, his breath hot on my skin.

I sighed. "I'm sorry, it's just difficult to be in the present with all of the impeding doom."

He kissed my cheek, then moved in front of me to turn on the shower. At some point he'd lost his shirt, and his dark hair cascaded down his pale, naked back enticingly. Always a sucker for nice hair, I reached out and ran my fingers through the velvety softness, marveling at its texture.

Faster than my eyes could see, Alaric whipped around and grabbed my wrist. He smiled wide enough to flash his little fangs. "Now that's the spirit."

My lips parted and suddenly I was no longer thinking

about the war we had pushed into motion. My thoughts turned to the hot water running in the shower, and how nice it would feel for it to stream down both our bodies pushed together.

The warm feeling growing in my belly was only increased by the emotions Alaric was projecting. I could feel strong emotions the best, and his thoughts were just as filled with heat as mine. Our clothes were off quickly, little more than a secondary distraction.

Alaric took my hand, then stepped back into the shower, leading me to join him. I followed willingly. Although some might label what happened next as a sin, I felt less like I was stepping into the abyss, and more like I was stepping out of it.

When the water finally ran cold, we both hurried out of the shower, wrapping towels around ourselves to warm back up. I watched Alaric as I dried off slowly, not at all wanting to leave the bathroom to face the outside world. I would have stayed in that bathroom all day, but alas, our current abode was only a waypoint.

Mikael had alluded that we'd be traveling somewhere far different, though he wouldn't say specifically where. I imagined we'd be staying in Norway, but maybe a more densely populated city area where it would be easier to hide, and escape should we be found. The only thing I knew for sure was that we'd be meeting with a group of people that could help get us to where we were going.

Finished drying, I looked over at the new clothes I was supposed to wear. The house we were in had come equipped with all sorts of clothing. Mikael had planned for all contingencies, and all manner of companions. I'd originally gone for a pair of dark wash jeans and a plain tee-shirt, but Mikael had stopped me. I now looked down on neatly folded, Viking-style clothing, just like what most of Mikael's clan wore, except without the fur.

I reached out a hand to find that the steam of our shower had dampened the dark brown, tunic-style linen shirt, and lighter brown leather pants that sat on the closed lid of the toilet. Would I never escape leather pants? The clothing all looked like it was sewn by hand, but expertly so. Not wanting to put the strange clothing on, but also not about to leave the bathroom in nothing but a towel like Sophie, I frowned and crossed my arms. The now wet cord of the charm weighed heavily on my neck, one more annoyance to contend with.

"I don't feel like we'll fit in very well in these clothes," I remarked. "Isn't the whole idea to blend in?"

Finished dressing, Alaric walked behind me and wrapped his arms around my waist. "My only guess is that perhaps those we intend to meet with will expect more traditional attire."

I raised an eyebrow, though he couldn't see it. "This attire isn't exactly traditional, it's *ancient*."

Alaric kissed the top of my damp head. "I like it. It makes me feel like a young man again."

I turned in his grasp and pulled slightly away so I could observe his clothing, which was similar to mine. "I always forget that you're old enough to have worn stuff like this."

He quirked his lip into a half smile. "I can help you into yours if you like."

I nodded, then turned back to my pile of clothing. I had at least been given a modern day bra and panty set, which I was grateful for. While I slipped them on, Alaric unfolded the pants, loosening the ties that would cinch them around my waist.

He held them out to me. "One foot after the other," he said encouragingly.

I smirked at him. "I know how to put on pants."

He chuckled. "And I know how to take them off."

I took the pants from him and stepped into each leg. "I'm very well aware of that," I replied evenly.

Without another word he stepped forward and pulled the pants the rest of the way up my legs and hips. He crisscrossed the ties, then knotted them at the base of my waist.

"Shirt now," he ordered.

I reached back and grabbed the linen shirt from the toilet lid. I could have put it on myself, but I was having fun with the little game we were playing, so I handed the heavy fabric to him, then held my arms out.

With a lascivious smile, he slid each sleeve slowly over my arms, then jokingly tugged the rest of the shirt haphazardly over my head. I ended up with half my damp hair caught in the collar, and had to pause my giggling long enough to tug the shirt straight. The hem fell half-way down my thighs, the fabric much more comfortable than it looked. The final touch was a pair of boots that would stay on with leather wrappings rather than laces or zippers. Alaric really did have to help me with those, as I never would have gotten them on correctly myself.

I turned to gaze in the mirror at my new attire, while Alaric retrieved my knife from my discarded clothes to hook it back at my waist. "Well it's much better than the clothes *you* picked out for me," I teased.

I watched Alaric in the mirror as he grinned, then stepped to the side and threw an arm around my shoulder. "We are a perfect pair of peasants," he commented. "Now I'll go till the field, while you stay home and raise our nine children."

I used my reflection in the mirror to glare at him. "You know, there has been a lot of speculation lately that some of the Viking warriors were women."

Alaric kissed my cheek, then turned to put his hand on the doorknob. "Perhaps that is why Mikael gave you pants instead of a dress, my little *land-skjálpti.*"

I grinned as I turned to follow him into the hall. I was liking the pet name of *little earthquake* more and more.

CHAPTER TWELVE

*S*ophie and James waited on the little floral couch, each glued to opposite ends.

"Why does he get normal clothes!" I exclaimed, looking down at James.

Sophie glared over at the man in question. "He's not coming to the mysterious *meeting*."

She was dressed in similar clothes to mine and Alaric's, except her linen shirt was deep blue, cinched close to her waist by an ornate leather belt as wide as my palm.

I turned as Mikael entered the room from the kitchen, followed closely by Aila. Mikael was back in his old-fashioned attire as well, only his had a little more leather than ours, and his sword had returned to his back. Aila was in street clothes like James, and didn't look comfortable with the situation at all.

"He cannot come because he is not involved in our plans," Mikael explained. "If he can't remember his own life, then he cannot choose a side,"

"He's practically an invalid," Aila commented, though

judging by her clothes she wasn't coming to the meeting either.

I glared at her, but James didn't jump up to defend himself. Oh how the mighty had fallen.

"We must eat, and then we will depart," Mikael announced. "Faas and Tabitha will remain here with your . . . friend."

The two people he'd referred to were nowhere to be seen, and in fact, hadn't been around since we'd arrived at the house, unfortunately. I'd gleaned the information that Faas was Mikael's executioner, and I was dying to talk to him.

Aila stood rigid as a pole, glaring at each of us throughout the exchange. I wasn't sure what she was still so bent out of shape about, but she made sullen Sophie look like the Queen of Sunshine.

Mikael opened his mouth to say something further, but a knock on the door interrupted him.

Chaotic emotions hit me like a ton of bricks. "Don't answer that," I ordered, my eyes glued to the door.

I didn't know who was waiting outside, but I could sense their energy. Normally I'd have to be within touching distance to feel someone's emotions, but what I sensed was overwhelmingly strong. I shook my head. No, the emotions weren't *that* strong, they were just coming from more than one person. My heart raced as I picked up on the feeling of anticipation and something akin to bloodlust, coming from all around the house.

The charm, almost forgotten, began to thrum with excitement. A battle was about to occur, and a battle would empower it.

James and Sophie both rose and came to stand near the rest of us. Everything was still and silent for several heartbeats. The metaphysical burning balls of excitement that were likely other Vaettir shifted around the house, preparing for the attack.

"They have us surrounded," I whispered.

I watched as Aila looked to Mikael. "Do we fight, or flee?"

Instead of answering, Mikael turned his perfectly calm eyes to me. "How many are there, Madeline?"

I frowned, not wanting any decisions to depend on me. The knock sounded at the door again. "Ten or so," I answered, "though it's hard to be sure."

"A scouting party then," Mikael commented thoughtfully.

If Faas and Tabitha showed up, we'd almost be evenly matched. Of course, having Alaric and Sophie on our side helped even the odds. I was yet to see Mikael or Aila fight, but something told me they would be proficient. James would do in a pinch, then there was *me*. I was useless in a fight.

The charm pulsed so rapidly it made my neck twitch. An indignant thought arguing against my uselessness echoed through my mind. The charm didn't view us as useless, and was offended I'd even question it. Alaric caught me as I swayed to the side, thrown off balance by the second presence in my head.

There was a loud thunk on the door, then another, drawing my attention back to reality. They were going to break it down.

"Fight apparently," Mikael commented.

The charm shared Mikael's attitude. Both would always rather fight than flee. I felt compelled against my will to move toward the door, but Alaric shoved me behind him. Sophie suddenly had two long blades in her hands, and she tossed one to Alaric as she came to stand in front of me by his side.

I finally got to see the long sword that Mikael wore across

his back as he drew it. The center of the blade was tarnished, but the sharp edges gleamed in the sunlight cast by the nearby window, belying its age.

James stood wordlessly, not needing a weapon, though in reality neither did Alaric or Sophie. Aila apparently didn't need one either as she stood next to Mikael empty handed, a deadpan expression on her face.

A much heavier thunk sounded and the door burst open. At the same time, the nearby window was shattered by a large rock, echoed by the sound of shattering glass in other areas of the house. Alaric and Sophie turned toward the first of our attackers. I was stunned to realize that I recognized one them, although last time I saw her she'd been missing a foot.

Maya now stood impossibly whole, framed in the doorway with several others standing behind her. More stood outside the now broken window, not entering, but the threat was there.

Maya's dark brown skin had all grown back to cover the burns James had given her, as had her curly deep umber hair. She quirked the corner of her mouth at me. "You're going to have to come with us, Madeline. Aislin would like you unharmed."

I stepped forward to stand between Alaric and Sophie, rather than behind them. Sophie was quivering slightly, and as I neared her I realized it was from rage. Sophie had risked everything to save Maya, and now I was pretty sure she was ready to kill her.

We will not be taken prisoner, the charm echoed in my head.

"No we will not," I murmured in reply.

Maya looked at me like I was crazy, and opened her mouth to say something else, but she didn't have time as

Sophie launched herself forward and crashed into her, sending them both out into the sunlight.

"Well that makes *that* decision," Mikael quipped, stepping forward to meet the other Vaettir who now entered the doorway.

My vision went blurry as the charm started feeding on the small amount of energy generated by Maya and Sophie, fighting beyond our sight outside.

I had a moment of regret for ruining the peacefulness of the quiet, safe, neighborhood, then the real fighting began. I backed away as my companions met with our opponents. I knew I'd do more harm than good if I tried to fight and got in the way, but the charm's energy sent a shiver of bloodlust through me, something I'd never felt before. It was like it awakened some deep, primal part of my brain. Kill or be killed. The charm wanted to get closer so I could take the lives of our enemies as soon as they were weakened.

Pain hit me, bringing me back to myself as Alaric tossed aside a man who'd almost made it past him to grab me. Mikael sliced another man nearly in half with his sword, and my pain increased. I doubled over, wracked with nausea, but the feeling was soon wiped away by the charm's excitement. It didn't care about pain, and wouldn't let me care about it either.

I shook my head over and over again, wanting to reach out to someone for help, but everyone was busy fighting for their lives. I watched as Alaric threw the same man he'd tossed before against the wall above the couch. The man thudded onto the couch cushions, then slipped down onto the floor. The entire backside of my body ached for a brief second, then the pain was once again blocked out by the charm.

I stared at his prostrate body, feeling oddly transfixed,

then hands wrapped around me from behind, covering my mouth and lifting me off my feet. In all the chaos I had forgotten about the other Vaettir I'd sensed behind and around the house. They'd come in through a back door or window to get the jump on us.

My attacker carried me backward into the hallway, then toward one of the bedrooms at the far end of the house. The charm screamed in my brain, more because it was being taken away from the battle, than because I was being kidnapped, though it wasn't happy about either. The key's will warred to overpower mine. It wanted to free us, but at what cost? Would relinquishing control mean I'd never gain it again?

Internally fighting the key, I weakly thrashed about, dragging my feet across the carpet, but was unable to free myself of my own volition. Whoever held me was massive, and had arms like steel traps. I looked down the empty hallway in despair, screaming against the hand that covered my mouth, then Aila appeared.

She watched thoughtfully as I was pulled into the bedroom. I turned my head briefly to see the wide open window that I'd likely be going through, then I was whipped around and tossed to the ground. I scooted away on the floor as Aila launched her foot into my captor's chest. Other than his size and the way he flailed about to avoid Aila's kick, he looked perfectly normal with his bald, gleaming head and punk-style street clothes.

It was almost comical to watch him fend off the attacks of the lightning-fast, blonde Viking who whipped about like she could walk on air. Her movements were so fast, I almost couldn't follow what was happening. Then the man suddenly stopped defending himself, and Aila stood still a few feet away. In painfully slow motion his body slumped, then fell sideways, narrowly missing the area where I was crouched.

Now that he was on the floor, I could see the little knife sticking out of his neck. Blood welled up around the blade from the artery Aila had perfectly severed.

I looked up at her. "You almost let him take me," I commented, remembering her expression when she'd first come into view.

She sneered. "Mikael would not have forgiven me, now out the window you go."

My eyes widened in surprise. I could still hear fighting in the other room, and both the charm and I wanted to get back to it.

"Are *you* kidnapping me now?" I asked, distracted as I listened to the chaos just a few rooms away.

"I will get you to safety," she stated. "Mikael will meet us."

I glanced around the room for a means of escape, not liking how she'd only mentioned Mikael meeting us and not the others. I needed to get back to the outer room to make sure Alaric and Sophie were okay.

Knowing I wasn't likely to get past her to the doorway on physical prowess alone, I decided to stall in hopes that the fighting would end and the others would come to find me. I'd use the key before I'd let her take me.

A dull, throbbing pain, drew my gaze down the large, bald man, with a pool of blood slowly forming underneath him on the beige carpet. Maybe I didn't need the key after all.

Misinterpreting my thoughts, Aila rolled her eyes. "Quickly," she demanded.

I reached out to the mostly dead man and released his soul, feeling the usual rush. I drew my hand away like I'd been burned, a little shocked at how easy the process had become, and how little I thought about the fact that I was taking a life, even if he was already dead in the most literal sense of the word.

"Now go," Aila prompted.

Police sirens wailed outside.

I stood. The sounds of fighting were cut through by a scream of anguish. "That was Sophie," I breathed, terrified that something had already happened to Alaric if he wasn't there to protect her. There was no way I was going out that window now.

Aila's eyes narrowed. "Don't even think about it," she warned, moving to block my way.

I shifted my weight from foot to foot, weighing my options. I had a little bit of power now, but I'd only have one shot at using it.

"Sorry," I mumbled, just before forcing the stolen energy in her direction.

It wasn't enough to send her flying, but it did knock her down. She fell on her butt with a surprised *yip*, then I launched myself over her long legs and out into the hall. With her speed I knew she'd only be moments behind me, but luckily I didn't have far to go.

Someone grabbed me as soon as I entered the room, and I realized with a start that it was Alaric. His pale face was dotted crimson with blood, and there were larger splashes on his clothes. "We have to go," he explained quickly. "Aislin's people fled at the sound of sirens, and we should do the same."

"Sophie—" I began, but then my eyes found her. She was hunched over, sobbing with her now-bloody knife held loosely in her hand. James was trying to help her up, but she kept swatting him away. The rest of the room had turned crimson, the work of Mikael's sword and Alaric and Sophie's blades.

I pulled away from Alaric and tried not to focus too hard on the bodies as I grazed my fingers across them, releasing that bit of energy that lingered in the Vaettir, even after death.

"Grab her," Alaric demanded of James as they both looked down at Sophie. He turned and guided me toward the kitchen and the back door as I wiped my bloody fingertips on my pants.

I looked back over my shoulder to see Sophie swat at James again, then Aila pushed him aside and picked Sophie up herself. She threw Sophie over her shoulder in a fireman's carry, ignoring the knife still clutched in Sophie's hand.

I turned to find Mikael already waiting in the kitchen, cleaning the blood off his sword with a dish towel. He stood grinning at us with crimson spatters in his hair and on his clothing.

"This is more fun than I've had in years!" he exclaimed.

"It won't be fun dealing with the human police," Alaric stated, pushing me forward.

The sirens closed in, accompanied by the sound of tires screeching to a halt.

"Shit," Alaric commented, tugging me away from the back door.

"To the tunnels!" Mikael exclaimed, a finger lifted in the air.

Aila shoved her way into the kitchen with Sophie hanging limply over her shoulder, still crying.

A megaphone screeched to life outside and we were flooded with the sound of a man speaking Norwegian.

I crossed my arms to suppress a shiver, looking to Aila. "Tell me he isn't joking and there really are escape tunnels in this place."

She glared at me. "He isn't, and there are."

She passed me to open a door into what I'd assumed was a laundry room, then held the door open and gestured for someone else to go first. Not wanting to be out in the open when the police stormed the building and saw the bodies, I obliged, finding myself in a small room with a washer, dryer, large basin sink, and tattered floral rug covering much of the linoleum floor.

His sword now sheathed, Mikael shooed me off the rug, then lifted the edge of the dusty fabric. He folded the whole thing back, revealing a trap door with its lid glued to the bottom of the carpet. It was quite clever really, as the rug would still cover the door once we escaped . . . *if* we escaped.

The megaphone had silenced and I could hear footsteps and shocked, murmuring voices in the living room. Not waiting for further instruction, I jumped down through the opening, barely catching my hands and feet onto the ladder inside. I made the short journey down, then waited in the near-dark as everyone else hurried down. Mikael came last, pausing on the ladder to shut the trap door quietly above him, leaving us in complete darkness. I heard a lock being slid into place, then lights flickered on.

We now stood in an old root cellar, complete with various jars of food and dusty barrels that might have once held apples or potatoes.

Aila, who'd carried Sophie down the ladder like she weighed nothing, now finally let her down to her feet to stand on her own. Sophie's eyes were red-rimmed and puffy, and her hands were still stained with blood. I wondered if it was Maya's.

"I tried to leave her to come back and help Alaric," she mumbled, "but she came after me. She came after me like I was just another enemy. She would have killed me if the sirens hadn't started. Even after I cut her, she wouldn't stop."

Alaric held a finger up to his lips to silence her as footsteps sounded above us. I cringed when I heard someone walk over the trap door, but they kept on walking normally, not noticing it.

Mikael went to open a door at the far end of the room, then waited for the rest of us to follow.

I hesitated, then put an arm around Sophie and guided her forward. "You know she's the enemy, right?" I whispered as everyone else waited on us. "You can't trust her."

Sophie shook her head. "I still thought she loved me, at least, but she would have killed me."

Not knowing what else to say, I gave Sophie's shoulders a squeeze as we walked through the doorway together. Alaric, James, and Aila followed us, then Mikael entered with an old kerosene lantern in hand. He shut the door behind him, and we were left with only the dull light from the lantern to guide our way.

Mikael took the lead and started forward while the rest of us formed a single file line behind him. What had started out as an extension of the cellar soon turned into a narrow tunnel like in a mineshaft. It had that damp, mineshaft smell too, making breathing unpleasant.

Sophie had walked ahead, directly behind Mikael, then came Aila, followed by Alaric. Their bodies blocked out most of the lantern light, leaving me blind. Luckily Alaric held my hand, guiding me with his superior low-light vision so I wouldn't be running into walls. James walked behind me, cursing to himself as he tried to keep up in the darkness.

"Where are we going?" he asked, out of breath.

"Away from the cops," Alaric replied sarcastically.

"Yeah, but *where*?" James asked, sounding annoyed.

It was a good question. I waited for someone else to

answer, but no one did, so eventually I answered, "I don't know."

"How can you not know?" James asked, making me regret saying anything. "Doesn't that little key you wear make you the person in charge?"

I snorted, but Alaric gave my hand a little squeeze before I said anything. I was *so* not in charge. Mikael may have knelt before me, but we all knew who was calling the shots on this little adventure. Well, everyone but James apparently.

Some of us may have been more blind than others, but we were all being led by the mischievous Viking in front of us.

CHAPTER THIRTEEN

We walked for over an hour before we finally reached the tunnel's end. The sunlight streaming in through the small, cave-like opening was a welcome relief, as Mikael's lantern had begun to dim twenty minutes prior.

We climbed out one by one into a wooded area to find Faas and Tabitha waiting for us.

Faas crossed his well-muscled arms as he looked each of us up and down. "We came to meet you and saw the police," he explained. "What happened?"

I observed Faas as he spoke. He had similar coloring to Aila, blond and pale, but was a good eight or nine inches shorter than her, putting him at around 5'7". His pin-straight hair was long on top and shaved on the sides, a hairstyle I didn't find terribly becoming, but who was I to judge with the frizzy mess on my head?

Tabitha was taller, with hair so blonde it looked white. Unlike the others, she was more lithe than muscled.

"A scouting party," Mikael explained with a roguish grin.

Faas quirked his lip in reply, then looked at the rest of us one by one. His small smile disappeared when his eyes met mine, deflating my excitement about finally spending some time around another executioner.

Estus had once explained to me that when an executioner was born into a clan where the position was already filled, the child was dumped into the human world to be raised not knowing what they were. He'd said it was a needed precaution, as executioners tended to compete and often ended up killing each other. The remembered words sent a chill through my bones as Faas stared at me.

Tabitha cleared her throat, cutting the tension. "Will we move on with things as planned?"

I turned to Mikael in time to see him nod. "Indeed. Those of you not coming will join the others in hiding. You will come out for *no* reason. I will not have you harmed while I'm away."

Tabitha nodded, as did Faas, though he was still staring at me. I avoided eye contact, too worried about the implications of what Mikael had said to focus on Faas. He'd made it sound like we were going to be *away* for a while. As far as I knew we were just going to a meeting, so why would Faas and Tabitha need to join the others in hiding?

Alaric cast a worried glance at his sister, clearly sharing my concerns. Sophie didn't return the look, and instead stared forward like she was pretending she was somewhere else, maybe somewhere with a non-traitorous Maya.

Tabitha nodded in James' direction. "You'll come with us now."

"*Now?*" I asked, wondering why we would part ways before reaching the meeting place.

"The place we seek is not far," Mikael explained.

Alaric snorted. "You planned on leaving through that tunnel all along, didn't you?"

Mikael accepted a satchel that Tabitha had been carrying, then turned to Alaric. "I did, though I had not planned on leaving in such a dramatic fashion."

"And you couldn't have told us beforehand?" Alaric pressed.

Mikael shrugged.

"You offered Madeline a partnership," Alaric went on. "*This* does not seem like a partnership."

Mikael turned his amber eyes to me. "If Madeline would like to know my plans, she need only ask."

I raised my eyebrows in surprise. "Okay, what are your plans?"

Mikael's lips curved into a mischievous smile. "I will tell you everything after the meeting."

Aila smiled smugly at me.

I sighed. "Let's get this over with."

"I don't want to go with them," James interrupted, referring to Faas and Tabitha.

"You have no choice in the matter," Mikael replied.

"Well if we're partners," I interrupted, "then I have a choice."

Mikael raised an eyebrow at me. "You really want him along?"

I didn't, but I did want to assert myself in the situation before it was too late. "No," I replied, not sure if a small lie would constitute a betrayal that would break my oath, "but he's coming to the meeting anyhow. If Estus or Aislin got a hold of him, they would find out much more information than we want them to know. I feel better with him in my sights."

James seemed unsure of how to react to what I'd said. I *almost* felt bad since I was the only one that made any effort to be nice to him, but I once again reminded myself that he was still James, and I was pretty sure the real James was evil. I had the scars to prove it.

"He can come to the meeting," Mikael agreed.

I narrowed my eyes at him. "What's the catch?"

He lifted a hand to his chest. "Why Madeline, you wound me. You know I cannot betray you."

I let out an irritated breath. "Fine, let's go."

Faas gave me a final rude glare, then turned to Mikael. "We shall await your return, and guard our people while you are away."

Mikael nodded curtly, dismissing Faas, who walked away, followed by Tabitha.

He gestured to a narrow path through the looming, snow-speckled trees. "Ladies first."

It seemed silly for me to lead the way since I had no idea where we were going, but I was tired of standing in the cold so I obliged. The leather wrapped boots had thin enough soles that I was grateful for the loamy, well-cushioned soil beneath my feet.

The further I walked down the well-worn path, further from the scene of the crime, the more at ease I felt. Still, we were rather conspicuous walking through the woods together when most of us were covered in blood. If any humans saw us, they would likely call the police, but the woods were fortunately silent and empty. If I never had another close call with the cops, it would be too soon.

As the path widened, Alaric and James caught up to walk on either side of me, while the other three walked behind. I could hear a hushed conversation between Aila and Sophie, but they were far enough back that I couldn't make out the words. I could tell they weren't angry though, which was a surprise coming from either of them.

James cleared his throat, glancing at me. "Thanks for what you did back there."

I shrugged, not wanting to say that I hadn't really done it for him. "Sure."

"You did well, Maddy," Alaric commented quietly. "If you give him an inch, he will leave you with nothing."

"Are you speaking from your own experiences?" I asked.

He kept his gaze on the woods ahead of us as he answered, "I'm speaking what I know. We cannot rely on his oath to you alone. He will find a way around it."

"Well then perhaps we shouldn't be blindly walking into this *meeting* with him," I whispered.

Alaric shrugged. "I believe this *meeting* is only a means to take us somewhere far away, judging by the way his people spoke. If we're to carry out *your* plan, we must find a way to not go through with his. We will accomplish nothing if you are not near the bloodshed, correct?"

"Up close and personal," I confirmed, feeling a little sick at the idea.

"Remind me again what you will do once we get you there?" he asked, knowing full well I had no real explanation for him.

"I'm still not sure," I replied hesitantly, not really wanting to discuss things around James, memory or no. "The Norn showed me pictures and emotions. I'm basing my plan more off a feeling than anything else."

Alaric pulled me close to him as we walked. "You know, Madeline, that is not at all comforting."

"It wasn't meant to be."

He gave me a squeeze and kissed my temple. "My offer to run away together still stands."

I smirked. "I'm pretty sure Mikael would view that as a betrayal, and I'd really like to avoid being *claimed by the earth*."

He laughed. "Pesky blood oaths, ruining all our fun."

I laughed in return, but it was cut short as the others increased their pace to catch up with us.

"We are nearing the meeting place," Mikael announced, moving past James to take the lead.

"I was expecting somewhere farther," I commented, feeling apprehensive and at the same time, a little excited.

Mikael looked over his shoulder and winked at me. "The location of my tunnel exit was not mere happenstance."

"Of course it wasn't," I sighed. "Will you at least tell us with whom we're meeting now?"

He stepped into a small clearing. "Nope."

The clearing didn't seem as touched by winter as the rest of the surrounding earth, and even boasted a few small purple flowers.

Mikael knelt to inspect the ground, then stood, took a few steps, and knelt again. "Madeline," he said, motioning for me to join him.

I only hesitated for a moment before moving to stand beside his crouched form.

"Lie here," he instructed, moving his hand across the grass to map out a specific area.

I crossed my arms. "Why?"

He looked up and rolled his eyes at me. "We're going to another Salr. This is the entrance."

I took a step back in surprise, making him sigh.

"What *now*?" he asked, clearly irritated.

I shook my head. "Nothing, just surprised you actually answered one of my questions."

He sighed again, then stood. "Lie down, *please*."

I did as he asked. The grass was cushy and comfortable, but there was no magic or extra energy that I could sense. If this was another Salr, it was very well hidden.

Mikael instructed the others one by one to lie in designated areas, then finally lowered himself to the ground. He was closer to me than I would have liked, but I didn't complain as the whole ordeal had already taken up a good twenty minutes, and I was ready to get it over with.

For a few minutes nothing happened, then the ground began to tremble. It took every ounce of my self restraint to not move as the soil shifted below us until we began sinking. Soon we were encased in the earth. I had a few horrifying seconds of thinking I might be buried alive, then we came out of a dirt wall, standing upright. I looked back at the wall, astonished to see it showed no sign of our entrance, then looked down at my miraculously clean clothing.

"I will *never* get used to Salr entrances," I commented, glancing around at my companions. The only one who seemed as stunned as me was James.

"How did you enter the Salr in your homeland?" Mikael questioned.

"Vines," I replied, moving to stand beside Alaric and Sophie.

The room we were in was cellar-like, and reminded me far too much of the entrance to where the charm had been held.

Aila waited for us to fall in line behind Mikael before she brought up the rear. We left the cellar room through a short wooden doorway, then continued along a narrow passageway. Our surroundings slowly began to look more like the other Salr with stone ceilings, walls, and floors, only these stones were red and brown, as opposed to gray.

"Are we visiting another clan?" I asked curiously, hoping Mikael would continue to be forthcoming with answers.

He chuckled. "Of a sort. You'll see soon enough."

This Salr seemed smaller and less complex than the

others. The halls of both Estus' and Mikael's Salr were like mazes, with countless twists and turns that were easy to get lost in. This one, though it had a few branches, had one long, straight hallway down the middle. I peeked around Mikael's broad shoulders to see a door at the very end of the hall. My heart jumped a bit when the door swung inward, but nobody emerged.

I gulped. "I take it that's where we're going."

"How very astute of you," Aila commented from the end of the line.

"You know what, Aila?" I said, finally getting irritated with her bad attitude. "*Shove it.*"

"Shove what?" she asked, truly perplexed and not at all offended.

"Nothing," I grumbled.

We reached the ominous door. Any other insults I might have tossed out froze on my tongue as I followed Mikael through the door and into a large room.

"Well I'll be damned," Alaric quietly mused, coming to stand beside me.

"I think we already are," Sophie replied, sounding awestricken.

I was fairly awestricken myself. In front of us stood seven Norns, all towering over even Mikael and Aila. They all looked similar to the Norn who'd guarded the charm, and all appeared female, but with slight variations. Some of their horns were deer-like, two had twisted goat horns, and one had horns resembling the long-horned cattle I'd only ever seen in pictures.

The Norns stood with no emotions playing across their angular, green-tinted faces. They all wore shapeless brown robes that made me wonder about the impossibly thin, tall bodies underneath. Hooved feet could be seen at the edge of some of the robes, some looking like goat hooves and some looking more like the hooves of a horse. They all clasped what passed for hands in front of them. A couple resembled the talons of a hawk, and the rest looked like paws of lions or tigers. The only thing all their hands had in common were razor-sharp, long claws.

"You could have given us some sort of warning," I said to Mikael in a strained voice.

Mikael shrugged. "I feared you would not want to come."

While I understood why he might assume that, I still would have come had I known what was in store. I had so many questions I would have liked to ask the Norn before she died, and now I was presented with seven more. If they truly were the weavers of fate, perhaps they could help.

Mikael began speaking loudly in Old Norsk, addressing each of the Norns in turn. In reply they each bowed their antlered heads.

"Old friends?" I questioned under my breath.

"Something like that," Mikael replied.

"Why is that one staring at you?" James asked over my shoulder.

I looked across the row of Norns to find that one was in fact staring at me. The cow-horned Norn tilted her head in thought, blinking large, almond shaped eyes at me. While Mikael walked forward to continue speaking to one of the other Norns in line, the one who'd been watching me held out a feline paw large enough to cover my entire face, with claws as long as my fingers.

I glanced at Alaric, then asked through clenched teeth, "What do I do?"

His brow furrowed with worry, he replied, "I wouldn't keep her waiting."

I looked back to the Norn. I'd just been wishing I could

"speak" with one of them, but the long claws and sharp horns suddenly looked daunting.

She bobbed her paw slightly in the air, impatient for me to obey her request. I forced myself forward, step by step until I was only about a foot away from her. The Norn closed that final gap herself, leaving me to either crane my neck awkwardly upward, or stare at her sternum. Before I could make a choice, she placed her heavy paw on my shoulder, and images began to play through my mind.

She showed me the place where the charm had been held, with the giant tree in the center and burial mounds surrounding it. Then she showed me an image of the Norn who'd watched over that place. The images were never quite still, and played more like glitchy videos in my mind.

I focused on the images and realized she was asking me what had happened there. I did my best to replay some of the scenes in my mind, unsure if the Norn would be able to see them like I could see hers.

She bowed her head as I pictured the Norn in my memory, ripping out her own heart and handing it to me. The Norn in front of me turned sad eyes to look down into mine, then placed her free paw on my chest so she could tap the charm beneath my shirt with one black claw.

I thought of the images the last Norn had shown me, but my memory had blurred them enough that they were difficult to convey. It was much more simple to picture things I had seen with my own eyes. The Norn tapped the charm again, not understanding.

Before I could think of a better way to convey what the Norn wanted to know, someone grabbed my arm and began pulling me away from the her. I lost contact with the Norn's paw, and turned to find that it was Alaric pulling me while Sophie waited by the door with a scared look on her face. What had happened while I was transfixed by the Norn?

I pulled against Alaric, scanning the room for the source of his fear, only to find Mikael smiling and looking perfectly calm next to the Norn he'd been speaking with.

"They're going to send us away," Alaric explained before tugging at my arm more forcefully, throwing me forward.

"He doesn't want to take us to another place, he wants to take us to another *time*," he continued, finally motivating me to run.

Sophie turned in the doorway as we reached her, and I could see James already waiting further down the hall. There was no sign of Aila. Had I lost time while "speaking" with the Norn? My brain felt like it was filled with cotton.

We all ran, though I still didn't fully understand what was happening. Yet something was wrong. Mikael wasn't coming after us. I learned why as my feet suddenly went out from under me, I hit the ground *hard*, and Alaric landed beside me. I tried to crawl forward, but my limbs wouldn't budge.

Sophie looked back at us in horror, and began to run back toward us, then abruptly disappeared from sight, as did the floor beneath us and the walls around us. I closed my eyes tight in fear, grateful that Alaric's hand was still on my arm, though he seemed just as frozen as I was. We endured several moments where it felt like we were floating in space, then everything stopped. I felt rough grass beneath my palms, tickling my face.

I took a deep breath and opened my eyes. We were in an expansive yellow field, and I could hear the ocean nearby. A wild wind tickled strands of hair away from my face. Alaric's hand squeezed my arm. He got to his knees, pulling me along with him, only I felt so suddenly dizzy that I immediately pulled myself back to the ground.

"Where are we?" I groaned, fighting the urge to vomit from motion sickness.

"We are still in Norway," Mikael said from somewhere behind us.

"And what year is it?" Alaric asked coldly.

Mikael chuckled. His voice was nearer when he said, "It is the year 820."

I curled up into a ball on the grass, not wanting to open my eyes again. "That's not possible."

"The Norns are the keepers of time," Mikael replied happily. "With them, anything is possible."

I finally opened my eyes to see Alaric shake his head. "How did you make them do it?"

Mikael came over and crouched beside me, then looked down at me curiously. "Dizzy?" he asked.

I cringed and nodded. It felt like I had the world's worst hangover. "Why aren't you two sick?"

Mikael smiled down at me warmly. "It affected you more because you're pregnant."

CHAPTER FOURTEEN

I sat up so quickly my vision went black, and I had to huddle in a little ball again until I could refocus. "Come again?" I asked weakly, still on the ground.

"How could you possibly know that?" Alaric asked incredulously.

I opened my eyes to see Mikael shrug. "One of the Norns told me. I take it this was unplanned?"

I felt like I was going to faint. We were allegedly in the year 820, and I was . . . pregnant? Mikael had to be lying. He was descended from the god of deception for crying out loud.

Alaric stood and offered me a hand up. Not sure if I was ready to stand, I took the hand anyway. I looked to Mikael, unable to summon the glare I wanted to give him, but he inclined his head like he knew what I was thinking.

"I will give you two a moment," he stated, then moved away toward the edge of a long cliff, the ocean thundering distantly below.

Oh crap, we were on a *cliff*, not down on solid, safe ground. Suddenly the wind made sense. Another wave of dizziness passed over me. We weren't anywhere near the edge, but I'm not great with heights at the best of times, and this definitely wasn't the best of times. I leaned against Alaric, not sure what to say.

"We were careful," he stated, focusing on the more mundane problem, rather than what Mikael had done to us.

I nodded. "He has to be lying."

Alaric shook his head. "That would be a direct betrayal, and would break his oath. If he'd told *me* that you were pregnant, he could have lied, but he told you directly."

I shook my head, unable to digest the idea of a living creature forming inside me with everything else going on. "I really can't focus on the magnitude of both of these situations at once, so I'm just going to pick the more pressing issue. How the hell is time travel possible? I mean, I know the Norns have a lot of magic, but this is ridiculous."

He sighed. I could tell he wanted to discuss the *other* situation, but still he answered, "The Norns are meant to weave the fates we choose ourselves, but they are capable of giving things a . . . shove from time to time."

"The fates we *choose?*" I asked, wondering at his word choice.

Alaric smiled slightly with a faraway look in his eyes. "Fate might guide us," he explained, "but there is always a choice."

I shook my head, not sure if I even believed in fate at all. "If the Norns can *shove* fate, then why aren't they ruling the world?"

Alaric wrapped his arms around me and shrugged. "They aren't motivated by power like the rest of us. Plus, for *shoves* this grand, they'd have to all agree. Rarely do so many of them work together."

"So whatever Mikael wants here is important," I deduced, "or else the Norns would never have helped."

Alaric sighed and kissed the top of my head. "Or else they owed him a very big favor."

I buried my face in his chest. "I like the first option better."

"About the pregnancy," he began hesitantly.

I looked up at him, trying my best to keep the tears building up in my eyes from falling. "Can we please just worry about getting back to our own time for now?"

He gave me a soft smile. "That's probably wise."

We both turned to where Mikael stood near the edge of the cliff, looking quite picturesque with his warrior's garb, and long auburn hair whipping about in the wind.

Alaric pulled away from me, then took my hand before walking in Mikael's direction. I went reluctantly, not wanting to go anywhere near the cliffside. We stopped a few steps behind him, close enough to see the dark ocean several hundred feet below. The angry waves whipped about like a storm was coming, and sure enough, one was. The sky further out in the ocean was gloomy and ominous. I pulled my hand free of Alaric's to wrap my arms around myself against the cold wind, but it did little good.

"Why are we here, Mikael?" Alaric asked.

Mikael turned to us with a secretive smile. "To help Madeline, of course."

I glared at him, because it was better than looking over the edge of the cliff. "If you really want to help me, you'll tell me what the hell is going on."

Mikael inclined his head in assent. "We're here to find one of the key's previous owners."

My eyes widened as I touched the key at my throat. It had

been so quiet I'd almost forgotten it was there. "Why would we want to do that?"

Mikael chucked. "Because she's the only one to have used it to its full potential, and lived to tell the tale, at least for a time."

My mouth went dry. No one had ever said anything about the charm killing me. As far as I knew, it wanted me to use it, and would work to stay in my possession until I could, but what then? I honestly hadn't thought that far ahead. If I was actually pregnant, I wasn't sure I could go through with any of it. I also wasn't sure I had a choice.

Not waiting for my reply, Mikael turned and walked back toward where we had originally appeared. Alaric and I trotted to catch up, and I was grateful to find that my stomach did not protest the extra movement. Mikael led us past that spot, then onward.

We reached the first of many sparse trees populating the meadow as we walked, but as they were short with little foliage, they provided no respite from the wind. The storm on the horizon was gaining on us too, and the wimpy trees would offer little shelter.

"Why did Sophie and James get left behind?" I asked, my voice breaking through the soft howls of the wind. "And what about Aila?"

Alaric glanced at me, then his gaze joined mine on Mikael's back.

"James was always going to be left behind," Mikael replied, glancing over his shoulder at us. "And Aila departed before the spell began to return to my people. Sophie simply ran too far and ended up outside the boundary of the spell."

I glared at his back as he turned. "You said that James could come. You *lied*."

Mikael laughed. "I said he could come to the meeting, and

he did. I made no promises after that. The Norns will watch over him until we return."

I bit my lip in irritation. I needed to improve my abilities at skirting around the truth if I was ever going to compete with Mikael.

"What about Aila?" I pressed. "Why did she leave? One would think you would have brought *her*."

"Someone must advise the troops while I'm away," he said simply.

I shook my head, irritated by his vague answers.

"So this person we're looking for," I began, hoping that a new angle would actually garner some useful information, "did you know her, you know, back in this time?"

"She was my wife," he replied

I stopped walking. "*Wife?*" I asked, really wishing I could see Mikael's expression. "You don't really seem like the love and marriage type."

Mikael chuckled, but kept walking, forcing Alaric and I to catch up. "You've got me there. Marriage in these times was more of a contractual obligation between two families, and this was a time when our people still lived amongst humans. We did our best to blend in."

"So the woman we're looking for is human?" I pressed, confused.

"No she is Vaettir, but to others it would have been strange if two youths from well-off families remained unwed."

"Did you have children?" I asked, then instantly regretted it. It was *so* not my business, and I really didn't want to think about the idea of children at that moment.

"Yes," he replied still not giving me any hint on how he was feeling.

His lack of emotion led me to suspect I'd hit a nerve. I had decided to just shut up when Alaric asked, "What happened to them?"

Mikael stopped walking, but his back remained turned. For a moment I thought he wouldn't answer, then with a tired sigh he said, "In this current time they are young men off to war. In our time, they have been ash for hundreds of years."

We were all silent then. Thunder rumbled behind us, pressing that we would soon be highly uncomfortable if we didn't find shelter.

We all kept walking. My hands absentmindedly went to my belly. With my particular . . . gifts, I'd kind of written off the idea of ever having kids. Wouldn't want to accidentally kill them.

I shivered. That could still be an issue.

The scent of distant woodsmoke filled my nose, and my shoulders relaxed. I'd never realized what a comforting scent smoke could be until that moment, when we were so far from anything we knew. The smoke smelled like civilization, and the comfort of others living with the same problems anyone else might face. In this case the *others* were likely fierce Vikings that would rather pillage the next town over than sit down for a nice cup of tea, but I'd take my comforts where I could find them.

We continued on as a path became clear in the grass. It seemed like Mikael knew exactly where we were going, even after all of the time that had passed since he'd last been there. I wondered if he would try to see his children while we were here, which led me to wonder how we were going to get back to our own era when the time came. I knew Mikael had to have a plan, but I really would have liked a preview.

I clenched my jaw, pushing uncomfortable thoughts about time travel out of my head, turning them back to

Mikael. If he was feeling nostalgic or sad about his kids, I couldn't tell. He seemed better at shutting out his emotions than most, and I had a feeling he'd lived that way for quite some time, focusing on plotting and intrigue instead. It would have been interesting to meet him as a young, unjaded man. That particular thought led me to a question.

"We're not going to run into your past self, are we?"

Mikael slowed his steps to walk on my side opposite Alaric. "Past me has long since fled this place. Now correct me if I'm wrong, but you don't seem angry that I brought you here."

"*I'm* angry," Alaric interrupted.

I shrugged. "I don't appreciate the way you went about it, but I wouldn't mind speaking with someone who fought the charm and won."

Mikael smiled bitterly and looked ahead. "I said she lived, for a time, I didn't say she *won*."

With that portentous tidbit, an odd thought dawned on me. "Back when we first came to your Salr, the charm knew your name. When it spoke through me, it was as if it *knew* you."

Mikael glared at me. It was the first time I'd seen any real anger in his expression. "That was not the only time I was forced to kneel before the *Lykill*."

I veered away from that expression as we walked, putting me closer to Alaric. "If you hate the charm so much, why are you involving yourself in any of this?"

His mood changed so suddenly it was a little unnerving. "We're here because I want to beat it. I want to use it for my own advancement, and then I want to show it that it has no power over me."

Alaric snorted. "So this is all about your centuries long vendetta against an object?"

Mikael's expression turned sour. "And how much of this is about your centuries long vendetta against me?"

"If it weren't for Maddy," Alaric began calmly, "I would have already killed you."

"You would have tried," Mikael snarled.

I was beginning to feel overwhelmed with both men's emotions so close to the surface, a mixture of pride, aggression, and underneath that, regret.

"You guys are making me dizzy," I complained. "Please shove that anger back below the surface where you usually keep it and Mikael, tell me more about your wife."

Mikael clenched his jaw, but did as I asked. "Erykah was —*is* a telepath. The charm used her in more subtle ways, gleaning information from the minds of others to use for its own devices."

"What made her decide to get rid of it?" I asked, since I'd considered just ditching the thing countless times, but for some reason, had never followed through.

Mikael looked at me like I was being silly. "Deciding to get rid of it is one thing, actually doing it is quite another."

I scrunched my face in confusion, then immediately stumbled over a rock. Alaric caught me before I could fall. "I don't follow," I replied, righting myself.

"Have you tried?" he asked.

I shook my head and began walking again. "I've thought about it, but I don't want to risk it falling into the wrong hands."

"Is that really the reason?" he pressed.

The smell of woodsmoke was growing nearer, and I really wanted him to get to his point before we reached where we were going.

"Of course it is," I replied without really thinking about it.

"Try taking it off and dropping it to the ground," he advised.

I gave him a *you wish* look. "Why, so you can take it?"

He raised an eyebrow at me. "Now why would I take it, when I've set into action this elaborate plan to help you learn how to control it?"

I bit my lip. Hadn't he already proven that he wasn't trying to take it, and hadn't he sworn an oath that prohibited him from betraying me?

"The reality is that you *can't* take it off," he explained. "It has chosen you, and any time you think of taking it off, you'll find an excuse not to."

"Try it," Alaric prompted.

I stopped walking and reached a shaky hand up to my throat. Mikael and Alaric both stopped a few steps ahead and turned to face me.

I closed my eyes and touched the cool metal with my fingertips, but all I could think about was that if I took it off, it might get lost in the grass, and then where would we be?

I forced my fingers to close around it, and tried to make myself tug down on it to undo the leather cord . . . but if I broke the cord, how would I re-affix it? Wasn't this just a test anyway? There was no need to undo the cord when I would just put it back on. I didn't need to *prove* I could do it.

I looked back up at the men in front of me. "I don't think I can do it," I breathed.

Alaric looked momentarily stunned, then he walked up to me and grabbed the charm at my neck. As soon as his fingers made contact with the metal, a burst of energy emanated from me, throwing him off his feet to land in a heap where he'd started, and knocking me down onto my butt.

Alaric sat up and looked at me from across the expanse between us. "Oh *fuck*."

I blinked at him. "You can say that again." I turned my frightened eyes up to Mikael. "How did she do it? How was your wife able to get rid of it?"

Mikael offered me a hand up as Alaric rose on his own. "I believe it would be better for Erykah to explain. The village is not far."

I nodded shakily and removed my hand from Mikael's. I had the urge to reach my fingers up to touch the charm, but I resisted. *That,* at least, I was able to do.

The first few raindrops from the storm pattered down around us. With a nervous look behind us, Mikael urged me ahead of him down the path. Alaric was soon at my side, and we continued onward with a storm licking at our heels, both literally and metaphorically.

CHAPTER FIFTEEN

We were soaked by the time we reached the village, and I was again awestricken by our situation. Many of the village structures were small, with wooden walls showing only on one or two sides. The other sides were covered by the green, loamy earth encasing the roofs, making it seem like the buildings had grown out of the ground like something straight from a fairytale. The layout of the buildings was circular, with the smaller buildings facing each other in a semi-arc.

While the small homes were enchanting in their own, rustic way, what really caught my attention was the longhouse. I'd taken enough history classes in college to know the longhouse was the main habitation in many ancient Scandinavian villages, and it definitely appeared to be the case in this village, judging by the size of the oblong structure. Animal skins covered the door of the wooden building, shielding whoever might be inside from the rain and wind.

The three of us stood together outside the village, but no one moved forward. I looked to Mikael, wondering what the hold up was. At first I thought it was just from the rain, since it had soaked his dusky red hair to drip onto his face and clothing, but then I realized his eyes held unshed tears. It completely caught me off guard, since his emotions were still shielded from me.

"Mikael?" I questioned softly.

He shook himself as if coming out of a dream. He laughed, but it came out more like a cough. "I had not considered what it might feel like to come back here," he admitted.

I glanced at Alaric, who watched Mikael suspiciously.

"Um," I began, not really sure what to say. "If you need a moment..." I trailed off.

I sincerely hoped he didn't *need a moment*, because my teeth were chattering so furiously I thought they might crack.

"Every extra moment spent in the past is a moment wasted," he announced, though the quiver in his voice betrayed the happy-go-lucky attitude he was trying to project.

I looked to Alaric again, who shook his head and looked back to the small village. His dark, loose hair was plastered to his back, but he of course still looked drool-worthy, if a little bedraggled. I really hoped the villagers didn't have mirrors, because I did *not* want to see what I looked like after our soggy, uncomfortable journey. If Alaric looked bedraggled, I surely looked something akin to a drowned rat.

Mikael finally walked forward without another word. He approached the longhouse like he owned the place, leaving his previous hesitation behind as if it had never existed. We followed like good little minions.

Reaching the structure, Mikael whipped aside the pelts covering the entrance, then went inside. Alaric held the skins aside for me to enter ahead of him.

Mikael waited to my left. I moved to stand at his shoulder, the warmth and soft murmur of conversation a welcome relief. Several small fires lined the center of the building, filtering smoke up through narrow holes in the roof. Rain dripped in through the holes, falling in a sizzling cacophony on the flames.

Four women near the entrance looked up at us. They had all been doing needlework, aided by the light emanating from little pots of oil with cotton wicks. The women's copper needles paused mid-motion as they looked us up and down, then one stood and gave Mikael a toothy grin.

The girl couldn't have been more than sixteen, with dark, curly hair held back in a mess of braids and leather clasps. She began speaking quickly in Old Norsk as she stepped closer to Mikael. Judging by her tone she was excited to see him, but the words were all beyond me.

He gave the girl a sad smile, then spoke back to her. I recognized the name Erykah, and realized he was asking the girl where his wife was. I was suddenly nervous to meet her, especially since I didn't know what terms she and Mikael were on in the current time.

While Mikael spoke to the girl, the other women retreated further into the building, then returned to wrap animal pelts around mine and Alaric's shoulders.

I liked being wrapped in the pelt even less than I liked wearing leather, but not wanting to insult anyone, I accepted the musty skin gratefully.

Finally Mikael and the girl finished speaking, and she led us back out into the rain to slog through the mud. Though the animal pelt deflected some of the moisture from my shoulders, water still dripped steadily down my face.

"Are they all Vaettir?" I whispered to Alaric as we followed Mikael and the girl to one of the smaller structures.

"Can't you tell?" he asked back at a regular volume.

Feeling silly for whispering considering those in the village likely wouldn't understand us, I considered his answer. Come to think of it, I *could* feel it. It wasn't like I could just look at someone and tell whether or not they were human, but there was a distinct energy in the air that I'd become used to since I was first taken to Estus' Salr. Most, if not all who dwelled in the village were Vaettir.

"Do you understand what they're saying?" I questioned.

Alaric nodded. "Nothing terribly interesting yet. The girl believes Mikael has returned from a long journey, which I suppose in a way, he has."

We reached the small building, and Mikael knocked on a door of thin logs, the lightweight wood held together by intricately woven twine. There was a faint answer from within, then Mikael opened the door.

The girl left us, examining Alaric curiously as she walked by. Her eyes only met mine briefly, then she looked away and hurried back to the longhouse.

Not taking time to ponder the girl's strange reaction, I walked behind Alaric as he entered the building behind Mikael.

I wrinkled my nose at the smell. I had expected another home-like environment, but the building was actually a cowshed. The cows inside were brown and fluffy, much smaller than the cows I was used to seeing. They were separated from each other by wooden bars, forming little pens. I covered my nose with my hand, but it was still hard to breathe.

A woman who had been feeding the cows turned toward us as she wiped her hands on the dark brown pinafore covering her lighter brown dress. She had yellow blonde hair, twisted in a messy braid falling all the way to her narrow waist. Large, aqua-blue eyes dominated a narrow, angular face.

At first she only saw me and Alaric and she looked confused, then she turned around fully and saw Mikael, standing almost meekly off to one side. At the sight of him she said something blandly in their language.

Mikael took a deep breath then began speaking rapidly back to her. Eventually both their voices raised to an uncomfortable volume.

"Translation, please?" I whispered to Alaric as we backed ourselves into a corner.

One of the cows reached out and nibbled at my damp sleeve as I waited for Alaric to answer me. He was quiet for a moment, listening to what was being said.

Finally he looked to me and answered, "Apparently we've arrived in a time where they have already parted ways. Erykah didn't expect him to return, and is quite upset that he did."

I opened my mouth into an *oh* of understanding. "I can't say I blame her for feeling that way," I whispered.

The cow nipped at my sleeve again. I shifted one hand to hold onto my pelt, then reached back with the other to pet it. Erykah eyed me sharply and I quickly retracted my hand from the animal's fuzzy forehead.

Erykah spoke rapidly as she turned away from Mikael to approach me. I tried to back away, but was blocked by the cow pen. Soon enough she had reached me. She lifted her hand toward my throat and I leaned away, scared despite the fact that she was much smaller than me.

She tsked and snapped her fingers at me until I straightened, then she gently pulled the charm free of my shirt. She tsked again, looking at the little key in disgust before letting it fall back against me.

She spoke to me again and I shook my head, not understanding.

"She asks if the key speaks to you," Mikael explained as he approached, looking sullen.

I bit my lip, unsure of how to answer. It didn't *speak* to me per se, but it did occasionally share its emotions, which sometimes translated clearly enough that I could tell what it was *thinking*.

"It doesn't use words," I explained, considering how I might convey what the charm's strange form of communication was like, "but I can tell what it wants, and when it's excited about something."

Alaric translated for me, and Erykah nodded, then said something else.

"She says if you can *hear* it, then you might be able to gain control over it, at least for a time," Mikael translated. "Erykah was able to do so because she's a telepath, I believe you can do so because you're an empath."

The charm was silent against my skin. If I didn't know better, I would have guessed its sentient nature had left it, but I did know better. Life was never that easy.

Erykah said something else, and Mikael rolled his eyes. "She says she will help you, for a price."

I looked down at the fierce little woman in front of me, then thought of the life brewing in my belly, and what might happen to me and . . . it, should I refuse.

"Honestly, at this point. I'm willing to do just about anything." I looked to Alaric, remembering how I'd almost been forced to sacrifice him. "Within reason," I added.

Rather than translating everything I'd just said, Alaric nodded to Erykah. She nodded in reply, then said something else, ending with a sneer.

Mikael sighed wearily. "She says first there will be a

welcome feast for me . . . though I deserve to eat with the cows."

I smiled, liking Erykah more and more. She quickly surveyed the rest of the cow pens, then led us back out into the rain.

I inhaled the clean air gratefully as Mikael shut the small wooden door behind us. Erykah led the way back to the longhouse amidst the scent of smoke. We all hurried inside out of the rain.

Erykah ventured away from us, while Alaric, Mikael, and I waited near the door, watching as two pairs of men hoisted cookpots over the fires. Mikael was drawn away, leaving Alaric and I to stand in the corner observing the scene.

Soon enough, savory smells filled the longhouse.

"This is *so* weird," I muttered, leaning against Alaric's damp shoulder. I glanced at him. "Well, I guess it probably isn't so weird for *you*."

He snorted. "I'm not *that* old, Madeline."

I laughed, feeling some of my tension easing away, then watched as several of the younger women carried stacks of wooden bowls toward the cookpots, then began filling them. One woman fetched a tray of hard little dinner rolls with dark brown outer crusts, which she began placing on top of each filled bowl.

Those already waiting near the fires seated themselves on long wooden benches, as more men and women filtered in from the rain. There were no tables that I could see, and those who already had bowls of food just held them in their laps.

One of the girls approached and handed me a serving of food, then took the slowly drying pelt from me. I looked down into the bowl to find several chunks of stringy meat, a few scrawny carrots, and one little loaf of bread that was too hard to soak up the thick brown gravy it rested in.

I gave Alaric a worried look. As a long-time vegetarian, the meal wasn't at all appealing to me, but my stomach was growling and there didn't seem to be any other options.

Alaric shrugged apologetically as the girl returned to hand him a bowl. Unlike me, he had no qualms with eating meat, and neither did Mikael judging by the way he began shoveling food into his mouth once he received his own bowl. He lounged on one of the benches next to the girl with the toothy grin, surrounded by several other teenagers speaking rapidly, begging him for stories of his adventures by the look of it.

Alaric nodded toward one of the less populated benches. Agreeing with the sentiment of relative solitude, I led the way over to the bench where we both seated ourselves.

Alaric began eating, then paused. "You could at least eat the bread."

I looked down at the hard little boulder in distaste. "It's all covered in the gravy."

"You don't know when the next meal will come along," he reminded me, "and you're eating for two now."

My pulse quickened at the thought. "So, are we talking about that now?"

"We have to talk about it sometime."

I looked down at the bread again. Before I could think too much about it, I snatched it up and took a bite. It was actually softer than it looked, but still took a bit of work to chew.

I swallowed, then looked to Alaric again. "Do you have any other children?"

He dropped his hunk of bread back into his bowl in surprise, then turned astonished eyes to me. "Why on earth would you think that?"

My face flushed. "I just thought, well, you've been alive a long time . . . "

He sighed and placed his bowl in his lap. "No, Madeline, I do not have any children. In fact, I was pretty sure by this point that I *couldn't* have children."

I took another bite of bread, feeling immensely relieved, and not really understanding why. "Is it common among the Vaettir?" I asked. "The not being able to have children?"

Alaric nodded. "Once bloodlines become muddled enough, it becomes easier, but if two from strong, yet opposing bloodlines try to conceive, the chances are very low. The different *tendencies* of each individual come from very different genetics, so a water spirit like Sivi would have little chance of conceiving a child from someone aligned with fire and heat, like James."

The thought of James and Sivi having a child made me shiver. I imagined Sivi's pointed teeth and translucent hair on James body, then quickly brushed the eerie thought away. Any child from those two would be an evil little bundle of doom.

"I've thought from the beginning that perhaps we are so drawn to each other because of our lineages," Alaric continued. "It would make sense that such a connection would make it easier to conceive."

"Yeah, death and war mix well, but that doesn't explain what we're going to *do*."

Alaric looked down at my stomach where this new creature allegedly dwelled. "Well, I'd say we're going to have a baby."

I raised an eyebrow at him. "We're going to have a baby, in the middle of a war, a war that we're at the center of, while I contend with a sentient key with a strong personality?"

"They're not the best of circumstances, but this is all happening whether we think it's rational or not."

I felt nervous again, because there was one more question I needed to ask. Okay, there were a million, but one was currently standing out above the others.

I swallowed the lump in my throat. "Do you want to get rid of it?"

Alaric dropped his bread again, and looked just as shocked as the first time. "Do *you*?"

Did I? It was a good question. The real question was, *could* I?

"I don't know what I *want* to do," I sighed, "but I don't think I could go through with anything that would snuff out a life inside of me. I have a hard enough time snuffing out the lives of others."

Alaric's shoulders slumped in relief. The fact that he was relieved made me feel infinitely more positive about the situation, even if the looming doubt that I'd even live through the entire pregnancy still nagged at me.

Someone plopped down on my other side. I turned to see Mikael, swilling something that smelled alcoholic out of an ornate silver cup.

He lowered the cup from his lips and smiled at me. "You've traveled through time for perhaps the only time in your life, and you two are sitting over here looking like someone ran over your cat." He winked at Alaric. "Pun intended."

"You're drunk," I accused.

He grinned. "No, dear Madeline, I'm just getting started. This might be the last time I see any of my kin alive, and I intend to make the most of it."

The thought was sobering. I was suddenly glad I had no kin to lose, at least not that I knew of. I looked around the room with a new perspective, realizing the happy, somewhat drunk people were all long since dead. Yet they somehow existed here in this time. The thought made me dizzy, and I suddenly felt like I might throw up.

I held up a finger, about to explain my situation to Alaric, but sensing I was running out of time, I shoved my bowl at him, stood, and hurried toward the door.

The chilly night air was like a slap in the face as I pushed the animal skins aside, but it was a welcome one. I fell to all fours and vomited what little food I'd eaten. As my queasiness subsided, I looked up at the sky, not quite ready to stand. The storm had moved away, leaving just a few clouds to partially obscure the moon. I felt a hand on my shoulder and turned, thinking it was Alaric. Instead of his welcome face, I got Erykah, looking stern and serious in the moonlight. Her yellow hair appeared white in the darkness, framing and equally white face.

Thoughts went through my mind suddenly, letting me know that she was aware of my pregnancy. Our language barrier was broken with this form of communication, just like with the Norns.

I groaned. I was really tired of being spoken to with no words, even if it was convenient.

Her return thought was that I was being childish. I had a gift and I should learn to use it to my advantage.

I attempted to climb to my feet, but felt so weak that Erykah had to give me a hand up. Her next thought was that I needed to eat. It was selfish to not eat when another life was depending on me.

She guided me away from the longhouse. I started to panic, thinking of Alaric.

Her thoughts assured me that he would join us soon, as she had asked him to give us a moment. My panic dampened.

I had no reason to trust her, but it was kind of hard not to when you were in each other's heads.

We walked over the soggy ground arm in arm to another one of the smaller structures. The doorway was covered with skins like the longhouse, which she held aside for me so I could enter.

The interior was small, but cozy, just three little benches covered in woolen cushions, and a large pelt over the center of the floor that I guessed once belonged to one of the little fluffy cows. Erykah held onto me until I sat on a cushions, then she began making a fire in a small pit in the back center of the room. When she was done, she sat on the bench beside me, rather than on any of the vacant seats, and handed me a small bowl of dried fruit. I munched on the fruit appreciatively until Erykah cut back into my thoughts.

I will die soon, she thought, though once again it wasn't with actual words.

I looked at her in surprise, and she conveyed that she had read her future in Mikael's mind. He was impeccable at shielding thoughts and emotions, but this one weighed on him enough that it leaked through.

My instinct was to comfort her in some way, to express my regrets, but as soon as I thought it, she already knew. She gave me a soft smile. She was glad she would at least die before her sons.

Not wanting to dwell on her impending demise, she reached out and once again pulled the charm free from my shirt. *This is the reason I will die,* she thought, sending a chill through my bones.

I could not destroy it, only release it, and eventually it went on to another. Its new owner will send forces to kill me, not knowing I am their only hope of freeing themselves. All here will die.

I stood up too quickly, thinking of the girl with the toothy grin, and everyone else having fun in the longhouse, worry free. "We have to warn them!" I blurted.

Erykah shook her head sadly. *You cannot change the past. No matter what you do, the same events will come to pass.*

I sat back down, defeated. I thought, *why are you telling me all of this?*

You must agree to the price I've asked for helping you, she explained. *You must swear to me the key will be destroyed, no matter the cost. It cannot move on to another owner. The destruction of the key will be my final revenge.*

I let my surprise project, not surprise at what she asked, but surprise she didn't already know my plans. I was going to destroy the key anyway.

She looked sad again. *You must promise me you will destroy it, no matter the cost.*

I nodded, thinking that it was an easy promise to make.

The destruction will likely kill you, and your child, she admitted.

My thoughts raced incoherently, which was good, because I didn't really want to share them with anyone at that moment. When they stilled, all I could think about was how she had mentally chastised me for not feeding my child. It didn't make sense if we were both going to die.

She patted my hand and smiled warmly. *Never give up hope. There is much to live for, much to fight for. I only wish I knew sooner.*

Someone knocked on the wood beside the door outside. Erykah said something in her language, then a moment later Alaric popped his head in.

"Is female bonding time over?" he asked, not sensing the weight of what had just transpired.

I forced a smile and nodded. "Erykah will teach me how to defeat the charm."

"And what of her price?" he pressed as he entered the room the rest of the way, letting the skins fall shut behind him.

I glanced back at Erykah, then returned my gaze to Alaric as I tried not to cry. "It will be paid."

CHAPTER SIXTEEN

As Alaric led me away from the little building where I'd sat with Erykah, her final thoughts echoed through my mind. *I will teach you at first light, then you must go. You cannot be here when we die.*

I shivered, and it wasn't just from the cold and my still damp clothing. The mud stuck to my boots uncomfortably, and I was overcome with the urge to just give up and lie down in the muck.

Alaric glanced at me every so often. "Are you okay? Did Erykah say something to upset you?"

I went over everything I'd learned, trying to figure out how to put into words that I might have to kill myself and our child, eventually coming to the conclusion that I shouldn't tell him at all. If he knew, he would try to stop me, but his efforts would be futile. There might be no other way. The charm would cling to me, and even if I managed to free myself like Erykah had, it would come back to destroy me. I *had* to destroy it first. If there was even the slightest chance I could survive that destruction, I had to take it.

I grasped Alaric's hand in mine and gave it a squeeze. "I'm

just tired. This morning back in our time seems like it happened weeks ago."

Alaric squeezed my hand in return. "It's hard to believe that a mere ten or twelve hours ago we were having a nice shower without a care in the world."

I laughed, but it sounded forced, even to me. "I'd say we still had plenty of cares. They were just easier to shut out."

We reached the longhouse again, and Alaric let go of my hand so he could hold the skins aside for me. There was now music being played inside, melding with raucous laughter and conversation. I peeked in to see half of the Vikings dancing around the fires, while the other half sat and clapped along to the music.

The warmth of the fires appealed to me, but I would have rather just gone to bed. I didn't want to be around people having fun, especially when I knew all of them would soon be dead. I took a step forward and hesitated in the doorway, wondering if we could find somewhere else to go.

My decision was made for me as Mikael swung by the doorway and grabbed my hand, pulling me into the center of the dancing. He twirled me around to the music, clearly drunk.

I leaned away, reaching my hands futilely toward the edge of the room.

"Just one dance!" he begged. "Let us celebrate while we still can."

Underneath his revelry I could sense his sadness, though I could probably only feel it because the alcohol had weakened his emotional shields. It gave me pause, and I shook my head at Alaric, who'd been coming to rescue me. He stopped and glared at Mikael, but didn't continue his approach.

Mikael pulled me close to him, swinging me in slow circles. Since he was eight inches taller than me, I had to crane my neck upward to look into his eyes. The same sadness I'd sensed from him was there in their amber depths.

He broke eye contact and leaned his face down to my ear. "She knows, doesn't she?"

"Erykah?" I whispered back.

He nodded, sliding his hair across my cheek.

For a moment I debated telling him, then not seeing the harm I answered, "Yes."

"You know you can't tell anyone," he whispered, still crouched so we'd be cheek to cheek.

"She told me I couldn't," I answered. "She said it wouldn't change anything."

He nodded again. "She was always wise beyond her years."

He pulled back and we both took in the people around us as we continued to dance half-heartedly.

"I came back when I heard what had happened," he explained leaning in, his arms loosely around my waist, "but I was several weeks too late. Since then I have been there each time the key was used, waiting for my chance at revenge. When it was sealed away, I thought it was over, then one of my spies brought word that the other clans were looking for it once again."

"You have spies among Estus' people?" I questioned.

He nodded. "Among Aislin's as well. I knew who you were before you even stepped foot in Norway."

I laughed despite the current mood of our conversation. "Of course you did. I'm sure you knew where the key was hidden all along as well?"

He let out a bitter laugh. "Just like many other things, the location of my chosen Salr was not mere happenstance. It was inevitable the charm would return, and I wanted to be near when that happened."

"And what about coming back here?" I pressed. "Was this all part of your master plan?"

He shrugged, and led me to dance in a more quiet part of the Salr. Alaric watched us like a hawk, ignoring the invitations he was receiving to dance.

"I had intended to come here on my own," Mikael explained, "once I knew the key might resurface. I wanted to speak with Erykah so that I would be prepared this time. I wanted to promise to avenge her."

"And when the key came to you, it just made things a little more convenient," I finished for him. "How did you get the Norns to agree to this?"

A wry smile crossed his face, reminding me of the less sad Mikael, hell-bent on becoming ruler. "When the Vaettir abandoned their old ways, they abandoned much of their magic, including the Norns. Under our new way of living, we were forbidden to shelter them."

I rolled my eyes. "And you suck at following rules."

He nodded. "The Salr were made for the Vaettir, and the Vaettir alone, but we can bring others there if we wish."

"You found them a home," I concluded, "and a trip back in time was your payment."

He pulled away from me, then led me to a vacant bench to sit. "A payment that took me several hundred years to call in. I've been waiting a long time for this."

Alaric finally took his cue to approach us as we looked out at the crowd. "You're sure we can't save them?" I asked, unable to let it go.

"I'm sure."

A group of young children ran in front of us, giggling as they shoved each other playfully.

I bit my lip, thinking of my own potential child. "How do you know?"

Mikael's eyes met mine just as Alaric reached us. "Because I've tried before. There are other magics that can alter time, and I tried to save them weeks after their deaths."

Alaric watched Mikael warily as he helped me to stand, then leaned down and kissed my cheek. "We should get some rest."

I nodded in reply, but felt unable to look away from the raw emotion in Mikael's gaze. Everyone he loved was about to die, a reality he'd already suffered twice, though I was sure he would suffer just as much the third time around.

It was all because of the little key around my neck. The key that chose that moment to buzz with energy against my skin, almost as if it wanted to remind me it was there.

I felt the key's satisfaction as the thought that I would never forget its existence danced through my mind. Our existences had been woven into one string of fate. When that string broke, we would both unravel.

CHAPTER SEVENTEEN

"Are you telling me I'm stuck here with you?" Sophie growled.

James frowned. "I'm telling you that Aila ran off ahead of us, and everyone else has disappeared. Those creatures are standing in there like statues, just waiting. They won't talk to me."

"The Norns," Sophie mumbled as she rose to her feet. Whatever the Norns had done had knocked her unconscious. Now as far as James was saying, her brother, Madeline, and Mikael were *gone*, leaving her only the silent creatures to question.

"What do we do now?" James asked, sounding frightened.

Sophie hated hearing that tone in his voice. She'd take the overly-confident, easy-to-hate James any day of the week. He stood tall, well muscled, and imposing, even with his golden, angelic hair. At one point he had lived up to his looks, except the angelic part. An angel of sadistic destruction perhaps.

Sophie strode confidently back into the room with the Norns, flipping her long black hair over her shoulder, trying to hide the fact that she didn't feel entirely steady on her feet.

She walked up to the nearest creature, one with little goat horns poking out of her head. The Norn didn't acknowledge her in the slightest.

Sophie jumped up and down, waving her hand in the air in front of the Norn's green-tinged face as James approached behind her.

"I already tried," he explained. "It's like they don't see us at all. I've been awake for hours."

Sophie ceased her jumping and huffed in irritation. "Why didn't you wake me sooner?"

James shook his head and backed away, seemingly frightened by her tone. "I tried. You were *out*, probably because you were closer to whatever happened."

"And what *did* happen?" she asked, hating the slight tremble in her voice.

James' gaze went distant, as if seeing the scene play out before him. "The air began to shimmer, ever so slightly, and the pressure dropped, like right before a storm. Then everything . . . shifted. The extreme change in pressure made it hard to breathe and I lost consciousness."

Sophie rolled her eyes. "Well that's of no help at all."

James looked truly apologetic.

Sophie grunted in frustration, wishing James would at least defend himself, then a thought came to her. "Aila," she growled, knowing she would likely get far more information out of the blonde Viking than she would the Norns. Without a word she left the room, heading toward the entrance of the Salr. Aila was Mikael's number two, and Sophie had no doubt he'd shared his plans with her. She'd known to run before the spell began.

James had to jog to catch up to her side. "But how will we find her?"

Not looking at him, Sophie raised a finger to tap her nose. "That won't be an issue."

James suddenly stopped walking.

Feeling increasingly irritated, Sophie spun on her heel to meet his astonished gaze.

"You're going to sniff her out?" he asked incredulously.

Sophie sighed, then turned to start walking again. The old James would have been useful in this situation. The new, impaired James was little more than dead weight. Maybe if she hit him over the head again, he'd regain his memory. If it didn't work, well, it would still be satisfying.

She reached the entrance of the Salr, and stared at a solid dirt wall. She shrugged, then pushed her fingers against the dirt, hoping this entrance was somewhat like the magical vines back in Estus' Salr. She held her breath as her finger sunk right through the wall. Next went her arm, and soon her entire body was encased in the earth. She panicked, unable to breathe, then she was lying on her back above ground, bathed in soft moonlight. A moment later, James rose up beside her.

Sophie was up in the blink of an eye, stalking off into the darkness with James trailing behind her. She'd find Aila, and she'd make her guide her to wherever Alaric had gone. For the past five hundred years, she and Alaric had always saved each other. She wasn't about to let him down now.

CHAPTER EIGHTEEN

I woke up cold, even though Alaric's arm was still wrapped tightly around me. I could feel the line of his warm body against my back, perfectly still in the thrall of deep sleep. He had even remained asleep as Erykah, appeared for an early morning visit. Such deep sleep was unusual for him. We'd had a trying few days though, so his coma-like state was understandable.

I, on the other hand, hadn't slept at all since Erykah departed. She had promised to teach me to control the key at first light, and that was what she'd done . . . sort of.

She'd shaken me awake in what felt like the middle of the night, then led me outside to see the barest hint of sunlight peeking over the horizon. There was an unbearable chill in the air, but Erykah seemed unfazed.

The lesson hadn't taken long, in fact, she never even spoke, since I wouldn't understand her. Still, the moment she placed her hand on my shoulder, gazing intently at me with her aqua eyes, I was overwhelmed with information. The images nearly knocked me off my feet, and I had to brace myself against her so I'd remain standing.

She showed me her entire struggle with the key, from when she first found it, to when she realized it was controlling her, to when she was finally able to rid herself of it. The whole ordeal felt akin to an abusive relationship, where the abused was so far in they believed their abuser when they said everything was for their own good.

I also saw some scenes with Mikael that made me blush. Erykah mentally tsked at my discomfort. He was her husband. What did I expect?

Erykah shook her head and got to the point. She had broken the key's hold over her by tricking it. She'd learned to shield her thoughts so the key couldn't convince her what she was thinking was wrong. The key was an effective adversary because it could insert thoughts into your mind until you couldn't tell the difference between your real thoughts, and the fake ones. Mentally shielding your thoughts meant the key would have nothing to work with.

I'd panicked at the revelation, because I hadn't learned to shield my thoughts, therefore the key would know I was planning to try. It would then manipulate me to keep itself fully in my mind.

At that moment, Erykah gripped my arms, conveying the thought, *If you are strong enough, it cannot stop you from shielding. It already knows you intend to destroy it. This game was begun when it first came into your possession. It may try to convince you otherwise, but all it will take is a moment of clarity, and the needed skills to defeat it.*

I nodded as her thoughts left my consciousness. She was right. It knew I wanted to destroy it, but wasn't willing to give me up as its host. I had to beat it at its own game by learning to shield my thoughts.

Then Erykah gave me what she thought was the answer

to my problems. *Mikael can teach you. Shielding is one of his gifts.*

Understanding played across my face, then confusion. *If he can teach me what I need, then why did we travel back in time?*

Erykah smiled sadly. *He doesn't understand how he does it, or that it's what you need to survive this. He won't be able to show you willingly, but if you can break down his shields like I did, you can gather that information for yourself. I would try to show you myself, but my shields are not as strong as his, not as complex. If you are to truly best the key, best it in a way I could not, you must learn to shield from the best. You must see inside Mikael's mind.*

I shook my head. *I'm an empath, I feel emotions. I can't read minds.*

She sighed. *Thoughts and feelings are more closely knit than you believe. How else would we be having this conversation?*

I gasped. *I'm reading your mind?*

Only because I'm letting you, she explained. *It will be much more difficult with Mikael. He lets no one in willingly, even if he says he will.*

She hugged me suddenly, catching me completely off guard. *Thank you for your promise. I can march toward death with honor, knowing that my adversary will not win. I was only able to shield long enough to rid myself of it. You will learn to shield well enough to destroy it fully. I have faith.*

I hugged her back as a few tears slipped from my eyes. They weren't tears just for her, as I'd only known her a short time. They were for the entire village. They would all die soon, even the children. I felt a pang of guilt for leaving, but in reality their deaths had occurred centuries ago. There was nothing I could do to stop them.

Erykah had left me then, and I'd returned to the small abode where Alaric still slept. I climbed silently back into bed with him, wrapping his arm around me like a life-line.

I could sense it the moment Alaric startled into wakefulness. His arm tensed around me, then relaxed as he maneuvered me more firmly against him.

"Good morning," he whispered in my ear, searching downward with his hand.

Realizing his intent, I pulled away and rolled over to face him.

He looked slightly hurt, then noting my expression, waited for me to explain.

I sat up, reluctantly pulling myself out of the warm bedding. "We have to go. Mikael will be here soon."

Alaric sat up, pulling free from the blankets to reveal his bare chest and the top of his dark brown, woolen pants. "What about the key? We still don't know how to destroy it."

I looked down at my lap as I tried to think of what to say. I knew I couldn't tell him the entire truth, that destroying the key might kill both me and our unborn child, but he wouldn't let me just brush him off.

"What is it, Maddy?" he said evenly.

I looked up to meet his dark eyes, then reached my hand out toward his black, silken hair.

He gripped my wrist softly, inches from his hair. "Answer me," he pressed.

I frowned, then shook his hand off my wrist so I could comb my fingers through his hair. He watched me cautiously with my hand inches from his face.

"I know what to do," I said finally, "but you're just going to have to trust me."

He grabbed my wrist again, but this time it was to press my palm against his lips. He kissed my skin gently, maintaining eye contact all the while. "I have ways of making you tell me," he said, only half-joking.

I pulled my hand away and let it fall to my lap, turning my head from him while I fought back tears. A moment later the bed shifted, and he wrapped his arms around me, bringing my face to rest in the crook of his shoulder.

We both jumped as the small, wooden door to our temporary home burst inward. Mikael stood framed in the doorway. His long, auburn hair flew forward in the cool morning breeze, but did nothing to obscure the intensity in his rich, chestnut eyes.

"It seems our manners have returned to medieval times as well," Alaric mumbled, but Mikael didn't seem to hear him.

Mikael's eyes met mine. He gave the barest of nods, which I returned without a second thought. We had to leave. There was no other choice.

"Meet me on the path," Mikael ordered, finally including Alaric in the scope of his gaze. "We don't have much time."

As Alaric and I disentangled ourselves, Mikael left us, leaving the door wide open behind him. I had kept on most of my clothing, so I only needed to put on the extra outerwear that had been provided by Mikael's village.

Alaric was dressed in an instant, and crouched down to help me with my boots while I secured the clasps on my short, leather and fur jacket, loose fitting with only half-sleeves. He had been given a wool cloak that swept down near his knees. I would have preferred a cloak like his, but I wasn't going to argue when I'd arrived with no coat at all. The furs were thick and warm, probably warmer than his cloak regardless.

Alaric pushed his hair out of his face as he began to wrap up my second boot. "Are you going to tell me what's going on, or do I have to guess?" he asked, clearly annoyed.

"I'll tell you as soon as we leave the village," I assured. "There's no time to explain now."

Alaric nodded as he stood, though it was clear by his expression he wasn't happy with the deal. He helped me to my feet, then placed his hand on my lower back as we squeezed through the doorway. He stayed protectively close as we made our way through the small village, likely sensing my nerves, but not knowing what they were about.

A few of the Vikings I'd met last night were already out and about, shaking out rugs and pelts, and moving in and out of the livestock huts. They paid us little mind, assuming we wouldn't actually be leaving them any time soon. Erykah was nowhere to be seen, luckily, as I wasn't sure I had the heart to face her. I was doing what she asked, but it still felt wrong.

I averted my gaze as a young girl walked by in front of us, oblivious to the peril that would soon befall her.

"You're shivering," Alaric commented, pulling me firmly against his side. "Do you want my cloak?"

I shook my head and looked down, unable to meet his gaze. It wasn't the chill in the morning air that was bothering me.

He let it go, though his expression remained concerned.

We neared the edge of the village without interruption. I could see Mikael further down the path, standing in a copse of trees with his back to us. His satchel looked bulky, likely stuffed with fresh supplies, but the rest of him appeared normal, at least to anyone who might be looking. To my secondary perceptions, he was brimming with a grief so powerful it leaked through his well-formed mental shields. His grief become more invasive as we neared his still form. At first it had been like a chill wind, but increased to the ferocity of an icy ocean wave as Alaric and I came to stand behind him.

He turned his face toward us, reddish brown eyes bland of emotion. I knew my face held just what he was feeling, and I knew he wouldn't appreciate that I knew, but I couldn't help it. I would have grieved even without his emotions helping me along. So many unnecessary deaths.

Alaric rubbed his tunic-clad arms like he had goosebumps, then looked over his shoulder at the now distant village. "Will someone please tell me what's going on?" he muttered, turning back to me. "We came all this way . . . "

I met his eyes and shook my head, urging him to stay quiet. Mikael was teetering on the brink, and I really didn't want to see what would happen if he uncaged all the emotion he was holding in.

Ignoring Alaric, Mikael turned to face me. "I trust you have the information you need."

Did I? What Erykah had given me was anything but clear, and definitely not what I *needed*, but I knew it was all she had to give. I nodded, and it seemed to be enough for Mikael. He turned from me to continue down the path. I grabbed Alaric's hand in mine and started forward, anxious to be away from the village before things started happening.

Alaric allowed me to pull him down the path, if a little reluctantly. He didn't ask any more questions, which got him major bonus points in my book. It was nice having someone actually trust that I knew what I was doing. Unfortunately, I didn't really trust it myself.

We'd only gone roughly a quarter of a mile when the first scream cut through the air. Mikael stopped in his tracks, forcing us to do the same on the narrow path.

"*What* is going on?" Alaric demanded, finally letting his anger seep through. His anger sent fiery sensations creeping up my hand where it rested in his.

Mikael didn't turn around as he answered, "It doesn't

matter. It's ancient history."

Unsatisfied with Mikael's answer, Alaric turned to me. Another scream cut through the air, followed by the sound of metal on metal. I could sense his tension, and knew he was only moments away from pulling out of my grasp to run back toward the village.

"Ignorance is bliss," I explained weakly, clutching onto his hand.

Ire crossed his face. He pulled his hand away from mine, but didn't run. His gaze was on Mikael's back as he replied, "Only to those willing to play the fool."

Finally Mikael turned around and took a step toward us. I instantly felt like a dwarf with his 6'5" frame so near, and Alaric only a few inches shorter. "They're already dead," he hissed, daring Alaric to argue with him. "It is not for us to tangle the strings of fate."

Alaric stared at Mikael for a heartbeat, then turned his astonished expression to me. "You knew," he whispered as more screams reached us.

"Let us leave this place," Mikael said through gritted teeth, flexing his hands impatiently.

We both stared at him, knowing we had no choice, but unable to make the decision to move forward.

He spun on his heel and marched away, leaving a cloud of angry emotions in his wake. The decision made for us, Alaric and I began walking while I did my best to shut out the sounds of battle in the distance. Instead I focused on Mikael's back. His emotions were slowly sliding away, being shut back behind his normally impenetrable shields.

I didn't need to be an empath to know how much the move had cost him, and I didn't need to be a psychic to know I'd have a hell of a time finding my way past those shields again.

CHAPTER NINETEEN

We continued walking as ominous clouds gathered overhead. The sounds of battle had faded long ago, leaving us with only the whistling of the wind to break the silence. Medieval Scandinavia might have been a blustery, rainy place in general, but as ice cold raindrops began to hit my face, it felt like the universe was mocking me. First, fate saw me kidnapped, then tortured, then nearly sacrificed to free the little key around my neck. As if that wasn't enough, Lady Fate continued on to see me shackled to said key, pregnant, and hunted by the majority of the Vaettir. Cold rain and no shelter was just icing on the cake.

The three of us continued on in silence, not remarking on the rain. Though it was uncomfortable, it was the least of our worries. I wanted to ask Mikael how we would travel through time without the Norns, and I wanted to ask him what we would do after that, but I was afraid to prod the beast. His raw emotions were still too fresh in my mind, though I felt nothing from him now as he walked beside me.

"What did she tell you?" Mikael asked suddenly, breaking the silence and making me jump.

Alaric and I both turned to watch him as we continued walking.

"I spoke to her after she met with you," Mikael went on, "but she wouldn't tell me. She simply said you knew what you needed to do."

I looked down at the ground ahead of us, still muddy from the previous day's rainfall, and bound to get muddier. My boots felt like they weighed a million pounds, and my clothing was beginning to take on the weight of moisture from the rain. I could at least unburden my thoughts and share everything Erykah had told me, but something stopped me. I had no doubt Mikael would allow me to sacrifice myself if it meant he would finally beat the sentient being that was the key, but Alaric would try to stop me. If not for my own well-being, then for our child's. I could just share the part about needing to break down Mikael's shields in order to learn how to build my own, but it might make Mikael close up even more. Still, I had no idea how to take down his shields without his help.

"I need you to teach me to shield my thoughts," I said finally, leaving out the implication that he needed to let his own shields down in order to show me.

Mikael stopped walking and turned to fully face me, while Alaric stood silently at my back. Mikael searched my face, as if to behold the importance of what I *wasn't* saying. Suddenly, he turned and began walking again.

Alaric and I had to jog to catch up with his long legs. "Well?" I pressed.

He wouldn't meet my eyes. "I don't know how. It's something that has always come naturally to me."

I grabbed his arm to halt his pace, then instantly regretted it. The angry look he gave me was nothing compared to the pain leaking through at my touch. My lips parted in surprise, and Mikael's eyes widened.

He shook my hand away and took a step back. "Stay out of my head," he growled.

I took a step back and bumped into Alaric's chest. "I didn't mean to," I replied instantly, feeling shaken.

I could almost *feel* Alaric smiling behind me as his hands protectively enveloped my upper arms. "But isn't that the whole point?" he taunted. "If she's to learn about your shields, you have to let her in. She must see inside your head, everything laid bare."

I was glad the look on Mikael's face was aimed above my head at Alaric and not at me. I *never* wanted to see an ancient Viking descended from a god glaring at me like that. Luckily, his expression softened as it dropped back down to my face. "Even if I *wanted* to let you into my head, I don't know how. Erykah broke my shields down without my consent. If you are not capable of doing that, then our plan has failed."

My head drooped. "Your shields come down in moments of extreme grief," I explained, avoiding eye contact. "In those moments I'm able to feel what you feel. If you can manage to rebuild that barrier more slowly next time, I might be able to learn how."

He gazed off in the direction we'd come. The village was miles away now. The carnage was likely over. He turned back to me. "The death of my people was the first and *last* grief I ever felt."

Alaric's hands flexed on my arms. "No grief for causing a woman's death after she helped to cover your tracks?" he snapped.

Mikael looked past me to Alaric. "I meant what I said," he stated, then turned and walked away.

I moved out of Alaric's grip and slid my hand around his waist. He obliged me by putting his arm around my shoulders. We gave each other a quick glance, then watched Mikael walk away.

Alaric's arm tightened around my shoulders. "He'll pay for his crimes before all this is over."

I watched Mikael round a bend in the wooded trail, disappearing from sight. Alaric and I had no choice but to follow. I wasn't so sure Mikael would be the one to pay. He was a survivor, after all. As we began walking, I could almost feel the noose of fate tightening around my neck.

"We're not going back in the direction we came," Alaric commented sometime later, as we continued to follow behind Mikael.

The Viking in question was still a good distance ahead of us, but occasional sightings of him let me know we were still heading in the right direction. I knew I should have been feeling a lot of emotions in that moment, but what I felt most was *hungry*. We had been walking for several hours, and were yet to stop to eat. Given Mikael was the one with a satchel full of supplies, and he didn't seem to be speaking to us, our prospects were not good.

"Does it matter?" I asked, narrowing my eyes as the trail straightened and Mikael once again came into view.

Alaric didn't seem tired or hungry in the least. In fact, he seemed at full alert, his eyes darting around the trail at the slightest hint of noise. The rain had subsided, but his dark hair still hung in wet clumps around his shoulders. "I had thought perhaps our way back to our time might lie in the spot we arrived, like a portal or some sort of vortex, but we've veered too far south. At this rate we'll miss that spot by several miles."

I shrugged. "Maybe we have to go somewhere else to get back."

"Or maybe we're not going back at all."

I stopped walking and faced him, feeling the barest hint of panic in my stomach. "Why would you say that? The whole point of coming here was for me to learn to control the key so we can use it to beat Estus. We can't beat him in a time where he doesn't even exist."

"Perhaps Estus is not Mikael's first priority," Alaric commented, grabbing my arm to guide me forward.

"B-but Mikael can't lie to me," I stammered, trying desperately to think of something that would mean Alaric wasn't right.

Alaric snorted. "And what has he told you of us being here? That you would gain information about the charm? Well, you have. He's told us nothing else."

I had the sudden urge to go running up the trail where I would violently shake Mikael until he told us what was going on, but I had a feeling it wouldn't turn out how I wanted. I thought back to the dance Mikael and I had shared the night before. He'd confided in me, and I'd felt bad for him. Was it all just manipulation? Did he intend to trap us here in a foreign time, where perhaps things were more to his liking?

I shook my head as I found my conclusion. "We're going back."

Alaric sighed. "And how do you know that?"

I smiled smugly. "Because Mikael hates to lose. Staying here would be too close to running."

Alaric stopped walking. At first I thought he was going to argue with me, but then I saw his expression. He held up a hand to keep me quiet while he tilted his head toward the twisting path in front of us, listening.

"I hear voices up ahead," he commented, face deep in concentration.

"Someone with Mikael?" I questioned, suddenly doubting my assertions of his intentions.

Instead of answering me, he continued to listen, though I couldn't hear a thing. I would forever be the feeble kid without any physical powers.

He straightened and turned to fully face me. "It seems like someone Mikael knows, but you should hide here just in case."

"I'm not going to stay here alone!" I rasped, taking a cue from Alaric on keeping my voice down.

Alaric quirked the corner of his mouth, revealing one of his dainty cat fangs. "Would you miss me?" he teased.

I glared at him. "I might miss you if a bear attacked me, but only then."

He grinned even wider and moved to put an arm around my shoulders. "Walk with me aways," he whispered, "but do not speak as we near their meeting place. You can hide out of sight before we reach them, far enough to not be seen, but close enough to not become bear food."

I nodded, too nervous to remark on the bear food comment. For all we knew, Mikael might be with more friendly people like those who'd perished in the village, but he also might have run into someone he didn't expect. Someone who might mean him, and by effect *us*, harm.

We continued walking. I did my best to be quiet, but my footsteps seemed thunderous next to Alaric's near-silent gait. Louder still was the groaning of my stomach. Back in the normal world I usually skipped breakfast, but I seemed unable to do that now. I wasn't sure if it was the pregnancy, or just stress, but my stomach was *not* happy with the situation.

Alaric chuckled softly at a particularly loud stomach growl, but didn't comment.

After a few more minutes I could finally hear the voices. Alaric stopped walking and gestured for me to hide. I glanced around for a good spot, but nothing jumped out at me. Finally, Alaric pointed to a bramble patch a few feet off the narrow path. I nodded, not liking the look of the plant's pointy leaves, but I could at least hide behind it and hope no one snuck up on me.

Alaric gave me a kiss on the cheek as I pulled away from him. With how he'd heard the distant voices, I knew he'd hear me if I screamed, and he ran faster than someone with a humanoid body should, so he'd reach me quickly. Of course, it would only take a few seconds for a bear, or other ancient woodland beast to break my neck. If I gave a bear in this time a hearty human meal, when it otherwise might have killed something else, would I alter the course of history? I shook my head at my thoughts as I crouched behind the brambles. I really needed to eat something.

I could still hear the voices as I waited in hiding. My clothes had nearly dried, but the ground was damp and loamy, making me not want to lower myself into a full seated position.

I heard the footsteps a moment too late. Before I could turn around, someone grabbed my arm and yanked upward. I was brought abruptly to my feet by a man roughly my height, wearing dirty wool clothing with leather bracers strapped over his forearms, and a wide, leather belt. His hair was even frizzier than mine, and its bright red color made it look like foamy fire.

He leaned his bearded face into mine and peered at me with one blue eye. Where the other eye should have been was nothing but a mass of scar tissue. He grinned, said something in Old Norsk that I didn't understand, then began dragging me toward the path.

Finally regaining my wits, I struggled against his grasp and yelled for Alaric. Though I was far from powerless, I couldn't steal the life from someone who wasn't weakened, and I hadn't taken the life of someone in a long time, so I had no pent up energy to wield. I cried out for Alaric, and moments later heard running footsteps thundering toward us.

The man jerked me violently forward, and I tugged back, screaming all the while. Before I knew what was coming, he had thrown back his arm, preparing to hit me.

Alaric, Mikael, and several other men reached us, just as my captor's fist was about to collide with my face. Without warning, the key around my neck came to life, and a burst of energy knocked the man backward, leaving me unscathed. I stumbled backward and raised my hand to clutch the little key at my throat without thinking. As soon as I realized what I was doing, I dropped my hand, but felt no less shaken.

One of the men standing with Mikael and Alaric muttered something under his breath that sounded like *völur*.

"She's not a witch," Alaric mumbled as he came to stand near me. He took my shaky hand in his and gave it a squeeze.

I leaned in close to him before I spoke, even though no one there besides Alaric and Mikael would understand me. "I take it they're not Vaettir?" I questioned, since they seemed somewhat astonished by what had transpired.

Alaric shook his head. The man I'd knocked down got to his feet and shot me a venomous, if somewhat frightened look, then went to stand with his comrades. One of the other men barked something vehemently at Mikael while pointing to me. All the other men watched me cautiously. I did *not* like where this was going.

The man speaking, apparently the leader, judging not only by the way he took command of the situation, but by the style of his clothing, took a step toward me. He swept aside a vibrant blue cloak, held in place by an oval, bronze broach at his shoulder. His golden blond hair was held back from his face, gathered in a bun at the nape of his neck. His beard was neat and well trimmed.

He said something that sounded scathing while he glared at me with dark gray eyes, his hand on the massive ax at his belt.

Mikael took a step forward and said something calmly, causing the lead Viking to turn and face him, a look of surprise on his face.

Alaric leaned in close to my ear. "Mikael revealed that he has sworn a blood oath to you, one that requires vengeance should anyone harm you."

I held my breath in surprise, then whispered, "That second part is a lie."

Alaric snorted. "And Mikael is the God of Lies."

I wasn't going to argue with Alaric, and I wasn't going to call Mikael out on his little fib. The men facing us all looked unsure now, including the leader. It was obvious they held a great deal of respect for Mikael, or at least knew his capabilities.

The leader gave me a final glare, then turned to Mikael and said something else.

"He says we will make camp with them tonight," Alaric explained. "But that the *witch* must agree to harness her powers."

The leader looked at me expectantly. I nodded, hoping the gesture meant the same thing in this time as it did in ours. It seemed to be enough for him, as he turned back in the direction most of the men had come from, expecting everyone to follow.

Mikael fell back in line beside me, while Alaric walked on my other side.

"Thank you," I muttered, hoping his sour mood had come to an end.

"I would have killed them," he replied, "but I fear the wrath of Lady Fate. I need you for my plans, so I had to protect you somehow."

His tone made it clear he was referring to me like a tool, just like many of the other Vaettir had done. I hated to admit it, but it stung. Until then, Mikael had at least treated me like a person. "And here I thought we were friends," I replied bitterly, unable to keep my emotions fully to myself.

"You are a means to an end, Madeline," he said coldly, then trudged on ahead to walk next to the lead Viking.

I looked to Alaric, expecting some sort of sarcastic remark, but his expression was serious as he turned his gaze from Mikael's back to my face. "He is a means to an end for us as well," he stated. "Let us not forget that."

I nodded, then looked down at the ground as we walked. Alaric was right, but I didn't like it. I wasn't used to using people like chess pieces. It was only in that moment that I realized how much I missed having friends. Alaric was the closest thing I had to a real friend, though our short history was obviously complicated. I considered Sophie a friend, but wasn't sure if she viewed me the same. I'd even somehow started to view Mikael as a friend, but he wasn't. It seemed all Vaettir would always view me as a tool first, and a person second, if at all. It was damn lonely.

I looked up at the cloudy sky, feeling numb and achy. No one would even care if I ever returned to the correct time. Sophie would be waiting for Alaric. Aila and the rest of

Mikael's people would be waiting for him. For me, there was only Estus, waiting to kill me. I glanced over at Alaric. I was pretty sure *he* cared what happened to me. The child inside me probably cared too. It was more than I'd had a month before, and would have to be enough for me now.

I glanced up at Mikael's back with renewed determination. If the Viking wanted to play, the least I could do was give him one hell of a game.

CHAPTER TWENTY

"Slow down," James pleaded.

"We can't let them get any farther away," Sophie snapped. "I won't risk them entering another Salr where I won't be able to find them."

"How do you know that hasn't already happened?" James huffed, stomping up beside her.

She'd stopped to scent the wind. James' sweaty man-smell was confusing her senses. She glared at him, and knew her feline eyes were likely reflecting in the moonlight by the way he gasped.

"I hate it when you go all cat-like," he grumbled, looking down at his shoes.

"Says the man that can sear flesh with a single touch," she quipped before starting off again. They were close.

Sophie had retraced their steps back to the tunnel entrance where they'd parted ways with Aila and a few other members of Mikael's clan. It hadn't even been a full twenty-four hours since that meeting, so the scent was still fresh. With the distant wail of sirens spurring her on, she'd traced the scent all the way to where they now searched, a remote area of the woods, far northeast of the Salr where they'd first met Mikael.

Sophie stopped to scent the air once more, then perked up at the sound of far off conversation. The voices were speaking Old Norsk, letting her know they were Vaettir, and not the police who were likely looking for the villains who'd left several corpses in a quaint, suburban neighborhood. The only question was if the people speaking belonged to Estus, Aislin, or Mikael.

She continued listening as she crept near, gesturing for James to stay behind. She didn't need his lumbering steps giving her away.

As the camp came into sight, the first form she saw was very tall, and very blonde. Sophie's smile was more of a snarl. She shouldn't go charging into the situation with brute force, but it was the only way she knew how.

I sat in a secluded area with Alaric, near the Viking camp. We were close enough to the sea that I could hear the waves crashing in the distance. A lot of people find the sound soothing, but it just made me nervous. I'd always been afraid of deep waters, even more than heights.

Not wanting to sit around while Mikael's human *friends* stared at me, Alaric and I had built a small fire of our own. We sat on a piece of driftwood, huddled near the flames for warmth.

I had a moment of wishing for our more comfortable lodgings of the night before. My heart lurched. Those lodgings were likely now burned to the ground. The people who had thrown Mikael a party the night before, dead in the cold night air.

"What are you thinking?" Alaric asked softly, startling me away from my morbid thoughts.

I jumped at his voice, then settled down to lean my shoulder against his. "What makes you think I was thinking anything?"

He put his arm around me and pulled me closer. "You had a look on your face like someone had just kicked your puppy. Were you thinking about the baby?"

I shivered. "It still sounds weird to hear you say that. We've travelled back in time, left a village full of people to their deaths, and were accosted by genuine Vikings, yet the pregnancy is the part that doesn't feel real."

He laughed. "I imagine it will begin to seem real as more time passes, and certain things begin to . . . show."

I turned my head and quirked an eyebrow at him. "You mean when I blow up like a balloon?"

He laughed again, using his free hand to push his tangled hair out of his face. "Something like that. Did you have enough to eat?"

I glanced over at the large wooden bowl we'd shared for our supper and wrinkled my nose. My vegetarian senses had not been pleased by the choice of fresh caught rabbit with hard, root vegetables, but I'd been so starved I ate anyway.

"More than enough," I replied, my distaste coloring my tone.

The sound of rustling branches and movement to our left caught our attention. Mikael appeared within the trees, then approached. I had no particular desire to share our fire with him, however, he might by slim chance tell us what we had to do to get home.

He looked right past me to Alaric. "I need to speak with Madeline."

Alaric didn't move. "No one is preventing you from doing so."

Mikael looked to me. I expected to see the harsh resentment I'd seen earlier, but there was an almost pleading feel to his expression.

I sighed, and looked to Alaric.

Picking up on what I wasn't saying, he frowned. "Are you sure?"

I smiled gratefully. "It's not like he's going to hurt me."

Alaric looked up at Mikael, then back to me. "If you say so." With that, he stood and walked off, not toward the rest of the camp, but further into the woods.

Mikael closed the distance between us, then took Alaric's vacated seat. I scooted away, but it was a small log. We still ended up shoulder to shoulder. I sat silently, partially turned away from him, waiting for him to speak.

He inhaled loudly, then exhaled with no words forthcoming.

I still didn't face him, feeling that it would somehow thwart his effort.

He finally spoke. "We can try working on the shielding thing."

The exasperated tone in his voice drew my eye to him. "What made you change your mind?"

He had the grace to look almost embarrassed. "If Erykah thinks—*thought* it's what needs to be done, then it will be done."

I knew it was a bad idea to say anything, especially with how he'd reacted earlier, but I couldn't help it. I placed my hand on top of his. "I'm sorry."

He didn't get angry, and instead smiled sadly. "Honestly, I was surprised you even told me the plan. Erykah manipulated my emotions and broke me down without warning. One would think it better to have me off guard."

I smirked. "Manipulate a descendant of Dolos, god of deceit and treachery? That seems like a losing battle."

Mikael laughed, and I suddenly realized that my hand was still on his. I withdrew it as inconspicuously as possible, though the act drew his gaze. "Dolos was simply misunderstood," he explained. "He was practically a slave to Prometheus, and copied his master's statue to show he was just as skilled. Prometheus stole the statue and claimed it was his own, and thus lies were formed."

I raised my eyebrows in disbelief. "Oh okay," I replied sarcastically. "So if deceit doesn't run in your blood, then how did you manipulate entire nations?"

He smiled, wiping away the rest of the sadness that had lingered on his face. "I see someone has been telling stories about me."

"That doesn't answer the question," I countered before he could change the subject.

He shrugged. "Through deceit and treachery."

I raised a finger in playful accusation. "But you just said that Dolos wasn't the god of those things."

Mikael grinned. "Did I? I'm pretty sure I just said he was misunderstood."

I frowned. He was playing games with me, and derailing the entire conversation from the original subject. "Misunderstood how?" I asked, giving in.

"By perceptions," he replied, holding up his hands to warm them by the fire. "Two men can commit the same *treacherous* act. One may be labeled a swindler, and the other, simply clever. There is no difference."

I stared into the fire. "The difference lies in how the man's actions affect others."

Mikael turned his gaze to me, and I suddenly had the feeling that I'd lost points in our verbal debate. "Oh?" he questioned. "And what about you? Should you be labeled a server of justice, a guiding hand, or a murderer?"

He was probably hoping to shock me with the term *murderer*, but I'd spent way too much time thinking upon it myself to be caught off guard. Without thinking, I replied, "If I was taking the life of someone who'd committed heinous crimes, then I'd be serving justice. If it was someone who wanted to die, a guiding hand. An innocent . . . well, I suppose that would be called murder."

"Yet each of those things depends on who you ask," he countered. "Say my best friend harmed someone in a crime of passion, and you took his life as justice. Most might call you the righteous executioner. I'd just call you a killer."

I grinned at him.

He leaned back slightly in surprise. "Whatever could have crossed your mind at that example?"

"I was just thinking that your example wasn't an accurate representation of the truth."

He seemed to think about my answer, then replied, "And why is that?"

I grinned even wider. "Because no one would want to be your best friend in the first place."

He threw his head back and laughed, obviously not offended. At that moment, a few flakes of snow began to fall. Mikael reached out a hand to catch them, seeming almost like a little kid marveling at the miracle of snow.

Seeing his good mood as an opportunity, I asked, "So where are we going now, *really*?"

He retained his smile as he replied, "We're going to seek a little more information, then hopefully find our way home."

"*Hopefully?*" I questioned, all of Alaric's observations rushing back to the forefront of my mind.

He patted my leg with his hand, and I shifted away, suddenly nervous. He sighed. "Everything in life is a gamble, my dear. The Norns in this time do not owe me favors like the ones in our present."

"Well I'm glad you've risked our lives, our futures, and the life of our child all in one fell swoop," a sarcastic voice called from within the tree line.

Mikael turned to me with a conspiratorial look. "Do you ever get tired of his kitty cat hearing?" he whispered.

Before I could answer, Alaric revealed himself and approached the fire. He seemed to fit right in with the surroundings in his dark, wool and linen clothing, and borrowed cloak. His loose, black hair had begun to gather snowflakes, little flecks of white amongst the solid darkness.

"Your lives, futures, and the life of your child were already at risk," Mikael said happily. "Can you really argue that you had anything to lose?"

"We left my sister in that time," Alaric replied coldly, gazing off into the distance rather than at Mikael.

"It was my intention to bring her," Mikael replied blandly.

I realized his hand had come to rest on my leg again, and I scooted away, trying not to draw attention to myself. I had a feeling Mikael would find a way to flirt even as the fires of the underworld leapt up to drag us all to our fate.

"So we could all die together?" Alaric asked, taking a step closer.

Mikael laughed. "On the contrary. There are far fewer people who want to kill us in this time. We could easily live out our days here."

Before I could blink, Alaric was standing directly in front of where Mikael sat. "You *do* intend to keep us here, don't you?" he accused. "If you wanted to come live in this time, that's one thing, but why drag us into it?"

Mikael sighed, seemingly unintimidated by the fact that Alaric's eyes had shifted to feline, and he was flexing his fists like he might suddenly sprout claws. "I was simply pointing out that your deaths are not on my agenda," Mikael answered tiredly, "and I have no intention of trapping either of you in this time. There is nothing for me here."

"Things are just as you want them in this time," Alaric countered. "You have your freedom. You can manipulate others into following you without fear of being struck down by the other Vaettir."

"I have already lived this life!" Mikael shouted as he suddenly stood, placing himself inches away from Alaric. More calmly, he continued, "In my mind, everything here is already ash. It pervades my senses with its acrid stench, with every step I take, with every word I breathe."

Alaric was silent. The two men stood there, inches away from each other, with Mikael's head towering slightly above Alaric's. Their anger made my skin itch, muddling my thoughts with their opposing energies. Mikael was like the angry seas he'd traveled in his youth, and Alaric was like a cool, still, night, his rage contained beneath the surface.

I started to feel nauseous, and at first thought it was from the overwhelming energy, then a sharp, stabbing pain seared through my abdomen. "Uh guys?" I questioned weakly, clutching at my middle.

They didn't seem to hear me, too enthralled in their stare-down. The key started thrumming at my neck, though I had no idea why. The pain grew, and I fell from the log I'd been seated on to my knees.

"Guys?" I said again, and they both finally turned to look at me, identical, questioning expressions on their faces.

I couldn't answer their questions as the pain doubled. The key at my neck felt like it had been resting in fire. I was sure it was burning my skin, but I couldn't lift a hand to reach it. I fell to the side, but Alaric knelt and caught me before my shoulder could hit the ground. He sat and pulled me backward into his lap.

Seconds later, Mikael was by my side. The pain exploded into a wracking nausea. I would have vomited if my body were able to move forward. I looked dizzily past Mikael to the falling snow, with Alaric's arms wrapped around me. I was pretty sure they were both speaking to me, but I couldn't hear them. Everything had gone numb. All I could think about was how pretty the snowflakes were, and how nice they felt on my hot skin.

CHAPTER TWENTY-ONE

I woke up feeling warm. A little *too* warm. I could feel bodies pressed against either side of me. Something was wrong with this picture. I opened my eyes, recalling the pain in my abdomen, and the key burning at my throat. I freed my hand from being pinned by someone's arm around my waist, then reached up to my throat. The key felt cool to the touch, and my skin was unmarred.

I turned my head to the side to see Mikael's sleeping face, only inches from mine.

"What the hell!" I shouted, turning on my side to shove him away from me.

He opened his eyes with a start, just as I felt arms convulse around me from behind.

"Oh come now," Mikael mocked, making no move to get up. "I was having the most marvelous dream." He waggled his eyebrows at me suggestively.

The person behind me shifted, and Alaric's face came into view beside mine. We were in a small hide tent, with rough bedding encasing us. Alaric stared past me at Mikael as he explained, "After you fainted, your entire body went cold. I felt it pertinent that you were warmed, no matter the cost."

He was being very polite, especially with how Mikael was still grinning beside us.

"Thank you for your warmth," I said through gritted teeth while I glared at Mikael, "now please go away."

Finally he scooted out of the blankets and crawled toward the covered opening to the tent. "You kids sit tight," he instructed. "I'll be back soon."

Once the thousand plus year old Viking had departed, I rolled over to look at Alaric, who still had an arm around my waist. "The warmth *so* wasn't worth it," I said sarcastically. "He'll be going on about this for days."

Alaric frowned. "Maddy, we thought you were dying, or at the very least that you were losing the baby. If *I* could deal with being that close to Mikael, I figured you could too."

I frowned in reply, not liking his serious tone. The pain in my stomach was gone, though I still felt a little weak. I reached down toward my abdomen, as if somehow I could tell that the baby was still there, then quickly retracted my hand. It was too early to be able to tell just by touching. Heck, I hadn't even known I was pregnant until Mikael told us.

"Do you think . . . " Alaric trailed off, and I knew he was trying to ask about the baby.

I shook my head. "I'm not sure."

His face fell. I really hadn't expected him to become so invested in the idea of a child. He was a being of war. He *lived* for violence and chaos, both of which weren't exactly conducive to raising a child.

"I'm sure it's fine," I lied, wanting to wipe the hurt expression from his face.

Not replying, he drew me into a tight hug.

I felt guilty even just admitting it to myself, but part of me would be relieved if the child was gone. Not only had I not planned on having children, but I was terrified of what this child in particular might turn out to be. I wouldn't wish my calling upon anyone. The idea of having to teach my child to take the lives of others was horrifying. Even if it didn't end up just like me, we were still Vaettir. Our child would be destined for a life of violence and death regardless.

"What are you thinking?" Alaric asked with his face still pressed against mine.

"Nothing," I lied again. "Just wondering what supplies Mikael is off . . . procuring."

Alaric pulled away from me to flash a knowing smile. "Dating an empath is quite unfair. You always know what I'm feeling, but I cannot read you in return."

I cringed. "Sorry?"

Alaric kissed me softly before I could say anything else. I kissed him back, glad to put an end to the conversation. For the moment, we would just have to worry about getting home, then we could use modern medicine to determine if the child was still present.

I heard footsteps and a snuffling sound outside of the tent, moments before Mikael called out, "Knock, knock!"

Alaric and I pulled away from each other and sat up. He reached the tent flap first, pulling it aside to reveal a landscape dusted with pure, white snow. Amidst the near blinding white of early morning reflecting off ice stood Mikael, holding the reins of three stout, shaggy ponies.

I let Alaric help me out of bed, thanking my lucky stars that I had been left fully clothed. I searched the bedding to find that my coat had been draped over the blankets that had covered my legs. I donned it quickly, shivering as a cold gust of snowy air filtered into the tent, then took the boots Alaric handed me just as he finished wrapping up his own boots.

I put the boots on quickly, grateful to find that I finally had the hang of neatly wrapping up the strips of leather to anchor the boots around my ankles. Alaric left the tent, then offered me a hand out. I took his hand gratefully and stood, waiting for Mikael to make whatever sarcastic remark he was holding in.

I watched his face as he stood there, still holding onto the ponies, but instead of speaking, he offered me a *knowing* smile. A smile that said, *I just slept next to you all night, my body pressed firmly against yours, and there's nothing you can do to take it back.*

I scowled and gave Alaric's hand a squeeze, almost wishing Mikael would go back to being mad at us.

"Am I expected to ride that thing?" I asked, turning my attention to one of the ponies.

"It's likely not wise to exert yourself after what you experienced last night," Mikael explained.

I frowned and looked back to the animals. One of the ponies was pure white, looking innocent and pristine, while the other two were muddy brown in color. Guess which one I got.

I took the offered reins from Mikael and rubbed my chilled fingers across the animal's white neck. She bumped against me obligingly, so I snuggled up to her side while Mikael and Alaric packed up the tent and bedding.

When we were ready to go, I stepped back and put the reins over the animal's head, then prepared to insert my foot into the stirrup to climb onto the pony's back, only there was no saddle, only a rough blanket. I wasn't quite sure how to climb up without a stirrup to guide me. The ponies were fairly short, so maybe I could have hoisted myself, but I was feeling shaky enough that I was afraid to try. Finally, Alaric moved to my side and gave me an effortless boost, allowing me to climb onto the horse with little to no exertion on my part. Once seated, I steadied myself. I would still have preferred a saddle, but at least the pony was wide enough to make me feel secure in my seat. I looked down at Alaric with a reassuring smile, then he left me to take his reins from Mikael.

Before climbing atop the final pony still in his possession, Mikael came to stand beside me, digging for something in the satchel hanging from his shoulder. With his height, and how short my pony was, we weren't that far from eye level. He pulled his hand out of the satchel and offered me something akin to a pastry, only larger and round.

I raised an eyebrow at him. "Sweets for breakfast?"

"Aren't pregnant woman supposed to crave this sort of stuff?" he teased.

He'd meant it in a joking way, but my mood instantly fell. Was I even still pregnant? Did I want to be? With the threat of the key, I'd probably be better off without a child growing inside of me, but I'd also become attached to the little life.

Not commenting on my sudden change of mood, Mikael left me with the pastry in my hand, then climbed atop his pony while Alaric did the same. They both made their way to the main path while I followed shortly behind. I took a large bite of the pastry-like item. I *was* craving sweets, not that I was about to admit it. It was likely just a result of the long periods I've gone without calories.

Eventually the path widened into a road, and we were all able to ride side-by-side.

"Where did your friends go?" I asked, tired of the silence that had drawn out when the path was narrow.

Mikael startled, as if deep in thought, then glanced over at me, pushing a lock of hair away from his face. "Friends?"

"The ones that wanted to kill me for being a witch," I clarified.

Alaric snorted from my other side, but didn't comment.

"Well," Mikael sighed, "I had to defend your honor, so I killed them."

My jaw dropped. He had to be joking, right?

He let me off the hook with his laughter, then explained. "They invited me to sail with them, but I told them I had prior obligations. They departed first thing this morning," He was silent for a moment, then added, "While we were all nestled, warm in our bed."

I scowled.

He winked in reply.

"How much farther until we reach our destination," Alaric interrupted tiredly. Mikael had attempted to give him a sweet roll too, but he'd refused, and had seemed dejected ever since.

Mikael pointed off into the distance to a rising hill covered in the same sparse trees surrounding us. I could barely make out stone ruins near the top of the hill, but little else.

"Are there more Norns in our near future?" I asked, hoping the ruins would mean an end to our journey, and a return to modern times.

"Just one," he answered, gazing off into the distance ahead.

"*One?*" Alaric asked incredulously. "And that will be enough to send us back?"

Mikael chuckled. "Absolutely not, but she might have something that will aid us. She did it for me once before . . . " he trailed off.

He had to be referring to the first time he went back in an attempt to save his village, but I wasn't about to bring that up again. Before I could say anything, Alaric grumbled, "This better not be a waste of time."

Mikael smiled. I really wished I knew what he was finding so damn funny. "All will be revealed once we reach the crest of the hill," he explained cryptically.

Yeah, that's what I was afraid of.

CHAPTER TWENTY-TWO

It had started snowing again. I did my best to stay warm, huddled against the cold on my white pony. The animal's breath fogged the air near its muzzle as it labored onward. We'd nearly reached the top of the hill. The roadside, sprinkled with chunks of old stone covered in moss, was becoming quickly obscured in white.

Mikael rode ahead of us. He seemed unfazed by the cold, even as little white snowflakes began to cling to his loose, dusky red hair. He looked odd atop the little pony, especially with the intimidating touch of his great sword's pommel jutting over his shoulder.

I looked to Alaric as his pony caught up to mine. He looked worried. "Are you warm enough?" he asked softly.

My teeth were on the verge of chattering, but I nodded. It didn't really matter how cold I was, since there was nothing I could do about it.

Mikael's pony turned away from the path ahead of us. From our vantage point, and with snow obscuring our vision, it appeared he was riding straight into the mountainside on one side of the path. I had a moment of confusion before realizing he was riding into a cavern.

Alaric and I urged our ponies forward, anxious to get out of the cold.

The cave came into view, its entrance roughly eight feet tall. The opening would have seemed man-made if we were in a time where dynamite was used for mining. I could see Mikael inside the cave, dismounting his pony, but I could make out little else. Alaric rode in first, while I followed cautiously behind him.

Once inside, I observed the deceivingly large space until we reached Mikael and dismounted. The cavern was empty. No Norn. No signs of inhabitance. Nothing.

"What gives?" I asked, finally giving in and letting my teeth chatter.

Mikael calmly crouched down and began building a fire in the center of the cave. The ceiling was high enough we likely wouldn't get smoked out, and upon closer inspection, I could see that fires had been built there in the past, and there was even spare wood that Mikael was using now.

"Sit down," he instructed. "We may have to wait a while, and in the meantime, I'd like to tell you a story."

"We don't want to hear any stories," Alaric said coldly. "We want to know why you've led us to a deserted cave."

Mikael looked up from what he was doing to smirk at Alaric. "The story is for Madeline's benefit, and trust me, she wants to hear it."

I sat down with a huff as Alaric took my pony's reins. Arguing would be futile, so it was best to just get it over with.

Mikael stared Alaric down until he grudgingly sat beside me, trailing the ponies' reins in his left hand. The animals seemed content to be out of the snow, showing no hints that they planned to run. Mikael had released his pony completely.

As Mikael's fire caught, he sat down across from us and cleared his throat. "In the beginning," he began, "there was Yggdrasil, the World Tree."

"I've heard of that before," I interrupted.

Mikael rolled his eyes. "Yes, Madeline, many myths are founded in truth, though they become convoluted over time. Now no more interruptions." He eyed me until I nodded. "In the myths," he continued, "the Norns gathered around Yggdrasil's roots, and tended the tree. Really, they *were* the tree."

"I don't remember that part of the story," Alaric interrupted.

Mikael glared at him. "That's because you've been told the convoluted version that was altered to suit those in power. Now please, no more interruptions."

Alaric gave a sarcastic roll of his hand for Mikael to go on.

"The Norns are the weavers of fate," Mikael continued, his face illuminated by the fire to look somewhat sinister, "and Yggdrasil held them in place, merging time and fate. Within the bounds of time and fate, there is polarity. Light and dark. Life and death."

It wasn't the first time polarity had been mentioned to me. Like Alaric had said, life needed death, peace needed war, and so forth.

"After many centuries," Mikael continued, "the Norns grew lonely. They plucked the strings of fate for humanity, watching people live and die, passing on their legacy to their children. The Norns wanted children of their own, and thus, the Vaettir were created."

I wrinkled my brow in confusion. So we were the Norns . . . children?

Mikael raised his eyebrows at me, daring me to interrupt him again. When I didn't, he continued, "The Norns embody all things in nature, as it is the divine force within us all. This energy also composed the old gods. Each of these new children embodied an aspect of the old gods the Norns missed so dearly, minor and major deities alike."

I glanced at Alaric, then back to Mikael, both embodiments of major deities, but not the highest tier.

"But the plan backfired," Mikael stated abruptly. "With each of the Vaettir embodying only one aspect of nature, they were far different from the Norns. The darker forces weren't directly balanced by the light. Forces of greed, the thirst for power, and stubborn independence led to the dismemberment of the World Tree."

I had become so enthralled in his story that I gasped, then held a hand to my mouth in embarrassment.

Alaric put an arm around my shoulder as Mikael flashed me a teasing grin.

We were divided, a voice said, but it wasn't Mikael speaking. The voice was in my head. I looked to Alaric to see if he'd heard it too, but he'd already turned to find the source of the voice.

I followed his gaze to a tall silhouette, blocking much of the cave's entrance.

The voice in my head continued, *Our children destroyed Yggdrasil, and separated us from time.*

The form stepped forward, revealing a Norn with the great antlers of a moose. I could make out little else of her figure.

The separation created myself and my sisters as we are now, she continued, speaking directly into our minds. *It let time dictate itself freely, while we remain in stasis. The division did little harm, but there was something else. There was the magic that held us together. Wild, chaotic magic, that had been tainted by the residue of those who dismembered the tree. It formed a key.*

This time I wasn't embarrassed when I gasped. I reached up to the key at my throat. Could it be?

The Norn took another step forward so that I could see her green-tinged skin and large, angular eyes clearly in the firelight. She had the paws of a wolf at the ends of her arms. Her thin lips offered me a confusing smile.

"I told you that you wanted to hear my story," Mikael mocked.

I shot him a glare, then turned back to the Norn, willing her to tell me what I needed to hear. Alaric had shifted his hand to my leg. He watched the Norn just as apprehensively as I.

Are you ready? the Norn's voice echoed through my head.

"For wha—" I began to ask, but it was too late.

The air of the cave pressed down on me. I felt like all of my bones were being crushed. I opened my mouth to scream, but there was too much pressure for me to even make a peep. Just when I felt like I might die, I was thrust upward. The cave was gone, and I was surrounded by darkness, speckled with lights that stretched oddly in my vision as I sped by them. Alaric had lost his hold on my leg, so I was alone in the dazzling emptiness.

Suddenly I thudded to the ground, and it was as if time and space were rushing to catch up to me. The scenery around me blurred with motion until it all came to a crashing halt, leaving me in my still surroundings.

Moist sand soaked into the knees of my pants, and I could hear the ocean not far off. The sky was a calm, perfect blue. I turned my gaze upward to what was towering over me. It was a tree, growing straight out of the beach, its roots twisting upward out of the sand to swirl in a dizzying pattern, forming the tree's bark. From the top, its branches spanned outward, obscuring the sky with their silvery, pointed leaves.

Somehow I knew the tree was an ash tree, and I knew its name. Yggdrasil. The Norn had transported me back in time to lie at the roots of the friggin World Tree, sometime before it was destroyed.

Even worse. I was alone.

Sophie sat on her butt in the dirt, glaring at those who surrounded her. James sat beside her, looking thoroughly cowed.

"What did you do?" Aila demanded, standing over Sophie like a Viking goddess of war.

Sophie frowned. She was descended from Bastet, a true goddess of war, not this, this *imposter*.

"You were supposed to go with Alaric and Madeline," Aila continued. "You shouldn't be back already. Where is Mikael?"

Faas and Tabitha stood behind Aila. Faas was short for a man at 5'7", and definitely short compared to Aila and Tabitha. He watched the conversation curiously, void of the venomous expression he'd had around Madeline. Sophie would never understand the rivalry all executioners seemed to hold to. She had little doubt Faas would kill Madeline, given the chance.

Noticing Sophie's gaze, he flipped the long portion of his blond hair to partially obscure his eyes. It would have worked better had all his hair been long, but the sides were shaved nearly to the skin.

Tabitha stepped up beside Aila, appearing slight near Aila's muscular form, despite their almost equal height. Tabitha's blonde hair was nearly white, a common color among Mikael's people. "Perhaps she escaped," Tabitha commented, not seeming to care much either way.

Sophie was growing increasingly irritated as those speaking continued to exclude her. She would have liked to stand, but the axes and spears of other Vaettir surrounding her and James kept her seated. She could probably take most of them on in a fight, but without her brother to watch her back, she didn't dare risk it.

"Where the hell is my brother!" she growled, interrupting the murmurs of conversation that had sprung up around her.

"See?" Tabitha replied, looking at Aila instead of Sophie. "She must have been left behind."

Aila replied with a sharp nod, then crouched down to grab Sophie's arm, hauling her to her feet. Sophie was built more like Tabitha, and was only a few inches taller than Faas. She found Aila's size slightly intimidating, though she would never admit it out loud.

"You will wait with us until Mikael returns with the others," Aila stated. She glanced down at James. "Him too," she added.

Sophie shook out of Aila's grasp, then scowled up at the imposing woman. "I will remain for the time being," Sophie agreed, "but if it takes too long, I'll find my brother myself."

Aila gave Sophie a wry smile. "As you wish," she agreed. "Now come with me. There are many plans to be made, and I will not turn down the advice of a descendant of Bastet."

Sophie stood a little straighter, glad her heritage had been acknowledged. "Really, I don't know how you ever intended to go to war *without* my advice."

Aila smirked, then turned to lead Sophie back toward one

of the many tents composing their camp. Sophie followed, leaving James where he sat, eyeing the Vaettir around him with apprehension. Sophie really would have to do something about his memory. Maybe she'd have Aila hit him. That amount of force would have to do *something*.

I stared up at the massive tree before me in complete awe. I didn't know at what point in history the tree had been destroyed, but I knew it had happened a very long time before the time I'd come from, and an unfathomable amount of time before the time I belonged in.

I rose to my feet and brushed the sand from my clothing. The key was silent at my throat. If I didn't know any better, I might have guessed it was afraid.

I turned and surveyed the empty beach, unsure of what I was supposed to do.

"Alaric!" I called out.

No answer.

"Mikael!"

All was silent.

I trudged through the sand toward the sound of the ocean, which came into sight as I crested a large dune. I would have liked to think Alaric and Mikael had been sent back with me, landing somewhere out of hearing range, but not too far off, yet for some reason I doubted it. Some sort of internal instinct screamed at me that I was completely alone.

I gazed out at the calm ocean. It was warmer here. The short leather and fur coat I wore was almost too much. I continued walking, stripping the coat off as I went.

I reached the shoreline and gazed down at the frothy water

as it lapped toward my feet, only to rescind with the tide. The water seemed normal enough. I found myself wishing I could see into its depths. If I was far back enough in time, all sorts of fascinating primordial creatures might lurk there.

I shook my head and stepped away from the water. I was back here to do *something*. Something important. I didn't have time to wonder about the mysteries of the deep.

I made my way back to the tree and stared up at it, not understanding how the Norns were *part* of the tree. I kept imagining them living inside of it, but I was pretty sure that wasn't how it worked.

I held my breath as the sound of hushed voices reached my ears, then suddenly silenced. I looked around, unsure of where they'd come from, then looked back to the tree. Not knowing what else to do, I reached up to the lowest branch and plucked a single leaf, then brought it close to my face. It looked like a normal leaf.

I gripped the leaf in my palm, then placed my other hand on the rough bark of the tree. The gentle ocean breeze pushed my hair back from my face, but everything else was still. I was about to remove my hand when I felt a gentle thrumming resonating from within the tree. The key at my neck echoed that resonance.

Excitement rushed through me, maybe I'd found what I was supposed to do. I felt the tree's energy flow up my arm as the key thrummed fervently. Wait. No! I watched in horror as the bark beneath my palm grew gray with death. The gray area spread, then pieces of the bark began to flake off, turning to ash before they hit the ground.

I tried to pull away, but my hand felt glued to the tree. The dead patch continued to spread. Hot tears streamed down my face. Panic crushed my chest. The Norn had sent me back to Yggdrasil to do who knows what, and now I was killing it. I was killing the World Tree.

I fell to my knees, but my hand remained firmly against the tree. I could feel the key's joy as we both filled up with energy. My thoughts turned to Alaric. What would he think if he could see me now? Killing the tree that gave life to his people. *Our* people.

Alaric's face filled my mind's eye as I focused all of my energy onto getting back to him. I needed to get back. There was still so much to do. Suddenly my hand fell from the tree, and I was overcome with a feeling of vertigo. I kept my eyes firmly shut as the sand beneath me seemed to solidify into hard, cold earth. Someone wrapped their arms around me, but I struggled away. I was a killer. The only thing I could offer anyone was death.

My entire body buzzed with the energy of Yggdrasil. I was pretty sure I'd broken away before I killed the tree entirely, but the only way to know for sure was to look at it.

I opened my eyes, and there was no tree. Suddenly the arms around me made sense. I was back in the cave with Alaric and Mikael. The latter of whom was standing a short distance away, looking at me like I'd grown a second head.

I slowly unfurled one of my closed palms to see the leaf still in my hand, still silvery-green with life. With the energy of Yggdrasil, I'd traveled forward through time. I craned my neck back at Alaric as he put his arms around me once more.

"I'm back," I whispered in astonishment.

"You never left," he explained. "The Norn came and you fainted."

I looked down at the leaf in my hand again. "That's not possible," I said distantly. It had all felt so real, and the leaf *definitely* was real. I could feel Yggdrasil's power running through my veins. It echoed in the little leaf.

"Hold on to me," I demanded, though my voice came out as the barest of whispers.

Alaric's arms tightened around me, but Mikael still stood a good distance off.

"Hold on to me," I stated again, this time with more force as I looked up at Mikael.

I tried to steady my thoughts, but all I could feel was anger. Anger at the Vaettir for being so screwed up. Anger at the key for controlling me. Most of all, I felt anger at myself, for being an instrument of death and destruction.

Both of the men did as I bade them. I closed my hand around the leaf, crushing the remaining life out of it. Its energy zinged up my arm, and I was disgusted at the satisfaction I felt. I would have liked to blame it on the key, but I knew part of it was my own emotion. Emotion springing from that deeply repressed instinct that makes us what we truly are. I was death, and I enjoyed it.

I squeezed my eyes shut as the remaining power from Yggdrasil lit up my veins to make me feel all-powerful. Unstoppable. It was a wonderful yet sickening feeling.

I thought of the Salr back in our current time where the Norns were. This time the movement was barely jarring. Before I knew it, I felt cold stone beneath me.

I opened my eyes and saw blood. The floor was drenched in it, and the stone walls were painted with it. The cool liquid began to soak into my pants as I sat there, stunned.

Mikael and Alaric were both more quick to react, dragging me to my feet and away from the macabre scene. As my eyes fully focused, I saw the first of the bodies, its antlered head twisted at a strange angle, its bestial paw reaching out past its body, as if begging for mercy.

Alaric held me close to him. "You have to release them," he whispered in my ear.

His voice seemed like it was a million miles away. My eyes darted around the room as I took in more corpses. "I can't," I replied numbly.

Alaric gave me a gentle shake as if trying to bring me back to reality. "Madeline," he coaxed, "you can't leave them in there. They're like us. They need to be released."

I shook my head. "No, I can't release them because someone already did."

It was the truth. I couldn't feel their pain, or their deaths. They were empty shells, nothing more. I recalled the amount of power I'd received from releasing a single Norn's life. Someone had come in here and released the lives of six. There were so many implications, but the one my mind honed in on was the fact that there was another executioner walking around out there with some serious juice.

Alaric had disappeared from my side without me realizing, and now returned to take my arm. "Sophie isn't here," he breathed, relief clear in his voice. "Neither is James."

Piecing things together, Mikael hoisted a small hand-ax up to his shoulder. "We need to make sure my people are alright."

I nodded, still feeling numb. I'd take numbness any day over the fear I knew would wash in eventually. "Where'd you get the ax?" I questioned.

Mikael smirked. "You didn't think I'd travel all the way back in time just to ask a few questions, did you?"

He turned on his heel and led the way out of the gory room. I did my best not to look at the corpses as we walked. If the Norns were, in a sense, our mothers, some serious matricide had just been committed. I felt a mixture of rage and guilt for their deaths. Rage, because they had been completely innocent, and guilt, because we had probably led the killer right to them. If we hadn't used the Norns to go back in time, they might still be alive.

Some might say pain and anger are the best fuels for vengeance, but in that moment, I knew better. Guilt fueled the fires of vengeance like nothing else. I had no doubt in my mind that taking the lives of the killers would be justice, not murder. I wouldn't be factoring anyone else's perspective into it.

There were many moments where I hated what I was, and what I had to do.

This moment was not one of them.

CHAPTER TWENTY-THREE

Sophie twirled around like a dancer, a long blade in each hand. This is what she lived for.

The attack came during the night. Aislin's people, by the look of it, given that Sophie didn't recognize any of them.

Sophie's blade met with flesh. She barely even registered whose life she had just taken, only that they were part of the enemy force. That was all that mattered. Aila had her back, swinging through the oncoming attackers with a giant ax.

To her left, Sophie barely registered Faas, releasing the souls from the fallen, and using that energy to injure or impede their enemies. With several attackers dead at her feet, Sophie took a moment to survey what had turned into a battlefield. Through the fighting, she thought she saw a glimpse of curly hair, and perfect, dark skin. Maya.

With a grunt of rage she rushed forward, leaving the ranks of Aila and the others. It was an unwise move as it left her back vulnerable to attack, but she couldn't help it. Maya had to pay for betraying her.

Sophie wove through the onslaught, darting around attackers like they were nothing. She knew her eyes and teeth had gone feline, and could feel her nails lengthening. She sheathed her dual blades at her waist as she ran. Killing Maya with her bare hands seemed a more fitting justice.

Just before she reached the area where Maya had been, something incredibly powerful knocked her off her feet. She fell to the bloody earth. There was a ringing in her ears, and she couldn't seem to move.

We raced forward as the first tents came into view. The sound of fighting was all around. Mikael had known exactly where to go. He let out a cry of rage as we reached the scene of the battle, and his people fighting for their lives. He rushed off, leaving me and Alaric on the outskirts, hidden in the trees.

We took a few steps closer, then the pain reached me. Bloodlust and fear were distant echoes, unable to rival the emotions of both physical pain, and the pain of losing friends and loved ones. It was all I could do to remain standing.

Alaric stayed back with me, though I could tell he wanted to race forward to find his sister. His resolve to protect me hung on a tenuous string, and I didn't blame him one bit. I would have rushed forward too if I could move.

Inside my head the key laughed, blocking out some of the pain. I stood a little straighter, grateful for the reprieve, but also fearful, knowing it was the key's influence that helped me shut things out.

I turned to Alaric, about to say we should move forward, then something swept across the battlefield like a shockwave. I watched in awe as the Vaettir in the distance were thrown like rag dolls.

Alaric stood immobile. "What was that?" he asked in

disbelief, finally taking another step forward.

I shook my head. I knew, but seemed unable to speak. I had felt that type of energy before, coming from my own hands.

"The power from the Norns," I said finally, as if it explained everything.

Apparently it did. Alaric grabbed my arm and dragged me backward. "You need to hide," he demanded. "If there's another executioner here with that much power, they'll kill you."

I knew he was going to leave me to see if Sophie was alright. "They'll kill you too!" I gasped.

He kissed me on the forehead, then pulled away. Before I could grab him, he was gone. To hell with that. I threw my body forward and ran after him, letting the key take control enough to block out everything on the battlefield. It was a mistake, but I saw no other choice.

I ran through the dark trees. Branches snagged at my clothing, inflicting superficial cuts on my flesh. It didn't matter. My lungs burned with exertion. Luckily the fight wasn't far off.

Moments later, I reached Alaric's side. He turned to scowl at me, but the moment was short lived as he returned his attention to more immediate threats. There were bodies all around us, many dead, but some still groaning in pain. It was like a giant wave had hit them, only there was no water. Judging by their clothing, it seemed like many of the victim's weren't Mikael's people. *Everyone* had been hit, with complete disregard for casualties.

At the center of the bodies stood a man, clothed in a form-fitting black coat, and matching black pants. Long hair that was either white or gray hung forward to cover his face.

Dark shapes milled about roughly twenty feet behind

him. More enemy troops, ready to kill off any survivors.

Distantly I could feel death around me. It was enough death to attempt destroying the key, but what then? If I could absorb all the power, I might be able to focus it, but if the destruction didn't take out the other executioner, surely he or the Vaettir waiting behind him would kill us soon after.

Alaric tried to tug me behind him, but I refused. I didn't deserve to be shielded. The key was muttering in my mind, near incoherent thoughts of excitement. It knew I couldn't destroy it then. I needed it to survive, or so it assured me. It was right.

Someone stepped around the still form of the other executioner, a small woman in an out of place ballgown. She even wore a little sparkly tiara on her head, glinting in the moonlight. Her face appeared middle-aged. Her hair, its color indistinguishable in the low light, was done in soft ringlets like a little girl would wear. I could feel the centuries she'd lived echoing outward as her cold eyes found me.

"Aislin, I presume," I called out, sounding much more confident than I felt. I could hear fighting in the distance, but it was far off. Those on the ground around us were all still.

"Smart girl," Aislin replied, a hint of English to her accent.

The key thrummed around my neck, and I knew the next words out of my mouth were not my own. "It would be wise for you to bow to your new ruler, little Doyen."

Rage crossed her face, but the emotion was almost instantly wiped away. She raised one delicate, gloved hand up to the executioner at her side, gesturing for him to act.

He threw back his arm, then began to bring it forward for another shockwave. In the split second I had to make a decision, I knew I had no choice. I opened my mind fully to the key. Suddenly, all I could feel were the dead around me. The key sucked in their energy, releasing their souls without me even having to touch them. The power flooded me, just as the other executioner's wave of energy shot forward.

My hand raised in front of me of its own volition. I felt Alaric at my side, trying to move me out of the path of the shockwave, but I was like a mighty tree rooted in the earth. He couldn't move me, and if he stayed where he was the shockwave would hit him too.

Just before the wave would have hit us, energy shot from my hand to intercept it. Though the individual energies would be invisible to the untrained eye, the collision caused an eruption of static electricity. It crackled blue in the darkness, from the ground to a good twenty feet up in the air. As the energy dissipated, both Aislin and the other executioner stared at me in awe, unharmed, but so were we.

The other executioner looked down at Aislin. His voice sounded strained as he said, "Her energy calls to me."

I had a feeling I wasn't supposed to hear him, but all of my senses were heightened. The key was still sucking in the life of everyone around me. Alaric stood at my side, strong and immune to my vampiric powers.

Both Aislin and the other executioner were staring at me. "Now is not the time," Aislin said finally.

They retreated, and I let them. Not allowing myself to think, I reached up and snapped the cord holding the key around my neck. I focused all the energy I'd absorbed onto the key dangling from my hand, spinning and glinting in the moonlight. Its screams of rage echoed through my mind.

It fought against me. Our similar powers ricocheted off each other, much like what had happened with the other executioner. I had the energy needed to destroy it, but I only had one piece of the puzzle. I knew how to do it, but if the key could predict my every thought, it could counter my every move.

I lowered the key and grunted in frustration.

Alaric came up behind me, pressing his hands tentatively on my shoulders. "Maddy," he said softly, "there are many injured. Maybe you can help them. I have to find Sophie."

I looked out across the fallen, ashamed that I had momentarily forgotten them. I tied the key around my neck as it gloated in my mind. I tried to send my stored energy out to Mikael's people, but the key blocked me.

I hissed in frustration. "We can't have a war if half of our army is dead," I said out loud.

"What?" Alaric called out as he scanned the dark for his sister.

I shook my head. What I'd said gave the key pause. A moment later, I was able to send my energy outward, searching for those who could be healed. I felt sick as I realized all the bodies nearest me were fully dead. I'd taken their lives without a second thought, even though some may have otherwise survived.

With a muffled sob, I turned my attention away from them and back to the wounded. I may have given death, but I could also heal. I could feel wounds being knit in the distance as if they were my own. I could even sense each individual, which was something entirely new. I sensed Mikael, and knew he had been injured in the blast, but would live, and I sensed Sophie, cradled in Alaric's arms as he found her, already healed, but dazed.

I stood in the cold moonlight, feeling two dozen lives in my mind, yet I felt entirely alone. I could sense the key above all else. It knew it had me. It knew I would never survive any of this without it. There was only one final choice to make, and the key offered it willingly. Would I be its partner, or its slave?

CHAPTER TWENTY-FOUR

We burned the bodies. The battle here had happened far from civilization, but some hiker would have discovered the grisly scene eventually. Heck, with the cops likely combing the land after we left them guessing back at Mikael's house, they might happen upon the scene sooner rather than later. We needed to minimize the evidence.

It felt odd to finally be back in modern times. The atrocities against Mikael's village would never be investigated. No one would ever be brought to justice. I had to say, I mostly appreciated the justice system of the modern times, even when it worked against me.

Hiding bodies was an anxiety inducing prospect, but wasn't the matter at the forefront of my mind. I'd missed my first chance to destroy the key. The whole purpose of starting a war was to give me enough energy to destroy it, but how do you destroy something that can see into your head? The answer, you don't. Erykah was right. I had to learn to shield my thoughts, else all was lost.

Aislin's people had retreated after I had neutralized her

executioner. Aislin knew exactly what the key was, I was sure of it. She knew she didn't stand a chance against it. I briefly wondered if she knew I'd killed her sister, or if she knew that her great-nephew James was among those her people had injured. He was fine now, except for the missing memory.

Alaric walked up beside me, stinking of smoke from burning the bodies. "We're done here."

I couldn't bring myself to meet his eyes. If only he'd known how close I'd come to losing myself entirely to the key. It was quiet now, but I was certain it could flood my thoughts again whenever it chose.

Sophie joined us, fully healed. Mikael and his people had marveled at the effect of my healing energy, since most executioners caused only destruction, but Sophie had merely been irritated. Maya had escaped her again, and that was all she had to express.

Mikael walked up out of the darkness, followed by Aila. Most of his people had been sent on ahead of us. "We need to move far from this place," Mikael stated. "I'm without many of my contacts, and can't cover up anything that's happened any more than we already have. The human police will likely be on a terrorist hunt quite soon."

I nodded, but didn't speak, thinking of the burned bodies. So much death had transpired, and only more would come.

"What will we do now?" I asked distantly.

Mikael gazed up at the moon. "Once we are safe, we plan the next battle. This time, it will be in a place and under terms of our choosing." He turned to Aila. "Scout the way ahead. Make sure no one waits in ambush."

Aila nodded sharply.

"I'll join her," Sophie volunteered, then looked to Alaric expectantly.

He waved sarcastically. "Have fun!"

Sophie placed her hands on her hips. "We have better eyes and ears than most. We'll be able to see any scouts before they see us."

Alaric grunted in reply, then glanced at me.

"I'll keep her safe," Mikael assured.

Alaric looked over my head at him. "Somehow, I don't find that comforting."

A moment later, Alaric, Sophie, and Aila slipped away. I felt the barest caress of Alaric's hand on my back as he left, leaving me with shivers as I stared back up at the moon.

"Your ability to heal . . ." Mikael trailed off.

I continued looking up at the sky. "Pretty good for a creature of death, eh?"

Mikael chuckled, then gently guided me forward as the few members of his clan left with us began walking.

Mikael glanced at me. "What exactly did you do right before that?"

Before I could answer, Faas walked past us, glaring all the while. He probably hated me even more now that I'd saved his life.

"Hmm?" I asked, watching Faas walk away. "Before what?"

"I've been told you defeated the other executioner. How?" he clarified. "He was a force to be reckoned with."

I winced, uncomfortable with what I'd done. Not only with *how* I'd saved us, but with the wary looks Mikael's people now gave me. They might be alive because of me, but it wouldn't stop them from being cautious. If I was a threat to Aislin, I was a threat to everyone.

I bit my lip, feeling uneasy about what I was going to admit. "The key took control. I let it."

At that moment I really wished I could sense Mikael's emotions, but he was giving me nothing. His face remained passive. "That was unwise, Madeline," he said finally.

Well, *duh*. "I tried to destroy it afterward," I explained, "but it knew my every move. I had the energy to do it, but the key had the energy too. When I attacked the other executioner, our energy collided. The same thing happened when I tried to attack the key. It fended off my every attack. I couldn't have even dropped it to the ground in that moment, that's how powerless I was."

Mikael sighed. "I suppose all of this is my fault."

I gave him a surprised look and almost tripped on a branch. He grabbed my forearm to keep me from falling, then let go as soon as I'd righted myself. "How so?"

"If I had taught you to shield when you first asked me, you might have been able to destroy the key."

I shook my head. "I doubt it's something I'll be able to learn in a day."

Alaric appeared in the woods ahead of us, then made his way toward us as we continued walking.

"All clear ahead," he explained upon reaching us, then fell into step beside me. "Sophie and Aila are looping back around to ensure we are not followed." He looked over my head at Mikael. "I'll scout further once you tell us where we're going."

"We'll need to split up again," Mikael explained. "We're too easy to track in a large group. We will only come together when we're ready to attack. There is another house at my disposal where we may hide."

"My sister stays with us," Alaric said instantly.

"Agreed," Mikael replied, "As will some of my people."

"What about James?" I interrupted. I hadn't even had a chance to talk to him since we'd gotten back. It seemed cruel to just leave him with a bunch of people he didn't know, even if he deserved it.

Mikael nodded. "Three for Madeline, and three for me."

"Aila, I'm assuming," Alaric guessed, "but who else?"

"Faas and Tabitha," Mikael answered.

I tripped again, and both men dove in to steady me. I seriously needed some rest. I was going to end up impaling myself on a branch. "Faas?" I questioned, feeling a nervous ripple in my chest. When I'd first met him, I'd been dying to ask him a ton of questions. Now, I would have preferred to be anywhere but near him.

Mikael gave me a knowing look. "There are few I would trust more."

I raised an eyebrow. "Do you trust him to not try to kill me?"

Mikael laughed.

Alaric grunted in irritation.

"I trust him to do as I command," Mikael replied.

I supposed that would have to be good enough. Really, with the forces currently gunning for me, one executioner with a bad attitude shouldn't worry me. I should be more worried about one who would kill the beings that created us just to ramp up his power, or about the two rulers hell-bent on gaining control over all. Still, it was Faas' cold, angry eyes that would haunt me that night.

CHAPTER TWENTY-FIVE

When Mikael had said *house*, I'd assumed he'd really meant a house. Something similar to the quaint little home we'd stayed in before being chased off by the police. The living room where our group now stood was as large as my entire little house back in Spokane.

The house's owners, an elderly couple, watched us excitedly from the entry room. The woman wore a classic sheath dress and pearls that made her look like an elderly version of Audrey Hepburn. Her husband was a little less dapper with his wrinkled plaid shirt and green trousers.

"Who are these people?" I whispered, leaning in close to Mikael's shoulder.

With us were Alaric, Sophie, James, Aila, Faas, and Tabitha. I thought again how I could have done without the latter three, or really, the latter four, but I hadn't chosen the arrangements. Mikael's people stood near him, and mine near me.

"They're my fan club," he answered mischievously, too far away for the old couple to hear.

I walked a few steps further into the living room. The

furniture was all over-stuffed, done in floral fabric heavy on the gold thread. The rug beneath our dirty boots probably cost several grand.

"Fan club?" I questioned softly as Alaric went to marvel at one of the painted landscapes on the wall. James stood near our hosts, seeming to prefer their less aggressive company.

"They're historians of mythology, more specifically of Dolos and Prometheus," Mikael explained. "They're quite fond of me."

"But they're human," I argued. I didn't really know that for a fact, but it seemed a safe guess considering how they were gawking at us.

Mikael snickered. "Some humans are more informed than others, choosing not to look blindly past what is right in front of their faces."

"But we haven't been right in front of their faces," I argued. "We've been hidden away within various Salr."

"Your beau and his little sister, perhaps, but not I," he said with a waggle of his eyebrows.

"I can hear you," Alaric said tiredly as he slumped across the cushy couch uninvited.

Sophie lowered herself to sit primly beside him. Mikael's people stood waiting near the entryway, silent like good little minions.

"Can we get you anything!" the elderly woman finally burst out, waving one of her frail hands in the air to gain our attention.

The old couple's excitement was palpable, yet there was no twinge of fear or anxiety. They trusted Mikael, though they probably shouldn't have.

The Viking in question gave a slight bow. "Dinner would be lovely."

My stomach growled at the mention of food. More

pressing still was my need for a shower. Between the time we'd spent in a livestock shed back in Viking days and the burning of my victim's bodies, I stunk.

Our hostess hurried off to the kitchen, dragging her husband behind her. James watched them forlornly as they disappeared down the hall. With our hosts' advanced age, and the size of the house, I knew they likely had help with the upkeep, but I saw nor sensed anyone else.

Sophie, still seated on the couch with her spine ramrod straight, aimed an icy glare at Mikael, "You should not let them worship you."

With Sophie's superior attitude, I was surprised she cared. It made me feel a little more warmly toward her. I didn't like taking advantage of the sweet old couple either, and I liked even less that our presence might be endangering them.

Before Mikael could make whatever sarcastic remark he had in mind, I cleared my throat. He turned his gaze away from Sophie to land on me. "Yes, Madeline?"

"I agree with Sophie," I stated, "but right now I'm more worried about someone finding us here, and our hosts getting caught in the crossfire."

"No one will find us here," Mikael assured.

"They found us last time," Sophie cut in before I could point out that fact.

Mikael suddenly looked angry, but he stored it away quickly. "We had a, what is the modern term?" He held up a finger. "Oh yes, a *mole*."

"Not exactly a modern term," I muttered.

Alaric stood abruptly. "One of your people gave us away?" he hissed.

Mikael tilted his head and gave a slight nod, remaining calm.

Alaric looked past Mikael to where Aila, Tabitha, and Faas stood. "And how do you know they will not do so again?"

Mikael glared at Alaric. "No one else knows we're here. Those who have accompanied us have been by my side longer than you've been alive. I trust them with my life."

"I hope so," Alaric replied, his voice low, "because you're trusting them with *ours*."

Tabitha shifted uncomfortably under Alaric's gaze, while Aila remained indifferent. Faas glared at *me*. I glared right back, wanting to flip him off, but knowing we were all close enough to a fight as it was.

"I need a shower," I grumbled. I looked to Mikael, "I trust our *hosts* won't mind?"

He gestured toward a hallway further into the house. "Up the stairs, third door on the left."

"Great," I muttered, then turned and walked away.

Alaric followed me out of the room, with Sophie close behind. We both stopped and turned questioning looks at her.

"Well I'm not staying with *them*," she explained, gesturing behind her at the Vikings.

"Whatever," I grumbled. I turned to continue walking, leaving James to take care of himself.

Mikael's directions held true. Up a very wide set of stairs covered in the cushiest carpet I'd ever felt, and past several closed doors, we found the bathroom.

Sophie leaned her back against the hallway wall and slid downward with bent knees until she was slumped into a seated position, her legs pulled up against her chest. "Don't take too long," she advised. "I reek of blood and burnt flesh."

Ignoring Sophie, Alaric followed me into the bathroom. Though some alone time would have been nice, I didn't mind the company. Somehow having Alaric close made me feel less frightened, as if his very presence could ward away the impossible task of destroying the key.

Once the door was locked behind us, he cranked up the hot water in the shower. The place we were supposed to bathe was one of those huge, glass-walled contraptions, big enough to fit five people. There were multiple shower heads angled down from the ceiling in different directions. The shower didn't go well with the rest of the house. It was the epitome of modernity, nestled in a house filled with old-world, wealthy charm.

I stared at myself in the massive mirror above the double sinks as Alaric began to undress. My dark hair was matted and dirty, hanging limply nearly to my waist. My face was just as dirty, the mottled colors of soot and grime blending in with the bags under my eyes. I stared at myself, and wasn't sure if I recognized the girl in the mirror at all.

Alaric moved to stand behind me, fully comfortable in his nude state. His hair was somehow in better condition than mine, but it was also pin straight. It didn't tangle as much as my wavy mass.

"We don't have any clean clothes," I muttered miserably, only then realizing it.

Alaric turned me away from the mirror and helped me out of my tunic and pants, bending to undo my boots to remove the pants fully from my legs. He stood again, and stared down not at me, but the key around my neck.

"I brushed it when I was removing your shirt," he commented, "but it didn't knock me away. Not like last time."

I sighed. "I'm an empath and it's linked to me. It can sense your intent. It had no need to exert the energy to repel you when you were simply trying to undress me."

Alaric raised a dark brow at me. "You speak as if you can read its thoughts."

I stared up at him, letting all of my worry shine through in my expression.

"Oh, Maddy," he said softly. He wrapped me in his arms, understanding what I was trying to tell him. I *could* read the key's thoughts, and it could read mine. We became closer every time I used its power.

"It tolerates you because it knows you'll protect me," I whispered against his shoulder as the first of my tears fell.

He stroked my matted hair. "You make it sound almost benevolent."

As my tears fell faster, I began to shake. The hot water from the shower was filling up the entire bathroom with thick steam, making it hard to breathe, or maybe it was just my anxiety. Either way, I felt so suffocated I could hardly keep my feet.

"Sometimes I forget it isn't around to help me," I sobbed. "I don't know how to block it out, and sometimes its thoughts seem like they're mine. Sometimes I can't tell our thoughts apart at all."

Alaric rubbed small, comforting circles across my bare back. The touch of his skin on mine was the only thing keeping me grounded, and I dreaded the moment I'd have to step away.

"We'll insist that Mikael teaches you to shield tonight," Alaric assured. "Once you can block it out, your thoughts will be your own again. You're strong enough to do this, Maddy. I know it."

The key laughed in my mind. Shielding wouldn't work. I didn't really want the key out of my mind, did I? It was a part of me. I should want it as close to me as I wanted Alaric. *Closer.*

Alaric, unaware of my thoughts, at least I thought they were *my* thoughts, guided me gently into the shower. I couldn't seem to stop crying. Once the hot water hit me I felt like I couldn't move. My entire body was exhausted, as was my mind. The idea of keeping my thoughts separate from the key's was always in the back of my head, and in that moment I realized just how much energy I'd been expending on that goal. It was a constant battle, whether I realized it or not.

Alaric began to wash my hair, gently combing out the tangles with his fingers. I could feel his worry, and his sadness. Underneath that was fear, though whether it was fear for my sanity, or something else, I wasn't sure. I did, however, get the impression he thought we'd lost the baby. My empathy at times was becoming eerily close to telepathy.

I shivered, despite the hot water running down my body. I had no definitive answer to soothe Alaric's mind either way. Part of me felt like I was maybe still pregnant, but I hadn't been sick or felt any other signs. It was just a feeling I had. I didn't want to get his hopes up based on a gut feeling. I could sense what the eventual disappointment might do to him.

Once Alaric had finished helping me wash, he positioned me so I'd be kept warm under the falling water, then moved to stand under one of the other shower heads so he could get clean. I watched as the water made his black hair even darker, cascading down his pale skin. Normally the sight would have put *other* thoughts in my mind, but all I craved was a good cuddle, and a long night's sleep.

I watched as he washed his hair, using the same shampoo he'd used in mine, something that looked and smelled pricey, and had probably been placed in the shower just for guests. As the foamy streaks washed down his body, I felt the sudden need to go to him. After all the scary crap that had happened, he was still here, doing his best to protect me. At some point I'd forgiven him fully for past betrayals. He had become my partner, in both name and action. It was a feeling I'd known little in my life.

I moved toward him and wrapped my arms around his waist, startling him since he'd closed his eyes to protect them from the shampoo. He responded seconds later, wrapping me in his embrace.

"Thank you for still being here," I said softly, huddling to share the single shower head with him.

"Thank you for existing," he replied.

I laughed, and it felt strange with all the emotions welling up in my chest. I pulled away slightly so I could look up at him. "That's not exactly something deserving of praise."

He pulled me tightly against his chest. "Yes it is," he whispered against my wet hair.

We stayed like that for a long while, until finally we had to admit we should probably get out of the shower. After shutting off the water, we stepped out and made use of the fluffy white towels stacked on a shelf near the door. With the towels wrapped around us, we both looked down at our dirty clothes with distaste.

"Any day now!" Sophie shouted from outside the bathroom door.

I frowned. "I can't decide if I'd be better off with dirty underwear, or no underwear at all."

Alaric gave me a mischievous grin. "I like the idea of no underwear."

I sighed. "You go without underwear in wool pants and tell me how much you like it."

Alaric chuckled and picked up the offending black panties. "Dirty underwear it is."

I grabbed them and put them on my clean body before I could think about it. I didn't care that we were in hiding. Tomorrow I'd be procuring some clean underwear, or else.

Sophie cleared her throat loudly.

We finished getting dressed and let ourselves out into the hall amidst a veil of steam. Sophie looked up at us from her seat on the carpet. "It's about damn time. It smells like dinner is ready."

Sophie rose to her feet and stalked past us, shutting herself in the bathroom. Alaric took my hand and gave it a squeeze before we prepared to head downstairs. I didn't fancy the idea of eating at the same table as Faas, but it was the least of my worries. When your life, free will, and perhaps your very soul were hanging in the balance, what was dinner with a mortal enemy?

CHAPTER TWENTY-SIX

Our meal was blissfully uneventful. Afterward, I found myself wandering the house alone while everyone else talked strategy. I'd never been involved in a war before, so my opinions weren't exactly valuable.

Our hosts, who I'd found out were named Clive and Marie, had dined with us. They were expats living in Norway, and they'd spent their lives tracking down the strange and unnatural, trying to find proof the old gods existed. Mikael had met them whilst drunk in a human bar, and had told them the story of his entire life. They didn't believe him, but remained friends. After twenty or so years of friendship with their eccentric comrade who thought he was a Viking, they started to realize he hadn't aged a day. The rest was history.

I shook my head as I trailed my hand up the gold-patterned wallpaper of the hall. I didn't blame Clive and Marie for searching for something magical. I'd done my fair share of wondering after accidentally killing Matthew, but had never come to any real conclusions until the Vaettir came for me. Luckily, Clive and Marie's initiation into Vaettir society had been a little more pleasant than mine.

I padded barefoot further down the upstairs hall, wondering if I'd find anything strange, or if our hosts, who had retired for the evening, were actually as normal and friendly as they seemed. Even James had stayed for the war planning, so I had no one to speculate with, leaving me only with the option of snooping. Okay, I could have just tried going to bed, but I knew I'd have trouble sleeping, and snooping seemed like a lot more fun.

One room in the hall drew my attention. It was guarded by a set of white double doors, one slightly ajar. I lifted a finger and pushed the door open a little further to reveal a large study, though all I could make out was a large desk in the center. Wanting to see more of the room than the hall light allowed, I flipped on the switch inside and quickly entered, then shut the door gently behind me.

The desk in the middle of the room looked antique, but that wasn't what held my attention. What caught my eye were the books. Lining both walls on either side of the desk were books that looked hundreds of years old. Some spines were cracked and fraying, while others, made of thick leather, held together a little better. Closer observation revealed the books were all on the occult, mythology, or ancient history. The collection had to be worth thousands, if not more, though I'm no book appraiser.

My fingers skimmed the shelves until a title caught my eye. I removed the book simply titled, *Norse Mythology*, figuring with everything that had happened, I could stand to brush up on the subject. I was glancing around for a comfortable place to sit when the door opened. I dropped the book in surprise and cursed, then bent down to pick it up.

Mikael beat me to it, crouching in front of me to cradle the book lovingly. We both stood.

"Doing some light reading?" he asked as he closed the heavy tome to look at the cover.

"I wasn't really needed down there," I said defensively, taking the book back from him. I took in his fresh clothing and damp hair. He must have snuck away from the group to take a shower. His clothing was just as Viking-esque as ever, making me worry that perhaps he was planning another visit to olden times.

He gestured to the book. "You won't find much of use in there," he explained, "just the human versions of the myths."

"You've read it?" I asked, unable to picture Mikael snuggling up contentedly with a good book.

"I've read them all," he answered, sweeping his hand to encompass the books surrounding us.

I smirked. "Is that why you've spent so much time with Marie and Clive, their books?"

He snatched the book away from me and thudded it onto the shelf, obviously offended.

"I didn't mean—" I began, realizing how bitchy my comment must have seemed.

"It's fine," he grumbled. "Spend several centuries using people for your own gain, and eventually that's all anyone will see."

I went silent, not sure what else I could say.

Mikael sighed and his anger leaked away. He gave me a knowing smile. "Your little kitty cat was quite insistent we work on your shielding tonight. It quickly became clear that we'd accomplish nothing else until I attended you."

I sighed. I had been hoping for a good night's rest before tackling *that* issue, but it probably was wise to do it sooner rather than later.

Yet, there was still a more immediate matter. "Where did you get a change of clothes?" I asked, shifting uncomfortably in my dirty tunic.

He looked me up and down and laughed. "I keep supplies anywhere I might end up. *Your* wardrobe will have to wait until the morning. Now back to the shielding . . . " he trailed off, as if he didn't really want to talk about it, but knew he had to.

"Go on," I urged, wondering if Mikael's temper would resurface at the previously touchy subject.

"I've been thinking," he began, moving away from me to pace around the room, "it's going to be a difficult task for me to let down my shields. Deceit is in my nature, and it's a trying task to fight one's nature."

"I didn't think it was going to be a cakewalk," I commented, not seeing his point.

He paused his pacing to smirk at me. "What if we try it while I'm asleep?"

I opened my mouth in surprise, then paused to think about what he'd said. It made sense. We were all at our most defenseless when we slept. "It's worth a shot," I agreed.

He smiled, but it was strained. If I didn't know any better, I'd say he was nervous. For someone like Mikael to be showing his nerves, they had to be pretty extreme. The only question was, what did the ever-confident Viking not want me to know, and would he forgive me if I found out?

He leaned in close to me, reaching his arm around me to retrieve the mythology book once more. He handed it to me.

I frowned. "I thought you said it wasn't any good."

He smiled, looming over me. "I said it wasn't accurate, not that it wasn't any good."

My frown deepened. I wasn't sure if he was just covering up for his nervous display, or if he was somehow mocking me. Men were complex enough to begin with. Give them a thousand plus years and they only got worse, like ever-growing labyrinths of smugness and bravado.

Mikael was the most complex labyrinth of all. I had a feeling he possessed many dead ends, and probably more than a few dark abysses. I sensed I might be seeing into one of those abysses when I tucked him into bed that night. I could only hope I'd find my way out again.

Eleven o'clock found me in Mikael's room. I had waited in the study alone, reading the mythology book, until Alaric appeared, looking for confirmation that Mikael had spoken with me. Alaric had warned me to be careful. Careful with what, I wasn't sure. Could a sleeping Viking really be so dangerous? Don't answer that.

When Mikael hadn't answered my knock, I'd let myself into his room, hoping he was already asleep. No such luck. He was, however, drinking straight from the bottle of some hundred year old bourbon. He leaned against the padded headboard of his bed as I stepped into the room, his lower half obscured by the blankets, but his bare chest plain for all to see. His deep, reddish hair was pushed back from his face, trapped between his back and the headboard.

He paused to regard me with the bottle's opening hovering near his lips. "No kitty cat?" he questioned, then immediately started giggling.

"You're drunk," I accused, still standing near the doorway. I would have told him to put a shirt on, but I knew the comment would only get turned against me.

Nervous, I looked around his room. It was just as grand as the rest of the house, with plush, beige carpeting and a queen-size, four-poster bed. A cushy chair had been placed beside the nightstand for my convenience.

"It helps with the defenses," he explained as he lifted the bottle, slightly slurring his words. "Plus, I doubt I'll be able to fall asleep whilst you're staring at me awake without it. I'd offer you some, but—" he glanced down at my belly.

"Yeah, yeah," I said tiredly, shutting the door behind me before approaching the bed.

"So he let you come alone?" he asked, looking up at me.

I sat. I didn't like the way he said *let*. Alaric hadn't wanted me to come alone, but he'd seen the logic in it. Mikael's defenses would be difficult enough to penetrate as it was. We didn't need someone that he disliked, and who hated him in return, in the room to make matters more difficult.

"You should probably close your eyes if you're going to fall asleep," I said sarcastically, knowing Mikael would go to sleep when he damn well pleased, if at all.

He took another deep swig of the bourbon, then lowered the bottle to his lap. "Perhaps it would help if you sung me a lullaby."

"I don't sing," I grumbled.

"All women sing," he stated matter-of-factly. "They just don't all admit it."

I glared at him. "Well if we never admit it, then how do you know that we sing?"

He crooked the corner of his lip into a half smile. "Well do you, when no one else is around?"

I did, but I wasn't about to admit it, and I sure as hell wouldn't make the admission for the entire female race, allowing Mikael to lump us into some antiquated stereotype.

"Do you have any advice?" I asked tiredly, attempting to change the subject.

"About singing?" he asked, before taking another deep swig of the bourbon.

"About what I should do," I clarified. "I've never tried to read someone's emotions while they're sleeping. I never really *try* at all. It just happens."

"Do the Erykah thingy," he suggesting, seeming more drunk by the second. I glanced down to see there was an extra empty bottle beside his bed. "The one where she puts her hands on either side of your face," he continued, "and suddenly knows everything you're thinking."

"She was a telepath," I sighed. "I read things a little differently than she did."

"*Was*," he sighed, suddenly sad. "Sometimes the past seems like it was just yesterday."

I smiled softly. "Probably because yesterday we were in the past."

"Oh yeah," he replied, still gazing forlornly across the room.

I took the bottle from his hands and placed it on the floor beside the empty one. "You know, you're a terrible drunk," I teased.

He turned to me and grinned. "Perhaps, but I'm awful good at most everything else."

I smirked and pushed my hair behind my ears. "Not good at sleeping, apparently."

Suddenly he was somber again. His mood swings were jarring, especially with my fatigue setting in.

When I just stared at him, he explained, "Sleep becomes a tiresome thing after a few centuries. You can only see so much evil before all of your dreams turn ugly."

It was an interesting thought. I only had twenty-some odd years of experiences to dream about, Mikael had centuries. "I'm sure you've seen a lot of good," I countered, "and beauty."

"I'm staring at some beauty right now," he said lasciviously, leaning forward to playfully leer at me.

I snorted. "Add flirting to the list of things you're bad at."

He sighed dramatically and resumed his comfortable position against the headboard. "If you keep up with the scathing remarks, I'll be up all night nursing my wounds."

I slouched back into my chair. "My guess is my remarks don't affect you in the slightest."

He smiled softly. "Words wound more fatally than swords my dear, for time may dull a blade, but words will never fade." He hiccuped and chuckled at his rhyme.

I rolled my eyes. "At least lie down properly," I instructed. "You're never going to fall asleep like that." I gestured to the headboard he was still propped against.

"It would be more comfortable if you laid with me," he teased. "Of course, a lullaby might warm me just as much."

He was being manipulative, but his past few days had been almost as rough as mine, and he'd been pretty nice to me about it. *Mostly*.

"Shut up and I'll sing you your damn lullaby."

He grinned. "I promise I won't tell anyone you sing. It will be our little secret."

"It better be," I grumbled, as I wracked my brain for something to sing. "Now close your eyes."

He did as I bade him, scooting down so his head rested on his pillow. I cleared my throat and began to sing the only song I could think of. It was a song I'd made up for myself as a child, because I didn't have a mother to sing it for me. I briefly wondered if Mikael had known his mother, and if she'd sung to him at night. I couldn't imagine it, but since I was about to dive into his head, maybe I'd find out.

CHAPTER TWENTY-SEVEN

"*P*regnant?" Sophie balked, letting her surprise and disdain show through in her voice. "Traveling back in time I can believe, but *you* being a father?"

Alaric put his arms behind his head, resting comfortably on the soft mattress. "You'd think you would be happy about being an auntie."

Sophie paced across the room. These cushy interiors were making her claustrophobic. "I'm more worried about what it might do to *you*," she grumbled.

Alaric snorted, increasing her ire. "Like what?"

"Like making idiotic decisions," she snapped. "Like trying to put yourself between Madeline and that executioner." This blasted pregnancy was going to get him *killed*.

The widening of Alaric's eyes gave her a great deal of satisfaction.

"Yeah," she went on, "I heard about *that*. Not everyone was unconscious when they had their little showdown."

"I would have done that, baby or no."

Sophie felt her expression soften, just as her resolve

wavered. She took a seat beside her brother. "You do have a penchant for stupid decisions."

Alaric shoved her playfully. "Luckily I have my practical sister to do wise things like rushing off in the middle of battle to chase after a certain little woman who somehow replaced her missing foot."

Sophie's mouth formed a hard line. She was still intent on killing Maya. Next time, she wouldn't get away. "I'm not ready to talk about that yet."

Alaric raised an eyebrow at her. "Remember, the longer you hold it in, the more your rage will get the better of you."

Sophie smirked. "Well then we'll both have something to inspire stupid decisions."

"That we will," Alaric mused.

Their conversation died off, but Sophie had a feeling Alaric still had something to tell her. She poked him in the arm, then looked at him expectantly.

He sighed. "You're almost as perceptive as Madeline."

She chuckled, her brother often brought out her better moods, though he just as often brought out her worst. "Tell me."

Alaric raised his hands to rake his hair away from his face. Hair that was just like hers. Many might mistake them for fraternal twins, though Alaric was actually several years older than her.

"She's hiding something from me," he said finally. "Something that has her frightened."

Sophie stroked her chin in thought. "She has plenty to be frightened of. It doesn't mean she's hiding something."

He shook his head. "It's worse than she's letting on. I'll watch her when she doesn't see me, and her eyes look so . . . haunted."

She frowned. She had noticed Madeline's mood after the

battle, but that was just Madeline. She was emotional about everything, and probably felt bad about sucking the life out of the injured at her feet, even though she used it to heal everyone else.

"She did just travel back in time and leave an entire village of people to die," she commented, repeating the information Alaric had told her while they scouted the woods.

"Exactly," Alaric replied. "She was shaken after that, but this new fear came after what happened with the other executioner."

Sophie pursed her lips. "What could have changed?"

Alaric shook his head. "She told me the key is in her thoughts. That sometimes, she cannot tell which thoughts are hers. I think the battle made it worse."

Sophie felt a small tickle of panic at the base of her spine. She didn't wish Madeline any harm, but she feared even more what it might do to her brother. "We need to destroy it," she said firmly, referring to the key.

Alaric smiled sadly. "I know. I would not have her alone in a room with Mikael if it could be any other way."

Sophie gave him a knowing look. There was some reason Alaric had it out for Mikael, though he wouldn't tell her why. She planned on figuring it out, no matter how adamantly he kept it from her. She laid her head on his shoulder, doing her best to belie her thoughts.

"I'll try to talk to her," she offered finally. "Perhaps she'll tell me how bad it really is."

Alaric laughed. "You might give her horrid flashbacks of when you were her social worker."

Sophie lifted her head to glare at him. "I was a damn good social worker, thank you very much."

He patted her shoulder. "If you say so."

They both laughed, then their conversation ebbed once

again. Sophie knew better than to leave her brother alone while Madeline cozied up with the Viking. He would go barging in there eventually, unable to take it anymore. Sophie would simply have to wait it out with him until Madeline broke down Mikael's shields and found what she needed.

"You love her, don't you?" she asked suddenly.

The idea of her brother in love was a little jarring. Sure, he'd dated, but love was neither Sophie's nor her brother's strong suit. It wasn't what they were made for.

He leaned forward to rest his chin in his hands, bracing his elbows against his knees and shielding his face with his hair. "I have from the start."

Her jaw dropped. She hadn't really expected him to admit it. "Why her?" she blurted out.

Alaric turned to her, looking slightly offended.

She bit her lip. "I didn't mean it like that. It's just, you've had plenty of opportunities to fall in love. What was different this time?" Her heart was racing, and she wasn't sure why.

Alaric shrugged, disappointing her. "It could be our similar natures," he explained, "death and war go together nicely, and I'm sure that's why she ended up pregnant. But—" he cut himself off, seeming deep in thought.

"But what?" she pressed, feeling elated once more. She was quite sure what she'd previously felt for Maya was love . . . or was it just affection? Attachment from knowing someone for long enough? She wasn't sure.

Alaric sat up straight and flexed his hands in the air, as if grasping at the words that would not come. "She cares about *everything*," he began hesitantly, but then the words began to tumble out of his mouth like a mudslide, just a few rocks at first, leading to an almost frantic downpour. "The Vaettir abandoned her with no knowledge of who she was, and our treatment after reclaiming her wasn't much better, yet she still cares what happens to us. She forgave me for letting James haul her off to a cell, and for letting him stab her. It's like she *understands*, even though she's only been a part of our world for a short time. She balks at even killing one of her enemies, but can accept the fact that I've killed thousands. She wants to save us all, even though none of us deserve it."

Sophie stared at him, surprised by his outburst. "So you love her because she's a martyr?" she asked skeptically.

He grunted in frustration. "It's more than that. How do you explain why you love someone? It's not just their smile, or the way they laugh, or how they look when they sleep. It's all of it. It's seeing that burning humanity inside them, a single light that's like no other. It's irreplaceable."

If Sophie was surprised before, now she was completely dumbfounded. Jaw agape, she watched her brother, waiting to see if he'd say more, but he didn't. He buried his face in his palms and sunk into a fugue.

She placed a hand on his back. She might not know romantic love, but she knew familial love for her brother. She hated seeing the pain of worry on his face. "We'll protect her," she assured. "You'll see."

He nodded, but not like he believed her.

"I'll talk to her," Sophie offered again. "We'll get to the bottom of her worries, then we'll find a way to fix them."

Alaric nodded again, seeming slightly hopeful this time. Sophie took a deep breath, sincerely hoping there was a way to help Maddy. She didn't like to think how her brother would be affected if there was not, and she had no doubt he'd do something stupid, even if he had no chance of coming out alive.

She didn't like the idea of living alone in such a painful world. It simply wasn't an option.

CHAPTER TWENTY-EIGHT

The song did the trick. Eventually Mikael's breathing slowed as he drifted off to sleep. I looked down at his passive face, illuminated only by the small amount of light given off by the bedside lamp. His dark lashes formed perfect crescents below his eyebrows. It was odd to see him in such a relaxed, almost helpless state.

Really, I was shocked he'd managed to fall asleep at all with me in the room, though the alcohol had definitely helped him along. Still, you don't survive for a thousand years by trusting people enough to fall asleep near them, especially people you'd only known for a little over a week.

I shook my head. Who was I kidding? If someone burst into the room to murder us, I had no doubt Mikael would be up in two seconds flat, skewering them with his sword.

Thinking of the sword, I searched around the room for it, finding it resting against the wall near the closet. The ax he'd brought back from the past was nowhere to be seen.

I took a deep, shaky breath. I was stalling. I really didn't want to see inside Mikael's head. I didn't want to see inside *anyone's* head. I looked back to Mikael's still form. I *had* to do this, and it was now or never.

I leaned forward in my seat, then placed my hands gently on either side of his face. His skin was soft and supple, not like what you'd expect after so many years of existence. I smoothed my hands up so they rested partially in his hair. It was an oddly intimate gesture, and I was glad he wasn't conscious for it.

As if sensing my thoughts, his eyelids began to flutter open.

"No, no," I soothed, my voice barely above a whisper. "It's just me."

Not fully waking, he lifted one of his hands to cradle my palm against his face for a moment. Either realizing it was just me, or perhaps thinking it was someone else he wished was there, his arm fell back to his side as he drifted back into drunken sleep.

I tried to focus on any emotions I might pick up on, but Mikael almost waking up had me panicked. It was well past midnight, and my thoughts were muddled with my need for sleep. My empathy wasn't something I used on purpose, which made it difficult to hone in.

With another shaky breath, I closed my eyes and thought back to my *conversation* with Erykah. It had been effortless, but then again, she had been purposefully projecting her thoughts for me. Mikael was projecting nothing but bourbon breath. I would have to *take* his thoughts, giving nothing in return.

I scrunched my eyes tightly shut and focused, internally begging and wishing, but nothing happened. I opened my eyes and was about to pull away, but something stopped me.

As if seeing a moment of weakness, the key came alive at my neck. Reading the key's intent, I tried again to pull away from Mikael, but seemed unable to move. It was like a voice inside my head was saying, *You want to see inside his head? Oh, I'll show you inside his head*, only there were no words.

My outward sight went blind as scenes began to play inside my mind. I was powerless to stop them. I saw Erykah and the village we'd left behind, but felt none of the guilt Mikael felt in the present. It was a time before the key destroyed them all. His lovely wife was yet to be twisted into the hard, calculating woman she'd become. A woman that would climb inside his head without permission.

I turned to the side in the vision, and it felt as if my actual body was turning. I turned from Erykah and saw Mikael's sons, running in and out of the livestock huts, frightening the cattle, then laughing maniacally as adults tried to catch and chastise them.

I felt my lips curve into a smile, and realized I was seeing through Mikael's eyes, inhabiting his mind during the memory. There was something in my arms. I looked down to see a baby girl. She smiled up at me with bright, reddish brown eyes, her delicate skin alabaster perfection. I felt a tear come to my eye. The scene blurred, and changed.

I was standing in the same spot, but was surrounded by corpses and ash. All the structures had been burned, and the people murdered. It was many years later. My daughter had long since been killed, now Erykah had joined her. My sons were far from that place, safe for the time being, but they would want revenge.

Fast forward again. Entire empires crumbling at my feet. I didn't care. Let them grieve as I'd grieved. The world was not a kind place.

I felt dizzy as Mikael woke. He'd realized what was happening, and was trying to force me out. I felt his shields raising, and the key fought them for control.

The struggle seemed to last for ages, but its end was sudden. Mikael forced his shields up, shutting me out. It was like iron gates slamming into place. The impact rattled my teeth. Mikael's eyes shot open, meeting mine as I still gripped the sides of his face. At some point I'd moved closer, my mouth was only inches from his.

Words that were not mine trickled from my lips, "You are a more worthy adversary than we thought, Agnarsson. "

Then I fainted.

I shot up in bed, panting as my breathing tried to catch up with my heart. The room was pitch black, and arms wrapped around me from behind. I screamed.

"Maddy, Maddy," a voice soothed. "Shh."

Part of me recognized that voice, but I didn't understand where I was.

"Madeline," the voice said again, then it clicked that it was Alaric. In my sleep I had been seeing images I never should have seen. They'd all happened long before I was born, in places far away.

As reality set in, a new panic hit me. "Oh my god, Mikael. I practically raped his memories."

A light flipped on at the bedside. I noted a sliver of sunlight at the window, though the curtains were heavy enough to block most of it out. I turned around and was able to see Alaric's face. It helped bring me the rest of the way into reality.

"He carried you here after you fainted," Alaric explained. "He would not say what happened."

I shook my head over and over again. "This is *not* good. He's going to kill me. I shouldn't have seen all of that."

Alaric scooted behind me and rubbed his hands up and down my arms. "If he was going to kill you, you wouldn't be sitting here. Whatever it is, it's okay."

I took a deep, shaky breath. "You don't understand. He wouldn't have wanted anyone to feel his emotions like that."

Alaric continued to rub my arms. "He knew the risks."

I nodded, but it didn't make me feel any better.

He hugged me against him. "Did you at least get what you needed?"

I pulled away, only then remembering my initial intent in reading Mikael's thoughts. I recalled the moment he shut me out, and how his shields felt going up. It was quite literally a physical barrier in his mind, created by sheer force of will, and a desperate desire to hide his emotions.

"I think I did," I whispered, feeling somewhat astonished by the notion.

In my mind I thought, *You didn't expect that, did you?* but there was no reply. The key had delved into Mikael's memories, thinking he wouldn't have the will to shut it out, but he did. Mikael had managed to catch the key off guard. I briefly wondered if he'd be able to do it again, now that the key knew what it was up against.

"What are you thinking?" Alaric asked softly.

I shook my head. "Ugly thoughts. I need to talk to Mikael."

"I'll go with you," he offered.

I nodded. It was probably a bad idea to take Alaric with me, but I wasn't sure I possessed the bravery needed to face the scary Viking on my own.

We left the room and walked down the hall as the first hints of dawn chased us through the window. I did *not* want to do this. I remembered how Mikael had felt when I'd picked up on just an ounce of his grief. Now I'd seen his memories first hand, instead of just focusing on his shields. He was going to be *pissed.*

We made our way to the room where I'd sat with Mikael. Maybe he would still be asleep and we could delay the inevitable conversation. I knocked on the closed door.

No answer.

With a deep, shaky breath, I turned the knob and peeked inside, with Alaric hovering over my shoulder. The room was perfectly clean, the bed made, with no sign of its inhabitant.

I turned wide eyes to Alaric as I pulled the door shut, leaving us out in the hall. "Do you think—" I began.

Alaric shook his head. "He wouldn't be able to abandon you. It would be too close to a betrayal, which would break his oath to you."

My strength left me as I leaned against the wall. Alaric was right. Part of me would have liked to think we'd be better off without Mikael, but that part wasn't very wise. Like it or not, we needed him, and we needed him not mad at me.

Movement at the end of the hall caught my attention. Mikael became fully visible as he ascended the last few stairs. "I'm surprised to hear you speaking on my behalf," he commented, eyeing Alaric as he approached us.

Alaric glared. "I was speaking upon your oath to Madeline, nothing more."

Mikael smirked, though it was half-hearted. "Of course," he said quietly.

I stayed where I was standing, waiting for Mikael to address me, but he was yet to meet my eyes. As silence engulfed us, I leaned more heavily against the wall. I was exhausted, and felt like I might lose the bile in my stomach.

Finally Mikael looked at me. "Are you well?" he asked, his

eyes focused somewhere in the vicinity of my mouth rather than further up my face.

"Are you?" I breathed. Yep, I was going to have to find the bathroom.

Alaric reached for me, but I sprung from the wall and rushed past him. I really didn't want to mess up Marie's hallway carpeting. I made my way down the hall and burst into the vacant bathroom, slamming the door against the wall as I threw it open.

I made it to the toilet and began heaving, though nothing came up. I hadn't managed to turn on the bathroom light, but I was grateful for the darkness. It felt somehow safe as I huddled over the toilet. I heard Alaric and Mikael speaking in the hallway, then Sophie's voice was added to the mix. A moment later someone was behind me, sweeping my hair back from my face just as another wave of nausea hit me.

"It seems you're still pregnant," the man holding my hair mumbled once my dry heaving had stilled.

I jumped when I realized it was Mikael.

"Where's Alaric?" I groaned, feeling like I might heave again.

"I requested that he allow me to tend to you," Mikael explained.

I wanted badly to turn around and look at him, but I was afraid to move away from the toilet. "And he listened?" I asked skeptically, my voice barely above a croak.

"No," Mikael said, a hint of laughter in his voice, "but his sister intervened."

I shook my head, then instantly regretted it as my stomach did a little flip-flop. "No offense," I began slowly, closing my eyes to still my dizziness, "but holding my hair while I heave really is a job for the father of my child."

Mikael was silent for a moment, but continued to hold

my hair. Little tugs of movement let me know he was twining it around his fingers. "You stole your way into the memories I hold most dear. The least you can do is let me sit here with you."

I sighed. It was time to have *that* talk, apparently. I would rather have had it somewhere other than the bathroom, with me able bodied and ready to run away, but I wouldn't deny him answers now.

"I didn't mean to," I explained. "It was the key."

I expected a wash of anger, or an accusation that I was making excuses, but Mikael just silently kept playing with my hair while I hovered over the toilet. Feeling slightly more steady, I moved away from the bowl and sat back to lean against the wall. I tugged my hair out of Mikael's grasp, then brought my knees to my chest.

He took a seat beside me, mirroring my position. "How much control has it gained?"

I turned my neck to look at him, feeling slightly stunned. "You're never angry when I most expect it."

He picked up a lock of my hair and started playing with it again. Not meeting my eyes, he explained, "I *was* angry, but my anger will do us no good now."

I sighed and slouched further down the wall, giving up on keeping my hair to myself. Not knowing what to say in response, I decided to answer his original question. "Even now, with the memory of how you build your shields in my head, I'm not sure I can fight it. At times, I'm not even sure I want to."

"What did Erykah really tell you that night, right before we shared our dance?" he asked softly.

The bathroom darkened, letting me know that clouds were moving in outside to obscure the sun. "I don't know what you mean."

His hand found its way to my knee, but it was more attention-getting than flirtatious. "Yes, Madeline, you do."

I placed my hand on my belly, wishing I could somehow feel the small life inside. I knew I shouldn't tell anyone what Erykah had told me, or if I did, Alaric should be the first to know. It was his child too, after all.

Still, the words began to tumble from my mouth. "I know how to destroy the key, and I think I might be able to shield from it," I began, just as a tiny voice in my head argued both of those points, "but in all likelihood the effort would kill me . . . " I trailed off, then patted my belly and added, "and *it*."

Mikael's face went slack, the shadows in the room emphasizing the subtle change. "Why would you not say anything?"

I shrugged, wondering where Alaric had gone, and hoping he wasn't close enough to hear anything I was saying. "It would do little good."

"Then why tell me now?" Mikael pressed.

I closed my eyes, suddenly feeling excruciatingly tired. "Because I can't tell Alaric. Sometimes I consider Sophie a friend, but I can't tell her either."

When Mikael didn't reply, I opened one eye to see him smiling. "Does this mean that *I'm* your friend?" he teased.

I smirked. "You don't have friends."

"No," he replied, "I don't. Yet somehow you're wiggling your way in."

"Your daughter," I began, remembering how he felt looking down at the baby girl in his arms.

"Gone," he said simply.

"Was she . . . " I trailed off, hoping he'd catch my meaning so I wouldn't have to say it out loud. She wasn't around when we visited the village, at least I didn't think . . .

He shook his head. "She wasn't in the village the day they all died. She was lost to us long before that."

"I'm sorry," I said, unsure of what else to say.

He nodded, looking suddenly determined. "I will not allow your child to suffer the same fate."

I cringed and smoothed my fingers over my hair, turning my head to hide my expression. "I shouldn't have told you," I whispered. "I thought you of all people would understand I have to do this, no matter the cost. If I cannot destroy it, the key will find a way to destroy me regardless. If dying is my only choice, you can bet your ass I'll be taking the key down with me."

I turned back to Mikael to see his jaw set in a firm line. I could tell he wanted to argue with me, but before he could I said, "You know I'm right. Erykah escaped it without destroying it, and look what happened. I won't let the key come back for us all with a new owner. What if it ends up with Aislin or Estus?"

Mikael sighed, signaling that I had won the argument. "Nothing is ever truly written in stone," he said finally, "and I will do everything possible to keep you alive."

"Because of our oath," I added. "Letting me die when you could save me would probably count as a betrayal."

He sighed again, and looked somehow sad. "Yes, Madeline, because of our oath."

He stood and offered me a hand up. I wasn't sure if I was ready to leave the bathroom yet, but it was worth a shot. Mikael took hold of my hand and lifted me effortlessly to my feet.

I felt more steady as I followed him out into the hall. The key had been silent during our entire exchange. I wasn't sure if it was a bad sign, or a good one. Did it fear Mikael, or was it simply lulling us into complacency?

Sophie was coming toward us down the hall, but I didn't see Alaric anywhere.

"We need to talk," was all she said as she reached us.

Mikael handed me off to her without a word.

"Where's Alaric?" I asked as Sophie led me away. I wanted to be the one to tell him that I thought the baby was still there. I didn't want to miss his reaction.

A look crossed over Sophie's face that I didn't quite understand, making me apprehensive. What did she want to talk about that she couldn't say in front of Mikael? I looked back over my shoulder to see that the Viking in question had disappeared down the stairs.

I went willingly with Sophie as she guided me the rest of the way down the hall and into the study. I felt oddly energized. Mikael's assurances were still hanging in my mind. I was probably just delirious and hormonal, but as Sophie shut the door of the study behind us, I was overcome by a strange surge of energy.

I opened my mouth to ask why she needed to talk to me in private, but what came out was, "Get me out of here."

I reflexively wanted to lift my hand to my mouth, surprised by my words, but my hand lifted toward Sophie instead. A dome of energy encircled my palm, though I wasn't sure if it would be visible to the naked eye, or just mine.

I tried to lower my hand as Sophie's dark eyes widened in shock. My heart should have been racing, but my body was no longer my own. I'd been pushed into the passenger seat as the key took over, but I couldn't tell its intent. I might have learned to shield my thoughts, but so had the key.

CHAPTER TWENTY-NINE

"Put your hand down, Madeline," Sophie scolded, not quite getting how serious the situation had become.

I wanted to call out to her, to warn her somehow, but it was like sitting in a dark projection room with my hands tied. I could see the scene playing before me, but was powerless to stop it.

"We are leaving this place," I said against my will.

I tried to shake my head, but it wouldn't work. I couldn't imagine why the key wanted to leave now. Its host was protected, and we were starting a war. It was getting everything it wanted.

Sophie took a step back toward the door. "We're not going anywhere," she said calmly.

I reached my arm back and threw the energy collecting in my palm at her. She dove out of the way gracefully, rolling across the plush carpet, only to rise to her feet near one of the book cases. The energy hit the door harmlessly, dissipating to spread back into the environment.

I turned, stalking Sophie like a predator, ready to anticipate her next move. I threw another ball of energy just as the door opened behind us.

"I apologize—" said a woman's voice before cutting off, realizing the situation she'd just walked into.

I didn't hear her approach, but suddenly my body was leaping aside right before Aila could wrap her arms around me from behind. I landed back near the door, slamming it shut to trap Aila and Sophie inside with me. The two moved to stand shoulder to shoulder, ready for my next attack.

"The key seems to have taken her over," Sophie explained, keeping her eyes firmly on me as she partially crouched, ready to move.

Worry crossed Aila's face. "I don't know what to do," she admitted.

I watched the exchange between the two women while my mind was screaming at me to do something. I still couldn't sense any of the key's thoughts. I had learned how to shut it out of my mind, but not my body.

"Get—" I managed to force out through gritted teeth, but the key sent a searing wave of pain through my brain. It dizzied me enough I couldn't see for a moment.

When I opened my eyes again, Sophie and Aila were flanking me. I could hear footsteps running down the hall. The women exchanged a subtle nod, then leapt for me at once. Sophie was going to reach me first, and the key turned my body to fend her off. At the last moment, Sophie sidestepped and Aila crashed into me from behind, knocking us both to the floor.

Energy coursed through me, attacking the weight on my back. Aila screamed, then I was free. I rose shakily to my feet, just as Alaric and Mikael came rushing into the room, followed by Faas, Tabitha, and James. With so many of us, the study became suddenly claustrophobic. A small measure of the key's panic leaked into my mind. I had thought it was completely in control of the situation, but it was scared. We didn't have much energy left, and wouldn't be able to fend our captors off for long.

Involuntarily, I backed away toward the large window that sat behind the desk, opposite the door to the room. Horror overcame me as I realized the key might try making us jump out the second story window to escape.

The key held up my hands in front of me as I continued backing away. Both of my hands were glowing, and I was pretty sure I wasn't the only one who could see it, given James' awestruck expression. However, no one else seemed surprised.

All at once, the room exploded into movement. Energy shot from my hands as I was attacked, harming some, but not enough to get them away from me. We hadn't received any new energy since we'd used it all up on the battlefield, and fighting Mikael had pushed us past our limit. I looked around frantically. No one here was weak enough to drain. We were too weak.

Just as I realized the key was no longer shielding its thoughts, Alaric and Sophie simultaneously tackled me, knocking me onto my back and pinning my arms against the carpet. Faas moved to stand over us, his blond top knot of hair falling forward to cover half his face. He reached his hands toward me, but didn't close the distance. At first I couldn't tell what he was doing, then my last bit of energy began to drain away. He was stealing it from me, like I could do from a corpse, but I wasn't a corpse, and I wasn't weak enough to die.

"Get it off of her," Mikael demanded, stepping into view beside Faas.

"We can't, remember?" Alaric growled. I could hear his

voice, but couldn't see his face. All I could see was Faas, and blearily, Mikael.

"They're both weakened. Try," Mikael demanded.

Not arguing, Sophie kept my arm pinned with one hand, while she used the other to lower the collar of my shirt, revealing the key. Alaric mirrored her pose, using his free hand to reach for the key itself.

Before Alaric's hand finished its descent, I was overcome with pain like I'd never known. It felt like the key was tearing apart the flesh and bones it laid upon.

"It cannot be," Faas said in shock as he hovered over me, struggling to keep the key from using me to lash out.

I had a moment to take in the awestricken faces around me, then I was out.

I woke up lying on cold stone, or maybe I wasn't awake. I didn't feel awake. In fact, I didn't feel real at all. I propped myself up into a seated position, then instinctively reached for my throat. I gasped. The key wasn't there.

Elation filled me, but it was brief. Why could I still sense its presence? I looked around the shadowy room. It was oddly familiar, but somehow not. Something shifted in the near-darkness and I leapt to my feet.

I let out a sigh of relief as a Norn came into view, the same one we'd met when we'd travelled back in time. Suddenly I realized where I was. I was in the cave where the Norn had sent me back to the World Tree.

"Am I really here?" I asked, though I knew I didn't need to ask out loud for the Norn to hear me.

Not entirely, a voice echoed in my head. *You are here visiting me, just as much as you were present in your visit with Yggdrasil.*

"Where is the key?" I asked shakily.

The Norn took a few steps forward to tower over me, then lowered her wolf-like paw to my chest. *You are one.*

I gasped and pulled away. That wasn't possible. "Why am I here?" I asked, feeling almost angry in my desperation.

I did not bring you here, the Norn answered.

I shook my head. The key could have brought me, but that wasn't right. It wouldn't want to be here, but I wasn't capable of any sort of subconscious travel myself, was I?

I took a shaky breath. How I'd gotten there wasn't important. There were far more pressing matters. "What do you mean, the key and I are one?"

The Norn approached me again and put her massive paw on my shoulder. *I can feel its energy, intermingling with yours. It was not always an object, but pure energy made when Yggdrasil was torn apart. It has reverted to that state, within you.*

The Norn caught me as I almost fell, holding on to my arms until I became steady once more. At some point I'd began to cry, but the tears didn't feel wet. I knew they were there, but they weren't entirely physical, just like I wasn't entirely physical.

"How do I get rid of it?" I sobbed.

You and the key may both die, she explained, *releasing your energies into the universe.*

My thoughts jumped from Alaric, to Mikael, to the child inside of me.

There may be another way, the Norn thought suddenly. She crouched to lower her paw to my belly. *Perhaps the foreign energy could be focused into your child, giving the wild magic human form.*

I pulled forcefully away from the Norn. "How dare you!" I gasped. "I won't sacrifice a child just to save myself."

The Norn didn't seem offended, and instead continued to look down at me impassively. *Then you all shall die.*

I closed my eyes and shook my head over and over again. I needed to get out of there. I knew my body was still back in the present time, but I didn't know how to reach it.

As you wish, the Norn thought sadly. I lurched backward as she shoved me, then sat bolt upright in a cushy bed, laboring to catch my breath.

Alaric had been in a hunched, seated position next to me, silhouetted by the moonlight peeking in through the window. As soon as I woke, he turned to face me and gripped both my arms in his hands, searching my face for some sign that I was myself.

He looked scared, and whether it was of me, or for me, I could not tell.

I was trying to think of how to explain everything to Alaric, when there was a knock on the door. Neither of us told the visitor to come in, but the door opened anyway.

There were several visitors I would have expected at that moment, but Faas wasn't one of them. He looked almost like a kicked puppy as he pushed the door aside and slowly entered the room to approach the bed. I would have glared at him if I'd had the strength.

"What do you want?" Alaric asked, his anger at the interruption clear in his voice.

Faas raked his swatch of blond hair away from his face, unperturbed by Alaric's tone, then turned his gaze to me. "I wanted to apologize."

If I'd been shocked by his appearance, now I was doubly shocked. "Come again?"

"I thought you unworthy to be the bearer of such a power as the *Lykill*," he explained. "For lack of a better word, I was jealous. Now I see what a burden it truly is. I pity you."

I wasn't sure I liked his explanation, but at least he was trying. "Thanks, I guess," I conceded. "And thanks for keeping me from killing anyone."

He replied with a sharp nod. "Before you lost consciousness, the key seemed to melt," he went on. "It slid across your skin like molten metal. Is it gone?"

I held my breath. I hadn't yet figured out how I would explain things to Alaric, but it looked like now was the time, whether I liked it or not.

I exhaled. "It's inside of me—part of me . . . or something."

Alaric inhaled sharply, then turned to meet my eyes. "Are you sure?"

I nodded. "While I was . . . out, I visited the Norn back in time, just like what happened when I visited Yggdrasil."

"Yggdrasil?" Faas hissed.

I waved him off and continued to speak to Alaric. "She told me the key was part of me now."

"I must inform Mikael," Faas interrupted again.

"*Go*," Alaric ordered, clearly not desiring any more interruptions. As Faas left, Alaric turned back to me. "Did she tell you how to undo it?"

I shook my head. I felt like I should be crying, but I was oddly calm. I couldn't help but wonder if it was the key exerting its influence over me. "She said the key and I could die together, or perhaps we could put the key's energy into our baby, thus giving it a physical form. I refused either option."

He took my hand in his, lifting it to kiss my knuckles. "Good," he breathed.

I closed my eyes, reveling in the simple sensation of his lips on my skin. Just that morning I could have killed him. I might still. I shivered.

"Is it good?" I asked softly. "I'm a danger to everyone.

Perhaps I should have let the Norn end things for me right then."

Alaric squeezed my hand and gave me a dark look. "Your risk is more than ours. At least we can choose to put ourselves in harm's way. This was all thrust upon you."

Movement caught my eye, and I turned to see Mikael standing in the doorway, his head nearly reaching the moulding. "How do you feel?" he asked.

I laughed, though it was more of a bitter grunt. "I'm sharing my body with a force of corrupted, wild magic that could take me over at any time. How do you think I feel?"

"There may still be a way to defeat it," he stated.

"How?" Alaric asked instantly, before I could close my gaping jaw.

"The key is an ancient power," Mikael began as he approached the bed. "It is a concentration of the forces of chaos and corruption that destroyed Yggdrasil, the dark to balance the light. The old gods left this world long before Yggdrasil, and that is why the Norns created so many of us in their image."

I clenched my fists in impatience. We needed an answer and Mikael was just standing around talking about long dead myths. Yggdrasil and the old gods were gone. There was nothing they could do to help us.

Mikael looked at me like he was reading my thoughts, then gave me a slightly mocking smile. "The power of Yggdrasil is still within the key, just as it still resides within the Norns. The power to jump through time, and to different worlds. That power is now within you."

"Please don't tell me your plan is for me to travel to a different world to find the old gods."

Mikael scoffed. "Of course not. That would be ridiculous. My plan is for you to bring the old gods to us, using the power of Yggdrasil, and the connection of our blood to draw them forth. You have a direct link to Bastet sitting right beside you."

Alaric looked stunned. "You're mad."

Mikael smiled at Alaric, then knelt on the floor in front of us to take my free hand in his. "And what about you, Madeline? As someone who has touched Yggdrasil itself, as someone who has tasted the power of the Norns, and in effect, of the old gods, do you think me mad?"

Fear tickled down my spine, but it wasn't my fear. I opened my mouth to speak, then closed it, feeling more than thinking about what he'd said.

After a moment, I smiled. "Quite the contrary, I think you're on to something."

Alaric turned to me in disbelief. I really didn't know if Mikael's plan could work, but the key seemed to think it might be a possibility. It shivered again. It was afraid of the old gods. Something about this new closeness let me sense its emotions more keenly. We were one in the same now, after all.

EPILOGUE

I finally obtained new clothes. The dark wash jeans fit me like a second skin, complementing the magenta silk blouse. It felt unbelievably good to be back in normal clothes, and even better to have clean underwear. Tabitha had done the shopping, though I could have trusted any of the women with us to get me jeans that were long enough. They all knew the tall girl struggle.

We were all packed up and planned to leave Clive and Marie's home later that evening, under the cover of night. According to Mikael, we were heading North, *far* North. Someplace remote, where police weren't looking for a group of murderers, and where another altercation with our enemies might go unnoticed. The only other hint I'd been given was that it would be cold. Full winter gear was laid out across mine and Alaric's bed.

We'd all gotten a full night's sleep, and the key seemed to be lying dormant within me. I knew it would resurface eventually, especially once it gained access to more energy, but hopefully by then we'd be able to fight it. We'd just have to keep me away from any dead bodies in the meantime. I didn't like the idea of weakening myself to weaken the key, but it was our only option until we could summon the old gods.

I laughed at how silly my thoughts felt as Alaric walked up behind me. "What is it?"

I shook my head and leaned forward to finger the sleeve of my new winter coat. It was one of those expensive, micro-down numbers, thin and light, but extremely warm.

"Just amusing myself with the fact that we actually think we stand a chance of summoning *gods* to help us," I explained.

Alaric kissed my cheek. "You're the one that encouraged the idea, my dear."

I smirked, though he couldn't see it. "We travelled back in time, I touched Yggdrasil, and now an ancient magic is housed within me. I'm pretty sure anything is possible at this point."

Alaric spun me around and kissed me, but as he pulled away, a dark look crossed his face.

"What is it?" I questioned, still wrapped in his embrace.

He half shrugged. "After what I've seen, I wouldn't put it past you or Mikael to summon the old gods. The real question is, will they want to help us once they're here?"

I quirked an eyebrow at him. "What do you think Bastet will say?"

He frowned. "I'm not sure. We can choose between Bastet and Dolos. War and deceit . . . not the most magnanimous pair."

"Freyja too," I added.

I got the reaction I was hoping for as surprise crossed Alaric's face. It wasn't often I got the jump on him. "Freyja?" he questioned.

I nodded. "Aila is her descendant," I explained. "She told Sophie while they were waiting for us to return from the past."

Alaric seemed thoughtful. "A goddess of war and death," he mused, "but also love and fertility. Perhaps a goddess that would fight to save an unborn child."

I smiled. It was a slim, jagged, tenuous ray of hope, but it was hope nonetheless.

Alaric lifted me in his arms, then carried me to the bed, laying me down gently atop our winter clothes. "We have hours to kill until dark . . . " he trailed off, his voice gone low with seduction.

I raised my eyebrows as I looked up at him. "I can think of a thing or two to pass the time."

He kissed down my neck. "Name them slowly, please."

I stated my first suggestion.

Alaric lifted his gaze to mine, a dark grin on his face. "Now that's my little *land-skjálpti.*"

Hours later, as the sun began to make its slow descent from the sky, we prepared to leave. Still in our room, Alaric helped me into my new coat, taking the time to zip it, and button the clasp that would hold the collar close to my neck.

He pulled the hood up over my head playfully, then used it to draw me in for a kiss.

"I love you," he breathed.

I pulled away, surprised. "Come again?" I asked with a wry grin.

He tilted his head downward and eyed me like I was a misbehaving child.

"No," I said innocently, "I really didn't hear you, I need you to repeat yourself."

"You know," he teased, "I don't even say that out loud to my sister."

I crossed my arms and looked up at him. "You know, I'm an out loud kind of girl."

He grabbed me and lifted me effortlessly into his arms, cradling me like a baby. He kissed me fiercely. "Madeline," he began, "you are incorrigible, head strong, you care far too much about everyone else, *and* I love you."

I laughed. "Alaric, you are single-focused, impulsive, and perhaps a bit wily, but I love you too."

He kissed me again, then walked us toward the door. "I'm holding you to that," he joked. "You can't take it back now."

I smiled up at him as we prepared to go join the rest of our group. "War is capable of love," I teased.

He returned my smile, flashing his little fangs. "And death has a heart."

I hope you enjoyed the first two installments of Bitter Ashes. Book three can be found here:

ROCK, PAPER, SHIVERS (BOOK 3)

To enter my monthly paperback giveaways, please consider checking out my newsletter:

SARA C. ROETHLE MAILING LIST

ROCK, PAPER, SHIVERS

BOOK THREE

CHAPTER ONE

The cold wind stung what was visible of my face, and my hands and feet were numb despite the thick gloves and heavy duty winter boots. As far as the eye could see in any direction was crisp, pure white, almost blinding as the sun made its slow descent toward the horizon. I stood alone, musing over everything that had gotten me to this point, camping out in a frozen wasteland, contemplating summoning gods.

It had taken us weeks to get to our location. Weeks of hiding from our enemies while we traveled through the larger cities. Weeks of plotting our next step. Weeks of waiting for the key to rear its ugly head in an attempt to possess me again. We'd made it all this way without conflict. I shouldn't have been surprised since we'd taken so many precautions, but still, by this point, I expected things to go wrong at every turn. More surprising than our success so far, was that the key had remained dormant within me.

Mikael appeared by my side, staring out at the cold landscape ahead of us as the breeze played with his long, auburn hair. "Are you ready?"

I shook my head. "No."

I rubbed the slight bump of my belly, still not fully believing I was growing a child inside me. My winter clothing was all cinched up around me, so my pregnancy didn't show, but the entire group knew regardless. Sophie had a big mouth.

"Freyja is, among other things, the goddess of childbirth," Mikael reassured, placing a hand on my shoulder. "She will not harm you or your child."

I turned and raised an eyebrow at him, though my eyebrows were mostly covered by the black hood of my jacket. While I wore a top of the line, full-length, micro-down coat, plus many layers underneath to keep me warm, Mikael had only added a heavy, fleece lined, knee length coat to his normal Viking-esque gear. His dusky red hair whipped about freely in the icy air, yet he seemed unfazed. I was freezing even with all the layers. Camping out in the Arctic Circle was no joke.

"She's an ancient goddess," I countered, "one who left our people long before you were even born. You have no idea what she'll do."

Mikael smirked. "No, I don't, but you know I wouldn't tell you that your child will be safe if I didn't think it was true."

"Because of our oath," I agreed.

Mikael rolled his strange, amber eyes. "I wouldn't lie to you about such a thing, even with a blood oath hanging over my head."

I sighed, not because I thought he was misleading me, but because I believed him. The past few weeks had been trying. I'd finally been reported missing back in the States, but luckily still had fake identification from Diana. Many of Mikael's people, living safe within the Salr, had never possessed any real forms of identification, so we'd had to purchase a batch of fake IDs for them. Never mind that Mikael already had *a guy* in place to make the transaction go smoothly, and had around ten different personas in place for himself, all with passports, bank accounts, and backstories. Some even owned property.

We'd done much of our traveling by train, with me gritting my teeth the entire time, waiting for the cops to storm in and take us all away. Mikael had been the one to keep me calm through it all, oddly enough, and I'd really come to depend on him to keep the panic away.

Alaric and Sophie had been there for me too, but they were both a little more blunt, a little less tactful. They said exactly what they thought, which usually wasn't very comforting, though I appreciated it in a whole other way.

I turned to see Alaric waiting in the distance near our camp. He wore a more modern coat like mine, and a stocking cap over his long, black hair. Even from the distance I could tell he was smiling at me, I could *feel* it. Alaric might not be the best with comforting words, but he offered me partnership. We could both be worried together about ourselves and our child, and we could both be brave together. At that moment, if I didn't have Alaric's bravery helping me along, I probably would have called off the whole thing. I wasn't fit to summon gods . . . but then again, who was?

Mikael walked by my side as we started back toward the tents. The dense snow beneath our feet crunched, but didn't give way. I'd slipped and fallen on my butt on some of the harder-packed patches more times than I'd like to admit, far less graceful than any of my companions.

As we reached Alaric, Sophie and Aila came into view, both in full winter gear with their hoods pulled up. Aila looked gargantuan, but dangerous with the added layers on her already tall, muscular physique. I just looked like a fat penguin.

The other members of our small group, Faas, Tabitha, and James, waited inside the large tent that was our main base. The snow mobiles we'd used to reach such a remote area were parked around the tent, covered by fitted tarps, but otherwise ready for a fast escape.

We hadn't wanted to risk bringing any more of Mikael's people into our plan, so it was just the eight of us. We needed to be as unfindable as possible.

Many had voted against even bringing James. He was the weakest link without his memories. The arguments had ended though as Mikael pointed out that James was the only one who could create heat from nothing. It was a useful backup skill when camping on the frozen tundra.

I reached Alaric and stepped into the cradle of his arms, feeling some of the tension leak out of my body at his nearness. If Freyja didn't work out, we'd be using Alaric and Sophie to summon Bastet. I really hoped Freyja worked. I had no desire to meet a cat-headed war goddess.

I looked to Aila, who we'd be using to summon Freyja. All we needed was a bit of her blood. Aila looked nervous, her eyes a little too wide, and I knew it wasn't the prospect of slicing her arm open that had her worried. She'd suffered countless injuries over her long life, but it wasn't every day you met your patron deity.

Faas appeared from within the tent, just as bundled up as me. As executioners, denizens of death, we were much stronger in the magical department, but slightly lacking in the physical. In other words, we were a lot more prone to the elements.

Faas' white hood covered his blond swatch of hair and eyebrows, leaving only his eyes and nose visible. His eyes no longer held intense hatred for me, but they were still wary. His job was to step in and drain my energy if the key took over again, and I didn't blame him for being nervous about it, and I was still just as nervous around him. Even though he was built smaller than any of the other men, and tended to be less aggressive, he'd mastered skills I'd only recently found out I even had, and he knew how to use them to kill, maim, and control. He couldn't heal though. That little quirk was mine alone, but he had a little quirk too. He could drain energy from those who were uninjured. I could only steal from someone who was already near death, or from a weakened human. Faas had been draining my energy for weeks, keeping me weak enough to prohibit the key from using me to murder everyone.

We'd also kept me away from any corpses so I couldn't get a quick boost, just in case, but the key was still a force all on its own. Even without anyone to drain, it could do a great deal of damage before running out of juice, despite Faas draining my energy.

Still, the key hadn't been present in my mind, except for the occasional emotion leaking through. It was deep in hiding, which made me even more nervous than when it was trying to take over. At least when it tried to take over, I knew what it wanted. When I had learned from Mikael how to shield my thoughts and emotions, the key had learned too. It had built a brick wall between us, letting me know that if I wouldn't let it in on my plans, it wouldn't let me in on its plans either. Of course, I had a feeling it could still *hear* everything that was said, so it probably knew what we were planning with Freyja. Either it agreed with the ritual, or it was waiting for the right moment to pop in and cause chaos.

"Is everything prepared?" Mikael asked as Faas went to stand near him.

Faas nodded, though the gesture was almost imperceptible in his thick coat. "We'll begin the ritual as soon as the sun sets."

We all nodded in agreement, because there was nothing else to do. We were about to use my connection to Yggdrasil, the World Tree, to pull one of the old gods through into our world. If we succeeded, we would ask for her aid. It would be her choice whether she helped us, as there was nothing we could really do to compel her.

We were banking on the small chance that Freyja was a magnanimous goddess. My hopes were not high. I couldn't claim to know much about the old gods, but I knew one thing for certain. No one does anything for free.

CHAPTER TWO

The thick wool blanket between my body and the ice didn't do much in the way of warmth, and sitting so close to Aila only increased my lack of personal comfort. She wasn't a warm and fuzzy person at the best of times, and her nervous energy was making me itch and sweat beneath my coat.

I would have complained, but even with my discomforts, I was in a better position than most everyone else. Aila and I sat in front of a large fire built in a circular pit James had melted in the ice. The fire illuminated the darkness around us, but only so far. Glancing out in any direction, there was only pure blackness dotted by occasional distant stars. Though the moon was full, clouds obscured much of its light.

Aila and I sat on the blanket by ourselves, while everyone else stood on the other side of the fire, watching us like we might sprout second heads any moment.

Worry creased Alaric's brow, while Sophie just looked bored. Since I had discovered long ago that Sophie's bored face was actually her worried face, I gained little confidence from either of them. Heck, even Mikael looked worried.

Next to him stood James, who continuously glanced over his shoulder, like we might be attacked at any moment. He was probably right.

Faas moved to crouch beside Aila, while Tabitha stood behind him, holding an ornate chalice, and a wicked looking, curved blade. Tabitha wore a coat similar to her brother's, the white fabric, nearly the same color as her long hair, blending in with the surrounding snow. She handed Faas the blade as he held his hand out for it, then crouched to hold the chalice underneath Aila's bare, outstretched arm.

I inhaled sharply and turned away as Faas sliced into Aila's forearm, then glanced back to watch her vibrant blood flow into the chalice. The liquid looked dark with only the firelight to illuminate it, flowing across her pale skin like ink.

Aila turned to me. "I hope you know what you're doing," she said flatly in her heavily accented, deep voice.

I tried to smile encouragingly, but really I had no idea what I was doing. We were basing our actions on legends Mikael had read about in a really old book. The ritual was based around using one of the leaves from Yggdrasil, the World Tree. None of us had ever actually performed such a ritual, since Yggdrasil had been destroyed long before any of us had been born, even Mikael. To many, the tree was nothing more than legend.

Even though I was the youngest amongst us, I'd managed to touch Yggdrasil in person, sort of. My spectral form had traveled back in time, leaving my body behind, but I'd still had the power to unintentionally drain energy from the tree. The power enabled me to return to my body, where Alaric and Mikael were, and to take us all back home from Viking times.

It was not a fond memory for me, because in that moment I'd realized I truly was *death*. The key might have influenced my actions, but *I* was the one that had nearly killed the tree without even trying. More frightening still, was that it had felt amazing.

Not only had some of that power remained within me, connecting me to Yggdrasil forever, but the key was also originally a part of Yggdrasil. The key's existence within me strengthened that connection, or so we'd hypothesized. The tree's untimely death, centuries after the time I'd seen it, created the Norns as they are now, in individual forms, but it also created residual chaotic energies of destruction. In other words, the key. It was as much a part of Yggdrasil as the fates.

Faas took my hands, drawing me out of my thoughts. He guided them toward the fire, close enough to burn. I winced, but held my hands steady above the flames as he pulled away.

Tabitha stood with the chalice full of blood clenched firmly in her gloved hand. She circled behind us, then crouched at my side opposite Aila. I closed my eyes, wanting nothing more than to retract my sore hands. The blood Tabitha poured over them actually came as a relief. It dripped from my skin, sizzling in the fire as it hit, but I barely heard it.

With the touch of blood and fire, my body came alive. Not only did my human senses seem more keen, I was hit with a sudden symphony of emotion. I could sense Alaric's anxiety and Mikael's apprehension. James' fear and frustration. I didn't have time to ponder my new clarity as Tabitha began to chant in Old Norsk over my bloody hands.

As her words dipped up and down in the cadence of an ancient chant, my entire body began to tingle with energy, enough to make me dizzy and a little sick. The key reacted, like I'd been terrified it would. I wasn't sure if it was to Tabitha's words or the blood. Maybe both. I'd never reacted to just blood before. Usually I needed the corpse that went with it.

My hands began to throb like they were filled with too much blood, and I realized that I'd leaned forward enough to completely encase them in the flames, yet they didn't burn. Tabitha continued to chant, while everyone else watched on silently.

Something was thrumming in my chest, but it wasn't my heart. I could feel energy building toward . . . something. I started to panic, worried the key was about to take over like it had done when it first retreated into my body. The energy reached its apex, throwing my head back as it surged upward.

There were a few silent moments where everything seemed still, and I couldn't hear over the ringing in my ears. Once I was able to breathe, I brought my head forward to see the veins in my arms lit up like molten fire. The air around my face shimmered with gold. At first I couldn't tell why, then my eyes focused on the night sky around me. The branches of a great tree formed in the air above me, shining like the sun. *Yggdrasil.*

I could no longer sense nor see anyone around me, just the tree. I wanted to reach out and touch the shining branches, but felt frozen in place, a prisoner to the power that had taken me over. As I continued to stare up at the branches, a bright bolt of light, like a giant shooting star, touched down on one tiny twig at the top of the spectral tree. As soon as it hit, I could sense an immense presence, the likes of which I had never felt.

It shot downward, traveling through the branches of the tree toward my face. I screamed as it came barreling toward me, but at the last minute, it veered down a lower branch and sped toward Aila. It hit her like a Semi truck, throwing her from the blanket to land on the hard ice with a thud.

The moment the energy hit her, the entire tree winked out of existence, and my hands, still in the fire, began to burn.

I screamed and withdrew my hands as everything came back into focus.

Alaric appeared at my side. "How do you feel?" he asked frantically. "Did it work?"

I turned wide eyes to him, holding my burned hands away from my body. I shook my head, not because I thought the ritual didn't work, but because I had no idea what the hell had just happened.

I looked over my shoulder to Aila, who was being helped to her feet by Mikael. She seemed stunned, but unharmed.

I gazed into Alaric's eyes. "Did you see that?" I asked, half-hoping it had all been a figment of my imagination.

"The tree?" he questioned. At my nod, he replied, "Honey, that tree is going to be emblazoned in my memory until the day I die."

I turned my gaze as Faas came to crouch on my other side, while Alaric wrapped his arms comfortingly around me.

"Aila?" I questioned. She'd seemed fine, but now she was mumbling something to Mikael behind us.

"She's fine," Faas replied, as he looked me up and down, likely probing with his magical senses to see if my energy was still the same after the strange occurrence. "You seem unchanged as well," he added finally.

"But whatever that was that came through the tree hit Aila," I argued. "I thought it was coming straight for me, but it veered from its course and hit her."

Faas raised his pale eyebrows. "Something came through the tree?"

I nodded, and turned to Alaric for verification. He *had* to have seen it.

Alaric frowned. "I saw only the tree, then Aila was suddenly knocked aside. Still, if whatever you saw intentionally went for Aila, perhaps Freyja attempted to join us after all."

We all moved to look back at Aila, who still stood in the darkness with Mikael. They had been joined by Tabitha.

Faas stood and approached them. "She doesn't seem any different," he commented as he glanced over Aila once again.

"It felt like whatever hit me bounced off," Aila replied, her deep voice seeming loud in the quiet night.

"Then we have failed," Faas replied somberly, his shoulders slouching in defeat.

I squeezed my eyes shut as a moment of panic hit me, then was gone. We would simply have to try again. The key's presence would *not* remain within me forever. I was still *me*.

Mikael left Aila to approach me. At 6' 5", he was one of the few people around that could make me feel small. Well, him and Aila.

"How do you feel?" he asked, concern clear in his voice. "Did the key react, or was that all *you*?"

I shook my head. "I don't know. It felt like it might have, but it was washed away as the tree formed. I think it was Yggdrasil's remaining energy within me that created the golden tree, and maybe the key too."

"The key was originally part of Yggdrasil," Mikael replied. "You might not be far off in your assumptions, but that doesn't explain why the ritual didn't work in the end."

"But why would the key even allow me to use it like that?" I asked, finally getting to my feet with Alaric's help. "You would think it would want no part in summoning one of the old gods, since they are the only ones powerful enough to separate it from me. *That* wasn't me controlling the key. That was me being taken over by something else. I was just along for the ride."

"Perhaps the key wants to be separated," he mused with a small smile. "It *did* seem to have more power as a separate entity. As things are, it will likely die with you."

I frowned. I'd considered that little metaphysical aspect more than I'd like to admit. The Norn had told me I could end the key by ending my life, and my child's. It was almost selfish to stay alive. Then again, I'd still be leaving everyone in the middle of a war. Estus would likely kill my companions once the key's threat was eliminated, and he would continue being a tyrant over his portion of the Vaettir.

Still, we were the ones who'd forced both Estus' and Aislin's hands. We'd taken the potential for bloodshed up a notch, throwing the two clans more fiercely into a competition they had begun on their own. I wondered how they would react to finding out the key was no longer a physical object. Would they go back into their hidey-holes, content that at least their enemies wouldn't possess such raw power, or would they still try to use me somehow? Perhaps they'd just band together to completely eliminate the threat I might pose.

I shook my head as Alaric gave me a tight squeeze. We'd sure muddled things up since our original plan. We'd gone from wanting to just give the key to Aislin, to starting wars and summoning old gods.

"You seem tired," Alaric commented.

I nodded. I *was* tired, physically, mentally, and emotionally. Having Faas constantly draining a small measure of my energy took its toll. With the added inconveniences of the cold, and the botched ritual, I was ready to sleep for a week.

"We'll try again tomorrow," Mikael assured, startling me

because I'd been so deep in thought, I'd forgotten he was still beside us.

Sophie and James waited in the shadows on the other side of the fire. Observing the whole situation silently.

"Let's go to bed," I mumbled.

Alaric nodded, moving just one arm around my waist so we could walk side by side away from the others. I couldn't wait to climb into my insulated sleeping bag, shielded from the cold air by our ridiculously expensive winter tent. My hands ached enough that I was afraid to look at them, and I probably still had remnants of Aila's blood on me. I was too tired to attempt washing it off with icy water, and I had no doubt the contact would increase the pain.

We climbed into the tent, and Alaric zipped it up behind us. The space inside was small, leaving just enough room for our double sleeping bag. I sat on my butt while Alaric helped me out of my coat and boots, avoiding my hands.

"Do you want to bandage them?" he asked, finally taking them tentatively in his grasp. "The burns don't look bad, but it might ease the pain."

I shook my head, barely able to keep my back erect. "Sleep now please."

With a small smile, Alaric helped me into our cushy cocoon, then climbed in beside me.

He rested on his back so I could spoon against him with my head on his shoulder. I buried my face against his neck, trying not to think about the key's presence, threatening to ruin the intimate moment.

"Maddy?" Alaric questioned softly.

"Yes?" I asked with my lips against his warm neck, breathing in the familiar scent of his skin and hair.

He was silent for a moment, then sighed, "Nothing. Rest well."

Normally I would have pushed the matter, but I was too bone tired to try. Instead I shut my eyes and let my mind spiral off into oblivion, because it was a heck of a lot more comforting than reality.

I awoke to the sound of the tent unzipping, but felt disoriented. With a start, I realized it was still dark, Alaric was still beside me, and someone else was unzipping our tent.

Without thinking, I reached for the large, sheathed knife I kept near my pillow, just in case, as Alaric finally awakened. We both sat up quickly, ready to face the person now leaning into our open tent.

"What the hell are you doing?" Alaric asked of the dark form.

Tension leaked out of me at his tone. This was obviously someone from our camp. I couldn't see a thing in the darkness, but with Alaric's catlike night vision, he probably saw them clearly.

"*Sophie,*" he demanded when there was no reply.

"Sophie?" I questioned, leaning closer to the dark form.

Alaric held me back. "Something's wrong."

As my eyes adjusted, I could see Sophie staring at us, but she wasn't speaking.

She leaned a little closer to peer at me. "That was a very rude summoning, child," she said in a tone of voice I'd never heard coming from Sophie.

"Oh shit," Alaric spat, "Do you think . . . " he trailed off.

My mind caught up to his way of thinking a moment later. "Oh *shit*," I echoed.

Sophie glared at us. "I would discontinue your disrespectful way of speaking immediately, if I were you. Now get out here." She disappeared from the opening.

We scrambled out of our blankets and out into the cold night air, quickly donning our coats and boots as we went. Sophie was obviously not Sophie anymore, something I might have found hard to believe if I hadn't experienced a sort of possession myself previously.

Once we were all out of the tent, we stood in a triangle with Alaric and I both staring at Sophie, and Sophie tapping her foot on the ice impatiently.

"Freyja?" I questioned, my voice tinged with disbelief.

Sophie rolled her eyes. "Freyja no longer answers the calls of her children, girl, and she's not who you need regardless. Most call me the Morrigan, though I go by many other names, and I have come to *your* call."

"What?" I gasped.

No one from the other tents had stirred yet, and I wasn't sure if we should be keeping our voices down for privacy, or if we should be shouting from the rooftops to wake everyone and tell them Sophie had been possessed.

Sophie/the Morrigan seemed confused. "You summoned Yggdrasil itself to light my path, child. Do not tell me you did so by accident."

Alaric was looking at his sister like she was some sort of monster. "This better not be permanent," he interjected.

Sophie glared at him, and it was so much like a normal Sophie glare it was unnerving. "Your sister will not be harmed," she replied dispassionately. "I would not disrespect Bastet in such a way." She turned back to me. "Now tell me why I'm here."

Her eyes sparkled in the moonlight. I had a feeling she knew a lot more than she was letting on, like she was testing me ... or toying with me.

My heart thundered in my chest, making it difficult to breathe. I was facing down a goddess, and regardless of her actual intentions, she was obviously not happy. It did not bode well.

"We were trying to summon Freyja," I explained weakly. "We need her help."

Sophie smirked. "You expect the help of the gods, when you have clearly forgotten us?"

I cringed. I'd heard legends of the Morrigan, and I wasn't even sure that she was a *god*, yet here she was.

"We had no other choice," I explained.

Sophie took a step closer to me, really *looking* at me. "There is a secondary energy within you," she observed. "What have you done? I will not have any daughter of mine turning herself into an abomination."

"Daughter?" I questioned, feeling even more confused.

I distantly heard the sound of another tent unzipping. Someone was coming to see what the commotion was.

Sophie smiled. "You truly have strayed far from your roots, my child, and I'm here to bring you back to them."

Her comment didn't quite make sense to me. Here she was acting like she had no idea what was going on, followed by an assumption that she knew quite a bit about me.

The figures of Faas and Tabitha became clear as they approached us, followed by everyone else in our party.

"Wha—" Faas began, then stopped as his eyes darted right to Sophie. "*You're* not Sophie."

Sophie sneered. "How very observant of you." She took in everyone as they came to join us, then shuddered in irritation, reminding me of a bird settling its feathers. "If you all don't mind, I would appreciate a moment alone with my daughter."

Alaric stepped beside me and wrapped an arm around my

shoulders, obviously unwilling to leave me alone with the Morrigan. Mikael came into view as he stalked around Sophie, observing her like she was an animal up for auction.

Sophie/the Morrigan frowned and met my eyes. We stared at each other, as she seemed to look into my very soul. I was still stuck on the fact that she'd called me *daughter.*

"Consort with your *man*," she said as a cold smile played across her face. She was ignoring everyone around us, her eyes remaining firmly on me. "I will take a moment to find my bearings in this much changed world."

I nodded a little too quickly. Alaric watched his possessed sister, looking worried as she turned and walked off into the darkness. I didn't blame him, I was worried about Sophie too, despite the Morrigan's reassurances.

"I can't believe it worked," Faas breathed as soon as the Morrigan had taken Sophie's body out of sight.

Mikael seemed pensive, so I turned my full attention to him, with Alaric's arm still wrapped around me.

"What is it?" I asked, wondering if he knew more about the Morrigan than the rest of us.

Mikael frowned. "I'm just not entirely sure why the Morrigan would be the one to answer our call. I wasn't even under the impression that she was a goddess."

The cold was seeping into my bones, and I felt wary being out in the darkness. The Morrigan could have returned to watch us and we might never know. Of course, Alaric would probably smell her if that were the case.

I gnawed on my lip. The Morrigan claimed I was her *daughter*, which as far as the Vaettir were concerned, simply meant descendant, and not even in the most literal sense of the word. There was no actual blood relation, but calling them our ancestors was the simplest way of voicing that information.

"If she's not a goddess," I whispered, "then what is she? How did she travel through Yggdrasil?"

Mikael took all of us into his gaze. "As far as the legends are concerned, the Morrigan is either a witch, some sort of fairy, or both. She was in this world more recently than the old gods, though she disappeared countless centuries ago. Regardless, as far as the stories are concerned, she's not very nice."

"The stories seem accurate," Alaric mumbled.

I sensed fear from Tabitha, surprising me. She was incredibly timid for someone who grew up amongst our people. It was easy to forget that not all Vaettir were as ruthless as the ones I was used to. "What if she's not here to help us? What if she wants the key?" she whispered.

I let out an abrupt laugh, more of an expression of the tension I was feeling than anything else. "Well," I replied, "she'll have to cut me open and sever it from my very being if she wants it for herself."

Tabitha's pale eyes met mine, letting her thoughts show through before she answered, "That's what I'm afraid of."

I caught my breath at the thought as Alaric squeezed me a little tighter. What if she really was there for the key, and I was just a mortal shell getting in her way? How do you stop an ancient witch or goddess from cutting you open?

The only answer I could come up with was, *you don't*.

CHAPTER THREE

The Morrigan wasn't gone for long, returning within twenty minutes. I could sense the first light of morning not far off, and my bones ached with tiredness, but there was no way I was going back to bed until we figured all of this out. In reality, I probably wasn't going back to bed period, but I'd soothe myself with comforting lies in the meantime.

We all stood waiting by the rebuilt fire as she approached, the firelight illuminating her slender form. Our eyes met. It was just as unnerving seeing someone else looking out at me from Sophie's eyes as it was the first time when she'd practically climbed into our tent.

As she closed the distance between herself and our group, I noticed she walked differently too. Sophie's gait was very direct. Graceful, but aggressive. The Morrigan walked with a slow sway, almost seductively. There was something reptilian about her. The way she moved sent a chill down my spine.

"May we speak in private now?" she asked, her tone making it clear she hadn't appreciated being kept waiting.

"I go where Madeline goes," Alaric answered for me.

The Morrigan/Sophie arched a dark brow at me, her pale face seeming to glow in the firelight. "You let a man speak for you?"

I grabbed Alaric's hand and gave it a squeeze. "Only when I agree with what he says."

The Morrigan sighed. "*You* brought me to this place, not anyone else here," she snapped. "You summoned me with fire, and a sacrifice of blood, and now you cannot be troubled to allow me a private audience?"

I let out a shaky breath. She had a point. I really didn't want to be alone with her, but I wanted her out of Sophie's body sooner rather than later. If Sophie had to deal with being possessed, I could deal with a few minutes alone with the scary witch goddess.

"Fine," I replied before I could think better of it.

Alaric's hand convulsed around mine at my answer. He glanced over at me. "Are you sure?"

I met his eyes and nodded. "If Bastet requested a private audience with you, would you tell her no?"

Alaric was clearly unhappy, but he let go of my hand and nodded for me to go, earning himself a big bag of bonus points.

The Morrigan/Sophie nodded, then turned and walked back in the direction she had come, expecting me to follow. Everyone else looked as worried as I felt. Their emotions crept over me, making me even more anxious to walk out into our dark, snowy surroundings. I crossed my fingers that at the very least, I wouldn't slip on the ice and embarrass myself in front of my alleged ancestor.

Pushing my worries to the back of my mind, I turned from the group and hurried to catch up to the Morrigan's side as she glided across the hard-packed snow. I felt clumsy next to her serpentine grace, but I felt that way around normal Sophie too, so it wasn't much of a change.

Her dark hair flitted about in the breeze as she asked, "Why have you chosen such an inhospitable environment?"

I watched my feet as we continued to walk. Our surroundings were nothing but white, with scraggly vegetation here and there. Everything was snow as far as the eye could see, which wasn't far in the darkness.

"We're hiding," I explained.

"From whom?"

I took a deep breath as I pondered the best way to explain it. "Basically from all of the Vaettir of the largest two clans."

"Why?"

I was getting tired of walking on the cold, hard ground, and I was getting hungry. The small life inside me demanded more nourishment than I would normally need, and I felt enormous guilt any time I denied it. Still, I did my best to remain patient.

"There exists a charm that was part of Yggdrasil," I explained, starting from the beginning. "When the Vaettir destroyed the tree, the Norns were formed. The leftover dark energy formed a tiny key. The ones after us want that key."

The Morrigan/Sophie laughed for some reason I didn't understand, then nodded as she stopped walking and turned to face me. "I remember that day," she explained. "Your brethren took away the gods' mode of transportation between worlds. You'd think they would have been more grateful to those they were modeled after."

I shrugged. "I wasn't there, so I can't really defend why they did it."

She took a step closer to me. "And yet, you have touched the tree. There is a part of it within you, else you would not have been able to summon me here."

I gulped. I glanced over my shoulder for some form of reassurance, but we'd walked far enough that our camp was entirely out of view. I turned back to meet the Morrigan's cold stare.

"I have touched Yggdrasil," I admitted. "One of the Norns pushed me back in time, not physically, but a part of me traveled there."

"There's more," she observed. "Tell me the rest."

I looked down at the ground. "The charm I mentioned, the dark energy left over when Yggdrasil was destroyed . . . " I trailed off.

The Morrigan gasped, showing the first real surprise I'd seen on her. "It's within you, isn't it? I knew I could feel it. This is wonderful. We can reopen the gates between the worlds!" She grinned. "Balance will be restored at last."

Her sudden shift to excitement left me reeling. I didn't want to reopen the gates to the old gods. Heck, I could barely comprehend that such gates existed. I just wanted to get rid of the key, while living to tell the tale.

Her eyes narrowed. "I see that is not your intent," she accused.

I shrugged. "We were trying to summon Freyja because we thought she might be compassionate to our cause. I don't want this energy inside me any longer. It took me over entirely before, and all it wants is power and destruction."

The Morrigan seemed to withdraw herself from me, deep in thought. I shivered and wrapped my arms around myself for several minutes while she continued to ponder our predicament.

Finally, her eyes lit up as she came to a conclusion. "We will take the energy from within you, and use it to regrow Yggdrasil. You will be free, and we will restore the natural order. You are wrong to think it only wants power and destruction. It wants chaos. The thing you call the charm is the embodiment of wild magics, and the concepts of luck and chance. War and destruction may come naturally to it, but they are not all that it signifies."

My heart skipped a beat. I wanted to press the *you will be free* comment, but I needed to actually understand the rest before making any real decisions.

I opened my mouth to speak, but she was so excited she didn't seem to notice. She clapped her hands together. "First, I must find a suitable host," she mused. "I would not use one of the children of the gods any longer than necessary."

I opened my mouth again to ask a million questions at once, but suddenly Sophie/the Morrigan shut her eyes and went limp. I darted forward to catch her before she hit the snow.

Cradled awkwardly in my arms, she opened her eyes. Her brow wrinkled.

"Sophie?" I questioned.

"Care to explain why you're cradling me like a child?" she asked, uneasy.

"Um," I began, licking my chapped lips. "You were possessed by the Morrigan."

Sophie pulled away from me and stood. She brushed off her already clean clothes like a cat smoothing its fur. "Come again?" she asked incredulously.

"The Morrigan came through the tree and possessed you," I stated, waiting for her reaction.

Her eyes narrowed. "The Morrigan? I always thought she was just a legend, not a goddess."

"We should get to camp," I advised, hoping for backup when I explained everything that had happened to Sophie.

She startled and looked around us, as if just then realizing we were standing alone on the frozen tundra. With a look of distaste, she nodded her agreement, and began walking in the direction of the camp without me having to tell her which way it was.

By the time we neared the smell of woodsmoke, the first light of morning had descended. I stifled a yawn, longing to go back to sleep, though I now doubted more than ever that it would happen.

Alaric jogged toward us as we came into sight. If I would have jogged on the snow, I would have broken an ankle, but he did so effortlessly, his feet barely making a sound.

"She's Sophie again," I explained as he reached us.

He let out a long sigh of relief, then swept his sister up in a hug. She struggled and fought him off, then huffed and smoothed her hair.

"Why the hell did she choose to possess *me?*" she questioned. "She could have taken Maddy, or Aila, or anyone actually standing near the ritual."

"Well," Alaric began, "she wanted to *talk* to Maddy, so she wasn't really an option."

Sophie glared at me as if it was all somehow my fault. I lifted my hands in defense. "Don't shoot the messengers."

Sophie sighed and turned back to her brother. "I didn't do anything horrible, did I?"

He shook his head. Just the fact that Sophie thought she'd done awful things while she was possessed made my mind jump back to Mikael's assessment of the Morrigan. He was the one who would likely have any more relevant details on her, so he was the one I needed to speak with.

I walked away from Alaric and Sophie, only to have them both jog to catch up as I approached the fire, which had been rebuilt even larger while I was gone, as if to ward away any more spirits. Everyone had remained awake, and now Aila, James, Faas, Tabitha, and

Mikael all sat gathered around the fire for warmth. Something was cooking near the edge of the fire in a large pot.

I looked down at Mikael as he leaned forward to stir the lumpy brown stew. Stew for breakfast. *Yummy*.

"I take it Sophie is Sophie again?" Mikael asked.

I nodded. "The Morrigan is gone, but I'm pretty sure she'll be back. I'd like you to tell me all you know about her before she returns."

He grinned, then patted an empty space on the blanket beside him. "Story time it is!"

Relieved Mikael had shifted back to his normal, joking self, I took a seat beside him. Alaric sat on my other side. Sophie walked across the fire to sit near Aila, who had the hood of her coat cinched over her mane of blonde hair, leaving only her eyes and part of her nose visible.

"There are many accounts of the Morrigan, from many different sources," Mikael began. "Some call her a goddess, some a witch, and some label her a member of the *Tuatha De Danann*, the Celtic fairy folk."

He shifted into a more comfortable position as he continued speaking. "The only thing most accounts seem to agree on, is that the Morrigan is vindictive, a woman scorned. Sometimes she is described as a single woman, sometimes as three, sometimes portrayed as the maiden, the mother, and the crone. In many myths, she's a shapeshifter, changing between the three female forms, as well as the form of a crow. The crow form chooses who will die on the battlefield."

"Well she thinks I was made in her image," I interrupted. "So the death thing kind of fits."

Mikael nodded. "As does your ability to heal."

Well *now* he really had my attention. No one had been

able to explain how I was an executioner, but also a healer. The two "gifts" seemed counterproductive.

"Go on," I pressed.

"In early myths, before the Morrigan became more of an ominous figure, she was a bringer of both life and death, keeping the balance. She was a protector of the land, and in some tales, was the earth herself. It was only in the later stories that she was portrayed as a bitter old witch."

"I wouldn't let her hear you say that," I cautioned as the gears began to turn in my head.

Perhaps I really was descended from the Morrigan, if the early stories were true. Just as Alaric, descended from a goddess of war, was skilled in combat and tactical thinking, and Mikael, descended from a god of deceit and treachery, was skilled in manipulation, I might have gained my skills from a goddess of life and death.

Tabitha moved to begin filling wooden bowls with stew. The meat inside looked brown, probably beef, making my stomach churn uncomfortably. My pregnancy had given me a taste for red meat, even though years of not eating it made me sick at the thought. Still, I took the offered bowl. If baby wanted beef, baby would get beef.

I felt almost cozy sitting by the fire, enveloped in the scent of woodsmoke, with a bowl of hot stew warming my hands through my gloves. The comforting illusion was shattered as I noticed the blood stain on the blanket beneath me. It was Aila's blood from the ritual. She seemed dejected this morning, and I wondered if it was because her goddess had rejected her call.

A sudden thought dawned on me. "The Morrigan claimed she wanted to regrow Yggdrasil to restore balance to the land."

Everyone suddenly seemed uneasy, and no one would meet my eyes.

"Why isn't anyone looking at me?" I questioned, not getting why such a notion would scare my companions.

Alaric placed a hand on my leg. "Maddy, when a goddess of death says she wants to restore balance to the land, you should be afraid. When she says she wants to regrow a tree that would allow the old gods to come and go as they please, you should be terrified. Think about it. Life as we know it would cease to exist."

My mouth formed an 'oh' of understanding. Suddenly the stew in my hands seemed even less appetizing. While balance sounded like a good thing, the Morrigan's version of balance might not be what one would expect. She might be even worse than Estus and Aislin combined, and I'd brought her here. Any disasters that might occur would be firmly placed on my head. I could only hope it would remain attached to my shoulders long enough to deal with the fallout.

"So what do we do?" I asked of no one in particular.

"She's here now," Mikael answered. "There's no undoing it, so we should try to move forward as planned. We knew our actions would have grand consequences from the start, so we cannot truly complain when those consequences aren't what we expected. She may not be Freyja, but the Morrigan is still a force to be reckoned with. She could make a formidable ally, and we need all the allies we can get."

I nodded. "So we try to bring her around to our way of thinking. She already wants to free me from the key, so we're halfway there."

Alaric gave my leg a squeeze at the new information. I turned to see him smiling. "If we can manage that much," he commented, "we can worry about the rest later. Separating you from the key takes priority."

Aila snorted, drawing everyone's attention to her. She hunkered further down into her coat.

"Is there a problem?" Alaric questioned.

Aila snuggled her arms tightly around herself, but didn't comment, seeming to regret her snort.

"If you have concerns, then voice them," Sophie pressed, compassionately rather than angrily. It wasn't a tone I heard often from Sophie.

Aila frowned. "Thinking of only the next step, and only how things affect Madeline, has not gotten us very far. Instead of fighting, we are hiding in the snow with our tails between our legs."

Mikael laughed, bringing everyone's attention to him. He grinned in Aila's direction. "What Aila is so eloquently trying to say, is that she hasn't gotten to kill enough things. We promised her war after many years of inaction, and she's seen little of it."

I sighed, not agreeing with the sentiment. "I'm going back to bed," I announced as I stood.

"It's morning," Aila argued.

Alaric stood with me. "I'll join you, in *bed*," he purred lasciviously.

Aila grunted in annoyance, but Alaric only smiled down at her. "There *are* a few things more exciting than battle," he teased. "Perhaps you should try them sometime."

Aila began to lunge forward, but Faas put a hand on her arm, holding her back. He was grinning, as was Tabitha. Something told me that teasing Aila was a favored pastime amongst the group of Vikings.

I urged Alaric forward before Aila decided to kill him, but I couldn't help my grin.

It's funny, just when you think the world has stolen away all your smiles, they tend to come back in the direst of times.

CHAPTER FOUR

Over the next few days, we bided our time, waiting for the Morrigan to return in her new host. Then we waited some more. Finally, on the third night, a woman appeared. She had long, fiery red, curly hair, and dark brown eyes. Her skin was pale, a little too pale, and lightly freckled. She was tall and lithe, with narrow hips and little meat to her. She would have been beautiful in a gaunt sort of way if she didn't look so much like a corpse.

Alaric and I were the only ones who hadn't gone to bed when she arrived, and suddenly I was kicking myself for wanting to stay out by our warm fire to look at the stars. On the other hand, since I knew she had no problem with letting herself into our tent while we were sleeping, maybe staying up had been the wise choice.

The red haired woman approached and sat by the fire, settling the loose, black fabric of her clothes around her. Her dress was partially covered by what could only be called a cloak. Her clothes looked vaguely medieval, but were crafted out of modern day fabrics with fine stitching. She waited as I observed her, staring at us with her dark eyes.

"Are you the new Morrigan?" I asked hopefully, because otherwise some crazy woman had found us in the middle of nowhere, and hoped to share our fire.

She nodded as she tucked her legs a little more firmly around her side. "I apologize for leaving you for so long. It took time to find an acceptable host in a stage where its soul had left it, but it still had not begun to rot. I cannot maintain anything with another soul in it for long, unless the vessel has welcomed me as its guest."

I cringed, since she'd basically just said that she'd taken over a dead body, though I supposed it was better than her stealing a live one.

"Aren't you cold?" I asked, not knowing what else to say.

She glanced at the dark snow around her, then shook her head. "This body is dead. It feels very little."

Well that was an uncomfortable thought, though I was a little envious that she didn't have to feel the cold. Alaric remained silent beside me, allowing me to do the talking, though his eyes were cautiously glued to the Morrigan.

The Morrigan began playfully swooping her hand through the fire, back and forth, quick enough to not let her skin burn.

I cleared my throat.

Her eyes met mine. "I forget how impatient children can be," she mused. "If we must speak, tell me more of this war. I haven't tasted war in quite some time."

I took a deep, even breath, picturing the Morrigan as a crow flying over the battlefield.

"There have only been small skirmishes so far," Alaric explained, letting me off the hook. "Madeline was to use the deaths to destroy the key, but complications arose."

I shivered. *Complications* was one way of putting it. A total lack of will power and follow through on my part was another.

The Morrigan's gaze went distant. "It was a sound plan, if only you'd known exactly what you were dealing with."

The way she spoke made it seem like we *still* didn't know what we were dealing with. If that was the case, I'd have to argue, since what we were dealing with was now a part of me.

Her eyes suddenly snapped to mine. "You were chosen for a reason. The fates may be scattered and unorganized, but have no doubt, it was fate that brought you together with such a divine force. This is not entirely a curse, though you may view it as such."

I wrapped my arms tightly around myself. I didn't believe in fate. Too many screwed up things had happened over the course of my life for me to believe they were *meant* to happen. No, I believed in *choice*, even if an alleged deity was arguing otherwise.

"Let's see," she continued, eyes once again going distant. I was beginning to get the impression she wasn't entirely sane. "First, we'll need to choose the location for the final battle," she continued. Her eyes returned to mine. "You will need enough energy to not only part yourself from what you refer to as *the key*, but enough to regrow Yggdrasil."

"In other words, we need a lot of death," I clarified. I definitely wasn't sold on regrowing Yggdrasil, but parting myself from the key seemed like a good start regardless.

She nodded. "We'll need to move on from this place in the morning. Your enemies are near."

Well that was news.

"How close are they?" Alaric cut in, suddenly all business. "Have you seen them?"

The Morrigan's eyes flicked to Alaric, then back to me.

Ignoring him while still answering his question, she said to me, "This corpse is not my only form," she gestured to her body, "and I saw much in my time away. Your enemies have left their holes to march forth. They search for *you* night and day, understanding the threat you pose. One still hopes to use you, while the other hopes to kill you, or so the rumors go amongst their troops."

I briefly wondered if it was Estus or Aislin that wanted to kill me, but really, it didn't matter. We couldn't wait around for either of them. We had to bring them together to fight each other, instead of us.

Echoing my thoughts, Alaric interjected, "We need to make Estus believe Aislin is close to success in her endeavors. We must force him to act against her, rather than focusing his resources on finding Madeline."

The Morrigan finally acknowledged Alaric with a nod. "I do not think such a feat will be overly difficult. They are all afraid. The Vaettir's way of life will be changing no matter the outcome of this war. It puts doubt in the minds of the soldiers. A non-unified army is an easy target."

I yawned. Not that I wasn't interested in the Morrigan's plans, but the cold made me tired, and if we were leaving first thing in the morning, I would rather discuss the plans while we traveled.

Seeming to sense my need for rest, the Morrigan stood. "I would appreciate another moment alone before you retire."

I nodded and stood. Alaric didn't argue this time. If the Morrigan had wanted to harm me, she would have done so the first time we were alone.

I reached down and gave Alaric's arm a squeeze, then followed the Morrigan into the chilly darkness. I hoped this wouldn't be a long talk, as every moment spent away from the fire seemed to increase my fatigue.

Once we were out of sight in the darkness, the Morrigan stopped and leaned close to me conspiratorially. "How well do you know the child of Bastet?" she whispered, surprising me.

I narrowed my eyes suspiciously. "Well enough."

She sighed and linked my arm in hers. I tensed initially, not liking the idea of buddying up with a goddess filled corpse. "In these matters, we must look out for ourselves. I need you to understand. He cannot comprehend the road before you, and will only cause you to fail."

I shook my head. "Alaric is one of the few reasons I'm still alive. He protects me."

The Morrigan smirked. "You are more than capable of protecting yourself. Your lack of belief in that point is part of the problem. You cannot rely on the help of others in this situation. You must find the strength within yourself."

My eyes narrowed even further, this time in suspicion. "But it's okay to accept *your* help?"

The Morrigan sighed, letting out a long stream of fog in the air. Whatever she'd done to the corpse she inhabited had given it true life, if it had the body heat and lung function for its breath to create fog.

"Accepting my help is different," she replied. "You must understand, I *am* you. We share the same energies. This has not occurred in a *very* long time. You're different from the Vaettir, *special*. I've waited for this day, but had begun to fear it would never come. I feared I was to remain one of a kind, and I was too weak to come back to this earth without aid. I explained to you that coming together with the key was fate. It was meant to be a part of you as much as anything else. You were brought into this world at this time on purpose."

I shook my head. None of what she was saying made sense, or did it? "Say you're right," I began, "what does it change? I'm going to do my best to part myself with the key regardless of whether or not I'm fated to do so."

I hadn't expected the look of sympathy that crossed the Morrigan's face. "I must remember that you are still very young. You have not seen the world as I have, so I cannot expect you to view things clearly."

I frowned, feeling like I'd missed something. "If we're to leave first thing in the morning, we should get some rest."

The Morrigan nodded. "I do not require rest, but go if you must. Just remember what I told you."

I crossed my arms, *so* ready to go to bed, but needing to clarify something first. "I trust Alaric," I stated.

The Morrigan offered me a humoring smile. "Just see that your *trust* does not come back to bite you. A lady should not depend on anyone more than she depends on herself."

With that, she walked off into the darkness. I had no idea where she was planning on going, but I thought it best not to question her. I just had to trust she wouldn't run off and tell Estus or Aislin where we were.

I shook my head as I began walking back toward our camp. The Morrigan didn't want me to trust Alaric, yet expected me to blindly trust her. The thing about blind trust, is that it can only be given by fools. Trust is earned by actions, not words, and I knew exactly who had gained mine, and who hadn't.

Alaric shook me awake early the next morning. I groaned as the warm sleeping bag was pulled down from my shoulders, exposing me to the harsh morning air.

He crouched and placed a light kiss on my cheek.

"Everyone is ready to leave," he explained. "The Morrigan demanded that we let you sleep in."

I groaned and pushed the bedding the rest of the way down my body. The cold within the tent was a shock, but it was nothing compared to how it would be outside. I sat up and quickly slid myself into my coat, zipping it up to my neck, then searched around for my boots.

Alaric grabbed them from the other end of the tent, then handed them to me one by one.

"You should have argued with her," I groaned, irritated that everyone would now be waiting on me.

Not offended, Alaric smiled, then crouched down to kiss my slight baby bump through my coat. "Rest is important," he muttered.

I groaned again and moved away from him to begin lacing up my boots. I was not looking forward to the day's travels. The wind was incredibly cold with the speed of the snow mobiles, and the seats were hard and uncomfortable.

We hadn't discussed where we would go next, since Mikael and the others would have only learned we needed to leave that morning, presumably. Of course, they'd probably figured everything out while I was still in the tent, snoring away.

Alaric held open the tent door for me so I could struggle out into the blinding whiteness. You'd think sunny days would be welcome in such a cold area, but the glare on the surrounding white was a discomfort, even with sunglasses.

Mikael was suddenly there, offering me a hand up out of the tent. His long, auburn hair was once again loose in the cold air, but his reddish eyes were hidden behind a pair of expensive looking sunglasses. The sunglasses made me smile. He could feel human discomforts after all.

Alaric climbed out of the tent after me, his black stocking cap now on his head, but no sunglasses to be seen.

I looked past Mikael to the others. All the other tents had been packed up, and their previous occupants were now cooking breakfast around a small fire. I didn't see the Morrigan.

As if sensing my forthcoming question, Mikael explained, "She went to see how close we are to being discovered. We'll depart as soon as she returns."

He still held on to my hand. I looked down in question.

With an uneasy air, he gave my hand a squeeze. "I want you to be careful around her," he advised, referring to the Morrigan.

That I could sense his unease even around his shields meant he was very nervous indeed.

"I'm careful around everyone," I assured, half joking.

Alaric moved close to my side and Mikael's hand dropped.

Mikael's gaze moved to encompass both of us. "There are many myths surrounding the Morrigan," he explained. "She's more *human* than the other gods, if she's even a god at all. If the tales are true, she's driven by human emotions and motivations. We have no idea what her true agenda might be."

"So you not only tell lies, but you sense them too?" Alaric replied snarkily.

While the rivalry between Mikael and Alaric had temporarily lightened due to our present circumstances, they occasionally let everyone know it wasn't forgotten. It was irritating, but it was better than them trying to kill each other.

I didn't blame Alaric for wanting Mikael to pay for the death of his and Sophie's mother, but now really wasn't the time. I hoped *never* would be the time, since one of them would probably end up dead. I briefly wondered if Mikael would kill the father of my child, knowing what it would do to me. Of course, Alaric might not give him a choice. Then again, maybe Alaric would win.

I shivered. According to the Morrigan, I was stronger than I knew. Maybe I could stop them altogether. It would be worth a shot, given that I'd try regardless.

Ignoring Alaric's rude comment, Mikael angled his face to me to say something, then suddenly his lips shut tight as his shielded gaze looked past me.

I glanced over my shoulder to see the Morrigan approaching, still in the red-headed corpse. I really couldn't imagine her turning into a crow to scout for us, and wouldn't fully believe it until I saw it. Even with all that had happened, there were still some things I couldn't quite wrap my mind around.

"They are not far off," the Morrigan said as she closed the distance between us. She tossed her dark cloak back over her shoulder to reveal the plain black dress underneath. "But they approach on foot. We should be able to stay ahead of them. For now."

Mikael's tension kicked up a notch at the Morrigan's appearance, giving me the sensation of tiny ants crawling across my skin.

The Morrigan waited for my response, staring only at me, as if I was somehow in charge.

"Do we have time to eat?" I questioned.

I didn't like the idea of letting the other Vaettir gain on us any more than necessary, but my stomach was growling painfully, and it would be nearly impossible to eat while atop the snow mobiles.

The Morrigan nodded sharply, then led the way to the fire where James, Tabitha, Faas, Sophie, and Aila waited. I followed with Mikael and Alaric walking on either side of me.

Mikael leaned his 6'5" frame toward my shoulder. "Promise me?" he questioned.

I nodded. "I'll be careful," I whispered back.

Alaric took my gloved hand and gave it a squeeze. I had a thirteen-hundred year old Viking, and a five-hundred year old descendant of a war goddess to protect me. What could go wrong?

I shook my head at my own thoughts. The answer was *everything*. Like usual.

CHAPTER FIVE

I had to admit, even with the discomfort, gliding across the ice on the snow mobiles was fun. I sat behind Alaric with my arms wrapped tightly around his waist. I watched the sparkling scenery drifting by until my nose was numb with cold, then ducked behind Alaric's broad shoulders to peer upward at a crow flying overhead.

My eyes narrowed into a glare as I watched the Morrigan's crow form drifting easily up and down on currents of chill air. I wouldn't have believed it was her if she hadn't changed right in front of us. The shift hadn't been the horrible limbs popping and cracking like in so many werewolf movies, rather, it was more like magic. The transformation only took seconds, and seemed painless. The result was a crow the size of a bald eagle, with gleaming black feathers slick as oil. Intelligence danced in those beady eyes, much more than was characteristic for the already intelligent species of bird.

I sighed and ducked my head back behind Alaric. If I was truly descended from the Morrigan, it would have been nice to inherit that bit of magic. Flying above everything where my enemies would never even recognize me was appealing . . . as long as I avoided any low-flying planes.

The machine beneath us slowed as the snow mobiles ahead of us came to a stop. I hoped it was lunchtime. We'd been riding for several hours. I'd grown hungry after one.

I swung my leg over the snow mobile, climbing down ahead of Alaric. I stretched my arms over my head, then flinched as a black shape swooped near. Just before hitting the ground, the Morrigan effortlessly transitioned back into human form, making me *more* than just a little jealous at how effortless the change was. Nothing was *that* effortless for me. Not even walking.

Sophie moved to stand at my side, glancing warily at the Morrigan. She tugged her black coat straight where it had bunched during her ride on the snowmobile, then leaned near my shoulder. "Are you absolutely sure she won't try to possess me again?"

I smirked. "Why don't you ask her?"

Sophie grumbled under her breath, dutifully ignoring the Morrigan's curious gaze.

Aila, who'd been riding with Sophie, joined us next. She seemed cranky, as usual, but didn't speak.

Finally Mikael joined us, glaring back at James. I refused the urge to smile patronizingly at them for being stuck together on the snow mobile when Sophie refused either of their company. Faas and Tabitha had ridden together, creepy siblings that they were.

Without a word, Mikael dug through a satchel slung across his shoulder, then began doling out protein bars. I took mine with a frown, then glared down at the brightly colored packaging. While we'd cooked much of our food during our time at camp, the protein bars had been our extra ration. They were thick, hard to chew, and tasted *delightfully* like wet cardboard.

I started to open the bar, then jumped when I realized the Morrigan was standing right beside me. "A moment, please?" she questioned.

I lowered the bar to my side. I was getting tired of these *moments*. Interacting with the Morrigan at all was unnerving, and speaking alone with her increased that anxiety tenfold. Of course, since we needed her help, I couldn't exactly say no. We had, after all, summoned her to us, and not the other way around.

I nodded, but Mikael caught my eye before we could walk away. His look said it all, *be careful*. Alaric watched me with much the same look, except with the added effect of biting his lip to keep himself from speaking. I could sense how much it cost him to hold himself back as I turned away with the Morrigan at my side.

Uncomfortable with everyone's worried gazes on my back, I followed the Morrigan out into the crisp white expanse. The stiffness slowly left my legs as we walked, and I grew more comfortable with every crunching step.

I looked at our feet as I realized I couldn't even hear the Morrigan's boots on the snow. My own gait in my heavy snow boots made an annoying *crunch* with every step, while she glided along like a dainty ballerina.

My shoulders slumped. *Someday* I'd meet another clumsy supernatural being. There *had* to be another one out there.

Unsure of how far we were going to walk, I unwrapped my protein bar and took a bite. I wasn't about to miss my only chance at sustenance.

My bar was half gone by the time she finally turned to me. I glanced back, even though I knew the others would be out of sight. Suddenly I felt nervous, Mikael's words echoing in my mind.

"We probably shouldn't be out here much longer," I said weakly, fiddling with the half-eaten bar in my gloved hands. "We want to be far away from our last camp before we end our travels for the night."

The Morrigan's dark eyes peered into mine for several seconds, then she held out her hand. "Take my hand, please," she instructed. "I will not harm you."

My instincts screamed at me to run. I took a step back instead. "Why do I feel like your version of harm is different from mine?"

She frowned, her hand still outstretched. "I'm here to *help* you. I would not do anything to keep my sole descendant from greatness."

I did *not* like the way she'd said *greatness*. I didn't want any greatness, period. I just wanted to stay, you know ... alive.

I lifted my foot to take another step back, then stumbled as she lunged forward, latching on to my hand.

"Hey!" someone shouted.

We both turned.

James ran toward us. "Let her go!"

Even though he was *James*, he looked for the life of me like a angel in that moment.

"Why did you follow us?" the Morrigan snapped, dropping my hand.

James looked smug as he reached us. "Everyone can keep me in the dark all they want. I'm not helpless, and I can find out information on my own."

"So you came to *spy?*" the Morrigan hissed.

I sighed. James wasn't a very good spy if he revealed himself at the first sign of trouble, not that I wasn't grateful for the interruption.

My gratitude came to a screeching halt as the Morrigan waved a hand in front of James' face, and he instantly dropped to the ground.

My jaw wide open, I looked from James' prostrate form, then back to the Morrigan. Before I could react, she grabbed my hand again. I tugged against her grip, but my limbs felt incredibly weak, then I couldn't feel anything at all.

My vision shifted like I was falling forward, but instead of hitting the ground, I was being pulled away from it. I watched the ground in horror as I rose higher and higher. I could see black wings in my peripheral vision, moving up and down as I gained altitude.

Though I could feel little else, I felt it as my heart sank down in realization. I was part of a crow, but I had no control. The Morrigan was steering. I was just an unwilling passenger along for the ride.

I screamed in my mind, but had no mouth to actually express it. She was taking me away from Alaric, and Mikael, and *everyone*, yet all I could think about was my baby. If I was no longer in my natural form, where had my baby gone? Could it be a part of the bird too? I cried with no eyes to shed tears as the Morrigan carried me farther away from everything I held dear.

"They've been gone for far too long," Alaric announced, restless for Madeline's return. He knew he never should have let Madeline walk off with the Morrigan to begin with. They'd done it twice before, but each time was still a risk, a risk he was a fool to take.

Mikael nodded, peering in the direction Madeline had gone. "Agreed."

Alaric hated that he and the Viking were agreeing on most things lately, but he could swallow his pride for now if it meant helping Madeline. He internally chastised himself again for letting her go. He'd convinced himself it was safe, but now they hadn't returned, and he couldn't argue with the sick feeling in his gut.

"Let's go," Mikael ordered, needing no further prompting.

Alaric did not appreciate how much Mikael had grown to care for Madeline, but if it meant extra protection for her, well, he could bear that too. For now. Madeline needed all the allies she could get.

Scenting the air for Maddy, Alaric hurried across the snow with Mikael at his side. Footsteps trotted up behind them, then Sophie was at his other side. The others stayed with the snow mobiles, not that there was anyone around the barren, frozen wasteland to steal them.

The snowy ground was hard packed enough that footprints were barely visible, but Alaric could smell where Madeline had walked. Her smell had become more familiar to him than any other, save that of his sister.

Sophie inhaled deeply through her nose. "Did anyone notice where James went? His scent is in this direction."

"He claimed he was going for a short walk," Mikael replied. "I thought little of it."

Alaric's eyes narrowed. There was little doubting by this point that James' memory was truly lost, it was no act, but what if it had suddenly returned to him? Would he try to harm or kidnap Madeline?

He walked faster, then picked up speed to run. Mikael and Sophie both kept pace with him easily. Something was very wrong. He shouldn't have let Madeline walk off without him.

A crumpled form came into view, but it was too big to be

Madeline. *James*. Alaric looked down as he reached him. He was clearly still alive, but unconscious. Beside him was a half-eaten protein bar. Alaric picked it up and could smell Madeline all over it, yet her scent ended there. It did not lead off into any other direction.

At first, he couldn't help but look around their snowy surroundings for some other clue, then he thought of the Morrigan's crow form, and how easily she shifted. Protein bar still gripped in his hand, he looked up at the sky as the pieces fell into place.

It seemed like we had flown for days, with me silently screaming all the while. The Morrigan never seemed to tire. We'd flown over the ocean, across an expanse of land, then another large expanse of water. Eventually a green, rocky coastline came into view. We continued onward, then began to lose altitude over a circular, rocky outcropping.

The moment we touched down, we separated. I fell to the loamy earth coughing and gasping for breath, shocked to have my body back.

"My baby!" I croaked, cradling my stomach.

The Morrigan looked down at me, her red hair whipping about in the wind. "The child is fine, though you could have told me of her presence sooner. It was quite a shock to realize we had an extra passenger."

Tears flowed down my face, as hard as I fought them. "I wasn't planning on being turned into a bird!" I shouted. Then it clicked what the Morrigan had just said. "Her?" I questioned weakly.

A small smile played across her face, but instead of answering me, she ordered, "Get to your feet. I'm tired from our journey, and desire shelter. Listening to you scream for such a long distance has given me a headache."

I stayed right where I was sitting, the damp grass unable to penetrate my black ski pants. "Take me back to Alaric," I demanded.

She shook her head. "It was too risky to remain with your companions. They would only slow you down. We're better off on our own."

"No," I argued. "We have to go back. We can at least bring them here."

The Morrigan smirked. "I would not share such an experience with any of them, even if I could, but it doesn't matter, because I cannot. I was only able to change your form because it is a gift you would have had if you were stronger."

I frowned, still holding a hand to my tummy to reassure myself that the baby was really still there. The idea of having such an amazing gift was appealing, but not if it would make me any more like the Morrigan than I already was.

"I will not take you back," she continued, "so your choices are to sit here in the grass and starve, or to come with me and take care of your child."

My frown deepened. She had a point. I didn't know where I was, but there were no signs of civilization. Who knew how far the nearest town might be? I would need to get my bearings, and hopefully some supplies, before I tried to escape.

My heart felt hollow as I realized that even if I escaped, I would have no way of finding Alaric and the others. They were in hiding, after all. My greatest hope was the small chance that the Morrigan might take me back to them.

She turned and walked away from me as I scrambled to my feet. Now that I was standing, I could see large jagged rocks spanning for miles, all covered in green moss and surrounded by lush grass. The air was chilly, but not as cold as where we'd been.

I followed the Morrigan as she led the way toward the circle of rocks I'd noticed from the air. Each of them was larger than a person, and they formed a perfect half-circle, almost as if they'd been placed there on purpose.

The Morrigan moved to the center of the circle, then crouched down to retrieve something from the ground. She came up with a stone in each hand, offering one to me as I reached her. Curiosity got the better of me, and I took the offered stone.

A moment later, I felt a strange sinking feeling, as if we'd stepped into quicksand. I panicked and tried to step away, but I was too late. We sunk into the earth, then came out the other side.

I gasped, crouching where I had landed as the space we were now in slowly illuminated. Familiar stone walls met my eyes.

"A Salr?" I questioned, slowly rising. "How did you bring us here? I thought only the Vaettir could find them."

The Morrigan smirked. "You really are an arrogant race. Who do you think *created* the Salr?"

I gave her a shocked look. Surely she couldn't mean—

She rolled her eyes. "No, not me, you silly thing, but the magic of the old gods. These sanctuaries were the last gift to their children before Yggdrasil was destroyed."

Her explanation made me more confused, not less. "I thought we were more like the Norns' children, not the gods'."

The Morrigan brushed off her cloak, though I could see no dirt on it, then walked past me, further into the Salr. "Many of you were made in the gods' images, and they loved you just as the Norns did. Then you destroyed Yggdrasil, and cast the Norns out to die."

I hurried to catch up. "Sorry?" I offered, even though I hadn't been alive when everything she'd recounted took place.

"Hrmf," was the Morrigan's only reply. She led us down a narrow, stone hall, trailing her fingertips across the stones as we walked.

I glanced around warily, ready for a Norn to pop out at any moment. "I notice you didn't include yourself when you were speaking about the gods. You said *they* not *we*."

"We are the same, and we are different," she replied.

I let out a long, frustrated sigh, not understanding, but sensing that I wouldn't be receiving any real explanation.

"How long are we staying here?" I grumbled.

"Long enough to prepare," she answered vaguely.

I stopped walking. "Prepare for what?"

She continued walking, forcing me to either catch up to her, or remain alone in the hall. I caught up.

"For war," she answered as soon as I reached her side.

I huffed. "I thought that's what we were already doing."

The Morrigan stopped walking and turned to fully face me with a stern expression, making me half-regret even speaking to begin with.

"My dear child," she said in a lecturing tone, "we can talk strategy until we all turn to dust. There is still one simple fact that cannot be ignored."

"And what is that?" I asked snidely, crossing my arms.

A small smile curled her lips. "For war you need an army," she replied. "And I'm going to help you build one."

I opened my mouth, then closed it, unsure of what to say. An army didn't sound like a terrible thing, depending on the soldiers. An army could protect us. It could keep Alaric and

Mikael out of the fighting altogether. An army could also turn on us and send us all to our graves, but there was no use dwelling on *ifs* in dire times such as these.

"So you agree?" she pressed, watching my expression as I muddled over what she'd said.

I shrugged, feeling sick and wanting nothing more than to lie down. "Do I have a choice?"

She grinned. "There is always a choice, Madeline. I'm here to show you that."

She turned and continued walking before I could argue that she was showing me quite the opposite.

CHAPTER SIX

James sat on the ice, glaring at everyone. Alaric and Mikael had dragged him back to camp while Sophie walked ahead, refusing to help. James had woken eventually. Alaric had expected him to be whiney and frightened, but he'd been in for quite the suprise.

"What happened to Madeline?" Alaric demanded, barely restraining himself from throttling the man at his feet.

James smiled coldly, a smile that was all old James, not the James without his memory. "I'll answer your questions when you answer mine."

James was outnumbered, surrounded by Alaric, Sophie, and Mikael and his people, yet he wouldn't tell them a damn thing. He sat smugly on the ice, warm and comfortable within his snow gear.

"I don't know what happened to Diana," Alaric lied for the fifth time.

If James found out Madeline had killed his grandmother, he'd likely not be inclined to help rescue her. Of course, now that James was back to his old self, he likely wouldn't be inclined to help either way.

"You're lying," James said simply.

Mikael grunted. "We could just torture him," he suggested.

Alaric shook his head. "It won't do any good."

He knew James better than that. They could cut off his fingers and toes one by one, and he wouldn't say a word. He turned back to James, his shoulders slumped in resignation. Nope, he wouldn't tell them a damn thing until his questions were answered.

"Diana is dead," Alaric explained. "She forced Madeline's hand, and Madeline killed her."

James surprised Alaric by smiling, then surprised him even more by erupting with laughter. "Little mouse has teeth after all," he mused.

Mikael let out a long whistle. "Not the reaction I was expecting."

Besides Sophie and Madeline, Mikael had been the only other who knew the truth about Diana. Maddy hadn't even wanted to admit to herself that she'd raised several corpses to tear Diana to pieces, all before the Norn cut out her heart to release the key. Aila's confused expression confirmed that Mikael had kept his mouth shut on all he'd been told.

"Diana was a tool to be used like any other," James explained.

Sophie huffed. "Do you truly care about no one?"

James glared at her. "Diana left me to be arrested back at the hotel, so she could escape and follow Madeline. Had I been killed, she would not have shed a tear. I owe her no loyalty."

Well that was good news, Alaric thought. Though he despised James, he might still prove useful. "Now tell us what happened," he demanded.

James smiled up at him. "*Fine.* I had followed Madeline

and the Morrigan, not trusting the Morrigan's intentions. I tried to interject when the Morrigan grabbed Madeline. Then the witch waved her hand and I was out like a light. When I woke up, I remembered everything. Everything from before, and everything since." His expression turned bitter at that, obviously displeased with the events after his memory loss.

Alaric smiled coldly. He sincerely hoped that was the case, and that James remembered acting like a scared little child. Judging by James' glare, he did. Alaric smiled wider.

"That tells us nothing," Mikael cut in. "How do we find her?"

James smirked up at him. "Why do you care, *Viking*?"

Mikael growled and lunged at James, but Aila darted in to hold him back. Seeming to regain his composure, Mikael straightened.

"Madeline and I have a blood oath," he said simply. "I must at least try to find her."

Alaric doubted that was the real reason, but said nothing to that effect. Arguing with Mikael would do no good, though it was hard to tell that to the burning ball of rage and jealousy in his gut.

Pushing back his emotions, he turned back to James. "You know we cannot let you go."

James laughed. "And I don't plan on leaving. I want to be on the team with the big scary charm and the evil witch."

"You would abandon Aislin, just like that?" Alaric questioned.

James rose to his feet, and no one stopped him. "I remained at Estus' side for thirty years on Aislin's orders, and look where that's gotten me. I was without my memory for weeks, and the people who took care of me were those I might consider enemies, not those I've sworn loyalty to. No, I'll take my chances with team wild card."

Sophie finally stepped forward. "What if we don't want you?"

James took a step toward Sophie, putting himself inches from her face. "If you didn't want me, then I wouldn't be here," he teased with an infuriating smile.

With a growl Sophie turned on her heel, then stalked off across the ice. Alaric shook his head, he would much rather kill James than bring him along, but he had an idea growing in his mind. One where James, now that he was James again, might prove very useful indeed.

"Pack everything up," Alaric ordered. "We need to get moving as soon as Sophie finishes her tantrum."

Mikael had turned to gaze off into the distance, keeping his thoughts on everything to himself. It was one of those moments where Alaric wished he had Madeline's unusual abilities. He would have very much liked to know what the Viking was thinking and feeling right at that time.

Not that Alaric cared about Mikael's emotions, but the game they played had just been irreparably altered. Alaric would not lose to the Morrigan, and he would not lose to Mikael. The prize for winning was simple. He would keep Madeline and his child safe. It was a prize worth more than any amount of riches.

After we'd settled into the Salr, the Morrigan had provided food and clothing more suited to our current environment. I had no idea where she'd gotten any of it, but I grudgingly appreciated that she'd actually taken into account my vegetarian sensibilities. The clothes weren't bad either. The gray jeans fit comfortably, as did the forest green, chunky knit sweater. The brown leather boots weren't what I would have chosen, but that was about it. I'd been able to take a hot bath, which was a huge luxury after my time spent in the icy wilds. I wasn't able to enjoy it like I would have if I knew everyone else was safe, but I hadn't turned my nose up at it either.

Besides the painful ball of worry in my gut, the only other thing wrong with the situation was the company. The Morrigan sat across from me at a large, plain wood table, ignoring me. She poured over an ancient looking book that had left a rectangle of dust on the table, while I gnawed at the remainder of my apple core and watched her every move.

My thoughts turned back to Alaric. Was he safe? Had our small party been found by our *enemies*, or had the Morrigan made the entire thing up? Would he and Sophie remain with Mikael's people, now that I'd disappeared, along with the charm that their plans relied on?

I shivered. I knew Alaric would look for me, but there was no way he'd be able to find me. It would be up to me to get back to him.

Looking up from her book to notice my shiver, the Morrigan waved her hand at the small fire in the stone fireplace, making the flames roar at full steam. She was gladly accommodating all of my needs, yet my pleas to take me back to my companions had fallen on deaf ears.

"What are you reading?" I asked, unable to sit in silence any longer. I grabbed the ends of my now-clean hair and pawed at them nervously.

"Rituals," she muttered absently. "We'll need to brush up to make sure we get everything right."

"What sort of rituals?" I pressed.

She slammed the book shut suddenly and gave me her full

attention. "What do you know of the legends concerning me?" she questioned abruptly.

"N-not much," I muttered, taken aback by the sudden attention.

She laughed bitterly. "Of course you don't. I'm sure if I asked you about Odin or Ra, you'd sing a different tune."

Not knowing what to say, I said nothing.

She sighed. "Many legends refer to me as the *Phantom Queen*. In many regards, they are right. It was not always so, but near the end of my time in these lands, I had the need for an army. I called to my side the banshees and other phantoms."

Just from what I'd learned of the Morrigan in the short time since I'd met her, I couldn't help but believe everything she was saying. She *seemed* just like a banshee queen.

"If things go according to my plans, you will have the power you need to rid yourself of the foreign energy inside you," she continued. "And our army shall protect you while your enemies are slain."

I shivered. This was the plan *I* had set into motion. I couldn't really pretend to be morally above it now.

"I have a question," I interjected, trying my best to ignore all of the bloody implications in favor of a question that had been vexing me.

She nodded. "Go on."

I bit my lip, not sure how to phrase what I wanted to know. Best to start from the beginning. "Several weeks before we summoned you, the key had taken me over. It kind of *possessed* me. When the others tried to remove it from my neck, it absorbed into my body. Long story short, I ended up meeting with one of the Norns. She conveyed that I could either die, thus taking the key with me, or I could put its energy into my child, thus giving the key human form. I rejected either option."

The Morrigan leaned forward over her old book, listening intently.

"The key has been dormant since then," I continued. "I felt it for a moment when you were summoned, but that's it. I'm frightened, because when I learned to shield myself from it, it learned the same. I feel like it's plotting something, but I have no way of telling."

She stood abruptly and walked around the table. I tensed as she moved behind me, then jumped as her hands landed gently on my shoulders.

She was silent for several heartbeats, then removed her hands. "I can sense its presence," she remarked as she moved around the table to reclaim her seat, "but little else. It is shielding very tightly."

"You're an empath too?" I asked breathlessly.

The Morrigan rolled her eyes. "As I said, you and I are the same. Any gifts you have are mine."

I let out a shaky sigh. The fire was making it too warm in the room, and I desperately wanted some fresh air.

"What about what the Norn said?" I forced myself to ask. "She claimed the only way for me to be rid of the key at this point was through death, or through my child."

The Morrigan smirked. "She was speaking in effect to who you were *then*, not to who you have the potential to become. Fate is a tricky thing. Her answer was in response to available solutions in that very moment, based on the person you were, and decisions you were capable of making."

My face fell in confusion. As far as I knew, I'd always been the same person, and always would be.

She tsked at me. "You are weak, Madeline. You look to

others to save you. You do not have the will to force the key out of you. You barely have the will to block it out of your thoughts. This weakness has shaped who you are, but it is also a choice."

My face burned with a blush. "I'm not weak," I argued. "You have no idea what I've been through."

"Those are the words of a child," the Morrigan snapped, then said sarcastically, "Poor me, I've fought so hard." Her eyes hardened. "None of it matters. What matters is the person you are today. When there is danger, you look first to others for protection. When there are decisions, you yield to others, believing your opinions are invalid. *You* are *weak*."

"Fine!" I shouted, just wanting her to shut up. "If I'm so weak, then why even waste your time on me? If I'm bound to fail, then why even try?"

Her stern expression suddenly transitioned to a sympathetic smile as her eyes went somewhat distant. "I was weak once too," she mused.

"What changed?" I asked shakily.

Her eyes met mine. "I was forced to stand on my own. The only way to break the cycle of depending on others is to stand on your own, *really* on your own. The only way you can become the person you need to be to control the power inside you, is to make the choice to do it yourself."

A few wretched tears slipped out. "That's why you took me away from the others," I accused. "It wasn't because they were slowing us down."

"They were slowing *you* down," she replied. "Holding you back."

I shook my head. "I wouldn't be alive if not for Alaric."

"Wouldn't you?" she questioned seriously. "Tell me, I've only been with you a short time, so tell me when he's saved you."

I thought about it. I'd escaped Estus' Salr with the help of

James. I'd defeated Diana with my magic. We'd travelled back to the present time with energy I'd stolen from Yggdrasil.

"When we were attacked in Estus' Salr," I blurted, trying to recall the exact event. All of the emergencies had somewhat blurred together in my mind. "One of Aislin's people had spotted me, and was coming toward me with an intent to harm. Alaric killed him."

"But this harmful man, he never actually reached you?" the Morrigan said as if she already knew the answer.

I frowned.

"How do you know you would not have saved yourself, had Alaric not been present? How do you know that if he had been somewhere else, that you wouldn't be alive today?"

My frown deepened. I didn't.

"Now tell me of the times you have saved yourself," she instructed.

I went back over everything I'd just gone through in my head, but didn't say any of it out loud.

Still, the Morrigan smiled, satisfied. "The truth is, though you've had help, you have no proof you couldn't have done all of it on your own. You feel you need a protector, without realizing you already have one inside you."

I went silent. I couldn't really argue, but I didn't exactly agree with her either. There might have been no proof I *couldn't* have done it all on my own, but there was also no proof that I could.

Really not wanting to discuss things further, I stood. "I'm going to take a look around," I announced, hoping she'd actually let me.

She nodded. "Think on what I've said."

I nodded quickly and hurried for the door.

"And Madeline?" she questioned, halting me mid-motion.

"I've sealed all entrances to this Salr. Don't waste your time trying to escape me."

I gritted my teeth and finished my advance toward the door. For someone who wanted me to stand on my own two feet, she sure was treating me like a child.

I let myself out into the hall and shut the door behind me. As soon as I was alone, I breathed a sigh of relief. I might not be able to leave, but it was nice to be away from the Morrigan's overwhelming presence.

I walked back toward the entrance we'd come through, unable to simply trust it was actually sealed. I at least had to *try*.

Sure enough, once I was in the entry room, there was no apparent way out. I touched the walls, and even used a rickety chair so I could touch the ceiling. There was no feel of magic to any of it.

Resigned, I journeyed back into the long hallway, not really paying attention to where I was going. I went through several twists and turns, occasionally checking behind closed doors, only to find barren rooms. I was just about to turn around and go back to find the Morrigan to ask her where I was supposed to sleep, when a noise caught my attention.

It sounded like a *psst*, followed by a giggle. More curious than I was afraid, I looked to my left. There was a door, slightly ajar. I'd ignored it since all the other rooms had been empty.

A small voice whispered, "Hey!"

My heart gave a little jump as I took a step closer and peered into the darkness seeping around the edges of the door. The rough wood slowly opened a little further inward, as if beckoning me inside.

Steeling myself for an attack, I pushed the door the rest of the way inward. The room within gradually lit of its own accord to reveal what was either a tiny woman or a child. It was hard to tell which. Her hair was dark green, but it was a green that looked natural, not dyed. It had highlights right where the sun would hit, and other subtle variations in color throughout. Rough-cut bangs obscured the upper portion of her face, which was delicate and angular, boasting large, sparkly hazel eyes that gave her a childlike appearance, though upon closer observation, I was pretty sure she was an adult.

Still, she couldn't have been more than five feet tall. Her clothes were a mishmash of different fabrics and styles, pairing a loose, long skirt with a button up tank top, and a pastel pink cardigan that clashed with the more vivid colors of her other clothing.

She gestured frantically with a tiny hand for me to step into the room, which I did without thinking. The door shut of its own accord behind me.

The room was clearly the small woman's living quarters, which meant she was likely Vaettir, if she was able to get inside to begin with. Her bed was made of straw, and the room was dotted with various crystals, shells, and other things that could be collected outside.

"What are you doing here?" she whispered. "No one has come to this place in a very long time."

"Who are you?" I whispered back, still feeling wary.

She looked slightly startled by the question. "I'm Kira," she answered, pointing at her chest.

"Are you Vaettir?" I asked, wondering just how long she'd been in the Salr alone.

"I know that word," she said thoughtfully.

I nodded. "I'm Vaettir too. How long have you been here alone?"

She shrugged. "I'm not sure, but I'm not alone. The

humans up above think I'm a fairy. They give me clothes and food, and they don't tell anyone about me."

My eyes widened. She'd somehow been living on her own and interacting with humans, while remaining off the radar of the other Vaettir.

"How on earth have you managed to live this way?" I marveled.

Misinterpreting my question, she answered. "The humans enjoy my gifts. I can make the flowers grow, and I watch over their gardens."

I shook my head. "I mean, how have you remained hidden from other Vaettir? We're not allowed to interact with humans any more than necessary."

Kira's eyes widened. "I didn't know! I'm good at hiding. I can hide from the humans too if that's what I'm supposed to do."

At the third mention of the humans, it finally clicked. Kira knew the way to civilization, and she knew the way in and out of the Salr.

She watched me silently as I thought things over, clearly panicked.

"I'm sorry," I blurted, realizing that she was waiting for me to explain things to her. "If you've remained hidden from the Vaettir this long, you probably don't need to hide from your human friends."

Kira heaved a sigh of relief, then asked, "Why are you with the Morrigan? I thought she left us long ago."

I inhaled sharply. "How do you know who she is?"

Kira seemed confused. "I remember her, somehow, from a very long time ago."

Woah. If Kira had seen the Morrigan before, that meant she was very, *very* old. Then something hit me that didn't quite make sense. "The Morrigan hasn't always looked like she does now. How did you recognize her?"

Kira's eyes widened. "Can you not feel her power? She's sealed us within the Salr with only a thought."

My hope deflated. If Kira was stuck here too, she couldn't show me the way out. "It won't be permanent," I soothed. "We're only staying here for a little while."

I didn't feel the need to mention we'd be using the Salr as a sanctuary while we summoned a dark army of phantoms.

Kira suddenly looked worried again. "Just be sure to do what she says while you're here," she warned. "You don't want to end up like Cúchulainn."

"Cúchulaiin?" I questioned, not having heard the name before.

Kira nodded and looked toward the door as if afraid the Morrigan would come bursting in at any moment. She turned back to me. "The Morrigan's only love. He seduced her, wanting her support in battle. She was once known as a great champion of warriors, protecting them in their endeavors. He eventually grew vain, and cast her aside, thinking he was powerful enough to make his conquests on his own. Outraged, the Morrigan hindered him in battle from that point forth. She could have killed him initially, but wanted his humiliation first. When he was finally slain, she appeared as a crow on his shoulder, showing him the darkness she would inflict upon his soul, even after death. She left this world shortly after. Many say she followed him into the underworld to torment him even there."

I shivered. I could see the Morrigan doing just as Kira claimed, and it explained her distaste for men.

"You should probably stay hidden," I advised, starting to worry that the Morrigan would come looking for me soon. "I'll come speak with you again, if I can."

Kira nodded as I turned to go.

"Hey!" she whispered before I could push the door open. "What's your name?"

I turned back to look at her. "Madeline," I answered, "but you can call me Maddy."

Kira nodded and smiled. "I can feel your power too, Maddy. Don't let the Morrigan change who you are."

With that unsettling warning, I nodded and turned to go. The Morrigan had said she wanted to make me strong. With the new information from Kira, I couldn't help but wonder just what that might entail.

On one hand, strength in times of conflict was necessary, but at what cost? Was it strong to sacrifice few for the good of many? Was it strong to risk summoning an army of spirits to save yourself and your child? I knew there were many differences, but at that moment, as I crept back down the hallway, strength and selfishness seemed to go hand in hand.

CHAPTER SEVEN

*A*laric glanced at James, creeping along silently in the darkness beside him toward the Salr. He felt uneasy with only James at his side, and even more uneasy with the plan in general.

Mikael was the one most skilled at negotiations, but he'd remained behind with the others. If things did not go as planned, *someone* would still need to save Madeline. Alaric hated the fact that it would have to be Mikael, but the Viking also stood the greatest chance of accomplishing the task, should Alaric perish.

He trusted Sophie to rescue Madeline too, but she wasn't as strong as Mikael, nor did she have the support of a clan. Mikael might have had many faults, but Alaric could almost guarantee he would protect Madeline, even though she carried Alaric's unborn child.

James gestured in the darkness, pointing toward the entrance. Alaric's eyes followed to where he pointed.

A large tree stump stood forlornly amidst the other trees, emitting a faint, familiar magic. He could only hope that past that entrance, would be Aislin. Since she had become Doyen for several clans, she had Salr in different countries, including this one in Norway. As Aislin's spy, James had known the location, though he couldn't guarantee Aislin would actually be there. Regardless, even if she was not somewhere below them, they might at least succeed in getting a message to her. A message filled with half-truths that might trick her into helping them, at least for the time being.

She didn't need to know James had turned on her, or that Alaric would sooner die than to give her Maddy. All Aislin needed to know was that Madeline had been kidnapped, and Alaric was desperate to find her. Desperate enough to join Aislin's clan, and to help her control Madeline. Hopefully the lie, being so bold and backed by his love for Madeline, would persuade Aislin to believe it.

The Norns' slaughter caused him to believe Aislin had a way of tracking Madeline, or perhaps of tracking them all, since she'd found them so easily. Then again, maybe she had just tracked the key. It made no difference as long as she could find Madeline or the key again.

Without tracking them, finding the Norn's Salr would have been near impossible. An idea supported by the fact that Mikael had kept it hidden for centuries. Aislin *had* to have a way to find Madeline for any of it to be possible.

James ran his hand over the surface of the tree stump. Moments later, a staircase appeared, level with the earth, leading downward. James went first. Alaric followed, relieved to not have the treacherous man at his back. Of course, Alaric supposed he was a treacherous man himself, shirking all former allegiances in the name of love. Estus had not been the first Doyen he'd served, but he would be the last, despite any consequences. He would never again stand by while someone he loved was tortured.

It *was* love, this thing he felt for Madeline. He wasn't sure if his draw to her was due to their similar natures, or to the fact that she was so different than other Vaettir. Either way, he was willing to die for her, a point he might well prove in the next few minutes.

Heading down the spiraling staircase, he found a Salr that looked much like any other. Nearing the bottom, two women came into view, clearly on guard duty judging by their stance, leather armor, and cold stares leveled at James and Alaric as they descended the stairs. Just one step above them, James halted. Alaric's stomach twisted as the ruse was about to begin.

One woman was small, with short gray hair, while the other was tall, with blonde hair cropped close to her head.

The gray haired woman smirked. "We never thought to see *you* again," she said to James. "Aislin will be pleased you yet live."

James nodded curtly. "Is she here?"

The blonde woman answered, "She is, but she grants audiences to very few."

"Trust me, she's going to want to hear what we have to say."

The older-looking woman smiled softly. "We shall see."

She turned and led the way deeper into the Salr, leaving the blonde woman behind to keep guard.

As James and Alaric followed, the blonde guard watched them warily. She was nervous about something, though whether it was due to Alaric's and James' presence, or something else, he did not know.

They left the entry room and continued walking. Other Vaettir watched as they passed by in the halls. Some nodded in recognition of James, but none spoke. Alaric did his best to quell his anxiety. There was no telling who else might have the gift of empathy, like Madeline, and he didn't want to give away any more information than necessary.

Eventually they reached a heavy wooden door with two more guards outside, one male and one female, both wearing the same leather armor as the stair guards.

The woman guard leaned against the wall casually, her long, red hair trailing across the stone, while the man stood at attention. Everything about him said *military*, from his crew-cut black hair to his ramrod straight spine, though he'd likely never been enlisted.

Vaettir were prohibited from joining human organizations unless it was to the direct benefit of the Vaettir, like in the case of police or social workers. Having a single soldier in the military wouldn't do any good, unless Aislin was gathering information. The thought made Alaric's stomach flip flop nervously.

Their escort looked the red haired woman up and down with distaste, then turned her attention to the male guard. "Tell the Doyen her spy is here, and that he is accompanied by . . . " She turned to Alaric.

"Alaric," he answered, assuming that with Aislin's intel, she would recognize his name.

The male guard turned and opened the door just enough to quickly slip into the room, careful to not let Alaric or James see inside.

Several painful moments later, he returned, opening the door fully. "She'll see you."

With a smug expression, James led the way inside. Alaric nodded to their chaperone and the red-haired guard, then followed.

The contrast between the room they entered compared to the rest of the Salr was jarring. Vintage lace and pastel velvet covered everything. The room edged on Victorian, but with hints of medieval, like the heavy wooden table where Aislin sat, pushed off to one side.

Ignoring them, Aislin lifted a spoon to her thin lips, calmly eating her supper despite the appearance of her visitors. Alaric's eyes narrowed as he scrutinized her. She wore a dressing gown that would have seemed casual, if not for the tiny gemstones sewn into the fabric. Her gray hair was curled into an ornate updo, topped by a simple tiara. Several attendants in leather armor surrounded her.

Aislin ate a final spoonful of her soup, set down her utensil, then dabbed her lips delicately with a cream colored napkin. With a regal air, she gestured for one of the attendants to remove her bowl. Once the attendant with the bowl silently let himself out of the room, Aislin stood.

"I thought perhaps you'd betrayed me," she said calmly to James, her lined face dispassionate.

"I was temporarily without my memory due to a blow on the head," he explained. "I only just recently regained knowledge of the past thirty years or so."

Aislin's lips sealed into a tight line. "You were there that night, the night Madeline used the charm to defeat my executioner. You fought for the wrong side."

If James was nervous, he didn't show it. "As I explained, I had lost my memory. Now that I have regained it, my allegiance is with you."

Aislin cocked her head in apparent deep thought. Alaric kept his breathing even, his stance relaxed, though he was quite sure he and James were about to die.

With a surprising nod of assent, Aislin turned her pale eyes to Alaric. "You were there that night as well, you stood at Madeline's side. I cannot believe that *you* have suddenly decided to choose the correct side."

Alaric glanced at James, then spoke. "Madeline and I had

hoped to use the charm as a bargaining tool to join your clan, as we desired protection from Estus. Siding with Mikael's people was a temporary allegiance, at best."

"Ah Mikael," Aislin mused. "How I would like to get my hands on him. Where is our Viking friend?"

Alaric didn't have to fake his frown in regards to Mikael. "We parted ways when Madeline was kidnapped. He did not view rescuing her as a feasible option."

Aislin laughed. "Now it all becomes clear. You hope I can find the girl, but why would I want to do such a thing?"

Alaric smiled. "Because you want to find the charm before Estus."

Aislin shrugged. "I spent centuries searching for the charm, until one of the Norns informed me that an executioner would use the dead to find it. Part of that information was relayed to Estus, unfortunately, setting this competition into motion."

"You speak to the Norns?" Alaric asked, truly astonished. Until recently, most Vaettir, except Mikael, had been under the impression the Norns no longer existed, and perhaps they never had.

Aislin fluttered her lashes, clearly bored. "That's besides the point. My point, is that I have waited for the charm for centuries, and I will wait centuries more if need be. Long enough for Madeline to perish, and for the charm to become fully available to *me*."

Alaric doubted Aislin had several more centuries in her. She'd aged a great deal over her long life, unlike him or Mikael. Her powers might be frightening, but she wasn't powerful enough to live forever. Still, it would likely be a moot point to argue with her, especially when he had valuable information to spur her into action.

"The charm has left behind its physical form," he

explained. "It now dwells within Madeline. When she dies, its energy will be released back into the universe. Whatever it is you intend to accomplish, it will have to be soon."

Aislin growled and slammed her dainty fist down onto the table, then turned ire-filled eyes to James. "Is this true?" she demanded.

James nodded. "I retained my memories during my lost time. I saw the charm withdraw into her body myself."

Aislin gritted her teeth. "I will kill the girl before I let her use the charm against me."

Panic washed through him. He debated killing Aislin then and there, heedless of her guards, but instead raised a finger into the air. "There is another way," he suggested, giving everything he had into keeping his voice calm.

"And *what* is that?" Aislin snapped.

Alaric took a step toward the terrifying little woman. "Madeline loves me, and she will trust what I tell her. All we desire is a safe home. She will use the charm to help you meet your goals."

Aislin's eyes lit up for a brief moment, then narrowed. "And how do I know she will not simply turn it against me as soon as I find her?"

"And how do you know she will not simply help Estus if he finds her first?" Alaric countered. "I've come to you in peace. If you help me, Madeline will do the same."

Aislin sighed and sunk back down to her chair, her anger suddenly gone. "So be it," she muttered. "I will help you find the girl. Just remember, your only hope for a clan lies with me, as Estus had already decided to have the girl killed."

Alaric smiled, though inside he felt sick. The Morrigan claimed that one clan still sought to use Madeline, while the other sought to kill her. He was actually surprised the one with murder on mind was Estus. Estus was an opportunist.

He would never eliminate someone useful. So what were his true intentions? Alaric's stomach tightened. He preferred dealing with an enemy he *knew,* not a stranger. For the first time, he was beginning to think he never knew his enemies at all.

CHAPTER EIGHT

A loud banging at the door woke me. Remembering I was still in the Morrigan's Salr, I yawned, then lifted my arms to rub my groggy eyes. I didn't want to get out of bed, even with a scary goddess hammering away at my door.

I stared at the ceiling for a moment, ignoring the banging. I hadn't slept much. Every time I drifted off, I was overcome by horrible nightmares. In most of them I was fleeing from unknown, dark forms. My pursuers remained vague, but I could sense their dark intents. Had the key wielded the dreams to mess with me? Maybe, but really, the dreams felt like more of a warning than a prank. Although I could still barely sense the key, I'd probably know if it awoke to terrorize me.

Another loud set of knocks sounded on the door. I sat up, groaning at the Morrigan's impatience, as the lights slowly came on in my fully furnished room. I had no idea where the Morrigan had gotten the furniture, and I didn't want to know. I didn't want to learn anything more from her. All I wanted was to be away from the goddess as soon as possible.

As my feet hit the cold floor, I realized I wasn't alone in

the room. My heart leapt into my throat, then settled back down as I realized the person crouching next to my heavy, wooden dresser was Kira. Leaning against the dresser's wooden siding, she held a finger to her lips, urging me to be quiet.

The Morrigan knocked again.

I cursed under my breath and stood, then gestured for Kira to hide under the bed. I hastily tugged the covers down to make sure she was fully concealed, then hurried to answer the door. It wasn't locked, and frankly I was surprised, yet grateful, that the Morrigan hadn't just come barging in. In fact, she even remained in the hall as I opened door.

She still wore her layers of dark clothing, with her red hair cascading nearly to her waist. However, unlike yesterday, she appeared *very* tired. Heavy bags marred the skin under her eyes, looking almost bruised against the near-translucence of her face.

"We must prepare for the ritual," she stated blandly, looking me up and down.

I instinctually wanted to take a step back, but that might invite her further into the room where she'd possibly sense Kira.

"You look tired," I commented, hoping she wouldn't take offense. "Are you sure you're up for it?"

She frowned. "This body was not made for the magic I possess. The things I've done have taken a toll."

"Maybe you should rest, er—" I paused. "You know, I really don't know what I'm supposed to call you. Is your name more of a title, or an actual name?"

She actually smiled. "You may call me Mara, and rest will not help me. I will draw strength from our army once they arrive."

I didn't like the sound of that.

She raised a red brow. "You know I can sense your emotions, my dear?"

I cringed, then shut my emotions down the way I'd learned from Mikael. I wasn't used to being around another empath, and it made me realize just how annoying I might be to everyone else.

My heart pattered nervously, but Mara didn't seem angry or offended.

"I will explain the ritual to you over breakfast," she said with a knowing smile. "Meet me when you are ready, but do not take too long."

She turned abruptly and swayed away down the hall, followed by the trail of her billowy dress and black cloak.

With a sigh of relief I shut the door, locked it, and turned back toward the room. Kira scurried out from underneath the bed, then slumped back against it in relief, still on the floor. Her green hair was alive with static from the underside of the boxspring, making her look just as frazzled as the emotions I was sensing from her. Emotions that echoed my own quite perfectly.

"What ritual?" Kira asked breathlessly. "What army?"

I moved to sit by her on the floor. "The Morrigan wants to summon an army of banshees and other phantoms to fight our enemies, other Vaettir."

I sensed a thrill of fear as it shot through her.

I turned to her. "Something tells me you know a bit about this phantom army."

Kira visibly shivered. "I remember something, from a long time ago. It seems like some distant dream."

First she remembered the Morrigan, and now this, both things that no one living should be able to recall? "Kira, just how old are you?"

She shrugged. "I remember when the lands were solid

green, and the few humans respected us. I made the crops plentiful in the spring, and my sister Sivi made the rivers flow. Our patron goddess, Coventina, gave us the gifts of the wells and springs, bringing life to the land."

I inhaled so sharply that I choked on my own spit. "Sivi?" I sputtered as I tried to regain some oxygen.

Kira nodded innocently, an expression I couldn't even imagine on Sivi's face. It had to be the same Sivi, who now that I thought about it, looked quite a bit like Kira. Sivi had translucent white hair and violet eyes, but their features were nearly identical.

Sivi had been the first one to offer me a way out of Estus' Salr after I arrived. She'd later offered me a way out of his dungeon, but it would have been at the expense of many innocent lives. Sivi wanted to put things back to how they were in Kira's memories.

"She's dead," Kira clarified, interrupting my thoughts.

"Are you sure about that?" I asked weakly.

Kira nodded. "The humans took her. They had started killing our people with fire, thinking us evil. Some of us were," she added. "Things had changed by then."

Well that explained Sivi's hatred of the humans. "Did you see her die?" I asked.

Kira shook her head. "No, but if she'd survived, she would have come back for me."

"Kira," I began, gently placing my hand on her boney shoulder. I didn't want to give her false hope, but some coincidences were just too great. "I'm pretty sure I've met your sister, and she was very much alive."

She startled, then looked like she might cry. "It cannot be. She would have come for me."

I shook my head. "I'm not sure she had a choice."

Kira shivered again, clearly holding tears in. "You should

go to the Morrigan," she muttered softly. "I worry she'll come back to fetch you soon."

I wanted to ask her more about the phantom army, but I'd just dropped a major bomb on her. It didn't seem right to push the subject. I sensed she wanted to be alone, so I nodded and removed my hand from her shoulder.

I stood and began to walk away, but felt compelled to turn around, overcome by a sudden wave of emotion from Kira. She remained huddled by the foot of the bed, covering her face to hide her tears, though her gentle sobs gave her away.

I wanted to go to her, but knew she wouldn't appreciate it. She'd been dealing with this pain on her own for a very long time.

I left the room, shutting the door gently behind me, then went straight to the bathroom. The small room lit up as I opened the door. Though the Salr all seemed somewhat similar, the bathroom fixtures in this one were different, more medieval. The tub was made heavy, dark metal, perhaps cast iron, and there was no toilet, just a chamber pot . . . not the most fun thing to use. On a small wooden bench by the tub were fresh clothes.

I paused to lock the door behind me, then leaned my back against it with a sigh. I'd taken a bath the previous day, and had mainly just been sitting around, so I rallied myself and went straight for the clothes. I donned the underwear and soft crimson sweater quickly. I lifted the next piece of fabric, which unfurled to reveal a long, flowy skirt, so not my style. I dropped it back to the bench, then went for the charcoal jeans I'd left in the bathroom the day before.

When I had done everything I needed in the bathroom, and could no longer stall, I left in search of the Morrigan. There had to be some way I could talk her out of the ritual. I wanted to beat Estus just as much as anyone, but I wasn't quite ready to summon a phantom army to do it.

I found Mara in the room where I'd eaten the day before. Her old book was lying open on the table, and several more had been added to it. I approached and touched one of the ancient pages while Mara remained seated by the fire.

"Where did you get these?" I asked, feeling somewhat enamored of the old books, even though they held information on a big, scary ritual.

"They were mine," she said, not turning to face me. "Preserved by my residual magic all this time. They waited for me here, hidden."

She still hadn't turned to face me, so I flipped through the pages of one of the books. The thick, waxy pages felt full of energy, making my fingertips tingle.

"Where is here, exactly?" I questioned.

I knew we were in a Salr, and that outside everything was very green, but that was the only information I had. In crow form I'd been able to perceive that we'd crossed oceans, but I wasn't sure which ones, or how far we'd actually traveled.

"This land is now called Ireland," she explained. "It is my homeland, and the land where my phantoms dwell, laid to rest within the earth."

Something about the tone of her voice was strange, almost sad, though she was shielding her emotions from me, so I couldn't be sure. There was an extra seat beside the fire, and feeling almost sympathetic, I moved away from the books and took it.

She offered me a sad smile as I sat, accepting my company. "You'll thank me for all of this in the end," she stated.

I wasn't so sure about that, but since she seemed in an information giving mood, I'd humor her.

"Why did you come back here?" I asked. At her sharp look I added, "Seriously. If this earth has changed so much from what it should have been, what value do you find in being here?"

She turned back to the fire. "You called to me."

I shook my head. "No I didn't. I didn't even know I was created in your image. Why did you come?"

She let out a long sigh, still staring into the fire. She seemed different with the fire illuminating areas of her face, almost *soft*.

"I saw an opportunity, and I took it," she answered quietly. "The old gods no longer hear the cries of their children, but I am not like them. I am no god."

Her revelation startled me. If she wasn't a goddess, how the hell had she traveled through the World Tree to get here? "If not a goddess, then what are you?"

She shrugged. "Over the centuries, many have labeled me a witch, some a goddess, and some have accused me of being one of the banshees. They are all correct, and they are all wrong."

Not fully understanding what she was saying, I waited for her to continue.

"I'm not explaining this well," she sighed, shifting in her seat. "The old gods are more like the Vaettir themselves, embodying different aspects of the earth, and of life itself, including civilization. I *am* this earth. It is a part of me. We come from the same natural balance of life, death, and emotion. It is what we are, and what you are meant to be. Harmonic balance, a never ending cycle of finding meaning, the spirit, then accepting death."

I blinked at her. " . . . *what?*"

She smiled, her gaze distant. "You will understand in time, once you have fully accepted your nature."

I shook my head, still not fully comprehending what she was, and by extension what *I* was. "But where did you *come* from? How did it happen that you were given physical form, if you *are* the earth?"

She smiled at me again. "I'm an accumulation of that energy, combined with humanity. I do not know just why I came into *physical* being, but becoming a part of humanity forced me to learn and grow as any human does. I'm the combination of humans and the earth, and all the greatnesses and terrors that such a combination can result in."

I let my breath out as I sank back into my chair.

"Do you understand?" she questioned.

I slouched down further into the cushion, feeling like I needed a hot bath, or a shot of whiskey, or *something* to take the edge off.

"Yes, and no. I mean, it makes sense to me, but if I think too hard about any of it, my brain just sort of *stops*."

Mara chuckled, then looked back toward the fire.

"I have one more question though, and I'm sorry if it sounds selfish."

She smiled and nodded.

I took her nod as a sign to go ahead and ask, "If you are the earth herself, and humanity, and emotion, then what the hell does that make me?"

She frowned for some reason, worrying me. "You are Vaettir. You are a member of your race just like any other, but you are also more. You can connect with the old, pure powers because even in this mortal form, they still flow through you. You can see things others cannot, such as the innate energy that courses through everything, and everyone, connecting us all."

I shivered despite the heat pouring forth from the fire. I *could* sense different energies, if that's what she meant, but I'd thought it was just part of being an empath. Emotion *was* energy. It was simply my gift, or my curse, nothing more.

Feeling more confused than ever, I shoved the information aside to be mulled over later. Her explanations had brought a more pertinent question to mind.

"If you are the earth and the connection within us all, why are you summoning an army to kill those we are somehow connected with?"

Her lips curved into a malicious grin, surprising me. "Because there is as much human nature in me as in any other, and vengeance and death are a part of life. We will cast our enemies down for ever thinking they are any more important than a frog, a leaf, or a tiny honey bee. I am light, but I am also darkness. We are good, but we are also evil."

I sunk even further into my chair as my heart began to race. I didn't want to be part of darkness or evil, but at that moment, I wasn't sure if I'd have a choice. All I wanted was to keep my child safe, and Alaric and Sophie. Heck, even Mikael. I was motivated by the urge to save my friends, not to crush my enemies. That was where the Morrigan and I differed.

If that made me a lesser being, then so be it. I'd never asked to be anything more than human.

Sensing my unease, Mara leaned forward, closing the space between us to put her hand over mine, which rested on the arm of my chair.

"You want to protect them, don't you?" she asked.

I inhaled deeply. I didn't know if she meant Alaric and my child, our traveling companions, or the Vaettir race in general. I was at the point where I couldn't care less about the Vaettir, but as for the others, the answer was *yes*. They had protected me, and now I needed to return the favor.

I nodded, hesitant to seal the deal with an actual *yes*.

"I can give you the power to save them all, and to save yourself," she explained, "but it has to be your choice. I was never given a choice in what came to me. I would not bestow the same fate upon you."

I quickly thought of my other options. Mikael's wife, Erykah, had said that in destroying the key, I would likely die, as would my child. One of the Norns had said the same. If I refused to put the key into my child, we would both die. Mara was the only one who'd actually given me an option where everyone would not only live, but I would be the one to save them. It would be a nice change from being such a monumental burden.

"Yes," I answered finally, placing my free hand on my belly. "I want to save them, and I will do whatever it takes."

Mara withdrew her hand and smiled. "Good. Now we must get to work. I have much to teach you before nightfall."

I let out a shaky breath and nodded. I could practically feel the gears of fate shifting. What we were going to do was against the laws of nature, and against the grim fate that had been laid before me.

So be it. I'd choose free will and survival over fate any day.

CHAPTER NINE

Crouched behind a distant tree, Sophie had watched in the darkness as her brother and James disappeared into the earth. Now, the first hints of sun were beginning to peek over the horizon. They'd been down there for hours. She glanced again through her binoculars impatiently, ignoring her weariness. She didn't like the binoculars, or anything that might hint her own senses weren't good enough, but she couldn't risk getting close enough to be seen. It could ruin everything.

If Alaric resurfaced, she would return to Mikael, setting their side of the plan into motion. If he did not, she would go in after him, despite the promises she'd made. Mikael would still be left to save Madeline, and that would have to be good enough.

She took another look through her binoculars and nearly gasped as the first figure climbed out of the earth. Luckily, she managed to remain silent. Even at such a far distance, certain Vaettir might hear her.

She didn't recognize the first person out of the ground, a man with dark hair and copper skin, but she did recognize

James as he surfaced next. She had to stifle her growl. *James.* She wished she'd had the heart to kill him, but she'd never been much of a killer unless circumstances truly called for it, despite her warlike nature. Alaric was the killer, Sophie was the tactician.

Sophie's body sagged in relief as Alaric surfaced next, followed by two other Vaettir she did not recognize. The plan must have worked. They would seek out Madeline, while Sophie and the others would prepare to aid them in any way possible, all while planning what might be the final battle for them all.

She rose and ran silently back in the direction of Mikael's current camp, wondering how her life had come to this. If only she would have stayed hidden when Alaric, Madeline, and James came looking for her in Spokane. She would have been safe . . . but no. That never would have been an option. Her brother was all she had. She'd rather follow him into hell than be alone.

She bounded across the earth tirelessly, following her own scent to find the hidden encampment. The ten miles went by quickly, though she had to stop and catch her breath right outside of the camp. Normally such a run wouldn't have fatigued her, but after the non-stop travel south, then a full night with no sleep, the long run took its toll.

Breathing easier, she ventured forth, feigning confidence to cover the aching anxiety zinging through her entire body.

Aila came into view first, her leather and fur clothing blending in well with the dried grass and oak of the forest. The only thing that stood out was her bright, blonde hair, up in its usual ponytail. Sophie observed her for a moment while Aila still couldn't see her.

The Viking warrioress hadn't spoken much since the night of the ritual. This saddened Sophie, as Aila had at some point crossed the line between traveling companion to friend. Yes, Aila had been rejected by her patron goddess, but Sophie suspected the result was based around Madeline, not Aila. Strange things had happened around Madeline since the beginning, and the attention always seemed to be on her. It wasn't surprising Madeline's goddess would come through instead of Aila's.

Finally spotting her, Aila lifted her hand in greeting. Sophie closed the distance between them as Faas and Tabitha crawled out of their tents. The few visible tents were low to the ground even when erect, their olive green coloring furthering their camouflage.

"It worked," Sophie informed Aila. "They are on the move."

"You and Mikael should go before the scent grows old," Aila advised.

Sophie nodded, not enjoying *that* aspect of the plan. She was the only one who could easily follow her brother's scent, and she would need to catch up before they reached civilization and the complications of automobiles and airplanes.

If they were able to continue following at that point, they would. If not, Mikael had given Alaric a number to call or text whenever he was able. *If* he was able. Sophie didn't like that aspect of the plan either. Aislin's people would be watching Alaric closely, and might not give him an opportunity to make contact. If that was the case, he and James would be on their own.

Mikael walked up beside Aila, wearing street clothes and a stern expression. Sophie wasn't used to seeing the expression on Mikael's face. She'd been under the impression that he'd tell jokes even if piranhas were eating him from the toes up.

"It worked?" he asked Sophie.

"James and Alaric came back out alive, with an escort," Sophie explained.

He accepted her answer with a nod. "Lead the way."

Before departing, both turned to Aila. She nodded. She would know what to do.

Sophie turned and ran back in the direction she had come, knowing Mikael would follow her.

Though she wasn't pleased with her brother being in danger, or with the ever-present threat of the key, and enemy forces, she had to admit that running through the woods felt *good*. It felt like what she was supposed to be doing. She was the embodiment of a war goddess, and also a part of nature. She was never meant to be trapped in some dark, depressing hole in the ground.

Alaric thought he caught a glimpse of his sister watching them as they walked through the forest. He clenched his jaw against his urge to look over his shoulder again. He would have to trust Sophie would be cautious enough to remain far out of sight. If one of Aislin's people spotted her following them, the plan would be ruined, and they would all likely die.

James walked at his side, showing no signs of worry. Part of Alaric was still waiting for James to betray him, throwing him to the wolves while he went to claim Madeline himself. Of course, the plan as they'd presented it to Aislin was contingent on the fact that Alaric would convince Madeline to use the key to do Aislin's bidding. If he were dead, the plan wouldn't exactly work.

The plan wouldn't work regardless, since Madeline had about as much control over the key as anyone, but Aislin didn't need to know that. All Alaric needed was to find

Madeline. If he could find her, then he'd have a chance of saving her.

When the opportunity presented itself, Mikael and Sophie would join them, and Aislin's people would likely need to be killed. *Or* the Morrigan would slaughter them all, and none of it would matter. No matter how likely such an end might be, he at least had to try.

Aislin had sent three people to accompany James and himself. He found sending such a small number odd. It was likely Aislin felt the plan might fail. She would not sacrifice any more of her people than she had to. If the plan he and James had presented was a trick, only three would die. If not, then Aislin would have Madeline and the key at her disposal. Either way, the Doyen had little to lose.

Alaric felt little guilt at the idea of killing those who accompanied them in cold blood. He knew they would do the same to him. Damon and Alejandro were the *muscle*, the former standing around six feet tall with short, honey blond hair and pale eyes, and the latter around 5'10" with perfectly copper skin, long, dark hair, and strong features hinting at his Native American heritage. Both men were well-muscled fighters. Alaric was unsure of Damon's nature, but he had learned from James that Alejandro was a descendant of Xolotl, the Aztec god of thunder.

Their third companion was Tallie, the tracker. She stood around 5'6", with straight black hair, porcelain skin, and features that spoke of the Far East. Her main talent was to track the energy signatures of others, though she could also take the form of a wolf, or so James claimed. Normally Tallie could only track someone she had interacted with, but the energy of the key was so great, she'd sensed it the moment it had been released from its former prison.

Aislin had used Tallie to track the key, and by association,

Madeline, wherever she had gone, but in most cases, the search took days. The locations Tallie sensed were not exact, and she could only gain a true feel for the place if the key and Madeline remained there for several days. She had also been the one to lead Aislin to the Salr where the Norns had been slaughtered, sensing the great amount of energy used to send Alaric, Madeline, and Mikael back in time.

Aislin's troops had been on their way to the campsite where the Morrigan had been summoned, just as the Morrigan claimed, so in effect the goddess *had* saved them from a confrontation. Alaric wondered at that, since she then took Madeline away. She could have done it without the warning, leaving Alaric and the others to die.

Alaric jumped back into the present as James asked, "Are you sure you know where to find Madeline?"

Tallie glared over her shoulder at him as she continued walking. "Just because I'm not willing to share that specific information with you, does not mean I don't know where she is."

Aislin's three emissaries had all changed from their leather armor to clothes that would blend in the human world, so Alaric guessed they were either on their way to an airport or train station. Hopefully he would be able to alert Sophie once tickets were purchased, and he had an idea of where they were going.

If not, he would save Madeline on his own. He would let no one stand in his way, even the Morrigan herself.

The ocean wind hit my face, soothing my nerves, if only slightly. I watched the fading sunlight flickering on the water, hesitant to move forward. Mara stood at my side, watching me. Had I *actually* agreed to this?

We had gone over the ritual to summon the banshees countless times. Once they surfaced, other phantoms would flock to their energy, and our army would be formed.

I shivered at the thought as I looked back at the circle of rocks that marked the entrance to the Salr. The air was icy, especially with the sun slowly sinking past the horizon. It seemed odd that a place so green could also be so cold. It reminded me of Mara herself, capable of warmth and beauty, but also ruthlessness.

At some point, I'd come to believe Mara truly had what she *thought* were my best interests at heart. The banshees would protect not only me, but Alaric, Sophie, and Mikael when the time for battle came. She claimed the phantoms would be under *my* control, and would not be loosed on humanity as a whole.

While I was still nervous about the idea of being surrounded by spirits, and I hadn't quite agreed to regrowing Yggdrasil, if it could even be done, the thought of being protected by an army of my own was enough to push me into performing the needed ritual, despite my reservations. I had to do whatever would give my child the best chance at survival, if nothing else.

Before ascending to the surface, I'd found the opportunity to leave a message for Kira. I'd hidden the note in my room in hopes she would go there after we left. Once we were gone, my new friend would be able come and go from the Salr as she pleased, and my only request was that she keep an eye out for Alaric or Mikael.

She didn't understand modern technologies like telephones, and wouldn't be able to contact them even if she tried, but at least her remaining behind to keep watch gave me a small hope of them finding me.

Of course, with an army of what basically amounted to ghosts at my disposal, perhaps I would be able to find them without Mara's direct help.

I stiffened as Mara's had alighted on my shoulder. She'd seemed melancholy at best since we'd started discussing the ritual, her eyes often going distant, as if witnessing things from the far past.

She removed her hand from my shoulder then offered it to me. I took it, wrapping my fingers around hers.

A moment later we were up in the air. I mentally screamed just as much as the first time, unable to come to terms with the feeling of not having a body of my own.

Luckily, we didn't need to travel near as far this time. Roughly ten minutes later, we swooped down toward an ancient, overgrown graveyard, separating into our human forms as our feet hit the ground. I took a deep, frantic breath, moving my hands up and down my body, then instinctually clutched my belly. It had grown dark while we travelled, but the moon was full, giving us enough light to see by.

The first thing I noticed, besides the crumbling headstones surrounding us, were the distant lights of houses. We were somewhere not far from civilization.

I looked to Mara, my worry clear on my face.

"The banshees will be under *your* command," she soothed. "They will not harm anyone unless you tell them to do so."

My shoulders slumped, but a measure of tension remained in my body. "Tell me why *I'll* be the one to command them again?"

Mara smiled patiently, her pale skin illuminated by the moonlight. "I may need to leave you for a short time. This body has weakened. I would not want to lose control of the phantoms because of my current state."

She wasn't lying. I had sensed her growing weakness like a weight pushing down on me. I knew it was almost unbearable for her, if I could sense it to such a great extent.

"You feel pity for me?" she asked, surprised.

I blushed in the darkness, still unused to keeping a constant shield up to protect my emotions.

"I can feel how tired you are," I explained.

She chuckled. "You hated me when I first took you away."

I shrugged. "I'm still mad, but I think you really do want to save me."

"And?" she pressed.

I sighed, empaths could be a real pain in the ass. "*And* maybe some of what you said about me always needing a protector somewhat made sense. It's refreshing to be around someone who thinks I'm capable of standing on my own two feet. I should never have *expected* others to help me like they have."

She grinned. "You could make the whole world bow at your feet, if you so chose."

I laughed. "Let's not get carried away. I want to save my loved ones, and sever my connection with the key. That's it."

She nodded. "Then that is what you will do, all on your own."

I nodded in return, then took a deep breath. "Are we ready?"

She let out a breath of her own, and if I didn't know any better, I would have said she was nervous.

She reached both of her hands out to me. I grasped them in my own, forming a circle with our arms. A cool breeze played with my loose hair. It tickled my face, distracting me, though my distraction only lasted for a moment as Mara closed her eyes and began to chant.

I joined in, repeating the words I'd memorized, first invoking the cardinal directions. The chant reminded me of something from modern day witch movies, except it was in Gaelic, the Morrigan's chosen tongue. The pronunciation had come more natural to me than Old Norsk, but it still had been difficult to get down. Fortunately it was a short chant, and having Mara say it with me helped.

I felt power growing around us, but words were only half the battle. Mara had explained that rituals weren't just about the words, they were about *intent*. You could mutter magic words all night long, but if you didn't have both the intent and power to back them up, all you would end up with was a lost voice from too much chanting.

We continued the chant, then started it anew from the beginning.

We finished, and repeated it a third time. That we were repeating it yet again was probably my fault. I wasn't focused. I still had reservations about what we were doing, and my mind was too consumed with thoughts of Alaric, and what might be going on with the budding war while I was with Mara.

She stopped chanting and eyed me in the darkness. "This body is too weak to complete the ritual on its own. I need your help."

I frowned. "I'm trying. I just can't seem to focus."

Mara sighed. "I can feel that you're trying, I apologize. Sometimes I forget you do not have the same experiences as I. Complete focus is a skill many mortals never attain. I can't expect you to have honed such a skill in your short lifetime."

I pulled away and dropped my hands to my sides. "So what do we do?"

Mara laughed, though it was weak. I could feel bone-aching tiredness wafting off her, making me feel tired too, though I was well rested.

"It weakens me being on this earth without my true form," she explained at my worried expression. "That form was lost to me long ago. I know it is wrong for me to be here, but I *needed* to help you. I needed to right the unbalance I helped create."

"But—" I began, wondering at her words.

She held up a hand to stop me. "We must try again."

I held my hands out to her reluctantly. If she didn't have the strength to perform such a ritual, there was no way I'd be able to do it.

Her eyes bored into mine as our arms formed a circle once more. "Close your eyes," she instructed.

I did as she bade me, feeling nervous. I'd always felt uncomfortable keeping my eyes closed when I wasn't going to sleep. Like something was going to jump out and attack me if I didn't keep an ever vigilant watch.

"Breathe deeply," she continued as I forced my eyes to remain shut. "Taste the moisture in the air. Feel the plants around us."

I took a deep breath, and felt a measure of calm. When I really focused, I *could* sense the plants around us, and the tiny little lives of animals and bugs. It was all energy, just like the force that flowed through humans and Vaettir alike.

"Good," Mara commented. "Continue to feel the energy. Search outward, and search downward. Focus on all that we're surrounded by."

I did as she bade, and eventually complete calm washed over my body.

"Now chant," she said softly.

I chanted, no longer worried about forgetting the foreign

words. They came naturally to my tongue, as if I'd been speaking them all my life. I felt pressure building as we named each direction once again, asking for the earth and sky to grant us their energy. I'd never been overly pagan in my spirituality, but the answering energies left little doubt there was something to the idea of earth magic. The energies were too tangible, too *real*, to be ignored.

The key remained quiet all the while, to my great relief. It hadn't chimed in for ages, as if afraid . . . or else it was just waiting for the right moment. Perhaps I was doing just as it wanted.

The thought gave me pause, momentarily severing my connection from nature, but it was too late. A final burst of energy erupted between our bodies, blowing our hair away from our faces in perfect unison.

The energy grew between us, but nothing else was happening. No phantoms came into existence.

Mara suddenly pulled away from me. I reached out for her, surprised. She hadn't said anything about pulling away during the ritual.

A gleaming knife appeared in her hand, held steady as the loose fabric of her clothing whipped around her like a mini hurricane. I reared away from her, fearful I'd been betrayed, then she plunged the blade through her ribcage, directly into her heart. I felt it as the blade connected with the vital organ, like I had been stabbed myself.

I coughed, thinking that it was only my empathy affecting me, but my hand came away with blood. I fell to my knees, mirroring Mara. Blood trickled from her lips as her eyes met mine.

"The ritual connects us, and it calls for death," she croaked. "Take my energy," she instructed. "Finish this."

We simultaneously coughed up more blood and I reached

out for her. My hands connected with her bloody chest. I could feel her frantic life force reaching out to me. It had nothing to do with whatever life had previously been in the corpse. It was all Mara, the same energy that had travelled through the spectral tree and into Sophie. I didn't understand how I could release that much life force, a life force capable of surviving on its own, and jumping from host to host.

Our faces were only inches away from each other. "I have grown too weak to maintain myself. Give me form when it is time," she whispered. "You are much stronger than I ever was."

Her life force rushed into me. The pain left me, and I knew just what I was supposed to do. I sent a wave of energy into the ground, just like I had done when I raised the corpses that initially protected the key. Something answered, a distant echo in my head, as Mara's body slumped to the earth beside me.

Misty shapes emerged from the soil, surrounding me so that I could barely see past them. They wore cloaks that seemed to be made of swirling smoke. Inside the cloaks, spectral features slowly formed. They were all women, with long, incorporeal hair swirling in the breeze to meld with their cloaks.

"Why have you awoken us?" several voices asked in my head. It felt like when I "spoke" to any other dead. There really were no words, but the point was conveyed regardless.

I opened my mouth to instruct the banshees, but was cut off as the key came to life inside me. I was held immobile as something that wasn't me said, "To spill the blood of my enemies."

"As you wish, Morrigan," the banshees echoed in my head.

I didn't know if the banshees were talking to me, the key, or the Morrigan's energy still within me, but I didn't have time to think about it. The three energies fought against each other, making me feel like they might burst through my skin any moment. I couldn't contain such immense power in my mortal form. There was no way.

As the energies collided with each other in one final shove, I screamed, clawing at my face in agony.

Still on my knees, I fell the rest of the way to the ground. The damp soil was moist and soothing, even though distantly I knew that my cheek was resting against a gravestone.

Beyond the immense energy within me, I could feel the energy of the earth below me. I reached out, focusing on that calm force instead of the war inside me. It soothed the three of us, as it called out to each form of energy equally. We were all different, yet we were all a part of the earth. We could work together. We were *supposed* to work together.

Suddenly all felt still. The earth, life, death, emotion, and chaos had suddenly found balance, just as they had found a purpose.

CHAPTER TEN

James and Alaric had been led to the Oslo Airport, where they now waited to board their flight. It was the same airport that had first welcomed them to Norway, and it brought back nostalgic memories for Alaric.

On that original flight, Madeline had slept on his shoulder almost the entire way, giving him hope she would forgive him. It had been one of the happiest moments he'd had in many years, and he'd always remember it fondly, especially because it was one of the last days before Madeline came in contact with the key. He wished he could rewind to that flight right in that moment. He doubted his upcoming flight would be anywhere near as enjoyable.

"What are you doing?" Alejandro demanded, walking up beside Alaric.

Alaric startled. He hadn't heard Alejandro's approach in the noisy airport boarding area. He raked his fingers through his hair and offered Alejandro a lazy smile, pretending he had just been daydreaming, when really he'd been trying to drop a note in a trash can for Sophie. He knew she would be somewhere near the airport, and would be able to smell out anything he left for her. She would not be pleased about digging through a trash can, but it seemed his best option if he didn't want Damon, Alejandro, or Tallie to notice the note before they departed.

He glanced over at James, relaxing in the first of several rows of waiting room seats. His muscled arms were spread out onto the seats on either side of him, taking up way more space than was necessary. He was so still he could have almost been asleep. It was hard to tell for sure with the dark sunglasses shielding his eyes. Either way, he wasn't likely to be much help.

"Just wondering why I'm not allowed to hold my own ticket," Alaric replied, letting his irritation show in his voice.

Really, he had no need to hold the ticket. Even though he'd had to wait near the airport's entrance while Tallie purchased plane tickets for all, with his heightened hearing he'd heard her booking their flight to Dublin, Ireland. That was what he'd written on the crumpled napkin that was now back within his pocket.

"You'll find out where we're going soon enough," Damon grumbled as he came to stand on Alaric's other side, nervously pushing his honey blond hair back from his face. "For now, we'd rather like to delay the moment where you try to kill us."

Alaric dramatically lifted a hand to his chest. "Do you truly think so little of me?"

Before Damon could reply, Alejandro smirked. "We are *all* on Aislin's bad side. This is our last chance to come through for her. If it's a trap, you'll just be saving Aislin the trouble of killing us herself."

"Shut up," Tallie ordered as she joined them, a large, soft pretzel in hand.

"What does it matter?" Alejandro sighed, glancing over at Tallie. "I'm sure he already figured out where we're going. We can fight to the death now, or later. What's the difference?"

Though Alejandro was correct, Alaric didn't quite feel the need to rub it in. Instead he kept quiet, hoping to keep the trio in an argumentative state where they might give away more information. His hopes were dashed as James chuckled from where he sat behind them, bringing everyone's attention to him.

"What is so damned funny?" Tallie asked hotly, turning away from Alejandro to aim her dark eyes at James.

James smirked, remaining in a relaxed, seated position. "You're all *so* worried that Aislin has purposefully put you into a position to be killed. Imagine what she'll do to *me* if I somehow end up fooling all of you. A quick death would be a reward compared to what might be in store for me. You all should be grateful."

"Is that an admission of guilt?" Tallie growled, turning away from the rest of the group to stalk toward James.

James grinned, though it was more a bearing of teeth, predator to predator. "Not quite."

Annoyed with the entire situation, Alaric looked up at the flight board. They were congregated in the wrong section of the airport, a weak attempt by Tallie to keep him and James in the dark. He knew which plane they needed to board, and when. Their flight was the next in line, and he hadn't managed to leave any clues for Sophie. With how Alejandro was watching him, he doubted he'd be given any opportunities.

"Why even try?" Alaric muttered, more voicing his own frustration than anything.

Tallie turned away from James to eye him dangerously. "If we succeed, we will be back in Aislin's good graces. If we fail, we will die. If we don't try at all, or if we run, we will end up with fates far worse than death. I have no doubt Aislin would find us, no matter where we hid, or with whom."

Damon and Alejandro silently nodded in agreement. Alaric was beginning to think Estus wasn't the only Doyen who didn't really care about the best interests of other Vaettir. He flashed back on the nervous blonde guard in Aislin's Salr, followed by the wary glances of her people as they walked through the halls. A tyrant is a tyrant is a tyrant. They might have come in different packages, but Estus and Aislin were very much the same.

A little beep sounded as the airport's intercom came to life. A voice announced it was time to board the flight to Dublin.

Alaric feigned surprise as Damon shoved him ahead of the rest of the group. They crossed the center hall to the correct waiting area. Damon smiled smugly as they filed into line with the other passengers. Alejandro moved up to Alaric's other side, giving him a look that said, *drop the act*. Alaric smiled knowingly at Alejandro and nodded.

Turning his gaze forward, Alaric fingered the napkin in his pocket. Since they were surrounded by distracting humans, he briefly considered dropping it on the ground, but it was too risky. If one of the others found it, they'd know the trap was coming that they already half-expected. He needed a more finite location on Madeline before that confrontation took place.

Gritting his teeth in annoyance, he boarded the plane.

I had no idea how much time had passed since the earth's soothing energy overcame me. When I finally sat up, it was still dark, and the banshees still watched me with hollow eyes.

Mara's dead body was beside me, and I knew I better high tail it out of the cemetery before any humans decided to visit their loved ones. As I looked down at her corpse, her words echoed in my head, *Give me form when it's time*.

I had no idea what she meant. The body she'd "killed" had already died once. It wasn't her real body, so maybe she'd just find a new one . . . but then, why had she asked *me* to give her form? Had her essence weakened too much for her to simply find another body, or was her last body's death some sort of sacrifice? Did she give up more in the ritual than just her borrowed form?

The questions were making my head spin, especially since I'd likely never get a definite answer. I rose to my feet as the banshees watched me curiously. Now that I was able to fully focus on them, I could tell their faces were actually very different, though they were all female. They floated above the earth in diaphanous robes, but I could still tell that some were taller than others, and some had larger or smaller frames. These were real women once, and now they were tortured souls. I could feel them just like I could feel the remaining energy in one of the Vaettir after their body had died. The banshees were trapped, anchored to the earth. It kept them from moving on.

I felt a connection to them, just like I did with other dead. I knew I could command them. I could sense their desire for a purpose. Thoughts suddenly flashed through my mind, and I wasn't sure if they came from the key, or from whatever part of the Morrigan was now inside me. It was confusing trying to decipher the difference, so instead I just listened to what the thoughts were trying to convey.

Our army must grow, they said.

I frowned. It was a thought both the Morrigan and the key would have, but I only wanted to listen if it was Mara telling me to do it. Anything the key wanted would be evil . . . yet it seemed to be going along with our plan. It had shown me it still had the ability to take over, to make me speak words that were not my own, yet it had kept quiet as we planned to summon Freyja, perhaps knowing we would get the Morrigan instead. Then it had kept quiet as Mara and I planned the ritual to summon the banshees. I was obviously playing right into what the key wanted, and I wasn't sure if that was a good thing or a bad thing.

"I don't know what comes next," I said out loud.

Realistically I needed to get out of that graveyard, and I needed to grow an army, but I didn't know *how* to do either of those things.

We know the way, one of the banshees chimed in, her voice an eerie whisper in my mind.

We can take you, another explained, her voice far deeper than the first.

"I need to find Alaric," I replied out loud.

No, not yet, a voice echoed in my head. It wasn't one of the banshees, rather a voice from within me. It made me dizzy to listen to so many forms of input directly into my brain. I clutched at my stomach, feeling nauseous.

"I need to do this on my own," I muttered, surprised, because I was pretty sure that it was *my* thought.

This fight had become extremely personal, especially with two foreign entities in my head, and one growing in my belly. It was the latter that made me realize I needed to step up to the plate.

My daughter would have Alaric, Sophie, and perhaps even others to protect her eventually, but right now, what she had was *me.* I needed to be strong enough to not only protect her, but to eventually show her that she could protect herself.

The banshees edged closer to me. I noticed a light swooping back and forth in the distance, and I realized with a start that someone was walking toward the graveyard with a flashlight. Someone had probably heard me talking to myself, and wanted to make sure no one was out here defacing the graves.

The banshees were suddenly very close. *We must go,* one of them urged. The image of a woman turning into a crow swept through my mind, but I shook my head. I wasn't the Morrigan. *That* gift was beyond me.

They seemed to sigh, then suddenly I was enveloped in mist. I had the sensation of flying, though I couldn't see nor feel much else. It wasn't as frightening as when I'd traveled with Mara. My body still felt whole as I was lifted into the air, just somewhat incorporeal.

The next thing I knew, I was standing in another dark graveyard. This one was deep within a forest. Most of the gravestones were nothing but chunks of stone on the ground, but I could feel the graves underneath. They weren't like regular graves. They were . . . restless.

They are not like us, one of the banshees explained, *but they will come if you call. They will fight.*

I felt confused again as reality seeped in. It was like I was alternating between a trance state, and the real me. The banshees' energy was overwhelming, as were the energies inside me. The spirits in the ground called out to the part of me that was *death*, but that was not all that I was. I was also life, and I couldn't forget that.

We only recognize death, one of the banshees whispered through my mind. *It holds us in its eternal embrace. It is all that we are.*

I sensed the truth in her words. The banshees would bring death and darkness, because it was all they knew. They followed me because they recognized one of their own, at least in part.

Call to them, the banshees instructed as one.

I did as they bade me. It hardly took any effort, since the spirits were already reaching out to me, begging to be released. I had a moment of worry over what might happen if I lost control of the dead I was collecting, but the thought washed away as the spirits joined us. Most were barely visible, but the change in energy was dramatic. It radiated through me, making me want *more*.

I could feel the key's excitement. It was no longer bothering to shield itself from me. We had a dual purpose now, even if we were acting for different reasons. It was sure it could take over if I faltered, though I didn't entirely agree. I was frightened by the idea, but I thought that maybe, just maybe, I'd be strong enough to fight it. The dead were mine, after all. They did not answer to the chaos that was the key.

Without another word, the banshees closed around me. After several dizzying moments, we reached the next set of ancient graves. These had no headstones at all. They'd never had them. It was a mass grave. The spirits were all tangled together underneath the earth.

I called to them, and they answered, pleased to be released from below.

We continued on, from graveyard to graveyard. I began to get a sense that *all* of these spirits recognized the Morrigan. She had used them before, and they had waited for centuries, anxious for the moment she would come again. Phantom Queen indeed.

They weren't normal spirits, either. Normal spirits found their peace and moved on. These wanted *more*. They could not let go of the lives they had once lived, just like the banshees.

We moved on to the next graveyard, traveling a much greater distance, then on to the next, growing my army every time my feet hit the ground. Eventually other creatures began to join us. Creatures that shouldn't exist in the modern day world flocked to the gathering energy, awoken from what should have been an eternal slumber.

I couldn't make them out clearly in the night. Most often, I would just catch a glimpse of bat-like wings in my peripheral vision, or perhaps a glowing set of eyes here and there.

As our communal power grew, I began to feel like we might actually succeed. We might win against Estus, and Aislin. My child and I might survive.

As I stood in another graveyard, looking around at the army I had amassed in record time, I felt almost smug. There was a new Phantom Queen in town.

CHAPTER ELEVEN

*A*fter arriving in Dublin well after midnight, Alaric, James, and Aislin's trio traveled by car to the North. *Far* North. Tallie drove, still unwilling to give away Madeline's location.

She seemed overly anxious during the car ride, giving Alaric the impression that more was wrong than previously stated. He hoped the *wrongness* had nothing to do with what Tallie could sense of the key and Madeline. At the very least, it could be that Madeline had already left wherever she had been, leaving Tallie to trace only the residual energy of her prolonged stay. At the very worst . . . well, he didn't like to think about the worst. He *couldn't* think about the worst.

After several hours, they arrived in a remote area near the coast, just as the first rays of morning sun appeared. Their plane had landed in the middle of the night, but none of them had voiced concern over rest as they immediately picked up their rental car and began driving. Luckily Ireland was a small country.

They emerged from the car to stand amongst a countryside awash with green. The ocean surf sounded in the distance. Alaric and the other men followed Tallie's lead like silent shadows.

She walked on for ten minutes, utterly absorbed in her task, but eventually stopped to look around, confused. Sensing Tallie's unease, Alaric surveyed the countryside anxiously. Had she lost the trail?

He scented the air. Madeline's scent was everywhere, but faint. She hadn't been there in several hours, if not more. He turned his gaze back to Tallie, searching amongst large chunks of rock for an exact location.

The search went on for another twenty minutes. Unable to stand idly by any longer, Alaric approached Tallie's side, leaving the other men to wait in silence behind him. She continued looking down at the ground. Alaric wasn't sure if she was actually looking for something, or just trying to bar any conversation.

"She's not here anymore, is she?" he asked softly, leaning forward into Tallie's gaze so she couldn't ignore him.

She tilted her chin down enough that her long, black hair covered her delicate features, then continued walking forward.

"Answer me," he demanded, catching up to her side once more.

She turned her panicked face up to him. "No," she breathed, "but we can at least look for clues to indicate where she went. She hasn't remained in one place long enough for me to locate her again."

Alaric let out the breath he'd been holding. At least she was still alive. He could deal with her not being where they'd hoped, as long as she still lived.

He looked over his shoulder, sensing eyes on him, but the others remained back where he'd left them, looking bored.

He glanced around the greenery and stones, sure there was someone else around, but his eyes found nothing.

"What is it?" Tallie asked suspiciously.

"Someone is here," he whispered.

The rustle of a nearby patch of brambles piqued his senses. He turned his gaze in search of the source, knowing he would feel extremely silly if it turned out to be an animal. Still, he couldn't shake the feeling that he'd had eyes on him.

Movement caught his attention once more. "There," he whispered, pointing to a copse of small, scraggly trees.

Before he could react, Tallie leapt through the air, shifting fluidly into a wolf before she hit the ground. Alaric had seen other Vaettir shift before, and was capable of small changes himself, but a shift like that . . . he'd only seen once.

His jaw clenched at the thought of the Morrigan turning effortlessly into a crow. He didn't know how she'd transported Madeline along with her in that form, but he was sure she did, given there was no scent trail to follow on the frozen ground back where Madeline had first disappeared.

He shook away his morose feelings as the giant wolf that was formerly Tallie darted around large stones, making a beeline for the copse of trees. Cursing his hesitation, he darted after her, hoping she wouldn't kill whatever she found. Distantly he heard the rest of their group jogging to catch up behind them.

He reached the copse of trees a moment later to find Tallie, still in wolf form, pinning something to the ground. No, not something, *someone*. The woman was tiny, with long green hair and angular features. She wore bulky, mismatched clothes, and seemed almost childlike. Judging by her scent, she was Vaettir.

Ignoring the snarling wolf on top of her, she turned wide eyes up to Alaric. "*You*," she whispered. "Are you really him?"

He took a step closer as the others reached them. "Am I really who?" he asked suspiciously.

"Maddy's boyfriend," the tiny woman answered, her voice strained from the crushing presence of the wolf.

Alaric's heart fell to his toes, then shot back up again in elation. "Get off her!" he demanded, shoving Tallie aside.

Tallie immediately returned to human form, her clothes reappearing as if by magic, just like the Morrigan's had. Her rump in the grass, she glared up at him.

Ignoring her, Alaric reached down to offer the small, frightened woman a hand up. She looked hesitantly at his outstretched hand, then took it. Once up on her feet, she took back her hand and stepped away from him.

"What do you know about Madeline?" he demanded, his heart still fighting to beat out of his chest. "Where did she go?"

The woman bit her lip. "So you're really him then? Alaric? Where is Mikael?"

Alaric frowned at the mention of Mikael, but quickly brushed the uncomfortable feeling aside. "Mikael is not here. Now *please* tell me where Madeline is. Time may be running out."

The woman nodded. Everyone stood silent as she explained, "The Morrigan took her away yesterday evening. I don't know where they were going, but Maddy left me a note. She said if I saw you or Mikael, I should tell you she's alright, that the Morrigan won't hurt her, but that she hopes to find you soon. She didn't know where they were going."

"One day," Alaric breathed. "We missed them by *one* day," he said more loudly, overwhelmingly frustrated.

"Will they return to this place?" Alejandro cut in as he took a step toward the small woman.

Alaric was glad for the interruption, and the logical question. He felt like he was about to lose his mind, or maybe he already had.

The little woman shook her head in response to Alejandro. "I don't know. The Morrigan left her books behind, maybe she'll come back for them."

"Books?" Alaric questioned, grasping at any small details that might tell him where Madeline had gone.

The woman's face lit up as she nodded, excited to be of use.

It was clear to Alaric that Madeline had befriended the strange woman, and he was not at all surprised. Madeline seemed to make friends under the most unusual of circumstances.

"Follow me," she said happily, then hurried right past Tallie, apparently unafraid that Tallie could shift back into a wolf and eat her.

Alaric was the first to run after her, followed a moment later by the others.

"My name is Kira," the woman explained as they jogged along over the loamy earth.

Her short legs belied the fact that she was incredibly fast. Alaric had to run at full speed to keep up with her as she darted around rocks, her long, green hair streaming behind her.

Kira suddenly came to such an abrupt stop that he ran right past her. He skidded to a halt, then turned to see her standing amongst a circle of large rocks. "And this is my home," she explained breathily.

Alaric took a step toward her, wondering what she was talking about. He had his answer a moment later as Kira bent down to touch something on the ground. Alaric tensed as he began to sink into the earth, then relaxed when he realized Kira was sinking too. Within a minute they were below the earth, standing in the entrance of a Salr.

"Are there other Vaettir here?" he asked cautiously.

He glanced around the dimly lit room. They'd entered the earth ahead of the others, leaving Alaric suddenly alone with Kira, vulnerable to an ambush.

She shook her head. "It was just me for a very long time, then Maddy and the Morrigan came. Maddy helped to keep me hidden. She didn't know what the Morrigan would do if she found me."

"Where can I find the books you mentioned?" he interrupted, anxious to look for clues now that he knew there was no danger, unless Kira was lying, but he didn't think she was.

Kira nodded, then started forward out of the small entry room, leading the way down a long hall. There was a commotion behind him as the others figured out how to enter the Salr, but he didn't bother waiting for them.

Kira led him to a large, cozy room with a heavy, wood table, comfy furniture, and a massive fireplace. He could still smell the smoke and ash of a recent fire. Books lined the large table, recently placed, judging by the dust that had been swept from them. He still couldn't believe he'd just barely missed Madeline, though the proof was all around.

The books now in his sights, Alaric rushed forward and began leafing though the pages while Kira stood aside. He could smell Madeline all over the ancient parchment, and the Morrigan too. They had studied these books together.

He frowned as the contents of the pages became clear. They were books of necromancy, or something like it, filled with rituals to summon the dead. He couldn't decipher them fully, as the text was in Gaelic, but he'd spent ample time in his five hundred years learning languages, and knew enough Gaelic to get the gist.

With a sigh, he stepped away from the books, hoping Madeline hadn't let the Morrigan talk her into something foolish. "Where is the note she left you?" he asked numbly, his back still to Kira.

"In her room," she answered, drawing Alaric's attention to her face. She suddenly seemed sad.

"Show me," he demanded.

She nodded, then ran off again with Alaric hot on her heels. A moment later they arrived in a bedroom. Madeline's scent was everywhere, and the bedding was still mussed from the last time she'd slept there. It was all almost too much. If they'd gone to Aislin just a little bit sooner . . .

Suddenly Kira was at his side, poking his arm to get his attention. She handed him a crumpled note.

He took it gingerly and flattened it in his hands. It read:

Kira,

I'm sorry I had to leave you here alone, but I'm guessing it's how you like things to be. You should be able to leave the Salr now to visit your human friends. I would like to let you just get back to normal life, but I have to ask you a favor.

My boyfriend, Alaric, is searching for me. I don't know if he will make it this far, but I can't miss the chance if he does. If he comes, you will recognize him by his long, black hair and dark eyes. He's very handsome, and is also Vaettir, like us. He might be with a woman who looks very similar to him, and another man, this one very tall, with long, reddish hair and eyes almost just as red. His name is Mikael. If you see either of them, please tell them that I'm okay. The Morrigan is trying to help me, and I think she knows what she's doing. I'm trusting in that idea, as I have no other choice. Once I am able, I will come looking for them. Alaric will have trouble finding me since we're traveling by . . . unusual means. If he still chooses to try, all I can tell him is that I believe we will remain on this continent for a while.

Tell him I love him, and that our daughter is doing just fine. At his stunned expression, clarify to him that yes, I said daughter. I think we might have a way to win this war, and to control the key, but I cannot say any more for fear this letter will fall into the wrong hands.

Once this is all over, if I am able, I will return here, and bring you to your sister if you so choose. Just be aware, she may not be the sister you once knew.

Your friend always,
Madeline

P.S. If you see any other Vaettir besides Alaric or Mikael, please do not approach them as you did me. They may mean you harm.

Alaric let out his breath as he reread the hastily scrawled words. They were a small consolation, but at least he knew Madeline and their child had been well when she wrote the letter. He shook his head. Not just their child. Their *daughter*. He felt an overwhelming mixture of elation, paired with crushing fear. He *would* save them.

Alaric reread the letter again, barely aware of James and Alejandro as they entered the room behind him.

"Did you see the books?" James questioned.

Alaric turned and nodded, almost wishing he had taken the time to hide the books from the others. He didn't want to give Aislin any clues as to what might happen in the near future.

"We need to find her quickly," he stated.

Both James and Alejandro nodded in reply. Alejandro looked worried. James just looked like James. Cold and dispassionate.

Tallie and Damon appeared in the doorway behind them.

"Let's go," Tallie ordered.

Alaric didn't like taking orders, but this one he had no problem obeying. He needed to find Madeline, to stop her from doing whatever she might be doing, before it was too late.

Sophie sat next to Mikael on the plane, breathing in the stale airplane air, tinged with a smell like antiseptic. She hated flying at the best of times, and her traveling companion wasn't making it any easier. He had requested numerous plastic cups of wine from the steward over the course of the flight, and was beginning to seem a little drunk.

"Is now really the time for that?" Sophie questioned, as he ordered what must have been his tenth glass. She'd lost count at some point, and had a suspicion he'd snuck more in while she'd been deep in thought.

He frowned at her, then sighed as he leaned back against his seat, reclining it the small amount allowed.

"Flying makes me nervous," he admitted.

Sophie's eyes widened.

"What?" he asked, sounding almost embarrassed, though Sophie felt he was incapable of *true* embarrassment.

She shook her head, then grabbed her seltzer water to take a sip. Flying made her queasy, just like riding in the backseat of a car, though she'd never outwardly admit weakness in either situation. "Nothing," she answered, returning her seltzer to the little tray attached to the seat in front of her, "just surprised you actually admitted that to me."

He grinned, transitioning easily back into the Mikael she was used to. "Come now, we're practically family."

Sophie glared, thinking she liked the embarrassed Mikael better. "*No* we are not. Alaric is my only family."

"And Madeline?" he pressed, leaning toward her, a small, knowing smile on his face. "She's carrying your niece or nephew. Is she not family?"

Sophie ground her teeth in annoyance. "Yes," she answered grudgingly. "Madeline is family."

It was the truth. When Sophie had found the note in the trash can, covered in James' scent, she had been elated by the idea that she'd be able to help rescue Madeline and her unborn child, especially since she'd almost given up hope.

She'd purchased a plane ticket just so she could follow Alaric's scent to the boarding area. But as she scoured everything he'd touched, she found no clue as to where he had gone. It was only when she switched gears and started scenting James that she found the note. It had been more than surprising. Perhaps leaving James alive hadn't been the *worst* idea after all.

"We better be able to find them," she muttered to herself, her thoughts turning back to Alaric and Madeline.

Thinking she was talking to him, Mikael replied, "I have many contacts in Ireland. Hopefully someone will have seen *something*. Unless you think you can sniff your brother out."

Sophie huffed. "Only if they're traveling on foot. If they rented a car at the airport, I have no way of locating him."

Mikael nodded. "My connections it is. Many reside in Dublin, so that will be our first stop."

Sophie frowned and leaned back against her seat. "They better be damn good connections."

Mikael looked smug as he received his umpteenth plastic cup of wine. "Everything I do is damn good," he replied. "You should know that by now."

Mikael *had* gotten them farther than Sophie had thought possible, so she supposed she could give credit where credit was due . . . though she'd never give it out loud.

CHAPTER TWELVE

Alaric inhaled the coastal breeze as they exited the Salr. The sky outside had grown cloudy, changing the pressure and making everything feel crisp with moisture. He gazed out toward the coastline as the others joined him.

Tallie wrapped her arms around herself, making the black leather of her coat groan. She gazed up at the clouds warily.

"That sure was an abrupt weather change," Damon commented.

Alaric ignored him, though he was thinking the same thing. He began walking back toward the car, expecting the others to follow. They'd searched the rest of the Salr to little avail, gaining nothing of use in their quest for Madeline. He was anxious to start searching elsewhere.

According to Tallie, Madeline had been on the move all night, and great amounts of energy were gathering wherever she went. Tallie felt the energy clusters were enough that she could probably lead them to one of the places, but it might be a worthless venture, as Madeline had not stayed put in any place for long, likely leaving few clues, if any.

They were going to the nearest site regardless, as it was

better than just waiting at the mostly-abandoned Salr. If Tallie sensed Madeline again, they would simply change course.

They were halfway to the car when the air pressure changed dramatically, making Alaric's ears pop. The temperature immediately dropped by ten degrees, and the sky darkened further.

"Do you feel that?" Tallie hissed, halting in her tracks.

Alejandro looked up at the sky, his long hair whipping away from his face as the wind picked up. "It feels like standing too close to lightning. Like there are electric currents running from the sky to the earth around us."

Alaric shifted from foot to foot uneasily as the hairs raised on his bare arms. His attention was drawn back to the coast. Something was moving out there, like a large, swirling mass of low, dark clouds.

After staring at the coastline for several minutes, he walked toward the dark scene. A horrible feeling compressed his lungs as his entire body erupted with goosebumps.

"Where are you going?" Tallie asked breathlessly. "Whatever this is, we don't want to confront it."

Ignoring her, Alaric increased his pace to a jog, trusting his intuition. Whatever the swirling mass was, it had something to do with Madeline. Once he had closed some of the distance, *she* came into view. He knew it was her, even without being close enough to see her features.

Dark shapes swirled around, darting in and out of the mass that seemed to move with Madeline's slender form. At first it had seemed like she was floating with them, almost melding with their diaphanous shapes, then she touched down onto the sandy shore and began to walk.

Alaric raced toward her, heedless of the phantoms.

"Madeline!" he called, loud enough to be heard over the

crashing ocean waves as he neared the beach where Madeline stood.

Her eyes rose to his as he halted his progress, about twenty feet away from her. She wore a crimson sweater and gray jeans that looked out of place with her supernatural entourage.

Panic clawed at his throat as Madeline stared at him. He feared she'd been taken over by the key, or worse, the Morrigan. Then she smiled.

"I knew you'd find me!" she called out.

He darted forward, closing the rest of the distance between them. His feet sunk into the soft sand as he wrapped her up in his arms. The phantoms swirled around them both as he kissed her, unable to help himself, though he had a million questions.

When he finally pulled away, he whispered, "What have you done?"

She smiled again. "I've built an army to protect us and our child."

"How?" he asked, glancing up at the dark forms. "*Why?*"

The unnatural wind played with his hair, melding it with Madeline's as he held her close. She didn't feel entirely real in his arms. Everything felt like a dream, at least, he hoped it was a dream, and not a nightmare.

He wasn't one to scare easily, but he had to admit, the phantoms had him on edge, even *if* they were under Madeline's control like they seemed to be. He didn't know how to fight phantoms, or if he even could. He was a warrior at heart, and intangible entities unnerved him.

She frowned. "What do you mean, *why*? I couldn't rely on you to protect me forever. I know you all think I'm weak, but I'm not."

"I know you're not weak," he gasped, confused by the

accusation in her words, "but this?" he added removing an arm from around her waist to gesture at the sky.

She watched him with a hurt expression, not bothering to glance up at the phantoms. Maybe she wasn't entirely herself after all.

Seeing that his current tactics were getting him nowhere, he changed his approach, though it pained him to do so.

"Where is the Morrigan?" he questioned evenly.

Her expression crumbled. "She sacrificed her human form to summon the banshees. I will bring her back when the time comes."

Her words didn't make sense. Something was *very* wrong, but Alaric felt it prudent not to comment. It would probably be a good thing if the Morrigan was truly gone, and stayed gone.

Not voicing his opinion was difficult, but he didn't want Madeline getting mad and taking off with her phantoms. The *real* Madeline wouldn't run, but he had no idea who he was actually dealing with in that moment.

He returned his arm to her waist to hold her a little tighter, just in case, then calmly asked, "What do you plan next?"

Relaxing into his embrace, she explained, "We must plan the final battle. From that I will gather enough energy to separate myself from both the Morrigan and the key."

The relief he'd felt when Madeline relaxed in his arms was instantly wiped away at her words. Had the Morrigan somehow shielded herself within Madeline, just like the key? That had to be the case if Madeline needed to *separate* herself from her.

"Where is Mikael?" she asked.

He clenched his jaw, wanting to say *something*, or to at

least lash out at the Morrigan in some way, but instead he answered Madeline's question.

"I wasn't able to send word to him before coming here. He is likely still back in Norway, waiting for a phone call."

She didn't seem to hear his words as she turned her gaze past him. Alaric glanced back to see Aislin's people, waiting on the crest of a hill, but James had left them and was heading their way.

"Who are they?" Madeline whispered, referring to those remaining on the hill.

"They belong to Aislin," he explained, turning his attention back to Madeline in his arms. "Joining with them was the only way I could find you."

She nodded, seeming to accept his answer, then pulled away as James approached. Alaric turned to stand beside her, facing James.

"He has his memories back," Madeline observed once James was within hearing range, surprising Alaric with her insight.

"I sure do," James said as he reached them, stopping before he reached the phantoms. "And I know who killed my grandmother."

Alaric turned his head to watch Madeline's expression. If she was nervous, it didn't show. The old Madeline would have been nervous.

"You'll get over it."

One of the phantoms darted toward James. He stumbled back, cowering as more of the dark forms swooped toward him, *threatening*.

"I suppose I will," he agreed, eyes remaining on the phantoms.

Alaric looked past James to Tallie, Alejandro, and Damon on the hill. They knew they were likely on a suicide mission from the start. If they tried to run now, Aislin would have them hunted and killed. If they tried to take Madeline by force, they would have to contend with an army of phantoms.

"Their choices are poor," Madeline commented, almost as if reading Alaric's mind.

He was used to her reading his emotions, but to pluck such a keen observation from emotions alone seemed far fetched at best. Perhaps she had not only gained an army, but a few new tricks as well.

She paused in thought, then said, "We cannot let them leave to spread word of what they've seen here. We can give them the choice to join us, but they cannot be set free."

James had finally braved the phantoms enough to stand near Alaric and Madeline. He lowered his voice as he commented, "If they join us, they're little more than mutineers."

Madeline smiled at him. "Aren't we all?"

James smirked. "I suppose we are, but the fact remains, they cannot be trusted. They might turn on you the moment you let down your guard."

Madeline laughed. "Then I will not let down my guard."

She walked forward, trailing her phantoms behind her, leaving Alaric and James behind to gawk at her back. She reached the edge of the rocky beach then walked across the lush grass toward the waiting trio. Alejandro seemed hesitant to remain where he was, but Tallie and Damon stood strong.

"You have two options," Madeline called out as she neared them. "Accept a new queen, or die."

Alaric's heart dropped as Damon abruptly threw himself toward Madeline, a blade gleaming in his hand. Alaric began to rush forward, but there was no need. Before the blade could strike, three banshees dropped down in front of him, letting out horrid cries.

Damon skidded to a halt, gazing at the spectral women before him, awestruck. As Alaric reached Madeline's side, Damon began to sputter while clutching at his throat. His hands moved to claw at his face, eyes still intent on the banshees before him. Everyone watched in silent horror as he fell to his knees, then keeled over, dead. It had all happened so quickly Alaric felt frozen. He'd had no time to act, and wasn't even sure what he would have done if he had.

Tallie and Alejandro dropped to their knees before Madeline. Not looking up, Tallie explained, "Our job was never to bring you back with us. It was to kill you. Aislin did not believe the charm is within you, and wants you dead so she may claim it for herself."

Thoughts raced through Alaric's mind as he tried to ignore the dead man at their feet. It was Estus who wanted Madeline alive after all. Had Estus learned the charm was within Madeline, or did he simply understand he couldn't take it from her regardless? Still, Alaric wasn't sure how Estus would hope to use her. She was a force to be reckoned with, and held no love for the aged Doyen. After the scene with Damon, he did not envy Estus' chances at survival.

Madeline crouched and released the life from Damon's body, not bothering to even look down at him, then stood to face Alaric, ignoring Tallie and Alejandro.

Alaric still longed to hold her, but she was not *his* Madeline, not right now at least. He hated that his first thought was that maybe Mikael would know what to do, but he really was their best hope in that moment. The Viking had been alive over 1,300 years, and had acquired a great deal of arcane knowledge in that time.

Alaric knew he should be setting some sort of plan in

motion, but he couldn't seem to fully focus on the details with Damon's dead body lying a few feet away. He wasn't bothered as much by the death, as Madeline's reaction to it. Madeline *always* cared about death. She valued the lives of heroes and villains alike.

Madeline seemed as if she were about to say something to him, but something else caught her attention. Alaric followed her gaze past the still waiting Tallie and Alejandro to two distant forms. Relief flooded through him. Mikael and Sophie.

He never thought he'd feel such happiness to see someone he utterly detested, but there it was. He was at a complete loss with Madeline, sensing that if he pointed out that she was being influenced into decisions that weren't her own, she'd simply leave. Whatever foreign energies were inside her likely held no love for him, so if the part of Madeline that was still Madeline wasn't strong enough, he didn't stand a chance.

Mikael and Sophie broke into a jog upon seeing them. Both wore modern clothing that would have blended in anywhere. Sophie's of course, was uniform black.

Neither hesitated at the sight of the phantoms still swirling around Madeline, though Sophie did watch them warily as they approached.

Tallie turned to their new company, then took a step back. "You're Mikael," she gasped. She turned back to Alaric. "You had planned to ambush us from the start," she accused, then quickly went pale as one of the phantoms darted a little too close to her, blowing her hair away from her face with the sudden gust.

Mikael stepped forward. "On the contrary." He winked at Tallie, then walked past her. "We caught word from my contacts on this continent of one of the Vaettir, a woman, raising the spirits of the restless dead across the countryside, paying little heed to any who might witness the odd sight." His eyes focused on Madeline. "Some of them were nearby, trying to figure out a way to kill you before I intervened. At that time, Sophie caught wind of her brother, leading us here."

Madeline's smile sent a chill down Alaric's spine. "Kill me?" she laughed. "Let them try."

Mikael's expression didn't change, though there was a certain wariness in his gaze. "There will be no need for that. Save your strength for our enemies."

Madeline smiled even wider. "If I expend my strength, I will simply gather more." She turned back to Alaric. "We've waisted enough time. We must choose the location of the final battle."

"We need to stop and think," he cautioned. There had to be a way to reach the *real* Madeline, to pull her back from the abyss.

James grunted in agreement, reminding Alaric that he was right beside him. He'd been so distracted that he'd forgotten his once friend, now long-time enemy had been there at all.

"I've made my choice," Madeline said evenly.

She turned away from Alaric to regard Tallie and Alejandro, both of whom went green with the new attention. "Send word to Aislin. I will await her on the battlefield, but tell her nothing else. If you betray me, I promise your deaths will be much worse than your Doyen could ever manage."

Before Alaric could reach out and grab her, the phantoms lifted Madeline back into the air. She didn't look at him at all as she was carried away, back toward the coast. Within moments, she faded from view, almost as if she'd been absorbed into the swirling fog composed of spirits.

Mikael closed the final distance between them with Sophie following shortly behind. His long, auburn hair blew back from his face as a particularly harsh, cold breeze came in from the coast.

The breeze prickled Alaric's skin with electricity, as if it carried unnatural energy with it.

Mikael glanced between Alaric and Sophie. "*That* was not Madeline."

Alaric turned away from Mikael and his sister to gaze off in the direction Madeline had gone. "At first I thought the key had taken her over again," he explained, "but there's something more. I believe the Morrigan has shielded herself inside her as well. They all now work toward the same purpose."

Alaric turned back to Mikael to find that he had been gazing at the coast with him.

Swallowing his pride, Alaric asked, "How do we fix this?"

Mikael shook his head. "We summoned a deity to *fix* this, and we've only succeeded in making things worse. I do not know how to fix this."

Alaric felt like he wanted to scream, to curse the entire planet for providing the one he loved with such a tumultuous existence. He couldn't lose her and their child now. He had promised to protect them both.

"We have to try," he urged, willing the Viking to agree with him.

If Mikael gave up, Alaric would force Tallie to find Madeline again. He did not know what he'd do when he found her, but he couldn't *not* find her.

"I swore an oath to her," Mikael said coldly, seeming to sense what Alaric was thinking. "Despite what you may think of me, I hold true to my oaths."

Alaric breathed a sigh of relief, then gestured back to the

waiting Tallie and Alejandro. "Tallie can find her, given enough time," he explained. "We just need to wait until Madeline remains in one place long enough for a perceptible amount of energy to build."

Mikael glanced back at Tallie, then turned away, seeming to dismiss her. "We cannot remain one step behind. We must anticipate Madeline's next move."

He clenched his fists. "No one could have anticipated any of this."

"She's going to gather more power," Mikael observed, not offended by Alaric's tone. "She wants a *final battle*, but which part of her wants it? The key would be motivated toward that goal. I don't see what the Morrigan would have to gain, but perhaps she would as well."

"What's your point?" Sophie growled, finally interjecting herself into the discussion.

Mikael shrugged. "I'm just trying to determine where Madeline is coming from. *Why* she has embarked on this endeavor."

"She's obviously been taken over by more powerful forces," Sophie grumbled. "Madeline is coming from nowhere. It's the key's actions we must predict."

Mikael shrugged again, but said nothing.

Sophie sighed. "What is it?" she asked tiredly. "What are you not saying?"

Mikael frowned. "I'm saying that the Morrigan and the key might both want the final battle, but Madeline might want it too. Was her original intent not to use the deaths from a large battle to destroy the key?"

"I don't think Madeline is willingly going along with this," Alaric countered. "It's not something she would do just to beat the key. The last time she raised the dead . . . " he trailed off, thinking of Diana. "She was horrified. You saw those *things* she summoned. That is *not* her."

Mikael snorted. "I think you give her too little credit."

"On the contrary," Alaric argued, "I give her the credit she deserves. Madeline would not be reckless enough, and selfish enough to summon an army of spirits just for a chance to rid herself of the key."

Mikael smiled. "Unless she truly thinks she can win."

Alaric shook his head at Mikael's foolishness, then looked back to Tallie and Alejandro. They could have tried to run during their discussion, but hadn't. Of course, they had nowhere to go. If they didn't return with news that Madeline was dead soon, Aislin would send others to hunt them.

James walked forward, encompassing Tallie and Alejandro in the span of his gaze. "I chose the side I think most likely to win," he explained to them. "Will you do the same, or will you ride Aislin's sinking ship to your deaths, which will probably happen tomorrow?"

Tallie stood tall and unyielding. "I can find Madeline again, given the time. I've weighed the odds, and think this route my most likely chance of survival, but I want a guarantee of protection from Aislin."

She'd looked to Mikael as she'd said the last, and he nodded in reply.

Alejandro stepped up beside her, though he didn't seem happy about it, especially since Damon's corpse was only a few feet away. "I have no desire to go near the Phantom Queen again, but I will fight for the side not planning on sending assassins after me."

Alaric shivered. *Phantom Queen*. It sounded familiar to him.

"They called the Morrigan the Phantom Queen," Mikael observed, "not long before she left this world."

Alaric crossed his arms against the cold seeping into his bones. He was rarely affected by cold, but he was sure feeling it now.

"There is a Salr here," Alaric explained to Mikael and Sophie. "We can wait until Tallie gets a sense of where Madeline is. Perhaps she'll even come back."

"I will send for my people to gather on this continent," Mikael replied, turning his gaze back to the coast. "We must be ready, should Madeline spring the *final* battle on us." His expression turned pensive. "I must speak to my contacts once more to see if they can grant me any further insight into what Madeline has done."

Before Alaric could accuse him of planning to run off, Mikael met his eyes firmly and said, "I will keep my oath to her."

Alaric sealed his lips into a tight line and nodded. "As will I."

The two men turned away from each other, Alaric marching in the direction of the Salr with the rest of their party following, while Mikael walked off alone.

The only other oaths Alaric had ever sworn were to protect his sister, and to kill Mikael to avenge his mother. This latest oath, to save Madeline and his child, would have to take precedence. He'd waited hundreds of years to kill Mikael, but it no longer mattered. He was now only concerned with who needed to live, not who needed to die. Death could come later.

They were going to have a daughter, Madeline had said, and no ancient Viking, nor vengeful deity could compare to the importance of that.

CHAPTER THIRTEEN

Mikael had lied when he said he was going to meet with his contacts once more. He'd already learned all he could from them, and what they suspected regarding Madeline's whereabouts.

Madeline had spent the previous evening visiting ancient graveyards, many of which could not be found on any map. Some were mass graves of victims who'd suffered ill fates due to famine and war. Others were simply old. They were places where the spirits didn't truly rest, unwilling to let go of their natural lives.

Given her chosen locations, Mikael's contacts had speculated on where she might go next, and he had to agree with them.

There was a well known sight in Dublin called Bully's Acre. Originally a priory, hundreds of thousands of people had been buried in the area, starting as early as the 1170s. The gravesite had eventually been leveled, leaving no record of most of the bodies beneath the earth. It was a perfect place for Madeline to fill out her ranks, with so many dead in one space.

He found the odds especially likely, since she had covered most of Northern Ireland during the previous night. It would only make sense for her to cover the South before moving on to other continents, if she moved on at all. Ireland was the Morrigan's chosen homeland, so it figured her phantoms would come from there, and only there.

Madeline had proven she could cover many graveyards in a single evening, and Bully's Acre would undoubtedly be on her list. So that was where Mikael would head, on his own. He knew Alaric would not forgive him for omitting him from his plans, but he also knew he could not take him. Madeline was not herself. If she harmed Alaric while possessed, it would kill her later. Mikael's only hope was their blood oath. If Madeline caused him harm, the earth would come to claim her. With any luck, he would have a chance to remind her of that fact before she killed him.

If it was in both the Morrigan's and the key's best interest to keep Madeline alive, they would at the very least exercise caution, or so he kept telling himself. In reality, any positive outcome would require a great deal of luck. He'd always been lucky, but this was pushing it.

Still, he didn't think twice before climbing into the car he and Sophie had driven to the countryside. He never reconsidered as he took the narrow country road toward the highway.

Dublin was several hours away, but it was barely midday. Madeline had visited the other graves under the cover of night, so it would stand to reason that if she did indeed visit Bully's Acre, it would not be until the sun went down. He had time.

Even so, as soon as he reached the end of the country road and turned onto the highway that would take him South, he sped down it like a bat out of hell. Once he reached an area where his cell had service, he called Aila, instructing her and Faas to catch the next flight to Ireland, leaving Tabitha to gather the rest of his people, urging them out of hiding.

Faas would not appreciate being separated from his sister, but he would be needed to determine just what was going on inside Madeline. Since he could drain and analyze the spiritual energy from others, he'd be able to tell Mikael just how much space the Morrigan and the key were now taking up . . . if Madeline didn't kill him first.

The key would most definitely see Faas as a threat, since Faas could weaken its vessel. The real Madeline would willingly let Faas take her energy. The other energies, most likely, would put up a fight.

He clenched his jaw and focused on the road. After all he had sacrificed, all he had lost, he would not lose to the key now. This was a battle begun long before Madeline was born, and he would see it through to the bitter end.

"You shouldn't have let Mikael go," James argued as soon as they were back within the Salr.

"He won't harm Madeline," Alaric sighed, scenting the air for Kira.

He knew he had already gotten all of the information out of her that he could, but he couldn't just sit and wait for Tallie to sense the key. He *had* to act. If Kira couldn't be found, he would read the Morrigan's books cover to cover, despite the language barrier. Perhaps their pages held some way to reverse what had been done to Madeline. If so, he'd do his best to decipher it.

"How can you be so sure?" James asked, following Alaric down the narrow hall.

Tallie and Alejandro had gone ahead, claiming a room to get some rest after disposing of Damon's body. Alaric probably should have gotten some rest himself, but even after not sleeping the previous night, he knew any efforts he made would be fruitless. There was no way he could sleep so soon after losing Maddy once again.

He had no answer for James, or rather, none he was willing to give. He sensed Mikael was either in love with Madeline, or he'd found some other sort of camaraderie within her that Alaric didn't quite understand. Either way, the Viking was intent on rescuing her. Mikael might betray Alaric and James, but he would not betray Madeline, even if there wasn't an oath holding him in line.

He decided to give up on his search for Kira, since James would probably pester him the entire way. Instead, he stopped at the room containing the Morrigan's books.

"You didn't answer me," James said evenly, following him in.

"He swore a blood oath to Madeline," Alaric explained. "You were there, if you recall."

James snorted. "All of that time seems like a dream to me."

Alaric lifted one of the heavy tomes from the table and slumped into a chair to peruse its contents. "It was more like a nightmare, seeing you cower in fear with only the slightest provocation."

"Yeah," James grumbled. "You must have *loved* seeing that."

"I'd rather not see you at all," Alaric replied simply.

He knew he was baiting James, but he was itching for a fight. Too much inaction and too much fear over Madeline's predicament left him grasping for something to focus his attention on. Why did James even want to converse with him in the first place?

James picked up a book himself, not really looking at it. "You say that," he argued, "but then why am I still here, and not in an unmarked grave with Diana?"

Alaric shrugged and focused on the book, not wanting to put Sophie in the spotlight. She was off exploring the rest of the new Salr on her own, and she'd not thank him for giving away her secret to James.

"Answer me," James demanded, raking his hands through his golden hair with an irritated flick.

Alaric glared at him. "We considered leaving you unconscious, but didn't want you relaying any information to Aislin."

"*And?*" James pressed.

Alaric shrugged again, giving in if it meant James would leave him alone. "And my sister didn't have the heart to kill a man while he was unable to defend himself. Sophie has never been much of a killer."

James smirked. "If she was, I'd be dead ten times over, though I'm not sure why you've never tried to do it for her."

Alaric looked back down at his book. "Sophie can fight her battles as she chooses."

"And Madeline?" James walked to the front of the empty fireplace, his back to Alaric. "Can *she* fight her battles as she chooses?"

Alaric frowned behind James' back. "If Madeline were in her right mind, I would respect her decisions. I *have* respected her decisions thus far. Yet I will not stand idly by while foreign energies use her body for their own purposes."

"And you're so sure that Madeline has no control in this situation?"

Unable to focus on reading, Alaric put down his book.

"You saw the same display as I. We both know Madeline would never speak like that. She would never have brushed off Damon's death so easily."

"Or maybe the little mouse is growing fangs," James taunted, turning away from the fireplace to face him, "and you're worried that they'll be bigger than yours."

Alaric raised an eyebrow at him. "You truly think that was Madeline speaking, and not the key or the Morrigan?"

James smirked again. "She was looking at you with the same sappy eyes she always does. *That* look didn't come from the key, and I doubt it came from the Morrigan, given how she feels about men. Madeline might not have been pulling all the strings, but my guess is she's a willing partner in this endeavor, not a prisoner." He turned back to the empty fireplace and began stacking some nearby logs in the center.

Alaric shook his head, turning his attention back to the book. The Madeline he knew would never summon a phantom army. Of course, the Madeline he first met would not have made it this far to begin with. Maybe he wasn't giving her enough credit. Or, perhaps he was giving her *too* much credit by assuming she'd take the moral high ground, despite the consequences. Perhaps Madeline was more like the other Vaettir than he'd originally thought.

He wasn't sure if it was a comforting thought, or a frightening one. On one hand, a callous outlook bettered her chances of survival. On the other, it changed who she was. Madeline's unyielding respect for life was a part of her. It had shaped who she was, and in many ways, it had shaped him during the time that he'd spent with her. He didn't want her to change, and he wasn't sure if his concern was for her, or for himself.

That thought alone troubled him. He wasn't used to the

dynamics of a committed relationship, and he wasn't sure how selfless or selfish he was supposed to be.

He pushed his thoughts away as he read the text in front of him. None of it mattered, really, since as far as the odds were concerned, neither of them would survive very long.

Forget phantoms, deities, and the key. A battle between the two largest clans of the Vaettir would mean bloodshed like their race had never seen, and it would undoubtedly spill over into the human world. There was no way to contain it.

Even if they lived, their lives would be changed forever. There was no telling in what way, but he was quite sure it wouldn't be good.

His attention was brought back to James as the fire roared to life. He looked a question at him as he rose, surprised that James would be considerate enough to build a fire.

Not meeting Alaric's eyes, James muttered, "I'm going to get some rest. I suggest you do the same."

Alaric nodded as James left him, turning his eyes back to the book. There was an image of a woman sacrificing a man before him. The accompanying chant called to death and darkness for power.

Though Madeline could bring death, that wasn't all she was. She was *light* and compassion. She wouldn't take part in a ritual that worshipped only death.

Would she?

CHAPTER FOURTEEN

Mikael walked amongst the gravestones dotting the grassy earth like the broken teeth of some long-dead giant. He thought he could almost *feel* the energy of the dead below, but it was probably just paranoia. Sensing the dead, or energies in general, was not one of his talents.

The sun was yet to set, so a few humans, tourists most likely, milled about the ancient gravesite. There weren't many since the winter months weren't the tourist high season. Hopefully they would leave before full dark. Witnessing what Madeline had to offer might be a bit more than the visitors had bargained for on their trip to Ireland.

He took a seat on a nearby bench to wait, fidgeting nervously. It wasn't often that his nerves got the better of him, but it also wasn't often he went into a situation he was unlikely to win. Best case scenario, Madeline would hop a ride with her phantoms to get away from him. Worst case, she would disregard her oath and kill him, then the earth would claim her in turn. Of course, there was a third option.

She might gather enough power to find a way around their oath, and would kill him with no consequences.

He could only hope enough of the real Madeline was still beneath the surface to not want to hurt him. Of course, if the key was in control, it might not kill him either. The key would use anyone it could, and Mikael was rather useful. However, if the Morrigan was in charge, he would die. He trusted that witch even less than he trusted the key.

He remained on his bench as darkness slowly crept across the countryside, chasing away the humans visiting the historical site. He felt more comfortable as the last of the visitors left, then grimaced at the thought of what might have happened had Madeline shown up with her phantoms in public.

Mikael wasn't worried about what the humans would think. Most humans wouldn't believe the story of a ghost army descending upon an ancient graveyard. It would be passed off as poisonous gasses seeping up from the ground to make people hallucinate, or some other such rationalization. He was more worried about the idea of Madeline harming people. Her conscience would destroy her in the end, if they ever managed to restore her to her original self at all.

As full darkness fell, he continued to wait, but there was no sign of Madeline. He decided to move to a less conspicuous spot, not only worried a security guard might approach, but also not wanting Madeline to see him first. If she saw him first, she might simply flee.

His mind made up, he moved silently to a more secluded area of the gravesite and crouched in the darkness, where he continued to wait.

The hours crept on. He'd left his cell phone in the rental car, and had no watch to tell the time, but he guessed it was somewhere around midnight. He cursed silently. He'd been so sure Madeline would want to utilize Bully's Acre, but perhaps he was wrong. Perhaps she went to another continent entirely, and he had no hope of finding her without Tallie's help.

Still, he would wait the night out in the graveyard, just in case. He pushed his hair back away from his face as a cool breeze hit him, sending goosebumps up and down his arms. Normally he was fairly tolerant to the cold, but there was something about this breeze that wasn't quite right. It felt like it was laced with electricity, yet there was no storm to provide lightning.

He continued to crouch as he heard light footsteps on the grass not far off.

"I didn't expect to find you hiding in a graveyard," a voice said, suddenly near him.

He rose abruptly and turned toward the voice. Madeline stood roughly twenty feet away, alone. At least, she appeared to be alone. Mikael had little doubt the phantoms could swoop in without a moment's notice.

He took a step toward her. "Well you left so suddenly this morning, we never got to finish our conversation."

Madeline closed the distance between them. Over her sweater and jean ensemble, she'd added a knee-length, black coat that billowed around her legs as she moved, adding to the *Phantom Queen* imagery quite nicely. Her long, wavy hair danced around her shoulders and waist as the breeze played with the loose tendrils. Standing before him, she turned her face upward, her expression calm.

Looking down at her smaller form, Mikael could have sworn she was the normal Madeline. The look in her pale blue eyes was familiar, unlike the presence of a foreign power.

"It really is you in there, isn't it?" he observed.

"Did you doubt it?" she asked, sounding like Madeline, only slightly off. He realized with a start that the new tone in her voice was confidence.

"But there are others inside of you as well . . . " he trailed off, feeling the urge to reach out and touch her to verify she was real.

She nodded, sending her hair forward over her shoulders. "You were already aware of the presence of the key. Now the Morrigan helps us too."

He sighed. He didn't want to contradict Madeline out of fear she'd take off again, but he also wanted to keep their civil conversation going. "Up until now, I was under the impression we were fighting *against* the key."

Madeline tilted her head to the side in thought, a very un-Madeline gesture. "For now, our purpose is the same. We must work together to achieve our goals. Once our enemies have been dealt with, the key and I can have a stand off of our own."

Mikael nodded, outwardly accepting her answer, even though he didn't accept it at all. "If we are to defeat our enemies, it would be nice to have you around to plan with us."

Madeline frowned. "I must finish summoning my army first."

His palms began to sweat. Something about the whole conversation was unnerving. He remembered when Erykah had been tied to the key. Sometimes it spoke through her, but not like this. This was like Madeline's personality had actually melded with the other forces.

"You're nervous," Madeline observed. "That's new."

Mikael was momentarily shocked that he'd let his mental shields down, or had he? His eyes widened slightly as he focused his attention inward. His shields were still firmly in place. Her empathic powers must have increased along with everything else.

"Can you blame me?" he asked.

She shook her head and smiled. "No, I don't blame you, but I must ask you to stand aside while I retrieve what I came here for."

Ignoring her request, Mikael asked. "Is it *you* that wants this, or is it the Morrigan?"

Madeline laughed, surprising him. "You all think I'm *so* weak. The Morrigan saw my strength. She knew I could do this on my own."

Mikael laughed in reply. "If I thought you were weak, I would never have allied myself with you to begin with. Our oath goes both ways, so you know I'm not lying."

That seemed to give Madeline pause. "If that is the case, then you can trust that I know what I'm doing."

"I do trust you," he replied. "I just want to make sure that this is *your* choice."

"It is, now please stand back."

"At least come reassure Alaric that you and your child are both okay!" he blurted out as she began to slowly raise her arms. "This uncertainty is killing him."

Her intent expression faltered, once again giving Mikael hope the real Madeline was reachable.

"I'm doing this for both of them," she replied. "This is the only chance we have to all survive."

"Then come back to the Salr and tell him that," Mikael urged.

He really didn't care about Alaric's well-being, and Madeline probably sensed that, but it was still something *she* would care about, or at least, the real Madeline would.

"I can't," she stated. "We're running out of time, and the banshees are growing restless."

Mikael shivered at the mention of banshees. He'd been alive when banshees still roamed the countryside, and had no desire to go up against one.

Madeline shut her eyes, as if trying to shut something out. She was beginning to seem panicked, letting Mikael know that he was running out of time himself. He couldn't let her flee.

"I need to remind you of something," he said calmly. "*All* of you," he added, including the key and the Morrigan in his statement.

Madeline turned suddenly bored eyes to him, like she had once again been taken over by the calm, confident energy.

"Madeline," he began slowly, putting emphasis on her name, "you and I have an oath. If you directly harm me, or if you order anyone, or *anything* else to harm me, the earth will claim you. Your mortal form will cease to be, and therefore the key, and perhaps even the Morrigan, will cease to be."

Madeline was so still, he couldn't even tell if she was breathing. He knew he had to act fast, otherwise the banshees would come and take her away.

He darted forward and scooped her up in his arms. The moment he touched her, the banshees darted down from the sky, letting out ear-piercing shrieks.

Mikael ran forward, throwing Madeline over his shoulders, holding on tight. The banshees swarmed them, but caused no harm. What he'd said about the oath must have worked. Whoever controlled the banshees also knew that harming Mikael with Madeline's powers or her army would break her oath, and hence end Madeline. It would all be over if Madeline no longer existed.

Darting through the cemetery, he tightened his grip on the back of her thighs, hoping she wouldn't view this kidnapping as a form of betrayal. He was also saving her, was he not? If he did not try to save her, would that not also be a form of betrayal? He was taking a risk, but saw no other choice.

He spotted the rental car ahead. Madeline hadn't fought back, she might yet as she hadn't had much time to react. When she did, she might reason that she could harm him without breaking their oath, as she'd just be defending herself. Reaching the car, he flung open the driver's side door, set her in, then quickly lifted her over the center console to the passenger seat. He slid in after her and slammed the door shut, then started the car to peel away before Madeline had time to rebel.

"What the hell do you think you're doing!" she shouted as she recovered.

Mikael tore out onto the empty, night-time street.

"Saving you from yourself," he replied calmly, keeping his eyes on the road.

"You can't betray me like this!" she shouted. "Our oath prevents it!"

He smiled. If it was a betrayal, he would be dead right now. "Saving you from yourself is not a betrayal. Allowing you to be controlled by other beings *is*."

"You're afraid," she spat back. "I can feel fear wafting from you like foul perfume."

He clenched his jaw. "I just kidnapped the *Phantom Queen*, not entirely knowing if doing so would break my oath and thus, would quickly end my life. Of course I'm afraid."

Madeline quieted at that. Her sudden shift in demeanor was unnerving. "Well you've stopped me from my task, for now, so what do you want? You can't keep me indefinitely. There are too many things in motion now."

His foot pressed more firmly on the gas pedal. "I just

wanted to talk with you without the risk of you getting angry and running away."

He couldn't bring her back to the Salr where Alaric and the others waited. Not yet. Still, he needed to take her somewhere the banshees couldn't reach them.

"So talk," she demanded. "I've got things to do."

Talking in the car was really probably as good a place as any. As long as they were moving, it would be difficult for her to escape.

"What happened with the Morrigan?" he asked, wanting the specifics of what was going on before he addressed any further issues.

Madeline sighed. "Why should I tell you?"

Mikael grunted in annoyance, flexing his fingers on the steering wheel. "Perhaps because we're friends. Or because we've been helping each other since this all began. If not for those reasons, let's go with the fact that I've saved your ass plenty of times, and you owe me."

Madeline was silent for several minutes, then finally answered, "She killed herself, at least in part, to summon the banshees. A portion of her energy is inside me now, so I can bring her back."

"How?" Mikael demanded, hating the idea that the Morrigan had become a part of Madeline, almost as much as he hated the key being a part of her. "How will you bring her back?" he clarified.

Madeline was silent again, then answered. "I don't know. I imagine she'll tell me when it's time."

Mikael frowned. "And the key?" he pressed. "You're now working with it, rather than against it?"

Out of the corner of his eye, he saw her shrug. "For now we all share the same goal. Any conflicts will be addressed after that goal has been met."

"After we destroy our enemies?" Mikael asked, then added, "Are you even thinking about the fallout of such a large scale battle? Don't get me wrong, I agree that it must happen, but it will change the world forever. There is no way to hide such a thing from the humans. Many lives will be lost after the fact. Everything will be out of balance. Are you willing to shoulder the consequences of that?"

"Our plan is to restore balance," she said immediately, then turned pleading eyes to him. "Don't you see?"

Glancing at her, he slowed down briefly to take a turn, then sped back up. There was still no sign of banshee pursuit. Perhaps Madeline had ordered them to fall back.

"I'll see if you tell me," he replied.

He fully understood that small actions could have very long term consequences. He'd been around long enough to see things that had happened a thousand years prior affect the present day. Things that had happened to *him* a thousand years prior.

"I can't," she replied softly. "You're just going to have to trust me."

He was surprised to realize that he *did* trust her, as he trusted very few people on this earth. Still, he didn't trust the warring forces inside her.

"I trust *you*," he replied, hoping she would get why he was putting emphasis on the *you*.

She was staring at him so intently, he glanced away from the road again.

"I'm not a slave, or merely a vehicle in this situation," she said evenly, meeting his gaze.

Her eyes were so intense, Mikael wondered if she was trying to tell him more than she was saying.

He turned his gaze back to the road with a sigh. "I can see

that. I just hope you can tell the difference between your thoughts and the *others*."

Mikael glanced at her again, catching a brief glimpse of worry before she wiped it away.

"Where are we going?" she demanded.

"Where do you want to go?"

She snorted. "I already went to where I needed to go, and you took me away."

"I asked where you *wanted* to go," he countered, "not where you needed to go."

When she didn't reply, he added, "You really should speak to Alaric. Assure him you're okay. He'll never believe it coming from me."

He glanced at her raising an eyebrow at him, her pale blue eyes soft. "So you believe that I'm okay?"

"I believe that you're strong enough to get through this," he replied evenly, "and lucky enough to perhaps come out alive. I believe fate has chosen you for this role, so as much as I'd like to fight it, I cannot."

"You've always struck me more as an *I make my own fate* kind of guy."

Mikael smirked. "In many ways yes, but far too much has happened for me to consider it mere happenstance. That the key would fall into the hands of a descendant of the Morrigan herself, that *has* to be fate."

She turned her gaze away from him to look out the passenger window. "I can't see Alaric," she said softly.

"Why?" he demanded.

Mikael hated that he was defending the man, but he really did believe it was in Madeline's best interests to be around him if she wanted to maintain the part of herself that was *her*.

She continued to gaze out the window, partially turned away from him. "I think you of all people can understand that he would distract me from what I need to do. If I'm with him, and we begin to think about our child, our *daughter*, I'll just want to run away and hide from everything to keep them safe. I can't do that. I have to be brave."

"That's one way to look at it," Mikael began, "*or* you could draw strength from him. There's nothing wrong with accepting help."

"I don't need it," she snapped, suddenly defensive, though Mikael sensed it was still Madeline talking, and Madeline who'd somehow been offended by what he'd said.

A thought dawned on him. Madeline's drastic attitude change could have been a defensive reaction to the Morrigan manipulating her. He fully understood the intricacies of manipulation. He was the descendant of Dolos after all.

"She made you feel weak, didn't she?" he asked before he could think better of it. The Morrigan was still inside Madeline, after all, but Madeline seemed to be the one doing the talking at the moment.

Madeline glared at him. "Perhaps at first. Then she showed me how strong I really am."

"It takes just as much strength to accept help as it does to do things on your own," he countered.

Madeline nodded. "Yes, but there is a difference between accepting someone's protection, and *needing* it."

He sighed. "You've come far from the Madeline I knew."

He'd meant it in part as a compliment, but Madeline obviously didn't take it that way.

"The Madeline you knew was weak," she snapped.

"The Madeline I knew made a promise to my wife," he snapped back, finally getting angry. Had she forgotten everything?

She seemed taken aback. "You're really just going to have to trust me," she said finally.

By her tone, he felt again she was trying to tell him more than she was saying. Was she perhaps shielding certain thoughts from the key, and thus unable to voice her true plans out loud?

"I'll trust you if you come back to the Salr with me," he offered, hoping he wasn't making the wrong decision.

Madeline sighed. "Fine, but I won't stay. I can't lose any more time."

He nodded. "Talk to Alaric, then we'll stand back while you do whatever you need to do."

Madeline went silent after that.

He took the turn that would lead them back toward the Salr. There was still no sign of any banshees. He almost wanted to ask Madeline if she was keeping them at bay, but he couldn't quite bring himself to do it. He wasn't sure if it was more frightening that she had control over things straight out of men's nightmares, or if she didn't. One option made Madeline a huge force to reckon with all on her own, and the other meant that they were all completely screwed.

CHAPTER FIFTEEN

My pulse picked up speed as the car slowed, then came to a stop. We'd driven as far as we could toward the Salr, and would have to walk the rest of the way. It would be dawn soon, meaning I had lost an entire night of progress, but that wasn't what had me frightened.

It had been hard enough for me to leave Alaric the first time. I wasn't sure if I could do it again. I wasn't sure if I could look away from the option of having him embrace me. To *protect* me.

Yet, I knew what I had to do. No one could help me with the task before me. If I wasn't strong enough to do it, then no one could save me regardless.

I startled when a blast of cold air hit me. The passenger car door was open, revealing Mikael. I'd been so absorbed in my thoughts I hadn't realized he'd exited the car. He stood there, leaning toward me, offering a hand to help me out, a much more polite gesture than when I'd been forced in. I took his hand and slid out of the car. Fatigue washed over me, more than I'd felt in days.

With a start, I realized I'd now gone two entire nights

without sleep, though the entire span of time seemed like a blurry dream. I needed rest. I had to keep my strength up if I hoped to not only survive, but to maintain my identity against the powerful forces within me.

Releasing my hand without a word, Mikael led the way toward the Salr. I followed, wrapping my coat tightly around myself in an attempt to shut out the freezing cold coastal wind. It was of little use. When I'd been among the banshees, I had barely felt the cold. Now without their presence, I felt human again. Weak and fragile.

The thought was almost enough for me to summon them forward. I had pushed them away once I'd arrived at Bully's Acre, not wanting to make a scene with any humans that might be hanging around the historical site late at night. My foresight had been to my detriment, since it had allowed Mikael time to grab me before the banshees could. Once I'd been thrown into the car, it only took a single thought to hold them back again. I'd known deep inside that this meeting was something I couldn't avoid, though it scared me half to death.

As I walked, I pictured Alaric's face when I told him he couldn't help me. He'd gone through hell for me, and had put me through a bit of hell himself. Still, I couldn't deny the fact that he'd proven his love, even if it was a love I didn't fully understand.

I'd thought what I'd experienced with Matthew, my first real boyfriend, had been love, especially after I'd accidentally released his life, but I'd been wrong. I knew now what love felt like. I knew what it was like to sit next to someone and feel utterly at home. I didn't know why that love had come so suddenly, and I could speculate until the cows came home whether it was fate, or just that Alaric and I had similar natures that drew us together, but it didn't really matter.

What mattered was that it was there, and there was no arguing with it . . . though I was about to try.

I unwrapped my arms from myself to rub the small bump of my belly as Mikael walked silently beside me in the darkness. Alaric wouldn't understand, but I was doing this as much for him as I was for myself and our daughter.

Eventually, we reached the circle of rocks leading to the Salr. There was no one there to greet us, not that I expected there to be. Mikael wasn't one to share his plans unless he thought it absolutely necessary.

He crouched and touched a small stone on the ground to trigger the entrance. The action would only work for one of the Vaettir, a little quirk possessed by every Salr. I clutched at my belly again, not wanting to descend into the earth, even as we began to sink.

Mikael gave me an encouraging smile in the moonlight, then suddenly we were underground. I turned to glance down the familiar hallway, expecting to see Alaric waiting right there, but he wasn't.

The person I did see was the woman, one of Aislin's people, who'd been with Alaric when I'd arrived at the Salr the previous morning.

Her eyes widened as she saw me, then she averted her gaze and hurried down the hall until she was out of sight, her long, dark hair whipping behind her.

I turned to Mikael in surprise, then suddenly realized why she was afraid. My banshees had killed a man she knew right in front of her. I barely even remembered the scene, and that thought alone made me shiver. Maybe being around the energy of the phantoms had altered me more than I'd realized.

Mikael gestured for me to move forward, and I did, since the only other choice was climbing back out of the Salr.

I walked down the familiar hall, half expecting to walk around a corner and see Mara, even though there was no way for that to happen.

Not knowing where Alaric was, but somehow sensing where I should go, I approached the room where Mara and I had gone over her books. The door was slightly ajar.

I turned to look at Mikael for reassurance, but he'd stopped following me at some point. I was alone, and I'd been too absorbed to even notice his departure.

I took a deep breath and slowly pushed the door open. A fire had been made to dimly light the otherwise dark room. By its light, I could see Alaric's hunched form. He was leaning over the table, asleep on a pile of ancient books. His black hair hid his face from sight.

I approached him quietly, wanting desperately to see his face, though I was afraid to wake him. Unable to restrain myself, I gently pushed his hair back behind his ear.

Lightning fast, his hand shot up to grab my wrist. I let out a little yip of surprise, then relaxed as his eyes opened and focused on me.

Within seconds, he was up out of his chair, wrapping me in his embrace.

"I had the most terrible dream," he whispered into my hair.

I laughed softly, relieving some of my tension, if only temporarily. "It probably wasn't a dream."

He pulled back just enough to look into my eyes, though his arms remained around my waist, keeping me close.

"What made you come back?" he asked, suddenly very serious.

"Mikael," I admitted. "The man has a way with words, I'll give him that."

Alaric accepted my answer with a nod. I wanted nothing

more than to kiss him in that moment, but I couldn't. I couldn't give in. Not yet.

His eyed me steadily. "Why do I have the feeling this is just a temporary reunion?"

I looked down, then forced myself to meet his eyes again. The room was too hot with the fire and my coat, but I didn't want to pull away long enough to remove it.

"Because it is," I forced myself to say. "There are some things I need to do on my own."

"I can help you," he argued, anger in his tone. "We're in this together."

I shook my head and forced myself to pull away. "I just wanted to let you know that I'm okay, and that everything will make sense once the time comes."

Seeing that I wasn't coming back to his embrace, his arms dropped to his sides. "You seem different than you were the other morning," he commented, voice void of emotion, though what I was sensing from him was hitting me like a tidal wave.

"Being around that much power affected me more than I realized," I admitted. I slumped into one of the nearby seats, too tired to stand any longer.

Alaric resumed his seat next to me. The distance between us now felt like a dagger in my heart, but I couldn't pull it out.

"Yet you'll put yourself back in that position?" he asked.

"I have to," I answered immediately. "You don't understand what needs to be done."

"Then tell me."

"Not yet," I answered, urging him to understand.

I was shielding like a son of a bitch against the key. The Morrigan's energy was helping me, but we could only shield so much. Anything I said out loud would be clearly conveyed.

The key shielded from us as well, so we had no idea how much it actually knew.

Alaric frowned. "At least stay here tonight. We can talk more about it in the morning."

I shook my head and looked down, fighting against the tears threatening to spill from my eyes.

"Have you eaten anything?" he asked, his voice suddenly cold.

I shook my head. "I need to go."

"You won't tell me what you plan, and you won't let me help you. The least you can do is let me feed you. You may have taken on extra power, but your body is still mortal, as is our child. You need to eat."

I nodded, suddenly feeling like a horrible person.

I thought he would leave the room to find food, but he only stood and went to a backpack I hadn't noticed previously, sitting in one of the chairs next to the fire.

He came back with two protein bars, an apple, a bag trail mix, and a bottle of water. He sat it all in front of me on the table, then resumed his seat.

My eyebrows raised as I looked down at the food. "Am I supposed to eat all of that?"

He nodded as I glanced over at him. "If you're only staying long enough to eat, then I'm going to feed you till you pop."

I smiled in spite of myself, glad for the excuse to stay, if only for a little while. I opened a protein bar. While I ate, Alaric took my free hand in his, watching me as if memorizing my every movement.

We gazed into each other's eyes often, as an unspoken agreement formed between us. He would trust while I climbed whatever mountains I needed, and would be there should I happen to fall.

"I've been looking for you everywhere," James said to Sophie, approaching her in the early morning light.

It was true. After speaking with Alaric, he'd gone to his room to rest. He'd fallen asleep only to wake in the wee hours of the morning with a single thought nagging at him. Why was he alive?

He didn't mean the thought in a existential sort of way. Instead, he just didn't understand why Sophie had insisted he come along after losing his memory. She'd been nothing but a bitch to him the entire time, yet here he was. He couldn't understand it, and he needed to know *why*.

Sophie turned, her face silhouetted by the barest hint of purple sunlight. He knew she'd smelled and heard him long before he reached her, but had only dignified him with acknowledgement once he'd made it clear he intended to speak with her.

She was just as beautiful as ever, and just as fierce, with her long, black hair framing her narrow, toned body, clad in black as usual. She leaned against a scraggly tree as if the weight of the world was pushing her down. Her ethereal features still took his breath away, just like always, though he'd never admit it now. She was the only girl he'd ever loved, and she'd torn his heart out.

"I have a question for you," he stated when she didn't speak.

"Go on," she said coldly.

"Why didn't you kill me? You've hated me since I killed Sammuel, and you had the perfect opportunity, so why didn't you kill me?"

She stared at him, and James suddenly felt like the vilest insect to have ever walked the face of the earth. She always made him feel like that. Like he wasn't worth nearly as much as she was.

"Well?" he growled, anger boiling in his stomach.

"I had just been left by Maya," she answered sadly, surprising him. "It left me feeling the slightest bit sentimental, but don't worry, it won't happen again."

He shook his head, tossing his golden hair forward to partially obscure his eyes. "I still don't get it. Don't you hate me?"

She turned away from him to gaze out at the slowly rising sun. "I hate you, and I always will. I can never forgive you. Don't get the wrong impression."

He took a step closer, wanting to reach out to her, but not wanting to lose a hand. "If your hatred is still that strong, then why not kill me?" he pressed, knowing he was taunting her, but unable to help himself.

Suddenly Sophie turned on him. "Because I'm not you!" she shouted. Her voice echoed across the land, carried far by the thin, morning air. In a more calm voice, she continued, "Just because I was betrayed by a monster, doesn't mean I have to become one."

James stepped back in shock. He didn't know what he'd expected, but it hadn't been *that*. All this time, he'd thought Sophie would enact her vengeance as soon as he gave her the chance, but in reality she'd never planned on it. She'd never planned on turning herself into exactly what he was. He realized with a start he'd been waiting around, hoping she would try. If she was just like him, then she couldn't hate him anymore.

He exhaled, suddenly feeling like he might just turn to dust to blow away on the breeze. He began to turn away, then mumbled, "You're a stronger person than I."

"What?" Sophie snapped, though James knew she'd heard him.

He turned to fully face her. "I thought you were a monster for leaving me for another man," he began, his anger threatening to spill over. His anger was always like that now, just below the surface, waiting to be unleashed. "So I became one in return," he continued. "I became a monster, because that's what I thought you were."

Sophie's eyes narrowed. "You were always a monster, James. I simply gave you to courage to be what you truly were."

James stared into her honest eyes, and couldn't quite handle what he saw there. It was easy to blame others for your actions. Accepting that you'd made your own choices was another thing entirely.

He turned abruptly and walked away, leaving Sophie to her thoughts.

Perhaps he *had* always been a monster. It didn't matter, as long as that's what he was now. Being a monster was a lot easier than feeling pain, and it was a hell of a lot less scary than experiencing heartbreak. Being a monster was the only thing that allowed him to walk away in that moment. It was the only thing that had allowed him to survive all this time around her. All this time being *hated* by her. A monster was all he would ever be, from that point forward.

He thought he heard Sophie crying as he walked away, but he shut the sound out. Monsters didn't care about the tears of others. They only cared about themselves.

"I have to go," I argued, rising to my feet as Alaric held onto my hand.

I'd done my best to convince him, but it really was my fault as much as his that I hadn't left yet. The Morrigan's energy had started with subtle prodding, but her force had become almost overwhelming as I'd stalled the early morning away.

Alaric's face held so many unsaid things as his shoulders sagged in resignation. Suddenly he knelt in front of me, putting his face level with my belly.

To my surprise, he started speaking to it. "Now daughter," he began, then smiled, still gazing at my stomach, "It feels very weird saying that, but I need you to listen." His eyes rolled up to me as he said the next part, "I trust your mother. I trust her not to listen to anyone's opinions but her own."

My breath caught. Did he understand? Did he know I could shield my thoughts from the key, but not my words?

He gave me solid eye contact as he continued, "I'll be counting the hours until I can see both of you again. All I need is the slightest sign, and I'll follow your mother to the ends of the earth. She and I will be together before you join us."

I held back tears as I used his hand to pull him to his feet. He hugged me hard enough it almost hurt, but I wouldn't have it any other way.

"I'll walk you out," he whispered in my ear.

I nodded, suddenly feeling afraid. Previously, I'd been so gung ho in my task, and so caught up in the energies that had surrounded me, I hadn't felt fear. It was all catching up with me now, but I knew what I needed to do. I would just have to be careful not to lose myself again.

We left the room and walked down the hall, hand in hand. I would have liked to thank Mikael, but I saw no sign of him, and I couldn't hold off the energies within me forever. I didn't want to risk riling them enough that they'd try to take over.

We reached the Salr's entrance with no obstacles, and ascended to the surface together.

Morning had come, the cheery sunlight contrasting with my mood. I heard footsteps and turned to see James stomping toward us, his energy chaotic. My attention was drawn away from him as the screech of a banshee sounded near the coast. As I watched, the phantoms sped toward me, even though I hadn't called for them. I'd kept them waiting too long, and they'd grown restless, ready to serve their purpose.

"I see you're both still pretending this can actually work out," James sniped.

Alaric and I turned back to see him scowling at our joined hands.

"I see you're still pretending we want to speak with you," Alaric replied coldly.

The banshees and other phantoms reached us, swirling around impatiently. Neither James nor Alaric seemed fazed, and I could sense some new tension between them that hadn't been there before.

I felt impatience welling up inside of me, but it wasn't mine. I was the opposite of impatient. I didn't want to go.

A wave of angry energy hit me, making me lose my grip on Alaric's hand. He snapped his head from James to me in surprise.

"I *felt* that," he gasped.

James' anger hit me a second later. I had no idea what he was so upset about, but I'd never felt his emotions like that. Usually, I hardly felt his emotions at all.

I looked at James in shock.

"Stop empathing me," he growled.

"I didn't mean—" I began, but was cut off as someone came into sight from the direction of the road. A moment later I realized it was Mikael, along with Aila and Faas, though I had no idea when the latter two had arrived.

Two of the banshees darted toward James, not liking the aim of his fury.

"Call them off," James demanded, his ire increasing.

"Maddy," Alaric said cautiously, grabbing my hand to give it a squeeze.

I closed my eyes and tried to let Alaric's calm seep in, but was met with the agitated energies of the key and the Morrigan. There was no calm to be found within me, and emotions were heightening all around me.

I sensed Sophie's approach without opening my eyes. She was angry, confused, and also scared. The more I sensed everyone's emotions, the more the feeling increased. I wasn't usually so easily overwhelmed, but my added power boost had increased my senses. It was becoming difficult to define where my feelings ended and everyone else's began.

Alaric was like a cool wind at my side, radiating calm because he knew that it helped me, but it wasn't enough.

The banshees darted at James again, trying to warn him away from me. I couldn't tell if they were being protective, or if they were just affected by his emotions as an extension of me.

"Stop it!" James shouted, not backing down, just as Mikael, Aila, and Faas reached us.

"You need to calm down," Faas said warily, looking at James, but James didn't seem to hear him.

James lashed out at the banshees whenever they came near, though mortal hands couldn't harm them. The only thing that could harm them was either someone who could control the dead, or who could control energy.

Suddenly panicked, I met Faas' eyes. "Don't," I said, "it will only make it worse."

His brow creased with worry, he nodded. If he tried to drain the energy from the banshees, it would only turn them toward attacking him instead.

I pulled away from Alaric and backed away from the group. It wasn't the goodbye I had in mind, but if I left, the banshees would leave with me.

Still, I felt like I was going to faint. The key's energy suddenly washed through me, awakened by the chaos of the moment.

"No," I breathed, a moment before I lost control.

My arm flung into the air, no longer controlled by my thoughts alone, sending the banshees forward. They swarmed their chosen target, James, knocking him to the ground. There was shouting all around, but I was too dizzy to make out what was happening.

I felt it the moment Faas began draining energy from the banshees, but it was too late. There were too many of them.

"Focus on me," I screamed to Faas, knowing it was the only way to stop what was happening. Just as I gained energy from the banshees, they gained energy from me. Draining my power would weaken us all.

At first I didn't think Fass heard me, but a moment later I began to feel weak as my life force drained away. He was taking more energy than he ever had before, trying to stop what was happening to James. As he drained what felt like the last of *my* energy away, the Morrigan rushed forward, unwilling to give her power to anyone but me.

I felt a flying sensation, right before I lost consciousness. The last thing I heard was Alaric shouting my name.

CHAPTER SIXTEEN

I came to as we landed, realizing Mara had turned us into a crow, though I hadn't thought such a feat possible with my body as the host.

I lay face up in the grass, panting as a voice in my head explained, *Faas weakened us. I could not carry us far.*

Good, I thought in reply, wanting nothing more than to run back to make sure Alaric was okay. Now, if only I could stand.

"Hello Madeline," a voice said.

I held my breath in panic as I realized the voice wasn't *in* my head, but somewhere *near* my head. The panic wasn't from the innocuous greeting itself, but the person who'd given it. I recognized that eerily calm voice. A voice I'd never hoped to hear again.

"Estus," I breathed.

He came into view as he moved to stand over me. He was small, several inches shorter than me, but at the current angle he looked enormous. He smiled down at me, his lined face framed by his loose, silver hair flowing to his ankles.

"I've been searching for you," he explained, still smiling.

A voice in my head whispered, *Run*, but I still felt unable to stand. I reached out metaphysically, searching for the banshees, but nothing answered my call. I felt somehow blocked off.

Another person stepped into view, and if I had the energy, I would have screamed. *Aislin*.

At her side stood her executioner. The only time I'd ever seen him had been by the light of the moon. His hair had looked pure white then, and now that I could see it in the daylight, I could tell that it really was that white, though his angular face was young. His eyes looked gray or hazel, and held little emotion as he looked down at me.

"Marcos is a necromancer," Aislin explained, fluffing the full skirts of her ornate white dress around her. "He is blocking your phantoms from finding you, as well as the spirit that seems to have taken up residence within you."

She had to mean the Morrigan, and come to think of it, I could no longer sense her. I could still sense the key, but it wasn't offering me any help. I knew I should have been afraid, but my fear was secondary to a shocking realization that made sense of everything.

James and I had escaped from Estus' Salr so easily, and Alaric had no trouble leaving to follow us. We'd found Diana, Aislin's sister, who led us right to the key. As much as we'd tried to create conflict between the two clans, they had continued to come after us, only attacking Mikael's people and not each other.

"You've both been working together all this time," I croaked, still feeling too weak to speak properly.

Aislin and Estus both smiled, while Marcos' face remained impassive.

"Clever girl," Aislin mocked. "You never stood a chance."

I glared at them. Even with the realization, I still had no

idea *why* they were working together, or what they hoped to achieve if their goals weren't to defeat one another. Aislin had wanted me dead, her people had said so themselves, so why weren't they killing me now?

"The charm truly is inside her," Marcos remarked, "though I do not understand the other energy."

Aislin frowned. "I didn't think it possible. I thought for sure her man was lying. The charm never entered any of its previous hosts."

"What do you want?" I whispered, feeling like a lab specimen.

"We're going to save our race, my dear," Estus explained, "but first we need to find a way to separate you from the charm." He crouched down, putting his face inches from mine. "Even if it means we must cut you open to scrape it from your very soul."

I mustered what little strength I had left to scoot away, wishing Faas hadn't drained me so violently. We hadn't flown far. Alaric and the others had to be somewhere near. There was still hope.

"Hope is a funny thing," Estus whispered, as if reading my mind. "It makes you strong in times of weakness, but leaves you when you truly need it most. This is a lesson you will learn very, very soon."

I struggled as Marcos crouched and lifted me up into his arms. I tried to lash out, to drain his energy, to do *something*, but he was like a brick wall to me. He began to carry me away, while I was still too weak to scream.

"They're gone," Aila panted, gazing up at the sky for any sign of the banshees.

They'd left moments after Madeline had gone. Alaric still couldn't quite believe what his eyes had shown him as Madeline fluidly shifted into the form of a crow. He'd seen the Morrigan do it, but had never guessed Madeline might be capable, even with the Morrigan's energy inside her.

Faas rose from his crouch, finished with releasing James' life. Madeline's abrupt departure had not come soon enough to save him.

Sophie now stood by Alaric, looking down at James' body with a strange expression. She leaned her head forward enough that her hair slithered over her shoulder to hide her face.

"I told him he was a monster," she muttered under her breath.

"He was," Alaric replied, not sure how to comfort his sister, if he should even comfort her at all. She might not need it, and she definitely wouldn't accept it.

Alaric looked up to Mikael, who stood by Aila. "How did you find her?" he asked. "She told me you were the one who brought her back here. So how did you find her?"

"Luck," Mikael grumbled, looking uncharacteristically angry. "That damn Morrigan. She's the cause of this. I know it. Madeline couldn't shift into a crow on her own. The Morrigan took over."

"Madeline was able to speak freely with me while we were in the Salr," Alaric explained, then backtracked, "As freely as she was able without giving anything away. I didn't get the feeling the Morrigan was who she was hiding things from."

Mikael frowned. "You noticed it too? Like she was afraid to say too much?"

"Or else the key might hear," Faas finished for them, quickly catching on to their train of thought.

Alaric turned back to his sister. "Go find Tallie. We need to know if she can sense anything."

Sophie didn't move. She just stared down at James.

"Sophie," Alaric demanded, "*go*."

She nodded a little too quickly, then left them to return to the Salr. Alaric knew Madeline had left in an attempt to call off the banshees, but something screamed in his mind that she wasn't safe. He felt a sense of urgency he couldn't quite explain. All he knew was that they needed to *act*. They could no longer wait.

Something green several miles off caught Alaric's eye. It was a darker green than the loamy ground, and sped toward them at an alarming speed.

"Kira," he observed as the tiny woman came fully into view.

She continued to run, impossibly fast like a bullet darting through the air, until she reached them and collapsed onto the ground at Alaric's feet.

"They took her!" she gasped, clutching at her throat for oxygen, her mishmash of bright clothing looking even more ridiculous in her current predicament.

She tossed her dark green hair out of her face, then began again, still panting, "Those people took Madeline. I wanted to help, but I thought I would help more by letting you know. You'll save her. You always do."

Kira's earnest eyes looked up into Alaric's, pleading.

"*Who* took her?" Alaric demanded, the screaming panic within him increasing tenfold.

"The old man and woman," Kira panted, "and the man with white hair. They said he was a necromancer."

Alaric was unsure what Kira meant by *the old man and woman*, but the white haired necromancer jogged something in his mind. Aislin's executioner had been white haired.

Necromancy was a skill known to very few. It differed from the skills of an executioner on levels of control, but both were still similar in many ways. If Aislin's executioner took Madeline, that had to mean that the old woman was Aislin, but then who was the old man? The only person who came to mind was Estus, but that didn't make sense. He and Aislin were mortal enemies.

"Take me to where you last saw her," Alaric demanded, his gaze intent on Kira.

Mikael was suddenly at his side. He glanced at Faas and Aila. "Have Sophie track us once she returns with the others," he ordered.

Kira rose to her feet, recovered from her long run. "Are you ready?" she asked in her small voice.

Both men nodded. Kira took off in the direction she had come with Alaric and Mikael right behind her. Distantly, Alaric could hear Aila shouting orders at Faas, but the words flowed past his ears like an insubstantial breeze. He was faster than any Vaettir he'd encountered over the course of his five hundred years. If those who'd taken Madeline wanted to race, they'd chosen the wrong opponent.

I'd lost consciousness at some point, and when I awoke, I felt cut off from everything. I couldn't feel the emotions around me, I couldn't sense the banshees, and I couldn't even *see*. Everything was pitch black.

I heard footsteps. I struggled to move, but it felt like I was tied to a wooden chair, each wrist bound to an arm, and each ankle bound to a leg. I could feel the pinch of another rope at my waist.

There was the familiar sound of a matchstick striking its

box, then candlelight illuminated the room. Marcos' face became harshly shadowed as he lit several more candles spaced around the area. As the room filled with pockets of light, Estus and Aislin approached from the darkness to stand in front of me.

Estus' dark, loose clothing seemed centuries away from Aislin's prim ballgown, though the pair appeared similar in age and stature. Aislin's expression was blank, while Estus' lined face held a small smile. Marcos moved to stand behind them, his face a pale oval in the deeper shadows of the room.

"Why can't I sense anything?" I rasped, unable to match their silence.

"It's Marcos' gift," Aislin explained, "though he is only able to contend with the charm because you allowed yourself to become so horribly weakened. Even gods need rest."

"I'm not a god," I grumbled, straining against my bonds to no avail.

Estus smirked. "Close enough. The energy of the charm makes you near immortal. It protects you from any that would cause you physical harm."

Remembering his earlier words, I asked, "If that's the case, then how do you intend to cleave it from my soul?"

Estus leaned forward to put his face near mine, gazing directly into my eyes. "First we will steal the charm from you, *then* we will do the cleaving."

I struggled again, making my hair fall into my face. Frustrated, I tried to blow it away with my mouth, then jerked back as Marcos stepped around Estus to move it for me. Marcos' hand dropped back to his side as he continued to eye me wordlessly, expression unchanged.

I turned my attention back to Estus and Aislin. "Why do you want it so badly?" I asked, trying to stall for time. "If you're working together, then it's obviously not to be the sole leader of the Vaettir."

Estus chuckled. "Since you are about to die, I will explain. No one should go to their grave confused. As you may have noticed, Aislin and I have become rather advanced in age. We are *dying*."

"Everyone dies," I snapped, unable to keep my rage and frustration to myself.

Unfazed, Estus countered, "Not *gods*. With the power of the charm within us, we will be as close to gods as possible. The charm needs its host to live on, and so it will provide us with the power needed to do so."

"Unless someone comes along and takes it away," I argued, "just like you're planning to do with me."

Estus tilted his head and gave me a look of pity. Like he was speaking with a rather dense child, he explained, "The charm will be divided between us. If someone wants it for themselves, they will have to catch us both."

Throbbing pain was building behind my skull. I needed to keep stalling. For what, I didn't know, but I couldn't just let them kill me.

"Divided?" I questioned. "I don't think that's going to work."

Estus grinned, scaring me. "It will work because our DNA is very similar. Our connection will allow the key to spread its energy between us seamlessly."

My brain came to a skidding halt. "W-wait," I stammered, "your DNA?"

"We're twins," Aislin explained, sounding bored, then added, "Triplets actually, but our sister seems to have met her untimely end."

If my brain had skidded before, now it crashed and exploded in a fiery wave of chaos. I already knew who

Aislin's sister was, but had been unaware of her relation to Estus.

"Diana?" I questioned.

Aislin nodded.

I knew I should have had a million questions, but the only one I could think to ask was, "Does James know?"

Aislin eyed me cooly. "He only knows that he was grandson to Diana, who was my big sister, born just a few minutes before me. He does not know of my relation to Estus."

I shook my head over and over. "But if you were just working with your brother from the start, why were you at war? Your people attacked us when I was still at Estus' Salr. The people we questioned, that James *tortured,* were working for *you.*"

Estus chuckled. "What better way to inspire ones troops than to threaten war? What better excuse to question our people for information on the charm, than to claim that they were traitors? The executioner before you had figured it out too. He had conversed with the dead, only to realize *why* I sought the charm. Knowing what fate awaited him, he told others the information he had found. They had to be questioned."

I shook my head and turned my attention to Aislin. "But you wanted me killed. You told your people to kill me as soon as they got the chance."

Aislin smirked. "I did not truly believe the charm was within you, so yes, I wanted you dead, though I did not intend for my people to actually succeed. Their true purpose was simply to locate you. If they died in the process, it would have saved me the trouble of killing them myself."

I squeezed my eyes shut at my own stupidity. "They let

you know where we were," I replied. "Even though they expected you to kill them, they still let you know."

Aislin laughed, chilling me to the bone. "They did not betray you. They swore oaths to me. I can sense all of my people at all times. It is my gift."

I turned to Estus. "But you believed the charm was within me? I was told only one of you wanted me dead."

"We want the charm," Estus explained. "We couldn't care less what happens to you afterward. All that matters is that we will be immortal. Still, if you can prove yourself useful after the charm is ours, I would be more than happy to let you live, though I doubt my sister would agree with me."

I shook my head at the senselessness of it all. "So this, *all* of this, was because you were afraid to die?"

"It's more than that," Aislin snapped, her thin lips forming an ugly snarl. "It's what the humans did to us, burning us alive, forcing us into hiding. The Vaettir *need* us to lead them back into the world. To right the wrongs inflicted upon us, so many centuries ago."

I shook my head. "But *you* were the ones keeping the Vaettir underground," I accused.

Estus frowned. "They would have been taken down by the humans eventually. We could not have our people running amuck and getting into trouble before we were prepared. The Vaettir need strong leaders, *invincible* leaders, to reclaim the world for them."

As I reeled over that new thought, I realized Marcos had disappeared. Suddenly I had the idea that perhaps *I* was the one being distracted, and not the other way around. They were giving me the information I wanted to stall me from trying to act.

I focused what little energy I had left inward, searching

for the key or for Mara. I felt a distant spark, but it was like I was being blocked from them. It had to be Marcos' doing.

"You're monsters," I grunted, finding no real sense of *anything*. I knew my banshees still had to be out there, likely looking for me, but if Marcos was able to cut me off from the energies *inside* me, it was probably no extra trouble to cut me off from outside ones.

Estus smirked. "Perhaps, but soon we'll be gods."

I shook my head. I knew they were distracting me, but from what? There was nothing I could do.

"So what about me?" I spat. "How did I become a part of this? What about my parents? Did you question and kill them too?"

"Your parents are inconsequential," Estus answered simply. "As you know, our people kept an eye on you while you lived amongst the humans. Over time, some began to expect you were not only an executioner, but an empath. I suspected you were imbued with the Morrigan's energy, but told no one of my suspicions. The Morrigan's energy is special, because she is not truly a god. You are not created in her image, you are *her*. Your lineage doesn't matter. You are likely descended from some common death deity, but your energy is *more*. We had already been searching for the charm for centuries, and I knew if it was going to come forth to anyone, it would be someone with her magic. The key chose you, just as it chose her."

I shook my head, even more confused as Marcos reentered the room, carrying a tray of ritual paraphernalia. I hadn't needed to keep the Morrigan's presence to myself after all. Estus had known all along that I'd been descended from her, and I'd probably only confirmed it for him by revealing I was an empath.

"What do you mean, chose her?" I asked while giving everything I had to fight against Marcos' blockade.

Estus grinned. "The moon has risen overhead, and so the ritual may now begin."

My mouth went dry. The moon? Had I been unconscious an entire day?

Estus smiled knowingly. "Let me tell you one last story before you die, just so you truly understand. When Yggdrasil was destroyed, it formed three things: the Norns, who were the embodiment of fate; the charm, the embodiment of chaotic energy and wild magics; and the Morrigan, who had formed the roots of the tree. She was the earth, and the balance between all things.

"When the parts of the tree were torn apart, they naturally wanted to go back together. The charm found the Morrigan, imbuing her with great powers. Many thought she was a god, though she wasn't. She came into existence long after the old gods had left the world of man. Still, together the charm and the Morrigan were unstoppable. She would have ruled over this earth even today, if she had not been overcome by human emotions.

"For within the Morrigan was the balance of life and death, dark and light, and all the emotions that drive the never ending cycles. She fell in love, and was betrayed. She turned to darkness, throwing off the balance that was part of her very being. It destroyed her, casting her energy out into the universe."

"No," I whispered. It was all too much. Why hadn't Mara told me?

"Yes," Estus replied. "When I realized just what you were, I knew the time had come. You were born to return balance, but you are too weak, too *human* for the job. My sister and I will have to take it from here."

"Enough talk," Aislin snapped. "We must complete the ritual while the moon is still fresh in the sky."

My heart raced. That was it. They'd been stalling until nightfall. I tried with all of my might to summon enough energy just to get them away from me, but it was no use. Marcos approached with the tray. On it sat an ornate dagger, what looked like a chalice of blood or some other dark liquid, and two lit candles, one white and one black.

He kneeled before me and set the tray on the ground as Estus and Aislin both took a step back.

Marcos lifted the dagger from the tray, and before I could even react, he sliced open my forearm, still tied to the arm of the chair. A moment later, the wound began to sting as blood poured forth. He lifted the chalice to my dripping blood, letting it mingle with the dark liquid already residing within.

"With the blood of the fates, I call you forth, *lykill*," Marcos chanted, using the old Norsk term for the key.

I panted in fear as his words flowed over me. *The blood of the fates*. If the Norns were the fates, did that mean . . . it all suddenly made sense. He hadn't killed the Norns who'd sent us back in time just to rob them of their energy. He'd needed their blood to call to the key. They were the other severed part of Yggdrasil. The key would naturally want to join with them.

He handed the chalice, now containing an ample amount of my blood to mix with the Norns', back to Aislin, who took a hearty swallow.

I gagged at the sight. Not only was she drinking *blood*, but half of it had been lying around for several weeks.

Next, she handed the chalice to Estus, who downed the rest of the liquid, leaving a red stain on his lips as he lowered the vessel. Estus crouched to return the chalice to the tray, then took up the candles, handing the black one to Aislin, while keeping the white for himself.

Marcos glanced back at them, then to me. "With the balance of light and dark, I call you."

He placed his hands on either side of my ribcage, and I began to feel a pulling sensation, much like how it felt when Faas drained my energy. The first sign I had that the key was even still inside of me at all, was its sudden reaction to the ritual. It was being called forth.

I gasped as the enormous energy of the key suddenly gushed outward through my skin. There was nothing to see with our eyes, but it felt like molten metal was flooding out of my pores. Marcos pulled his hands away, and they glowed with energy.

"I cannot remove every trace from her," he said through gritted teeth, "but it should be enough."

Still kneeling, he turned his upper body toward Estus and Aislin. They each took one of his hands, with the candles held in their free palms.

I could sense the energy as it transferred to them, and suddenly I could sense everything else too. Aislin and Estus threw their heads back in identical expressions of rapture while Marcos bowed before them. The transfer of energies seemed to be taking all of Marcos' attention, because his mental hold on me had loosened. Before I could act, Mara's energy rushed forth, jumping into the nearest target, Marcos.

In the blink of an eye, Marcos stood, grabbing the dagger from the tray on his way up. While Aislin and Estus were still overcome by the euphoria of their newly acquired power, Marcos shoved the dagger into the bodice of Aislin's dress, searching upward for her heart.

She screamed as her body collapsed, and blood blossomed on the white fabric of her dress like a red rose in winter. The candle flames flickered from the abrupt movements as Marcos withdrew the blade, leaving Aislin sputtering on the ground. He turned to where Estus had been, but he was already backing away, looking down at his sister's corpse.

Estus smiled coldly, then met my eyes, not seeming to view Marcos as a threat. "I never liked sharing power anyhow," he muttered, then turned and ran, far too nimble for a man of his apparent age.

I expected Marcos, possessed by Mara, to follow him, but his body began to quiver as he dropped back to his knees before me. The dagger clattered to the floor beside him as his hands gripped my thighs almost painfully. His head bowed near my lap.

"I don't have much longer," he said, turning his gaze upward to meet my eyes. "This body still has a soul, and I am too weak to maintain my hold. My time here is through."

Though I was looking down at a man, Mara's fierce energy shone through his gray eyes. I wanted to reach out to cradle his face, but my hands were still bound.

Suddenly Alaric and Mikael came crashing into the room, followed by Faas.

"What the—" Faas began, just as Alaric leapt toward Marcos.

"No!" I shouted, stopping him mid-motion.

I looked back down to Marcos as he lifted a hand to cradle my face instead. "You are so much stronger than I ever was," he whispered. "I know you will complete the cycle. You will restore balance, where I failed."

Marcos slumped onto my lap as Mara's energy left him. I couldn't tell if he was unconscious or dead, and I didn't really care. Mara was gone. I was now alone in my body for the first time in what seemed like years. I should have been ecstatic, but all I could feel was loss.

Alaric took a step forward while Mikael and Faas stood back. Not asking questions, he gently pushed Marcos aside, allowing him to slump down to the floor before he began untying my bonds. He tensed as he noticed my bloody arm, but continued his work.

When I was free, he helped me stand, and I *needed* the help. Despite all that had happened, I'd still been drained of energy, and I'd still gone two nights without sleep. Faas wasn't the only one who'd weakened me to the point of vulnerability. I'd done just as much damage myself.

As I leaned against Alaric, we both looked down at Aislin. She was still alive, though blood splattered out of her mouth as she tried to breath, lying immobile on her back.

"Do we let her die?" Mikael questioned. There was a wicked smile on his face, as if he was very pleased with the notion.

I looked down at Aislin, for the first time feeling absolutely no sympathy for someone's death. I could distantly feel her pain, but it was nothing compared to the enormous loss I felt within me. Emotional pain trumps physical pain without fail.

"Everything dies," I answered coldly as I stared at Aislin's bloody chest.

Her eyes darted around the room frantically until they met mine. I instructed Alaric to help me kneel beside her and added, "Even gods," just as I placed my hand on her cheek and stole her life away.

CHAPTER SEVENTEEN

Stealing Aislin's energy gave me a measure of strength, but I was still painfully weary. Alaric helped me back to my feet to face Mikael and Fass.

"Estus was here," I explained.

"I thought I smelled him," Alaric growled, maintaining a tight grip around my waist.

"He took the key," I added, not sure how I felt about that fact.

Marcos had claimed that some of the key's energy still remained inside me, though I couldn't sense it, nor could I sense any lingering energy from Mara.

Faas gasped, then looked me up and down. "I sense traces of its energy, but it's more like part of you, not a foreign entity. How is that possible?"

I shrugged. I had an idea, but nothing was concrete. "One of the Norns once told me she could transfer the key from me to my child. Marcos used the blood of the Norn's he helped kill for the ritual. They are the fates, part of Yggdrasil, so their blood calls to the key."

"Marcos?" Alaric questioned softly.

I turned partially to look down at the executioner. I could see the rise and fall of his chest. Just unconscious then, not dead. *Pity*.

"So you're free," Alaric muttered in awe as we all stared down at Marcos.

"But Estus has the key," I added.

Alaric turned to me, grabbing both my arms in his so I would meet his eyes directly. "This doesn't have to be your fight anymore."

What I was about to say made me want to cry, but I had to say it. "I made a promise. This is my fight until the bitter end."

Mikael stepped into view. "Do not do this just for Erykah. I will find Estus and avenge her myself."

I could sense the truth in his words. He would go after Estus and the key, even if it meant his death.

I shook my head. "Erykah wasn't the only one I made a promise to. I have to set things right." I turned back to Alaric. "I will *not* bring my child into a world where Estus is the omnipotent leader. He wants to enact vengeance against all of mankind. The death of one tyrant has not ended this war."

Alaric pulled me close, wrapping his arms tightly around me. I almost thought he was crying, but when he pulled away, his eyes were dry.

Still, his tortured expression made my heart hurt. "It will be okay," I soothed.

He nodded. "I know."

A tear did slip down his face then.

I lifted a finger and wiped it away. "Then why are you sad?"

He smiled despite his tears and pulled me into another crushing hug. His body moved with laughter as he held me close. "The moment that you said you still had to fight, not out of vengeance, but because it's the right thing to do. In that moment, I knew you were fully yourself again. Part of me thought I had lost you."

I wrapped my arms around him and squeezed just as tightly as I let out a few tears of my own. "Did you really think that small things like the root of chaos and an ancient deity could keep me away from you?" I joked.

He stroked my hair, still holding me tight. "Not for a moment, but it's a relief either way."

"Oh enough cuddling," someone said from behind us.

I pulled away from Alaric enough to see Sophie clattering down a set of stairs leading into the room, which led me to actually look around the rest of the room. It wasn't a Salr, that much was clear. The room just looked like a plain old cellar, except for the corpse and the blood everywhere.

Sophie was followed by Aila, and both of Aislin's people, whose names I was yet to catch.

I lost my breath as I suddenly recalled just how I'd fallen into Estus' and Aislin's hands.

"Where is James?" I asked weakly.

I was met with silence.

I looked to Sophie, knowing she of all people would be brutally honest with me.

"He finally got what he deserved," she said coldly.

One of Aislin's people, the man with coppery skin and long dark hair, stepped around us to look at his former Doyen. He nudged the arm of her corpse with the toe of his boot, making it flop lifelessly.

"She's much less scary this way," he commented. His eyes met mine. "I owe you for my newfound freedom, and will help you if I can, but I do not desire a new leader."

"Nor do I," the female chimed in, keeping her distance, "though I'm also grateful."

I looked to Mikael, Faas, and Aila, who now stood side by side.

"Well you know *I'm* not going anywhere," Mikael teased.

Aila sighed, but nodded her assent, while Faas smiled softly.

"To the bitter end?" I questioned.

Mikael reached out his hand with a wry grin. Smiling, I put my hand on top of his. Alaric followed suit, then came Aila and Faas. With a sigh loud enough to make sure everyone knew how annoyed she was, Sophie marched across the room and slapped her hand down on top of Faas'.

"To the *bitter* end," she sighed.

We all echoed her, pushing our palms down before lifting them all up in unison.

"The fellowship lives!" Mikael exclaimed.

I laughed at the *Lord of the Rings* reference as one of Aislin's people muttered to the other, "What have we gotten ourselves into?"

Alaric suddenly pulled me aside. Staying within his grasp, I turned to see Marcos climbing to his feet, using the chair I'd been tied to for balance.

Mikael came to stand on my other side, observing the executioner. "Do we kill him?"

I gritted my teeth as I glared at Marcos, who now stood silently, bravely awaiting his fate. "We might need him to tear the key out of Estus."

"But will he cooperate?" Mikael asked quizzically, continuing to speak about Marcos like he wasn't even there.

The necromancer's face remained stony. I couldn't sense a single drop of emotion from him. He was either capable of completely shutting me out, or he just didn't feel anything.

I sighed, feeling guilty because I kind of wished Marcos had just died in all of the commotion, making the tough decision for us. The memory of the Morrigan looking out at me from his eyes was still fresh on my mind, making me feel a measure of compassion toward him that I shouldn't have.

Plus, he'd been able to block me from my banshees, so he was dangerous ... but perhaps it had only been since I was so weakened. Would he be able to do it now that I'd regained my strength from Aislin's energy.

I startled. Mara was gone. Did I even still have banshees? They were supposed to be under *my* command, so I should. The thought of them frightened me now that I was more myself, but we still needed an upper hand against Estus. Using the Norn's blood, he'd lured the key into himself. I wasn't sure if the key would work for him now, but it would still want to survive. Now that it was in Estus' body, it would *need* him to survive as well.

First thing was first though, I needed to see if the phantoms would still answer my call.

I pulled away from Alaric and headed for the stairs. As I approached, a gust of fresh air hit me, drawing my gaze to the stars above.

Alaric appeared behind me a moment later as I climbed the stairs out into the moonlight.

I took in our surroundings, since I'd been unconscious when I'd first entered the cellar. Sparse trees surrounded us, and to my left was an old homestead, long since fallen into disrepair.

Alaric and I stepped forward as the rest of our party joined us. Mikael and Aila came to stand beside me, each holding on to one of Marcos' arms. Suddenly I felt like maybe we *should* kill him. If I was still able to call to the banshees, he might try to take control of them. I had no idea what necromancers were capable of.

Alaric wrapped his arm around my shoulders as he said, "You should probably wait on certain *things* until we have this one locked away." He nodded toward Marcos.

I nodded in agreement, though it would be hard to wait. I really wanted to know how much Mara's departure had affected our plans.

Suddenly a shiver of what felt like electricity zinged down my spine. Alaric pulled his arm away as if he'd felt it too.

"What was that?" he asked warily.

I gasped as I realized what I was sensing. "Get Marcos away from here," I ordered breathlessly.

Mikael and Aila began to tug him away, but it was too late. The air grew even colder as dark shapes darted between us and the moon. The banshees were still around, and they'd found me.

They descended as we all stood in awe. I wasn't sure if they would listen to me now that Mara was gone, but it was our only hope.

The banshees reached the ground and surrounded us, accompanied by other phantoms, their nightmare shapes only perceivable in my peripheral vision.

We are sorry, my queen, a voice echoed through my head. *We could not find you.*

I heaved a sigh of relief, and could sense Alaric relaxing beside me, though he hadn't heard the voice.

You are different, my queen, another banshee with a deeper voice observed.

I cringed, and just as my mind flitted across the fact that Mara and the key had left me, the banshees suddenly knew, just as they knew my fears that they would no longer follow me.

You are who we followed, the first one who'd spoken explained. *You called us from the earth, and only you can return us.*

I sighed again. We had a chance. We could do this. The key might have been all powerful, but an army of phantoms was nothing to laugh at either. We would hunt Estus down and restore balance, no matter the cost. It was the least I could do, now that Mara was gone.

Before I could explain to my living companions that we were in the clear, I felt something tugging at my consciousness. No, it was tugging at the phantoms.

I felt sick as I remembered Marcos. I'd been so consumed with my inner dialogue I'd almost forgotten my initial fears. They were coming to life now as he tried to steal my phantoms.

My eyes met his. Aila and Mikael had stopped their movements when the banshees appeared, and didn't seem able to sense what Marcos was doing. It made sense. They had no affiliation with the dead. This struggle was between Marcos and I alone.

A small, knowing smile curved the necromancer's lips.

Ever perceptive, even if he couldn't feel the dead, Mikael asked, "Is he doing something that he shouldn't be doing? I'll gladly kill him."

"No," I answered. "I mean yes, but don't kill him."

I was no longer a scared little mouse, and this man was not stronger than me. I repeated the words like a mantra in my head, willing them to be true as I marched up to where Marcos stood, sandwiched between Mikael and Aila.

His smile faltered, only to be replaced by his normal, stony expression. He gasped as I shut my shields into place, cutting him off from *my* phantoms.

I came to stand before him, feeling smug. "I was weakened when you found me," I explained, looking up since he was several inches taller than me.

I was close enough to invade his personal bubble, but he couldn't back away from Mikael and Aila's iron grips.

"And you may have taken the key from me," I continued.

A small measure of his sudden fear leaked through, then was shut away as he realized it.

"But *I*," I went on, "am not weak. I am the Morrigan incarnate, and lowly necromancers like you should be bowing at my feet."

He audibly gulped, surprising me almost as much as I'd just surprised myself.

Mikael raised an eyebrow at me. "Are you *sure* the Morrigan left you?"

I smiled as I turned to walk back to my waiting banshees, then thought better of it. My smile still in place, I spun back around and punched Marcos in the face.

The impact reeled him backward, and the only thing that kept him from falling was Mikael's grip as Aila stepped back.

"*That's* for kidnapping me and cutting my arm open," I said evenly.

Righting himself, Marcos nodded. "Yes, my queen," he said evenly.

Oh good grief, I thought, turning away as I tried to slow my speeding heart. Sophie had joined Alaric, and they were both grinning at me. Aislin's minions, whose names I would have to learn at some point, just looked scared.

Ignoring them, I approached Alaric.

"Permission to kiss you, *my queen*?" he asked jokingly.

"Permission granted," I replied.

As Alaric leaned in for a kiss, I heard one of Aislin's people whisper, "I think they're *crazy*."

I laughed, then Alaric smothered my lips with his. I wrapped my arms around his neck, not caring that we had strangers and a gaggle of banshees watching us, and kissed him for all I was worth.

See? I told you I'm no creampuff.

CHAPTER EIGHTEEN

We retreated back to the Salr. I hoped Kira wouldn't mind the extra company. Something told me she'd be okay with it.

We took Marcos with us. It was a dangerous move to leave him alive, but I didn't want to risk losing a possibly useful resource. We needed all the resources we could get.

He hadn't spoken a word since the scene outside the cellar, but had come with us willingly. Something told me he had an entire internal plot of his own, but there was nothing I could do about it short of killing him, so we would just have to wait and see.

The main reason I wanted Marcos around was simple. If we could capture Estus, then maybe Marcos would be able to transfer the key back to me. I hadn't voiced to anyone yet that this was my hope, since they would all call me crazy. Maybe I was. All I knew was that I would need the key to restore balance. I would also need the Morrigan's energy, the energy of the earth, which hopefully I possessed on my own. The final piece was fate. All of Mikael's Norns had been killed, but there had to still be some out there, and we would need to find them.

Once I had gathered all of those pieces, I would hopefully know what to do. Mara had claimed I would know. I wasn't sure if I would regrow Yggdrasil, or if putting all of those energies together would be enough to achieve anything of worth. Really, I didn't know much at all. At the moment I was just grateful to be back with my friends, in a relatively safe, warm environment, my belly filled with food, and my skin draped in silky blue pajamas.

I rolled over in bed to see Alaric, who had apparently been watching me as I mulled over my thoughts.

He reached out a hand and stroked my hair. "You know Estus might come back here for you."

I smiled. "Let him. It would save us the trouble of finding him."

"You truly think you can subdue him, even though he now has the key?" he pressed.

I placed my hand over his and brought it to rest against my cheek. "Your worry is making me anxious," I teased.

He smiled. "You know, teasing in dire situations is supposed to be *my* thing."

I snuggled a little closer. "The banshees will come to my call the moment I step foot outside. Mara, the Morrigan," I corrected, realizing Alaric didn't know her true name, "was a force equal to the key. The key was chaos, and she was the earth, and the balance between all things."

"But you're not *her*," he countered.

I frowned. "No, but I'm all we've got. Plus Marcos and the banshees."

"That's the other thing," he sighed. "I think we should have killed Marcos. He was able to block you from calling the phantoms, and he tried to call them from you, even after he'd been captured."

"And he failed," I added.

"This time," he argued.

I rolled onto my back, pulling away from him. "You really have no faith in me, do you?"

He turned and wrapped his arms around my ribcage, pulling me back toward him, then propped himself up so he could look at me. "Madeline, you are the *only* thing I have faith in."

I smiled. "Then trust me on this."

He leaned forward and laid a gentle kiss on my lips, but seemed perplexed as he pulled away.

Suddenly worried, I asked, "What is it?"

He frowned. "I just realized you never told me what it was you were trying to hide from the key. Why you couldn't say all that you needed to while it was still inside you."

My heart warmed. "So you understood? I was hoping you would. It was so hard trying to leave without being able to explain."

He gave me a tight squeeze. "I understood you couldn't say certain things in front of the key, not what they were."

I smiled, content in the fact that Alaric had known me well enough to understand what I'd been trying to convey. "The Morrigan and I were working with the key, with the intent of regrowing Yggdrasil."

Alaric tensed, but didn't speak.

"What the key didn't understand, was that it would have to become a part of the tree again, and hence, a part of the earth. It would no longer be a sentient being."

Alaric nodded in understanding. "So you wanted to keep the key in favor of your plan. If you'd told me you were going to regrow Yggdrasil, I would have questioned you, and you might have said the wrong thing."

"Exactly," I replied.

"But that doesn't explain why you wouldn't let me help you," he countered. "I would have gone along, even without an explanation."

I sighed. "That was the Morrigan's side of the deal, that I needed to do things on my own. I couldn't be distracted by wanting to keep you safe."

"So you were shielding certain things from the Morrigan too," he said.

I cringed.

He raised a dark eyebrow at me. "Or maybe you weren't?"

I let out a long breath, preparing myself to be honest. "I agreed with her. I would have never been able to go around raising spirits from their graves if I was worried about you coming to harm."

"And?" he pressed, knowing me too well to let the explanation drop at that.

"And," I continued, "I needed to prove to myself that I could do it on my own. My entire life I've run from things. I've run from my past, from love, and even from *you*. I don't want our daughter to ever feel like she can't handle things on her own. I need to be a living example of that."

Alaric laid a gentle kiss on my temple, then held me close. "Our *daughter*," he mused. "I still can't get used to it."

I smiled. "So you forgive me for leaving you out of things?"

He chuckled. "There is nothing to forgive. It was always your choice to make, as much as I would have liked to fight against it."

I smiled and relaxed into his embrace as I rubbed a hand

across my belly. "I'm glad my daughter will have a father that won't tell her she can't do things on her own."

His hand covered mine to feel the small bump underneath the fabric of my pajamas. "Oh I'll try," he joked, "but with the perfect role model of her mother around, I doubt I'll have much luck."

"So you're fine with her being just like me?" I asked slyly.

He laughed. "I'm fine with her being whatever she wants, as long as she's not too much like my sister."

I jumped as the door to our room suddenly flew open to reveal Sophie, standing in the doorway with her hip cocked, and a bottle of champagne in her hand.

"That's not very nice, *brother*," she chided.

Mikael appeared in the doorway behind her with a paper shopping bag in each hand.

Sophie entered the room uninvited, then came to sit on the foot of our bed while Alaric and I moved to seated positions. Alaric let out a long sigh.

I combed my fingers through my hair to make sure I didn't look like too much of a mess, but gave up. When people like Sophie and Mikael barged into your room, you had little choice but to go along with it. I raised an eyebrow at the bags in Mikael's hands as he approached us.

"We're never letting the Viking do the supply shopping again," Sophie commented as Mikael set the bags on the bedside table. "It's almost all booze," she added, lifting the champagne bottle in her hand for emphasis.

"Well I for one think we deserve to celebrate," Mikael teased, removing a bottle of whiskey from the bag, followed by a package of plastic cups.

He handed me the cups while Alaric glared at him, then produced another champagne bottle from the bag, handing it to me.

"Sparkling cider," he explained, "for little Mikaela junior," he added, gesturing to my belly.

"Hah *hah*," I replied sarcastically, tearing open the plastic encasing the cups. "Where are Aila and the others?"

"Watching our new friend Marcos to make sure he doesn't get any funny ideas," Mikael explained as he pulled the corked top out of the whiskey.

I smirked. "Maybe we should invite him too. He might be nicer when he's drunk."

Alaric looked at me seriously, for once the only one in the conversation *not* joking.

I offered him a smile as I handed him the sparkling cider to uncork.

He rolled his eyes then smiled, giving in to the situation. He popped the cork into his hand, then took the cup I handed him to pour me a glass. After handing the filled cup and bottle back to me, he accepted a cup of champagne from Sophie. I scooted closer to Alaric and leaned against the headboard beside him. He put his arm around me obligingly, and I felt it as the tension drained from him.

Whiskey in hand, Mikael stood before us and raised his glass. "To traveling through time, cavorting with deities, getting possessed and unpossessed, and still coming out alive."

I lifted my glass. "To the living, to the dead, and to fate herself."

Alaric lifted his glass toward the center of the group, but his eyes were all for me as he said, "To Madeline, for being both strong and kind, light and dark, and everything in between, *and* to our daughter, who will not be named Mikaela."

Sophie snorted at Alaric's toast, then lifted her glass. "To family," she said, encompassing both Alaric and I in her gaze, "and to friends, sort of," she added, looking to Mikael, who accepted the inclusion with a slight bow, "and to James," she sighed, "may he find peace in death, even if he doesn't deserve it."

We all touched the rims of our glasses, then took a sip. Well, Mikael took more than a sip, then poured himself another glass.

I snuggled closer to Alaric and placed a hand on my belly, enjoying the simple moment. I felt like I'd quite literally been through hell and back, and maybe, just maybe, I was better for the experience.

It was odd to think about how my life had been before, living alone in my little house, avoiding close relationships. Avoiding *life*. Now I not only had friends, but I had a true partner in Alaric, and eventually we would have a daughter.

What were a few unparalleled forces of nature to contend with, when you had rewards like those?

NOTE FROM THE AUTHOR

I hope you enjoyed the first three installments in the Bitter Ashes series! Book four, Duck, Duck, Noose, is available now. For news and updates, please sign up for my mailing list by visiting:

www.saracroethle.com

Printed in Poland
by Amazon Fulfillment
Poland Sp. z o.o., Wrocław

34107346R00423